BRANDON SANDERSON

THE WAY OF KINGS

PART TWO

Book One of

THE STORMLIGHT ARCHIVE

First published in Great Britain in 2010 by
Gollancz
An imprint of the Orion Publishing Group
Orion House, 5 Upper St Martin's Lane, London WC2H 9EA
An Hachette UK Company

This edition published in Great Britain in 2011 by Gollancz

11

A CIP catalogue record for this book is available
from the British Library

ISBN 978 0 575 10248 4

Typeset by Input Data Services Ltd, Bridgwater, Somerset

Printed in Great Britain by Clays Ltd, St Ives plc

The Or[illegible] natural,
renewable [illegible] sustainable
forests. Th[illegible] conform to
[illegible]n.

FOREWORD BY
BRANDON SANDERSON

Welcome to Part 2 of this Gollancz edition of *The Way of Kings*.

The Way of Kings has been a long time in the making. It's been some twenty years that I've worked on this book now, in one form or another. The original draft was completed in 2002, though I decided it was not yet good enough for publication. It took me another seven years to get the characters, world, and plot to the level I wanted.

During all those years, I waited eagerly for the chance to finally do a grand epic on the scale I'd dreamed of achieving. One of the difficulties over the last few years has been knowing that the first book – in order to set the stage appropriately, yet include a complete story of its own – was going to have to be long. The longest book in the series, most likely. I knew this size would make it difficult to print the book in a single volume.

I debated this for a great long time. I toyed with cutting sequences completely to make the book shorter, toyed with removing characters. In the end, I decided that couldn't be done. At least, not while creating the story I wanted. And so, when I wrote the book in 2009 (and did so from scratch, throwing away previous drafts) I wrote it at the length I knew it needed to be. I also gave publishers the option to split the book if they absolutely had to.

I chose the breaking point myself. While it would have been easiest to break at the end of one of the five 'Parts' within the book, this didn't feel right. Those breaks were chosen to signify the end of a sequence and the beginning of a new one, but were not intended to be satisfying ends unto themselves. Instead, I broke the novel in the middle of one of the parts. I strongly feel that, if we are going to end one half and begin another, this is the best place.

The break point was chosen for its fulfillment of several plot cycles while beginning the whispers of the true challenges ahead. I want you to understand, however, that this is a single story with a single arc, not meant to be taken as two divided parts. I encourage readers to view them as a single whole.

I apologize for the need to do this, but it was what the story demanded. As always, you have my sincere thanks for reading and for supporting me in my writing.

If you have yet to read Part 1 of this edition of *The Way of Kings*, I would encourage you to do so first.

CONTENTS

ILLUSTRATIONS

Roshar

Endless Ocean
Rall Elorim
Reshi
Kasitor
Iri
Rira
Kurth
Eila
Babatharnam
Panatham
Shinovar
Desh
Azir
Yulay
Alm
Yezier
Azimir
Emul
Liafor
Steen
Tashikk
Sesemalex Dar
Tukar
Icewater
Aimian Sea
Aimia

Southern Depths

Steamwater Ocean

Isles

Akak

Sumi

Sea

Akak

Northgrip

Herdaz

Mourn's Vault

Varikev

u Parat

Elanar

Jah Keved

HornEater Peaks

Kholinar

Shulin

Alethkar

Unclaimed Hills

Valath

Bavland

Rathalas

Dawn's Shadow

Silnasen

Triax

Vedenar

Dumadari

Tarat Sea

Karanak

Shattered Plains

New Natanan

Kharbranth

Frostlands

Longbrow's Straits

The Shallow Crypts

Thaylenah

Ocean of Origins

For His Royal Majesty King Gavilar Kholin

By His Royal High Cartographer

Isasik Shulin

1167

Shalebark
Shale snail ?
3"
4½"
Cremlings

PART THREE: DYING (CONTINUED)

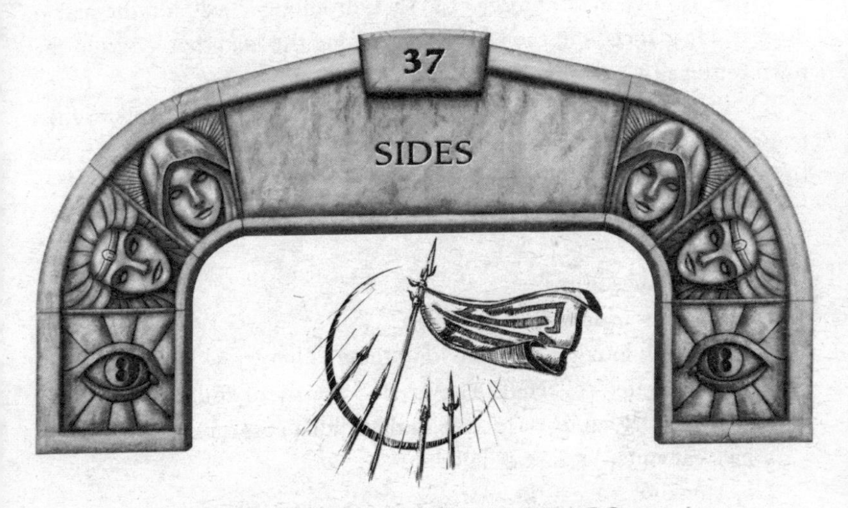

37

SIDES

FIVE AND A HALF YEARS AGO

'Kaladin, look at this rock,' Tien said. 'It changes colors when you look at it from different sides.'

Kal looked away from the window, glancing at his brother. Now thirteen years of age, Tien had turned from an eager boy into an eager adolescent. Though he'd grown, he was still small for his age, and his mop of black and brown hair still refused all attempts at order. He was squatting beside the lacquered cobwood dinner table, eyes level with the glossy surface, looking at a small, lumpish rock.

Kal sat on a stool peeling longroots with a short knife. The brown roots were dirty on the outside and sticky when he sliced into them, so working on them coated his fingers with a thick layer of crem. He finished a root and handed it up to his mother, who washed it off and sliced it into the stew pot.

'Mother, look at this,' Tien said. Late-afternoon sunlight streamed through the leeside window, bathing the table. 'From this side, the rock sparkles red, but from the other side, it's green.'

'Perhaps it's magical,' Hesina said. Chunk after chunk of longroot plunked into the water, each splash with a slightly different note.

'I think it must be,' Tien said. 'Or it has a spren. Do spren live in rocks?'

'Spren live in everything,' Hesina replied.

'They can't live in *everything*,' Kal said, dropping a peel into the pail at his feet. He glanced out the window, watching the road that led from the town to the citylord's mansion.

'They do,' Hesina said. 'Spren appear when something changes – when fear appears, or when it begins to rain. They are the heart of change, and therefore the heart of all things.'

'This longroot,' Kal said, holding it up skeptically.

'Has a spren.'

'And if you slice it up?'

'Each bit has a spren. Only smaller.'

Kal frowned, looking over the long tuber. They grew in cracks in the stone where water collected. They tasted faintly of minerals, but were easy to grow. His family needed food that didn't cost much, these days.

'So we eat spren,' Kal said flatly.

'No,' she said, 'we eat the roots.'

'When we *have* to,' Tien added with a grimace.

'And the spren?' Kal pressed.

'They are freed. To return to wherever it is that spren live.'

'Do I have a spren?' Tien said, looking down at his chest.

'You have a soul, dear. You're a person. But the pieces of your body may very well have spren living in them. Very small ones.'

Tien pinched at his skin, as if trying to pry the tiny spren out.

'Dung,' Kal said suddenly.

'Kal!' Hesina snapped. 'That's not talk for mealtime.'

'Dung,' Kal said stubbornly. 'It has spren?'

'I suppose it does.'

'Dungspren,' Tien said, then snickered.

His mother continued to chop. 'Why all of these questions, suddenly?'

Kal shrugged. 'I just— I don't know. Because.'

He'd been thinking recently about the way the world worked, about what he was to do with his place in it. The other boys his age, they didn't wonder about their place. Most *knew* what their future held. Working in the fields.

Kal had a choice, though. Over the last several months, he'd finally made that choice. He would become a soldier. He was fifteen now, and could volunteer when the next recruiter came through town. He planned to do just that. No more wavering. He would learn to fight. That was the end of it. Wasn't it?

'I want to understand,' he said. 'I just want everything to make sense.'

His mother smiled at that, standing in her brown work dress, hair pulled back in a tail, the top hidden beneath her yellow kerchief.

'What?' he demanded. 'Why are you smiling?'

'You *just* want everything to make sense?'

'Yes.'

'Well next time the ardents come through the town to burn prayers and Elevate people's Callings, I'll pass the message along.' She smiled. 'Until then, keep peeling roots.'

Kal sighed, but did as she told him. He checked out the window again, and nearly dropped the root in shock. The carriage. It was coming down the roadway from the mansion. He felt a flutter of nervous hesitation. He'd planned, he'd thought, but now that the time was upon him, he wanted to sit and keep peeling. There would be another opportunity, surely. . . .

No. He stood, trying to keep the anxiety from his voice. 'I'm going to go rinse off.' He held up crem-covered fingers.

'You should have washed the roots off first as I told you,' his mother noted.

'I know,' Kal said. Did his sigh of regret sound fake? 'Maybe I'll just wash them all off now.'

Hesina said nothing as he gathered up the remaining roots, crossed to the door, heart thumping, and stepped out into the evening light.

'See,' Tien said from behind, 'from this side it's green. I don't think it's a spren, Mother. It's the light. It makes the rock change. . . .'

The door swung closed. Kal set down the tubers and charged through the streets of Hearthstone, passing men chopping wood, women throwing out dishwater, and a group of grandfathers sitting on steps and looking at the sunset. He dunked his hands into a rain barrel, but didn't stop as he shook the water free. He ran around Mabrow Pigherder's house, up past the commonwater – the large hole cut into the rock at the center of the town to catch rain – and along the breakwall, the steep hillside against which the town was built to shield it from storms.

Here, he found a small stand of stumpweight trees. Knobby and about as tall as a man, they grew leaves only on their leeward sides, running down the length of the tree like rungs on a ladder, waving in the cool breeze. As Kal got close, the large, bannerlike leaves snapped up close to the trunks, making a series of whipping sounds.

Kal's father stood on the other side, hands clasped behind his back. He was waiting where the road from the manor turned past Hearthstone. Lirin turned with a start, noticing Kal. He wore his finest clothing: a blue coat, buttoning up the sides, like a lighteyes's coat. But it was over a pair of white trousers that showed wear. He studied Kal through his spectacles.

'I'm going with you,' Kal blurted. 'Up to the mansion.'

'How did you know?

'Everyone knows,' Kal said. 'You think they wouldn't talk if Brightlord Roshone invited you to dinner? You, of all people?'

Lirin looked away. 'I told your mother to keep you busy.'

'She tried.' Kal grimaced. 'I'll probably hear a storm of it when she finds those longroots sitting outside the front door.'

Lirin said nothing. The carriage rolled to a stop nearby, wheels grinding against the stone.

'This will not be a pleasant, idle meal, Kal,' Lirin said.

'I'm not a fool, Father.' When Hesina had been told there was no more need for her to work in the town . . . Well, there was a reason they'd been reduced to eating longroots. 'If you're going to confront him, then you should have someone to support you.'

'And that someone is you?'

'I'm pretty much all you have.'

The coachman cleared his throat. He didn't get down and open the door, the way he did for Brightlord Roshone.

Lirin eyed Kal.

'If you send me back, I'll go,' Kal said.

'No. Come along if you must.' Lirin walked up to the carriage and pulled open the door. It wasn't the fancy, gold-trimmed vehicle that Roshone used. This was the second carriage, the older brown one. Kal climbed in, feeling a surge of excitement at the small victory – and an equal measure of panic.

They were going to face Roshone. Finally.

The benches inside were amazing, the red cloth covering them softer than anything Kal had ever felt. He sat down, and the seat was surprisingly springy. Lirin sat across from Kal, pulling the door closed, and the coachman snapped his whip at the horses. The vehicle turned around and rattled back up the road. As soft as the seat was, the ride was terribly bumpy, and it rattled Kal's teeth against one another. It was worse than riding in a wagon, though that was probably because they were going faster.

'Why didn't you want us to know about this?' Kal asked.

'I wasn't certain I'd go.'

'What else would you do?'

'Move away,' Lirin said. 'Take you to Kharbranth and escape this town, this kingdom, and Roshone's petty grudges.'

Kal blinked in shock. He'd never thought of that. Suddenly everything seemed to expand. His future changed, wrapping upon itself, folding into a new form entirely. Father, Mother, Tien . . . *with* him. 'Really?'

Lirin nodded absently. 'Even if we didn't go to Kharbranth, I'm sure many Alethi towns would welcome us. Most have never had a surgeon to care for them. They do the best they can with local men who learned most of what they know from superstition or working on the occasional wounded chull. We could even move to Kholinar; I'm skilled enough to get work as a physician's assistant there.'

'Why don't we go, then? Why *haven't* we gone?'

Lirin watched out the window. 'I don't know. We should leave. It makes sense. We have the money. We aren't wanted here. The citylord hates us, the people mistrust us, the Stormfather himself seems inclined to knock us down.' There was something in Lirin's voice. Regret?

'I tried very hard to leave once,' Lirin said, more softly. 'But there's a tie between a man's home and his heart. I've cared for these people, Kal. Delivered their children, set their bones, healed their scrapes. You've seen the worst of them, these last few years, but there was a time before that, a good time.' He turned to Kal, clasping his hands in front of him, the carriage rattling. 'They're mine, son. And I'm theirs. They're my responsibility, now that Wistiow has gone. I can't leave them to Roshone.'

'Even if they *like* what he's doing?'

'Particularly because of that.' Lirin raised a hand to his head. 'Stormfather. It sounds more foolish now that I say it.'

'No. I understand. I think.' Kal shrugged. 'I guess, well, they still come to us when they're hurt. They complain about how unnatural it is to cut into a person, but they still come. I used to wonder why.'

'And did you come to a conclusion?'

'Kind of. I decided that in the end, they'd rather be alive to curse at you a few more days. It's what they do. Just like healing them is what you do. And they *used* to give you money. A man can say all kinds of things, but where he sets his spheres, that's where his heart is.' Kal frowned. 'I guess they *did* appreciate you.'

Lirin smiled. 'Wise words. I keep forgetting that you're nearly a man, Kal. When did you go and grow up on me?'

That night when we were nearly robbed, Kal thought immediately. *That night when you shone light on the men outside, and showed that bravery had nothing to do with a spear held in battle.*

'You're wrong about one thing, though,' Lirin said. 'You told me that they *did* appreciate me. But they still do. Oh, they grumble – they've always done that. But they also leave food for us.'

Kal started. 'They do?'

'How do you think we've been eating these last four months?'

'But—'

'They're frightened of Roshone, so they're quiet about it. They left it for your mother when she went to clean or put it in the rain barrel when it's empty.'

'They tried to rob us.'

'And those very men were among the ones who gave us food as well.'

Kal pondered that as the carriage arrived at the manor house. It had been a long time since he'd visited the large, two-story building. It was constructed with a standard roof that sloped toward the stormward side, but was much larger. The walls were of thick white stones, and it had majestic square pillars on the leeward side.

Would he see Laral here? He was embarrassed by how infrequently he thought about her these days.

The mansion's front grounds had a low stone wall covered with all kinds of exotic plants. Rockbuds lined the top, their vines draping down the outside. Clusters of a bulbous variety of shalebark grew along the inside, bursting with a variety of bright colors. Oranges, reds, yellows, and blues. Some outcroppings looked like heaps of clothing, with folds spread like fans. Others grew out like horns. Most had tendrils like threads that waved in the wind. Brightlord Roshone paid much more attention to his grounds than Wistiow had.

They walked up past the whitewashed pillars and entered between the thick wooden stormdoors. The vestibule inside had a low ceiling and was decorated with ceramics; zircon spheres gave them a pale blue cast.

A tall servant in a long black coat and a bright purple cravat greeted them. He was Natir, the steward now that Miliv had died. He'd been brought in from Dalilak, a large coastal city to the north.

Natir led them to a dining room where Roshone sat at a long darkwood table. He'd gained weight, though not enough to be called fat. He still had that grey-flecked beard, and his hair was greased back down to his collar. He wore white trousers and a tight red vest over a white shirt.

He'd already begun his meal, and the spicy scents made Kal's stomach rumble. How long had it been since he'd had pork? There were five different dipping sauces on the table, and Roshone's wine was a deep, crystalline orange. He ate alone, no sign of Laral or his son.

The servant gestured toward a side table set up in a room next to the dining hall. Kal's father took one look at it, then walked to Roshone's table and sat down. Roshone paused, skewer halfway to his lips, spicy brown sauce dripping to the table before him.

'I'm of the second nahn,' Lirin said, 'and I have a personal invitation to dine with you. Surely you follow the precepts of rank closely enough to give me a place at your table.'

Roshone clenched his teeth, but did not object. Taking a deep breath, Kal sat down beside his father. Before he left to join the war on the Shattered Plains, he *had* to know. Was his father a coward or a man of courage?

By the light of spheres at home, Lirin had always seemed weak. He worked in his surgery room, ignoring what the townspeople said about him. He told his son he couldn't practice with the spear and forbade him to think of going to war. Weren't those the actions of a coward? But five months ago, Kal had seen courage in him that he'd never expected.

And in the calm blue light of Roshone's palace, Lirin met the eyes of a man far above him in rank, wealth, and power. And did not flinch. How did he do it? Kal's heart thumped uncontrollably. He had to put his hands in his lap to keep them from betraying his nervousness.

Roshone waved to a serving man, and within a short time, new places had been set. The periphery of the room was dark. Roshone's table was an illuminated island amid a vast black expanse.

There were bowls of water for dipping one's fingers and stiff white cloth napkins beside them. A lighteyes's meal. Kal had rarely eaten such fine food; he tried not to make a fool of himself as he hesitantly took a skewer and imitated Roshone, using his knife to slide down the bottommost chunk of meat, then raising it and biting. The meat was savory and tender, though the spices were much hotter than he was accustomed to.

Lirin did not eat. He rested his elbows on the table, watching the Brightlord dine.

'I wished to offer you the chance to eat in peace,' Roshone said eventually, 'before we talked of serious matters. But you don't seem inclined to partake of my generosity.'

'No.'

'Very well,' Roshone said, taking a piece of flatbread from the basket and wrapping it around his skewer, pulling off several vegetable chunks at once and eating them with the bread. 'Then tell me. How long do you think you can defy me? Your family is destitute.'

'We do just fine,' Kal cut in.

Lirin glanced at him, but did not chastise him for speaking. 'My son is correct. We can live. And if that doesn't work, we can leave. I will not bend to your will, Roshone.'

'If you left,' Roshone said, holding up a finger, 'I would contact your new citylord and tell him of the spheres stolen from me.'

'I would win an inquest over that. Besides, as a surgeon, I am immune to most demands you could make.' It was true; men and their apprentices who served an essential function in towns were afforded special protection, even from lighteyes. The Vorin legal code of citizenship was complex enough that Kaladin still had difficulty understanding it.

'Yes, you would win an inquest,' Roshone said. 'You were so meticulous, preparing the exact right documents. You were the only one with Wistiow when he stamped them. Odd, that none of his clerks were there.'

'Those clerks read him the documents.'

'And then left the room.'

'Because they were ordered to leave by Brightlord Wistiow. They have admitted this, I believe.'

Roshone shrugged. 'I don't need to *prove* that you stole the spheres, surgeon. I simply have to continue doing as I have been. I know that your family eats scraps. How long will you continue to make them suffer for your pride?'

'They won't be intimidated. And neither will I.'

'I'm not asking if you're intimidated. I'm asking if you're *starving*.'

'Not by any means,' Lirin said, voice growing dry. 'If we lack for something to eat, we can feast upon the attention you lavish upon us, *Brightlord*. We feel your eyes watching, hear your whispers to the townspeople. Judging from the degree of your concern with us, it would seem that *you* are the one who is intimidated.'

Roshone fell still, skewer held limply in his hand, brilliant green eyes narrowed, lips pursed tight. In the dark, those eyes almost seemed to *glow*. Kal had to stop himself from cringing under the weight of that disapproving gaze. There was an air of command about lighteyes like Roshone.

He's not a real *lighteyes! He's a reject. I'll see real ones eventually. Men of honor.*

Lirin held the gaze evenly. 'Every month we resist is a blow to your authority. You can't have me arrested, since I would win an inquest. You've tried to turn the other people against me, but they know – deep down – that they need me.'

Roshone leaned forward. 'I do not like your little town.'

Lirin frowned at the odd response.

'I do not like being treated like an *exile*,' Roshone continued. 'I do not like living so far from anything – everything – important. And most of all, I do not like darkeyes who think themselves above their stations.'

'I have trouble feeling sympathy for you.'

Roshone sneered. He looked down at his meal, as if it had lost any flavor. 'Very well. Let us make an ... accommodation. I will take nine-tenths of the spheres. You can have the rest.'

Kal stood up indignantly. 'My father will never—'

'Kal,' Lirin cut in. 'I can speak for myself.'

'Surely you won't make a deal, though.'

Lirin didn't reply immediately. Finally, he said, 'Go to the kitchens, Kal. Ask them if they have some food more to your tastes.'

'Father, no—'

‘Go, son.’ Lirin’s voice was firm.

Was it true? After all of this, would his father simply *capitulate*? Kal felt his face grow red, and he fled the dining room. He knew the way to the kitchens. During his childhood, he’d often dined there with Laral.

He left not because he was told to, but because he didn’t want his father or Roshone to see his emotions: chagrin at having stood to denounce Roshone when his father planned to make a deal, humiliation that his father would *consider* a deal, frustration at being banished. Kal was mortified to find himself crying. He passed a couple of Roshone’s house soldiers standing at the doorway, lit only by a very low-trimmed oil lamp on the wall. Their rough features were highlighted in amber hues.

Kal hastened past them, turning a corner before pausing beside a plant stand, struggling with his emotions. The stand displayed an indoor vinebud, one bred to remain open; a few conelike flowers climbed up from its vestigial shell. The lamp on the wall above it burned with a tiny, strangled light. These were the back rooms of the mansion, near the servant quarters, and spheres were not used for light here.

Kal leaned back, breathing in and out. He felt like one of the ten fools – specifically Cabine, who acted like a child though he was adult. But what was he to think of Lirin’s actions?

He wiped his eyes, then pushed his way through the swinging doors into the kitchens. Roshone still employed Wistiow’s chef. Barm was a tall, slender man with dark hair that he wore braided. He walked down the line of his kitchen counter, giving instructions to his various subchefs as a couple of parshmen walked in and out through the mansion’s back doors, carrying in crates of food. Barm carried a long metal spoon, which he banged on a pot or pan hanging from the ceiling each time he gave an order.

He barely spared Kal a brown-eyed glance, then told one of his servants to go fetch some flatbread and fruited tallew rice. A child’s meal. Kal felt even more embarrassed that Barm had known instantly why he had been sent to the kitchens.

Kal walked to the dining nook to wait for the food. It was a whitewashed alcove with a slate-topped table. He sat down, elbows on the stone, head on his hands.

Why did it make him so angry to think that his father might bargain away most of the spheres in exchange for safety? True, if that happened, there wouldn't be enough to send Kal to Kharbranth. But he'd already decided to become a soldier. So it didn't matter. Did it?

I am going to join the army, Kal thought. *I'll run away, I'll . . .*

Suddenly, that dream – that plan – seemed incredibly childish. It belonged to a boy who ought to eat fruited meals and deserved to be sent away when the men talked of important topics. For the first time, the thought of not training with the surgeons filled him with regret.

The door into the kitchens banged open. Roshone's son, Rillir, sauntered in, chatting with the person behind him. '. . . don't know *why* Father insists on keeping everything so dreary around here all the time. Oil lamps in the hallways? Could he be any more provincial? It would do him some real good if I could get him out on a hunt or two. We might as well get some use out of being in this remote place.'

Rillir noticed Kal sitting there, but passed over him as one might register the presence of a stool or a shelf for wine: noting it, but otherwise ignoring it.

Kal's own eyes were on the person who followed Rillir. Laral. Wistiow's daughter.

So much had changed. It had been so long, and seeing her brought up old emotions. Shame, excitement. Did she know that his parents had been hoping to marry him to her? Merely seeing her again almost flustered him completely. But no. His father could look Roshone in the eyes. He could do the same with her.

Kal stood up and nodded to her. She glanced at him, and blushed faintly, walking in with an old nurse in tow – a chaperone.

What had happened to the Laral he'd known, the girl with the loose yellow and black hair who liked climbing on rocks and running through fields? Now she was wrapped up in sleek yellow silk, a stylish lighteyed woman's dress, her neatly coiffed hair dyed black to hide the blond. Her left hand was hidden modestly in her sleeve. Laral *looked* like a lighteyes.

Wistiow's wealth – what was left of it – had gone to her. And when Roshone had been given authority over Hearthstone and granted the mansion and surrounding lands, Highprince Sadeas had given Laral a dowry in compensation.

'You,' Rillir said, nodding to Kal and speaking in a smooth, city accent. 'Be a good lad and fetch us some supper. We'll take it here in the nook.'

'I'm not a kitchen servant.'

'So?'

Kal flushed.

'If you're expecting some kind of tip or reward for just fetching me a meal . . .'

'I'm not – I mean—' Kal looked to Laral. 'Tell him, Laral.'

She looked away. 'Well, go on, boy,' she said. 'Do as you're told. We're hungry.'

Kal gaped at her, then felt his face redden even more. 'I'm . . . I'm not going to fetch you anything!' he managed to say. 'I wouldn't do it no matter how many spheres you offer me. I'm not an errand boy, I'm a surgeon.'

'Oh, you're *that* one's son.'

'I am,' Kal said, surprised at how proudly he felt those words. 'I'm not going to be bullied by you, Rillir Roshone. Just like my father isn't bullied by yours.'

Except, they are making a deal right now. . . .

'Father didn't mention how amusing you were,' Rillir said, leaning back against the wall. He seemed a decade older than Kal, not a mere two years. 'So you find it shameful to fetch a man his meal? Being a surgeon makes you that much better than the kitchen staff?'

'Well, no. It's just not my Calling.'

'Then what is your Calling?'

'Making sick people well.'

'And if I don't eat, won't I be sick? So couldn't you call it your duty to see me fed?'

Kal frowned. 'It's . . . well, it's not the same thing at all.'

'I see it as being very similar.'

'Look, why don't you just go get yourself some food?'

'It's not my Calling.'

'Then what *is* your Calling?' Kal returned, throwing the man's own words back at him.

'I'm cityheir,' Rillir said. 'My duty is to lead – to see that jobs get done and that people are occupied in productive work. And as such, I give important tasks to idling darkeyes to make them useful.'

Kal hesitated, growing angry.

'You see how his little mind works,' Rillir said to Laral. 'Like a dying fire, burning what little fuel it has, pumping out smoke. Ah, and look, his face grows red from the heat of it.'

'Rillir, please,' Laral said, laying her hand on his arm.

Rillir glanced at her, then rolled his eyes. 'You're as provincial as my father sometimes, dear.' He stood up straight and – with a look of resignation – led her past the nook and into the kitchen proper.

Kal sat back down hard, nearly bruising his legs on the bench with the force of it. A serving boy brought him his food and set it on the table, but that only reminded Kal of his childishness. So he didn't eat it; he just stared at it until, eventually, his father walked into the kitchen. Rillir and Laral were gone by then.

Lirin walked to the alcove and surveyed Kal. 'You didn't eat.'

Kal shook his head.

'You should have. It was free. Come on.'

They walked in silence from the mansion into the dark night. The carriage awaited them, and soon Kal again sat facing his father. The driver climbed into place, making the vehicle quiver, and a snap of his whip set the horses in motion.

'I want to be a surgeon,' Kal said suddenly.

His father's face – hidden in shadow – was unreadable. But when he spoke, he sounded confused. 'I know that, son.'

'No. I want to be a surgeon. I don't want to run away to join the war.'

Silence in the darkness.

'You were *considering* that?' Lirin asked.

'Yes,' Kal admitted. 'It was childish. But I've decided for myself that I want to learn surgery instead.'

'Why? What made you change?'

'I need to know how *they* think,' Kal said, nodding back toward the mansion. 'They're trained to speak their sentences in knots, and I have to be able to face them and talk back at them. Not fold like . . .' He hesitated.

'Like I did?' Lirin asked with a sigh.

Kal bit his lip, but had to ask. 'How many spheres did you agree to give him? Will I still have enough to go to Kharbranth?'

'I didn't give him a thing.'

'But—'

'Roshone and I talked for a time, arguing over amounts. I pretended to grow hotheaded and left.'

'Pretended?' Kal asked, confused.

His father leaned forward, whispering to make certain the driver couldn't hear. With the bouncing and the noise of the wheels on the stone, there was little danger of that. 'He has to think that I'm willing to bend. Today's meeting was about giving the *appearance* of desperation. A strong front at first, followed by frustration, letting him think that he'd gotten to me. Finally a retreat. He'll invite me again in a few months, after letting me "sweat."'

'But you won't bend then, either?' Kal whispered.

'No. Giving him any of the spheres would make him greedy for the rest. These lands don't produce as they used to, and Roshone is nearly broke from losing political battles. I still don't know which highlord was behind sending him here to torment us, though I wish I had him for a few moments in a dark room. . . .'

The ferocity with which Lirin said that shocked Kal. It was the closest he'd ever heard his father come to threatening real violence.

'But why go through this in the first place?' Kal whispered. 'You said that we can keep resisting him. Mother thinks so too. We won't eat well, but we won't starve.'

His father didn't reply, though he looked troubled.

'You need to make him think that we're capitulating,' Kal said. 'Or that we're close to doing so. So that he'll stop looking for ways to undermine us? So he'll focus his attention on making a deal and not—'

Kal froze. He saw something unfamiliar in his father's eyes. Something like guilt. Suddenly it made sense. Cold, terrible sense.

'Stormfather,' Kal whispered. 'You *did* steal the spheres, didn't you?'

His father remained silent, riding in the old carriage, shadowed and black.

'That's why you've been so tense since Wistiow died,' Kal whispered. 'The drinking, the worrying . . . You're a thief! We're a family of thieves.'

The carriage turned, and the violet light of Salas illuminated Lirin's face. He didn't look half so ominous from that angle – in fact, he looked fragile. He clasped his hands before him, eyes reflecting moonlight. 'Wistiow was not lucid during the final days, Kal,' he whispered. 'I knew that, with his death, we would lose the promise of a union. Laral had not reached her day of majority, and the new citylord wouldn't let a darkeyes take her inheritance through marriage.'

'So you *robbed* him?' Kal felt himself shrinking.

'I made certain that promises were kept. I had to do something. I couldn't trust to the generosity of the new citylord. Wisely, as you can see.'

All of this time, Kal had assumed that Roshone was persecuting them out of malice and spite. But it turned out he was *justified*. 'I can't believe it.'

'Does it change so much?' Lirin whispered. His face looked haunted in the dim light. 'What is different now?'

'Everything.'

'And yet nothing. Roshone still wants those spheres, and we still deserve them. Wistiow, if he'd been fully lucid, would have given us those spheres. I'm certain.'

'But he didn't.'

'No.'

Things were the same, yet different. One step, and the world flipped upside down. The villain became the hero, the hero the villain. 'I—' Kal said. 'I can't decide if what you did was incredibly brave or incredibly wrong.'

Lirin sighed. 'I know how you feel.' He sat back. 'Please, don't tell Tien what we've done.' What *we've* done. Hesina had helped him. 'When you are older, you'll understand.'

'Maybe,' Kal said, shaking his head. 'But one thing hasn't changed. I want to go to Kharbranth.'

'Even on stolen spheres?'

'I'll find a way to pay them back. Not to Roshone. To Laral.'

'She'll be a Roshone before too long,' Lirin said. 'We should expect an engagement between her and Rillir before the year is out. Roshone will not let her slip away, not now that he's lost political favor in Kholinar. She represents one of the few chances his son has for an alliance with a good house.'

Kal felt his stomach turn at the mention of Laral. 'I have to learn. Perhaps I can . . .'

Can what, he thought. *Come back and convince her to leave Rillir for me? Ridiculous.*

He looked up suddenly at his father, who had bowed his head, looking sorrowful. He *was* a hero. A villain too. But a hero to his family. 'I won't tell Tien,' Kal whispered. 'And I'm going to use the spheres to travel to Kharbranth and study.'

His father looked up.

'I want to learn to face lighteyes, like you do,' Kal said. 'Any of them can make a fool of me. I want to learn to talk like them, think like them.'

'I want you to learn so that you can help people, son. Not so you can get back at the lighteyes.'

'I think I can do both. If I can learn to be clever enough.'

Lirin snorted. 'You're plenty clever, son. You've got enough of your mother in you to talk circles around a lighteyes. The university will show you how, Kal.'

'I want to start going by my full name,' he replied, surprising himself. 'Kaladin.' It was a man's name. He'd always disliked how it sounded like the name of a lighteyes. Now it seemed to fit.

He wasn't a darkeyed farmer, but he wasn't a lighteyed lord either. Something in between. Kal had been a child who wanted to join the army because it was what other boys dreamed of. Kaladin would be a man who learned surgery and all the ways of the lighteyes. And someday he would return to this town and prove to Roshone, Rillir, and Laral herself that they had been wrong to dismiss him.

'Very well,' Lirin said. 'Kaladin.'

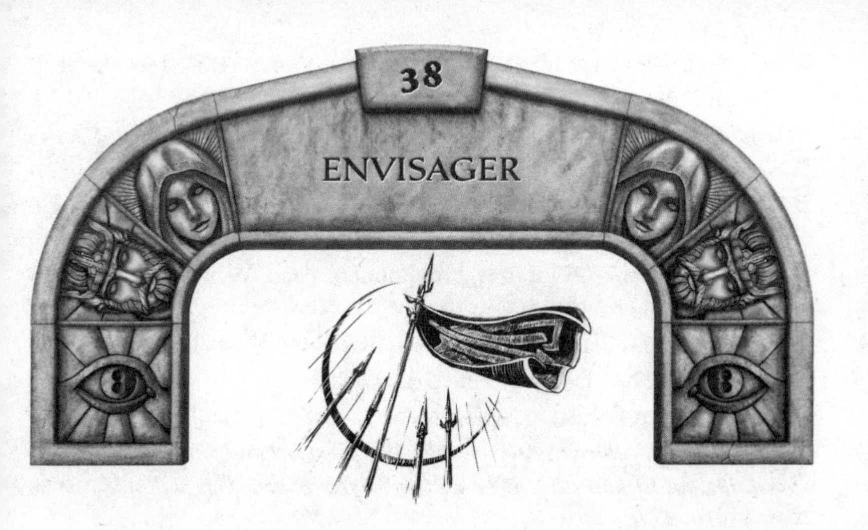

38

ENVISAGER

'Born from the darkness, they bear its taint still, marked upon their bodies much as the fire marks their souls.'

—I consider Gashash-son-Navammis a trustworthy source, though I'm not certain about this translation. Find the original quote in the fourteenth book of *Seld* and retranslate it myself, perhaps?

Kaladin floated.

Persistent fever, accompanied by cold sweats and hallucinations. Likely cause is infected wounds; clean with antiseptic to ward away rotspren. Keep the subject hydrated.

He was back in Hearthstone with his family. Only he was a grown man. The soldier he had become. And he didn't fit with them anymore. His father kept asking, How did this happen? You *said* you wanted to become a surgeon. A surgeon . . .

Broken ribs. Caused by trauma to the side, inflicted by a beating. Wrap the chest and prevent the subject from taking part in strenuous activity.

Occasionally, he'd open his eyes and see a dark room. It was cold, the walls made of stone, with a high roof. Other people lay in lines, covered in blankets. Corpses. They were corpses. This was a warehouse where they were lined up for sale. Who bought corpses?

Highprince Sadeas. He bought corpses. They still walked after he bought them, but they *were* corpses. The stupid ones refused to accept it, pretending they were alive.

Lacerations on face, arms, and chest. Outer layer of skin stripped away in several patches. Caused by prolonged exposure to highstorm winds. Bandage wounded areas, apply a denocax salve to encourage new skin growth.

Time was passing. A lot of it. He should be dead. Why wasn't he dead? He wanted to lie back and let it happen.

But no. *No*. He had failed Tien. He had failed Goshel. He had failed his parents. He had failed Dallet. Dear Dallet.

He would not fail Bridge Four. He would *not*!

Hypothermia, caused by extreme cold. Warm subject and force him to remain seated. Do not let him sleep. If he survives a few hours, there will likely be no lasting aftereffects.

If he survives a few hours . . .

Bridgemen weren't supposed to survive.

Why would Lamaril say that? What army would employ men who were supposed to die?

His perspective had been too narrow, too shortsighted. He needed to understand the army's objectives. He watched the battle's progress, horrified. What had he done?

He needed to go back and change it. But no. He was wounded, wasn't he? He was bleeding on the ground. He was one of the fallen spearmen. He was a bridgeman from Bridge Two, betrayed by those fools in Bridge Four, who diverted all of the archers.

How dare they? How *dare* they?

How dare they survive by killing me!

Strained tendons, ripped muscles, bruised and cracked bones, and pervasive soreness caused by extreme conditions. Enforce bed rest by any means necessary. Check for large and persistent bruises or pallor caused by internal hemorrhaging. That can be life-threatening. Be prepared for surgery.

He saw the deathspren. They were fist-size and black, with many legs and deep red eyes that glowed, leaving trails of burning light. They clustered around him, skittering this way and that. Their voices were whispers, scratchy sounds like paper being torn. They terrified him, but he couldn't escape them. He could barely move.

Only the dying could see deathspren. You saw them, then died. Only the very, very lucky few survived after that. Deathspren knew when the end was close.

Blistered fingers and toes, caused by frostnip. Make sure to apply antiseptic to any blisters that break. Encourage the body's natural healing. Permanent damage is unlikely.

Standing before the deathspren was a tiny figure of light. Not translucent, as she had always appeared before, but of pure white light. That soft, feminine face had a nobler, more angular cast to it now, like a warrior from a forgotten time. Not childlike at all. She stood guard on his chest, holding a sword made of light.

That glow was so pure, so sweet. It seemed to be the glow of life itself. Whenever one of the deathspren got too close, she would charge at it, wielding her radiant blade.

The light warded them off.

But there were a lot of deathspren. More and more each time he was lucid enough to look.

Severe delusions caused by trauma to the head. Maintain observation of subject. Do not allow alcohol intake. Enforce rest. Administer fathom bark to reduce cranial swelling. Firemoss can be used in extreme cases, but beware letting the subject form an addiction.

If medication fails, trepanning the skull may be needed to relieve pressure. Usually fatal.

⁂

Teft entered the barrack at midday. Ducking into the shadowy interior was like entering a cave. He glanced to the left, where the other wounded usually slept. They were all outside at the moment, getting some sun. All five were doing well, even Leyten.

Teft passed the lines of rolled-up blankets at the sides of the room, walking to the back of the chamber where Kaladin lay.

Poor man, Teft thought. *What's worse, being sick near to death, or having to stay all the way back here, away from the light?* It was necessary. Bridge Four walked a precarious line. They had been allowed to cut Kaladin down, and so far nobody had tried to stop them from caring for him. Practically the entire army had heard Sadeas give Kaladin to the Stormfather for judgment.

Gaz had come to see Kaladin, then had snorted to himself in

amusement. He'd likely told his superiors that Kaladin would die. Men didn't live long with wounds like those.

Yet Kaladin hung on. Soldiers were going out of their way to try to get a peek at him. His survival was incredible. People were talking in camp. Given to the Stormfather for judgment, then spared. A miracle. Sadeas wouldn't like that. How long would it be before one of the lighteyes decided to relieve their brightlord of the problem? Sadeas couldn't take any overt action – not without losing a great deal of credibility – but a quiet poisoning or suffocation would abbreviate the embarrassment.

So Bridge Four kept Kaladin as far from outside eyes as possible. And they always left someone with him. Always.

Storming man, Teft thought, kneeling beside the feverish patient in his tousled blankets, eyes closed, face sweaty, body bound with a frightful number of bandages. Most were stained red. They didn't have the money to change them often.

Skar kept watch currently. The short, strong-faced man sat at Kaladin's feet.

'How is he?' Teft asked.

Skar spoke softly. 'He seems to be getting worse, Teft. I heard him mumble about dark shapes, thrashing and telling them to keep back. He opened his eyes. He didn't seem to see me, but he saw *something*. I swear it.'

Deathspren, Teft thought, feeling a chill. *Kelek preserve us.*

'I'll take a turn,' Teft said, sitting. 'You go get something to eat.'

Skar stood, looking pale. It would crush the others' spirit for Kaladin to survive the highstorm, then die of his wounds. Skar shuffled from the room, shoulders slumped.

Teft watched Kaladin for a long while, trying to gather his thoughts, his emotions. 'Why now?' he whispered. 'Why here? After so many have watched and waited, you come here?'

But of course, Teft was getting ahead of himself. He didn't *know* for certain. He only had assumptions and hopes. No, not hopes – *fears*. He had rejected the Envisagers. And yet, here he was. He fished in his pocket and pulled out three small diamond spheres. It had been a long, long while since he'd saved anything of his wages, but he'd held on to these, thinking, worrying. They glowed with Stormlight in his hand.

Did he really want to know?

Gritting his teeth, Teft moved closer to Kaladin's side, looking down at the unconscious man's face. 'You bastard,' he whispered. 'You storming bastard. You took a bunch of hanged men and lifted them up just enough to breathe. Now you're going to leave them? I won't have it, you hear. I *won't.*'

He pressed the spheres into Kaladin's hand, wrapping the limp fingers around them, then laying the hand on Kaladin's abdomen. Then Teft sat back on his heels. What would happen? All the Envisagers had were stories and legends. Fool's tales, Teft had called them. Idle dreams.

He waited. Of course, nothing happened. *You're as big a fool as any, Teft*, he told himself. He reached for Kaladin's hand. Those spheres would buy a few drinks.

Kaladin gasped suddenly, drawing in a short, quick, powerful breath.

The glow in his hand faded.

Teft froze, eyes widening. Wisps of Light began to rise from Kaladin's body. It was faint, but there was no mistaking that glowing white Stormlight streaming off his frame. It was as if Kaladin had been bathed in sudden heat, and his very skin steamed.

Kaladin's eyes snapped open, and they leaked light too. He gasped again loudly, and the trailing wisps of light began to twist around the exposed cuts on his chest. A few of them pulled together and knit themselves up.

Then it was gone, the Light of those tiny chips expended. Kaladin's eyes closed and he relaxed. His wounds were still bad, his fever still raging, but some color had returned to his skin. The puffy redness around several cuts had diminished.

'My God,' Teft said, realizing he was trembling. 'Almighty, cast from heaven to dwell in our hearts . . . It is true.' He bowed his head to the rock floor, squeezing his eyes shut, tears leaking from their corners.

Why now? he thought again. *Why here?*

And, in the name of all heaven, why me?

He knelt for a hundred heartbeats, counting, thinking, worrying. Eventually, he pulled himself to his feet and retrieved the spheres – now dun – from Kaladin's hand. He'd need to trade them for spheres with Light in them. Then he could return and let Kaladin drain those as well.

He'd have to be careful. A few spheres each day, but not too many. If the boy healed too quickly, it would draw too much attention.

And I need to tell the Envisagers, he thought. *I need to . . .*

The Envisagers were gone. Dead, because of what he had done. If there were others, he had no idea how to locate them.

Who would he tell? Who would believe him? Kaladin himself probably didn't understand what he was doing.

Best to keep it quiet, at least until he could figure out what to do about it.

'Within a heartbeat, Alezarv was there, crossing a distance that would have taken more than four months to travel by foot.'

—Another folktale, this one recorded in *Among the Darkeyed*, by Calinam. Page 102. Stories of instantaneous travel and the Oathgates pervade these tales.

Shallan's hand flew across the drawing board, moving as if of its own accord, charcoal scratching, sketching, smudging. Thick lines first, like trails of blood left by a thumb drawn across rough granite. Tiny lines like scratches made by a pin.

She sat in her closetlike stone chamber in the Conclave. No windows, no ornamentation on the granite walls. Just the bed, her trunk, the nightstand, and the small desk that doubled as a drawing table.

A single ruby broam cast a bloody light on her sketch. Usually, to produce a vibrant drawing, she had to consciously memorize a scene. A blink, freezing the world, imprinting it into her mind. She hadn't done that during Jasnah's annihilation of the thieves. She'd been too frozen by horror or morbid fascination.

Despite that, she could see each of those scenes in her mind just as vividly as if she'd deliberately memorized them. And these memories didn't vanish when she drew them. She couldn't rid her mind of them. Those deaths were burned into her.

She sat back from her drawing board, hand shaking, the picture before her an exact charcoal representation of the suffocating nightscape, squeezed between alley walls, a tortured figure of flame rising toward the sky. At that moment, its face still held its shape, shadow eyes wide and burning lips agape. Jasnah's hand was toward the figure, as if warding, or worshipping.

Shallan drew her charcoal-stained fingers to her chest, staring at her creation. It was one of dozens of drawings she'd done during the last few days. The man turned into fire, the other frozen into crystal, the two transmuted to smoke. She could only draw one of those two fully; she'd been facing down the alleyway to the east. Her drawings of the fourth man's death were of smoke rising, clothing already on the ground.

She felt guilty for being unable to record his death. And she felt stupid for that guilt.

Logic did not condemn Jasnah. Yes, the princess had gone willingly into danger, but that didn't remove responsibility from those who had chosen to hurt her. The men's actions were reprehensible. Shallan had spent the days poring through books on philosophy, and most ethical frameworks exonerated the princess.

But Shallan had been there. She'd watched those men die. She'd seen the terror in their eyes, and she *felt* terrible. Hadn't there been another way?

Kill or be killed. That was the Philosophy of Starkness. It exonerated Jasnah.

Actions are not evil. Intent is evil, and Jasnah's intent had been to stop men from harming others. That was the Philosophy of Purpose. It lauded Jasnah.

Morality is separate from the ideals of men. It exists whole somewhere, to be approached – but never truly understood – by the mortal. The Philosophy of Ideals. It claimed that removing evil was ultimately moral, and so in destroying evil men, Jasnah was justified.

Objective must be weighed against methods. If the goal is worthy, then the steps taken are worthwhile, even if some of them – on their own – are reprehensible. The Philosophy of Aspiration. It, more than any, called Jasnah's actions ethical.

Shallan pulled the sheet from her drawing board and tossed it down beside the others scattered across her bed. Her fingers moved again, clutching the charcoal pencil, beginning a new picture on the blank sheet strapped in place on the table, unable to escape.

Her theft nagged at her as much as the killings did. Ironically, Jasnah's demand that Shallan study moralistic philosophy forced her to contemplate her own, terrible actions. She'd come to Kharbranth to steal the fabrial, then use it to save her brothers and their house from massive debt and destruction. Yet in the end, this wasn't why Shallan had stolen the Soulcaster. She'd taken it because she was angry with Jasnah.

If the intentions were more important than the action, then she had to condemn herself. Perhaps the Philosophy of Aspiration – which stated that objectives were more important than the steps taken to achieve them – would agree with what she'd done, but that was the philosophy she found most reprehensible. Shallan sat here sketching, condemning Jasnah. But Shallan was the one who had betrayed a woman who had trusted her and taken her in. Now she was planning to commit heresy with the Soulcaster by using it although she was not an ardent.

The Soulcaster itself lay in the hidden part of Shallan's trunk. Three days, and Jasnah had said nothing about the disappearance. She wore the fake each day. She said nothing, acted no differently. Maybe she hadn't tried Soulcasting. Almighty send that she didn't go out and put herself into danger again, expecting to be able to use the fabrial to kill men who attacked her.

Of course, there was one other aspect of that night that Shallan had to think of. She carried a concealed weapon that she hadn't used. She felt foolish for not even thinking of getting it out that night. But she wasn't accustomed to—

Shallan froze, realizing for the first time what she'd been drawing. Not another scene from the alleyway, but a lavish room with a thick, ornamented rug and swords on the walls. A long dining table, set with a half-eaten meal.

And a dead man in fine clothing, lying face-first on the floor, blood pooling around him. She jumped back, tossing aside the charcoal, then crumpled up the paper. Shaking, she moved over and sat down on the bed among the pictures. Dropping the crumpled drawing, she raised her fingers to her forehead, feeling the cold sweat there.

Something was wrong with her, with her drawings.

She had to get out. Escape the death, the philosophy and the questions. She stood and hurriedly strode into the main room of Jasnah's quarters. The princess herself was away researching, as always. She hadn't demanded that Shallan come to the Veil today. Was that because she realized that her ward needed time to think alone? Or was it because she suspected Shallan of stealing the Soulcaster, and no longer trusted her?

Shallan hurried through the room. It was furnished only with the basics provided by King Taravangian. Shallan pulled open the door to the hallway, and nearly ran into a master-servant who had been reaching up to knock.

The woman started, and Shallan let out a yelp. 'Brightness,' the woman said, bowing immediately. 'Apologies. But one of your spanreeds is flashing.' The woman held up the reed, affixed on the side with a small blinking ruby.

Shallan breathed in and out, stilling her heart. 'Thank you,' she said. She, like Jasnah, left her spanreeds in the care of servants because she was often away from her rooms, and was likely to miss any attempt to contact her.

Still flustered, she was tempted to leave the thing and continue on her way. However, she did need to speak with her brothers, Nan Balat particularly, and he'd been away the last few times she'd contacted home. She took the spanreed and closed the door. She didn't dare return to her rooms, with all of those sketches accusing her, but there was a desk and a spanreed board in the main room. She sat there, then twisted the ruby.

Shallan? the reed wrote. *Are you comfortable?* It was a code phrase, meant to indicate to her that it was indeed Nan Balat – or, at least, his betrothed – on the other side.

My back hurts and my wrist itches, she wrote back, giving the other half of the code phrase.

I'm sorry I missed your other communications, Nan Balat sent. *I had to attend a feast in Father's name. It was with Sur Kamar, so it wasn't really something I could miss, despite the day of traveling each way.*

It's all right, Shallan wrote. She took a deep breath. *I have the item*. She turned the gem.

The reed was still for a long moment. Finally, a hurried hand wrote, *Praise the Heralds. Oh, Shallan. You've done it! You are on your way back to us, then? How can you use the spanreed on the ocean? Are you in port?*

I haven't left, Shallan wrote.

What? Why?

Because it would be too suspicious, she wrote. *Think about it, Nan Balat. If Jasnah tries the item and finds it broken, she might not immediately decide that she's been had. That changes if I've suddenly and suspiciously left for home.*

I have to wait until she's made the discovery, then see what she does next. If she realizes that her fabrial was replaced with a fake, then I can deflect her toward other culprits. She's already suspicious of the ardentia. If – on the other hand – she assumes that her fabrial has broken somehow, I'll know we're free.

She twisted the gem, setting the spanreed in place.

The question she'd been expecting came next. *And if she immediately assumes that you did it? Shallan, what if you can't deflect her suspicion? What if she orders a search of your chambers and they find the hidden compartment?*

She picked up the pen. *Then it is still better for me to be here*, she wrote. *Balat, I have learned much about Jasnah Kholin. She is incredibly focused and determined. She will not let me escape if she thinks I have robbed her. She will hunt me down, and will use* all *of her resources to exact retribution. We'd have our own king and highprinces on our property in days, demanding that we turn over the fabrial. Stormfather! I'll bet Jasnah has contacts in Jah Keved that she could reach before I got back. I'd find myself in custody the moment I landed.*

Our only hope is to deflect her. If that doesn't work, better for me to be here and suffer her wrath quickly. Likely she would take the Soulcaster and banish me from her sight. If we make her work and chase after me, though . . . She can be very ruthless, Balat. It would not go well for us.

The response was long in coming. *When did you get so good at logic, small one?* he finally sent. *I see that you've thought this through. Better than I have, at least. But Shallan, our time is running out.*

I know, she wrote. *You said you could hold things together for a few more months. I ask you to do that. Give me two or three weeks, at least, to see what Jasnah does. Besides, while I am here, I can look into how the thing works. I haven't found any books that give hints, but there are so many here, maybe I just haven't found the right one yet.*

Very well, he wrote. *A few weeks. Be careful, small one. The men who gave Father his fabrial visited again. They asked after you. I'm worried about them.*

Even more than I worry about our finances. They disturb me in a profound way. Farewell.

Farewell, she wrote back.

So far, there had been no hint of reaction from the princess. She hadn't even mentioned the Soulcaster. That made Shallan nervous. She wished that Jasnah would just say something. The waiting was excruciating. Each day, while she sat with Jasnah, Shallan's stomach churned with anxiety until she was nauseated. At least – considering the killings a few days ago – Shallan had a very good excuse for looking disturbed.

Cold, calm logic. Jasnah herself would be proud.

A knock came at the door, and Shallan quickly gathered up the conversation she'd had with Nan Balat and burned it in the hearth. A palace maid entered a moment later, carrying a basket in the crook of her arm. She smiled at Shallan. It was time for the daily cleaning.

Shallan had a strange moment of panic at seeing the woman. She wasn't one of the maids Shallan recognized. What if Jasnah had sent her or someone else to search Shallan's room? Had she done so already? Shallan nodded to the woman and then – to assuage her worries – she walked to her room and closed the door. She rushed to the chest and checked the hidden compartment. The fabrial was there. She lifted it out, inspecting it. Would she know if Jasnah somehow reversed the exchange?

You're being foolish, she told herself. *Jasnah's subtle, but she's not* that *subtle.* Still, Shallan stuffed the Soulcaster in her safepouch. It just barely fit inside the envelope-like cloth container. She'd feel safer knowing she had it on her while the maid cleaned her room. Besides, the safepouch might be a better hiding place for it than her trunk.

By tradition, a woman's safepouch was where she kept items of intimate or very precious import. To search one would be like strip-searching her – considering her rank, either would be virtually unthinkable unless she were obviously implicated in a crime. Jasnah could probably force it. But if Jasnah could do that, she could order a search of Shallan's room, and her trunk would be under particular scrutiny. The truth was, if Jasnah chose to suspect her, there would be little Shallan could do to hide the fabrial. So the safepouch was as good a place as any.

She gathered up the pictures she'd drawn and put them upside-down on the desk, trying not to look at them. She didn't want those to be seen by the maid. Finally, she left, taking her portfolio. She felt that she needed to get outside and escape for a while. Draw something other than death and murder. The conversation with Nan Balat had only served to upset her more.

'Brightness?' the maid asked.

Shallan froze, but the maid held up a basket. 'This was dropped off for you with the master-servants.'

She hesitantly accepted it, looking inside. Bread and jam. A note, tied to one of the jars, read: *Bluebar jam. If you like it, it means you're mysterious, reserved, and thoughtful.* It was signed Kabsal.

Shallan placed the basket's handle in the crook of her safearm's elbow. Kabsal. Maybe she should go find him. She always felt better after a conversation with him.

But no. She was going to leave; she couldn't keep stringing him, or herself, along. She was afraid of where the relationship was going. Instead, she made her way to the main cavern and then to the Conclave's exit. She walked out into the sunlight and took a deep breath, looking up into the sky as servants and attendants parted around her, swarming in and out of the Conclave. She held her portfolio close, feeling the cool breeze on her cheeks and the contrasting warmth of the sunlight pressing down on her hair and forehead.

In the end, the most disturbing part was that Jasnah had been right. Shallan's world of simple answers had been a foolish, childish place. She'd clung to the hope that she could find truth, and use it to explain – perhaps justify – what she had done back in Jah Keved. But if there was such a thing as truth, it was far more complicated and murky than she'd assumed.

Some problems didn't seem to have any good answers. Just a lot of wrong ones. She could choose the source of her guilt, but she couldn't choose to be rid of that guilt entirely.

⁂

Two hours – and about twenty quick sketches – later, Shallan felt far more relaxed.

She sat in the palace gardens, sketchpad in her lap, drawing snails. The gardens weren't as extensive as her father's, but they were far more varied, not to mention blessedly secluded. Like many modern gardens, they were designed with walls of cultivated shalebark. This one's made a maze of living stone. They were short enough that, when standing, she could see the way back to the entrance. But if she sat down on one of the numerous benches, she could feel alone and unseen.

She'd asked a groundskeeper the name of the most prominent shalebark plant; he'd called it 'plated stone.' A fitting name, as it grew in thin round sections that piled atop one another, like plates in a cupboard. From the sides, it looked like weathered rock that exposed hundreds of thin strata. Tiny little tendrils grew up out of pores, waving in the wind. The stonelike casings had a bluish shade, but the tendrils were yellowish.

Her current subject was a snail with a low horizontal shell edged with little ridges. When she tapped, it would flatten itself into a rift in the shalebark, appearing to become part of the plated stone. It blended in perfectly. When she let it move, it nibbled at the shalebark – but didn't chew it away.

It's cleaning the shalebark, she realized, continuing her sketch. *Eating off the lichen and mold*. Indeed, a cleaner trail extended behind it.

Patches of a different kind of shalebark – with fingerlike protrusions growing up into the air from a central knob – grew alongside the plated stone. When she looked closely, she noted little cremlings – thin and multilegged – crawling along it, eating at it. Were they too cleaning it?

Curious, she thought, beginning a sketch of the miniature cremlings. They had carapaces shaded like the shalebark's fingers, while the snail's shell was a near duplicate of the yellow and blue colorings of the plated stone. It was as if they had been designed by the Almighty in pairs, the plant giving safety to the animal, the animal cleaning the plant.

A few lifespren – tiny, glowing green specks – floated around the shalebark mounds. Some danced amid the rifts in the bark, others in the air like dust motes zigzagging up, only to fall again.

She used a finer-tipped charcoal pencil to scribble some thoughts about the relationship between the animals and the plants. She didn't know of any books that spoke of relationships like this one. Scholars seemed to prefer studying big, dynamic animals, like greatshells or whitespines. But this seemed a beautiful, wondrous discovery to Shallan.

Snails and plants can help one another, she thought. *But I betray Jasnah.*

She glanced toward her safehand, and the pouch hidden inside. She felt more secure having the Soulcaster near. She hadn't yet dared try to use it. She'd been too nervous about the theft, and had worried about using the object near Jasnah. Now, however, she was in a nook deep within the maze, with only one curving entrance into her dead end. She stood up casually, looking around. No one else was in the gardens, and she was far enough inside that it would take minutes for anyone to get to her.

Shallan sat back down, setting aside her drawing pad and pencil. *I might as well see if I can figure out how to use it*, she thought. *Maybe there's no need to keep searching the Palanaeum for a solution.* So long as she stood up and glanced about periodically, she could be certain she wouldn't be approached or seen by accident.

She removed the forbidden device. It was heavy in her hand. Solid. Taking a deep breath, she looped the chains over her fingers and around her wrist, the gemstones set against the back of her hand. The metal was cold, the chains loose. She flexed her hand, pulling the fabrial tight.

She'd anticipated a feeling of power. Prickles on her skin, perhaps, or a sense of strength and might. But there was nothing.

She tapped the three gemstones – she'd placed her smokestone into the third setting. Some other fabrials, like spanreeds, worked when you tapped the stones. But that was foolish, as she'd never seen Jasnah do that. The woman just closed her eyes and touched something, Soulcasting it. Smoke, crystal, and fire were what this Soulcaster was best at. Only once had she seen Jasnah create anything else.

Hesitant, Shallan took a piece of broken shalebark from the base of one of the plants. She held it up in her freehand, then closed her eyes.

Become smoke! she commanded.

Nothing happened.

Become crystal! she commanded instead.

She cracked an eye. There was no change.

Fire. Burn! You're fire! You—

She paused, realizing the stupidity of that. A mysteriously burned hand? No, that wouldn't be *at all* suspicious. Instead, she focused on crystal. She closed her eyes again, holding the image of a piece of quartz in her mind. She tried to *will* the shalebark to change.

Nothing happened, so she just tried focusing, imagining the shalebark transforming. After a few minutes of failure, she tried making the pouch change instead, then tried the bench, then tried one of her hairs. Nothing worked.

Shallan checked to make certain she was still alone, then sat down, frustrated. Nan Balat had asked Luesh how the devices worked, and he'd said that it was easier to show than explain. He'd promised to give them answers if she actually managed to steal Jasnah's.

Now he was dead. Was she doomed to carry this one back to her family, only to immediately give it away to those dangerous men, never using it to gain wealth to protect her house? All because they didn't know how to activate it?

The other fabrials she'd used had been simple to activate, but those were constructed by contemporary artifabrians. Soulcasters were fabrials from ancient times. They wouldn't employ modern methods of activation. She stared at the glowing gemstones suspended on the back of her hand. How would she figure out the method of using a tool thousands of years old, one forbidden to any but ardents?

She slid the Soulcaster back into her safepouch. It seemed she was back to searching the Palanaeum. That or asking Kabsal. But would she manage that without looking suspicious? She broke out his bread and jam, eating and thinking idly. If Kabsal didn't know, and if she couldn't find the answers by the time she left Kharbranth, were there other options? If she took the artifact to the Veden king – or maybe the ardents – might they be able to protect her family in exchange for the gift? After all, she couldn't really be blamed for stealing from a heretic, and so long as Jasnah didn't know who had the Soulcaster, they would be safe.

For some reason, that made her feel even worse. Stealing the Soulcaster to save her family was one thing, but turning it over to the very ardents whom Jasnah disdained? It seemed a greater betrayal.

Yet another difficult decision. *Well then*, she thought, *it's a good thing Jasnah is so determined to train me in how to deal with those. By the time all this is done, I should be quite the expert. . . .*

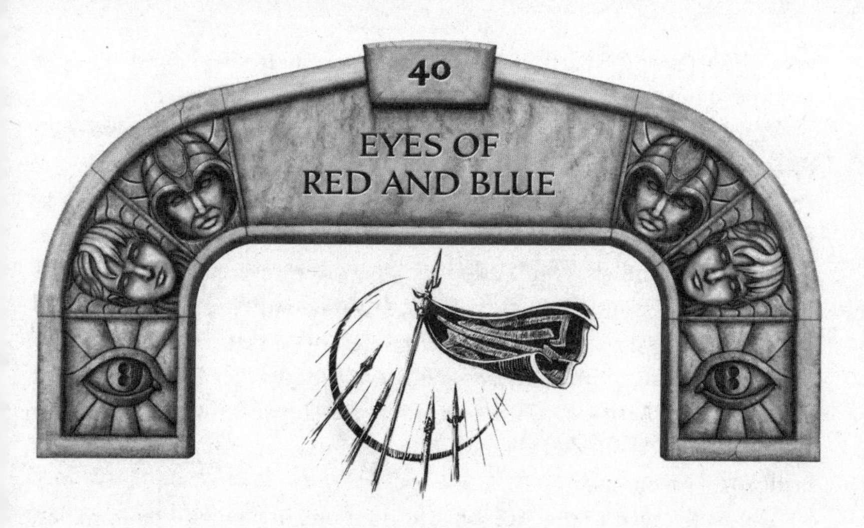

'Death upon the lips. Sound upon the air. Char upon the skin.'

—From 'The Last Desolation' by Ambrian, line 335.

Kaladin stumbled into the light, shading his eyes against the burning sun, his bare feet feeling the transition from cold indoor stone to sun-warmed stone outside. The air was lightly humid, not muggy as it had been in previous weeks.

He rested his hand on the wooden doorframe, his legs quivering rebelliously, his arms feeling as if he'd carried a bridge for three days straight. He breathed deeply. His side should have blazed with pain, but he felt only a residual soreness. Some of his deeper cuts were still scabbed over, but the smaller ones had vanished completely. His head was surprisingly clear. He didn't even have a headache.

He rounded the side of the barrack, feeling stronger with each step, though he kept his hand on the wall. Lopen followed behind; the Herdazian had been watching over Kaladin when he awoke.

I should be dead, Kaladin thought. *What is going on?*

On the other side of the barrack he was surprised to find the men carrying their bridge in daily practice. Rock ran at the front center, giving the marching beat as Kaladin had once done. They reached the other side of the lumberyard and turned around, charging back. Only when they were almost past the barrack did one of the men in front – Moash – notice Kaladin. He froze, nearly causing the entire bridge crew to trip.

'What is wrong with you?' Torfin yelled from behind, head enveloped by the wood of the bridge.

Moash didn't listen. He ducked out from under the bridge, looking at Kaladin with wide eyes. Rock gave a hasty shout for the men to put down the bridge. More saw him, adopting the same reverent expressions as Moash. Hobber and Peet, their wounds sufficiently healed, had started practicing with the others. That was good. They'd be drawing pay again.

The men walked up to Kaladin, silent in their leather vests. They kept their distance, hesitant, as if he were fragile. Or holy. Kaladin was bare-chested, his nearly healed wounds exposed, and wore only his knee-length bridgeman's trousers.

'You really need to practice what to do if one of you trips or stumbles, men,' Kaladin said. 'When Moash stopped abruptly, you all about fell over. That could be a disaster on the field.'

They stared at him, incredulous, and he couldn't help but smile. In a moment, they crowded around him, laughing and thumping him on the back. It wasn't an entirely appropriate welcome for a sick man, particularly when Rock did it, but Kaladin did appreciate their enthusiasm.

Only Teft didn't join in. The aging bridgeman stood at the side, arms folded. He seemed concerned. 'Teft?' Kaladin asked. 'You all right?'

Teft snorted, but showed a hint of a grin. 'I just figure those lads don't bathe often enough for me to want to get close enough for a hug. No offense.'

Kaladin laughed. 'I understand.' His last 'bath' had been the highstorm.

The highstorm.

The other bridgemen continued to laugh, asking how he felt, proclaiming that Rock would have to fix something *extra* special for their nightly fireside meal. Kaladin smiled and nodded, assuring them he felt well, but he was remembering the storm.

He recalled it distinctly. Holding to the ring atop the building, his head down and eyes closed against the pelting torrent. He remembered Syl, standing protectively before him, as if she could turn back the storm itself. He couldn't see her about now. Where was she?

He also remembered the face. The Stormfather himself? Surely not. A delusion. Yes . . . yes, he'd certainly been delusional. Memories of deathspren were blended with relived parts of his life – and both mixed with strange, sudden *shocks* of strength – icy cold, but refreshing. It had been like the cold air of a crisp morning after a long night in a stuffy room, or like rubbing the sap of gulket leaves on sore muscles, making them feel warm and cold at the same time.

He could remember those moments so clearly. What had caused them? The fever?

'How long?' he said, checking over the bridgemen, counting them. Thirty-three, counting Lopen and the silent Dabbid. Almost all were accounted for. Impossible. If his ribs were healed, then he must have been unconscious for four weeks, at least. How many bridge runs?

'Ten days,' Moash said.

'Impossible,' Kaladin said. 'My wounds—'

'Is why we're so surprised to see you up and walking!' Rock said, laughing. 'You must have bones like granite. Is my name you should be having!'

Kaladin leaned back against the wall. Nobody corrected Moash. An entire crew of men couldn't lose track of the weeks like that. 'Idolir and Treff?' he asked.

'We lost them,' Moash said, growing solemn. 'We did two bridge runs while you were unconscious. Nobody badly wounded, but two dead. We . . . we didn't know how to help them.'

That made the men grow subdued. But death was the way of bridgemen, and they couldn't afford to dwell for long on the lost. Kaladin did decide, however, that he'd need to train a few of the others in healing.

But how was he up and walking? Had he been less injured than he'd assumed? Hesitantly, he prodded at his side, feeling for broken ribs. Just a little sore. Other than the weakness, he felt as healthy as he ever had. Perhaps he should have paid a little more attention to his mother's religious teachings.

As the men turned back to talking and celebrating, he noticed the looks they gave him. Respectful, reverent. They remembered what he'd said before the highstorm. Looking back, Kaladin realized he'd been a little delirious. It now seemed an incredibly arrogant proclamation, not to mention that it smelled of prophecy. If the ardents discovered that . . .

Well, he couldn't undo what he'd done. He'd just have to continue. *You were already balancing over a chasm*, Kaladin thought to himself. *Did you have to scale an even* higher *cliffside?*

A sudden, mournful horn call sounded across the camp. The bridgemen fell silent. The horn sounded twice more.

'Figures,' Natam said.

'We're on duty?' Kaladin asked.

'Yeah,' Moash said.

'Line up!' Rock snapped. 'You know what to do! Let's show Captain Kaladin that we haven't forgotten how to do this.'

'"Captain" Kaladin?' Kaladin asked as the men lined up.

'Sure, gancho,' Lopen said from beside him, speaking with that quick accent that seemed so at odds with his nonchalant attitude. 'They tried to make Rock bridgeleader, sure, but we just started calling you "captain" and him "squadleader." Made Gaz angry.' Lopen grinned.

Kaladin nodded. The other men were so joyous, but he was finding it difficult to share their mood.

As they formed up around their bridge, he began to realize the source of his melancholy. His men were right back where they'd started. Or worse. He was weakened and injured, and had offended the highprince himself. Sadeas would not be pleased when he learned that Kaladin had survived his fever.

The bridgemen were still destined to be cut down one by one. The side carry had been a failure. He hadn't saved his men, he'd just given them a short stay of execution.

Bridgemen aren't supposed to survive. . . .

He suspected why that was. Gritting his teeth, he let go of the barrack wall and crossed to where the bridgemen stood in line, leaders of the subsquads doing a quick check of their vests and sandals.

Rock eyed Kaladin. 'And what is this thing you believe you are doing?'

'I'm joining you,' Kaladin said.

'And what would you tell one of the men if *they* had just gotten up from a week with the fevers?'

Kaladin hesitated. *I'm not like the other men*, he thought, then regretted it. He couldn't start believing himself invincible. To run now with the crew, as weak as he was, would be sheer idiocy. 'You're right.'

'You can help me and the moolie carry water, gancho,' Lopen said. 'We're a team now. Go on every run.'

Kaladin nodded. 'All right.'

Rock eyed him.

'If I'm feeling too weak at the end of the permanent bridges, I'll go back. I promise.'

Rock nodded reluctantly. The men marched under the bridge to the staging area, and Kaladin joined Lopen and Dabbid, filling waterskins.

⁂

Kaladin stood at the edge of the precipice, hands clasped behind his back, sandaled toes at the very edge of the cliff. The chasm stared up at him, but he did not meet its gaze. He was focused on the battle being waged on the next plateau.

This approach had been an easy one; they'd arrived at the same time as the Parshendi. Instead of bothering to kill bridgemen, the Parshendi had taken a defensive position in the center of the plateau, around the chrysalis. Now Sadeas's men fought them.

Kaladin's brow was slick with sweat from the day's heat, and he still felt a lingering exhaustion from his sickness. Yet it wasn't nearly as bad as it should have been. The surgeon's son was baffled.

For the moment, the soldier overruled the surgeon. He was transfixed by the battle. Alethi spearmen in leathers and breastplates pressed a curved line against the Parshendi warriors. Most Parshendi used battle-axes or hammers, though a few wielded swords or clubs. They all had that red-orange armor growing from their skin, and they fought in pairs, singing all the while.

It was the worst kind of battle, the kind that was close. Often, you'd lose far fewer men in a skirmish where your enemies quickly gained the upper hand. When that happened, your commander would order the retreat to cut his losses. But close battles . . . they were brutal, blood-soaked things. Watching the fighting – the bodies dropped to the rocks, the weapons flashing, the men pushed off the plateau – reminded him of his first fights as a spearman. His commander had been shocked at how easily Kaladin dealt with seeing blood. Kaladin's father would have been shocked at how easily Kaladin spilled it.

There was a big difference between his battles in Alethkar and the fights on the Shattered Plains. There, he'd been surrounded by the worst – or at least worst-trained – soldiers in Alethkar. Men who didn't hold their lines. And yet, for all their disorder, those fights had made sense to him. These here on the Shattered Plains still did not.

That had been his miscalculation. He'd changed battlefield tactics before understanding them. He would not make that mistake again.

Rock stepped up beside Kaladin, joined by Sigzil. The thick-limbed Horneater made for quite a contrast to the short, quiet Azish man. Sigzil's skin was a deep brown – not true black, like some parshmen's. He tended to keep to himself.

'Is bad battle,' Rock said, folding his arms. 'The soldiers will not be happy, whether or not they win.'

Kaladin nodded absently, listening to the yells, screams, and curses. 'Why do they fight, Rock?'

'For money,' Rock said. 'And for vengeance. You should know this thing. Is it not your king who Parshendi killed?'

'Oh, I understand why *we* fight,' Kaladin said. 'But the Parshendi. Why do *they* fight?'

Rock grinned. 'Is because they don't very much like the idea of being beheaded for killing your king, I should think! Very unaccommodating of them.'

Kaladin smiled, though he found mirth unnatural while watching men die. He had been trained too long by his father for any death to leave him unmoved. 'Perhaps. But, then, why do they fight for the gemhearts? Their numbers are dwindling because of skirmishes like these.'

'You know this thing?' Rock asked.

'They raid less frequently than they used to,' Kaladin said. 'People talk about it in camp. And they don't strike as close to the Alethi side as they once did.'

Rock nodded thoughtfully. 'It seems logical. Ha! Perhaps we will soon win this fight and be going home.'

'No,' Sigzil said softly. He had a very formal way of speaking, with barely a hint of an accent. What language did the Azish speak, anyway? Their kingdom was so distant that Kaladin had only ever met one other. 'I doubt that. And I can tell you why they fight, Kaladin.'

'Really?'

'They must have Soulcasters. They need the gemstones for the same reason we do. To make food.'

'It sounds reasonable,' Kaladin said, hands still clasped behind his back, feet in a wide stance. Parade rest still felt natural to him. 'Just conjecture, but a reasonable one. Let me ask you something else, then. Why can't bridgemen have shields?'

'Because this thing makes us too slow,' Rock said.

'No,' Sigzil said. 'They could send bridgemen with shields out in front of the bridges, running in front of us. It wouldn't slow anyone down. Yes, you would have to field more bridgemen – but you'd save enough lives with those shields to make up for the larger roster.'

Kaladin nodded. 'Sadeas fields more of us than he needs already. In most cases, more bridges land than he needs.'

'But why?' Sigzil asked.

'Because we make good targets,' Kaladin said softly, understanding. 'We're put out in front to draw Parshendi attention.'

'Of course we are,' Rock said, shrugging. 'Armies always do these things. The poorest and the least trained go first.'

'I know,' Kaladin said, 'but usually, they're at least given some measure of protection. Don't you see? We're not just an expendable initial wave. We're *bait*. We're exposed, so the Parshendi can't help but fire at us. It allows the regular soldiers to approach without being hurt. The Parshendi archers are aiming at the bridgemen.'

Rock frowned.

'Shields would make us less tempting,' Kaladin said. 'That's why he forbids them.'

'Perhaps,' Sigzil said from the side, thoughtful. 'But it seems foolish to waste troops.'

'Actually, it *isn't* foolish,' Kaladin said. 'If you have to repeatedly attack fortified positions, you can't afford to lose your trained troops. Don't you see? Sadeas has only a limited number of trained men. But untrained ones are easy to find. Each arrow that strikes down a bridgeman is one that *doesn't* hit a soldier you've spent a great deal of money outfitting and training. That's why it's better for Sadeas to field a large number of bridgemen, rather than a smaller – but protected – number.'

He should have seen it earlier. He had been distracted by how important bridgemen were to the battles. If the bridges didn't arrive at the chasms, then the army couldn't cross. But each bridge crew was kept well stocked with bodies, and twice as many bridge crews were sent on an assault as were needed.

Seeing a bridge fall must give the Parshendi a great sense of satisfaction, and they usually got to drop two or three bridges on every bad chasm run. Sometimes more. So long as bridgemen were dying, and the Parshendi didn't spend their time firing on soldiers, Sadeas had reason to keep the bridgemen vulnerable. The Parshendi should have seen through it, but it was very hard to turn your arrow away from the unarmored man carrying the siege equipment. The Parshendi were said to be unsophisticated fighters. Indeed, watching the battle on the other plateau – studying it, focusing – he saw that was true.

Where the Alethi maintained a straight, disciplined line – each man protecting his partners – the Parshendi attacked in independent pairs. The Alethi had superior technique and tactics. True, each of the Parshendi was superior in strength, and their skill with those axes was remarkable. But Sadeas's Alethi troops were well trained in modern formations. Once they got a foothold – and if they could prolong the battle – their discipline often saw them to victory.

The Parshendi haven't fought in large-scale battles before this war, Kaladin decided. *They're used to smaller skirmishes, perhaps against other villages or clans.*

Several of the other bridgemen joined Kaladin, Rock, and Sigzil. Before long, the majority of them were standing there, some imitating Kaladin's stance. It took another hour before the battle was won. Sadeas proved victorious, but Rock was right. The soldiers were grim; they'd lost many friends this day.

It was a tired, battered group of spearmen that Kaladin and the others led back to camp.

A few hours later, Kaladin sat on a chunk of wood beside Bridge Four's nightly fire. Syl sat on his knee, having taken the form of a small, translucent blue and white flame. She'd come to him during the march back, spinning around gleefully to see him up and walking, but had given no explanation for her absence.

The real fire crackled and popped, Rock's large pot bubbling on top of it, some flamespren dancing on the logs. Every couple of seconds, someone asked Rock if the stew was done yet, often banging on his bowl with a good-natured smack of the spoon. Rock said nothing, stirring. They all knew that nobody ate until he declared the stew finished; he was very particular about not serving 'inferior' food.

The air smelled of boiling dumplings. The men were laughing. Their bridgeleader had survived execution and today's bridge run hadn't cost a single casualty. Spirits were high.

Except for Kaladin's.

He understood now. He understood just how futile their struggle was. He understood why Sadeas hadn't bothered to acknowledge Kaladin's survival. He was already a bridgeman, and being a bridgeman was a death sentence.

Kaladin had hoped to show Sadeas that his bridge crew could be efficient and useful. He'd hoped to prove that they deserved protection – shields, armor, training. Kaladin thought that if they acted like soldiers, maybe they would be *seen* as soldiers.

None of that would work. A bridgeman who survived was, by definition, a bridgeman who had failed.

His men laughed and enjoyed the fire. They trusted him. He'd done the impossible, surviving a highstorm, wounded, tied to a wall. Surely he would perform another miracle, this time for them. They were good men, but they thought like foot soldiers. The officers and the lighteyes would worry about the long term. The men were fed and happy, and that was enough for now.

Not for Kaladin.

He found himself face-to-face with the man he'd left behind. The one he'd abandoned that night he'd decided not to throw himself into the chasm. A man with haunted eyes, a man who had given up on caring or hoping. A walking corpse.

I'm going to fail them, he thought.

He couldn't let them continue running bridges, dying off one by one. But he also couldn't think of an alternative. And so their laughter tore at him.

One of the men – Maps – stood, holding up his arms, quieting the others. It was the time between moons, and so he was lit mostly by the firelight; there was a spray of stars in the sky above. Several of those moved about, the tiny pinpricks of light chasing after one another, zipping around like distant, glowing insects. Starspren. They were rare.

Maps was a flat-faced fellow, his beard bushy, his eyebrows thick.

Everyone called him Maps because of the birthmark on his chest that he swore was an exact map of Alethkar, though Kaladin hadn't been able to see the resemblance.

Maps cleared his throat. 'It's a good night, a special night, and all. We've got our bridgeleader back.'

Several of the men clapped. Kaladin tried not to show how sick he felt inside.

'We've got good food coming,' Maps said. He eyed Rock. 'It *is* coming, ain't it, Rock?'

'Is coming,' Rock said, stirring.

'You're sure about that? We could go on another bridge run. Give you a little extra time, you know, five or six more hours. . . .'

Rock gave him a fierce look. The men laughed, several banging their bowls with their spoons. Maps chuckled, then he reached to the ground behind the stone he was using for a seat. He pulled out a paper-wrapped package and tossed it to Rock.

Surprised, the tall Horneater barely caught it, nearly dropping it into the stew.

'From all of us,' Maps said, a little awkwardly, 'for making us stew each night. Don't think we haven't noticed how hard you work on it. We relax while you cook. And you always serve everyone else first. So we bought you something to thank you.' He wiped his nose on his arm, spoiling the moment slightly, and sat back down. Several of the other bridgemen thumped him on the back, complimenting his speech.

Rock unwrapped the package and stared into it for a long while. Kaladin leaned forward, trying to get a look at the contents. Rock reached in and held the item up. It was a straight razor of gleaming silvery steel; there was a length of wood covering the sharp side. Rock pulled this off, inspecting the blade. 'You airsick fools,' he said softly. 'Is beautiful.'

'There's a piece of polished steel too,' said Peet. 'For a mirror. And some beard soap and a leather strop for sharpening.'

Amazingly, Rock grew teary-eyed. He turned away from the pot, bearing his gifts. 'Stew is ready,' he said. Then he ran into the barrack building.

The men sat quietly. 'Stormfather,' youthful Dunny finally said, 'you think we did the right thing? I mean, the way he complains and all . . .'

'I think it was perfect,' Teft said. 'Just give the big lout some time to recover.'

'Sorry we didn't get you nothin', sir,' Maps said to Kaladin. 'We didn't know you'd be awake and all.'

'It's all right,' Kaladin said.

'Well,' Skar said. 'Is someone going to serve that stew, or will we all just sit here hungry until it burns?'

Dunny jumped up, grabbing the ladle. The men gathered around the pot, jostling one another as Dunny served. Without Rock there to snap at them and keep them in line, it was something of a melee. Only Sigzil did not join in. The quiet, dark-skinned man sat to the side, eyes reflecting the flames.

Kaladin rose. He was worried – terrified, really – that he might become that wretch again. The one who had given up on caring because he saw no alternative. So he sought conversation, walking over toward Sigzil. His motion disturbed Syl, who sniffed and buzzed up onto his shoulder. She still held the form of a flickering flame; having that on his shoulder was even *more* distracting. He didn't say anything; if she knew it bothered him, she'd be likely to do it more. She *was* still a windspren, after all.

Kaladin sat down next to Sigzil. 'Not hungry?'

'They are more eager than I,' Sigzil said. 'If previous evenings are a reliable guide, there will still be enough for me once they have filled their bowls.'

Kaladin nodded. 'I appreciated your analysis out on the plateau today.'

'I am good at that, sometimes.'

'You're educated. You speak like it and you act like it.'

Sigzil hesitated. 'Yes,' he finally said. 'Among my people, it is not a sin for a male to be keen of mind.'

'It isn't a sin for Alethi either.'

'My experience is that you care only about wars and the art of killing.'

'And what have you seen of us besides our army?'

'Not much,' Sigzil admitted.

'So, a man of education,' Kaladin said thoughtfully. 'In a bridge crew.'

'My education was never completed.'

'Neither was mine.'

Sigzil looked at him, curious.

'I apprenticed as a surgeon,' Kaladin said.

Sigzil nodded, thick dark hair falling around his shoulders. He'd been one of the only bridgemen who bothered shaving. Now that Rock had a razor, maybe that would change. 'A surgeon,' he said. 'I cannot say that is surprising, considering how you handled the wounded. The men say that you're secretly a lighteyes of very high rank.'

'*What?* But my eyes are dark brown!'

'Pardon me,' Sigzil said. 'I didn't speak the right word – you don't *have* the right word in your language. To you, a lighteyes is the same as a leader. In other kingdoms, though, other things make a man a . . . curse this Alethi language. A man of high birth. A brightlord, only without the eyes. Anyway, the men think you must have been raised outside of Alethkar. As a leader.'

Sigzil looked back at the others. They were beginning to sit back down, attacking their stew with vigor. 'It's the way you lead so naturally, the way you make others want to listen to you. These are things they associate with lighteyes. And so they have invented a past for you. You will have a difficult time disabusing them of it now.' Sigzil eyed him. 'Assuming it is a fabrication. I was there in the chasm the day you used that spear.'

'A spear,' Kaladin said. 'A darkeyed soldier's weapon, not a lighteyes's sword.'

'To many bridgemen, the difference is minimal. All are so far above us.'

'So what is your story?'

Sigzil smirked. 'I wondered if you were going to ask. The others mentioned that you have pried into their origins.'

'I like to know the men I lead.'

'And if some of us are murderers?' Sigzil asked quietly.

'Then I'm in good company,' Kaladin said. 'If it was a lighteyes you killed, then I might buy you a drink.'

'Not a lighteyes,' Sigzil said. 'And he is not dead.'

'Then you're not a murderer,' Kaladin said.

'Not for want of trying.' Sigzil's eyes grew distant. 'I thought for certain I had succeeded. It was not the wisest choice I made. My master . . .' He trailed off.

'Is he the one you tried to kill?'

'No.'

Kaladin waited, but no more information was forthcoming. *A scholar,* he thought. *Or at least a man of learning. There has to be a way to use this.*

Find a way out of this death trap, Kaladin. Use what you have. There has *to be a way.*

'You were right about the bridgemen,' Sigzil said. 'We are sent to die. It is the only reasonable explanation. There is a place in the world. Marabethia. Have you heard of it?'

'No,' Kaladin said.

'It is beside the sea, to the north, in the Selay lands. The people are known for their great fondness for debate. At each intersection in the city they have small pedestals on which a man can stand and proclaim his arguments. It is said that everyone in Marabethia carries a pouch with an overripe fruit just in case they pass a proclaimer with whom they disagree.'

Kaladin frowned. He hadn't heard so many words from Sigzil in all the time they'd been bridgemen together.

'What you said earlier, on the plateau,' Sigzil continued, eyes forward, 'it made me think of the Marabethians. You see, they have a curious way of treating condemned criminals. They dangle them over the seaside cliff near the city, down near the water at high tide, with a cut sliced in each cheek. There is a particular species of greatshell in the depths there. The creatures are known for their succulent flavor, and of course they have gemhearts. Not nearly as large as the ones in these chasmfiends, but still nice. So the criminals, they become bait. A criminal may demand execution instead, but they say if you hang there for a week and are not eaten, then you can go free.'

'And does that often happen?' Kaladin asked.

Sigzil shook his head. 'Never. But the prisoners almost always take the chance. The Marabethians have a saying for someone who refuses to see the truth of a situation. "You have eyes of red and blue," they say. Red for the blood dripping. Blue for the water. It is said that these two things are all the prisoners see. Usually they are attacked within one day. And yet, most still wish to take that chance. They prefer the false hope.'

Eyes of red and blue, Kaladin thought, imagining the morbid picture.

'You do a good work,' Sigzil said, rising, picking up his bowl. 'At first, I hated you for lying to the men. But I have come to see that a false hope makes them happy. What you do is like giving medicine to a sick man to ease his pain until he dies. Now these men can spend their last days in laughter. You are a healer indeed, Kaladin Stormblessed.'

Kaladin wanted to object, to say that it wasn't a false hope, but he couldn't. Not with his heart in his stomach. Not with what he knew.

A moment later, Rock burst from the barrack. 'I feel like a true *alil'tiki'i* again!' he proclaimed, holding aloft his razor. 'My friends, you cannot know what you have done! Someday, I will take you to the Peaks and show you the hospitality of kings!'

Despite all of his complaining, he hadn't shaved his beard off completely. He had left long, red-blond sideburns, which curved down to his chin. The tip of the chin itself was shaved clean, as were his lips. On the tall, oval-faced man, the look was quite distinctive. 'Ha!' Rock said, striding up to the fire. He grabbed the nearest men there and hugged them both to him, causing Bisig to nearly spill his stew. 'I will make you all family for this. A peak dweller's *humaka'aban* is his pride! I feel like a true man again. Here. This razor belongs not to me, but to us all. Any who wishes to use it must do so. Is my honor to share with you!'

The men laughed, and a few took him up on the offer. Kaladin wasn't one of them. It just . . . didn't seem to matter to him. He accepted the bowl of stew Dunny brought him, but didn't eat. Sigzil chose not to sit back down beside him, retreating to the other side of the campfire.

Eyes of red and blue, Kaladin thought. *I don't know if that fits us*. For him to have eyes of red and blue, Kaladin would have to believe that there was at least a small chance the bridge crew could survive. This night, Kaladin had trouble convincing himself.

He'd never been an optimist. He saw the world as it was, or he tried to. That was a problem, though, when the truth he saw was so terrible.

Oh, Stormfather, he thought, feeling the crushing weight of despair as he stared down at his bowl. *I'm falling back to the wretch I was. I'm losing my grip on this, on myself.*

He couldn't carry the hopes of all the bridgemen.

He just wasn't strong enough.

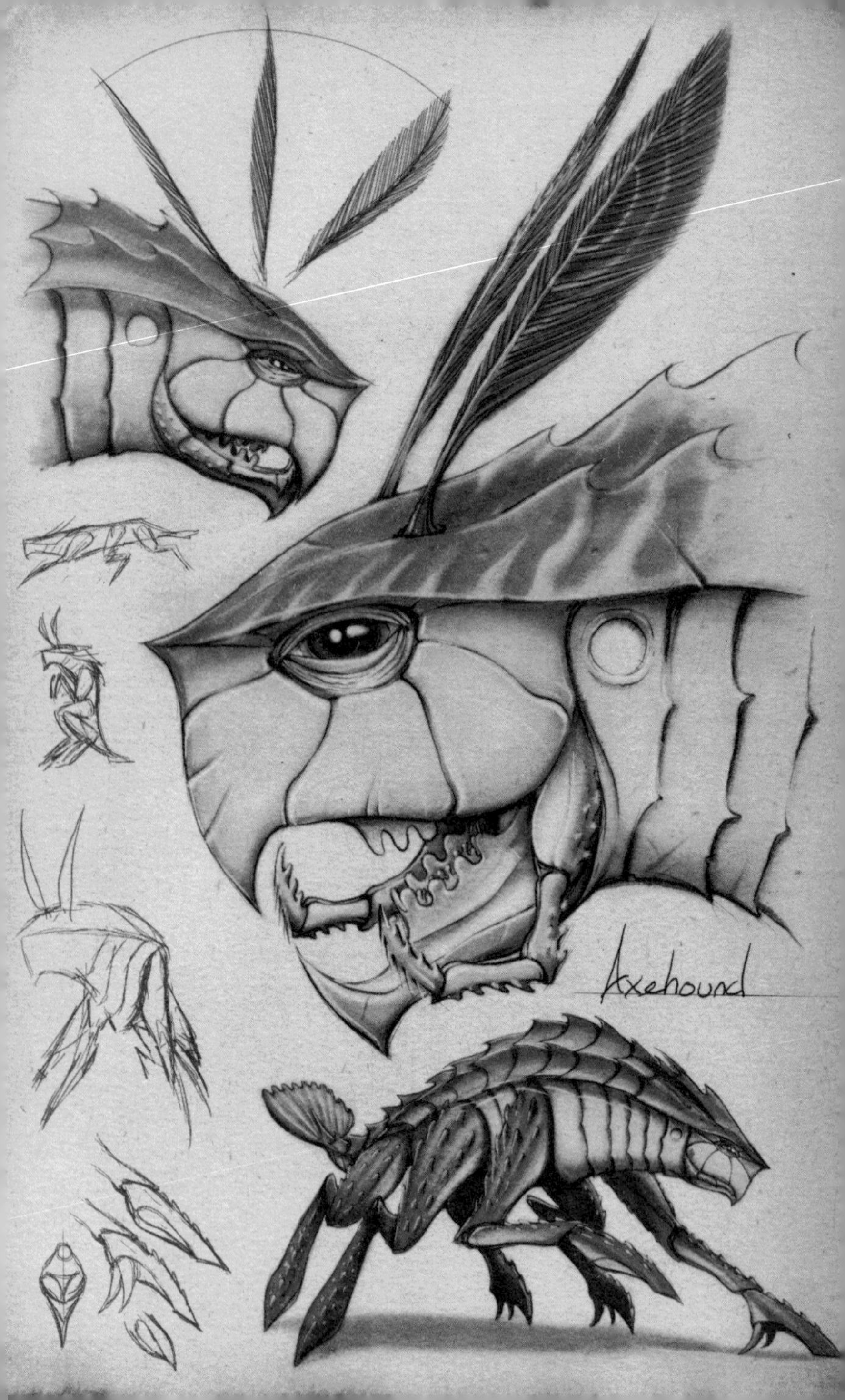
Axehound

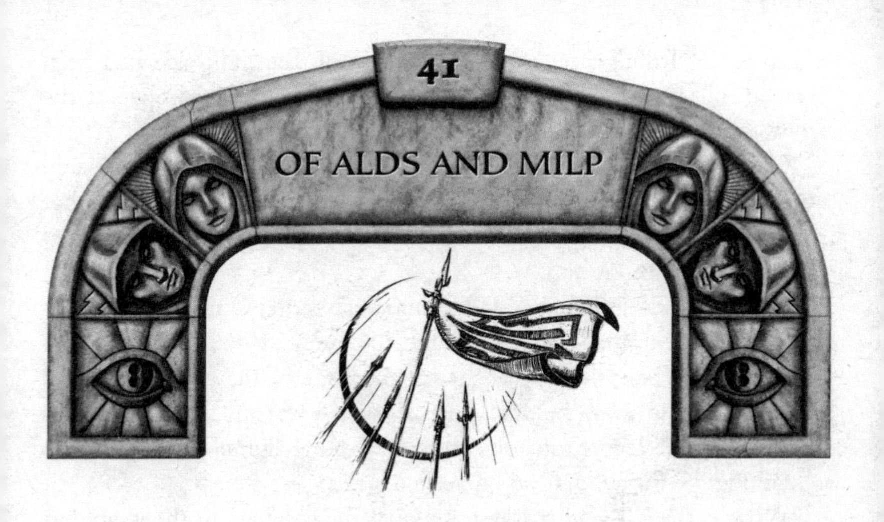

41

OF ALDS AND MILP

FIVE AND A HALF YEARS AGO

Kaladin pushed past the shrieking Laral and stumbled into the surgery room. Even after years working with his father, the amount of blood in the room was shocking. It was as if someone had dumped out a bucket of bright red paint.

The scent of burned flesh hung in the air. Lirin worked frantically on Brightlord Rillir, Roshone's son. An evil-looking, tusklike thing jutted from the young man's abdomen, and his lower right leg was crushed. It hung by only a few tendons, splinters of bone poking out like reeds from the waters of a pond. Brightlord Roshone himself lay on the side table, groaning, eyes squeezed shut as he held his leg, which was pierced by another of the bony spears. Blood leaked from his improvised bandage, flowed down the side of the table, and dripped to the floor to mix with his son's.

Kaladin stood in the doorway gaping. Laral continued to scream. She clutched the doorframe as several of Roshone's guards tried to pull her away. Her wails were frantic. 'Do something! Work harder! He can't! He was where it happened and I don't care and let me go!' The garbled phrases degenerated into screeches. The guards finally got her away.

'Kaladin!' his father snapped. 'I need you!'

Shocked into motion, Kaladin entered the room, scrubbing his hands then gathering bandages from the cabinet, stepping in blood. He caught a glimpse of Rillir's face; much of the skin on the right side had been scraped off. The eyelid was gone, the blue eye itself sliced open at the front, deflated like the skin of a grape pressed for wine.

Kaladin hastened to his father with the bandages. His mother appeared at the doorway a moment later, Tien behind her. She raised a hand to her mouth, then pulled Tien away. He stumbled, looking woozy. She returned in a moment without him.

'Water, Kaladin!' Lirin cried. 'Hesina, fetch more. Quickly!'

His mother jumped to help, though she rarely assisted in the surgery anymore. Her hands shook as she grabbed one of the buckets and ran outside. Kaladin took the other bucket, which was full, to his father as Lirin eased the length of bone from the young lighteyes's gut. Rillir's remaining eye fluttered, head quivering.

'What *is* that?' Kaladin asked, pressing the bandage to the wound as his father tossed the strange object aside.

'Whitespine tusk,' his father said. 'Water.'

Kaladin grabbed a sponge, dunked it in the bucket, and used it to squeeze water into Rillir's gut wound. That washed away the blood, giving Lirin a good look at the damage. He quested with his fingers as Kaladin got some needle and thread ready. There was already a tourniquet on the leg. Full amputation would come later.

Lirin hesitated, fingers inside the gaping hole in Rillir's belly. Kaladin cleaned the wound again. He looked up at his father, concerned.

Lirin pulled his fingers out and walked to Brightlord Roshone. 'Bandages, Kaladin,' he said curtly.

Kaladin hurried over, though he shot a look over his shoulder at Rillir. The once-handsome young lighteyes trembled again, spasming. 'Father ...'

'Bandages!' Lirin said.

'What are you doing, surgeon?' Roshone bellowed. 'What of my son?' Painspren swarmed around him.

'Your son is dead,' Lirin said, yanking the tusk free from Roshone's leg.

The lighteyes bellowed in agony, though Kaladin couldn't tell if that was because of the tusk or his son. Roshone clenched his jaw as Kaladin pressed the bandage down on his leg. Lirin dunked his hands in the water bucket, then quickly wiped them with knobweed sap to frighten off rotspren.

'My son *is not dead*,' Roshone growled. 'I can see him moving! Tend to him, surgeon.'

'Kaladin, get the dazewater,' Lirin ordered gathering his sewing needle.

Kaladin hurried to the back of the room, steps splashing blood, and threw open the far cupboard. He took out a small flask of clear liquid.

'What are you doing?' Roshone bellowed, trying to sit up. 'Look at my son! Almighty above, *look* at him!'

Kaladin turned hesitantly, pausing as he poured dazewater on a bandage. Rillir was spasming more violently.

'I work under three guidelines, Roshone,' Lirin said, forcibly pressing the lighteyes down against his table. 'The guidelines every surgeon uses when choosing between two patients. If the wounds are equal, treat the youngest first.'

'Then see to my son!'

'If the wounds are not equally threatening,' Lirin continued, 'treat the worst wound first.'

'As I've been *telling you*!'

'The third guideline supersedes them both, Roshone,' Lirin said, leaning down. 'A surgeon must know when someone is beyond their ability to help. I'm sorry, Roshone. I would save him if I could, I promise you. But I cannot.'

'No!' Roshone said, struggling again.

'Kaladin! Quickly!' Lirin said.

Kaladin dashed over. He pressed the bandage of dazewater to Roshone's chin and mouth, just below the nose, forcing the lighteyed man to breathe the fumes. Kaladin held his own breath, as he'd been trained.

Roshone bellowed and screamed, but the two of them held him down, and he was weak from blood loss. Soon, his bellows became softer. In seconds, he was speaking in gibberish and grinning to himself. Lirin turned back to the leg wound while Kaladin went to throw away the dazewater bandage.

'No. Administer it to Rillir.' His father didn't look away from his work. 'It's the only mercy we can give him.'

Kaladin nodded and used the dazewater bandage on the wounded youth. Rillir's breathing grew less frantic, though he didn't seem conscious enough to notice the effects. Then Kaladin threw the bandage with the dazewater into the brazier; heat negated the effects. The white, puffy bandage wrinkled and browned in the fire, steam streaming off it as the edges burst into flame.

Kaladin returned with the sponge and washed out Roshone's wound as Lirin prodded at it. There were a few shards of tusk trapped inside, and Lirin muttered to himself, getting out his tongs and razor-sharp knife.

'Damnation can take them all,' Lirin said, pulling out the first sliver of tusk. Behind him, Rillir fell still. 'Isn't sending half of us to war enough for them? Do they have to seek death even when they're living in a quiet township? Roshone should never have gone looking for the storming whitespine.'

'He was *looking* for it?'

'They went hunting it,' Lirin spat. 'Wistiow and I used to joke about lighteyes like them. If you can't kill men, you kill beasts. Well, this is what you found, Roshone.'

'Father,' Kaladin said softly. 'He's not going to be pleased with you when he awakes.' The brightlord was humming softly, lying back, eyes closed.

Lirin didn't respond. He yanked out another fragment of tusk, and Kaladin washed out the wound. His father pressed his fingers to the side of the large puncture, inspecting it.

There was one more sliver of tusk, jutting from a muscle inside the wound. Right beside that muscle thumped the femoral artery, the largest in the leg. Lirin reached in with his knife, carefully cutting free the sliver of tusk. Then he paused for a moment, the edge of his blade just hairs from the artery.

If that were cut . . . Kaladin thought. Roshone would be dead in minutes. He was only alive right now because the tusk had missed the artery.

Lirin's normally steady hand quivered. Then he glanced up at Kaladin. He withdrew the knife without touching the artery, then reached in with his tongs to pull the sliver free. He tossed it aside, then calmly reached for his thread and needle.

Behind them, Rillir had stopped breathing.

That evening, Kaladin sat on the steps to his house, hands in his lap.

Roshone had been returned to his estate to be cared for by his personal servants. His son's corpse was cooling in the crypt below, and a messenger had been sent to request a Soulcaster for the body.

On the horizon, the sun was red as blood. Everywhere Kaladin looked, the world was red.

The door to the surgery closed, and his father – looking as exhausted as Kaladin felt – tottered out. He eased himself down, sighing as he sat beside Kaladin, looking at the sun. Did it look like blood to him too?

They didn't speak as the sun slowly sank before them. Why was it most colorful when it was about to vanish for the night? Was it angry at being forced below the horizon? Or was it a showman, giving a performance before retiring?

Why was the most colorful part of people's bodies – the brightness of their blood – hidden beneath the skin, never to be seen unless something went wrong?

No, Kaladin thought. *The blood isn't the most colorful part of a body. The eyes can be colorful too.* The blood and the eyes. Both representations of one's heritage. And one's nobility.

'I saw inside a man today,' Kaladin finally said.

'Not for the first time,' Lirin said, 'and certainly not for the last. I'm proud of you. I expected to find you here crying, as you usually do when we lose a patient. You're learning.'

'When I said I saw inside a man,' Kaladin said, 'I wasn't talking about the wounds.'

Lirin didn't respond for a moment. 'I see.'

'You would have let him die if I hadn't been there, wouldn't you?'

Silence.

'Why didn't you?' Kaladin said. 'It would have solved so much!'

'It wouldn't have been letting him die. It would have been murdering him.'

'You could have just let him bleed, then claimed you couldn't save him. Nobody would have questioned you. You *could* have done it.'

'No,' Lirin said, staring at the sunset. 'No, I couldn't have.'

'But why?'

'Because I'm not a killer, son.'

Kaladin frowned.

Lirin had a distant look in his eyes. 'Somebody has to start. Somebody has to step forward and do what is right, *because* it is right. If nobody starts, then others cannot follow. The lighteyes do their best to kill themselves, and to kill us. The others still haven't brought back Alds and Milp. Roshone just left them there.'

Alds and Milp, two townsmen, had been on the hunt but hadn't returned with the party bearing the two wounded lighteyes. Roshone had been so worried about Rillir that he'd left them behind so he could travel quickly.

'The lighteyes don't care about life,' Lirin said. 'So I must. That's another reason why I wouldn't have let Roshone die, even if you hadn't been there. Though looking at you did strengthen me.'

'I wish it hadn't,' Kaladin said.

'You mustn't say such things.'

'Why not?'

'Because, son. We have to be *better* than they are.' He sighed, standing. 'You should sleep. I may need you when the others return with Alds and Milp.'

That wasn't likely; the two townsmen were probably dead by now. Their wounds were said to be pretty bad. Plus, the whitespines were still out there.

Lirin went inside, but didn't compel Kaladin to follow.

Would I have let him die? Kaladin wondered. *Maybe even flicked that knife to hasten him on his way?* Roshone had been nothing but a blight since his arrival, but did that justify killing him?

No. Cutting that artery wouldn't have been justified. But what obligation had Kaladin to help? Withholding his aid wasn't the same thing as killing. It just *wasn't.*

Kaladin thought it through a dozen different ways, pondering his father's words. What he found shocked him. He honestly would have let Roshone die on that table. It would have been better for Kaladin's family; it would have been better for the entire town.

Kaladin's father had once laughed at his son's desire to go to war. Indeed, now that Kaladin had decided he would become a surgeon on his own terms, his thoughts and actions of earlier years felt childish to him. But Lirin thought Kaladin incapable of killing. *You can hardly step on a cremling without feeling guilty, son*, he'd said. *Ramming your spear into a man would be nowhere near as easy as you seem to think.*

But his father was wrong. It was a stunning, frightening revelation.

This wasn't idle fancy or daydreaming about the glory of battle. This was real.

At that moment, Kaladin knew he *could* kill, if he needed to. Some people – like a festering finger or a leg shattered beyond repair – just needed to be removed.

'Like a highstorm, regular in their coming, yet always unexpected.'

—The word Desolation is used twice in reference to their appearances. See pages 57, 59, and 64 of *Tales by Hearthlight*.

'I've made my decision,' Shallan declared.

Jasnah looked up from her research. In an unusual moment of deference, she put aside her books and sat with her back to the Veil, regarding Shallan. 'Very well.'

'What you did was both legal and right, in the strict sense of the words,' Shallan said. 'But it was not moral, and it *certainly* wasn't ethical.'

'So morality and legality are distinct?'

'Nearly all of the philosophies agree they are.'

'But what do *you* think?'

Shallan hesitated. 'Yes. You can be moral without following the law, and you can be immoral while following the law.'

'But you also said what I did was "right" but not "moral." The distinction between those two seems less easy to define.'

'An action can be right,' Shallan said. 'It is simply something done, viewed without considering intent. Killing four men in self-defense is right.'

'But not moral?'

'Morality applies to your intent and the greater context of the situation. Seeking out men to kill is an immoral act, Jasnah, regardless of the eventual outcome.'

Jasnah tapped her desktop with a fingernail. She was wearing her glove, the gemstones of the broken Soulcaster bulging beneath. It had been two weeks. Surely she'd discovered that it didn't work. How could she be so calm?

Was she trying to fix it in secret? Perhaps she feared that if she revealed it was broken, she would lose political power. Or had she realized that hers had been swapped for a different Soulcaster? Could it be, despite all odds, that Jasnah just hadn't tried to use the Soulcaster? Shallan needed to leave before too long. But if she left before Jasnah discovered the swap, she risked having the woman try her Soulcaster just after Shallan vanished, bringing suspicion directly on her. The anxious waiting was driving Shallan near to madness.

Finally, Jasnah nodded, then returned to her research.

'You have nothing to say?' Shallan said. 'I just accused you of murder.'

'No,' Jasnah said, 'murder is a legal definition. You said I killed unethically.'

'You think I'm wrong, I assume?'

'You are,' Jasnah said. 'But I accept that you believe what you are saying and have put rational thought behind it. I have looked over your notes, and I believe you understand the various philosophies. In some cases, I think that you were quite insightful in your interpretation of them. The lesson was instructive.' She opened her book.

'Then that's it?'

'Of course not,' Jasnah said. 'We will study philosophy further in the future; for now, I'm satisfied that you have established a solid foundation in the topic.'

'But I still decided you were wrong. I still think there's an absolute Truth out there.'

'Yes,' Jasnah said, 'and it took you two weeks of struggling to come to that conclusion.' Jasnah looked up, meeting Shallan's eyes. 'It wasn't easy, was it?'

'No.'

'And you still wonder, don't you?'

'Yes.

'That is enough.' Jasnah narrowed her eyes slightly, a consoling smile appearing on her lips. 'If it helps you wrestle with your feelings, child, understand that I *was* trying to do good. I sometimes wonder if I should accomplish more with my Soulcaster.' She turned back to her reading. 'You are free for the rest of the day.'

Shallan blinked. 'What?'

'Free,' Jasnah said. 'You may go. Do as you please. You'll spend it drawing beggars and barmaids, I suspect, but you may choose. Be off with you.'

'Yes, Brightness! Thank you.'

Jasnah waved in dismissal and Shallan grabbed her portfolio and hastened from the alcove. She hadn't had any free time since the day she'd gone sketching on her own in the gardens. She'd been gently chided for that; Jasnah had left her in her rooms to rest, not go out sketching.

Shallan waited impatiently as the parshman porters lowered her lift to the Veil's ground floor, then hurried out into the cavernous central hall. A long walk later, she approached the guest quarters, nodding to the master-servants who served there. Half guards, half concierges, they monitored who entered and left.

She used her thick brass key to unlock the door to Jasnah's rooms, then slipped inside and locked the door behind her. The small sitting chamber – furnished with a rug and two chairs beside the hearth – was lit by topazes. The table still contained a half-full cup of orange wine from Jasnah's late research the night before, along with a few crumbs of bread on a plate.

Shallan hurried to her own chamber, then shut the door and took the Soulcaster out of her safepouch. The warm glow of the gemstones bathed her face in white and red light. They were large enough – and therefore bright enough – that it was hard to look at them directly. Each would be worth ten or twenty broams.

She'd been forced to hide them outside in the recent highstorm to infuse them, and that had been its own source of anxiety. She took a deep breath, then knelt and slid a small wooden stick from under the bed. A week and a half of practice, and she still hadn't managed to make the Soulcaster do ... well, anything at all. She'd tried tapping the gems, twisting them, shaking her hand, and flexing her hand in exact mimicry of Jasnah. She'd studied picture after picture she'd drawn of the process. She tried speaking, concentrating, and even begging.

However, she'd found a book the day before that had offered what seemed like a useful tip. It claimed that humming, of all things, could make a Soulcasting more effective. It was just a passing reference, but it was more than she'd found anywhere else. She sat down on her bed and forced herself to concentrate. She closed her eyes, holding the stick, imagining it transforming into quartz. Then she began humming.

Nothing happened. She kept on humming though, trying different notes, concentrating as hard as she could. She kept her attention on the task for a good half hour, but eventually her mind began to wander. A new worry began to nibble at her. Jasnah was one of the most brilliant, insightful scholars in the world. She'd put the Soulcaster out where it could be taken. Had she intentionally duped Shallan with a fake?

It seemed an awful lot of trouble to go through. Why not just spring the trap and reveal Shallan as a thief? The fact that she couldn't get the Soulcaster to work left her straining plausibility for explanations.

She stopped humming and opened her eyes. The stick had not changed. *So much for that tip*, she thought, setting the stick aside with a sigh. She'd been so hopeful.

She lay back on the bed, resting, staring up at the brown stone ceiling, cut – like the rest of the Conclave – directly out of the mountain. Here, the stone had been left intentionally rough, evoking the roof of a cave. It was quite beautiful in a subtle way she'd never noticed before, the colors and contours of the rock rippling like a disturbed pond.

She took a sheet from her portfolio and began to sketch the rock patterns. One sketch to calm her, and then she would get back to the Soulcaster. Perhaps she should try it on her other hand again.

She couldn't capture the colors of the strata, not in charcoal, but she could record the fascinating way the strata wove together. Like a work of art. Had some stoneworker cut this ceiling intentionally, crafting this subtle creation, or was it an accident of nature? She smiled, imagining some overworked stonecutter noticing the beautiful grain of the rock and deciding to form a wave pattern for his own personal wonder and sense of beauty.

'What are you?'

Shallan yelped, sitting up, sketchpad bouncing free of her lap. Someone had whispered those words. She'd heard them distinctly!

'Who is there?' she asked.

Silence.

'Who's there!' she said more loudly, her heart beating quickly.

Something sounded outside her door, from the sitting room. Shallan jumped, hiding the hand wearing the Soulcaster under a pillow as the door creaked open, revealing a wizened palace maid, darkeyed and dressed in a white and orange uniform.

'Oh dear!' the woman exclaimed. 'I had no idea you were here, Brightness.' She bowed low.

A palace maid. Here to clean the room, an everyday occurrence. Focused on her meditation, Shallan hadn't heard her enter. 'Why did you speak to me?'

'Speak to you, Brightness?'

'You . . .' No, the voice had been a whisper, and it had quite distinctly come from *inside* Shallan's room. It couldn't have been the maid.

She shivered and glanced about. But that was foolish. The tiny room was easily inspected. There were no Voidbringers hiding in the corners or under her bed.

What, then, had she heard? *Noises from the woman cleaning, obviously.* Shallan's mind had just interpreted those random sounds as words.

Forcing herself to relax, Shallan looked out past the maid into the sitting room. The woman had cleaned up the wineglass and crumbs. A broom leaned against the wall. In addition, Jasnah's door was cracked open. 'Were you in Brightness Jasnah's room?' Shallan demanded.

'Yes, Brightness,' the woman said. 'Tidying up the desk, making the bed—'

'Brightness Jasnah does *not* like people entering her room. The maids have been told not to clean in there.' The king had promised that his maids were very carefully chosen, and there had never been issues of theft, but Jasnah still insisted that none enter her bedchamber.

The woman paled. 'I'm sorry, Brightness. I didn't hear! I wasn't told—'

'Hush, it's all right,' Shallan said. 'You'll want to go tell her what you've done. She always notices if her things were moved. It will be better for you if you go to her and explain.'

'Y-Yes, Brightness.' The woman bowed again.

'In fact,' Shallan said, something occurring to her. 'You should go now. No point putting it off.'

The elderly maid sighed. 'Yes, of course, Brightness.' She withdrew. A few seconds later, the outside door closed and locked.

Shallan leapt up, pulling off the Soulcaster and stuffing it back in her safepouch. She hurried outside, heart thumping, the strange voice forgotten as she seized the opportunity to look into Jasnah's room. It was unlikely that Shallan would discover anything useful about the Soulcaster, but she couldn't pass up the chance – not with the maid to blame for moving things.

She felt only a glimmer of guilt for this. She'd already stolen from Jasnah. Compared with that, poking through her room was nothing.

The bedroom was larger than Shallan's, though it still felt cramped because of the unavoidable lack of windows. Jasnah's bed, a four-poster monstrosity, took up half the space. The vanity was against the far wall, and beside it the dressing table from which Shallan had originally stolen the Soulcaster. Other than a dresser, the only other thing in the room was the desk, books piled high on the left side.

Shallan never got a chance to look at Jasnah's notebooks. Might she, perhaps, have taken notes on the Soulcaster? Shallan sat at the desk, hurriedly pulling open the top drawer and poking through the brushpens, charcoal pencils, and sheets of paper. All were organized neatly, and the paper was blank. The bottom right drawer held ink and empty notebooks. The bottom left drawer had a small collection of reference books.

That left the books on the top of the table. Jasnah would have the majority of her notebooks with her as she worked. But . . . yes, there were still a few here. Heart fluttering, Shallan gathered up the three thin volumes and set them before her.

Notes on Urithiru, the first one declared inside. The notebook was full – it appeared – of quotes from and notations about various books Jasnah had found. All spoke of this place, Urithiru. Jasnah had mentioned it earlier to Kabsal.

Shallan put that book aside, looking at the next, hoping for mention of the Soulcaster. This notebook was also filled to capacity, but there was no title on it. Shallan picked through, reading some entries.

'The ones of ash and fire, who killed like a swarm, relentless before the Heralds . . .' Noted in Masly, page 337. Corroborated by Coldwin and Hasavah.

'They take away the light, wherever they lurk. Skin that is burned.' Cormshen, page 104.

Innia, in her recordings of children's folktales, speaks of the Voidbringers as being 'Like a highstorm, regular in their coming, yet always unexpected.' The word Desolation is used twice in reference to their appearances. See pages 57, 59, and 64 of Tales by Hearthlight.

'They changed, even as we fought them. Like shadows they were, that can transform as the flame dances. Never underestimate them because of what you first see.' Purports to be a scrap collected from Talatin, a Radiant of the Order of Stonewards. The source – Guvlow's Incarnate *– is generally held as reliable, though this is from a copied fragment of* The Poem of the Seventh Morning, *which has been lost.*

They went on like that. Pages and pages. Jasnah had trained her in this method of note taking – once the notebook was filled, each item would be evaluated again for reliability and usefulness and copied to different, more specific notebooks.

Frowning, Shallan looked through the final notebook. It focused on Natanatan, the Unclaimed Hills, and the Shattered Plains. It collected records of discoveries by hunters, explorers, or tradesmen searching for a river passage to New Natanan. Of the three notebooks, the largest was the one that focused on the Voidbringers.

The Voidbringers again. Many people in more rural places whispered of them and other monsters of the dark. The raspings, or stormwhispers, or even the dreaded nightspren. Shallan had been taught by stern tutors that these were superstition, fabrications of the Lost Radiants, who used tales of monsters to justify their domination of mankind.

The ardents taught something else. They spoke of the Lost Radiants – called the Knights Radiant then – fighting off Voidbringers during the war to hold Roshar. According to these teachings, it was only after defeating the Voidbringers – and the departure of the Heralds – that the Radiants had fallen.

Both groups agreed that the Voidbringers were gone. Fabrications or long-defeated enemies, the result was the same. Shallan could believe that some people – some scholars, even – might believe that the Voidbringers still existed, haunting mankind. But Jasnah the skeptic? Jasnah, who denied the existence of the Almighty? Could the woman really be so twisted as to deny the existence of God, but *accept* the existence of his mythological enemies?

A knock came at the outer door. Shallan jumped, raising her hand to her breast. She hurriedly replaced the notebooks on the desk in the same order and orientation. Then, flustered, she hurried out to the door. *Jasnah wouldn't knock, you silly fool*, she told herself, unlocking and opening the door a crack.

Kabsal stood outside. The handsome, lighteyed ardent held up a basket. 'I've heard reports that you have the day free.' He shook the basket temptingly. 'Would you like some jam?'

Shallan calmed herself, then glanced back at Jasnah's open quarters. She really should investigate more. She turned to Kabsal, meaning to tell him no, but his eyes were so inviting. That hint of a smile on his face, that good-natured and relaxed posture.

If Shallan went with Kabsal, maybe she could ask him what he knew regarding Soulcasters. That wasn't what decided it for her, however. The truth was, she *needed* to relax. She'd been so on edge lately, brain stuffed with philosophy, every spare moment spent trying to make the Soulcaster work. Was it any wonder she was hearing voices?

'I'd love some jam,' she declared.

⁂

'Truthberry jam,' Kabsal said, holding up the small green jar. 'It's Azish. Legends there say that those who consume the berries speak only the truth until the next sunset.'

Shallan raised an eyebrow. They were seated on cushions atop a blanket in the Conclave gardens, not far from where she'd first experimented with the Soulcaster. 'And is it true?'

'Hardly,' Kabsal said, opening the jar. 'The berries are harmless. But the leaves and stalks of the truthberry plant, if burned, give off a smoke that makes people intoxicated and euphoric. It appears that people often gathered the stalks for making fires. They'd eat the berries around the campfire and have a rather . . . interesting night.'

'It's a wonder—' Shallan began, then bit her lip.

'What?' he prodded.

She sighed. 'It's a wonder they didn't become known as birthberries, considering—' She blushed.

He laughed. 'That's a good point!'

'Stormfather,' she said, blushing further. 'I'm terrible at being proper. Here, give me some of that jam.'

He smiled, handing over a slice of bread with green jam slathered across the top. A dull-eyed parshman – appropriated from inside the Conclave – sat on the ground beside a shalebark wall, acting as an impromptu chaperone. It felt so strange to be out with a man near her own age with only a single parshman in attendance. It felt liberating. Exhilarating. Or maybe that was just the sunlight and the open air.

'I'm *also* terrible at being scholarly,' she said, closing her eyes, breathing deeply. 'I like it outside far too much.'

'Many of the greatest scholars spent their lives traveling.'

'And for each one of them,' Shallan said, 'there were a hundred more stuck back in a hole of a library, buried in books.'

'And they wouldn't have had it any other way. Most people with a bent for research *prefer* their holes and libraries. But you do not. That makes you intriguing.'

She opened her eyes, smiling at him, then took a luscious bite of her jam and bread. This Thaylen bread was so fluffy, it was more like cake.

'So,' she said as he chewed on his bite, 'do you feel any more truthful, now that you've had the jam?'

'I am an ardent,' he said. 'It is my duty and calling to be truthful at all times.'

'Of course,' she said. 'I'm always truthful as well. *So* full of truth, in fact, that sometimes it squeezes the lies right out my lips. There isn't a place for them inside, you see.'

He laughed heartily. 'Shallan Davar. I can't imagine anyone as sweet as yourself uttering a single untruth.'

'Then for the sake of your sanity, I'll keep them coming in pairs.' She smiled. 'I'm having a terrible time, and this food is awful.'

'You've just disproven an entire body of lore and mythology surrounding the eating of truthberry jam!'

'Good,' Shallan said. 'Jam should not have lore or mythology. It should be sweet, colorful, and delicious.'

'Like young ladies, I presume.'

'Brother Kabsal!' She blushed again. 'That wasn't at *all* appropriate.'

'And yet you smile.'

'I can't help it,' she said. 'I'm sweet, colorful, and delicious.'

'You have the colorful part right,' he said, obviously amused at her deep blush. 'And the sweet part. Can't speak for your deliciousness. . . .'

'Kabsal!' she exclaimed, though she wasn't entirely shocked. She'd once told herself that he was interested in her only in order to protect her soul, but that was getting more and more difficult to believe. He stopped by at least once a week.

He chuckled at her embarrassment, but that only made her blush further.

'Stop it!' She held her hand up in front of her eyes. 'My face must be the color of my hair! You shouldn't say such things; you're a man of religion.'

'But still a man, Shallan.'

'One who said his interest in me was only academic.'

'Yes, academic,' he said idly. 'Involving many experiments and much firsthand field research.'

'Kabsal!'

He laughed deeply, taking a bite of his bread. 'I'm sorry, Brightness Shallan. But it gets such a reaction!'

She grumbled, lowering her hand, but knew that he said the things – in part – because she encouraged him. She couldn't help it. Nobody had ever shown her the kind of interest that he, increasingly, did. She liked him – liked talking with him, liked listening to him. It was a wonderful way to break the monotony of study.

There was, of course, no prospect for a union. Assuming she could protect her family, she'd be needed to make a good political marriage. Dallying with an ardent owned by the king of Kharbranth wouldn't serve anyone.

I'll soon have to start hinting to him the truth, she thought. *He has to know that this won't go anywhere. Doesn't he?*

He leaned toward her. 'You really are what you seem, aren't you, Shallan?'

'Capable? Intelligent? Charming?'

He smiled. 'Genuine.'

'I wouldn't say that,' she said.

'You are. I see it in you.'

'It's not that I'm genuine. I'm naive. I lived my entire childhood in my family's manor.'

'You don't have the air of a recluse about you. You're so at ease at conversation.'

'I had to become so. I spent most of my childhood in my own company, and I *detest* boring conversation partners.'

He smiled, though his eyes held concern. 'It seems a shame that one such as you would lack for attention. That's like hanging a beautiful painting facing the wall.'

She leaned back on her safehand, finishing off her bread. 'I wouldn't say I lacked for attention, not *quantitatively*, for certain. My father paid me plenty of attention.'

'I've heard of him. A stern man, by reputation.'

'He's . . .' She had to pretend he was still alive. 'My father is a man of passion and virtue. Just never at the same time.'

'Shallan! That might just be the wittiest thing I've heard you say.'

'And perhaps the most truthful. Unfortunately.'

Kabsal looked into her eyes, searching for something. What did he see? 'You don't seem to care for your father much.'

'Another truthful statement. The berries are working on both of us, I see.'

'He's a hurtful man, I gather?'

'Yes, though never to me. I'm too precious. His ideal, perfect daughter. You see, my father is *precisely* the type of man to hang a picture facing the wrong way. That way, it can't be soiled by unworthy eyes or touched by unworthy fingers.'

'That's a shame. As you look very touchable to me.'

She glared. 'I told you, no more of that teasing.'

'That wasn't teasing,' he said, regarding her with deep blue eyes. Earnest eyes. 'You intrigue me, Shallan Davar.'

She found her heart thumping. Oddly, a panic rose within her at the same time. 'I shouldn't be intriguing.'

'Why not?'

'Logic puzzles are intriguing. Mathematical computations can be intriguing. Political maneuvers are intriguing. But women . . . they should be nothing short of baffling.'

'And what if I think I'm beginning to understand you?'

'Then I'm at a severe disadvantage,' she said. 'As I don't understand myself.'

He smiled.

'We shouldn't be talking like this, Kabsal. You're an ardent.'

'A man can leave the ardentia, Shallan.'

She felt a jolt. He looked steadily at her, not blinking. Handsome, soft-spoken, witty. *This could grow very dangerous very quickly,* she thought.

'Jasnah thinks you're getting close to me because you want her Soulcaster,' Shallan blurted out. Then she winced. *Idiot!* That's *your response when a man hints that he might leave the service of the Almighty in order to be with you?*

'Brightness Jasnah is quite clever,' Kabsal said, slicing himself another piece of bread.

Shallan blinked. 'Oh, er. You mean she's *right*?'

'Right and wrong,' Kabsal said. 'The devotary would very, very much like to get that fabrial. I planned to ask your help eventually.'

'But?'

'But my superiors thought it was a *terrible* idea.' He grimaced. 'They think the king of Alethkar is volatile enough that he'd march to war with Kharbranth over that. Soulcasters aren't Shardblades, but they can be equally important.' He shook his head, taking a bite of bread. 'Elhokar Kholin should be ashamed to let his sister use that fabrial, particularly so trivially. But if we were to steal it . . . Well, the repercussions could be felt across all of Vorin Roshar.'

'Is that so?' Shallan said, feeling sick.

He nodded. 'Most people don't think about it. I didn't. Kings rule and war with Shards – but their armies subsist through Soulcasters. Do you have any idea the kinds of supply lines and support personnel Soulcasters replace? Without them, warfare is virtually *impossible.* You'd need hundreds of wagons filled with food every month!'

'I guess . . . that would be a problem.' She took a deep breath. 'They fascinate me, these Soulcasters. I've always wondered what it would feel like to use one.'

'I as well.'

'So you've never used one?'

He shook his head. 'There aren't any in Kharbranth.'

Right, she thought. *Of course. That's why the king needed Jasnah to help his granddaughter.* 'Have you ever heard anyone talk about using one?' She cringed at the bold statement. Would it make him suspicious?

He just nodded idly. 'There's a secret to it, Shallan.'

'Really?' she asked, heart in her throat.

He looked up at her, seeming conspiratorial. 'It's really not that difficult.'

'It . . . What?'

'It's true,' he said. 'I've heard it from several ardents. There's so much shadow and ritual surrounding Soulcasters. They're kept mysterious, aren't used where people can see. But the truth is, there's not much to them. You just put one on, press your hand against something, and tap a gemstone with your finger. It works that simply.'

'That's not how Jasnah does it,' she said, perhaps too defensively.

'Yes, that confused me, but supposedly if you use one long enough, you learn how to control them better.' He shook his head. 'I don't like the mystery that has grown up around them. It smells too much like the mysticism of the old Hierocracy. We'd better not find ourselves treading down *that* path again. What would it matter if people knew how simple the Soulcasters are to use? The principles and gifts of the Almighty are often simple.'

Shallan barely listened to that last part. Unfortunately, it seemed that Kabsal was as ignorant as she. More ignorant, even. She'd tried the exact method he spoke of, and it didn't work. Perhaps the ardents he knew were lying to protect the secret.

'Anyway,' Kabsal said, 'I guess that's a tangent. You asked me about stealing the Soulcaster, and rest assured, I wouldn't put you in that position. I was foolish to think of it, and I was shortly forbidden to attempt it. I *was* ordered to care for your soul and see that you weren't corrupted by Jasnah's teachings, and perhaps try to reclaim Jasnah's soul as well.'

'Well, that last one is going to be difficult.'

'I hadn't noticed,' he replied dryly.

She smiled, though she couldn't quite decide how to feel. 'I kind of killed the moment, didn't I? Between us?'

'I'm glad you did,' he said, dusting off his hands. 'I get carried away, Shallan. At times, I wonder if I'm as bad at being an ardent as you are at being proper. I don't want to be presumptuous. It's just that the way you speak, it gets my mind churning, and my tongue starts saying whatever comes to it.'

'And so . . .'

'And so we should call it a day,' Kabsal said, standing. 'I need time to think.'

Shallan stood as well, holding out her freehand for his assistance; standing up in a sleek Vorin dress was difficult. They were in a section of the gardens where the shalebark wasn't quite so high, so once standing, Shallan could see that the king himself was passing nearby, chatting with a middle-aged ardent who had a long, narrow face.

The king often went strolling through the gardens on his midday walk. She waved to him, but the kindly man didn't see her. He was deep in conversation with the ardent. Kabsal turned, noticed the king, then ducked down.

'What?' Shallan said.

'The king keeps careful track of his ardents. He and Brother Ixil think I'm on cataloging duty today.'

She found herself smiling. 'You're scrapping your day's work to go on a picnic with me?'

'Yes.'

'I thought you were *supposed* to spend time with me,' she said, folding her arms. 'To protect my soul.'

'I was. But there are those among the ardents who worry that I'm a little *too* interested in you.'

'They're right.'

'I'll come see you tomorrow,' he said, peeking up over the top of the shalebark. 'Assuming I'm not stuck in indexing all day as a punishment.' He smiled at her. 'If I decide to leave the ardentia, that is my choice, and they cannot forbid it – though they may try to distract me.' He scrambled away as she prepared herself to tell him that he was presuming too much.

She couldn't get the words out. Perhaps because she was growing less and less certain *what* she wanted. Shouldn't she be focused on helping her family?

By now, Jasnah likely had discovered that her Soulcaster didn't work, but saw no advantage in revealing it. Shallan should leave. She could go to Jasnah and use the terrible experience in the alleyway as an excuse to quit.

And yet, she was terribly reluctant. Kabsal was part of that, but he wasn't the main reason. The truth was that, despite her occasional complaints, she *loved* learning to be a scholar. Even after Jasnah's philosophical training, even after spending days reading book after book. Even with the confusion and the stress, Shallan often felt fulfilled in a way she'd never been before. Yes, Jasnah had been wrong to kill those men, but Shallan wanted to know enough about philosophy to cite the correct reasons why. Yes, digging through historical records could be tedious, but Shallan appreciated the skills and patience she was learning; they were sure to be of value when she got to do her own deep research in the future.

Days spent learning, lunches spent laughing with Kabsal, evenings chatting and debating with Jasnah. *That* was what she wanted. And those were the parts of her life that were complete lies.

Troubled, she picked up the basket of bread and jam, then made her way back to the Conclave and Jasnah's suite. An envelope addressed to her sat in the waiting bin. Shallan frowned, breaking the seal to look inside.

Lass, it read. *We got your message. The* Wind's Pleasure *will soon be at port in Kharbranth again. Of course we'll give you passage and return to your estates. It would be my pleasure to have you aboard. We are Davar men, we are. Indebted to your family.*

We're making a quick trip over to the mainland, but will hurry to Kharbranth next. Expect us in one week's time to pick you up.

—Captain Tozbek

The undertext, written by Tozbek's wife, read even more clearly. *We'd happily give you free passage, Brightness, if you're willing to do some scribing for us during the trip. The ledgers badly need to be rewritten.*

Shallan stared at the note for a long time. She'd wanted to know where he was and when he was planning to return, but he'd apparently taken her letter as a request to come and pick her up.

It seemed a fitting deadline. That would put her departure at three weeks after stealing the Soulcaster, as she'd told Nan Balat to expect. If Jasnah hadn't reacted to the Soulcaster switch by then, Shallan would have to take it to mean that she wasn't under suspicion.

One week. She *would* be on that ship. It made her break inside to realize it, but it had to be done. She lowered the paper and left the guest hallway, her steps taking her through the twisting corridors into the Veil.

Shortly, she stood outside Jasnah's alcove. The princess sat at her desk, reed scratching at a notebook. She glanced up. 'I thought I told you that you could do whatever you want today.'

'You did,' Shallan said. 'And I realized that what I want to do is study.'

Jasnah smiled in a sly, understanding way. Almost a *self-satisfied* way. If she only knew. 'Well, I'm not going to chide you for that,' Jasnah said, turning back to her research.

Shallan sat, offering the bread and jam to Jasnah, who shook her head and continued researching. Shallan cut herself another slice and topped it with jam. Then she opened a book and sighed in satisfaction.

In one week, she'd have to leave. But in the meantime, she would let herself pretend a little while longer.

43

THE WRETCH

'They lived out in the wilds, always awaiting the Desolation – or sometimes, a foolish child who took no heed of the night's darkness.'

—A child's tale, yes, but this quote from *Shadows Remembered* seems to hint at the truth I seek. See page 82, the fourth tale.

Kaladin awoke to a familiar feeling of dread.

He'd spent much of the night lying awake on the hard floor, staring up into the dark, thinking. *Why try? Why care? There is no hope for these men.*

He felt like a wanderer seeking desperately for a pathway into the city to escape wild beasts. But the city was atop a steep mountain, and no matter how he approached, the climb was always the same. Impossible. A hundred different paths. The same result.

Surviving his punishment would not save his men. Training them to run faster would not save them. They were bait. The efficiency of the bait did not change its purpose or its fate.

Kaladin forced himself to his feet. He felt ground down, like a millstone used far too long. He still didn't understand how he'd survived. *Did you preserve me, Almighty? Save me so that I could watch them die?*

You were supposed to burn prayers to send them to the Almighty, who waited for his Heralds to recapture the Tranquiline Halls. That had never made sense to Kaladin. The Almighty was supposed to be able to see all and know all. So why did he need a prayer burned before he would do anything? Why did he need people to fight for him in the first place?

Kaladin left the barrack, stepping into the light. Then he froze.

The men were lined up, waiting. A ragged bunch of bridgemen, wearing brown leather vests and short trousers that only reached their knees. Dirty shirts, sleeves rolled to the elbows, lacing down the front. Dusty skin, mops of ragged hair. And yet now, because of Rock's gift, they all had neatly trimmed beards or clean-shaven faces. Everything else about them was worn. But their faces were clean.

Kaladin raised a hesitant hand to his face, touching his unkempt black beard. The men seemed to be waiting for something. 'What?' he asked.

The men shifted uncomfortably, glancing toward the lumberyard. They were waiting for him to lead them in practice, of course. But practice was futile. He opened his mouth to tell them that, but hesitated as he saw something approaching. Four men, carrying a palanquin. A tall, thin man in a violet lighteyes's coat walked beside it.

The men turned to look. 'What's this?' Hobber asked, scratching at his thick neck.

'It will be Lamaril's replacement,' Kaladin said, gently pushing his way through the line of bridgemen. Syl flitted down and landed on his shoulder as the palanquin bearers stopped before Kaladin and turned to the side, revealing a dark-haired woman wearing a sleek violet dress decorated with golden glyphs. She lounged on her side, resting on a cushioned couch, her eyes a pale blue.

'I am Brightness Hashal,' she said, voice lightly touched by a Kholinar accent. 'My husband, Brightlord Matal, is your new captain.'

Kaladin held his tongue, biting back a remark. He had some experience with lighteyes who got 'promoted' to positions like this one. Matal himself said nothing, simply standing with his hand resting on the hilt of his sword. He was tall – nearly as tall as Kaladin – but spindly. Delicate hands. That sword hadn't seen much practice.

'We have been advised,' Hashal said, 'that this crew has been troublesome.' Her eyes narrowed, focusing on Kaladin. 'It seems that you have survived the Almighty's judgment. I bear a message for you from your betters. The Almighty has given you another chance to prove yourself as a bridgeman. That is all. Many are trying to read too much into what happened, so Highprince Sadeas has forbidden gawkers to come see you.

'My husband does not intend to run the bridge crews with his predecessor's laxness. My husband is a well-respected and honored associate of Highprince Sadeas himself, not some near-darkeyed mongrel like Lamaril.'

'Is that so?' Kaladin said. 'Then how did he end up in *this* latrine pit of a job?'

Hashal didn't display a hint of anger at the comment. She flicked her fingers to the side, and one of the soldiers stepped forward and rammed the butt of his spear toward Kaladin's stomach.

Kaladin caught it, old reflexes still too keen. Possibilities flashed through his mind, and he could see the fight before it took place.

Yank on the spear, throw the soldier off guard.

Step forward and ram an elbow into his forearm, making him drop the weapon.

Take control, spin the spear up and slam the soldier on the side of the head.

Spin into a sweep to drop the two who came to help their companion.

Raise the spear for the—

No. That would only get Kaladin killed.

Kaladin released the butt of the spear. The soldier blinked in surprise that a mere bridgeman had blocked his blow. Scowling, the soldier jerked the butt up and slammed it into the side of Kaladin's head.

Kaladin let it hit him, rolling with it, allowing it to toss him to the ground. His head rang from the shock, but his eyesight stopped spinning after a moment. He'd have a headache, but probably no concussion.

He took in a few deep breaths, lying on the ground, hands forming fists. His fingers seemed to burn where he had touched the spear. The soldier stepped back into position beside the palanquin.

'No laxness,' Hashal said calmly. 'If you must know, my husband *requested* this assignment. The bridge crews are essential to Brightlord Sadeas's advantage in the War of Reckoning. Their mismanagement under Lamaril was disgraceful.'

Rock knelt down, helping Kaladin to his feet while scowling at the lighteyes and their soldiers. Kaladin stumbled up, holding his hand to the side of his head. His fingers felt slick and wet, and a trickle of warm blood ran down his neck to his shoulder.

'From now on,' Hashal said, 'aside from doing normal bridge duty, each crew will be assigned only *one* type of work duty. Gaz!'

The short bridge sergeant poked out from behind the palanquin. Kaladin hadn't noticed him there, behind the porters and the soldiers. 'Yes, Brightness?' Gaz bowed several times.

'My husband wishes Bridge Four to be assigned chasm duty permanently. Whenever they are not needed for bridge duty, I want them working in those chasms. This will be far more efficient. They will know which sections have been scoured recently, and will not cover the same ground. You see? Efficiency. They will start immediately.'

She rapped on the side of her palanquin, and the porters turned, bearing her away. Her husband continued to walk alongside her without saying a word, and Gaz hurried to keep up. Kaladin stared after them, holding his hand to his head. Dunny ran and fetched him a bandage.

'Chasm duty,' Moash grumbled. 'Great job, lordling. She'd see us dead from a chasmfiend if the Parshendi arrows don't take us.'

'What are we going to do?' asked lean, balding Peet, his voice edged with worry.

'We get to work,' Kaladin said, taking the bandage from Dunny.

He walked away, leaving them in a frightened clump.

◆◆◆

A short time later, Kaladin stood at the edge of the chasm, looking down. The hot light of the noon sun burned the back of his neck and cast his shadow downward into the rift, to join with those below. *I could fly*, he thought. *Step off and fall, wind blowing against me. Fly for a few moments. A few, beautiful moments.*

He knelt and grabbed the rope ladder, then climbed down into the darkness. The other bridgemen followed in a silent group. They'd been infected by his mood.

Kaladin knew what was happening to him. Step by step, he was turning back into the wretch he had been. He'd always known it was a danger. He'd clung to the bridgemen as a lifeline. But he was letting go now.

As he stepped down the rungs, a faint translucent figure of blue and white dropped beside him, sitting on a swinglike seat. Its ropes disappeared a few inches above Syl's head.

'What is wrong with you?' she asked softly.

Kaladin just kept climbing down.

'You should be happy. You survived the storms. The other bridgemen were so excited.'

'I itched to fight that soldier,' Kaladin whispered.

Syl cocked her head.

'I could have beaten him,' Kaladin continued. 'I probably could have beaten all four of them. I've always been good with the spear. No, not good. Durk called me amazing. A natural born soldier, an artist with the spear.'

'Maybe you should have fought them, then.'

'I thought you didn't like killing.'

'I hate it,' she said, growing more translucent. 'But I've helped men kill before.'

Kaladin froze on the ladder. '*What?*'

'It's true,' she said. 'I can remember it, just faintly.'

'How?'

'I don't know.' She grew paler. 'I don't want to talk about it. But it was right to do. I feel it.'

Kaladin hung for a moment longer. Teft called down, asking if something was wrong. He started to descend again.

'I didn't fight the soldiers today,' Kaladin said, eyes toward the chasm wall, 'because it wouldn't work. My father told me that it is impossible to protect by killing. Well, he was wrong.'

'But—'

'He was wrong,' Kaladin said, 'because he implied that you could protect people in *other* ways. You can't. This world wants them dead, and trying to save them is pointless.' He reached the bottom of the chasm, stepping into darkness. Teft reached the bottom next and lit his torch, bathing the moss-covered stone walls in flickering orange light.

'Is that why you didn't accept it?' Syl whispered, flitting over and landing on Kaladin's shoulder. 'The glory. All those months ago?'

Kaladin shook his head. 'No. That was something else.'

'What did you say, Kaladin?' Teft raised the torch. The aging bridgeman's face looked older than usual in the flickering light, the shadows it created emphasizing the furrows in his skin.

'Nothing, Teft,' Kaladin said. 'Nothing important.'

Syl sniffed at that. Kaladin ignored her, lighting his torch from Teft's as the other bridgemen arrived. When they were all down, Kaladin led the way out into the dark rift. The pale sky seemed distant here, like a far-off scream. This place was a tomb, with rotting wood and stagnant pools of water, good only for growing cremling larvae.

The bridgemen clustered together unconsciously as they always did in this fell place. Kaladin walked in front, and Syl fell silent. He gave Teft the chalk to mark directions, and didn't pause to pick up salvage. But neither did he walk too quickly. The other bridgemen were hushed behind them, speaking in occasional whispers too low to echo. As if their words were strangled by the gloom.

Rock eventually moved up to walk beside Kaladin. 'Is difficult job, we have been given. But we are bridgemen! Life, it is difficult, eh? Is nothing new. We must have plan. How do we fight next?'

'There is no next fight, Rock.'

'But we have won grand victory! Look, not days ago, you were delirious. You should have died. I know this thing. But instead, you walk, strong as any other man. Ha! Stronger. Is miracle. The *Uli'tekanaki* guide you.'

'It's not a miracle, Rock,' Kaladin said. 'It's more of a curse.'

'How is that a curse, my friend?' Rock asked, chuckling. He jumped up and into a puddle and laughed louder as it splashed Teft, who was walking just behind. The large Horneater could be remarkably childlike at times. 'Living, this thing is no curse!'

'It is if it brings me back to watch you all die,' Kaladin said. 'Better I shouldn't have survived that storm. I'm just going to end up dead from a Parshendi arrow. We all are.'

Rock looked troubled. When Kaladin offered nothing more, he withdrew. They continued, uncomfortably passing sections of scarred wall where chasmfiends had left their marks. Eventually they stumbled across a heap of bodies deposited by the highstorms. Kaladin stopped, holding up his torch, the other bridgemen peeking around him. Some fifty people had been washed into a recess in the rock, a small dead-end side passage in the stone.

The bodies were piled there, a wall of the dead, arms hanging out, reeds and flotsam stuck between them. Kaladin saw at a glance that the corpses were old enough to begin bloating and rotting. Behind him, one of the men retched, which caused a few of the others to do so as well. The scent was terrible, the corpses slashed and ripped into by cremlings and larger carrion beasts, many of which scuttled away from the light. A disembodied hand lay nearby, and a trail of blood led away. There were also fresh scrapes in the lichen as high as fifteen feet up the wall. A chasmfiend had ripped one of the bodies loose to devour. It might come back for the others.

Kaladin didn't retch. He shoved his half-burned torch between two large stones, then got to work, pulling bodies from the pile. At least they weren't rotted enough to come apart. The bridgemen slowly filled in around him, working. Kaladin let his mind grow numb, not thinking.

Once the bodies were down, the bridgemen laid them in a line. Then they began pulling off their armor, searching their pockets, taking knives from belts. Kaladin left gathering the spears to the others, working by himself off to the side.

Teft knelt beside Kaladin, rolling over a body with a head smashed by the fall. The shorter man began to undo the straps on the fallen man's breastplate. 'Do you want to talk?'

Kaladin didn't say anything. He just kept working. *Don't think about the future. Don't think about what will happen. Just survive.*

Don't care, but don't despair. Just be.

'Kaladin.' Teft's voice was like a knife, digging into Kaladin's shell, making him squirm.

'If I wanted to talk,' Kaladin grumbled, 'would I be working here by myself?'

'Fair enough,' Teft said. He finally got the breastplate strap undone. 'The other men are confused, son. They want to know what we're going to do next.'

Kaladin sighed, then stood, turning to look at the bridgemen. 'I don't know what to do! If we try to protect ourselves, Sadeas will have us punished! We're bait, and we're going to die. There's nothing I can do about it! It's hopeless.'

The bridgemen regarded him with shock.

Kaladin turned from them and went back to work, kneeling beside Teft. 'There,' he said. 'I explained it to them.'

'Idiot,' Teft said under his breath. 'After all you've done, you're abandoning us now?'

To the side, the bridgemen turned back to work. Kaladin caught a few of them grumbling. 'Bastard,' Moash said. 'I said this would happen.'

'Abandoning you?' Kaladin hissed to Teft. *Just let me be. Let me go back to apathy. At least then there's no pain.* 'Teft, I've spent hours and hours trying to find a way out, but there isn't one! Sadeas *wants* us dead. Lighteyes get what they want; that's the way the world works.'

'So?'

Kaladin ignored him, turning back to his work, pulling at the boot on a soldier whose fibula looked to have been shattered in three different places. That made it storming awkward to get the boot off.

'Well, maybe we will die,' Teft said. 'But maybe this isn't about surviving.'

Why was *Teft* – of all people – trying to cheer him up? 'If survival isn't the point, Teft, then what is?' Kaladin finally got the boot off. He turned to the next body in line, then froze.

It was a bridgeman. Kaladin didn't recognize him, but that vest and those sandals were unmistakable. He lay slumped against the wall, arms at his sides, mouth slightly open and eyelids sunken. The skin on one of the hands had slipped free and pulled away.

'I don't know what the point is,' Teft grumbled. 'But it seems pathetic to give up. We should keep fighting. Right until those arrows take us. You know, "journey before destination."'

'What does *that* mean?'

'I don't know,' Teft said, looking down quickly. 'Just something I heard once.'

'It's something the Lost Radiants used to say,' Sigzil said, walking past.

Kaladin glanced to the side. The soft-spoken Azish man set a shield on a pile. He looked up, brown skin dark in the torchlight. 'It was their motto. Part of it, at least. "Life before death. Strength before weakness. Journey before destination."'

'Lost Radiants?' Skar said, carrying an armful of boots. 'Who's bringing *them* up?'

'Teft did,' Moash said.

'I did not! That was just something I heard once.'

'What does it even mean?' Dunny asked.

'I said I don't know!' Teft said.

'It was supposedly one of their creeds,' Sigzil said. 'In Yulay, there are groups of people who talk of the Radiants. And wish for their return.'

'Who'd want them to return?' Skar said, leaning back against the wall, folding his arms. 'They betrayed us to the Voidbringers.'

'Ha!' Rock said. 'Voidbringers! Lowlander nonsense. Is campfire tale told by children.'

'They were real,' Skar said defensively. 'Everyone knows that.'

'Everyone who listens to campfire stories!' Rock said with a laugh. 'Too much air! Makes your minds soft. Is all right, though – you are still my family. Just the dumb ones!'

Teft scowled as the others continued to talk about the Lost Radiants.

'Journey before destination,' Syl whispered on Kaladin's shoulder. 'I like that.'

'Why?' Kaladin asked, kneeling down to untie the dead bridgeman's sandals.

'Because,' she replied, as if that were explanation enough. 'Teft is right, Kaladin. I know you want to give up. But you can't.'

'Why not?'

'Because you *can't*.'

'We're assigned to chasm duty from now on,' Kaladin said. 'We won't be able to collect any more reeds to make money. That means no more bandages, antiseptic, or food for the nightly meals. With all of these bodies, we're bound to run into rotspren, and the men will grow sick – assuming chasmfiends don't eat us or a surprise highstorm doesn't drown us. And we'll have to keep running those bridges until Damnation ends, losing man after man. It's hopeless.'

The men were still talking. 'The Lost Radiants helped the other side,' Skar argued. 'They were tarnished all along.'

Teft took offense at that. The wiry man stood up straight, pointing at Skar. 'You don't know anything! It was too long ago. Nobody knows what really happened.'

'Then why do all the stories say the same thing?' Skar demanded. 'They abandoned us. Just like the lighteyes are abandoning us right now. Maybe Kaladin's right. Maybe there *is* no hope.'

Kaladin looked down. Those words haunted him. *Maybe Kaladin is right . . . maybe there is no hope. . . .*

He'd done this before. Under his last owner, before being sold to Tvlakv and being made a bridgeman. He'd given up on a quiet night after leading Goshel and the other slaves in rebellion. They'd been slaughtered. But somehow he'd survived. Storm it all, why did *he* always survive? *I can't do it again*, he thought, squeezing his eyes shut. *I can't help them.*

Tien. Tukks. Goshel. Dallet. The nameless slave he'd tried to heal in Tvlakv's slave wagons. All had ended up the same. Kaladin had the touch of failure. Sometimes he gave them hope, but what was hope except another opportunity for failure? How many times could a man fall before he no longer stood back up?

'I just think we're ignorant,' Teft grumbled. 'I don't like listening to what the lighteyes say about the past. Their women write all the histories, you know.'

'I can't believe you're arguing about this, Teft,' Skar said, exasperated. 'What next? Should we let the Voidbringers steal our hearts? Maybe they're just misunderstood. Or the Parshendi. Maybe we should just *let* them kill our king whenever they want.'

'Would you two just storm off?' Moash snapped. 'It doesn't matter. You heard Kaladin. Even *he* thinks we're as good as dead.'

Kaladin couldn't take their voices anymore. He stumbled away, into the darkness, away from the torchlight. None of the men followed him. He entered a place of dark shadows, with only the distant ribbon of sky above for light.

Here, Kaladin escaped their eyes. In the darkness he ran into a boulder, stumbling to a stop. It was slick with moss and lichen. He stood with his hands pressed against it, then groaned and turned around to lean back against it. Syl alighted in front of him, still visible, despite the darkness. She sat down in the air, arranging her dress around her legs.

'I can't save them, Syl,' Kaladin whispered, anguished.

'Are you certain?'

'I've failed every time before.'

'And so you'll fail this time too?'

'Yes.'

She fell silent. 'Well then,' she eventually said. 'Let's say that you're right.'

'So why fight? I told myself that I would try one last time. But I failed before I began. There's no saving them.'

'Doesn't the fight itself mean anything?'

'Not if you're destined to die.' He hung his head.

Sigzil's words echoed in his head. *Life before death. Strength before weakness. Journey before destination.* Kaladin looked up at the crack of sky. Like a faraway river of pure, blue water.

Life before death.

What did the saying mean? That men should seek life before seeking death? That was obvious. Or did it mean something else? That life came before death? Again, obvious. And yet the simple words spoke to him. Death comes, they whispered. Death comes to all. But life comes first. Cherish it.

Death is the destination. But the journey, that is life. That is what matters.

A cold wind blew through the corridor of stone, washing over him, bringing crisp, fresh scents and blowing away the stink of rotting corpses.

Nobody cared for the bridgemen. Nobody cared for those at the bottom, with the darkest eyes. And yet, that wind seemed to whisper to him over and over. *Life before death. Life before death. Live before you die.*

His foot hit something. He bent down and picked it up. A small rock. He could barely make it out in the darkness. He recognized what was happening to him, this melancholy, this sense of despair. It had taken him often when he'd been younger, most frequently during the weeks of the Weeping, when the sky was hidden by clouds. During those times, Tien had cheered him up, helped him pull out of his despair. Tien had always been able to do that.

Once he'd lost his brother, he'd dealt with these periods of sadness more awkwardly. He'd become the wretch, not caring – but also not despairing. It had seemed better not to feel at all, as opposed to feeling pain.

I'm going to fail them, Kaladin thought, squeezing his eyes shut. *Why try?*

Wasn't he a fool to keep grasping as he did? If only he could win once. That would be enough. As long as he could believe that he could help someone, as long as he believed that some paths led to places other than darkness, he could hope.

You promised yourself you would try one last time, he thought. *They aren't dead yet.*

Still alive. For now.

There was one thing he hadn't tried. Something he'd been too frightened of. Every time he'd tried it in the past, he'd lost everything.

The wretch seemed to be standing before him. He meant release.

Apathy. Did Kaladin really want to go back to that? It was a false refuge. Being that man hadn't protected him. It had only led him deeper and deeper until taking his own life had seemed the better way.

Life before death.

Kaladin stood up, opening his eyes, dropping the small rock. He walked slowly back toward the torchlight. The bridgemen looked up from their work. So many questioning eyes. Some doubtful, some grim, others encouraging. Rock, Dunny, Hobber, Leyten. They believed in him. He had survived the storms. One miracle granted.

'There is something we could try,' Kaladin said. 'But it will most likely end with us all dead at the hands of our own army.'

'We're bound to end up dead anyway,' Maps noted. 'You said so yourself.' Several of the others nodded.

Kaladin took a deep breath. 'We have to try to escape.'

'But the warcamp is guarded!' said Earless Jaks. 'Bridgemen aren't allowed out without supervision. They know we'd run.'

'We'd die,' Moash said, face grim. 'We're miles and miles from civilization. There's nothing out here but greatshells, and no shelter from high-storms.'

'I know,' Kaladin said. 'But it's either this or the Parshendi arrows.'

The men fell silent.

'They're going to send us down here every day to rob corpses,' Kaladin said. 'And they don't send us with supervision, since they fear the chasmfiends. Most bridgeman work is busywork, to distract us from our fate, so we only have to bring back a small amount of salvage.'

'You think we should choose one of these chasms and flee down it?' Skar asked. 'They've tried to map them all. The crews never reached the other side of the Plains – they got killed by chasmfiends or highstorm floods.'

Kaladin shook his head. 'That's not what we're going to do.' He kicked at something on the ground before him – a fallen spear. His kick sent it into the air toward Moash, who caught it, surprised.

'I can train you to use those,' Kaladin said softly.

The men fell silent, looking at the weapon.

'What good would this thing do?' Rock asked, taking the spear from Moash, looking it over. 'We cannot fight an army.'

'No,' Kaladin said. 'But if I train you, then we can attack a guard post at night. We might be able to get away.' Kaladin looked at them, meeting each man's eyes in turn. 'Once we're free, they'll send soldiers after us. Sadeas won't let bridgemen kill his soldiers and get away with it. We'll have to hope he underestimates us and sends a small group at first. If we kill them, we might be able to get far enough away to hide. It will be dangerous. Sadeas will go to great lengths to recapture us, and we'll likely end with an entire company chasing us down. Storm it, we'll probably never escape the camp in the first place. But it's something.'

He fell silent, waiting as the men exchanged uncertain glances.

'I'll do it,' Teft said, straightening up.

'Me too,' Moash said, stepping forward. He seemed eager.

'And I,' Sigzil said. 'I would rather spit in their Alethi faces and die on their swords than remain a slave.'

'Ha!' Rock said. 'And I shall cook you all much food to keep you full while you kill.'

'You won't fight with us?' Dunny asked, surprised.

'Is beneath me,' Rock said raising his chin.

'Well, I'll do it,' Dunny said. 'I'm your man, Captain.'

Others began to chime in, each man standing, several grabbing spears from the wet ground. They didn't yell in excitement or roar like other troops Kaladin had led. They were frightened by the idea of fighting – most had been common slaves or lowly workmen. But they were willing.

Kaladin stepped forward and began to outline a plan.

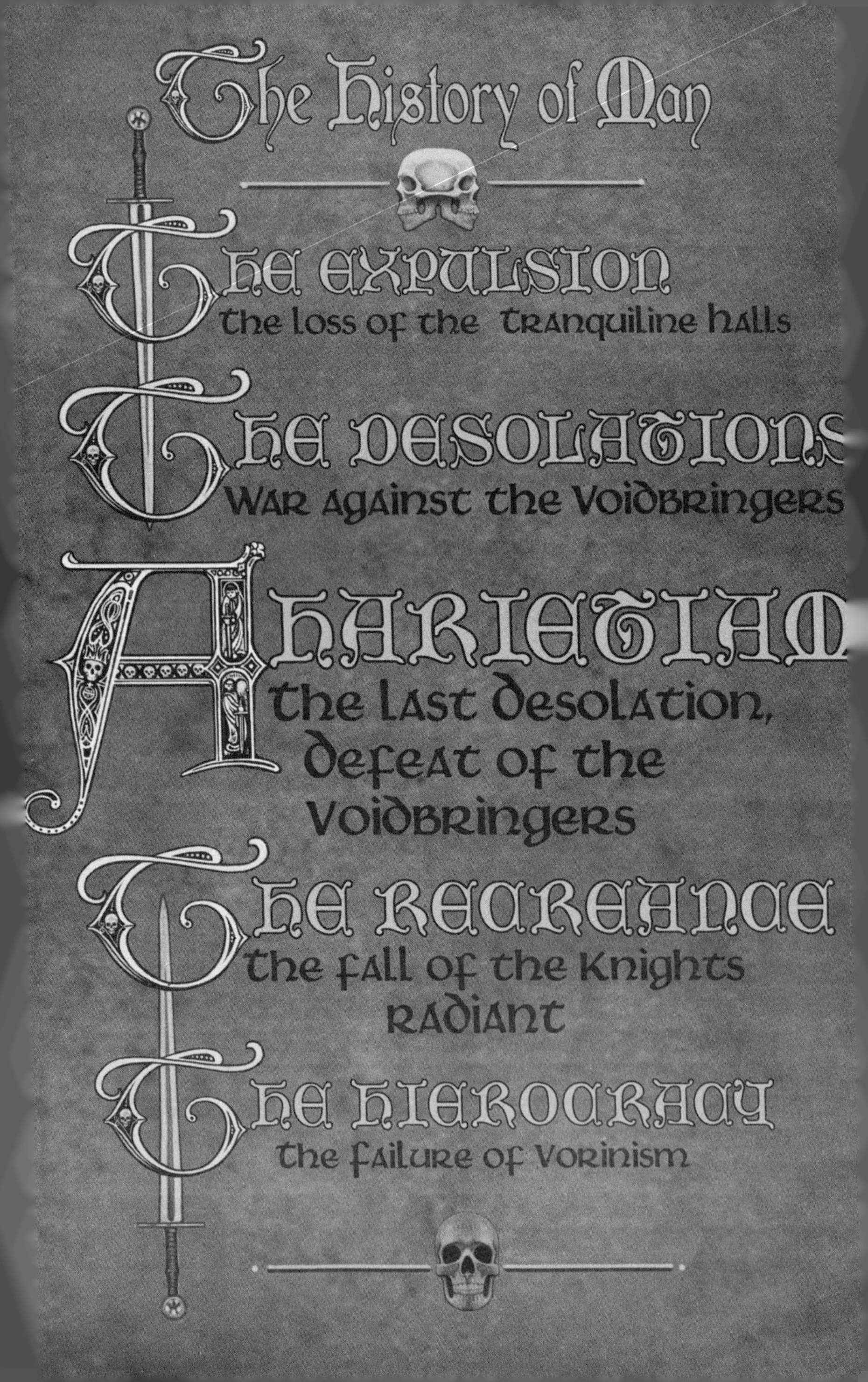
The History of Man
The Expulsion
the loss of the Tranquiline halls
The Desolations
War against the Voidbringers
Aharietiam
the last desolation,
defeat of the
Voidbringers
The Recreance
the fall of the Knights
Radiant
The Hierocracy
the failure of Vorinism

44 THE WEEPING

FIVE YEARS AGO

Kaladin hated the Weeping. It marked the end of an old year and the coming of a new one, four solid weeks of rain in a ceaseless cascade of sullen drops. Never furious, never passionate like a highstorm. Slow, steady. Like the blood of a dying year that was taking its last few shambling steps toward the cairn. While other seasons of weather came and went unpredictably, the Weeping never failed to return at the same time each year. Unfortunately.

Kaladin lay on the sloped roof of his house in Hearthstone. A small pail of pitch sat next to him, covered by a piece of wood. It was almost empty now that he'd finished patching the roof. The Weeping was a miserable time to do this work, but it was also when a persistent leak could be most irritating. They'd repatch when the Weeping ended, but at least this way they wouldn't have to suffer a steady stream of drips onto their dining table for the next weeks.

He lay on his back, staring up at the sky. Perhaps he should have climbed down and gone inside, but he was already soaked through. So he stayed. Watching, thinking.

Another army was passing through the town. One of many these days – they often came during the Weeping, resupplying and moving to new battlefields. Roshone had made a rare appearance to welcome the warlord: Highmarshal Amaram himself, apparently a distant cousin as well as head of Alethi defense in this area. He was one of the most renowned soldiers still in Alethkar; most had left for the Shattered Plains.

The small raindrops misted Kaladin. Many of the others liked these weeks – there were no highstorms, save for one right in the middle. To the townspeople, it was a cherished time to rest from farming and relax. But Kaladin longed for the sun and the wind. He actually missed the high-storms, with their rage and vitality. These days were dreary, and he found it difficult to get anything productive done. As if the lack of storms left him without strength.

Few people had seen much of Roshone since the ill-fated whitespine hunt and the death of his son. He hid in his mansion, increasingly reclusive. The people of Hearthstone trod very lightly, as if they expected that any moment he could explode and turn his rage against them. Kaladin wasn't worried about that. A storm – whether from a person or the sky – was something you could react to. But this suffocation, this slow and steady dousing of life . . . That was far, far worse.

'Kaladin?' Tien's voice called. 'Are you still up there?'

'Yeah,' he called back, not moving. The clouds were so *bland* during the Weeping. Could anything be more lifeless than that miserable grey?

Tien rounded to the back of the building, where the roof sloped down to touch the ground. He had his hands in the pockets of his long raincoat, a wide-brimmed hat on his head. Both looked too large for him, but clothing always seemed too large for Tien. Even when it fit him properly.

Kaladin's brother climbed up onto the roof and walked up beside him, then lay down, staring skyward. Someone else might have tried to cheer Kaladin up, and they would have failed. But somehow Tien knew the right thing to do. For the moment, that was keeping silent.

'You like the rain, don't you?' Kaladin finally asked him.

'Yeah,' Tien said. Of course, Tien liked pretty much everything. 'Hard to stare up at like this, though. I keep blinking.'

For some reason, that made Kaladin smile.

'I made you something,' Tien said. 'At the shop today.'

Kaladin's parents were worried; Ral the carpenter had taken Tien, though he didn't really need another apprentice, and was reportedly dissatisfied with the boy's work. Tien got distracted easily, Ral complained.

Kaladin sat up as Tien fished something out of his pocket. It was a small wooden horse, intricately carved.

'Don't worry about the water,' Tien said, handing it over. 'I sealed it already.'

'Tien,' Kaladin said, amazed. 'This is *beautiful*.' The details were amazing – the eyes, the hooves, the lines in the tail. It looked just like the majestic animals that pulled Roshone's carriage. 'Did you show this to Ral?'

'He said it was good,' Tien said, smiling beneath his oversized hat. 'But he told me I should have been making a chair instead. I kind of got into trouble.'

'But how . . . I mean, Tien, he's got to see this is amazing!'

'Oh, I don't know about that,' Tien said, still smiling. 'It's just a horse. Master Ral likes things you can use. Things to sit on, things to put clothes in. But I think I can make a good chair tomorrow, something that will make him proud.'

Kaladin looked at his brother, with his innocent face and affable nature. He hadn't lost either, though he was now into his teenage years. *How is it you can always smile?* Kaladin thought. *It's dreadful outside, your master treats you like crem, and your family is slowly being strangled by the citylord. And yet you smile. How, Tien?*

And why is it that you make me want to smile too?

'Father spent another of the spheres, Tien,' Kaladin found himself saying. Each time their father was forced to do that, he seemed to grow a little more wan, stand a little less tall. Those spheres were dun these days, no light in them. You couldn't infuse spheres during the Weeping. They all ran out, eventually.

'There are plenty more,' Tien said.

'Roshone is trying to wear us down,' Kaladin said. 'Bit by bit, smother us.'

'It's not as bad as it seems, Kaladin,' his brother said, reaching up to hold his arm. 'Things are never as bad as they seem. You'll see.'

So many objections rose in his mind, but Tien's smile banished them. There, in the midst of the dreariest part of the year, Kaladin felt for a moment as if he had glimpsed sunshine. He could swear he felt things grow brighter around them, the storm retreating a shade, the sky lightening.

Their mother rounded the back of the building. She looked up at them, as if amused to find them both sitting on the roof in the rain. She stepped onto the lower portion. A small group of haspers clung to the stone there; the small two-shelled creatures proliferated during the Weeping. They seemed to grow out of nowhere, much like their cousins the tiny snails, scattered all across the stone.

'What are you two talking about?' she asked, walking up and sitting down with them. Hesina rarely acted like the other mothers in town. Sometimes, that bothered Kaladin. Shouldn't she have sent them into the house or something, complaining that they'd catch a cold? No, she just sat down with them, wearing a brown leather raincoat.

'Kaladin's worried about Father spending the spheres,' Tien said.

'Oh, I wouldn't worry about that,' she replied. 'We'll get you to Kharbranth. You'll be old enough to leave in two more months.'

'You two should come with me,' Kaladin said. 'And Father too.'

'And leave the town?' Tien said, as if he'd never considered that possibility. 'But I like it here.'

Hesina smiled.

'What?' Kaladin said.

'Most young men your age are trying everything they can to be *rid* of their parents.'

'I can't go off and leave you here. We're a family.'

'He's trying to strangle us,' Kaladin said, glancing at Tien. Talking with his brother had made him feel a lot better, but his objections were still there. 'Nobody pays for healing, and I know nobody will pay you for work anymore. What kind of value does Father get for those spheres he spends anyway? Vegetables at ten times the regular price, moldy grain at double?'

Hesina smiled. 'Observant.'

'Father taught me to notice details. The eyes of a surgeon.'

'Well,' she said, eyes twinkling, 'did your surgeon's eyes notice the first time we spent one of the spheres?'

'Sure,' Kaladin said. 'It was the day after the hunting accident. Father had to buy new cloth to make bandages.'

'And did we *need* new bandages?'

'Well, no. But you know how Father is. He doesn't like it when we start to run even a little low.'

'And so he spent one of those spheres,' Hesina said. 'That he'd hoarded for months and months, butting heads with the citylord over them.'

Not to mention going to such lengths to steal them in the first place, Kaladin thought. *But you know all about that.* He glanced at Tien, who was watching the sky again. So far as Kaladin knew, his brother hadn't discovered the truth yet.

'So your father resisted so long,' Hesina said, 'only to finally break and spend a sphere on some cloth bandages we wouldn't need for months.'

She had a point. Why *had* his father suddenly decided to … 'He's letting Roshone think he's winning,' Kaladin said with surprise, looking back at her.

Hesina smiled slyly. 'Roshone would have found a way to get retribution eventually. It wouldn't have been easy. Your father ranks high as a citizen, and has the right of inquest. He *did* save Roshone's life, and many could testify to the severity of Rillir's wounds. But Roshone would have found a way. Unless he felt he'd broken us.'

Kaladin turned toward the mansion. Though it was hidden by the shroud of rain, he could just make out the tents of the army camped on the field below. What would it be like to live as a soldier, often exposed to storms and rain, to winds and tempests? Once Kaladin would have been intrigued, but the life of a spearman had no call for him now. His mind was filled with diagrams of muscles and memorized lists of symptoms and diseases.

'We'll keep spending the spheres,' Hesina said. 'One every few weeks. Partially to live, though my family has offered supplies. More to keep Roshone thinking that we're bending. And then, we send you away. Unexpectedly. You'll be gone, the spheres safely in the hands of the ardents to use as a stipend during your years of study.'

Kaladin blinked in realization. They weren't losing. They were *winning*.

'Think of it, Kaladin,' Tien said. 'You'll live in one of the grandest cities in the world! It will be so exciting. You'll be a man of learning, like Father. You'll have clerks to read to you from any book you want.'

Kaladin pushed wet hair off his forehead. Tien made it sound a lot grander than he'd been thinking. Of course, Tien could make a cremfilled puddle sound grand.

'That's true,' his mother said, still staring upward. 'You could learn mathematics, history, politics, tactics, the sciences …'

'Aren't those things women learn?' Kaladin said, frowning.

'Lighteyed women study them. But there are male scholars as well. If not as many.'

'All this to become a surgeon.'

'You wouldn't have to become a surgeon. Your life is your own, son. If you take the path of a surgeon, we will be proud. But don't feel that you need to live your father's life for him.' She looked down at Kaladin, blinking rainwater from her eyes.

'What else would I do?' Kaladin said, stupefied.

'There are many professions open to men with a good mind and training. If you really wished to study all the arts, you could become an ardent. Or perhaps a stormwarden.'

Stormwarden. He reached by reflex for the prayer sewn to his left sleeve, waiting for the day he'd need to burn it for aid. 'They seek to predict the future.'

'It's not the same thing. You'll see. There are so many things to explore, so many places your mind could go. The world is changing. My family's most recent letter describes amazing fabrials, like pens that can write across great distances. It might not be long before men are taught to read.'

'I'd never want to learn something like that,' Kaladin said, aghast, glancing at Tien. Was their own *mother* really saying these things? But then, she'd always been like this. Free, both with her mind and her tongue.

Yet, to become a stormwarden ... They studied the highstorms, predicted them – yes – but learned about them and their mysteries. They studied the winds themselves.

'No,' Kaladin said. 'I want to be a surgeon. Like my father.'

Hesina smiled. 'If that's what you choose, then – as I said – we will be proud of you. But father and I just want you to know that you *can* choose.'

They sat like that for some time, letting rainwater soak them. Kaladin kept searching those grey clouds, wondering what it was that Tien found so interesting in them. Eventually, he heard splashing below, and Lirin's face appeared at the side of the house.

'What in the ...' he said. 'All *three* of you? What are you doing up here?'

'Feasting,' Kaladin's mother said nonchalantly.

'On what?'

'On irregularity, dear,' she said.

Lirin sighed. 'Dear, you can be very odd, you know.'

'And didn't I just say that?'

'Point. Well, come on. There's a gathering in the square.'

Hesina frowned. She rose and walked down the slope of the roof. Kaladin glanced at Tien, and the two of them stood. Kaladin stuffed the wooden horse in his pocket and picked his way down, careful on the slick rock, his shoes squishing. Cool water ran down Kaladin's cheeks as he stepped off onto the ground.

They followed Lirin toward the square. Kaladin's father looked worried, and he walked with the beaten-down slouch he was prone to lately. Maybe it was an affectation to fool Roshone, but Kaladin suspected there was some truth to it. His father didn't like having to give up those spheres, even if it was part of a ruse. It was too much like giving in.

Ahead, a crowd was gathering at the town square, everyone holding umbrellas or wearing cloaks.

'What is it, Lirin?' Hesina asked, sounding anxious.

'Roshone is going to put in an appearance,' Lirin said. 'He asked Waber to gather everyone. Full town meeting.'

'In the *rain*?' Kaladin asked. 'Couldn't he have waited for Lightday?'

Lirin didn't reply. The family walked in silence, even Tien growing solemn. They passed some rainspren standing in puddles, glowing with a faint blue light, shaped like ankle-high melting candles with no flame. They rarely appeared except during the Weeping. They were said to be the souls of raindrops, glowing blue rods, seeming to melt but never growing smaller, a single blue eye at their tops.

The townspeople were mostly assembled, gossiping in the rain, by the time Kaladin's family arrived. Jost and Naget were there, though neither waved to Kaladin; it had been years since they'd been anything resembling friends. Kaladin shivered. His parents called this town home, and his father refused to leave, but it felt less and less like 'home' by the day.

I'll be leaving it soon, he thought, eager to walk out of Hearthstone and leave these small-minded people behind. To go to a place where lighteyes were men and women of honor and beauty, worthy of the high station given them by the Almighty.

Roshone's carriage approached. It had lost much of its luster during his years in Hearthstone, the golden paint flaking off, the dark wood chipped by road gravel. As the carriage pulled into the square, Waber and his boys finally got a small canopy erected. The rain had strengthened, and drops hit the cloth with a hollow drumming sound.

The air smelled different with all of these people around. Up on the roof, it had been fresh and clean. Now it seemed muggy and humid. The carriage door opened. Roshone had gained more weight, and his lighteyes's suit had been retailored to fit his increased girth. He wore a wooden peg on his right stump, hidden by the cuff of his trouser, and his gait was stiff as he climbed out of the carriage and ducked beneath the canopy, grumbling.

He hardly seemed the same person, with that beard and wet, stringy hair. But his eyes, they were the same. More beady now because of the fuller cheeks, but still seething as he studied the crowd. As if he had been hit with a rock when he wasn't looking, and now searched for the culprit.

Was Laral inside the carriage? Someone else moved inside, climbing out, but it turned out to be a lean man with a clean-shaven face and light tan eyes. The dignified man wore a neatly pressed, green formal military uniform and had a sword at his hip. Highmarshal Amaram? He certainly looked impressive, with that strong figure and square face. The difference between him and Roshone was striking.

Finally, Laral did appear, wearing a light yellow dress of an antique fashion, with a flaring skirt and thick bodice. She glanced up at the rain, then waited for a footman to hurry over with an umbrella. Kaladin felt his heart thumping. They hadn't spoken since the day she'd humiliated him in Roshone's mansion. And yet, she was *gorgeous*. As she had grown through her adolescence, she had gotten prettier and prettier. Some might find that dark hair sprinkled with foreigner blond to be unappealing for its indication of mixed blood, but to Kaladin it was alluring.

Beside Kaladin, his father stiffened, cursing softly.

'What?' Tien asked from beside Kaladin, craning to see.

'Laral,' Kaladin's mother said. 'She's wearing a bride's prayer on her sleeve.'

Kaladin started, seeing the white cloth with its blue glyphpair sewn onto the sleeve of her dress. She'd burn it when the engagement was formally announced.

But . . . who? Rillir was dead!

'I'd heard rumors of this,' Kaladin's father said. 'It appears Roshone wasn't willing to part with the connections she offers.'

'Him?' Kaladin asked, stunned. Roshone *himself* was marrying her? Others in the crowd had begun speaking as they noticed the prayer.

'Lighteyes marry much younger women all the time,' Kaladin's mother said. 'For them, marriages are often about securing house loyalty.'

'*Him?*' Kaladin asked again, incredulous, stepping forward. 'We have to stop it. We have to—'

'Kaladin,' his father said sharply.

'But—'

'It is their affair, not ours.'

Kaladin fell silent, feeling the larger raindrops hit his head, the smaller ones blowing by as mist. The water ran through the square and pooled in depressions. Near Kaladin, a rainspren sprang up, forming as if out of the water. It stared upward, unblinking.

Roshone leaned on his cane and nodded to Natir, his steward. The man was accompanied by his wife, a stern-looking woman named Alaxia. Natir clapped his slender hands to quiet the crowd, and soon the only sound was that of the soft rain.

'Brightlord Amaram,' Roshone said, nodding to the lighteyed man in the uniform, 'is absendiar highmarshal of our princedom. He is in command of defending our borders while the king and Brightlord Sadeas are away.'

Kaladin nodded. Everyone knew of Amaram. He was far more important than most military men who passed through Hearthstone.

Amaram stepped forward to speak.

'You have a fine town here,' Amaram said to the gathered darkeyes. He had a strong, deep voice. 'Thank you for hosting me.'

Kaladin frowned, glancing at the other townspeople. They seemed as confused as he by the statement.

'Normally,' Amaram said, 'I would leave this task to one of my subordinate officers. But as I was visiting with my cousin, I decided to come down in person. It is not so onerous a task that I need delegate it.'

'Excuse me, Brightlord,' said Callins, one of the farmers. 'But what duty is that?'

'Why, recruitment, good farmer,' Amaram said, nodding to Alaxia, who stepped forward with a sheet of paper strapped to a board. 'The king took most of our armies with him on his quest to fulfill the Vengeance Pact. My forces are undermanned, and it has become necessary to recruit young men from each town or village we pass. I do this with volunteers whenever possible.'

The townspeople fell still. Boys talked of running off to the army, but few of them would actually do it. Hearthstone's duty was to provide food.

'My fighting is not as glorious as the war for vengeance,' Amaram said, 'but it is our sacred duty to defend our lands. This tour will be for four years, and upon completing your duty, you will receive a war bonus equal to one-tenth your total wages. You may then return, or you may sign up for further duty. Distinguish yourself and rise to a high rank, and it could mean an increase of one nahn for you and your children. Are there any volunteers?'

'I'll go,' Jost said, stepping forward.

'Me too,' Abry added.

'Jost!' Jost's mother said, grabbing his arm. 'The crops—'

'Your crops are important, darkwoman,' Amaram said, 'but not nearly as important as the defense of our people. The king sends back riches from the plundered Plains, and the gemstones he has captured can provide food for Alethkar in emergency. You two are both welcome. Are there any others?'

Three more boys from the town stepped forward, and one older man – Harl, who had lost his wife to the scarfever. He was the man whose daughter Kaladin hadn't been able to save after her fall.

'Excellent,' Amaram said. 'Are there any others?'

The townspeople were still. Oddly so. Many of the boys Kaladin had heard talk so often about joining the army looked away. Kaladin felt his heart beating, and his leg twitched, as if itching to propel him forward.

No. He was to be a surgeon. Lirin looked at him, and his dark brown eyes displayed hints of deep concern. But when Kaladin didn't make any moves forward, he relaxed.

'Very well,' Amaram said, nodding to Roshone. 'We will need your list after all.'

'List?' Lirin asked loudly.

Amaram glanced at him. 'The need of our army is great, darkborn. I will take volunteers first, but the army *must* be replenished. As citylord, my cousin has the duty and honor of deciding which men to send.'

'Read the first four names, Alaxia,' Roshone said, 'and the last one.'

Alaxia looked down at her list, speaking with a dry voice. 'Agil, son of Marf. Caull, son of Taleb.'

Kaladin looked up at Lirin with apprehension.

'He can't take you,' Lirin said. 'We're of the second nahn and provide an essential function to the town—I as surgeon, you as my only apprentice. By the law, we are exempt from conscription. Roshone knows it.'

'Habrin, son of Arafik,' Alaxia continued. 'Jorna, son of Loats.' She hesitated, then looked up. 'Tien, son of Lirin.'

There was a stillness across the square. Even the rain seemed to hesitate for a moment. Then, all eyes turned toward Tien. The boy looked dumbfounded. Lirin was immune as town surgeon, Kaladin immune as his apprentice.

But not Tien. He was a carpenter's third apprentice, not vital, not immune.

Hesina gripped Tien tightly. 'No!'

Lirin stepped in front of them, defensive. Kaladin stood stunned, looking at Roshone. Smiling, self-satisfied Roshone.

We took his son, Kaladin realized, meeting those beady eyes. *This is his revenge.*

'I . . .' Tien said. 'The military?' For once, he seemed to lose his confidence, his optimism. His eyes opened wide, and he grew very pale. He fainted when he saw blood. He hated fighting. He was still small and spindly despite his age.

'He's too young,' Lirin declared. Their neighbors sidled away, leaving Lirin's family to stand alone in the rain.

Amaram frowned. 'In the cities, youths as young as eight and nine are accepted into the military.'

'Lighteyed sons!' Lirin said. 'To be trained as officers. They aren't sent into battle!'

Amaram frowned more deeply. He stepped out into the rain, walking up to the family. 'How old are you, son?' he asked Tien.

'He's thirteen,' Lirin said.

Amaram glanced at him. 'The surgeon. I've heard of you.' He sighed, glancing back at Roshone. 'I haven't the time to engage in your petty, small-town politics, cousin. Isn't there another boy that will do?'

'It is my choice!' Roshone insisted. 'Given me by the dictates of law. I send those the town can spare – well, that boy is the *first* one we can spare.'

Lirin stepped forward, eyes full of anger. Highmarshal Amaram caught him by the arm. 'Do not do something you would regret, darkborn. Roshone has acted according to the law.'

'You hid behind the law, sneering at me, surgeon,' Roshone called to Lirin. 'Well, now it turns against *you*. Keep those spheres! The look on your face at this moment is worth the price of every one of them!'

'I . . .' Tien said again. Kaladin had never seen the boy so terrified.

Kaladin felt powerless. The crowd's eyes were on Lirin, standing with his arm in the grip of the lighteyed general, locking his gaze with Roshone.

'I'll make the lad a runner boy for a year or two,' Amaram promised. 'He won't be in combat. It is the best I can do. Every body is needed in these times.'

Lirin slumped, then bowed his head. Roshone laughed, motioning Laral toward the carriage. She didn't glance at Kaladin as she climbed back in. Roshone followed, and though he was still laughing, his expression had grown hard. Lifeless. Like the dull clouds above. He had his revenge, but his son was still dead and he was still stuck in Hearthstone.

Amaram regarded the crowd. 'The recruits may bring two changes of clothing and up to three stoneweights of other possessions. They *will* be weighed. Report to the army in two hours and ask for Sergeant Hav.' He turned and followed Roshone.

Tien stared after him, pale as a whitewashed building. Kaladin could see his terror at leaving his family. His brother, the one who always made him smile when it rained. It was physically painful for Kaladin to see him so scared. It wasn't *right*. Tien should smile. That was who he was.

He felt the wooden horse in his pocket. Tien always brought him relief when he felt pained. Suddenly, it occurred to him that there was something he could do in turn. *It's time to stop hiding in the room when someone else holds up the globe of light*, Kaladin thought. *It's time to be a man.*

'Brightlord Amaram!' Kaladin yelled.

The general hesitated, standing on the stepstool into the carriage, one foot in the door. He glanced over his shoulder.

'I want to take Tien's place,' Kaladin said.

'Not allowed!' Roshone said from inside the carriage. 'The law says I may choose.'

Amaram nodded grimly.

'Then what if you take me *as well*,' Kaladin said. 'Can I volunteer?' That way, at least, Tien wouldn't be alone.

'Kaladin!' Hesina said, grabbing him on one arm.

'It is allowed,' Amaram said. 'I will not turn away any soldier, son. If you want to join, you are welcome.'

'Kaladin, no,' Lirin said. 'Don't both of you go. Don't—'

Kaladin looked at Tien, the boy's face wet beneath his wide-brimmed hat. He shook his head, but his eyes seemed hopeful.

'I volunteer,' Kaladin said, turning back to Amaram. 'I'll go.'

'Then you have two hours,' Amaram said, climbing into the carriage. 'Same possession allotment as the others.'

The carriage door shut, but not before Kaladin got a glimpse of an even *more* satisfied Roshone. Rattling, the vehicle splashed away, dropping a sheet of water from its roof.

'Why?' Lirin said, turning back to Kaladin, his voice ragged. 'Why have you done this to me? After all of our plans!'

Kaladin turned to Tien. The boy took his arm. 'Thank you,' Tien whispered. 'Thank you, Kaladin. *Thank you.*'

'I've lost both of you,' Lirin said hoarsely, splashing away. 'Storm it! Both of you.' He was crying. Kaladin's mother was crying too. She clutched Tien again.

'Father!' Kaladin said, turning, amazed at how confident he felt.

Lirin paused, standing in the rain, one foot in a puddle where rainspren clustered. They inched away from him like vertical slugs.

'In four years, I will bring him home safely,' Kaladin said. 'I promise it by the storms and the Almighty's tenth name itself. I will *bring him back.*'

I promise. . . .

'Yelig-nar, called Blightwind, was one that could speak like a man, though often his voice was accompanied by the wails of those he consumed.'

—The Unmade were obviously fabrications of folklore. Curiously, most were not considered individuals, but instead personifications of kinds of destruction. This quote is from Traxil, line 33, considered a primary source, though I doubt its authenticity.

They are an oddly welcoming group, these wild parshmen, Shallan read. It was King Gavilar's account again, recorded a year before his murder. *It has now been nearly five months since our first meeting. Dalinar continues to pressure me to return to our homeland, insisting that the expedition has stretched too long.*

The parshmen promise that they will lead me on a hunt for a great-shelled beast they call an ulo mas vara, *which my scholars say translates roughly to 'Monster of the Chasms.' If their descriptions are accurate, these creatures have large gemhearts, and one of their heads would make a truly impressive trophy. They also speak of their terrible gods, and we think they must be referring to several particularly large chasm greatshells.*

We are amazed to find religion among these parshmen. The mounting evidence of a complete parshman society – with civilization, culture, and a unique language – is astounding. My stormwardens have begun calling this people 'the Parshendi.' It is obvious this group is very different from our ordinary servant parshmen, and may not even be the same race, despite the skin patterns. Perhaps they are distant cousins, as different from ordinary parshmen as Alethi axe-hounds are from the Selay breed.

The Parshendi have seen our servants, and are confused by them. 'Where is their music?' Klade will often ask me. I do not know what he means. But our servants do not react to the Parshendi at all, showing no interest in emulating them. This is reassuring.

The question about music may have to do with the humming and chanting the Parshendi often do. They have an uncanny ability to make music together. I swear that I have left one Parshendi singing to himself, then soon passed another out of earshot of the first, yet singing the very same song – eerily near to the other in tempo, tune, and lyric.

Their favored instrument is the drum. They are crudely made, with hand-prints of paint marking the sides. This matches their simple buildings, which they construct of crem and stone. They build them in the craterlike rock formations here at the edge of the Shattered Plains. I ask Klade if they worry about high-storms, but he just laughs. 'Why worry? If the buildings blow down, we can build them again, can we not?'

On the other side of the alcove, Jasnah's book rustled as she turned a page. Shallan set aside her own volume, then picked through the books on the desk. Her philosophy training done for the time being, she had returned to her study of King Gavilar's murder.

She slid a small volume out from the bottom of the stack: a record dictated by Stormwarden Matain, one of the scholars who had accompanied the king. Shallan flipped through the pages, searching for a specific passage. It was a description of the very first Parshendi hunting party they encountered.

It happened after we set up beside a deep river in a heavily wooded area. It was an ideal location for a long-term camp, as the dense cobwood trees would protect against highstorm winds, and the river's gorge eliminated the risk of flooding. His Majesty wisely took my advice, sending scouting parties both upriver and down.

Highprince Dalinar's scouting party was the first to encounter the strange, untamed parshmen. When he returned to camp with his story, I – like many others – refused to believe his claims. Surely Brightlord Dalinar had simply run across the parshman servants of another expedition like our own.

Once they visited our camp the next day, their reality could no longer be denied. There were ten of them – parshmen to be sure, but bigger than the familiar ones. Some had skin marbled black and red, and others were marbled white and red, as is more common in Alethkar. They carried magnificent weapons, the bright steel etched with complex decorations, but wore simple clothing of woven narbin cloth.

Before long, His Majesty became fascinated by these strange parshmen, insisting that I begin a study of their language and society. I'll admit that my original intent was to expose them as a hoax of some kind. The more we learned, however, the more I came to realize how faulty my original assessment had been.

Shallan tapped the page, thinking. Then she pulled out a thick volume, titled *King Gavilar Kholin, a Biography*, published by Gavilar's widow, Navani, two years before. Shallan flipped through pages, scanning for a particular paragraph.

My husband was an excellent king – an inspiring leader, an unparalleled duelist, and a genius of battlefield tactics. But he didn't have a single scholarly finger on his left hand. He never showed an interest in the accounting of high-storms, was bored by talk of science, and ignored fabrials unless they had an obvious use in battle. He was a man built after the classical masculine ideal.

'Why was he so interested in them?' Shallan said out loud.

'Hmmm?' Jasnah asked.

'King Gavilar,' Shallan said. 'Your mother insists in her biography that he wasn't a scholar.'

'True.'

'But he *was* interested in the Parshendi,' Shallan said. 'Even before he could have known about their Shardblades. According to Matain's account, he wanted to know about their language, their society, and their music. Was that just embellishment, to make him sound more scholarly to future readers?'

'No,' Jasnah said, lowering her own book. 'The longer he remained in the Unclaimed Hills, the more fascinated by the Parshendi he became.'

'So there's a discrepancy. Why would a man with no prior interest in scholarship suddenly become so obsessed?'

'Yes,' Jasnah said. 'I too have wondered about this. But sometimes, people change. When he returned, I was encouraged by his interest; we spent many evenings talking about his discoveries. It was one of the few times when I felt I really connected with my father.'

Shallan bit her lip. 'Jasnah,' she finally asked. 'Why did you assign me to research this event? You *lived* through this; you already know everything I'm "discovering."'

'I feel a fresh perspective may be of value.' Jasnah put down her book, looking over at Shallan. 'I don't intend for you to find specific answers. Instead, I hope that you will notice details I've missed. You are coming to see how my father's personality changed during those months, and that means you are digging deeply. Believe it or not, few others have caught the discrepancy you just did – though many do note his later changes, once he returned to Kholinar.'

'Even so, I feel a little odd studying it. Perhaps I'm still influenced by my tutors' idea that only the classics are a proper realm of study for young ladies.'

'The classics do have their place, and I will send you to classical works on occasion, as I did with your study of morality. But I intend such tangents to be adjuncts to your current projects. *Those* must be the focus, not long-lost historical conundrums.'

Shallan nodded. 'But Jasnah, aren't you a *historian*? Aren't those long-lost historical conundrums the meat of your field?'

'I'm a Veristitalian,' Jasnah said. 'We search for answers in the past, reconstructing what truly happened. To many, writing a history is not about truth, but about presenting the most flattering picture of themselves and their motives. My sisters and I choose projects that we feel were misunderstood or misrepresented, and in studying them hope to better understand the present.'

Why, then, are you spending so much time studying folktales and looking for evil spirits? No, Jasnah was searching for something real. Something so important that it drew her away from the Shattered Plains and the fight to avenge her father. She intended to do something with those folktales, and Shallan's research was part of it, somehow.

That excited her. It was the sort of thing she'd wanted since she'd been a child, looking through her father's few books, frustrated that he'd chased off yet another tutor. Here, with Jasnah, Shallan was part of something – and, knowing Jasnah, it was something *big*.

And yet, she thought. *Tozbek's ship arrives tomorrow morning. I'll be leaving.*

I need to start complaining. I need to convince Jasnah that this was all so much harder than I anticipated, so that when I leave she won't be surprised. I need to cry, break down, give up. I need to—

'What is Urithiru?' Shallan found herself asking instead.

To her surprise, Jasnah answered without hesitation. 'Urithiru was said to be the center of the Silver Kingdoms, a city that held ten thrones, one for each king. It was the most majestic, most amazing, most important city in all the world.'

'Really? Why hadn't I heard of it before?'

'Because it was abandoned even before the Lost Radiants turned against mankind. Most scholars consider it just a myth. The ardents refuse to speak of it, due to its association with the Radiants, and therefore with the first major failure of Vorinism. Much of what we know about the city comes from fragments of lost works quoted by classical scholars. Many of those classical works have, themselves, survived only in pieces. Indeed, the single complete work we have from early years is *The Way of Kings*, and that is only because of the Vanrial's efforts.'

Shallan nodded slowly. 'If there were ruins of a magnificent, ancient city hidden somewhere, Natanatan – unexplored, overgrown, wild – would be the natural place to find them.'

'Urithiru is *not* in Natanatan,' Jasnah said, smiling. 'But it is a good guess, Shallan. Return to your studies.'

'The weapons,' Shallan said.

Jasnah raised an eyebrow.

'The Parshendi. They carried beautiful weapons of fine, etched steel. Yet they used skin drums with crude handprints on the sides and lived in huts of stone and crem. Doesn't that strike you as incongruous?'

'Yes. I would certainly describe that as an oddity.'

'Then—'

'I assure you, Shallan,' Jasnah said. 'The city is not there.'

'But you *are* interested in the Shattered Plains. You spoke of them with Brightlord Dalinar through the spanreed.'

'I did.'

'What were the Voidbringers?' Now that Jasnah was actually answering, perhaps she'd say. 'What were they *really*?'

Jasnah studied her with a curious expression. 'Nobody knows for sure. Most scholars consider them, like Urithiru, mere myths, while theologians accept them as counterparts of the Almighty – monsters that dwelled in the hearts of men, much as the Almighty once lived there.'

'But—'

'Return to your studies, child,' Jasnah said, raising her book. 'Perhaps we will speak of this another time.'

There was an air of finality about that. Shallan bit her lip, keeping herself from saying something rude just to draw Jasnah back into conversation. *She doesn't trust me*, she thought. Perhaps with good reason. *You're leaving*, Shallan told herself again. *Tomorrow. You're sailing away from this.*

But that meant she had only one day left. One more day in the grand Palanaeum. One more day with all of these books, all of this power and knowledge.

'I need a copy of Tifandor's biography of your father,' Shallan said, poking through the books. 'I keep seeing it referenced.'

'It's on one of the bottom floors,' Jasnah said idly. 'I might be able to dig out the index number.'

'No need,' Shallan said, standing. 'I'll look it up. I need the practice.'

'As you wish,' Jasnah said.

Shallan smiled. She knew exactly where the book was – but the pretense of searching for it would give her time away from Jasnah. And during that time, she'd see what she could discover about the Voidbringers on her own.

⁂

Two hours later, Shallan sat at a cluttered desk at the back of one of the Palanaeum's lower-level rooms, her sphere lantern illuminating a stack of hastily gathered volumes, none of which had proven much use.

It seemed that everybody knew something about the Voidbringers. People in rural areas spoke of them as mysterious creatures that came out at night, stealing from the unlucky and punishing the foolish. Those Void-bringers seemed more mischievous than evil. But then there would be the odd story about a Voidbringer taking on the form of a wayward traveler who – after receiving kindness from a tallew farmer – would slaughter the entire family, drink their blood, then write voidish symbols across the walls in black ash.

Most people in the cities, however, saw the Voidbringers as spirits who stalked at night, a kind of evil spren that invaded the hearts of men and made them do terrible things. When a good man grew angry, it was the work of a Voidbringer.

Scholars laughed at all these ideas. Actual historical accounts – the ones she could find quickly – were contradictory. Were the Voidbringers the denizens of Damnation? If so, wouldn't Damnation now be empty, as the Voidbringers had conquered the Tranquiline Halls and cast out mankind to Roshar?

I should have known that I'd have trouble finding anything solid, Shallan thought, leaning back in her chair. *Jasnah's been researching this for months, maybe years. What did I expect to find in a few hours?*

The only thing the research had done was increase her confusion. What errant winds had brought Jasnah to this topic? It made no sense. Studying the Voidbringers was like trying to determine if deathspren were real or not. What was the point?

She shook her head, stacking her books. The ardents would reshelve them for her. She needed to fetch Tifandor's biography and return to their balcony. She rose and walked toward the room's exit, carrying her lantern in her freehand. She hadn't brought a parshman; she intended to carry back only the one book. As she reached the exit, she noticed another light approaching out on the balcony. Just before she arrived, someone stepped up to the doorway, holding aloft a garnet lantern.

'Kabsal?' Shallan asked, surprised to see his youthful face, painted violet by the light.

'Shallan?' he asked, looking up at the index inscription atop the entryway. 'What are you doing here? Jasnah said you were looking for Tifandor.'

'I . . . got turned around.'

He raised an eyebrow at her.

'Bad lie?' she asked.

'Terrible,' he said. 'You're two floors up and about a thousand index numbers off. After I couldn't find you below, I asked the lift porters to take me where they brought you, and they took me here.'

'Jasnah's training can be exhausting,' Shallan said. 'So I sometimes find a quiet corner to relax and compose myself. It's the only time I get to be alone.'

Kabsal nodded thoughtfully.

'Better?' she asked.

'Still problematic. You took a break, but for *two hours*? Besides, I remember you telling me that Jasnah's training wasn't so terrible.'

'She'd believe me,' Shallan said. 'She thinks she's far more demanding than she is. Or . . . well, she *is* demanding. I just don't mind as much as she thinks I do.'

'Very well,' he said. 'But what *were* you doing down here, then?'

She bit her lip, causing him to laugh.

'What?' she demanded, blushing.

'You just look so blasted *innocent* when you do that!'

'I *am* innocent.'

'Didn't you just lie to me twice in a row?'

'Innocent, as in the opposite of sophisticated.' She grimaced. 'Otherwise, they'd have been more convincing lies. Come. Walk with me while I fetch Tifandor. If we hurry, I won't have to lie to Jasnah.'

'Fair enough,' he said, joining her and strolling around the perimeter of the Palanaeum. The hollow inverted pyramid rose toward the ceiling far above, the four walls expanding outward at a slant. The topmost levels were brighter and easier to make out, tiny lights bobbing along railings in the hands of ardents or scholars.

'Fifty-seven levels,' Shallan said. 'I can't even imagine how much work it must have been for you to create all this.'

'We didn't create it,' Kabsal said. 'It was here. The main shaft, at least. The Kharbranthians cut out the rooms for the books.'

'This formation is *natural*?'

'As natural as cities like Kholinar. Or have you forgotten my demonstration?'

'No. But why didn't you use this place as one of your examples?'

'We haven't found the right sand pattern yet,' he said. 'But we're sure the Almighty himself made this place, as he did the cities.'

'What about the Dawnsingers?' Shallan asked.

'What about them?'

'Could they have created it?'

He chuckled as they arrived at the lift. 'That isn't the kind of thing the Dawnsingers did. They were healers, kindly spren sent by the Almighty to care for humans once we were forced out of the Tranquiline Halls.'

'Kind of like the opposite of the Voidbringers.'

'I suppose you could say that.

'Take us down two levels,' she told the parshman lift porters. They began lowering the platform, the pulleys squeaking and wood shaking beneath her feet.

'If you think to distract me with this conversation,' Kabsal noted, folding his arms and leaning back against the railing, 'you won't be successful. I sat up there with your disapproving mistress for well over an hour, and let me say that it was *not* a pleasant experience. I think she knows I still intend to try and convert her.'

'Of course she does. She's Jasnah. She knows practically everything.'

'Except whatever it is she came here to study.'

'The Voidbringers,' Shallan said. 'That's what she's studying.'

He frowned. A few moments later, the lift came to a rest on the appropriate floor. 'The Voidbringers?' he said, sounding curious. She'd have expected him to be scornful or amused. *No*, she thought. *He's an ardent. He believes in them.*

'What were they?' she asked, walking out. Not far below, the massive cavern came to a point. There was a large infused diamond there, marking the nadir.

'We don't like to talk about it,' Kabsal said as he joined her.

'Why not? You're an ardent. This is part of your religion.'

'An unpopular part. People prefer to hear about the Ten Divine Attributes or the Ten Human Failings. We accommodate them because we, also, prefer that to the deep past.'

'Because . . .' she prodded.

'Because,' he said with a sigh, 'of our failure. Shallan, the devotaries – at their core – are still classical Vorinism. That means the Hierocracy and the fall of the Lost Radiants are *our* shame.' He held up his deep blue lantern. Shallan strolled at his side, curious, letting him just talk.

'We believe that the Voidbringers were *real*, Shallan. A scourge and a plague. A hundred times they came upon mankind. First casting us from the Tranquiline Halls, then trying to destroy us here on Roshar. They weren't just spren that hid under rocks, then came out to steal someone's laundry. They were creatures of terrible destructive power, forged in Damnation, created from hate.'

'By whom?' Shallan asked.

'What?'

'Who made them? I mean, the *Almighty* wasn't likely to have "created something from hate." So what made them?'

'Everything has its opposite, Shallan. The Almighty is a force of good. To balance his goodness, the cosmere needed the Voidbringers as his opposite.'

'So the more good that the Almighty did, the more evil he created as a by-product? What's the point of doing any good at all if it just creates more evil?'

'I see Jasnah has continued your training in philosophy.'

'That's not philosophy,' Shallan said. 'That's simple logic.'

He sighed. 'I don't think you want to get into the deep theology of this. Suffice it to say that the Almighty's pure goodness created the Voidbringers, but *men* may choose good without creating evil because as mortals they have a dual nature. Thus the only way for good to increase in the cos-mere is for men to create it – in that way, good may come to outweigh evil.'

'All right,' she said. 'But I don't buy the explanation about the Voidbringers.'

'I thought you were a believer.'

'I *am*. But just because I honor the Almighty doesn't mean I'm going to accept any explanation, Kabsal. It might be religion, but it still has to make sense.'

'Didn't you once tell me that you didn't understand your own self?'

'Well, yes.'

'And yet you expect to be able to understand the exact workings of the *Almighty*?'

She drew her lips into a line. 'All right, fine. But I still want to know more about the Voidbringers.'

He shrugged as she guided him into an archive room, filled with shelves of books. 'I told you the basics, Shallan. The Voidbringers were an embodiment of evil. We fought them off ninety and nine times, led by the Heralds and their chosen knights, the ten orders we call the Knights Radiant. Finally, Aharietiam came, the Last Desolation. The Voidbringers were cast back into the Tranquiline Halls. The Heralds followed to force them out of heaven as well, and Roshar's Heraldic Epochs ended. Mankind entered the Era of Solitude. The modern era.'

'But why is everything from before so fragmented?'

'This was thousands and thousands of years ago, Shallan,' Kabsal said. 'Before history, before men even knew how to forge steel. We had to be given Shardblades, otherwise we would have had to fight the Voidbringers with clubs.'

'And yet we had the Silver Kingdoms and the Knights Radiant.'

'Formed and led by the Heralds.'

Shallan frowned, counting off rows of shelves. She stopped at the correct one, handed her lantern to Kabsal, then walked down the aisle and plucked the biography off the shelf. Kabsal followed her, holding up the lanterns.

'There's more to this,' Shallan said. 'Otherwise, Jasnah wouldn't be digging so hard.'

'I can tell you why she's doing it,' he said.

Shallan glanced at him.

'Don't you see?' he said. 'She's trying to prove that the Voidbringers weren't real. She wants to demonstrate that this was all a fabrication of the Radiants.' He stepped forward and turned to face her, the lanternlight rebounding from the books to either side, making his face pale. 'She wants to prove once and for all that the devotaries – and Vorinism – are a gigantic fraud. *That's* what this is all about.'

'Maybe,' Shallan said thoughtfully. It did seem to fit. What better goal for an avowed heretic? Undermining foolish beliefs and disproving religion? It explained why Jasnah would study something as seemingly inconsequential as the Voidbringers. Find the right evidence in the historical records, and Jasnah might well be able to prove herself right.

'Haven't we been scourged enough?' Kabsal said, eyes angry. 'The ardents are no threat to her. We're not a threat to anyone these days. We can't own property . . . Damnation, we're property *ourselves*. We dance to the whims of the citylords and warlords, afraid to tell them the truths of their sins for fear of retribution. We're whitespines without tusks or claws, expected to sit at our master's feet and offer praise. Yet this is real. It's *all* real, and they ignore us and—'

He cut off suddenly, glancing at her, lips tight, jaw clenched. She'd never seen such fervor, such *fury* from the pleasant ardent. She wouldn't have thought him capable of it.

'I'm sorry,' he said, turning from her, leading the way back down the aisle.

'It's all right,' she said, hurrying after him, suddenly feeling depressed. Shallan had expected to find something grander, something more mysterious, behind Jasnah's secretive research. Could it all really just be about proving Vorinism false?

They walked in silence out to the balcony. And there, she realized she had to tell him. 'Kabsal, I'm leaving.'

He looked at her, surprised.

'I've had news from my family,' she said. 'I can't speak of it, but I can stay no longer.'

'Something about your father?'

'Why? Have you heard something?'

'Only that he's been reclusive lately. More than normal.'

She suppressed a flinch. News had gotten this far? 'I'm sorry to go so suddenly.'

'You'll return?'

'I don't know.'

He looked into her eyes, searching. 'Do you know when you'll be leaving?' he said in a suddenly cool voice.

'Tomorrow morning.'

'Well then,' he said. 'Will you at least do me the honor of sketching me? You've never given me a likeness, though you've done many of the other ardents.'

She started, realizing that was true. Despite their time together, she'd never done a sketch of Kabsal. She raised her freehand to her mouth. 'I'm sorry!'

He seemed taken aback. 'I didn't mean it bitterly, Shallan. It's really not that important—'

'Yes it *is*,' she said, grabbing his hand, towing him along the walkway. 'I left my drawing things up above. Come on.' She hurried him to the lift, instructing the parshmen to carry them up. As the lift began to rise, Kabsal looked at her hand in his. She dropped it hastily.

'You're a very confusing woman,' he said stiffly.

'I warned you.' She held the retrieved book close to her breast. 'I believe you said you had me figured out.'

'I rescind that statement.' He looked at her. 'You're really leaving?'

She nodded. 'I'm sorry. Kabsal . . . I'm not what you think I am.'

'I think you're a beautiful, intelligent woman.'

'Well, you have the woman part right.'

'Your father is sick, isn't he?'

She didn't answer.

'I can see why you'd want to return to be with him,' Kabsal said. 'But surely you won't abandon your wardship forever. You'll be back with Jasnah.'

'And she won't be staying in Kharbranth forever. She's been moving from place to place almost constantly for the last two years.'

He looked ahead, staring out the front of the lift as they rose. Soon, they had to transfer to another lift to carry them up the next group of floors. 'I shouldn't have been spending time with you,' he finally said. 'The senior ardents think I'm too distracted. They never like it when one of us starts looking outside the ardentia.'

'Your right to court is protected.'

'We're property. A man's rights can be protected at the same time that he is discouraged from exercising them. I've avoided work, I've disobeyed my superiors . . . In courting you, I've also courted trouble.'

'I didn't ask you for any of that.'

'You didn't discourage me.'

She had no response for that, other than to feel a rising worry. A hint of panic, a desire to run away and hide. During her years of near-solitude on her father's estate, she had never dreamed of a relationship like this one. *Is that what this is?* she thought, panic swelling. *A relationship?* Her intentions in coming to Kharbranth had seemed so straightforward. How had she gotten to the point where she risked breaking a man's heart?

And, to her shame, she admitted to herself that she would miss the research more than Kabsal. Was she a horrible person for feeling that way? She *was* fond of him. He was pleasant. Interesting.

He looked at her, and there was longing in his eyes. He seemed . . . Stormfather, he seemed to really be in love with her. Shouldn't she be falling in love with him too? She didn't think she was. She was just confused.

When they reached the top of the Palanaeum's system of lifts, she practically ran out into the Veil. Kabsal followed, but they needed another lift up to Jasnah's alcove, and soon she found herself trapped with him once more.

'I could come,' Kabsal said softly. 'Return with you to Jah Keved.'

Shallan's panic increased. She barely knew him. Yes, they had chatted frequently, but rarely about the important things. If he left the ardentia, he'd be demoted to tenth dahn, almost as low as a darkeyes. He'd be without money or house, in almost as bad a position as her family.

Her family. What would her brothers say if she brought a virtual stranger back with her? Another man to become part of their problems, privy to their secrets?

'I can see from your expression that it's not an option,' Kabsal said. 'It seems that I've misinterpreted some very important things.'

'No, it's not that,' Shallan said quickly. 'It's just . . . Oh, Kabsal. How can you expect to make sense of my actions when even *I* can't make sense of them?' She touched his arm, turning him toward her. 'I have been dishonest with you. And with Jasnah. And, most infuriatingly, with myself. I'm sorry.'

He shrugged, obviously trying to feign nonchalance. 'At least I'll get a sketch. Won't I?'

She nodded as the lift finally shuddered to a halt. She walked down the dark hallway, Kabsal following with the lanterns. Jasnah looked up appraisingly as Shallan entered their alcove, but did not ask why she'd taken so long. Shallan found herself blushing as she gathered her drawing tools. Kabsal hesitated in the doorway. He'd left a basket of bread and jam on the desk. The top of it was still wrapped with a cloth; Jasnah hadn't touched it, though he always offered her some as a peace offering. Without jam, since Jasnah hated it.

'Where should I sit?' Kabsal asked.

'Just stand there,' Shallan said, sitting down, propping her sketchpad against her legs and holding it still with her covered safehand. She looked up at him, leaning with one hand against the doorframe. Head shaved, light grey robe draped around him, sleeves short, waist tied with a white sash. Eyes confused. She blinked, taking a Memory, then began to sketch.

It was one of the most awkward experiences of her life. She didn't tell Kabsal that he could move, and so he held the pose. He didn't speak. Perhaps he thought it would spoil the picture. Shallan found her hand shaking as she sketched, though – thankfully – she managed to hold back tears.

Tears, she thought, doing the final lines of the wall around Kabsal. *Why should I cry? I'm not the one who just got rejected. Can't my emotions make sense once in a while?*

'Here,' she said, pulling the page free and holding it up. 'It will smudge unless you spray it with lacquer.'

Kabsal hesitated, then walked over, taking the picture in reverent fingers. 'It's wonderful,' he whispered. He looked up, then hurried to his lantern, opening it and pulling out the garnet broam inside. 'Here,' he said, proffering it. 'Payment.'

'I can't take that! For one thing, it's not yours.' As an ardent, anything Kabsal carried would belong to the king.

'Please,' Kabsal said. 'I want to give you something.'

'The picture is a gift,' she said. 'If you pay me for it, then I haven't given you anything.'

'Then I'll commission another,' he said, pressing the glowing sphere into her fingers. 'I'll take the first likeness for free, but do another for me, please. One of the two of us together.'

She paused. She rarely did sketches of herself. They felt strange to draw. 'All right.' She took the sphere, then furtively tucked it into her safe-pouch, beside her Soulcaster. It was a little odd to carry something so heavy there, but she'd gotten accustomed to the bulge and weight.

'Jasnah, do you have a mirror?' she asked.

The other woman sighed audibly, obviously annoyed by the distraction. She felt through her things, taking out a mirror. Kabsal fetched it.

'Hold it up beside your head,' Shallan said, 'so I can see myself.'

He walked back over, doing so, looking confused.

'Angle it to the side a little,' Shallan said, 'all right, there.' She blinked, freezing in her mind the image of her face beside his. 'Have a seat. You don't need the mirror any longer. I just wanted it for reference – it helps me for some reason to place my features into the scene I want to sketch. I'll put myself sitting beside you.'

He sat on the floor, and Shallan began to work, using it to distract herself from her conflicting emotions. Guilt at not feeling as strongly for Kabsal as he did for her, yet sorrow that she wouldn't be seeing him anymore. And above it all, anxiety about the Soulcaster.

Sketching herself in beside him was challenging. She worked furiously, blending the reality of Kabsal sitting and a fiction of herself, in her flower-embroidered dress, sitting with her legs to the side. The face in the mirror became her reference point, and she built her head around it. Too narrow to be beautiful, with hair too light, cheeks dotted with freckles.

The Soulcaster, she thought. *Being here in Kharbranth with it is a danger. But leaving is dangerous too. Could there be a third option? What if I sent it away?*

She hesitated, charcoal pencil hovering above the picture. Dared she send the fabrial – packaged, delivered to Tozbek in secret – back to Jah Keved without her? She wouldn't have to worry about being incriminated if her room or person were searched, though she'd want to destroy all pictures she'd drawn of Jasnah with the Soulcaster. And she wouldn't risk suspicion by vanishing when Jasnah discovered her Soulcaster didn't work.

She continued her drawing, increasingly withdrawn into her thoughts, letting her fingers work. If she sent the Soulcaster back alone, then she could stay in Kharbranth. It was a golden, tempting prospect, but one that threw her emotions further into a jumbled mess. She'd been preparing herself to leave for so long. What would she do about Kabsal? And Jasnah. Could Shallan really remain here, accepting Jasnah's freely given tutelage, after what she'd done?

Yes, Shallan thought. *Yes, I could.*

The fervency of that emotion surprised her. She would live with the guilt, day by day, if it meant continuing to learn. It was terribly selfish of her, and she was ashamed of it. But she would do it for a little longer, at least. She'd have to go back eventually, of course. She couldn't leave her brothers to face danger alone. They needed her.

Selfishness, followed by courage. She was nearly as surprised by the latter as she had been by the former. Neither was something she often associated with who she was. But she was coming to realize that she hadn't *known* who she was. Not until she left Jah Keved and everything familiar, everything she'd been expected to be.

Her sketching grew more and more fervent. She finished the figures and moved to the background. Quick, bold lines became the floor and the archway behind. A scribbled dark smudge for the side of the desk, casting a shadow. Crisp, thin lines for the lantern sitting on the floor. Sweeping, breezelike lines to form the legs and robes of the creature standing behind—

Shallan froze, fingers drawing an unintended line of charcoal, breaking away from the figure she'd sketched directly behind Kabsal. A figure that wasn't really there, a figure with a sharp, angular symbol hovering above its collar instead of a head.

Shallan stood, throwing back her chair, sketchpad and charcoal pencil clutched in the fingers of her freehand.

'Shallan?' Kabsal said, standing.

She'd done it again. Why? The peace she'd begun to feel during the sketching evaporated in a heartbeat, and her heart started to race. The pressures returned. Kabsal. Jasnah. Her brothers. Decisions, choices, problems.

'Is everything all right?' Kabsal said, taking a step toward her.

'I'm sorry,' she said. 'I— I made a mistake.'

He frowned. To the side, Jasnah looked up, brow wrinkled.

'It's all right,' Kabsal said. 'Look, let's have some bread and jam. We can calm down, then you could finish it. I don't care about a—'

'I need to go,' Shallan cut in, feeling suffocated. 'I'm sorry.'

She brushed past the dumbfounded ardent, hurrying from the alcove, giving a wide berth to the place where the figure stood in her sketch. What was *wrong* with her?

She rushed to the lift, calling for the parshmen to lower her. She glanced over her shoulder. Kabsal stood in the hallway, looking after her. Shallan reached the lift, drawing pad clutched in her hand, her heart racing. *Calm yourself*, she thought, leaning back against the lift platform's wooden railing as the parshmen began to take her down. She looked up at the empty landing above her.

And found herself blinking, memorizing that scene. She began sketching again.

She drew with concise motions, sketchpad held against her safearm. For illumination, she had just two very small spheres at either side, where the taut ropes quivered. She moved without thought, just *drawing*, staring upward.

She looked down at what she had drawn. Two figures stood on the landing above, wearing the too-straight robes, like cloth made from metal. They leaned down, watching her go.

She looked up again. The landing was empty. *What's happening to me?* she thought with increasing horror. When the lift hit the ground, she scrambled away, her skirt fluttering. She all but ran to the exit of the Veil, hesitating beside the doorway, ignoring the master-servants and ardents who gave her confused looks.

Where to go? Sweat trickled down the sides of her face. Where to run when you were going mad?

She cut into the main cavern's crowd. It was late afternoon, and the dinner rush had begun – servants pushing dining carts, lighteyes strolling to their rooms, scholars walking with hands behind their backs. Shallan dashed through their midst, her hair coming free of its bun, the hairspike dropping to the rock behind her with a high-pitched clink. Her loose red hair streamed behind. She reached the hallway leading to their rooms, panting, hair askew, and glanced over her shoulder. Amid the flow of traffic she'd left a trail of people looking after her in confusion.

Almost against her will, she blinked and took a Memory. She raised her pad again, gripping her charcoal pencil in slick fingers, quickly sketching the crowded cavern scene. Just faint impressions. Men of lines, women of curves, walls of sloping rock, carpeted floor, bursts of light in sphere lanterns on the walls.

And five symbol-headed figures in black, too-stiff robes and cloaks. Each had a different symbol, twisted and unfamiliar to her, hanging above a neckless torso. The creatures wove through the crowd unseen. Like predators. Focused on Shallan.

I'm just imagining it, she tried to tell herself. *I'm overtaxed, too many things weighing on me.* Did they represent her guilt? The stress of betraying Jasnah and lying to Kabsal? The things she had done before leaving Jah Keved?

She tried to stand there, waiting, but her fingers refused to remain still. She blinked, then started drawing again on a new sheet. She finished with a shaking hand. The figures were almost to her, angular not-heads hanging horrifically where faces should have been.

Logic warned that she was overreacting, but no matter what she told herself, she couldn't believe it. These were *real*. And they were coming for her.

She dashed away, surprising several servants who had been approaching her to offer assistance. She ran, slippered feet sliding on the hallway carpets, eventually reaching the door to Jasnah's rooms. Sketchpad under her arm, she unlocked it with quivering fingers, then pushed through and slammed it behind her. She locked it again and ran for her chamber. She slammed that door closed too, then turned, backing away. The only light in the room came from the three diamond marks in the large crystal goblet on her nightstand.

She got on the bed, then scrambled back as far from the door as she could, until she was against the wall, breathing through her nose with frantic breaths. She still had her sketchpad under her arm, though she'd lost the charcoal. There was more in her nightstand.

Don't do it, she thought. *Just sit and calm yourself.*

She felt a growing chill, a rising terror. She *had* to know. She scrambled to pull out the charcoal, then blinked and began to sketch her room.

Ceiling first. Four straight lines. Down the walls. Lines at the corners. Her fingers kept moving, drawing, depicting the pad itself, held before her, safehand shrouded and bracing the pad from behind. And then on. To the beings standing around her – twisted symbols unconnected to their uneven shoulders. Those not-heads had unreal angles, surfaces that melded in weird, impossible ways.

The creature at the front was reaching too-smooth fingers toward Shallan. Just inches from the right side of the sketchpad.

Oh, Stormfather ... Shallan thought, charcoal pencil falling still. The room was empty, yet depicted right in front of her was an image of it crowded full of sleek figures. They were close enough that she should be able to feel them breathing, if they breathed.

Was there a chill in the room? Hesitantly – terrified but unable to stop herself – Shallan dropped her pencil and raised her freehand to the right.

And felt something.

She screamed then, jumping to her feet on her bed, dropping the pad, backing against the wall. Before she could consciously think of what she was doing, she was struggling with her sleeve, trying to get the Soulcaster out. It was the only thing she had resembling a weapon. No, that was stupid. She didn't know how to use it. She was helpless.

Except ...

Storms! she thought, frantic. *I can't use that. I promised myself.*

She began the process anyway. Ten heartbeats, to bring forth the fruit of her sin, the proceeds of her most horrific act. She was interrupted midway through by a voice, uncanny yet distinct:

What are you?

She clutched her hand to her chest, losing her balance on the soft bed, falling to her knees on the rumpled blanket. She put one hand to the side, steadying herself on the nightstand, fingers brushing the large glass goblet that sat there.

'What am I?' she whispered. 'I'm terrified.'

This is true.

The bedroom transformed around her.

The bed, the nightstand, her sketchpad, the walls, the ceiling – everything seemed to *pop*, forming into tiny, dark glass spheres. She found herself in a place with a black sky and a strange, small white sun that hung on the horizon, too far away.

Shallan screamed as she found herself in midair, falling backward in a shower of beads. Flames hovered nearby, dozens of them, perhaps hundreds. Like the tips of candles floating in the air and moving in the wind.

She hit something. An endless dark sea, except it wasn't wet. It was made of the small beads, an entire ocean of tiny glass spheres. They surged around her, moving in an undulating swell. She gasped, flailing, trying to stay afloat.

You want me to change? a warm voice said in her mind, distinct and different from the cold whisper she had heard earlier. It was deep and hollow and conveyed a sense of great age. It seemed to come from her hand, and she realized she was grasping something there. One of the beads.

The movement of the ocean of glass threatened to tow her down; she kicked frantically, somehow managing to stay afloat.

I've been as I am for a great long time, the warm voice said. *I sleep so much. I will change. Give me what you have.*

'I don't know what you mean! Please, help me!'

I will change.

She felt suddenly cold, as if the warmth were being drawn from her. She screamed as the bead in her fingers flared to sudden warmth. She dropped it just as a shift in the ocean swell towed her under, beads rolling over one another with a soft clatter.

She fell back and hit her bed, back in her room. Beside her, the goblet on her nightstand *melted*, the glass becoming red liquid, dropping the three spheres inside to the nightstand's flooded top. The red liquid poured over the sides of the nightstand, splashing to the floor. Shallan pulled back, horrified.

The goblet had been changed into blood.

Her shocked motion thumped the nightstand, shaking it. An empty glass water pitcher had been sitting beside the goblet. Her motion knocked it over, toppling it to the ground. It shattered on the stone floor, splashing the blood.

That was a Soulcasting! she thought. She'd changed the goblet into blood, which was one of the Ten Essences. She raised her hand to her head, staring at the red liquid expanding in a pool on her floor. There seemed to be quite a lot of it.

She was so bewildered. The voice, the creatures, the sea of glass beads and the dark, cold sky. It had all come upon her so quickly.

I Soulcast, she realized again. *I did it!*

Did it have something to do with the creatures? But she'd begun seeing them in her drawings before she'd ever stolen the Soulcaster. How ... what ... ? She looked down at her safehand and the Soulcaster hidden in the pouch inside her sleeve.

I didn't put it on, she thought. *Yet I used it anyway.*

'Shallan?'

It was Jasnah's voice. Just outside Shallan's room. The princess must have followed her. Shallan felt a spike of terror as she saw a line of blood leaking toward the doorway. It was almost there, and would pass underneath in a heartbeat.

Why did it have to be blood? Nauseated, she leaped to her feet, slippers soaking up the red liquid.

'Shallan?' Jasnah said, voice closer. 'What was that sound?'

Shallan looked frantically at the blood, then at the sketchpad, filled with pictures of the strange creatures. What if they *did* have something to do with the Soulcasting? Jasnah would recognize them. There was a shadow under the door.

She panicked, tucking the sketchpad away in her trunk. But the blood, *it* would condemn her. There was enough that only a life-threatening wound could have created it. Jasnah would see. She'd know. Blood where there should be none? One of the Ten Essences?

Jasnah was going to know what Shallan had done!

A thought struck Shallan. It wasn't a brilliant thought, but it was a way out, and it was the only thing that occurred to her. She went to her knees and grabbed a shard of the broken glass pitcher in her safehand, through the fabric of her sleeve. She took a breath and pulled up her right sleeve, then used the glass to cut a shallow gash in her skin. In the panic of the moment, it barely even hurt. Blood welled out.

As the doorknob turned and the door opened, Shallan dropped the glass shard and lay on her side. She closed her eyes, feigning unconsciousness. The door swung open.

Jasnah gasped, immediately calling for help. She rushed to Shallan's side, grabbing her arm and putting pressure on the wound. Shallan mumbled, as if she were barely conscious, gripping her safepouch – and the Soulcaster inside – with her safehand. They wouldn't open it, would they? She pulled her arm closer to her chest, cowering silently as more footsteps and calls sounded, servants and parshmen running into the room, Jasnah shouting for more help.

This, Shallan thought, *will not end well.*

'Though I was due for dinner in Veden City that night, I insisted upon visiting Kholinar to speak with Tivbet. The tariffs through Urithiru were growing quite unreasonable. By then, the so-called Radiants had already begun to show their true nature.'

—Following the firing of the original Palanaeum, only one page of Terxim's autobiography remained, and this is the only line of any use to me.

Kaladin dreamed he was the storm.

He raged forward, the stormwall behind him his trailing cape, soaring above a heaving, black expanse. The ocean. His passing churned up a tempest, slamming waves into one another, lifting white caps to be caught in his wind.

He approached a dark continent and soared upward. Higher. Higher. He left the sea behind. The vastness of the continent spread out before him, seemingly endless, an ocean of rock. *So large*, he thought, awed. He hadn't understood. How could he have?

He roared past the Shattered Plains. They looked as if something very large had hit them at the center, sending rippling breaks outward. They too were larger than he'd expected; no wonder nobody had been able to find their way through the chasms.

There was a large plateau at the center, but with the darkness and the distance, he could not see much. There were lights, though. Someone lived there.

He did see that the eastern side of the plains was very different from the western side, marked by tall, spindly pillars, plateaus that had nearly been worn away. Despite that, he could see a symmetry to the Shattered Plains. From high above, the plains resembled a work of art.

In a moment, he was past them, continuing north and west to soar across the Sea of Spears, a shallow inland sea where broken fingers of rock jutted above the water. He passed over Alethkar, catching a glimpse of the great city of Kholinar, built amid formations of rock like fins rising from the stone. Then he turned southward, away from anything he knew. He crested majestic mountains, densely populated at their tips, with villages clustered near vents that emitted steam or lava. The Horn-eater Peaks?

He left them with rain and winds, rumbling down into foreign lands. He passed cities and open plains, villages and twisting waterways. There were many armies. Kaladin passed tents pulled flat against the leeward sides of rock formations, stakes driven into the rock to hold them taut, men hidden inside. He passed hillsides where soldiers huddled in clefts. He passed large wooden wagons, built to house lighteyes while at war. How many wars was the world fighting? Was there nowhere that was at peace?

He took a path to the southwest, blowing toward a city built in long troughs in the ground that looked like giant claw marks ripped across the landscape. He was over it in a flash, passing a hinterland where the stone itself was ribbed and rippled, like frozen waves of water. The people in this kingdom were dark-skinned, like Sigzil.

The land went on and on. Hundreds of cities. Thousands of villages. People with faint blue veins beneath their skin. A place where the pressure of the approaching highstorm blew water out of spouts in the ground. A city where people lived in gigantic, hollowed-out stalactites hanging beneath a titanic sheltered ridge.

Westward he blew. The land was so vast. So enormous. So many different people. It dazzled his mind. War seemed far less prevalent in the West than it was in the East, and that comforted him, but still he was troubled. Peace seemed a scarce commodity in the world.

Something drew his attention. Strange flashes of light. He blew toward them at the forefront of the storm. What *were* those lights? They came in bursts, forming the strangest patterns. Almost like physical things that he could reach out and touch, spherical bubbles of light that vibrated with spikes and troughs.

Kaladin crossed a strange city laid out in a triangular pattern, with tall peaks rising like sentries at the corners and center. The flashes of light were coming from a building on the central peak. Kaladin knew he would pass quickly, for as the storm, he could not retreat. Ever westward he blew.

He threw open the door with his wind, entering a long hallway with bright red tile walls, mosaic murals that he passed too quickly to make out. He rustled the skirts of tall, golden-haired serving women who carried trays of food or steaming towels. They called in a strange language, perhaps wondering who had left a window unbarred in a highstorm.

The flashes of light came from directly ahead. So transfixing. Brushing past a pretty gold- and red-haired woman who huddled frightened in a corner, Kaladin burst through a door. He had one brief glimpse of what lay beyond.

A man stood over two corpses. His pale head shaved, his clothing white, the murderer held a long, thin sword in one hand. He looked up from his victims and almost seemed to *see* Kaladin. He had large Shin eyes.

It was too late to see anything more. Kaladin blew out the window, throwing shutters wide and streaking into the night.

More cities, mountains, and forests passed in a blur. At his advent, plants curled up their leaves, rockbuds closed their shells, and shrubs withdrew their branches. Before long, he neared the western ocean.

CHILD OF TANAVAST. CHILD OF HONOR. CHILD OF ONE LONG SINCE DEPARTED. The sudden voice shook Kaladin; he floundered in the air.

THE OATHPACT WAS SHATTERED.

The booming sound made the stormwall itself vibrate. Kaladin hit the ground, separating from the storm. He skidded to a stop, feet throwing up sprays of water. Stormwinds crashed into him, but he was enough a part of them that they neither tossed nor shook him.

MEN RIDE THE STORMS NO LONGER. The voice was thunder, crashing in the air. THE OATHPACT IS BROKEN, CHILD OF HONOR.

'I don't understand!' Kaladin screamed into the tempest.

A face formed before him, the face he had seen before, the aged face as wide as the sky, its eyes full of stars.

ODIUM COMES. MOST DANGEROUS OF ALL THE SIXTEEN. YOU WILL NOW GO.

Something blew against him. 'Wait!' Kaladin said. 'Why is there so much war? Must we always fight?' He wasn't sure why he asked. The questions simply came out.

The storm rumbled, like a thoughtful aged father. The face vanished, shattering into droplets of water.

More softly, the voice answered, ODIUM REIGNS.

⁂

Kaladin gasped as he awoke. He was surrounded by dark figures, holding him down against the hard stone floor. He yelled, old reflexes taking over. Instinctively, he snapped his hands outward to the sides, each grabbing an ankle and jerking to pull two assailants off balance.

They cursed, crashing to the ground. Kaladin used the moment to twist while bringing an arm up in a sweep. He knocked free the hands pushing him down, rocked and threw himself forward, lurching into the man directly in front of him.

Kaladin rolled over him, tucking and coming up on his feet, free of his captives. He spun, flinging sweat from his brow. Where was his spear? He clutched for the knife at his belt.

No knife. No spear.

'Storm you, Kaladin!' That was Teft.

Kaladin raised a hand to his breast, breathing deliberately, dispelling the strange dream. Bridge Four. He was with Bridge Four. The king's stormwardens had predicted a highstorm in the early morning hours.

'It's all right,' he said to the cursing, twisting clump of bridgemen who had been holding him down. 'What were you doing?'

'You tried to go out in the storm,' Moash said accusingly, extricating himself. The only light was a single diamond sphere one of the men had set in the corner.

'Ha!' Rock added, standing up and brushing himself off. 'Had the door open to the rain, staring out, as if you'd been hit on the head with stone.

We had to pull you back. Is not good for you to spend another two weeks sick in bed, eh?'

Kaladin calmed himself. The riddens – the quiet rainfall at the trailing end of a highstorm – continued outside, drops sprinkling the roof.

'You wouldn't wake up,' Sigzil said. Kaladin glanced at the Azish man, sitting with his back to the stone wall. He hadn't tried to hold Kaladin down. 'You were having some kind of fever dream.'

'I feel just fine,' Kaladin said. That wasn't quite true; his head ached and he was exhausted. He took a deep breath and threw back his shoulders, trying to force the fatigue away.

The sphere in the corner flickered. Then its light faded away, leaving them in darkness.

'Storm it!' Moash muttered. 'That eel Gaz. He's been giving us dun spheres again.'

Kaladin crossed the pitch-black barrack, stepping carefully. His headache faded away as he felt for the door. He pushed it open, letting in the faint light of an overcast morning.

The winds were weak, but the rain still fell. He stepped out, and was shortly soaked through. The other bridgemen followed him out, and Rock tossed Kaladin a small chunk of soap. Like most of the others, Kaladin wore only his loincloth, and he lathered himself up in the cold downpour. The soap smelled of oil and was gritty with the sand suspended in it. No sweet, soft soaps for bridgemen.

Kaladin tossed the bit of soap to Bisig, a thin bridgeman with an angular face. He took it gratefully – Bisig didn't say much – and began to lather up as Kaladin let the rain wash the soap from his body and hair. To the side, Rock was using a bowl of water to shave and trim his Horneater beard, long on the sides and covering the cheeks, but clean below the lips and chin. It made an odd counterpoint to his head, which he shaved up the center, from directly above the eyebrows back. He trimmed the rest of his hair short.

Rock's hand was smooth and careful, and he didn't so much as nick himself. Once finished, he stood up and waved to the men waiting behind him. One by one, he shaved any who wanted it. He occasionally paused to sharpen the razor using his whetstone and leather strop.

Kaladin raised his fingers to his own beard. He hadn't been clean-shaven since he'd been in Amaram's army, so long ago. He walked forward to join those waiting in line. When Kaladin's time came, the large Horneater laughed. 'Sit, my friend, sit! Is good you have come. Your face is more like scragglebark branches than a proper beard.'

'Shave it clean,' Kaladin said, sitting down on the stump. 'And I'd rather not have a strange pattern like yours.'

'Ha!' Rock said, sharpening his razor. 'You are a lowlander, my good friend. Is not right for you to wear a *humaka'aban*. I would have to thump you soundly if you tried this thing.'

'I thought you said fighting was beneath you.'

'Is allowed several important exceptions,' Rock said. 'Now stop with your talking, unless you wish to be losing a lip.'

Rock began by trimming the beard down, then lathered and shaved, starting at the left cheek. Kaladin had never let another shave him before; when he'd first gone to war, he'd been young enough that he'd barely needed to shave at all. He'd grown into doing it himself as he got older.

Rock's touch was deft, and Kaladin didn't feel any nicks or cuts. In a few minutes, Rock stood back. Kaladin raised his fingers to his chin, touching smooth, sensitive skin. His face felt cold, strange to the touch. It took him back, transformed him – just a little – into the man he had been.

Strange, how much difference a shave could make. *I should have done this weeks ago.*

The riddens had turned to drizzle, heralding the storm's last whispers. Kaladin stood up, letting the water wash bits of shorn hair from his chest. Baby-faced Dunny – the last of those waiting – sat down for his turn at being shaven. He hardly needed it at all.

'The shave suits you,' a voice said. Kaladin turned to see Sigzil leaning against the wall of the barrack, just under the roof's overhang. 'Your face has strong lines. Square and firm, with a proud chin. We would call it a leader's face among my people.'

'I'm no lighteyes,' Kaladin said, spitting to the side.

'You hate them so much.'

'I hate their lies,' Kaladin said. 'I hate it that I used to believe they were honorable.'

'And would you cast them down?' Sigzil asked, sounding curious. 'Rule in their place?'

'No.'

This seemed to surprise Sigzil. To the side, Syl finally appeared, having finished frolicking in the winds of the highstorm. He always worried – just a little – that she'd ride away with them and leave him.

'Have you no thirst to punish those who have treated you so?' Sigzil asked.

'Oh, I'm happy to punish them,' Kaladin said. 'But I have no desire to take their place, nor do I wish to join them.'

'I'd join them in a heartbeat,' Moash said, walking up behind. He folded his arms across his lean, well-muscled chest. 'If I were in charge, things would change. The lighteyes would work the mines and the fields. They would run bridges and die by Parshendi arrows.'

'Won't happen,' Kaladin said. 'But I won't blame you for trying.'

Sigzil nodded thoughtfully. 'Have either of you ever heard of the land of Babatharnam?'

'No,' Kaladin said, glancing toward the camp. The soldiers were moving about now. More than a few were washing too. 'That's a funny name for a country, though.'

Sigzil sniffed. 'Personally, I always thought Alethkar sounded like a ridiculous name. I guess it depends on where you were raised.'

'So why bring up Babab . . .' Moash said.

'Babatharnam,' Sigzil said. 'I visited there once, with my master. They have very peculiar trees. The entire plant – trunk and all – lies down when a highstorm approaches, as if built on hinges. I was thrown in prison three times during our visit there. The Babath are quite particular about how you speak. My master was quite displeased at the amount he had to pay to free me. Of course, I think they were using any excuse to imprison a foreigner, as they knew my master had deep pockets.' He smiled wistfully. 'One of those imprisonments *was* my fault. The women there, you see, have these patterns of veins that sit shallowly beneath their skin. Some visitors find it unnerving, but I found the patterns beautiful. Almost irresistible . . .'

Kaladin frowned. Hadn't he seen something like that in his dream?

'I bring up Babath because they have a curious system of rule there,' Sigzil continued. 'You see, the elderly are given office. The older you are, the more authority you have. Everyone gets a chance to rule, if they live long enough. The king is called the Most Ancient.'

'Sounds fair,' Moash said, walking over to join Sigzil beneath the overhang. 'Better than deciding who rules based on eye color.'

'Ah yes,' Sigzil said. 'The Babath are very fair. Currently, the Monavakah Dynasty reigns.'

'How can you have a dynasty if you choose your leaders based on their age?' Kaladin asked.

'It's actually quite easy,' Sigzil said. 'You just execute anyone who gets old enough to challenge you.'

Kaladin felt a chill. 'They *do* that?'

'Yes, unfortunately,' Sigzil said. 'There is a great deal of unrest in Babatharnam. It was dangerous to visit when we did. The Monavakahs make very certain that *their* family members live the longest; for fifty years, no one outside their family has become Most Ancient. All others have fallen through assassination, exile, or death on the battlefield.'

'That's horrible,' Kaladin said.

'I doubt many would disagree. But I mention these horrors for a purpose. You see, it has been my experience that no matter where you go, you will find some who abuse their power.' He shrugged. 'Eye color is not so odd a method, compared to many others I have seen. If you were to overthrow the lighteyes and place yourselves in power, Moash, I doubt that the world would be a very different place. The abuses would still happen. Simply to other people.'

Kaladin nodded slowly, but Moash shook his head. 'No. I'd change the world, Sigzil. And I mean to.'

'And how are you going to do that?' Kaladin asked, amused.

'I came to this war to get myself a Shardblade,' Moash said. 'And I still mean to do it, somehow.' He blushed, then turned away.

'You joined up assuming they'd make you a spearman, didn't you?' Kaladin asked.

Moash hesitated, then nodded. 'Some of those who joined with me did become soldiers, but most of us got sent to the bridge crews.' He glanced at Kaladin, expression growing dark. 'This plan of yours had better work, lordling. Last time I ran away, I got a beating. I was told if I tried again, I'd get a slave's mark instead.'

'I never promised it would work, Moash. If you've got a better idea, go ahead and share it.'

Moash hesitated. 'Well, if you really do teach us the spear like you promised, then I guess I don't care.'

Kaladin glanced about, warily checking to see if Gaz or any bridgemen from other crews were nearby. 'Keep quiet,' Kaladin muttered to Moash. 'Don't speak of that outside of the chasms.' The rain had almost stopped; soon the clouds would break.

Moash glared at him, but remained silent.

'You don't really think they'd let you have a Shardblade, do you?' Sigzil said.

'Any man can win a Shardblade.' Moash said. 'Slave or free. Lighteyes or dark. It's the law.'

'Assuming they follow the law,' Kaladin said with a sigh.

'I'll do it somehow,' Moash repeated. He glanced to the side, where Rock was closing up his razor and wiping the rainwater from his bald head.

The Horneater approached them. 'I have heard of this place you spoke of, Sigzil,' Rock said. 'Babatharnam. My cousin cousin cousin visited there one time. They have very tasty snails.'

'That is a long distance to travel for a Horneater,' Sigzil noted.

'Nearly same distance as for an Azish,' Rock said. 'Actually, much more, since you have such little legs!'

Sigzil scowled.

'I have seen your kind before,' Rock said, folding his arms.

'What?' Sigzil asked. 'Azish? We are not so rare.'

'No, not your race,' Rock said. 'Your type. What is it they are called? Visiting places around the land, telling others of what they have seen? A Worldsinger. Yes, is the right name. No?'

Sigzil froze. Then he suddenly stood up straight and stalked away from the barrack without looking back.

'Now why is he acting like this thing?' Rock asked. 'I am not ashamed of being cook. Why is he ashamed of being Worldsinger?'

'Worldsinger?' Kaladin asked.

Rock shrugged. 'I do not know much. Are strange people. Say they must travel to each kingdom and tell the people there of other kingdoms. Is a kind of storyteller, though they are thinking of themselves as much more.'

'He's probably some kind of brightlord in his country,' Moash said. 'The way he talks. Wonder how he ended up with us cremlings.'

'Hey,' Dunny said, joining them. 'What'd you do to Sigzil? He promised to tell me about my homeland.'

'Homeland?' Moash said to the younger man. 'You're from Alethkar.'

'Sigzil said these violet eyes of mine aren't native to Alethkar. He thinks I must have Veden blood in me.'

'Your eyes aren't violet,' Moash said.

'Sure they are,' Dunny said. 'You can see it in bright sunlight. They're just really dark.'

'Ha!' Rock said. 'If you are from Vedenar, we are cousins! The Peaks are near Vedenar. Sometimes the people there have good red hair, like us!'

'Be glad that someone didn't mistake your eyes for red, Dunny,' Kaladin said. 'Moash, Rock, go gather your subsquads and pass the word to Teft and Skar. I want the men oiling their vests and sandals against the humidity.'

The men sighed, but did as ordered. The army provided the oil. While the bridgemen were expendable, good hogshide and metal for buckles were not cheap.

As the men gathered to work, the sun broke through the clouds. The warmth of the light felt good on Kaladin's rain-wet skin. There was something refreshing about the chill of a highstorm followed by the sun. Tiny rockbud polyps on the side of the building opened, drinking in the wet air. Those would have to be scraped free. Rockbuds would eat away the stone of the walls, creating pockmarks and cracks.

The buds were a deep crimson. It was Chachel, third day of the week. The slave markets would show new wares. That would mean new bridgemen. Kaladin's crew was in serious danger. Yake had caught an arrow in the arm during their last run, and Delp had caught one in the neck. There'd been nothing Kaladin could do for him, and with Yake wounded, Kaladin's team was down to twenty-eight bridge-capable members.

Sure enough, about an hour into their morning activities – caring for equipment, oiling the bridge, Lopen and Dabbid running to fetch their morning gruel pot and bring it back to the lumberyard – Kaladin caught sight of soldiers leading a line of dirty, shuffling men toward the lumberyard. Kaladin gestured to Teft, and the two of them marched up to meet Gaz.

'Afore you yell at me,' Gaz said as Kaladin arrived, 'understand that I can't change anything here.' The slaves were bunched up, watched over by a pair of soldiers in wrinkled green coats.

'You're bridge sergeant,' Kaladin said. Teft stepped up beside him. He hadn't gotten a shave, though he'd begun keeping his short, grey beard neatly trimmed.

'Yeah,' Gaz said, 'but I don't make assignments any more. Brightness Hashal wants to do it herself. In the name of her husband, of course.'

Kaladin gritted his teeth. She'd starve Bridge Four of members. 'So we get nothing.'

'I didn't say *that*,' Gaz said, then spat black spittle to the side. 'She gave you one.'

That's something, at least, Kaladin thought. There were a good hundred men in the new group. 'Which one? He'd better be tall enough to carry a bridge.'

'Oh, he's tall enough,' Gaz said, gesturing a few slaves out of the way. 'Good worker too.' The men shuffled aside, revealing one man standing at the back. He was a little shorter than average, but he *was* still tall enough to carry a bridge.

But he had black and red marbled skin.

'A *parshman*?' Kaladin asked. To his side, Teft cursed under his breath.

'Why not?' Gaz said. 'They're perfect slaves. Never talk back.'

'But we're at *war* with them!' Teft said.

'We're at war with a tribe of oddities,' Gaz said. 'Those out on the Shattered Plains are right different from the fellows who work for us.'

That much, at least, was true. There were a lot of parshmen in the warcamp, and – despite their skin markings – there was little similarity between them and the Parshendi warriors. None had the strange growths of armorlike carapace on their skin, for instance. Kaladin eyed the sturdy, bald man. The parshman stared at the ground; he wore only a loincloth, and he had a *thickness* about him. His fingers were thicker than those of human men, his arms stouter, his thighs wider.

'He's domesticated,' Gaz said. 'You don't need to worry.'

'I thought parshmen were too valuable to use in bridge runs,' Kaladin said.

'This is just an experiment,' Gaz said. 'Brightness Hashal wants to know her options. Finding enough bridgemen has been difficult lately, and parshmen could help fill in holes.'

'This is foolishness, Gaz,' Teft said. 'I don't care if he's "domesticated" or not. Asking him to carry a bridge against others of his kind is pure idiocy. What if he betrays us?'

Gaz shrugged. 'We'll see if that happens.'

'But—'

'Leave it, Teft,' Kaladin said. 'You, parshman, come with me.' He turned to walk back down the hill. The parshman dutifully followed. Teft cursed and did so as well.

'What trick are they trying on us, do you think?' Teft asked.

'I suspect it's just what he said. A test to see if a parshman can be trusted to run bridges. Perhaps he'll do as he's told. Or perhaps he'll refuse to run, or will try to kill us. She wins regardless.'

'Kelek's breath,' Teft cursed. 'Darker than a Horneater's stomach, our situation is. She'll see us dead, Kaladin.'

'I know.' He glanced over his shoulder at the parshman. He was a little taller than most, his face a little wider, but they all looked about the same to Kaladin.

The other members of Bridge Four had lined up by the time Kaladin returned. They watched the approaching parshman with surprise and disbelief. Kaladin stopped before them, Teft at his side, the parshman behind. It made him itch, to have one of them behind him. He casually stepped to the side. The parshman just stood there, eyes downward, shoulders slumped.

Kaladin glanced at the others. They had guessed, and they were growing hostile.

Stormfather, Kaladin thought. *There* is *something lower in this world than a bridgeman. A parshman bridgeman.* Parshmen might cost more than most slaves, but so did a chull. In fact, the comparison was a good one, because parshmen were worked like animals.

Seeing the reaction of the others made Kaladin pity the creature. And that made him mad at himself. Did he *always* have to react this way? This parshman was dangerous, a distraction for the other men, a factor they couldn't depend on.

A liability.

Turn a liability into an advantage whenever you can. Those words had been spoken by a man who cared only for his own skin.

Storm it, Kaladin thought. *I'm a fool. A downright, sodden idiot. This isn't the same. Not at all.* 'Parshman,' he asked. 'Do you have a name?'

The man shook his head. Parshmen rarely spoke. They could, but you had to prod them into it.

'Well, we'll have to call you something,' Kaladin said. 'How about Shen?'

The man shrugged.

'All right then,' Kaladin said to the others. 'This is Shen. He's one of us now.'

'A parshman?' Lopen asked, lounging beside the barrack. 'I don't like him, gancho. Look how he stares at me.'

'He'll kill us while we sleep,' Moash added.

'No, this is *good*,' Skar said. 'We can just have him run at the front. He'll take an arrow for one of us.'

Syl alighted on Kaladin's shoulder, looking down at the parshman. Her eyes were sorrowful.

If you were to overthrow the lighteyes and place yourselves in power, abuses would still happen. They'd just happen to other people.

But this was a *parshman*.

Gotta do what you can to stay alive . . . .

'No,' Kaladin said. 'Shen is one of *us* now. I don't care what he was before. I don't care what any of you were. We're Bridge Four. So is he.'

'But—' Skar began.

'*No*,' Kaladin said. 'We not going to treat him like the lighteyes treat us, Skar. That's all there is to it. Rock, find him a vest and sandals.'

The bridgemen split up, all save Teft. 'What about . . . our plans?' Teft asked quietly.

'We proceed,' Kaladin said.

Teft looked uncomfortable about that.

'What's he going to do, Teft?' Kaladin asked. 'Tell on us? I've never heard a parshman say more than a single word at a time. I doubt he could act as a spy.'

'I don't know,' Teft grumbled. 'But I've never liked them. They seem to be able to talk to each other, without making any sounds. I don't like the way they look.'

'Teft,' Kaladin said flatly, 'if we rejected bridgemen based on their looks, we'd have kicked you out weeks ago for that face of yours.'

Teft grunted. Then he smiled.

'What?' Kaladin asked.

'Nothing,' he said. 'Just . . . for a moment, you reminded me of better days. Afore this storm came crashing down on me. You realize the odds, don't you? Fighting our way free, escaping a man like Sadeas?'

Kaladin nodded solemnly.

'Good,' Teft said. 'Well, since you aren't inclined to do it, I'll keep an eye on our friend "Shen" over there. You can thank me after I stop him from sticking a knife in your back.'

'I don't think we have to worry.'

'You're young,' Teft said. 'I'm old.'

'That makes you wiser, presumably?'

'Damnation no,' Teft said. 'The only thing it proves is that I've more experience staying alive than you. I'll watch him. You just train the rest of this sorry lot to . . .' He trailed off, looking around. 'To keep from tripping over their own feet the moment someone threatens them. You understand?'

Kaladin nodded. That sounded much like something one of Kaladin's old sergeants would say. Teft was insistent on not talking about his past, but he never *had* seemed as beaten down as most of the others.

'All right,' Kaladin said, 'make sure the men take care of their equipment.'

'What will you be doing?'

'Walking,' Kaladin said. 'And thinking.'

◆
◆ ◆

An hour later, Kaladin still wandered Sadeas's warcamp. He'd need to return to the lumberyard soon; his men were on chasm duty again, and had been given only a few free hours to care for equipment.

As a youth, he hadn't understood why his father had often gone walking to think. The older Kaladin grew, the more he found himself imitating his father's habits. Walking, moving, it did something to his mind. The constant passing of tents, colors cycling, men bustling – it created a sense of change, and it made his thoughts want to move as well.

Don't hedge bets with your life, Kaladin, Durk had always said. *Don't put in a chip when you have a pocket full of marks. Bet them all or leave the table.*

Syl danced before him, jumping from shoulder to shoulder in the crowded street. Occasionally she'd land on the head of someone passing in the other direction and sit there, legs crossed, as she passed Kaladin.

All his spheres were on the table. He was determined to help the bridgemen. But something itched at him, a worry that he couldn't yet explain.

'You seem troubled,' Syl said, landing on his shoulder. She wore a cap and jacket over her usual dress, as if imitating nearby shopkeepers. They passed the apothecary's shop. Kaladin barely bothered to glance at it. He had no knobweed sap to sell. He'd run out of supplies soon.

He'd told his men that he'd train them to fight, but that would take time. And once they were trained, how would they get spears out of the chasms to use in the escape? Sneaking them out would be tough, considering how they were searched. They could just start fighting at the search itself, but that would only put the entire warcamp on alert.

Problems, problems. The more he thought, the more impossible his task seemed.

He made way for a couple of soldiers in forest-green coats. Their brown eyes marked them as common citizens, but the white knots on their shoulders meant they were citizen officers. Squadleaders and sergeants.

'Kaladin?' Syl asked.

'Getting the bridgemen out is as large a task as I've ever faced. Much more difficult than my other escape attempts as a slave, and I failed at each of those. I can't help wondering if I'm setting myself up for another disaster.'

'It will be different this time, Kaladin,' Syl said. 'I can feel it.'

'That sounds like something Tien would have said. His death proves that words don't change anything, Syl. Before you ask, I'm not sinking into despair again. But I *can't* ignore what has happened to me. It started with Tien. Since that moment, it seems that every time I've specifically picked people to protect, they've ended up dead. Every time. It's enough to make me wonder if the Almighty himself hates me.'

She frowned. 'I think you're being foolish. Besides, if anything, he'd hate the people who died, not you. *You* lived.'

'I suppose it's self-centered to make it all about me. But, Syl, I survive, every time, when almost nobody else does. Over and over again. My old spearman squad, the first bridge crew I ran with, numerous slaves I tried to help escape. There's a pattern. It's getting harder and harder to ignore.'

'Maybe the Almighty is preserving you,' Syl said.

Kaladin hesitated on the street; a passing soldier cursed and shoved him aside. Something about this whole conversation was wrong. Kaladin moved over beside a rain barrel set between two sturdy stone-walled shops.

'Syl,' he said. 'You mentioned the Almighty.'

'You did first.'

'Ignore that for now. Do you believe in the Almighty? Do you know if he really exists?'

Syl cocked her head. 'I don't know. Huh. Well, there are a lot of things I don't know. But I should know this one. I think. Maybe?' She seemed very perplexed.

'I'm not sure if I believe,' Kaladin said, looking out at the street. 'My mother did, and my father always spoke of the Heralds with reverence. I think he believed too, but maybe just because of the traditions of healing that are said to have come from the Heralds. The ardents ignore us bridge-men. They used to visit the soldiers, when I was in Amaram's army, but I haven't seen a single one in the lumberyard. I haven't given it much thought. Believing never seemed to help any of the soldiers.'

'So if you don't believe, then there's no reason to think that the Almighty hates you.'

'Except,' Kaladin said, 'if there *is* no Almighty, there might be something else. I don't know. A lot of the soldiers I knew were superstitious. They'd talk about things like the Old Magic and the Nightwatcher, things that could bring a man bad luck. I scoffed at them. But how long can I continue to ignore that possibility? What if all of these failures can be traced to something like that?'

Syl looked disturbed. The cap and jacket she'd been wearing dissolved to mist, and she wrapped her arms around herself as if chilled by his comments.

Odium reigns . . . .

'Syl,' he said, frowning, thinking back to his strange dream. 'Have you ever heard of something called Odium? I don't mean the feeling, I mean . . . a person, or something called by that name.'

Syl suddenly hissed. It was a feral, disturbing sound. She zipped off his shoulder, becoming a darting streak of light, and shot up underneath the eaves of the next building.

He blinked. 'Syl?' he called, drawing the attention of a couple of passing washwomen. The spren did not reappear. Kaladin folded his arms. That word had set her off. Why?

A loud series of curses interrupted his thoughts. Kaladin spun as a man burst out of a handsome stone building across the street and shoved a half-naked woman out in front of him. The man had bright blue eyes, and his forest green coat – carried over one arm – had red knots on the shoulder. A lighteyed officer, not very high-ranking. Perhaps seventh dahn.

The half-dressed woman fell to the ground. She held the loose front of the dress to her chest, crying, her long black hair down and tied with two red ribbons. The dress was that of a lighteyed woman, except that both sleeves were short, safehand exposed. A courtesan.

The officer continued to curse as he pulled on his coat. He didn't do up the buttons. Instead, he stepped forward and kicked the whore in the belly. She gasped, painspren pulling from the ground and gathering around her. Nobody on the street paused, though most did hurry on their way, heads down.

Kaladin growled, jumping into the roadway, pushing his way past a group of soldiers. Then he stopped. Three men in blue stepped out of the crowd, moving purposefully between the fallen woman and the officer in green. Only one was lighteyed, judging by the knots on his shoulders. Golden knots. A high-ranking man indeed, second or third dahn. These obviously weren't from Sadeas's army, not with those well-pressed blue coats.

Sadeas's officer hesitated. The officer in blue rested his hand on the hilt of his sword. The other two were holding fine halberds with gleaming half-moon heads.

A group of soldiers in green moved out of the crowd and began to surround those in blue. The air grew tense, and Kaladin realized that the street – bustling just moments ago – was quickly emptying. He stood practically alone, the only one watching the three men in blue, now surrounded by seven in green. The woman was still on the ground, sniffling. She huddled next to the blue-garbed officer.

The man who had kicked her – a thick-browed brute with a mop of uncombed black hair – began to button up the right side of his coat. 'You don't belong here, friends. It seems you wandered into the wrong warcamp.'

'We have legitimate business,' said the officer in blue. He had light golden hair, speckled with Alethi black, and a handsome face. He held his hand before him as if wishing to shake hands with Sadeas's officer. 'Come now,' he said affably. 'Whatever your problem with this woman, I'm sure it can be resolved without anger or violence.'

Kaladin moved back under the overhang where Syl had hidden.

'She's a whore,' Sadeas's man said.

'I can see that,' replied the man in blue. He kept his hand out.

The officer in green spat on it.

'I see,' said the blond man. He pulled his hand back, and twisting lines of mist gathered in the air, coalescing in his hands as he raised them to an offensive posture. A massive sword appeared, as long as a man is tall.

It dripped with water that condensed along its cold, glimmering length. It was beautiful, long and sinuous, its single edge rippled like an eel and curved up into a point. The back bore delicate ridges, like crystal formations.

Sadeas's officer stumbled away and fell, his face pale. The soldiers in green scattered. The officer cursed at them – as vile a curse as Kaladin had ever heard – but none returned to help him. With a final glare, he scrambled up the steps back into the building.

The door slammed, leaving the roadway eerily silent. Kaladin was the only one on the street besides the soldiers in blue and the fallen courtesan. The Shardbearer gave Kaladin a glance, but obviously judged him no threat. He thrust his sword into the stones; the Blade sank in easily and stood with its hilt toward the sky.

The young Shardbearer then gave his hand to the fallen whore. 'What did you do to him, out of curiosity?'

Hesitantly, she took his hand and let him pull her to her feet. 'He refused to pay, claiming his reputation made it a pleasure for me.' She grimaced. 'He kicked me the first time after I made a comment about his "reputation." It apparently wasn't what he thought he was known for.'

The brightlord chuckled. 'I suggest you insist on being paid *first* from now on. We'll escort you to the border. I advise against returning to Sadeas's warcamp anytime soon.'

The woman nodded, holding the front of her dress to her chest. Her safehand was still exposed. Sleek, with tan skin, the fingers long and delicate. Kaladin found himself staring at it and blushing. She sidled up to the brightlord while his two comrades watched the sides of the streets, halberds ready. Even with her hair disheveled and her makeup smudged, she was quite pretty. 'Thank you, Brightlord. Perhaps I could interest you? There would be no charge.'

The young brightlord raised an eyebrow. 'Tempting,' he said, 'but my father would kill me. He has this thing about the old ways.'

'A pity,' she said, pulling away from him, awkwardly covering her chest as she slipped her arm into its sleeve. She took out a glove for her safehand. 'Your father is quite prudish, then?'

'You might say that.' He turned toward Kaladin. 'Ho, bridgeboy.'

Bridgeboy? This lordling looked to be just a few years older than Kaladin himself.

'Run and give word to Brightlord Reral Makoram,' the Shardbearer said, flipping something across the street toward Kaladin. A sphere. It sparkled in the sunlight before Kaladin caught it. 'He's in the Sixth Battalion. Tell him that Adolin Kholin won't make today's meeting. I'll send word to reschedule another time.'

Kaladin looked down at the sphere. An emerald chip. More than he normally earned in two weeks. He looked up; the young brightlord and his two men were already retreating, the whore following.

'You rushed to help her,' a voice said. He looked up as Syl floated down to rest on his shoulder. 'That was very noble of you.'

'Those others got there first,' Kaladin said. *And one of them a lighteyes, no less. What was in it for him?*

'You still tried to help.'

'Foolishly,' Kaladin said. 'What would I have done? Fought down a lighteyes? That would have drawn half the camp's soldiers down on me, and the whore would just have been beaten more for causing such a fracas. She could have ended up dead for my efforts.' He fell silent. That sounded too much like what he'd been saying before.

He couldn't give in to assuming he was cursed, or had bad luck, or whatever it was. Superstition never got a man anywhere. But he had to admit, the pattern *was* disturbing. If he acted as he always had before, how could he expect different results? He had to try something new. Change, somehow. This was going to take more thought.

Kaladin began walking back toward the lumberyard.

'Aren't you going to do what the brightlord asked?' Syl said. She didn't show any lingering effects of her sudden fright; it was as if she wanted to pretend it hadn't happened.

'After how he treated me?' Kaladin snapped.

'It wasn't that bad.'

'I'm not going to bow to them,' Kaladin said. 'I'm done running at their whims just because they *expect* me to do so. If he was so worried about this message, then he should have waited to make certain I was willing.'

'You took his sphere.'

'Earned by the sweat of the darkeyes he exploits.'

Syl fell silent for a moment. 'This darkness about you when you talk of them frightens me, Kaladin. You stop being yourself when you think about lighteyes.'

He didn't respond, just continuing on his way. He owed that brightlord nothing, and besides, he had orders to be back in the lumberyard.

But the man *had* stepped up to protect the woman.

No, Kaladin told himself forcefully. *He was just looking for a way to embarrass one of Sadeas's officers. Everyone knows there's tension between the camps.*

And that was all he let himself think on the subject.

ONE YEAR AGO

Kaladin turned the rock over in his fingers, letting the facets of suspended quartz catch the light. He leaned against a large boulder, one foot pressed back against the stone, his spear next to him.

The rock caught the light, spinning it in different colors, depending on the direction he turned it. Beautiful, miniature crystals shimmered, like the cities made of gemstones mentioned in lore.

Around him, Highmarshal Amaram's army prepared for battle. Six thousand men sharpened spears or strapped on leather armor. The battlefield was nearby, and, with no highstorms expected, the army had spent the night in tents.

It had been nearly four years since he'd joined Amaram's army on that rainy night. Four years. And an eternity.

Soldiers hurried this way and that. Some raised hands and called greetings to Kaladin. He nodded to them, pocketing the stone, then folded his arms to wait. In the near distance, Amaram's standard was already flying, a burgundy field blazoned with a dark green glyphpair shaped like a white-spine with tusks upraised. *Merem* and *khakh*, honor and determination. The banner fluttered before a rising sun, the morning's chill starting to give way to the heat of the day.

Kaladin turned, looking eastward. Toward a home to which he could never return. He'd decided months ago. His enlistment would be up in a few weeks, but he would sign on again. He couldn't face his parents after having broken his promise to protect Tien.

A heavyset darkeyed soldier trotted up to him, an axe strapped to his back, white knots on his shoulders. The nonstandard weapon was a privilege of being a squadleader. Gare had beefy forearms and a thick black beard, though he'd lost a large section of scalp on the right side of his head. He was followed by two of his sergeants – Nalem and Korabet.

'Kaladin,' Gare said. 'Stormfather, man! Why are you pestering me? On a battle day!'

'I'm well aware of what's ahead, Gare,' Kaladin said, arms still folded. Several companies were already gathering, forming ranks. Dallet would see Kaladin's own squad into place. At the front, they'd decided. Their enemy – a lighteyes named Hallaw – was fond of long volleys. They'd fought his men several times before. One time in particular was burned into Kaladin's memory and soul.

He had joined Amaram's army expecting to defend the Alethi borders – and defend them he did. Against other Alethi. Lesser landlords who sought to slice off bits of Highprince Sadeas's lands. Occasionally, Amaram's armies would try to seize territory from other highprinces – lands Amaram claimed really belonged to Sadeas and had been stolen years before. Kaladin didn't know what to make of that. Of all lighteyes, Amaram was the only one he trusted. But it did seem like they were doing the same thing as the armies they fought.

'Kaladin?' Gare asked impatiently.

'You have something I want,' Kaladin said. 'New recruit, just joined yesterday. Galan says his name is Cenn.'

Gare scowled. 'I'm supposed to play this game with you *now*? Talk to me after the battle. If the boy survives, maybe I'll give him to you.' He turned to leave, cronies following.

Kaladin stood up straight, picking up his spear. The motion stopped Gare in his tracks.

'It's not going to be a trouble to you,' Kaladin said quietly. 'Just send the boy to my squad. Accept your payment. Stay quiet.' He pulled out a pouch of spheres.

'Maybe I don't want to sell him,' Gare said, turning back.

'You're not selling him. You're transferring him to me.'

Gare eyed the pouch. 'Well then, maybe I don't like how everyone does what *you* tell them. I don't care how good you are with a spear. My squad is my own.'

'I'm not going to give you any more, Gare,' Kaladin said, dropping the pouch to the ground. The spheres clinked. 'We both know the boy is useless to you. Untrained, ill-equipped, too small to make a good line soldier. Send him to me.'

Kaladin turned and began to walk away. Within seconds, he heard a clink as Gare recovered the pouch. 'Can't blame a man for trying.'

Kaladin kept walking.

'What do these recruits mean to you, anyway?' Gare called after Kaladin. 'Your squad is half made up of men too small to fight properly! Almost makes a man think you *want* to get killed!'

Kaladin ignored him. He passed through the camp, waving to those who waved at him. Most everyone kept out of his way, either because they knew and respected him or they'd heard of his reputation. Youngest squadleader in the army, only four years of experience and already in command. A darkeyed man had to travel to the Shattered Plains to go any higher in rank.

The camp was a bedlam of soldiers hurrying about in last-minute preparations. More and more companies were gathering at the line, and Kaladin could see the enemy lining up on the shallow ridge across the field to the west.

The enemy. That was what they were called. Yet whenever there was an *actual* border dispute with the Vedens or the Reshi, those men would line up beside Amaram's troops and they would fight together. It was as if the Nightwatcher toyed with them, playing some forbidden game of chance, occasionally setting the men on his gameboard as allies, then setting them to kill one another the next day.

That wasn't for spearmen to think about. So he'd been told. Repeatedly. He supposed he should listen, as he figured that his duty was to keep his squad alive as best he could. Winning was secondary to that.

You can't kill to protect. . . .

He found the surgeon's station easily; he could smell the scents of antiseptics and of small fires burning. Those smells reminded him of his youth, which now seemed so far, far away. Had he ever really planned to go become a surgeon? What had happened to his parents? What of Roshone?

Meaningless, now. He'd sent word to them via Amaram's scribes, a terse note that had cost him a week's wages. They knew he'd failed, and they knew he didn't intend to return. There had been no reply.

Ven was the chief of the surgeons, a tall man with a bulbous nose and a long face. He stood watching as his apprentices folded bandages. Kaladin had once idly considered getting wounded so he could join them; all of the apprentices had some incapacitation that prevented them from fighting. Kaladin hadn't been able to do it. Wounding himself seemed cowardly. Besides, surgery was his old life. In a way, he didn't deserve it anymore.

Kaladin pulled a pouch of spheres from his belt, meaning to toss it to Ven. The pouch stuck, however, refusing to come free of the belt. Kaladin cursed, stumbling, tugging at the pouch. It came free suddenly, causing him to lose his balance again. A translucent white form zipped away, spinning with a carefree air.

'Storming windspren,' he said. They were common out on these rocky plains.

He continued past the surgery pavilion, tossing the pouch of spheres to Ven. The tall man caught it deftly, making it vanish into a pocket of his voluminous white robe. The bribe would ensure that Kaladin's men were served first on the battlefield, assuming there were no lighteyes who needed the attention.

It was time to join the line. He sped up, jogging along, spear in hand. Nobody gave him grief for wearing trousers under his leather spearman's skirt – something he did so his men could recognize him from behind. In fact, nobody gave him grief about much of anything these days. That still felt odd, after so many struggles during his first years in the army.

He still didn't feel as if he belonged. His reputation set him apart, but what was he to do? It kept his men from being taunted, and after several years of dealing with disaster after disaster, he could finally pause and *think*.

He wasn't certain he liked that. Thinking had proven dangerous lately. It had been a long while since he'd taken out that rock and thought of Tien and home.

He made his way to the front ranks, spotting his men right where he'd told them to go. 'Dallet,' Kaladin called, as he trotted over to the mountainous spearman who was the squad's sergeant. 'We're soon going to have a new recruit. I need you to ...' He trailed off. A young man, maybe fourteen, stood beside Dallet, looking tiny in his spearman's armor.

Kaladin felt a flash of recall. Another lad, one with a familiar face, holding a spear he wasn't supposed to need. Two promises broken at once.

'He found his way here just a few minutes ago, sir,' Dallet said. 'I've been gettin' him ready.'

Kaladin shook himself out of the moment. Tien was dead. But *Stormfather*, this new lad looked a lot like him.

'Well done,' Kaladin said to Dallet, forcing himself to look away from Cenn. 'I paid good money to get that boy away from Gare. That man's so incompetent he might as well be fighting for the other side.'

Dallet grunted in agreement. The men would know what to do with Cenn.

All right, Kaladin thought, scanning the battlefield for a good place for his men to stand their ground, *let's get to it.*

He'd heard stories about the soldiers who fought on the Shattered Plains. The *real* soldiers. If you showed enough promise fighting in these border disputes, you were sent there. It was supposed to be safer there – far more soldiers, but fewer battles. So Kaladin wanted to get his squad there as soon as possible.

He conferred with Dallet, picking a place to hold. Eventually, the horns blew.

Kaladin's squad charged.

◆
◆ ◆

'Where's the boy?' Kaladin said, yanking his spear out of the chest of a man in brown. The enemy soldier fell to the ground, groaning. 'Dallet!'

The burly sergeant was fighting. He couldn't turn to acknowledge the yell.

Kaladin cursed, scanning the chaotic battlefield. Spears hit shields, flesh, leather; men yelled and screamed. Painspren swarmed the ground, like small orange hands or bits of sinew, reaching up from the ground amid the blood of the fallen.

Kaladin's squad was all accounted for, their wounded protected at the center. All except the new boy. Tien.

C*enn*, Kaladin thought. *His name is Cenn.*

Kaladin caught sight of a flash of green in the middle of the enemy brown. A terrified voice somehow cut through the commotion. It was him.

Kaladin threw himself out of formation, prompting a call of surprise from Larn, who had been fighting at his side. Kaladin ducked past a spear thrust by an enemy, dashing over the stony ground, hopping corpses.

Cenn had been knocked to the ground, spear raised. An enemy soldier slammed his weapon down.

No.

Kaladin blocked the blow, deflecting the enemy spear and skidding to a stop in front of Cenn. There were six spearmen here, all wearing brown. Kaladin spun among them in a wild offensive rush. His spear seemed to flow of its own accord. He swept the feet out from under one man, took down another with a thrown knife.

He was like water running down a hill, flowing, always moving. Spear-heads flashed in the air around him, hafts hissing with speed. Not one hit him. He could not be stopped, not when he felt like this. When he had the energy of defending the fallen, the power of standing to protect one of his men.

Kaladin snapped his spear into a resting position, crouching with one foot forward, one behind, spear held under his arm. Sweat trickled from his brow, cooled by the breeze. Odd. There hadn't been a breeze before. Now it seemed to envelop him.

All six enemy spearmen were dead or incapacitated. Kaladin breathed in and out once, then turned to see to Cenn's wound. He dropped his spear beside him, kneeling. The cut wasn't that bad, though it probably pained the lad terribly.

Getting out a bandage, Kaladin gave the battlefield one quick glance. Nearby, an enemy soldier stirred, but he was wounded badly enough that he wouldn't be trouble. Dallet and the rest of Kaladin's team were clearing the area of enemy stragglers. In the near distance, an enemy lighteyes of high rank was rallying a small group of soldiers for a counterattack. He wore full plate. Not Shardplate, of course, but silvery steel. A rich man, judging from his horse.

In a heartbeat, Kaladin was back to binding Cenn's leg – though he kept watch on the wounded enemy soldier from the corner of his eye.

'Kaladin, sir!' Cenn exclaimed, pointing at the soldier who had stirred.

Stormfather! Had the boy only just noticed the man? Had Kaladin's battle senses ever been as dull as this boy's?

Dallet pushed the wounded enemy away. The rest of the squad made a ring formation around Kaladin, Dallet, and Cenn. Kaladin finished his binding, then stood, picking up his spear.

Dallet handed him back his knives. 'Had me worried there, sir. Running off like that.'

'I knew you'd follow,' Kaladin said. 'Raise the red banner. Cyn, Korater, you're going back with the boy. Dallet, hold here. Amaram's line is bulging this direction. We should be safe soon.'

'And you, sir?' Dallet asked.

In the near distance, the lighteyes had failed to rally enough troops. He was exposed, like a stone left behind by a stream running dry.

'A Shardbearer,' Cenn said.

Dallet snorted. 'No, thank the Stormfather. Just a lighteyed officer. Shardbearers are far too valuable to waste on a minor border dispute.'

Kaladin clenched his jaw, watching that lighteyed warrior. How mighty the man thought himself, sitting on his expensive horse, kept safe from the spearmen by his majestic armor and tall mount. He swung his mace, killing those around him.

These skirmishes were caused by ones like him, greedy minor lighteyes who tried to steal land while the better men were away, fighting the Parshendi. His type had far, far fewer casualties than the spearmen, and so the lives under his command became cheap things.

More and more over the last few years, each and every one of these petty lighteyes had come to represent Roshone in Kaladin's eyes. Only Amaram himself stood apart. Amaram, who had treated Kaladin's father so well, promising to keep Tien safe. Amaram, who always spoke with respect, even to lowly spearmen. He was like Dalinar and Sadeas. Not this riffraff.

Of course, Amaram had failed to protect Tien. But so had Kaladin.

'Sir?' Dallet said hesitantly.

'Subsquads Two and Three, pincer pattern,' Kaladin said coldly, pointing at the enemy lighteyes. 'We're taking a brightlord off his throne.'

'You sure that's wise, sir?' Dallet said. 'We've got wounded.'

Kaladin turned toward Dallet. 'That's one of Hallaw's officers. He might be the one.'

'You don't know that, sir.'

'Regardless, he's a battalionlord. If we kill an officer that high, we're all but guaranteed to be in the next group sent to the Shattered Plains. We're taking him. Imagine it, Dallet. Real soldiers. A warcamp with discipline and lighteyes with integrity. A place where our fighting will *mean* something.'

Dallet sighed, but nodded. At Kaladin's wave, two subsquads joined him, as eager as he. Did they hate these squabbling lighteyes of their own accord, or had they picked up Kaladin's loathing?

The brightlord was surprisingly easy to take down. The problem with them – almost to a man – was that they underestimated darkeyes. Perhaps this one had a right. How many had he killed, in his years?

Subsquad three drew off the honor guard. Subsquad two distracted the lighteyes. He didn't see Kaladin approaching from a third direction. The man dropped with a knife to the eye; his face was unprotected. He screamed as he clattered to the ground, still alive. Kaladin rammed his spear down into the fallen man's face, striking three times as the horse galloped off.

The man's honor guard panicked and fled to rejoin their army. Kaladin signaled to the two subsquads by banging his spear against his shield, giving the 'hold position' sign. They fanned out, and short Toorim – a man Kaladin had rescued from another squad – made as if to confirm the lighteyes was dead. He was really covertly looking for spheres.

Stealing from the dead was strictly prohibited, but Kaladin figured that if Amaram wanted the spoils, he could storming well kill the enemy himself. Kaladin respected Amaram more than most – well, more than *any* – lighteyes. But bribes weren't cheap.

Toorim walked up to him. 'Nothing sir. Either he didn't bring any spheres into battle, or he has them hidden somewhere under that breastplate.'

Kaladin nodded curtly, surveying the battlefield. Amaram's forces were recovering; they'd win the day before long. In fact, Amaram would probably be leading a direct surge against the enemy by now. He generally entered the battle at the end.

Kaladin wiped his brow. He'd have to send for Norby, their captainlord, to prove their kill. First he needed those healers to—

'Sir!' Toorim said suddenly.

Kaladin glanced back at the enemy lines.

'Stormfather!' Toorim exclaimed. '*Sir!*'

Toorim wasn't looking at the enemy lines. Kaladin spun, looking back at friendly ranks. There – bearing down through the soldiers on a horse the color of death itself – was an impossibility.

The man wore shining golden armor. *Perfect* golden armor, as if this were what every other suit of armor had been designed to imitate. Each piece fit perfectly; there were no holes showing straps or leather. It made the rider look enormous, powerful. Like a god carrying a majestic blade that should have been too big to use. It was engraved and stylized, shaped like flames in motion.

'Stormfather ...' Kaladin breathed.

The Shardbearer broke out of Amaram's lines. He'd been riding through them, cutting down men as he passed. For a brief moment, Kaladin's mind refused to acknowledge that this creature – this beautiful *divinity* – could be an enemy. The fact that the Shardbearer had come through their side reinforced that illusion.

Kaladin's confusion lasted right up until the moment the Shardbearer trampled Cenn, Shardblade dropping and cutting through Dallet's head in a single, easy stroke.

'No!' Kaladin bellowed. '*No!*'

Dallet's body fell back to the ground, eyes seeming to catch alight, smoke rising from them. The Shardbearer cut down Cyn and trampled Lyndel before moving on. It was all done with nonchalance, like a woman pausing to wipe a spot on the counter.

'*NO!*' Kaladin screamed, charging toward the fallen men of his squad. He hadn't lost anyone this battle! He was going to protect them all!

He fell to his knees beside Dallet, dropping his spear. But there was no heartbeat, and those burned-out eyes ... He was dead. Grief threatened to overwhelm Kaladin.

No! said the part of his mind trained by his father. *Save the ones you can!*

He turned to Cenn. The boy had taken a hoof to the chest, cracking his sternum and shattering ribs. The boy gasped, eyes upward, struggling for breath. Kaladin pulled out a bandage. Then he paused, looking at it. A bandage? To mend a smashed chest?

Cenn stopped wheezing. He convulsed once, eyes still open. 'He watches!' the boy hissed. 'The black piper in the night. He holds us in his palm . . . playing a tune that no man can hear!'

Cenn's eyes glazed over. He stopped breathing.

Lyndel's face had been smashed in. Cyn's eyes smoldered, and he wasn't breathing either. Kaladin knelt in Cenn's blood, horrified, as Toorim and the two subsquads formed around him, looking as stunned as Kaladin felt.

This isn't possible. I . . . I . . .

Screaming.

Kaladin looked up. Amaram's banner of green and burgundy flew just to the south. The Shardbearer had cut through Kaladin's squad heading straight for that banner. Spearmen fled in disarray, screaming, scattering before the Shardbearer.

Anger boiled inside of Kaladin.

'Sir?' Toorim asked.

Kaladin picked up his spear and stood. His knees were covered with Cenn's blood. His men regarded him, confused, worried. They stood firm in the midst of the chaos; as far as Kaladin could tell, they were the only men who weren't fleeing. The Shardbearer had turned the ranks to mush.

Kaladin thrust his spear into the air, then began to run. His men bellowed a war cry, falling into formation behind him, charging across the flat rocky ground. Spearmen in uniforms of both colors scrambled out of the way, dropping spears and shields.

Kaladin picked up speed, legs pumping, his squad barely keeping pace. Just ahead – right before the Shardbearer – a pocket of green broke and ran. Amaram's honor guard. Faced by a Shardbearer, they abandoned their charge. Amaram himself was a solitary man on a rearing horse. He wore silvery plate armor that looked so *commonplace* when compared with the Shardplate.

Kaladin's squad charged against the flow of the army, a wedge of soldiers going the wrong way. The *only* ones going the wrong way. Some of the fleeing men paused as he charged past, but none joined.

Ahead, the Shardbearer rode past Amaram. With a sweep of the Blade, the Shardbearer slashed through the neck of Amaram's mount. Its eyes burned into two great pits, and it toppled, jerking fitfully, Amaram still in its saddle.

The Shardbearer wheeled his destrier in a tight circle, then threw himself from horseback at full speed. He hit the ground with a grinding sound, somehow remaining upright and skidding to a halt.

Kaladin redoubled his speed. Was he running to get vengeance, or was he trying to protect his highmarshal? The only lighteyes who had ever shown a modicum of humanity? Did it matter?

Amaram struggled in his bulky plate, the carcass of the horse on his leg.

The Shardbearer raised his Blade in two hands to finish him off.

Coming at the Shardbearer from behind, Kaladin screamed and swung low with the butt of his spear, putting momentum and muscle behind the blow. The spear haft shattered against the Shardbearer's back leg in a spray of wooden slivers.

The jolt of it knocked Kaladin to the ground, his arms shaking, the broken spear clutched in his hands. The Shardbearer stumbled, lowering his Blade. He turned a helmed face toward Kaladin, posture indicating utter surprise.

The twenty remaining men of Kaladin's squad arrived a heartbeat later, attacking vigorously. Kaladin scrambled to his feet and ran for the spear from a fallen soldier. He tossed his broken one away after snatching one of his knives from its sheath, snatched the new one off the ground, then turned back to see his men attacking as he had taught. They came at the foe from three directions, ramming spears between joints in the Plate. The Shardbearer glanced around, as a bemused man might regard a pack of puppies yapping around him. Not a single one of the spear thrusts appeared to pierce his armor. He shook a helmed head.

Then he struck.

The Shardblade swept out in a broad sweeping series of deadly strokes, cutting through ten of the spearmen.

Kaladin was paralyzed in horror as Toorim, Acis, Hamel, and seven others fell to the ground, eyes burning, their armor and weapons sheared completely through. The remaining spearmen stumbled back, aghast.

The Shardbearer attacked again, killing Raksha, Navar, and four others. Kaladin gaped. His men – his friends – dead, just like that. The last four scrambled away, Hab stumbling over Toorim's corpse and falling to the ground, dropping his spear.

The Shardbearer ignored them, stepping up to the pinned Amaram again.

No, Kaladin thought. *No, no, NO!* Something drove him forward, against all logic, against all sense. Sickened, agonized, *enraged.*

The hollow where they fought was empty save for them. Sensible spearmen had fled. His four remaining men achieved the ridge a short distance away, but didn't run. They called for him.

'Kaladin!' Reesh yelled. 'Kaladin, no!'

Kaladin screamed instead. The Shardbearer saw him, and spun – impossibly quick – swinging. Kaladin ducked under the blow and rammed the butt of his spear against the Shardbearer's knee.

It bounced off. Kaladin cursed, throwing himself backward just as the Blade sliced the air in front of him. Kaladin rebounded and lunged forward. He made an expert thrust at his enemy's neck. The neck brace rebuffed the attack. Kaladin's spear barely scratched the Plate's paint.

The Shardbearer turned on him, holding his Blade in a two-handed grip. Kaladin dashed past, just out of range of that incredible sword. Amaram had finally pulled himself free, and he was crawling away, one leg dragging behind him – multiple fractures, from the twist of it.

Kaladin skidded to a stop, spinning, regarding the Shardbearer. This creature wasn't a god. It was everything the most petty of lighteyes represented. The ability to kill people like Kaladin with impunity.

Every suit of armor had a chink. Every man had a flaw. Kaladin thought he saw the man's eyes through the helm's slit. That slit was just big enough for a dagger, but the throw would have to be perfect. He'd have to be close. Deadly close.

Kaladin charged forward again. The Shardbearer swung his Blade out in the same wide sweep he'd used to kill so many of Kaladin's men. Kaladin threw himself downward, skidding on his knees and bending backward. The Shardblade flashed above him, shearing the top of his spear free. The tip flipped up into the air, tumbling end over end.

Kaladin strained, hurling himself back onto his feet. He whipped his hand up, flinging his knife at the eyes watching from behind impervious armor. The dagger hit the faceplate just slightly off from the right angle, bouncing against the sides of the slit and ricocheting out.

The Shardbearer cursed, swinging his huge Blade back at Kaladin.

Kaladin landed on his feet, momentum still propelling him forward. Something flashed in the air beside him, falling toward the ground.

The spearhead.

Kaladin bellowed in defiance, spinning, snatching the spearhead from the air. It had been falling tip-down, and he caught it by the four inches of haft that remained, gripping it with his thumb on the stump, the sharp point extending down beneath his hand. The Shardbearer brought his weapon around as Kaladin skidded to a stop and flung his arm to the side, *slamming* the spearhead right in the Shardbearer's visor slit.

All fell still.

Kaladin stood with his arm extended, the Shardbearer standing just to his right. Amaram had pulled himself halfway up the side of the shallow hollow. Kaladin's spearmates stood on the edge of the scene, gawking. Kaladin stood there, gasping, still gripping the haft of the spear, hand before the Shardbearer's face.

The Shardbearer creaked, then fell backward, crashing to the ground. His Blade dropped from his fingers, hitting the ground at an angle and digging into the stone.

Kaladin stumbled away, feeling drained. Stunned. Numbed. His men rushed up, halting in a group, staring at the fallen man. They were amazed, even a little reverent.

'Is he dead?' Alabet asked softly.

'He is,' a voice said from the side.

Kaladin turned. Amaram still lay on the ground, but he had pulled offhis helm, dark hair and beard slicked with sweat. 'If he were still alive, his Blade would have vanished. His armor is falling off of him. He is dead. Blood of my ancestors . . . you killed a Shardbearer!'

Oddly, Kaladin wasn't surprised. Just exhausted. He looked around at the bodies of men who had been his dearest friends.

'Take it, Kaladin,' Coreb said.

Kaladin turned, looking at the Shardblade, which sprouted at an angle into the stone, hilt toward the sky.

'Take it,' Coreb said again. 'It's yours. Stormfather, Kaladin. You're a *Shardbearer*!'

Kaladin stepped forward, dazed, raising his hand toward the hilt of the Blade. He hesitated just an inch away from it.

Everything felt *wrong*.

If he took that Blade, he'd become one of them. His eyes would even change, if the stories were right. Though the Blade glistened in the light, clean of the murders it had performed, for a moment it seemed red to him. Stained with Dallet's blood. Toorim's blood. The blood of the men who had been alive just moments before.

It was a treasure. Men traded kingdoms for Shardblades. The handful of darkeyed men who had won them lived forever in song and story.

But the thought of touching that Blade sickened him. It represented everything he'd come to hate about the lighteyes, and it had just slaughtered men he loved dearly. He could not become a legend because of something like that. He looked at his reflection in the Blade's pitiless metal, then lowered his hand and turned away.

'It's yours, Coreb,' Kaladin said. 'I give it to you.'

'*What?*' Coreb said from behind.

Ahead, Amaram's honor guard had finally returned, apprehensively appearing at the top of the small hollow, looking ashamed.

'What are you doing?' Amaram demanded as Kaladin passed him. 'What— Aren't you going to take the Blade?'

'I don't want it,' Kaladin said softly. 'I'm giving it to my men.'

Kaladin walked away, emotionally exhausted, tears on his cheeks as he climbed out of the hollow and shoved his way through the honor guard.

He walked back to the warcamp alone.

'They take away the light, wherever they lurk. Skin that is burned.'

—Cormshen, page 104.

Shallan sat quietly, propped up in a sterile, white-sheeted bed in one of Kharbranth's many hospitals. Her arm was wrapped in a neat, crisp bandage, and she held her drawing board in front of her. The nurses had reluctantly allowed her to sketch, so long as she did not 'stress herself.'

Her arm ached; she'd sliced herself more deeply than she'd intended. She'd hoped to simulate a wound from breaking the pitcher; she hadn't thought far enough ahead to realize how much like a suicide attempt it might seem. Though she'd protested that she'd simply fallen from bed, she could see that the nurses and ardents didn't accept it. She couldn't blame them.

The results were embarrassing, but at least nobody thought she might have Soulcast to make that blood. Embarrassment was worth escaping suspicion.

She continued her sketch. She was in a large, hallwaylike room in a Kharbranthian hospital, the walls lined with many beds. Other than obvious aggravations, her two days in the hospital had gone fairly well. She'd had a lot of time to think about that strangest of afternoons, when she'd seen ghosts, transformed glass to blood, and had an ardent offer to resign the ardentia to be with her.

She'd done several drawings of this hospital room. The creatures lurked in her sketches, staying at the distant edges of the room. Their presence made it difficult for her to sleep, but she was slowly growing accustomed to them.

The air smelled of soap and lister's oil; she was bathed regularly and her arm washed with antiseptic to frighten away rotspren. About half of the beds held sick women, and there were wheeled fabric dividers with wooden frames that could be rolled around a bed for privacy. Shallan wore a plain white robe that untied at the front and had a long left sleeve that tied shut to protect her safehand.

She'd transferred her safepouch to the robe, buttoning it inside the left sleeve. Nobody had looked in the pouch. When she'd been washed, they'd unbuttoned it and given it to her without a word, despite its unusual weight. One did not look in a woman's safepouch. Still, she kept hold of it whenever she could.

In the hospital, her every need was seen to, but she could not leave. It reminded her of being at home on her father's estates. More and more, that frightened her as much as the symbolheads did. She'd tasted independence, and she didn't want to go back to what she had been. Coddled, pampered, displayed.

Unfortunately, it was unlikely she'd be able to return to studying with Jasnah. Her supposed suicide attempt gave her an excellent reason to return home. She had to go. To remain, sending the Soulcaster away on its own, would be selfish considering this opportunity to leave without arousing suspicion. Besides, she'd used the Soulcaster. She could use the long trip home to figure out how she'd done it, then be ready to help her family when she arrived.

She sighed, and then with a few shadings, she finished her sketch. It was a picture of that strange place she had gone. That distant horizon with its powerful yet cold sun. Clouds running toward it above, endless ocean below, making the sun look as if it were at the end of a long tunnel. Above the ocean hovered hundreds of flames, a sea of lights above the sea of glass beads.

She lifted the picture up, looking at the sketch underneath. It depicted her, huddled on her bed, surrounded by the strange creatures. She didn't *dare* tell Jasnah what she had seen, lest it reveal that she had Soulcast, and therefore committed the theft.

The next picture was one of her, lying on the ground amid the blood. She looked up from the sketchpad. A white-clothed female ardent sat against the wall nearby, pretending to sew but really keeping watch in case Shallan decided to harm herself again. Shallan made a thin line of her lips.

It's a good cover, she told herself. *It works perfectly. Stop being so embarrassed.*

She turned to the last of her day's sketches. It depicted one of the symbolheads. No eyes, no face, just that jagged alien symbol with points like cut crystal. They *had* to have something to do with the Soulcasting. Didn't they?

I visited another place, she thought. *I think . . . I think I spoke with the spirit of the goblet.* Did a *goblet*, of all things, have a soul? Upon opening her pouch to check on the Soulcaster, she'd found that the sphere Kabsal had given her had stopped glowing. She could remember a vague feeling of light and beauty, a raging storm inside of her.

She'd taken the light from the sphere and given it to the goblet – the *spren* of the goblet – as a bribe to transform. Was that how Soulcasting worked? Or was she just struggling to make connections?

Shallan lowered the sketchpad as visitors entered the room and began moving among the patients. Most of the women sat up excitedly as they saw King Taravangian, with his orange robes and kindly, aged air. He paused at each bed to chat. She'd heard that he visited frequently, at least once a week.

Eventually he reached Shallan's bedside. He smiled at her, sitting as one of his many attendants placed a padded stool for him. 'And young Shallan Davar. I was so terribly saddened to hear of your accident. I apologize for not coming earlier. Duties of state kept me.'

'It is quite all right, Your Majesty.'

'No, no, it is not,' he said. 'But it is what must be. There are many who complain that I spend too much of my time here.'

Shallan smiled. Those complaints were never vociferous. The landlords and houselords who played politics in court were quite content with a king who spent so much of his time outside the palace, ignoring their schemes.

'This hospital is amazing, Your Majesty,' she said. 'I can't believe how well everyone is cared for.'

He smiled widely. 'My great triumph. Lighteyes and darkeyes alike, nobody turned away – not beggar, not whore, not sailor from afar. It's all paid for by the Palanaeum, you know. In a way, even the most obscure and useless record is helping heal the sick.'

'I'm glad to be here.'

'I doubt that, child. A hospital such as this one is, perhaps, the only thing a man could pour so much money into and be delighted if it were never used. It is a tragedy that you must become my guest.'

'What I meant was that I'd rather be sick here than somewhere else. Though I suppose that's a little like saying it's better to choke on wine than on dishwater.'

He laughed. 'What a sweet thing you are,' he said, rising. 'Is there anything I can do to improve your stay?'

'End it?'

'I'm afraid that I can't allow that,' he said, eyes softening. 'I must defer to the wisdom of my surgeons and nurses. They say that you are still at risk. We must think of your health.'

'Keeping me here gives me health at the expense of my wellness, Your Majesty.'

He shook his head. 'You mustn't be allowed to have another accident.'

'I . . . I understand. But I promise that I'm feeling much better. The episode that struck me was caused by overwork. Now that I'm relaxed, I'm not in any further danger.'

'That is good,' he said. 'But we still need to keep you for a few more days.'

'Yes, Your Majesty. But could I at least have visitors?' So far, the hospital staff had insisted that she was not to be bothered.

'Yes . . . I can see how that might help you. I'll speak to the ardents and suggest that you be allowed a few visitors.' He hesitated. 'Once you are well again, it might be best for you to suspend your training.'

She pasted a grimace on her face, trying not to feel sick at the charade. 'I hate to do that, Your Majesty. But I have been missing my family greatly. Perhaps I should return to them.'

'An excellent idea. I'm certain the ardents will be more likely to release you if they know you'll be going home.' He smiled in a kindly way, resting a hand on her shoulder. 'This world, it is a tempest sometimes. But remember, the sun always rises again.'

'Thank you, Your Majesty.'

The king moved away, visiting other patients, then speaking quietly with the ardents. Not five minutes passed before Jasnah walked through the doorway with her characteristic straight-backed stride. She wore a beautiful dress, deep blue with golden embroidery. Her sleek black hair was done in braids and pierced by six thin golden spikes; her cheeks glowed with blush, her lips bloodred with lip paint. She stood out in the white room like a flower upon a field of barren stone.

She glided toward Shallan on feet hidden beneath the loose folds of her silk skirt, carrying a thick book under her arm. An ardent brought her a stool, and she sat down where the king had just stood.

Jasnah regarded Shallan, face stiff, impassive. 'I have been told that my tutelage is demanding, perhaps harsh. This is one reason why I often refuse to take wards.'

'I apologize for my weakness, Brightness,' Shallan said, looking down.

Jasnah seemed displeased. 'I did not mean to suggest fault in you, child. I was attempting the opposite. Unfortunately I'm . . . unaccustomed to such behavior.'

'Apologizing?'

'Yes.'

'Well, you see,' Shallan said, 'in order to grow proficient at apologizing, you must first make mistakes. That's your problem, Jasnah. You're absolutely terrible at making them.'

The woman's expression softened. 'The king mentioned to me that you would be returning to your family.'

'What? When?'

'When he met me in the hallway outside,' she said, 'and finally gave me permission to visit you.'

'You make it sound as if you were waiting out there.'

Jasnah didn't reply.

'But your research!'

'Can be done in the hospital waiting chamber.' She hesitated. 'It has been somewhat difficult for me to focus these last few days.'

'Jasnah! That's quite nearly *human* of you!'

Jasnah regarded her reprovingly, and Shallan winced, immediately regretting the words. 'I'm sorry. I've learned poorly, haven't I?'

'Or perhaps you are just practicing the art of the apology. So that you will not be unsettled when the need arises, as I am.'

'How very clever of me.'

'Indeed.'

'Can I stop now, then?' Shallan asked. 'I think I've had quite enough practice.'

'I should think,' Jasnah said, 'that apology is an art of which we could use a few more masters. Do not use me as a model in this. Pride is often mistaken for faultlessness.' She leaned forward. 'I am sorry, Shallan Davar. In overworking you, I may have done the world a disservice and stolen from it one of the great scholars of the rising generation.'

Shallan blushed, feeling more foolish and guilty. Shallan's eyes flickered to her mistress's hand. Jasnah wore the black glove that hid the fake. In the fingers of her safehand, Shallan grasped the pouch holding the Soulcaster. If Jasnah only knew.

Jasnah took the book from beneath her arm and set it on the bed beside Shallan. 'This is for you.'

Shallan picked it up. She opened to the front page, but it was blank. The next one was as well, as were all inside of it. Her frown deepened, and she looked up at Jasnah.

'It's called the *Book of Endless Pages*,' Jasnah said.

'Er, I'm pretty sure it's not endless, Brightness.' She flipped to the last page and held it up.

Jasnah smiled. 'It's a metaphor, Shallan. Many years ago, someone dear to me made a very good attempt at converting me to Vorinism. This was the method he used.'

Shallan cocked her head.

'You search for truth,' Jasnah said, 'but you also hold to your faith. There is much to admire in that. Seek out the Devotary of Sincerity. They are one of the very smallest of the devotaries, but this book is their guide.'

'One with blank pages?'

'Indeed. They worship the Almighty, but are guided by the belief that there are always more answers to be found. The book cannot be filled, as there is always something to learn. This devotary is a place where one is never penalized for questions, even those challenging Vorinism's own tenets.' She shook her head. 'I cannot explain their ways. You should be able to find them in Vedenar, though there are none in Kharbranth.'

'I . . .' Shallan trailed off, noticing how Jasnah's hand rested fondly on the book. It was precious to her. 'I hadn't thought to find ardents who were willing to question their own beliefs.'

Jasnah raised an eyebrow. 'You will find wise men in any religion, Shallan, and good men in every nation. Those who *truly* seek wisdom are those who will acknowledge the virtue in their adversaries and who will learn from those who disabuse them of error. All others – heretic, Vorin, Ysperist, or Maakian – are equally closed-minded.' She took her hand from the book, moving as if to stand up.

'He's wrong,' Shallan said suddenly, realizing something.

Jasnah turned to her.

'Kabsal,' Shallan said, blushing. 'He says you're researching the Voidbringers because you want to prove that Vorinism is false.'

Jasnah sniffed in derision. 'I would not dedicate four years of my life to such an empty pursuit. It's idiocy to try to prove a negative. Let the Vorin believe as they wish – the wise among them will find goodness and solace in their faith; the fools would be fools no matter what they believed.'

Shallan frowned. So why *was* Jasnah studying the Voidbringers?

'Ah. Speak of the storm and it begins to bluster,' Jasnah said, turning toward the room's entrance.

With a start, Shallan realized that Kabsal had just arrived, wearing his usual grey robes. He was arguing softly with a nurse, who pointed at the basket he carried. Finally, the nurse threw up her hands and walked away, leaving Kabsal to approach, triumphant. 'Finally!' he said to Shallan. 'Old Mungam can be a real tyrant.'

'Mungam?' Shallan asked.

'The ardent who runs this place,' Kabsal said. 'I should have been allowed in immediately. After all, I know what you need to make you better!' He pulled out a jar of jam, smiling broadly.

Jasnah remained on her stool, regarding Kabsal across the bed. 'I would have thought,' she said dryly, 'that you would allow Shallan a respite, considering how your attentions drove her to despair.'

Kabsal flushed. He looked at Shallan, and she could see the pleading in his eyes.

'It wasn't you, Kabsal,' Shallan said. 'I just . . . I wasn't ready for life away from my family estate. I still don't know what came over me. I've never done anything like that before.'

He smiled, pulling a stool over for himself. 'I think,' he said, 'that the lack of color in these places is what keeps people sick so long. That and the lack of proper food.' He winked, turning the jar toward Shallan. It was deep, dark red. 'Strawberry.'

'Never heard of it,' Shallan said.

'It's exceedingly rare,' Jasnah said, reaching for the jar. 'Like most plants from Shinovar, it can't grow other places.'

Kabsal looked surprised as Jasnah removed the lid and dipped a finger into the jar. She hesitated, then raised a bit of the jam to her nose to sniff at it.

'I was under the impression that you disliked jam, Brightness Jasnah,' Kabsal said.

'I do,' she said. 'I was simply curious about the scent. I've heard that strawberries are very distinctive.' She screwed the lid back on, then wiped her finger on her cloth handkerchief.

'I brought bread as well,' Kabsal said. He pulled out a small loaf of the fluffy bread. 'It's nice of you not to blame me, Shallan, but I can see that my attentions were too forward. I thought, maybe, I could bring this and . . .'

'And what?' Jasnah asked. 'Absolve yourself? "I'm sorry I drove you to suicide. Here's some bread."'

He blushed, looking down.

'Of course I'll have some,' Shallan said, glaring at Jasnah. 'And she will too. It was very kind of you, Kabsal.' She took the bread, breaking off a chunk for Kabsal, one for herself, then one for Jasnah.

'No,' Jasnah said. 'Thank you.'

'Jasnah,' Shallan said. 'Would you please at least try some?' It bothered her that the two of them got on so poorly.

The older woman sighed. 'Oh, very well.' She took the bread, holding it as Shallan and Kabsal ate. The bread was moist and delicious, though Jasnah grimaced as she put hers in her mouth and chewed it.

'You should really try the jam,' Kabsal said to Shallan. 'Strawberry is hard to find. I had to make quite a number of inquiries.'

'No doubt bribing merchants with the king's money,' Jasnah noted.

Kabsal sighed. 'Brightness Jasnah, I realize that you are not fond of me. But I'm working very hard to be pleasant. Could you at least *pretend* to do likewise?'

Jasnah eyed Shallan, probably recalling Kabsal's guess that undermining Vorinism was the goal of her research. She didn't apologize, but also made no retort.

Good enough, Shallan thought.

'The jam, Shallan,' Kabsal said, handing her a slice of bread for it.

'Oh, right.' She removed the lid of the jar, holding it between her knees and using her freehand.

'You missed your ship out, I assume,' Kabsal said.

'Yes.'

'What's this?' Jasnah asked.

Shallan cringed. 'I was planning to leave, Brightness. I'm sorry. I should have told you.'

Jasnah settled back. 'I suppose it was to be expected, all things considered.'

'The jam?' Kabsal prodded again.

Shallan frowned. He was particularly insistent about that jam. She raised the jar and sniffed at it, then pulled back. 'It smells terrible! This is jam?' It smelled like vinegar and slime.

'What?' Kabsal said, alarmed. He took the jar, sniffing at it, then pulled away, looking nauseated.

'It appears you got a bad jar,' Jasnah said. 'That's not how it's supposed to smell?'

'Not at all,' Kabsal said. He hesitated, then stuck his finger into the jam anyway, shoving a large glob into his mouth.

'Kabsal!' Shallan said. 'That's revolting!'

He coughed, but forced it down. 'Not so bad, really. You should try it.'

'What?'

'Really,' he said, forcing it toward her. 'I mean, I wanted this to be special, for you. And it turned out so horribly.'

'I'm *not* tasting that, Kabsal.'

He hesitated, as if considering forcing it upon her. Why was he acting so strangely? He raised a hand to his head, stood up, and stumbled away from the bed.

Then he began to rush from the room. He made it only halfway before crashing to the floor, his body sliding a little way across the spotless stone.

'Kabsal!' Shallan said, leaping out of the bed, hurrying to his side, wearing only the white robe. He was shaking. And . . . and . . .

And so was she. The room was spinning. Suddenly she felt very, very tired. She tried to stand, but slipped, dizzy. She barely felt herself hit the floor.

Someone was kneeling above her, cursing.

Jasnah. Her voice was distant. 'She's been poisoned. I need a garnet. Bring me a garnet!'

There's one in my pouch, Shallan thought. She fumbled with it, managing to undo the tie of her safehand's sleeve. *Why . . . why does she want . . .*

But no, I can't show her that. The Soulcaster!

Her mind was so fuzzy.

'Shallan,' Jasnah's voice said, anxious, very soft. 'I'm going to have to Soulcast your blood to purify it. It will be dangerous. *Extremely* dangerous. I'm not good with flesh or blood. It's not where my talent lies.'

She needs it. To save me. Weakly, she reached in and pulled out her safe-pouch with her right hand. 'You . . . can't . . .'

'Hush, child. Where is that garnet!'

'You can't Soulcast,' Shallan said weakly, pulling the ties of her pouch open. She upended it, vaguely seeing a fuzzy golden object slip out onto the floor, alongside the garnet that Kabsal had given her.

Stormfather! Why was the room spinning so much?

Jasnah gasped. Distantly.

Fading . . .

Something happened. A flash of warmth burned through Shallan, something *inside* her skin, as if she had been dumped into a steaming hot cauldron. She screamed, arching her back, her muscles spasming.

All went black.

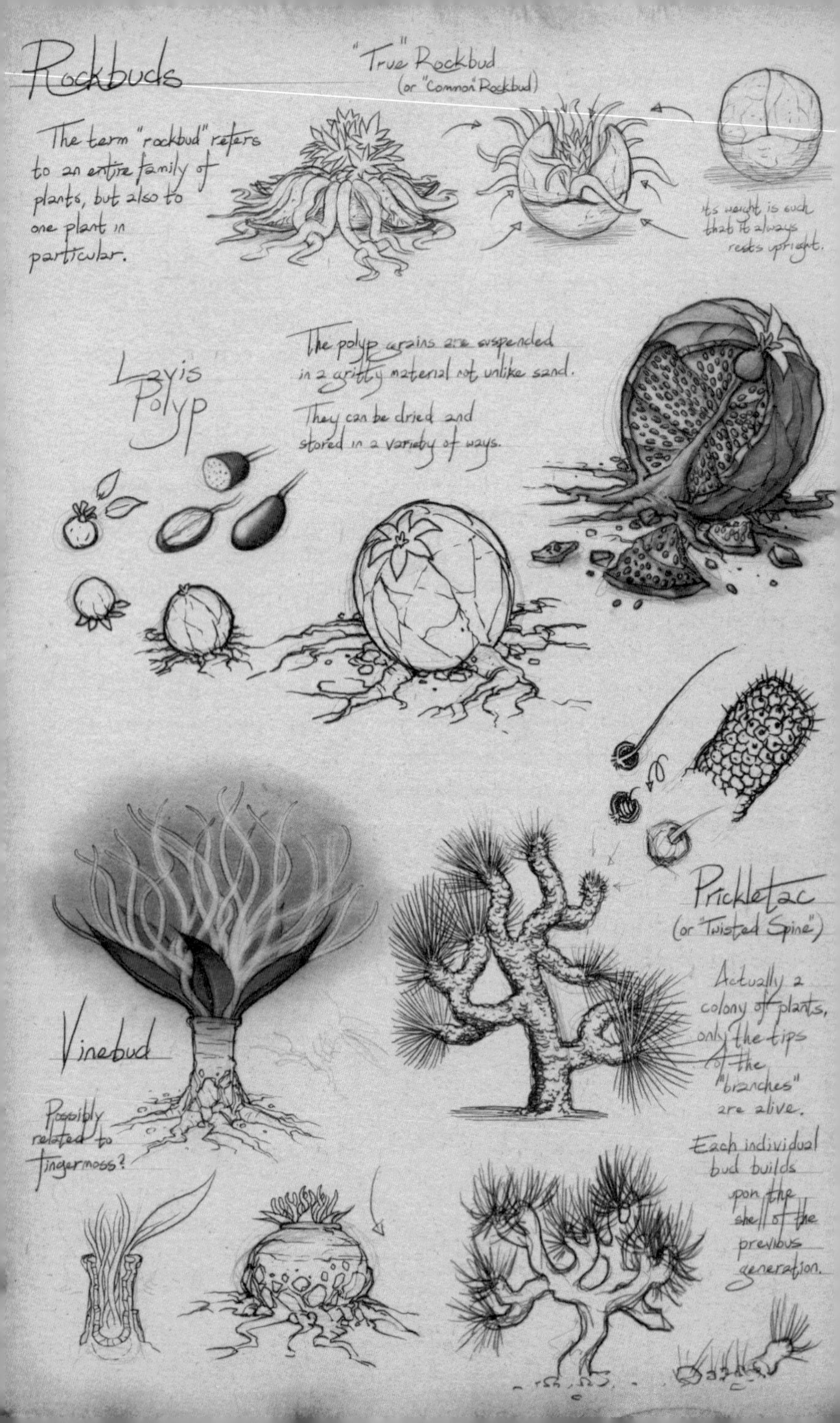

Rockbuds
"True" Rockbud
(or "Common" Rockbud)
The term "rockbud" refers to an entire family of plants, but also to one plant in particular.
Its weight is such that it always rests upright.
Layis Polyp
The polyp grains are suspended in a gritty material not unlike sand.
They can be dried and stored in a variety of ways.
Prickletac
(or "Twisted Spine")
Actually a colony of plants, only the tips of the "branches" are alive.
Each individual bud builds upon the shell of the previous generation.
Vinebud
Possibly related to fingermoss?

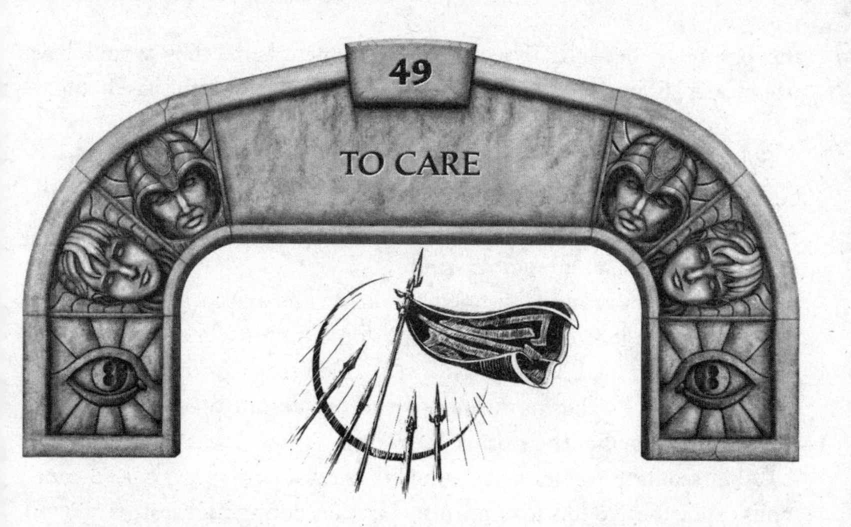

49 TO CARE

'Radiant / of birthplace / the announcer comes / to come announce / the birthplace of Radiants.'

—Though I am not overly fond of the ketek poetic form as a means of conveying information, this one by Allahn is often quoted in reference to Urithiru. I believe some mistook the home of the Radiants for their birthplace.

The towering walls of the chasm rising on either side of Kaladin dripped with greenish grey moss. His torch's flames danced, light reflecting on slick, rain-wetted sections of stone. The humid air was chilly, and the highstorm had left puddles and ponds. Spindly bones – an ulna and a radius – poked from a deep puddle Kaladin passed. He didn't look to see if the rest of the skeleton was there.

Flash floods, Kaladin thought, listening to the scraping steps of the bridgemen behind him. *That water has to go somewhere, otherwise we'd have canals to cross instead of chasms.*

Kaladin didn't know if he could trust his dream or not, but he'd asked around, and it was true that the eastern edge of the Shattered Plains was more open than the western side. The plateaus had been worn away. If the bridgemen could get there, they might be able to flee to the east.

Might. Many chasmfiends lived in that area, and Alethi scouts patrolled the perimeter beyond. If Kaladin's team met them, they would have trouble explaining what a group of armed men – many with slave brands – was doing there.

Syl walked along the wall of the chasm, about level with Kaladin's head. Groundspren didn't pull her downward as they did everything else. She walked with her hands clasped behind her back, her tiny, knee-length skirt fluttering in an intangible wind.

Escape to the east. It seemed unlikely. The highprinces had tried *very*hard to explore that way, looking for a route to the center of the Plains. They'd failed. Chasmfiends had killed some groups. Others had been caught in the chasms during highstorms, despite precautions. It was impossible to predict the storms perfectly.

Other scouting parties had avoided those two fates. They'd used enormous extensible ladders to climb atop plateaus during highstorms. They'd lost many men, though, as the plateau tops provided poor cover during storms, and you couldn't bring wagons or other shelter with you into the chasms. The bigger problem, he'd heard, had been the Parshendi patrols. They'd found and killed dozens of scouting parties.

'Kaladin?' Teft asked, hustling up, splashing through a puddle where bits of empty cremling carapace floated. 'You all right?'

'Fine.'

'You look thoughtful.'

'More breakfast-full,' Kaladin said. 'That gruel was particularly dense this morning.'

Teft smiled. 'I never took you for the glib type.'

'I used to be more so. I get it from my mother. You could rarely say anything to her without getting it twisted about and tossed back to you.'

Teft nodded. They walked in silence for a time, the bridgemen behind laughing as Dunny told a story about the first girl he'd ever kissed.

'Son,' Teft said, 'have you felt anything strange lately?'

'Strange? What kind of strange?'

'I don't know. Just . . . anything odd?' He coughed. 'You know, like odd surges of strength? The . . . er, feeling that you're light?'

'The feeling that I'm *what*?'

'Light. Er, maybe, like your head is light. Light-headed. That sort of thing. Storm it, boy, I'm just checking to see if you're still sick. You were beat up pretty badly by that highstorm.'

'I'm fine,' Kaladin said. 'Remarkably so, actually.'

'Odd, eh?'

It *was* odd. It fed his nagging worry that he was subject to some kind of supernatural curse of the type that were supposed to happen to people who sought the Old Magic. There were stories of evil men made immortal, then tortured over and over again – like Extes, who had his arms torn off each day for sacrificing his son to the Voidbringers in exchange for knowledge of the day of his death. It was just a tale, but tales came from somewhere.

Kaladin lived when everyone else died. Was that the work of some spren from Damnation, toying with him like a windspren, but infinitely more nefarious? Letting him think that he might be able to do some good, then killing everyone he tried to help? There were supposed to be thousands of kinds of spren, many that people never saw or didn't know about. Syl followed him. Could some kind of evil spren be doing the same?

A very disturbing thought.

Superstition is useless, he told himself forcefully. *Think on it too much, and you'll end up like Durk, insisting that you need to wear your lucky boots into every battle.*

They reached a section where the chasm forked, splitting around a plateau high above. Kaladin turned to face the bridgemen. 'This is as good a place as any.' The bridgemen stopped, bunching up. He could see the anticipation in their eyes, the excitement.

He'd felt that once, back before he'd known the soreness and the pain of practice. Oddly, Kaladin felt he was now both more in awe of *and* more disappointed in the spear than he'd been as a youth. He loved the focus, the feeling of certainty that he felt when he fought. But that hadn't saved those who followed him.

'This is where I'm supposed to tell you what a sorry group you are,' Kaladin said to the men. 'It's the way I've always seen it done. The training sergeant tells the recruits that they are pathetic. He points out their weakness, perhaps spars with a few of them, tossing them on their backsides to teach them humility. I did that a few times myself when training new spearmen.'

Kaladin shook his head. 'Today, that's not how we'll begin. You men don't need humbling. You don't dream of glory. You dream of survival.

Most of all, you *aren't* the sad, unprepared group of recruits most sergeants have to deal with. You're tough. I've seen you run for miles carrying a bridge. You're brave. I've seen you charge straight at a line of archers. You're determined. Otherwise you wouldn't be here, right now, with me.'

Kaladin walked to the side of the chasm and extracted a discarded spear from some flood-strewn rubble. Once he had it, however, he realized that the spearhead had been knocked off. He almost tossed it aside, then reconsidered.

Spears were dangerous for him to hold. They made him want to fight, and might lead him to think he was who he'd once been: Kaladin Stormblessed, confident squadleader. He wasn't that man any longer.

It seemed that whenever he picked up weapons, the people around him died – friends as well as foes. So, for now, it seemed good to hold this length of wood; it was just a staff. Nothing more. A stick he could use for training.

He could face returning to the spear another time.

'It's good that you're already prepared,' Kaladin said to the men. 'Because we don't have the six weeks I was given to train a new batch of recruits. In six weeks, Sadeas will have half of us dead. I intend to see you all drinking mudbeer in a tavern somewhere safe by the time six weeks have passed.'

Several of them gave a kind of half-cheer at that.

'We'll have to be fast,' Kaladin said. 'I'll have to push you hard. That's our only option.' He glanced at the spear haft. 'The first thing you need to learn is that it's all right to care.'

The thirty-three bridgemen stood in a double row. All had wanted to come. Even Leyten, who had been hurt so badly. They didn't have any who were wounded so badly they couldn't walk, although Dabbid continued to stare off at nothing. Rock stood with his arms folded, apparently with no intention of learning to fight. Shen, the parshman, stood at the very back. He looked at the ground. Kaladin didn't intend to put a spear in his hands.

Several of the bridgemen seemed confused by what Kaladin had said about emotions, though Teft just raised an eyebrow and Moash yawned. 'What do you mean?' Drehy asked. He was a lanky blond man, long-limbed and muscled. He spoke with a faint accent; he was from somewhere far to the west, called Rianal.

'A lot of soldiers,' Kaladin said, running his thumb across the pole, feeling the grain of the wood, 'they think that you fight the best if you're passionless and cold. I think that's stormleavings. Yes, you need to be focused. Yes, emotions are dangerous. But if you don't care about anything, what are you? An animal, driven only to kill. Our passion is what makes us human. We *have* to fight for a reason. So I say that it's all right to care. We'll talk about controlling your fear and anger, but remember this as the first lesson I taught you.'

Several of the bridgemen nodded. Most seemed confused still. Kaladin remembered being there, wondering why Tukks wasted time talking about emotions. He'd thought he understood emotion – his drive to learn the spear had come *because* of his emotions. Vengeance. Hatred. A lust for the power to exact retribution on Varth and the soldiers of his squad.

He looked up, trying to banish those memories. No, the bridgemen didn't understand his words about caring, but perhaps they would remember later, as Kaladin had.

'The second lesson,' Kaladin said, slapping the decapitated spear to the rock beside him with a crack that echoed down the chasm, 'is more utilitarian. Before you can learn to fight, you're going to have to learn how to stand.' He dropped the spear. The bridgemen watched him with frowns of disappointment.

Kaladin fell into a basic spearman's stance, feet wide apart – but not too wide – turned sideways, knees bent in a loose crouch. 'Skar, I want you to come try to push me backward.'

'What?'

'Try and throw me off balance,' Kaladin said. 'Force me to stumble.'

Skar shrugged and walked forward. He tried to shove Kaladin back, but Kaladin easily knocked his hands aside with a quick snap of the wrist. Skar cursed and came at him again, but Kaladin caught his arm and shoved him backward, causing Skar to stumble.

'Drehy, come help him,' Kaladin said. 'Moash, you too. Try to force me off balance.'

The other two joined Skar. Kaladin stepped around the attacks, staying squarely in the middle of them, adjusting his stance to rebuff each attempt. He grabbed Drehy's arm and yanked him forward, nearly causing him to fall. He stepped into Skar's shoulder-rush, deflecting the weight of the man's body and throwing him backward. He pulled back as Moash got his arms on him, causing Moash to overbalance himself.

Kaladin remained completely unfazed, weaving between them and adjusting his center of balance by bending his knees and positioning his feet. 'Combat begins with the legs,' Kaladin said as he evaded the attacks. 'I don't care how fast you are with a jab, how accurate you are with a thrust. If your opponent can trip you, or make you stumble, you'll lose. Losing means dying.'

Several of the watching bridgemen tried to imitate Kaladin, crouching down. Skar, Drehy, and Moash had finally decided to try a coordinated rush, planning to all tackle Kaladin at once. Kaladin held up his hand. 'Well done, you three.' He motioned them back to stand with the others. They reluctantly broke off their attacks.

'I'm going to split you into pairs,' Kaladin said. 'We're going to spend all day today – and probably each day this week – working on stances. Learning to maintain one, learning to not lock your knees the moment you're threatened, learning to hold your center of balance. It will take time, but I promise you if we start here, you'll learn to be deadly far more quickly. Even if it seems that all you're doing at first is standing around.'

The men nodded.

'Teft,' Kaladin ordered. 'Split them into pairs by size and weight, then run them through an elementary forward spear stance.'

'Aye, sir!' Teft barked. Then he froze, realizing what he'd given away. The speed at which he'd responded made it obvious that Teft had been a soldier. Teft met Kaladin's eyes and saw that Kaladin knew. The older man scowled, but Kaladin returned a grin. He had a veteran under his command; that was going to make this all a lot easier.

Teft didn't feign ignorance, and easily fell into the role of the training sergeant, splitting the men into pairs, correcting their stances. *No wonder he never takes off that shirt*, Kaladin thought. *It probably hides a mess of scars.*

As Teft instructed the men, Kaladin pointed to Rock, gesturing him over.

'Yes?' Rock asked. The man was so broad of chest that his bridgeman's vest could barely fasten.

'You said something before,' Kaladin said. 'About fighting being beneath you?'

'Is true. I am not a fourth son.'

'What does that have to do with it?'

'First son and second son are needed for making food,' Rock said, raising a finger. 'Is most important. Without food, nobody lives, yes? Third son is craftsman. This is me. I serve proudly. Only fourth son can be warrior. Warriors, they are not needed as much as food or crafts. You see?'

'Your profession is determined by your birth order?'

'Yes,' Rock said proudly. 'Is best way. On the Peaks, there is always food. Not every family has four sons. So not always is a soldier needed. I cannot fight. What man could do this thing before the *Uli'tekanaki*?'

Kaladin shot a glance at Syl. She shrugged, not seeming to care what Rock did. 'All right,' he said. 'I've got something else I want you to do, then. Go grab Lopen, Dabbid . . .' Kaladin hesitated. 'And Shen. Get him too.'

Rock did so. Lopen was in the line, learning the stances, though Dabbid – as usual – stood off to the side, staring at nothing in particular. Whatever had taken him, it was far worse than ordinary battle shock. Shen stood beside him, hesitant, as if not certain of his place.

Rock pulled Lopen out of the line, then grabbed Dabbid and Shen and walked back to Kaladin.

'Gancho,' Lopen said, with a lazy salute. 'Guess I'll make a poor spearman, with one hand.'

'That's all right,' Kaladin said. 'I have something else I need you to do. We'll see trouble from Gaz and our new captain – or at least his wife – if we don't bring back salvage.'

'We three cannot do the work of thirty, Kaladin,' Rock said, scratching at his beard. 'Is not possible.'

'Maybe not,' Kaladin said. 'But most of our time down in these chasms is spent looking for corpses that haven't been picked clean. I think we can work a lot faster. We *need* to work a lot faster, if we're going to train with the spear. Fortunately, we have an advantage.'

He held out his hand, and Syl alighted on it. He'd spoken to her earlier, and she'd agreed to his plan. He didn't notice her doing anything special, but Lopen suddenly gasped. Syl had made herself visible to him.

'Ah . . .' Rock said, bowing in respect to Syl. 'Like gathering reeds.'

'Well flick my sparks,' Lopen said. 'Rock, you never said it was so pretty!'

Syl smiled broadly.

'Be respectful,' Rock said. 'Is not for you to speak of her in that way, little person.'

The men knew about Syl, of course. Kaladin didn't speak of her, but they saw him talking to the air, and Rock had explained.

'Lopen,' Kaladin said. 'Syl can move far more quickly than a bridgeman. She will search out places for you to gather, and you four can pick through things quickly.'

'Dangerous,' Rock said. 'What if we meet chasmfiend while alone?'

'Unfortunately, we can't come back empty-handed. The *last* thing we want is Hashal deciding to send Gaz down to supervise.'

Lopen snorted. 'He'd never do that, gancho. Too much work down here.'

'Too dangerous too,' Rock added.

'Everyone says that,' Kaladin said. 'But I've never seen more than these scrapes on the walls.'

'They're down here,' Rock said. 'Is not just legend. Just before you came, half a bridge crew was killed. Eaten. Most beasts come to the middle plateaus, but there are some who come this far.'

'Well, I hate to put you in danger, but unless we try this, we'll have chasm duty taken from us and we'll end up cleaning latrines instead.'

'All right, gancho,' Lopen said. 'I'll go.'

'As will I,' Rock said. 'With *ali'i'kamura* to protect, perhaps it will be safe.'

'I intend to teach you to fight eventually,' Kaladin said. Then as Rock frowned, Kaladin hastily added, 'You, Lopen, I mean. One arm doesn't mean you're useless. You'll be at a disadvantage, but there are things I can teach you to deal with that. Right now a scavenger is more important to us than another spear.'

'Sounds swift to me.' Lopen gestured to Dabbid, and the two walked over to gather sacks for the collecting. Rock moved to join them, but Kaladin took his arm.

'I haven't given up on finding an easier way out of here than fighting,' Kaladin said to him. 'If we never returned, Gaz and the others would probably just assume that a chasmfiend got us. If there's some way to reach the other side . . .'

Rock looked skeptical. 'Many have searched for this thing.'

'The eastern edge is open.'

'Yes,' Rock said, laughing, 'and when you are able to travel that far without being eaten by chasmfiend or killed in floods, I shall name you my *kaluk'i'iki*.'

Kaladin raised an eyebrow.

'Only a woman can be *kaluk'i'iki*,' Rock said, as if that explained the joke.

'Wife?'

Rock laughed even louder. 'No, no. Airsick lowlanders. Ha!'

'Great. Look, see if you can memorize the chasms, perhaps make a map of some kind. I suspect that most who come down here stick to the established routes. That means we're much more likely to find salvage down side passages; that's where I'll be sending Syl.'

'Side passages?' Rock said, still amused. 'One might begin to think you *want* me to be eaten. Ha, and by a greatshell. They are supposed to be tast*ed*, not tast*ing*.'

'I—'

'No, no,' Rock said. 'Is a good plan. I only jest. I can be careful, and this will be good for me to do, since I do not wish to fight.'

'Thank you. Maybe you'll happen upon a place we could climb out.'

'I will do this thing,' Rock said, nodding. 'But we cannot simply climb out. The army has many scouts on the Plains. Is how they know when chasmfiends come to pupate, eh? They will see us, and we will not be able to cross chasms without bridge.'

It was a good argument, unfortunately. Climb up here, and they'd be seen. Climb out in the middle, and they'd be stuck on plateaus without anywhere to go. Climb out closer to the Parshendi areas, and they'd be found by their scouts. That was assuming they *could* get out of the chasms. Though some were as shallow as forty or fifty feet, many were well over a hundred feet deep.

Syl zipped away to lead Rock and his crew, and Kaladin moved back to the main body of bridgemen to help Teft correct stances. It was difficult work; the first day always was. The bridgemen were sloppy and uncertain.

But they also showed remarkable resolve. Kaladin had never worked with a group who made fewer complaints. The bridgemen didn't ask for a break. They didn't shoot him resentful glances when he pushed them harder. The scowls they bore were at their own foibles, angry at themselves for not learning faster.

And they got it. After just a few hours, the more talented of them – Moash at the forefront – started to change into fighting men. Their stances grew firmer, more confident. When they should have been feeling exhausted and frustrated, they were more determined.

Kaladin stepped back, watching Moash fall into his stance after Teft shoved him. It was a resetting exercise – Moash would let Teft knock him backward, then would scramble back and set his feet. Time and time again. The purpose was to train oneself to revert to the stance without thinking. Kaladin normally wouldn't have started resetting exercises until the second or third day. Yet here, Moash was drinking it in after only two hours. There were two others – Drehy and Skar – who were nearly as quick to learn.

Kaladin leaned back against the stone wall. Cold water leaked down the rock beside him, and a frillbloom plant hesitantly opened its fanlike fronds beside his head: two wide, orange leaves, with spines on the tips, unfolding like opening fists.

Is it their bridgeman training? Kaladin wondered. *Or is it their passion?* He had given them a chance to fight back. That kind of opportunity changed a man.

Watching them stand resolute and capable in stances they had only just been taught, Kaladin realized something. These men – cast off by the army, forced to work themselves near to death, then fed extra food by Kaladin's careful planning – were the most fit, training-ready recruits he'd ever been given.

By seeking to beat them down, Sadeas had prepared them to excel.

'Flame and char. Skin so terrible. Eyes like pits of blackness.'

—A quote from the *Iviad* probably needs no reference notation, but this comes from line 482, should I need to locate it quickly.

Shallan awoke in a small white room.

She sat up, feeling oddly healthy. Bright sunlight illuminated the window's gossamer white shades, bursting through the cloth and into the room. Shallan frowned, shaking her muddled head. She felt as if she should be burned toes to ears, her skin flaking off. But that was just a memory. She had the cut on her arm, but otherwise she felt perfectly well.

A rustling sound. She turned to see a nurse hurrying away down a white hallway outside; the woman had apparently seen Shallan sit up, and was now taking the news to someone.

I'm in the hospital, Shallan thought. *Moved to a private room.*

A soldier peeked in, inspecting Shallan. It was apparently a guarded room.

'What happened?' she called to him. 'I was poisoned, wasn't I?' She felt a sudden shock of alarm. 'Kabsal! Is he all right?'

The guard just turned back to his post. Shallan began to crawl out of bed, but he looked in again, glaring at her. She yelped despite herself, pulling up the sheet and settling back. She still wore one of the hospital robes, much like a soft bathing robe.

How long had she been unconscious? Why was she—

The Soulcaster! she realized. *I gave it back to Jasnah.*

The next half hour was one of the most miserable in Shallan's life. She spent it suffering the periodic glares of the guard and feeling nauseated. What had happened?

Finally, Jasnah appeared at the other end of the hallway. She was wearing a different dress, black with light grey piping. She strode toward the room like an arrow and dismissed the guard with a single word as she passed. The man hurried away, his boots louder on the stone floor than Jasnah's slippers.

Jasnah came in, and though she made no accusations, her glare was so hostile that Shallan wanted to crawl under her covers and hide. No. She wanted to crawl under the bed, dig down into the floor itself, and put stone between herself and those eyes.

She settled for looking downward in shame.

'You were wise to return the Soulcaster,' Jasnah said, voice like ice. 'It saved your life. *I* saved your life.'

'Thank you,' Shallan whispered.

'Who are you working with? Which devotary bribed you to steal the fabrial?'

'None of them, Brightness. I stole it of my own volition.'

'Protecting them does you no good. Eventually you *will* tell me the truth.'

'It is the truth,' Shallan said, looking up, feeling a hint of defiance. 'It's why I became your ward in the first place. To steal that Soulcaster.'

'Yes, but for whom?'

'For *me*,' Shallan said. 'Is it so hard to believe that I could act for myself? Am I such a miserable failure that the only rational answer is to assume I was duped or manipulated?'

'You have no grounds to raise your voice to me, child,' Jasnah said evenly. 'And you have *every* reason to remember your place.'

Shallan looked down again.

Jasnah was silent for a time. Finally, she sighed. 'What were you *thinking*, child?'

'My father is dead.'

'So?'

'He was not well liked, Brightness. Actually, he was *hated*, and our family is bankrupt. My brothers are trying to put up a strong front by pretending he still lives. But . . .' Dared she tell Jasnah that her father had possessed a Soulcaster? Doing so wouldn't help excuse what Shallan had done, and might get her family more deeply into trouble. 'We needed something. An edge. A way to earn money quickly, or *create* money.'

Jasnah was silent again. When she finally spoke, she sounded faintly amused. 'You thought your salvation lay in enraging not only all the entire ardentia, but Alethkar? Do you realize what my brother would have done if he'd learned of this?'

Shallan looked away, feeling both foolish and ashamed.

Jasnah sighed. 'Sometimes I forget how young you are. I can see how the theft might have looked tempting to you. It was stupid nonetheless. I've arranged passage back to Jah Keved. You will leave in the morning.'

'I—' It was more than she deserved. 'Thank you.'

'Your friend, the ardent, is dead.'

Shallan looked up, dismayed. 'What happened?'

'The bread was poisoned. Backbreaker powder. Very lethal, dusted over the bread to look like flour. I suspect the bread was similarly treated every time he visited. His goal was to get me to eat a piece.'

'But I ate a *lot* of that bread!'

'The jam had the antidote,' Jasnah said. 'We found it in several empty jars he'd used.'

'It can't be!'

'I've begun investigating,' Jasnah said. 'I should have done so immediately. Nobody quite remembers where this "Kabsal" came from. Though he spoke familiarly of the other ardents to you and me, they knew him only vaguely.'

'Then he . . .'

'He was playing you, child. The whole time, he was using you to get to me. To spy on what I was doing, to kill me if he could.' She spoke of it so evenly, so emotionlessly. 'I believe he used much more of the powder during this last attempt, more than he'd ever used before, perhaps hoping to get me to breathe it in. He realized this would be his last opportunity. It turned against him, however, working more quickly than he'd anticipated.'

Someone had almost killed her. Not someone, *Kabsal.* No wonder he'd been so eager to get her to taste the jam!

'I'm very disappointed in you, Shallan,' Jasnah said. 'I can see now why you tried to end your own life. It was the guilt.'

She *hadn't* tried to kill herself. But what good would it do to admit that? Jasnah was taking pity on her; best not to give her reason not to. But what of the strange things Shallan had seen and experienced? Might Jasnah have an explanation for them?

Looking at Jasnah, seeing the cold rage hidden behind her calm exterior, frightened Shallan enough that her questions about the symbolheads and the strange place she'd visited died on her lips. How had Shallan ever thought of herself as brave? She wasn't brave. She was a fool. She remembered the times her father's rage had echoed through the house. Jasnah's quieter, more justified anger was no less daunting.

'Well, you will need to learn to live with your guilt,' Jasnah said. 'You might not have escaped with my fabrial, but you *have* thrown away a very promising career. This foolish scheme will stain your life for decades. No woman will take you as a ward now. You *threw it away*.' She shook her head in distaste. 'I hate being wrong.'

With that, she turned to leave.

Shallan raised a hand. *I have to apologize. I have to say something.* 'Jasnah?'

The woman did not look back, and the guard did not return.

Shallan curled up under the sheet, stomach in knots, feeling so sick that – for a moment – she wished that she'd actually dug that shard of glass in a little deeper. Or maybe that Jasnah hadn't been quick enough with the Soulcaster to save her.

She'd lost it all. No fabrial to protect her family, no wardship to continue her studies. No Kabsal. She'd never actually had him in the first place.

Her tears dampened the sheets as the sunlight outside faded, then vanished. Nobody came to check on her.

Nobody cared.

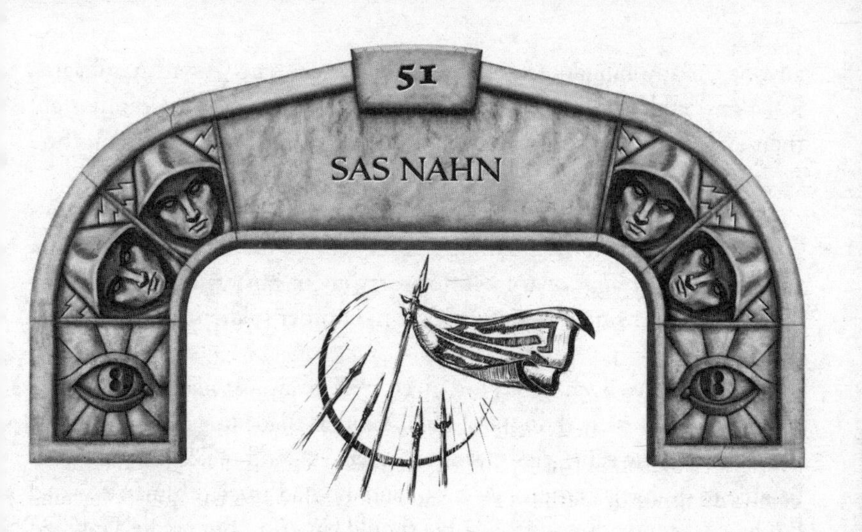

ONE YEAR AGO

Kaladin sat quietly in the waiting room of Amaram's wooden warcenter. It was constructed of a dozen sturdy sections that could be disconnected and pulled by chulls. Kaladin sat beside a window, looking out at the camp. There was a hole where Kaladin's squad had been housed. He could make it out from where he sat. Their tents had been broken down and given to other squads.

Four of his men remained. Four, out of twenty-six. And men called him lucky. Men called him Stormblessed. He'd begun to believe that.

I killed a Shardbearer today, he thought, mind numb. *Like Lanacin the Surefooted, or Evod Markmaker. Me. I killed one*.

And he didn't care.

He crossed his arms on the wooden windowsill. There was no glass in the window and he could feel the breeze. A windspren flitted from one tent to another. Behind Kaladin, the room had a thick red rug and shields on the walls. There were a number of padded wooden chairs, like the one Kaladin sat in. This was the 'small' waiting chamber of the warcenter – small, yet larger than his entire house back in Hearthstone, the surgery included.

I killed a Shardbearer, he thought again. *And then I gave away the Blade and Plate*.

That single event had to be the most monumentally stupid thing anyone, in any kingdom, in any era, had ever done. As a Shardbearer, Kaladin would have been more important than Roshone – more important than Amaram. He'd have been able to go to the Shattered Plains and fight in a real war.

No more squabbling over borders. No more petty lighteyed captains belonging to unimportant families, bitter because they'd been left behind. He would never again have had to worry about blisters from boots that didn't fit, dinner slop that tasted of crem, or other soldiers who wanted to pick a fight.

He could have been rich. He'd given it all away, just like that.

And *still*, the mere thought of touching that Blade turned his stomach. He didn't want wealth, titles, armies, or even a good meal. He wanted to be able to go back and protect the men who had trusted him. Why had he chased after the Shardbearer? He should have run. But no, he'd insisted on charging at a storming *Shardbearer.*

You protected your highmarshal, he told himself. *You're a hero.*

But why was Amaram's life worth more than those of his men? Kaladin served Amaram because of the honor he had shown. He let spearmen share his comfort in the warcenter during highstorms, a different squad each storm. He insisted that his men be well fed and well paid. He didn't treat them like slime.

He did let his subordinates do so, though. And he'd broken his promise to shelter Tien.

So did I. So did I. . . .

Kaladin's insides were a twisted mess of guilt and sorrow. One thing remained clear, like a bright spot of light on the wall of a dark room. He wanted nothing to do with those Shards. He didn't even want to touch them.

The door thumped open, and Kaladin turned in his chair. Amaram entered. Tall, lean, with a square face and long martial coat of deep green. He walked on a crutch. Kaladin eyed the wrappings and splint with a critical eye. *I could have done better.* He'd also have insisted that the patient remain in bed.

Amaram was talking to one of his stormwardens, a middle-aged man with a square beard and robes of deep black.

'. . . why Thaidakar would risk this?' Amaram was saying, speaking in a soft voice. 'But who else would it be? The Ghostbloods grow more bold.

We'll need to find out who he was. Do we know anything about him?'

'He was Veden, Brightlord,' the stormwarden said. 'Nobody I recognize. But I will investigate.'

Amaram nodded, falling silent. Behind the two, a group of lighteyed officers entered, one of them carrying the Shardblade, holding it on a pure white cloth. Behind this group came the four surviving members of Kaladin's squad: Hab, Reesh, Alabet, and Coreb.

Kaladin stood up, feeling exhausted. Amaram remained by the door, arms folded, as two final men entered and closed the door. These last two were also lighteyes, but lesser ones – officers in Amaram's personal guard.

Had these been among those who had fled?

It was the smart thing to do, Kaladin thought. *Smarter than what I did.*

Amaram leaned on his walking staff, inspecting Kaladin with bright tan eyes. He'd been in conference with his counselors for several hours now, trying to discover who the Shardbearer had been. 'You did a brave thing today, soldier,' Amaram said to Kaladin.

'I . . .' What did you say to that? *I wish I'd left you to die, sir.* 'Thank you.'

'Everyone else fled, including my honor guard.' The two men closest to the door looked down, ashamed. 'But you charged in for the attack. Why?'

'I didn't really think about it, sir.'

Amaram seemed displeased by the answer. 'Your name is Kaladin, is it?'

'Yes, Brightlord. From Hearthstone? Remember?'

Amaram frowned, looking confused.

'Your cousin, Roshone, is citylord there. He sent my brother into the army when you came recruiting. I . . . I joined with my brother.'

'Ah yes,' Amaram said. 'I believe I remember you.' He didn't ask after Tien. 'You still haven't answered my question. Why attack? It wasn't for the Shardblade. You rejected that.'

'Yes, sir.'

To the side, the stormwarden raised his eyebrows, as if he hadn't believed that Kaladin had turned down the Shards. The soldier holding the Shardblade kept glancing at it in awe.

'Why?' Amaram said. 'Why did you reject it? I have to know.'

'I don't want it, sir.'

'Yes, but why?'

Because it would make me one of you. Because I can't look at that weapon and not see the faces of the men its wielder slaughtered so offhandedly.

Because . . . because . . .

'I can't really answer that, sir,' Kaladin said, sighing.

The stormwarden walked over to the room's brazier, shaking his head. He began warming his hands.

'Look,' Kaladin said. 'Those Shards are mine. Well, I said to give them to Coreb. He's the highest ranked of my soldiers, and the best fighter among them.' The other three would understand. Besides, Coreb would take care of them, once he was a lighteyes.

Amaram looked at Coreb, then nodded to his attendants. One closed the window shutters. The others pulled out swords, then began moving toward the four remaining members of Kaladin's squad.

Kaladin yelled, leaping forward, but two of the officers had positioned themselves close to him. One slammed a punch into Kaladin's gut as soon as he started moving. He was so surprised that it connected directly, and he gasped.

No.

He fought off the pain, turning to swing at the man. The man's eyes opened wide as Kaladin's fist connected, throwing him backward. Several other men piled on him. He had no weapons, and he was so tired from the battle that he could barely stay upright. They knocked him to the ground with punches to his side and back. He collapsed to the floor, pained, but still able to watch as the soldiers came at his men.

Reesh was cut down first. Kaladin gasped, stretching out a hand, struggling to his knees.

This can't happen. Please, no!

Hab and Alabet had their knives out, but fell quickly, one soldier gutting Hab as two others hacked down Alabet. Alabet's knife thumped as it hit the ground, followed by his arm, then finally his corpse.

Coreb lasted the longest, backing away, hands held forward. He didn't scream. He seemed to understand. Kaladin's eyes were watering, and soldiers grabbed him from behind, stopping him from helping.

Coreb fell to his knees and began to beg. One of Amaram's men took him at the neck, neatly severing his head. It was over in seconds.

'You bastard!' Kaladin said, gasping against his pain. 'You storming bastard!' Kaladin found himself weeping, struggling uselessly at the four men holding him. The blood of the fallen spearmen soaked the boards.

They were dead. All of them were dead. Stormfather! All of them!

Amaram stepped forward, expression grim. He went down on one knee before Kaladin. 'I'm sorry.'

'Bastard!' Kaladin screamed as loud as he could.

'I couldn't risk them telling what they saw. This is what must be, soldier. It's for the good of the army. They're going to be told that your squad helped the Shardbearer. You see, the men must believe that *I* killed him.'

'You're taking the Shards for yourself!'

'I am trained in the sword,' Amaram said, 'and am accustomed to plate. It will serve Alethkar best if I bear the Shards.'

'You could have asked me for them! Storm you!'

'And when news got around camp?' Amaram said grimly. 'That you'd killed the Shardbearer but I had the Shards? Nobody would believe that you'd given them up of your own free choice. Besides, son. You wouldn't have let me keep them.' Amaram shook his head. 'You'd have changed your mind. In a day or two, you'd have wanted the wealth and prestige – others would convince you of it. You'd have *demanded* that I return them to you. It took hours to decide, but Restares is right – this is what must be done. For the good of Alethkar.'

'It's not about Alethkar! It's about you! Storm it, you're supposed to be better than the others!' Tears dripped from Kaladin's chin.

Amaram looked guilty suddenly, as if he knew what Kaladin had said was true. He turned away, waving to the stormwarden. The man turned from the brazier, holding something he'd been heating in the coals. A small branding iron.

'It's all an act?' Kaladin asked. 'The honorable brightlord who cares about his men? Lies? All of it?'

'This *is* for my men,' Amaram said. He took the Shardblade from the cloth, holding it in his hand. The gemstone at its pommel let out a flash of white light. 'You can't begin to understand the weights I carry, spearman.' Amaram's voice lost some of its calm tone of reason. He sounded defensive. 'I can't worry about the lives of a few darkeyed spear-men when thousands of people may be saved by my decision.'

The stormwarden stepped up to Kaladin, positioning the branding iron. The glyphs, reversed, read *sas nahn*. A slave's brand.

'You came for me,' Amaram said, limping to the door, stepping around Reesh's body. 'For saving my life, I spare yours. Five men telling the same story would have been believed, but a single slave will be ignored. The warcamp will be told that you didn't try to help your fellows – but you didn't try to stop them, either. You fled and were captured by my guard.'

Amaram hesitated by the door, resting the blunt edge of the stolen Shardblade on his shoulder. The guilt was still there in his eyes, but he grew hard, covering it. 'You are being discharged as a deserter and branded as a slave. But you are spared death by my mercy.'

He opened the door and walked out.

The branding iron fell, searing Kaladin's fate into his skin. He let out a final, ragged scream.

THE END OF

Part Three

INTERLUDES

BAXIL • GERANID • SZETH

I-7

BAXIL

Baxil hastened down the lavish palace corridor, clutching the bulky bag of tools. A sound like a footfall came from behind him and he jumped, spinning. He didn't see anything. The corridor was empty, a golden carpet lining the floor, mirrors on the walls, arched ceiling inlaid with elaborate mosaics.

'Would you *stop* that?' Av said, walking beside him. 'Every time you jump I nearly cuff you one out of surprise.'

'I can't help it,' Baxil said. 'Shouldn't we be doing this at night?'

'Mistress knows what she's doing,' Av said. Like Baxil, Av was Emuli, with dark skin and hair. But the taller man was far more self-confident. He sauntered down the halls, acting as if they'd been invited, thick-bladed sword slung in a sheath over his shoulder.

If the Prime Kadasix may provide, Baxil thought, *I'd rather Av never have to draw that weapon. Thank you.*

Their mistress walked ahead of them, the only other person in the hallway. She wasn't Emuli – she didn't even seem Makabaki, though she had dark skin and long, beautiful black hair. She had eyes like a Shin, but she was tall and lean, like an Alethi. Av thought she was a mixed breed. Or so he said when they dared talk about such things. The mistress had good ears. Strangely good ears.

She stopped at the next intersection. Baxil caught himself glancing over his shoulder again. Av elbowed him, but he couldn't help looking. Yes, the mistress claimed that the palace servants would be busy getting the new guest wing ready, but this was the home of Ashno of Sages himself. One of the richest and holiest men in all of Emul. He had hundreds of servants. What if one of them walked down this hallway?

The two men joined their mistress at the intersection. He forced his eyes forward so he wouldn't keep looking over his shoulder, but then found himself staring at the mistress. It was dangerous, being employed by a woman as beautiful as she was, with that long black hair, worn free, hanging down to her waist. She never wore a proper woman's robe, or even a dress or skirt. Always trousers, usually sleek and tight, a thin-bladed sword at her hip. Her eyes were so faintly violet they were almost white.

She was amazing. Wonderful, intoxicating, overwhelming.

Av elbowed him in the ribs again. Baxil jumped, then glared at his cousin, rubbing his belly.

'Baxil,' the mistress said. 'My tools.'

He opened the bag, handing over a folded tool belt. It clinked as she took it, not looking at him, then she strode down the hallway to their left.

Baxil watched, uncomfortable. This was the Hallowed Hall, the place where a wealthy man placed images of his Kadasix for reverence. The mistress walked up to the first piece of art. The painting depicted Epan, Lady of Dreams. It was beautiful, a masterpiece of gold leaf on black canvas.

The mistress took a knife from her bundle and slashed the painting down the front. Baxil cringed, but said nothing. He'd almost gotten used to the casual way she destroyed art, though he was baffled by it. She did pay the two of them very well, however.

Av leaned back against the wall, picking his teeth with a fingernail. Baxil tried to imitate his relaxed pose. The large hallway was lit with topaz chips set in beautiful chandeliers, but they made no move to take them. The mistress did not approve of stealing.

'I've been thinking of seeking the Old Magic,' Baxil said, partially to keep himself from cringing as the mistress moved on to gouge out the eyes of a fine bust.

Av snorted. 'Why?'

'I don't know,' Baxil said. 'Seems like something to do with myself. I've never sought it, you know, and they say every man gets one chance. Ask a boon of the Nightwatcher. Have you used yours?'

'Nah,' Av said. 'Don't fancy making the trip all the way to the Valley. Besides, my brother went. Came back with two numb hands. Never could feel anything with them again.'

'What was his boon?' Baxil asked as the mistress wrapped up a vase with a cloth, then quietly shattered it on the floor and crushed the pieces.

'Don't know,' Av said. 'He never said. Seemed embarrassed. Probably asked for something silly, like a good haircut.' Av smirked.

'I was thinking I'd make myself more useful,' Baxil said. 'Ask for courage, you know?'

'If you want,' Av replied. 'I figure there are better ways than the Old Magic. You never know what kind of curse you'll end up with.'

'I could phrase my request perfectly,' Baxil said.

'Doesn't work that way,' Av said. 'It's not a game, no matter how the stories try to put it. The Nightwatcher doesn't trick you or twist your words. You ask a boon. She gives what *she* feels you deserve, then gives you a curse to go along with it. Sometimes related, sometimes not.'

'And you're an expert?' Baxil asked. The mistress was slashing another painting. 'I thought you said you never went.'

'I didn't,' Av said. 'On account of my father going, my mother going, and each of my brothers going. A few got what they wanted. Most all of them regretted the curse, save my father. He got a heap of good cloth; sold it to keep us from starving during the lurnip famine a few decades ago.'

'What was his curse?' Baxil said.

'Saw the world upside down from then on.'

'Really?'

'Yeah,' Av said. 'Twisted all about. Like people walk on the ceilings and the sky was underneath him. Said he got used to it pretty quickly, though, and didn't really think it a curse by the time he died.'

Even thinking about that curse made Baxil feel sick. He looked down at his sack of tools. If he weren't such a coward, would he – maybe – be able to convince the mistress to see him as something more than just hired muscle?

If the Prime Kadasix could provide, he thought, *it would be very nice if I could know the right thing to do. Thank you.*

The mistress returned, hair somewhat disheveled. She held out a hand. 'Padded mallet, Baxil. There's a full statue back there.'

He responded, pulling the mallet out of the sack and handing it to her.

'Perhaps I should get myself a Shardblade,' she said absently, putting the tool up on her shoulder. 'But that might make this too easy.'

'I wouldn't mind if it were too easy, mistress,' Baxil noted.

She sniffed, walking back down the hallway. Soon she began to pound on a statue at the far end, breaking off its arms. Baxil winced. 'Someone's *going* to hear that.'

'Yeah,' Av said. 'Probably why she waited to do it last.'

At least the pounding was muffled by the padding. They had to be the only thieves who sneaked into the homes of rich men without taking anything.

'Why *does* she do this, Av?' Baxil found himself asking.

'Don't know. Maybe you should ask her.'

'I thought you said I should never do that!'

'Depends,' Av said. 'How attached to your limbs are you?'

'Rather attached.'

'Well, if you ever want that changed, start asking the mistress prying questions. Until then, shut up.'

Baxil said nothing further. *The Old Magic*, he thought. *It* could *change me. I will go looking for it.*

Knowing his luck, though, he wouldn't be able to find it. He sighed, resting back against the wall as muted thuds continued to come from the mistress's direction.

'I'm thinking of changing my Calling,' Ashir said from behind.

Geranid nodded absently as she worked on her equations. The small stone room smelled sharply of spices. Ashir was trying another new experiment. It involved some kind of curry powder and a rare Shin fruit that he'd caramelized. Something like that. She could hear it sizzling on his new fabrial hotplate.

'I'm tired of cooking,' Ashir continued. He had a soft, kindly voice. She loved him for that. Partially because he liked to talk – and if you were going to have someone talk while you were attempting to think, they might as well have a soft, kindly voice.

'I don't have *passion* for it as I once did,' he continued. 'Besides, what good will a cook be in the Spiritual Realm?'

'Heralds need food,' she said absently, scratching out a line on her writing board, then scribbling another line of numbers beneath it.

'Do they?' Ashir asked. 'I've never been convinced. Oh, I've read the speculations, but it just doesn't seem rational to me. The body must be fed in the Physical Realm, but the spirit exists in a completely different state.'

'A state of ideals,' she replied. 'So, you could create ideal foods, perhaps.'

'Hmm . . . What would be the fun in that? No experimentation.'

'I could do without,' she said, leaning forward to inspect the room's hearth, where two flamespren danced on the logs' fire. 'If it meant never again having to eat something like that green soup you made last month.'

'Ah,' he said, sounding wistful. 'That was something, wasn't it? Completely revolting, yet made entirely from appetizing ingredients.' He seemed to consider it a personal triumph. 'I wonder if they eat in the Cognitive Realm. Is a food there what it sees itself as being? I'll have to read and see if anyone has ever eaten while visiting Shadesmar.'

Geranid responded with a noncommittal grunt, getting out her calipers and leaning closer to the heat to measure the flamespren. She frowned, then made another notation.

'Here, love,' Ashir said, walking over, then knelt beside her and offered a small bowl. 'Give this a try. I think you'll like it.'

She eyed the contents. Bits of bread covered with a red sauce. It was men's food, but they were both ardents, so that didn't matter.

From outside came the sounds of waves gently lapping against the rocks. They were on a tiny Reshi island, technically sent to provide for the religious needs of any Vorin visitors. Some travelers did come to them for that, occasionally even some of the Reshi. But really, this was a way of getting away and focusing on their experiments. Geranid with her spren studies. Ashir with his chemistry – through cooking, of course, as it allowed him to eat the results.

The portly man smiled affably, head shaven, grey beard neatly squared off. They both kept to the rules of their stations, despite their seclusion. One did not write the ending of a lifetime of faith with a sloppy last chapter.

'No green,' she noted, taking the bowl. 'That's a good sign.'

'Hmmm,' he said, leaning down and adjusting his spectacles to inspect her notations. 'Yes. It really was fascinating the way that Shin vegetable caramelized. I'm so pleased that Gom brought it to me. You'll have to go over my notes. I think I got the figures right, but I could be wrong.' He wasn't as strong at mathematics as he was at theory. Conveniently, Geranid was just the opposite.

She took a spoon and tried the food. She didn't wear a sleeve on her safehand – another one of the advantages of being an ardent. The food was actually quite good. 'Did you *try* this, Ashir?'

'Nope,' he said, still looking over her figures. 'You're the brave one, my dear.'

She sniffed. 'It's terrible.'

'I can see that from how you're taking another large bite at this moment.'

'Yes, but you'd hate it. No fruit. Is this fish you added?'

'A dried handful of the little minnows I caught outside this morning. Still don't know what species they are. Tasty, though.' He hesitated, then looked up at the hearth and its spren. 'Geranid, what *is* this?'

'I think I've had a breakthrough,' she said softly.

'But the figures,' he said, tapping the writing board. 'You said they were erratic, and they still are.'

'Yes,' she said, narrowing her eyes at the flamespren. 'But I can predict when they will be erratic and when they won't be.'

He looked at her, frowning.

'The spren change when I measure them, Ashir,' she said. 'Before I measure, they dance and vary in size, luminosity, and shape. But when I make a notation, they immediately freeze in their current state. Then they remain that way permanently, so far as I can tell.'

'What does it mean?' he asked.

'I'm hoping you'll be able to tell me. I have the figures. You've got the imagination, dear one.'

He scratched at his beard, sitting back, and produced a bowl and spoon for himself. He'd sprinkled dried fruit over his portion; Geranid was half convinced he'd joined the ardentia because of his sweet tooth. 'What happens if you erase the figures?' he asked.

'The spren go back to being variable,' she said. 'Length, shape, luminosity.'

He took a bite of his mush. 'Go into the other room.'

'What?'

'Just do it. Take your writing board.'

She sighed, standing up, joints popping. Was she getting *that* old? Starlight, but they'd spent a long time out on this island. She walked to the other room, where their cot was.

'What now?' she called.

'I'm going to measure the spren with your calipers,' he called back. 'I'll take three measurements in a row. Only write down one of the figures I give you. Don't tell me which one you're writing down.'

'All right,' she called back. The window was open, and she looked out over a darkening, glassy expanse of water. The Reshi Sea wasn't as shallow as the Purelake, but it was quite warm most of the time, dotted with tropical islands and the occasional monster of a greatshell.

'Three inches, seven tenths,' Ashir called.

She didn't write down the figure.

'Two inches, eight tenths.'

She ignored the number this time too, but got her chalk ready to write – as quietly as possible – the next numbers he called out.

'Two inches, three ten – Wow.'

'What?' she called.

'It stopped changing sizes. I assume you wrote down that third number?'

She frowned, walking back into their small living chamber. Ashir's hotplate sat on a low table to her right. After the Reshi style, there were no chairs, just cushions, and all the furniture was flat and long, rather than tall.

She approached the hearth. One of the two flamespren danced about atop a log, shape changing and length flickering like the flames themselves. The other had taken on a far more stable shape. Its length no longer changed, though its form did slightly.

It seemed *locked* somehow. It almost looked like a little person as it danced over the fire. She reached up and erased her notation. It immediately began pulsing and changing erratically like the other one.

'Wow,' Ashir repeated. 'It's as if it knows, somehow, that it has been measured. As if merely *defining* its form traps it somehow. Write down a number.'

'What number?'

'Any number,' he said. 'But one that might be the size of a flamespren.'

She did so. Nothing happened.

'You have to *actually* measure it,' he said, tapping his spoon softly against the side of his bowl. 'No pretending.'

'I wonder at the precision of the instrument,' she said. 'If I use one that is less precise, will that give the spren more flexibility? Or is there a threshold, an accuracy beyond which it finds itself bound?' She sat down, feeling daunted. 'I need to research this more. Try it for luminosity, then compare that to my general equation of flamespren luminosity as compared to the fire they're drawn to dance around.'

Ashir grimaced. 'That, my dear, sounds a lot like math.'

'Indeed.'

'Then I shall make you a snack to occupy you while you create new marvels of calculation and genius.' He smiled, kissing her forehead. 'You just found something wonderful,' he said more softly. 'I don't know what it means yet, but it might very well change everything we understand about spren. And maybe even about fabrials.'

She smiled, turning back to her equations. And for once, she didn't mind at all as he began chatting about his ingredients, working out a new formula for some sugary confection he was *sure* she'd love.

Szeth-son-son-Vallano, Truthless of Shinovar, spun between the two guards as their eyes burned out. They slumped quietly to the floor. With three quick strokes, he slashed his Shardblade through the hinges and latch of the grand door. Then he took a deep breath, absorbing the Stormlight from a pouch of gemstones at his waist. He burst alight with renewed power and kicked the door with the force of a Light-enhanced foot.

It flew backward into the room, hinges no longer holding it in place, then crashed to the floor, skidding on the stone. The large feast hall inside was filled with people, crackling hearths, and clattering plates. The heavy door slid to a halt, and the room grew quiet.

I am sorry, he thought. Then he dashed in to start the slaughter.

Chaos ensued. Screams, yells, panic. Szeth leaped atop the nearest dining table and started spinning, cutting down everyone nearby. As he did so, he made certain to listen to the sounds of the dying. He did not shut his ears to the screams. He did not ignore the wails of pain. He paid attention to each and every one.

And hated himself.

He moved forward, leaping from table to table, wielding his Shard-blade, a god of burning Stormlight and death.

'Armsmen!' yelled the lighteyed man at the edge of the room. 'Where are my armsmen!' Thick of waist and shoulder, the man had a square brown beard and a prominent nose. King Hanavanar of Jah Keved.

Not a Shardbearer, though some rumors said that he secretly kept a Shardblade.

Near Szeth, men and women scrambled away, stumbling over one another. He dropped among them, his white clothing rippling. He cut through a man who was drawing his sword – but also sliced through three women who wanted only to escape. Eyes burned and bodies collapsed.

Szeth reached behind himself, infusing the table he'd leaped from, then Lashing it to the far wall with a Basic Lashing, the type that changed which direction was down. The large wooden table fell to the side, tumbling into people, causing more screams and more pain.

Szeth found himself crying. His orders were simple. Kill. Kill as you have never killed before. Lay the innocent screaming at your feet and make the lighteyes weep. Do so wearing white, so all know who you are. Szeth did not object. It was not his place. He was Truthless.

And he did as his masters demanded.

Three lighteyed men got up the nerve to attack him, and Szeth raised his Shardblade in salute. They screamed battle cries as they charged. He was silent. A flick of his wrist cut the blade from the first one's sword. The length of metal spun in the air as Szeth stepped between the other two, his Blade swishing through their necks. They dropped in tandem, eyes shriveling. Szeth struck the first man from behind, ramming the Blade through his back and out his chest.

The man dropped forward – a hole in his shirt, but his skin unmarred. As he hit the floor, his severed sword blade clanged to the stones beside him.

Another group came at Szeth from the side, and he drew Stormlight into his hand and flung it in a Full Lashing across the floor at their feet. This was the Lashing that bonded objects; when the men crossed it, their shoes stuck to the floor. They tripped, and found their hands and bodies Lashed to the floor as well. Szeth stepped through them mournfully, striking.

The king edged away, as if to round the chamber and escape. Szeth sprayed a table's top with a Full Lashing, then infused the entire thing with a Basic Lashing as well, pointed at the doorway. The table flipped into the air and crashed against the exit – the side bearing the Full Lashing sticking it to the wall. People tried to pry it out of the way, but that only made them bunch up as Szeth waded into them, Shardblade sweeping.

So many deaths. Why? What purpose did it fulfill?

When he'd assaulted Alethkar six years before, he'd thought that had been a massacre. He hadn't known what a true massacre was. He reached the door and found himself standing over the bodies of some thirty people, his emotions caught up in the tempest of Stormlight within him. He hated that Stormlight, suddenly, as much as he hated himself. As much as the cursed Blade he held.

And . . . and the king. Szeth spun on the man. Irrationally, his confused, broken mind blamed this man. Why had he called a feast on this night? Why couldn't he have retired early? Why had he invited so many people?

Szeth charged at the king. He passed the dead, who lay twisted on the floor, burned-out eyes staring in lifeless accusation. The king cowered behind his high table.

That high table shuddered, quivering oddly.

Something was wrong.

Instinctively, Szeth Lashed himself to the ceiling. From his viewpoint, the room flipped, and the floor was now the ceiling. Two figures burst out from beneath the king's table. Two men in Plate, carrying Shardblades, swinging.

Twisting in the air, Szeth evaded their swings, then Lashed himself back to the floor, landing on the king's table just as the king summoned a Shardblade. So the rumors were true.

The king struck, but Szeth jumped backward, landing beyond the Shardbearers. Outside, he could hear footfalls. Szeth glanced to see men pouring into the room. The newcomers carried distinctive, diamond-shaped shields. Half-shards. Szeth had heard of the new fabrials, capable of stopping a Shardblade.

'You think I didn't know you were coming?' the king yelled at him. 'After you killed three of my highprinces? We're ready for you, assassin.' He lifted something from beneath the table. Another of those half-shard shields. They were made of metal embedded with a gemstone hidden at the back.

'You are a fool,' Szeth said, Stormlight leaking from his mouth.

'Why?' the king called. 'You think I should have run?'

'No,' Szeth replied, meeting his eyes. 'Because you set a trap for me during a feast. And now I can blame you for their deaths.'

The soldiers fanned out through the room while the two fully armored

Shardbearers stepped toward him, Blades out. The king smiled.

'So let it be,' Szeth said, breathing deeply, sucking in the Stormlight of the many gemstones tied in the pouches at his waist. The Light began to rage within him, like a highstorm in his chest, burning and screaming. He breathed in more than he'd ever held before, holding it until he was barely able to keep the Stormlight from ripping him apart.

Were those still tears in his eyes? Would that they could hide his crimes. He yanked the strap free at his waist, releasing his belt and the heavy spheres.

Then he dropped his Shardblade.

His opponents froze in shock as his Blade vanished to mist. Who would drop a Shardblade in the middle of a battle? It defied reason.

And so did Szeth.

You are a work of art, Szeth-son-Neturo. A god.

It was time to see.

The soldiers and Shardbearers charged. Mere heartbeats before they reached him, Szeth spun into motion, liquid tempest in his veins. He dodged between the initial sword strikes, spinning into the midst of the soldiers. Holding this much Stormlight made it easier to infuse things; the light wanted out, and it pushed against his skin. In this state, the Shardblade would only be a distraction. Szeth himself was the real weapon.

He grabbed the arm of an attacking soldier. It took only an instant to infuse and Lash him upward. The man cried out, falling into the air as Szeth ducked another sword thrust. He touched the attacker's leg, inhumanly lithe. With a look and a blink, he Lashed that man to the ceiling as well.

Soldiers cursed, slashing at him, their bulky half-shards suddenly becoming hindrances as Szeth moved among them, graceful as a skyeel, touching arms, legs, shoulders, sending a dozen, then two dozen, men flying in all directions. Most went up, but he sent a barrage of them toward the approaching Shardbearers, who cried out as squirming bodies smashed into them.

He jumped backward as a squad of soldiers came at him, Lashing himself to the far wall and spinning into the air. The room changed orientations, and he landed on the wall – which was now down for him. He ran along it toward the king, who waited behind his Shardbearers.

'Kill him!' the king said. 'Storm you all! What are you doing? Kill him!'

Szeth leaped off the wall, Lashing himself downward as he flipped, landing with one knee on the dining table. Silverware and plates clinked as he grabbed a dining knife and infused once, twice, three times. He used a triple Basic Lashing, pointing it in the direction of the king, then dropped it and Lashed himself backward.

He lurched away as one of the Shardbearers struck, cutting the table in half. Szeth's released knife fell far more quickly than it should have, flashing toward the king. He barely got his shield up in time, eyes wide as the knife clanged against the metal.

Damnation, Szeth thought, Lashing himself upward with a quarter of a Basic Lashing. That didn't pull him upward, it just made him much lighter. A quarter of his weight was now pulled upward instead of downward. In essence, he became half as heavy as he had been.

He twisted, white clothing flapping gracefully as he dropped amid the common soldiers. Soldiers he'd Lashed earlier began to fall from the high ceiling, their Stormlight running out. A rain of broken bodies, crashing one by one to the floor.

Szeth came at the soldiers again. Some men fell as he sent others flying. Their expensive shields clanged to the stones, falling from dead or stunned fingers. Soldiers tried to reach him, but Szeth danced between them, using the ancient martial art of kammar, which used only the hands. It was meant as a less deadly form of fighting, focused on grabbing enemies and using their weight against them, immobilizing them.

It was also ideal when one wanted to touch and infuse someone.

He was the storm. He was destruction. At his will, men flipped into the air, fell, and died. He swept outward, touching a table and Lashing it upward with half a Basic Lashing. With half its mass pulled upward, half downward, it became weightless. Szeth sprayed it with a Full Lashing, then kicked it toward the soldiers; they stuck to it, their clothing and skin bonding to the wood.

A Shardblade hissed through the air beside him, and Szeth exhaled lightly, Stormlight rising from his lips as he ducked out of the way. The two Shardbearers attacked as bodies fell from above, but Szeth was too quick, too limber. The Shardbearers didn't work together. They were accustomed to dominating a battlefield or dueling with a single enemy. Their powerful weapons made them sloppy.

Szeth ran on light feet, held to the ground only half as much as other men. He easily leaped another swipe, Lashing himself to the ceiling to give himself just a little more lift before quarter-Lashing to make himself weighted down again. The result was an effortless leap of ten feet into the air.

The missed swing hit the ground and cut through the belt he'd dropped earlier, opening one of his large pouches. Spheres and bare gemstones sprayed across the floor. Some infused. Some dun. Szeth pulled Stormlight from those that rolled close.

Behind the Shardbearers, the king himself approached, weapon ready. He should have tried to run.

The two Shardbearers swung their oversized Blades at Szeth. He spun away from the attacks, reaching out and snatching a shield from the air as it tumbled toward the ground. The man who had been holding it crashed to the floor a second later.

Szeth leaped at one of the Shardbearers – a man in gold armor – deflecting his weapon with the shield and pushing past him. The other man, whose Plate was red, swung too. Szeth caught the Blade on his shield, which cracked, barely holding. Still pushing it against the Blade, Szeth Lashed himself behind the Shardbearer while jumping forward.

The move flipped Szeth up and over the man. Szeth went on, falling toward the far wall as the second wave of soldiers began to drop to the floor. One crashed into the Shardbearer in red, making him stumble.

Szeth hit the wall, landing against the stones. He was so full of Stormlight. So much power, so much life, so much terrible, terrible destruction.

Stone. It was sacred. He never thought about that anymore. How could anything be sacred to him, now?

As bodies crashed into the Shardbearers, he knelt and placed his hand on a large stone in the wall before him, infusing it. He Lashed it time and time again in the direction of the Shardbearers. Once, twice, ten times, fifteen times. He kept pouring Stormlight into it. It glowed brightly. Mortar cracked. Stone ground against stone.

The red Shardbearer turned just as the massive, infused rock fell toward him, moving with twenty times the normal acceleration of a falling stone. It crashed into him, shattering his breastplate, spraying molten bits in all directions. The block hurled him across the room, crushing him against the far wall. He did not move.

Szeth was nearly out of Stormlight now. He quarter-Lashed himself to reduce his weight, then loped across the ground. Men were crushed, broken, dead around him. Spheres rolled on the floor, and he drew in their Stormlight. The Light streamed up, like the souls of those he had killed, infusing him.

He began to run. The other Shardbearer stumbled backward, holding up his Blade, stepping onto the wood of a shattered tabletop, the legs of which had broken free. The king finally realized his trap was failing. He started to flee.

Ten heartbeats, Szeth thought. *Return to me, you creation of Damnation.*

Szeth's heartbeats began to thump in his ears. He screamed – Light bursting from his mouth like radiant smoke – and threw himself to the ground as the Shardbearer swung. Szeth Lashed himself toward the far wall, skidding through the Shardbearer's legs. He immediately Lashed himself upward.

He soared into the air as the Shardbearer rounded on him again. But Szeth wasn't there. He Lashed himself back downward, dropping behind the Shardbearer to land on the broken tabletop. He stooped and infused it. A man in Shardplate might be protected from Lashings, but the things he stood upon were not.

Szeth Lashed the plank upward with a multiple Lashing. It lurched into the air, tossing aside the Shardbearer like a toy soldier. Szeth himself stayed atop the board, riding it upward in a rush of air. As it reached the lofty ceiling he threw himself off, Lashing himself downward once, twice, three times.

The tabletop crashed to the ceiling. Szeth fell with incredible speed toward the Shardbearer, who lay dazed on his back.

Szeth's Blade formed in his fingers just as he hit, driving the weapon down through Shardplate. The breastplate exploded and the Blade sank deeply through the man's chest and into the floor underneath.

Szeth stood, pulling his Shardblade free. The fleeing king looked over his shoulder with a cry of disbelieving horror. Both of his Shardbearers had fallen in a matter of seconds. The last of the soldiers nervously moved in to protect his retreat.

Szeth had stopped crying. It seemed like he couldn't cry any longer. He felt numb. His mind ... it just couldn't think. He hated the king.

Hated him so badly. And it hurt, physically hurt him, how strong that irrational hatred was.

Stormlight rising from him, he Lashed himself toward the king.

He fell, feet just above the ground, as if he were floating. His clothing rippled. To those guards still alive, he would seem to be gliding across the ground.

He Lashed himself downward at a slight angle and began to swing his Blade as he reached the ranks of the soldiers. He ran through them as if he were moving down a steep slope. Swirling and spinning, he dropped a dozen men, graceful and terrible, drawing in more Stormlight from spheres that had been scattered on the floor.

Szeth reached the doorway, men with burning eyes falling to the ground behind him. Just outside, the king ran amid a final small group of guards. He turned and cried out as he saw Szeth, then threw up his half-shard shield.

Szeth wove through the guards, then hit the shield twice, shattering it and forcing the king backward. The man tripped, dropping his Blade. It puffed away to mist.

Szeth leaped up and Lashed himself downward with a double Basic Lashing. He hit atop the king, his increased weight breaking an arm and pinning the man to the ground. Szeth swept his Blade through the surprised soldiers, who fell as their legs died beneath them.

Finally, Szeth raised his Blade over his head, looking down at the king.

'What are you?' the man whispered, eyes watering with pain.

'Death,' Szeth said, then drove his Blade point-first through the man's face and into the rock below.

PART FOUR

Storm's Illumination

DALINAR • KALADIN • ADOLIN • NAVANI

'I'm standing over the body of a brother. I'm weeping. Is that his blood or mine? What have we done?'

–Dated Vevanev, 1173, 107 seconds pre-death. Subject: an out-of-work Veden sailor.

'Father,' Adolin said, pacing in Dalinar's sitting room. 'This is *insane.*'

'That is appropriate,' Dalinar replied dryly. 'As – it appears – I am as well.'

'I never claimed you were insane.'

'Actually,' Renarin noted, 'I believe that you did.'

Adolin glanced at his brother. Renarin stood beside the hearth, inspecting the new fabrial that had been installed there just a few days ago. The infused ruby, encased in a metal enclosure, glowed softly and gave offa comfortable heat. It was convenient, though it felt wrong to Adolin that no fire lay crackling there.

The three were alone in Dalinar's sitting room, awaiting the advent of the day's highstorm. It had been one week since Dalinar had informed his sons of his intention to step down as highprince.

Adolin's father sat in one of his large, high-backed chairs, hands laced before him, stoic. The warcamps didn't know of his decision yet – bless the Heralds – but he intended to make the announcement soon. Perhaps at tonight's feast.

'All right, fine,' Adolin said. 'Perhaps I said it. But I didn't mean it. Or at least I didn't mean for it to have this effect on you.'

'We had this discussion a week ago, Adolin,' Dalinar said softly.

'Yes, and you promised to think over your decision!'

'I have. My resolve has not wavered.'

Adolin continued to pace; Renarin stood up straight, watching him as he stalked past. *I'm a fool*, Adolin thought. *Of* course *this is what Father would do. I should have seen it.*

'Look,' Adolin said, 'just because you might have some problems doesn't mean you have to abdicate.'

'Adolin, our enemies will use my weakness against us. In fact, you believe that they are *already* doing so. If I don't give up the princedom now, matters could grow much worse than they are now.'

'But I don't *want* to be highprince,' Adolin complained. 'Not yet, at least.'

'Leadership is rarely about what we want, son. I think too few among the Alethi elite realize that fact.'

'And what will happen to you?' Adolin asked, pained. He stopped and looked toward his father.

Dalinar was so *firm*, even sitting there, contemplating his own madness. Hands clasped before him, wearing a stiff blue uniform with a coat of Kholin blue, silver hair dusting his temples. Those hands of his were thick and callused, his expression determined. Dalinar made a decision and stuck to it, not wavering or debating.

Mad or not, he was what Alethkar needed. And Adolin had – in his haste – done what no warrior on the battlefield had ever been able to do: chop Dalinar Kholin's legs out from under him and send him away in defeat.

Oh, Stormfather, Adolin thought, stomach twisting in pain. *Jezerezeh, Kelek, and Ishi, Heralds above. Let me find a way to right this. Please.*

'I will return to Alethkar,' Dalinar said. 'Though I hate to leave our army here down a Shardbearer. Could I . . . but no, I could not give them up.'

'Of course not!' Adolin said, aghast. A Shardbearer, giving up his Shards? It almost never happened unless the Bearer was too weak and sickly to use them.

Dalinar nodded. 'I have long worried that our homeland is in danger, now that every single Shardbearer fights out here on the Plains. Well, perhaps this change of winds is a blessing. I will return to Kholinar and aid the queen, make myself useful fighting against border incursions. Perhaps the Reshi and the Vedens will be less likely to strike against us if they know that they'd be facing a full Shardbearer.'

'That's possible,' Adolin said. 'But they could also escalate and start sending a Shardbearer of their own on raids.'

That seemed to worry his father. Jah Keved was the only other kingdom in Roshar that owned a substantial number of Shards, nearly as many as Alethkar. There hadn't been a direct war between them in centuries. Alethkar had been too divided, and Jah Keved was little better. But if the two kingdoms clashed in force, it would be a war the like of which hadn't been seen since the days of the Hierocracy.

Distant thunder rumbled outside, and Adolin turned sharply toward Dalinar. His father remained in his chair, staring westward, away from the storm. 'We will continue this discussion afterward,' Dalinar said. 'For now, you two should tie my arms to the chair.'

Adolin grimaced, but did as he was told without complaint.

⁂

Dalinar blinked, looking around. He was on the battlement of a single-walled fortress. Crafted from large blocks of deep red stone, the wall was sheer and straight. It was built across a rift in the leeward side of a tall rock formation overlooking an open plain of stone, like a wet leaf stuck across a crack in a boulder.

These visions feel so real, Dalinar thought, glancing at the spear he held in his hand and then down at his antiquated uniform: a cloth skirt and leather jerkin. It was hard to remember that he was really sitting in his chair, arms tied down. He couldn't feel the ropes or hear the highstorm.

He considered waiting out the vision, doing nothing. If this wasn't real, why should he participate? Yet he didn't completely believe – *couldn't* completely believe – that he was coming up with these delusions on his own. His decision to abdicate to Adolin was motivated by his doubts. Was he mad? Was he misinterpreting? At the very least, he could no longer trust himself. He didn't know what was real and what wasn't. In such a situation a man should step down from his authority and sort things through.

Either way, he felt he needed to *live* these visions, not ignore them. A desperate piece of him still hoped to come to a solution before he had to abdicate formally. He didn't let that piece gain too much control – a man had to do what was right. But Dalinar would give it this much: He would treat the vision as real while he was part of it. If there were secrets to be found here, only by playing along would he find them.

He looked about him. What was he being shown this time, and why? The spearhead on his weapon was of good steel, though his cap appeared to be bronze. One of the six men with him on the wall wore a breastplate of bronze; two others had poorly patched leather uniforms, sliced and resewn with wide stitches.

The other men lounged about, idly looking out over the wall. *Guard duty*, Dalinar thought, stepping up and scanning the landscape outside. This rock formation was at the end of an enormous plain – the perfect situation for a fortress. No army could approach without being seen long before its arrival.

The air was cold enough that clumps of ice clung to the stone in shadowed corners. The sunlight did little to dispel the cold, and the weather explained the lack of grass; the blades would be retracted into their holes, awaiting the relief of spring weather.

Dalinar pulled his cloak closer, prompting one of his companions to do the same.

'Storming weather,' the man muttered. 'How long's it going to last? Been eight weeks already.'

Eight weeks? Forty days of winter at once? That was rare. Despite the cold, the other three soldiers looked anything but engaged by their guard duties. One was even dozing.

'Stay alert,' Dalinar chided them.

They glanced at him, the one who had been dozing blinking awake. All three seemed incredulous. One – a tall, red-haired man – scowled. 'This from you, Leef?'

Dalinar bit back a retort. Who did they see him as?

The chill air made his breath steam, and from behind him he could hear metal clanging as men worked at forges and anvils below. The gates to the fortress were closed, and the archer towers were manned to the left and right. They were at war, but guard duty was always boring work. It took well trained soldiers to remain alert for hours on end. Perhaps that was why there were so many soldiers here; if the quality of eyes watching could not be assured, then quantity would serve.

However, Dalinar had an advantage. The visions never showed him episodes of idle peace; they threw him into times of conflict and change. Turning points. So it was that, despite dozens of other eyes watching, he was the first to spot it.

'There!' he said, leaning out over the side of the rough-stone crenellation. 'What is that?'

The redheaded man raised a hand, shading his eyes. 'Nothing. A shadow.'

'No, it's moving,' said one of the others. 'Looks like people. Marching.'

Dalinar's heart began to thump in anticipation as the red-haired man called the alert. More archers rushed onto the battlement, stringing bows. Soldiers gathered in the ruddy courtyard below. Everything was made of that same red rock, and Dalinar caught one of the men referring to this place as 'Feverstone Keep.' He'd never heard of it.

Scouts galloped from the keep on horses. Why didn't they have outriders already?

'It has to be the rear defense force,' one soldier muttered. 'They can't have gotten through our lines. Not with the Radiants fighting. . . .'

Radiants? Dalinar stepped closer to listen, but the man gave him a scowl and turned away. Whoever Dalinar was, the others didn't much care for him.

Apparently, this keep was a fallback position behind the front lines of a war. So either that approaching force was friendly, or the enemy had punched through and sent an advance element to besiege the keep. These were reserves, then, which was probably why they had been left with few horses. They still should have had outriders.

When the scouts finally did gallop back to the keep, they bore white flags. Dalinar glanced at his companions, confirming his suspicions as they relaxed. White meant friends. Yet would he have been sent here if it were that simple? If it *was* just in his mind, would it fabricate a simple, boring vision when it never had before?

'We need to be alert for a trap,' Dalinar said. 'Someone find out what those scouts saw. Did they identify banners only, or did they get a close look?'

The other soldiers – including some of the archers who now filled the wall top – gave him strange looks. Dalinar cursed softly, glancing back out at the shadowy oncoming force. He had a foreboding itch in the back of his skull. Ignoring the odd looks, he hefted his spear and ran down the walkway of the wall top, reaching a set of stairs. They were built in switchbacks, running in zigzags straight down the tall wall, with no railing. He'd been on such fortifications before, and knew how to keep his eyes focused on the steps to avoid vertigo.

He reached the bottom and – spear resting on his shoulder – struck out to find someone in charge. The buildings of Feverstone Keep were blocky and utilitarian, built up against one another along the rock walls of the natural rift. Most had square raincatchers on top. With good food stores – or, if lucky, a Soulcaster – such a fortification could withstand a siege for years.

He couldn't read the rank insignias, but he could recognize an officer when he saw one standing in a blood-red cloak with a group of honor guards. He had no mail, just a shiny bronze breastplate over leather, and was conferring with one of the scouts. Dalinar hurried up.

Only then did he see that the man's eyes were dark brown. That gave Dalinar a shock of incredulity. Those around him treated the man like a brightlord.

'. . . the Order of the Stonewards, my lord,' the still-mounted scout was saying. 'And a large number of Windrunners. All on foot.'

'But why?' the darkeyed officer demanded. 'Why are Radiants coming here? They should be fighting the devils on the front lines!'

'My lord,' the scout said, 'our orders were to return as soon as we identified them.'

'Well, go back and find out why they're here!' the officer bellowed, causing the scout to flinch, then turn to ride away.

The Radiants. They were usually connected to Dalinar's visions in one way or another. As the officer began to call commands to his attendants, telling them to prep empty bunkers for the knights, Dalinar followed the scout toward the wall. Men crowded near the kill slits there, peering out at the plain. Like those above, these wore motley uniforms that looked pieced together. They weren't a ragged bunch, but were obviously wearing secondhand leavings.

The scout rode through a sally port as Dalinar entered the shadow of the enormous wall, walking up to the back of a crowd of soldiers. 'What is it?' he asked.

'The Radiants,' one of the men said. 'They've broken into a run.'

'It's almost like they're going to attack,' said another. He chuckled at how ridiculous that sounded, though there was an edge of uncertainty to his voice.

What? Dalinar thought, anxious. 'Let me through.'

Surprisingly, the men parted. As Dalinar pushed by, he could sense their confusion. He'd given the command with the authority of a highprince and a lighteyes, and they'd obeyed instinctively. Now that they saw him, they were uncertain. What was this simple guardsman doing ordering them about?

He didn't give them a chance to question him. He climbed onto the platform against the wall, where a rectangular kill slit looked through the wall and onto the plain. It was too small for a man to get through, but wide enough for archers to fire out. Through it, Dalinar saw that the approaching soldiers had formed a distinct line. Men and women in gleaming Shardplate charged forward. The scout pulled to a halt, looking at the charging Shardbearers. They ran shoulder to shoulder, not a single one out of place. Like a crystalline wave. As they drew closer, Dalinar could see that their Plate was unpainted, but it glowed either blue or amber at the joints and across glyphs at the front, as with other Radiants he'd seen in his visions.

'They don't have their Shardblades out,' Dalinar said. 'That's a good sign.'

The scout outside backed his horse up. There looked to be a good two hundred Shardbearers out there. Alethkar owned some twenty Blades, Jah Keved a similar number. If one added up all the rest in the world, there might be enough total to equal the two powerful Vorin kingdoms. That meant, so far as he knew, there were less than a hundred Blades in all of the world. And here he saw *two hundred* Shardbearers gathered in one army. It was mind-numbing.

The Radiants slowed, falling into a trot, then a walk. The soldiers around Dalinar grew still. The leading Radiants stopped in a line, immobile. Suddenly, others began to fall from the sky. They hit with the sound of rock cracking, puffs of Stormlight blossoming from their figures. These all glowed blue.

Soon, there were some three hundred Radiants out on the field. They began summoning their Blades. The weapons appeared in their hands, like fog forming and condensing. It was done in silence. Their visors were down.

'If them charging without swords was a good sign,' whispered one of the men beside Dalinar, 'then what does this mean?'

A suspicion began to rise within Dalinar, the horror that he might know what this vision was about to show him. The scout, at last unnerved, turned his horse and galloped back to the keep, screaming for the door to be opened to him. As if a little wood and stone would be a protection against hundreds of Shardbearers. A single man with Plate and Blade was almost an army unto himself, and that wasn't accounting for the strange powers these people had.

The soldiers pulled the sally port open for the scout. Making a snap decision, Dalinar leaped down and charged to the opening. Behind, the officer Dalinar had seen earlier was clearing a path for himself to walk up to the kill slit.

Dalinar reached the open door, darting through it just after the scout charged back into the courtyard. Men called after Dalinar, terrified. He ignored them, running out onto the open plain. The expansive, straight wall stretched above him, like a highway up to the sun itself. The Radiants were still distant, though they'd stopped within bowshot. Transfixed by the beautiful figures, Dalinar slowed, then stopped about a hundred feet away.

One knight stepped ahead of his companions, his brilliant cape a rich blue. His Shardblade of rippling steel had intricate carvings along the center. He held it toward the keep for a moment.

Then he drove it point-first into the stone plain. Dalinar blinked. The Shardbearer removed his helm, exposing a handsome head with blond hair and pale skin, light as that of a man from Shinovar. He tossed the helm to the ground beside his Blade. It rolled slightly as the Shardbearer made fists in his gauntlets, arms at his sides. He opened his palms wide, and the gauntlets fell free to the rocky ground.

He turned, his Shardplate falling off his body – breastplate dropping free, greaves slipping off. Underneath, he wore a rumpled blue uniform. He stepped free of his bootlike sabatons and continued to walk away, Shardplate and Shardblade – the most precious treasures any man could own – tossed to the ground and abandoned like refuse.

The others began to follow suit. Hundreds of men and women, driving Shardblades into the stone and then removing their Plate. The sound of metal hitting stone came like rain. Then like thunder.

Dalinar found himself running forward. The door behind him opened and some curious soldiers left the keep. Dalinar reached the Shardblades. They sprouted from the rock like glittering silver trees, a forest of weapons. They glowed softly in a way his own Shardblade never had, but as he dashed among them, their light started to fade.

A terrible feeling struck him. A sense of immense tragedy, of pain and betrayal. Stopping where he stood, he gasped, hand to his chest. What was happening? What *was* that dreadful feeling, that screaming he swore he could almost hear?

The Radiants. They walked away from their discarded weapons. They all seemed individuals now, each walking alone despite the crowd. Dalinar charged after them, tripping over discarded breastplates and chunks of armor. He finally stumbled free of it all.

'Wait!' he called.

None of them turned.

He could now see others in the distance, far off. A crowd of soldiers, not wearing Shardplate, waiting for the Radiants to return. Who were they, and why hadn't they come forward? Dalinar caught up to the Radiants – they weren't walking very quickly – and grabbed one by the arm. The man turned; his skin was tan and his hair dark, like an Alethi. His eyes were of the palest blue. Unnaturally so, in fact – the irises were nearly white.

'Please,' Dalinar said. 'Tell me why you are doing this.'

The former Shardbearer pulled his arm free and continued to walk away. Dalinar cursed, then ran into the midst of the Shardbearers. They were of all races and nationalities, dark skin and light, some with white Thaylen eyebrows, others with the skin ripples of the Selay. They walked with eyes forward, not speaking to one another, steps slow but resolute.

'Will someone tell me why?' Dalinar bellowed. 'This is it, isn't it? The

Day of Recreance, the day you betrayed mankind. But why?' None of them spoke. It was as if he didn't exist.

People spoke of betrayal, of the day the Knights Radiant turned their backs on their fellow men. What were they fighting, and why had they stopped? *Two orders of knights were mentioned*, Dalinar thought. *But there were ten orders. What of the other eight?*

Dalinar fell to his knees in the sea of solemn individuals. 'Please. I must know.' Nearby, some of the keep's soldiers had reached the Shardblades – but rather than chasing after the Radiants, these men were cautiously pulling the Blades free. A few officers scrambled out of the keep, calling for the Blades to be put down. They were soon outnumbered by men who began boiling out of side gates and rushing toward the weapons.

'They are the first,' a voice said.

Dalinar looked up to see that one of the knights had stopped beside him. It was the man who looked Alethi. He looked over his shoulder at the crowd gathering around the Blades. Men had begun to scream at one another, everyone scrambling to get a Blade before they were all claimed.

'They are the first,' the Radiant said, turning to Dalinar. Dalinar recognized the depth of that voice. It was the voice that always spoke to him in these visions. 'They were the first, and they were also the last.'

'Is this the Day of Recreance?' Dalinar asked.

'These events will go down in history,' the Radiant said. 'They will be infamous. You will have many names for what happened here.'

'But why?' Dalinar asked. 'Please. Why did they abandon their duty?'

The figure seemed to study him. 'I have said that I cannot be of much help to you. The Night of Sorrows will come, and the True Desolation. The Everstorm.'

'Then answer my questions!' Dalinar said.

'Read the book. Unite them.'

'The book? *The Way of Kings*?'

The figure turned and walked from him, joining the other Radiants as they crossed the stone plain, walking toward places unknown.

Dalinar looked back at the melee of soldiers rushing for Blades. Many had already been claimed. There weren't enough Blades for everyone, and some had begun raising theirs up, using them to fend off those who got too close. As he watched, a bellowing officer with a Blade was attacked by two men behind him.

The glow from within the weapons had completely vanished.

The killing of that officer made others bold. Other skirmishes started, men scrambling to attack those who had Blades, hoping to get one. Eyes began to burn. Screams, shouts, death. Dalinar watched until he found himself in his quarters, tied to his chair. Renarin and Adolin watched nearby, looking tense.

Dalinar blinked, listening to the rain of the passing highstorm on the roof. 'I've returned,' he said to his sons. 'You may calm yourselves.' Adolin helped untie the ropes while Renarin stood up and fetched Dalinar a cup of orange wine.

Once Dalinar was free, Adolin stood back. The youth folded his arms. Renarin came back, his face pale. He looked to be having one of his episodes of weakness; indeed, his legs were trembling. As soon as Dalinar took the cup, the youth sat down in a chair and rested his head in his hands.

Dalinar sipped the sweet wine. He had seen wars in his visions before. He had seen deaths and monsters, greatshells and nightmares. And yet, for some reason, this one disturbed him more than any. He found his own hand shaking as he raised the cup for a second sip.

Adolin was still looking at him.

'Am I that bad to watch?' Dalinar asked.

'The gibberish you speak is unnerving, Father,' Renarin said. 'Unearthly, strange. Skewed, like a wooden building pushed to a slant by the wind.'

'You thrash about,' Adolin said. 'You nearly tipped over the chair. I had to hold it steady until you stilled.'

Dalinar stood up, sighing as he walked over to refill his cup. 'And you still think I don't need to abdicate?'

'The episodes are containable,' Adolin said, though he sounded disturbed. 'My point was *never* to get you to abdicate. I just didn't want you relying upon the delusions to make decisions about our house's future. So long as you accept that what you see isn't real, we can move on. No reason for you to give up your seat.'

Dalinar poured the wine. He looked eastward, toward the wall, away from Adolin and Renarin. 'I don't accept that what I see isn't real.'

'What?' Adolin said. 'But I thought I convinced—'

'I accept that I'm no longer reliable,' Dalinar said. 'And that there's a chance I might be going mad. I accept that something is happening to me.' He turned around. 'When I first began seeing these visions, I believed them to be from the Almighty. You have convinced me that I may have been too hasty in my judgment. I don't know enough to trust them. I could be mad. Or they could be supernatural without being of the Almighty.'

'How could that happen?' Adolin said, frowning.

'The Old Magic,' Renarin said softly, still sitting.

Dalinar nodded.

'What?' Adolin said pointedly. 'The Old Magic is a myth.'

'Unfortunately, it is not,' Dalinar said, then took another drink of the cool wine. 'I know this for a fact.'

'Father,' Renarin said. 'For the Old Magic to have affected you, you'd have had to travel to the West and seek it. Wouldn't you?'

'Yes,' he said, ashamed. The empty place in his memories where his wife had once existed had never seemed as obvious to him as it did at that moment. He tended to ignore it, with good reason. She'd vanished completely, and it was sometimes difficult for him to remember that he *had* been married.

'These visions are not in line with what I've understood about the Nightwatcher,' Renarin said. 'Most consider her to be just some kind of powerful spren. Once you've sought her out and been given your reward and your curse, she's supposed to leave you alone. When did you seek her?'

'It's been many years now,' Dalinar said.

'Then this probably isn't due to her influence,' Renarin said.

'I agree,' Dalinar said.

'But what did you ask for?' Adolin said, frowning.

'My curse and boon are my own, son,' Dalinar said. 'The specifics are not important.'

'But—'

'I agree with Renarin,' Dalinar said, interrupting. 'This is probably not the Nightwatcher.'

'All right, fine. But why bring it up?'

'Because, Adolin,' Dalinar said, feeling exasperated. 'I *don't know* what is happening to me. These visions seem far too detailed to be products of my mind. But your arguments made me think. I could be wrong. Or *you* could be wrong, and it could be the Almighty. Or it could be something entirely different. We don't know, and that is why it is dangerous for me to be left in command.'

'Well, what I said still holds,' Adolin said stubbornly. 'We can contain it.'

'No, we can't,' Dalinar said. 'Just because it has come only during highstorms in the past doesn't mean it couldn't expand to other times of stress. What if I were struck with an episode on the battlefield?' That was the very same reason they didn't let Renarin ride into battle.

'If that happens,' Adolin said, 'we'll deal with it. For now, we could just ignore—'

Dalinar threw a hand up into the air. 'Ignore? I *cannot* ignore something like this. The visions, the book, the things I feel – they're changing every aspect of me. How can I rule if I do not follow my conscience? If I continue as highprince, I second-guess my every decision. Either I decide to trust myself, or I step down. I cannot *stomach* the thought of something in-between.'

The room fell silent.

'So what do we do?' Adolin said.

'We make the choice,' Dalinar said. '*I* make the choice.'

'Step down or keep heeding the delusions,' Adolin spat. 'Either way we're letting them rule us.'

'And you have a better option?' Dalinar demanded. 'You've been quick to complain, Adolin, which seems a habit of yours. But I don't see you offering a legitimate alternative.'

'I gave you one,' Adolin said. 'Ignore the visions and move on!'

'I said a *legitimate* option!'

The two stared at one another. Dalinar fought to keep his anger contained. In many ways, he and Adolin were too similar. They understood one another, and that enabled them to push in places that hurt.

'Well,' Renarin said, 'what if we proved whether or not the visions were true?'

Dalinar glanced at him. 'What?'

'You say these dreams are detailed,' Renarin said, leaning forward with hands clasped in front of him. 'What, exactly, do you see?'

Dalinar hesitated, then gulped down the rest of his wine. For once he wished he had intoxicating violet instead of orange. 'The visions are often of the Knights Radiant. At the end of each episode, someone – I think one of the Heralds – comes to me and commands me to unite the highprinces of Alethkar.'

The room fell silent, Adolin looking disturbed, Renarin just sitting quietly.

'Today, I saw the Day of Recreance,' Dalinar continued. 'The Radiants abandoned their Shards and walked away. The Plate and Blades . . . faded somehow when they were abandoned. It seems such an odd detail to have seen.' He looked at Adolin. 'If these visions are fantasies, then I am a great deal more clever than I once thought myself.'

'Do you remember any specifics we could check on?' Renarin asked. 'Names? Locations? Events that might be traced in history?'

'This last one was of a place called Feverstone Keep,' Dalinar said.

'I've never heard of it,' Adolin said.

'Feverstone Keep,' Dalinar repeated. 'In my vision, there was some kind of war going on near there. The Radiants had been fighting on the front lines. They withdrew to this fortress, then abandoned their Shards there.'

'Perhaps we could find something in history,' Renarin said. 'Proof that either this keep existed or that the Radiants didn't do what you saw there. Then we'd know, wouldn't we? If the dreams are delusions or truth?'

Dalinar found himself nodding. Proving them had never occurred to him, in part because he had assumed they were real at the start. Once he'd started questioning, he'd been more inclined to keep the nature of the visions hidden and silent. But if he knew that he was seeing real events . . . well, that would at least rule out the possibility of madness. It wouldn't solve everything, but it would help a great deal.

'I don't know,' Adolin said, more skeptical. 'Father, you're talking about times before the Hierocracy. Will we be able to find anything in the histories?'

'There are histories from the time when the Radiants lived,' Renarin said. 'That's not as far back as the shadowdays or the Heraldic Epochs. We could ask Jasnah. Isn't this what she does? As a Veristitalian?'

Dalinar looked at Adolin. 'It sounds like it's worth a try, son.'

'Maybe,' Adolin said. 'But we can't take the existence of a single place as proof. You could have heard of this Feverstone Keep, and therefore included it.'

'Well,' Renarin said, 'that may be true. But if what Father sees are just delusions, then certainly we'll be able to prove some parts of them untrue. It seems impossible that every detail he imagines is one that he got from a story or history. *Some* aspects of the delusions would have to be pure fancy.'

Adolin nodded slowly. 'I . . . You're right, Renarin. Yes, it's a good plan.'

'We need to get one of my scribes,' Dalinar said. 'So I can dictate the vision I just had while it is fresh.'

'Yes,' Renarin said. 'The more details we have, the easier it will be to prove – or disprove – the visions.'

Dalinar grimaced, setting aside his cup and walking over to the others. He sat down. 'All right, but who would we use to record the dictation?'

'You have a great number of clerks, Father,' Renarin said.

'And they're all either wife or daughter to one of my officers,' Dalinar said. How could he explain? It was painful enough for him to expose weakness to his sons. If news of what he saw got around to his officers, it could weaken morale. There might come a time to reveal these things to his men, but he would need to do so carefully. And he'd much rather know for himself whether or not he was mad before he approached others.

'Yes,' Adolin said, nodding – though Renarin still looked perplexed. 'I understand. But, Father, we can't afford to wait for Jasnah to return. It could be months yet.'

'Agreed.' Dalinar said. He sighed. There was another option. 'Renarin, send a runner for your aunt Navani.'

Adolin glanced at Dalinar, raising an eyebrow. 'It's a good idea. But I thought you didn't trust her.'

'I trust her to keep her word,' Dalinar said, resigned. 'And to keep confidence. I told her of my plans to abdicate, and she didn't tell a soul.' Navani was excellent at keeping secrets. Far better than the women of his court. He trusted them to an extent, but keeping a secret like this would require someone supremely exacting in their words and thoughts.

That meant Navani. She would probably find a way to manipulate him using the knowledge, but at least the secret would be safe from his men.

'Go, Renarin,' Dalinar said.

Renarin nodded and stood. He had apparently recovered from his fit, and walked surefooted to the door. As he left, Adolin approached Dalinar. 'Father, what will you do if we prove that I'm right, and it's just your own mind?'

'A part of me wishes for that to happen,' Dalinar said, watching the door swing closed after Renarin. 'I fear madness, but at least it is something familiar, something that can be dealt with. I will give you the princedom, then seek help in Kharbranth. But if these things are *not* delusions, I face another decision. Do I accept what they tell me or not? It may very well be better for Alethkar if I prove to be mad. It will be easier, at the least.'

Adolin considered that, his brow furrowed, his jaw tense. 'And Sadeas? He seems to be nearing the completion of his investigation. What do we do?'

It was a legitimate question. Troubles over Dalinar trusting the visions in relation to Sadeas had been what had drawn Dalinar and Adolin to argument in the first place.

Unite them. That wasn't just a command from the visions. It had been Gavilar's dream. A unified Alethkar. Had Dalinar let that dream – combined with guilt over failing his brother – drive him to construct supernatural rationalizations for seeking his brother's will?

He felt uncertain. He *hated* feeling uncertain.

'Very well,' Dalinar said. 'I give you leave to prepare for the worst, just in case Sadeas moves against us. Prepare our officers and call back the companies sent to patrol for bandits. If Sadeas denounces me as having tried to kill Elhokar, we will lock down our warcamp and go on alert. I don't intend to let him bring me in for execution.'

Adolin looked relieved. 'Thank you, Father.'

'Hope it doesn't come to that, son,' Dalinar said. 'The moment Sadeas and I go to war in earnest, Alethkar as a nation will shatter. Ours are the two princedoms that uphold the king, and if we turn to strife, the others will either pick sides or turn to wars of their own.'

Adolin nodded, but Dalinar sat back, disturbed. *I'm sorry,* he thought to whatever force was sending the visions. *But I have to be wise.*

In a way, this seemed like a second test to him. The visions had told him to trust Sadeas. Well, he would see what happened.

◆ ◆ ◆

'. . . and then it faded,' Dalinar said. 'After that, I found myself back here.'

Navani raised her pen, looking thoughtful. It hadn't taken him long to talk through the vision. She'd scribed expertly, picking out details from him, knowing when to prod for more. She hadn't said a thing about the irregularity of the request, nor had she seemed amused by his desire to write down one of his delusions. She'd been businesslike and careful. She sat at his writing desk now, hair bound up in curls and crossed with four hair-spikes. Her dress was red, matched by her lip paint, and her beautiful violet eyes were curious.

Stormfather, Dalinar thought, *but she's beautiful.*

'Well?' Adolin asked. He stood leaning against the door out of the chamber. Renarin had gone off to collect a highstorm damage report. The lad needed practice at that sort of activity.

Navani raised an eyebrow. 'What was that, Adolin?'

'What do you think, Aunt?' Adolin asked.

'I have never heard of any of these places or events,' Navani said. 'But I believe you weren't expecting me to know of them. Didn't you say you wished me to contact Jasnah?'

'Yes,' Adolin said. 'But surely you have an analysis.'

'I reserve judgment, dear,' Navani said, standing up and folding the paper by pressing down with her safehand, holding it in place while she creased the fold tight. She smiled, walking by Adolin and patting him on the shoulder. 'Let's see what Jasnah says before we do any analyzing, shall we?'

'I suppose,' Adolin said. He sounded dissatisfied.

'I spent some time talking with that young lady of yours yesterday,' Navani noted to him. 'Danlan? I think you've made a wise choice. She's got a mind in that head of hers.'

Adolin perked up. 'You like her?'

'Quite a bit,' Navani said. 'I also discovered that she is very fond of avramelons. Did you know that?'

'I didn't, actually.'

'Good. I would have hated to do all that work to find you a means of pleasing her, only to discover that you already knew it. I took the liberty of purchasing a basket of the melons on my way here. You'll find them in the antechamber, watched over by a bored soldier who didn't look like he was doing anything important. If you were to visit her with them this afternoon, I think you'd find yourself very well received.'

Adolin hesitated. He probably knew that Navani was deflecting him from worrying over Dalinar. However, he relaxed, then started smiling.

'Well, that might make for a pleasant change, considering events lately.'

'I thought it might,' Navani said. 'I'd suggest going soon; those melons are perfectly ripe. Besides, I wish to speak with your father.'

Adolin kissed Navani fondly on the cheek. 'Thank you, Mashala.' He allowed her to get away with some things that others could not; around his favored aunt, he was much like a child again. Adolin's smile widened as he made his way out the door.

Dalinar found himself smiling as well. Navani knew his son well. His smile didn't last long, however, as he realized that Adolin's departure left him alone with Navani. He stood up. 'What is it you wished to ask of me?' he asked.

'I didn't say I wanted to *ask* anything of you, Dalinar,' she said. 'I just wanted to talk. We are family, after all. We don't spend enough time together.'

'If you wish to speak, I shall fetch some soldiers to accompany us.' He glanced at the antechamber outside. Adolin had shut the second door at the end, closing off his view of his guards – and their view of him.

'Dalinar,' she said, walking up to him. 'That *would* kind of defeat the point of sending Adolin away. I was after some privacy.'

He felt himself growing stiff. 'You should go now.'

'Must I?'

'Yes. People will think this is inappropriate. They will talk.'

'You imply that something inappropriate *could* happen, then?' Navani said, sounding almost girlishly eager.

'Navani, you are my *sister*.'

'We aren't related by blood,' she replied. 'In some kingdoms, a union between us would be mandated by tradition, once your brother died.'

'We aren't in other countries. This is Alethkar. There are rules.'

'I see,' she said, strolling closer to him. 'And what will you do if I *don't* go? Will you call for help? Have me hauled away?'

'Navani,' he said sufferingly. 'Please. Don't do this again. I'm tired.'

'Excellent. That might make it easier to get what I want.'

He closed his eyes. *I can't take this right now.* The vision, the confrontation with Adolin, his own uncertain emotions . . . He didn't know what to make of things any longer.

Testing the visions was a good decision, but he couldn't shake the disorientation he felt from being unable to decide what to do next. He liked to make decisions and stick to them. He couldn't do that.

It grated on him.

'I thank you for your scribing and for your willingness to keep this quiet,' he said, opening his eyes. 'But I really must ask you to leave *now*, Navani.'

'Oh, Dalinar,' she said softly. She was close enough that he could smell her perfume. Stormfather, but she was beautiful. Seeing her brought to his mind thoughts of days long past, when he'd desired her so strongly that he'd nearly grown to hate Gavilar for winning her affection.

'Can't you just relax,' she asked him, 'just for a little while?'

'The rules—'

'Everyone else—'

'I cannot be *everyone else*!' Dalinar said, more sharply than he intended. 'If I ignore our code and ethics, what am I, Navani? The other highprinces and lighteyes deserve recrimination for what they do, and I have let them know it. If *I* abandon my principles, then I become something far worse than they. A hypocrite!'

She froze.

'Please,' he said, tense with emotion. 'Just go. Do not taunt me today.'

She hesitated, then walked away without a word.

She would never know how much he wished her to have made one more objection. In his state, he likely would have been unable to argue further. Once the door shut, he let himself sit down in his chair, exhaling. He closed his eyes.

Almighty above, he thought. *Please. Just let me know what I am to do.*

53
DUNNY

'He must pick it up, the fallen title! The tower, the crown, and the spear!'

–Dated Vevahach, 1173, 8 seconds pre-death. Subject: a prostitute. Background unknown.

A razor-edged arrow snapped into the wood next to Kaladin's face. He could feel warm blood seep from a gash on his cheek, creeping down his face, mixing with the sweat dripping from his chin.

'Stay firm!' he bellowed, charging over the uneven ground, the bridge's familiar weight on his shoulders. Nearby – just ahead and to the left – Bridge Twenty floundered, four men at the front falling to arrows, their corpses tripping up those behind.

The Parshendi archers knelt on the other side of the chasm, singing calmly despite the hail of arrows from Sadeas's side. Their black eyes were like shards of obsidian. No whites. Just that emotionless black. In those moments – listening to men scream, cry, yell, howl – Kaladin hated the Parshendi as much as he hated Sadeas and Amaram. How could they sing while they killed?

The Parshendi in front of Kaladin's crew pulled and aimed. Kaladin screamed at them, feeling a strange surge of strength as the arrows were loosed.

The shafts zipped through the air in a focused wave. Ten shafts struck the wood near Kaladin's head, their force throwing a shudder through it, chips of wood splintering free. But not a one struck flesh.

Across the chasm, several of the Parshendi lowered their bows, breaking off their chanting. Their demonic faces bore looks of stupefaction.

'Down!' Kaladin yelled as the bridge crew reached the chasm. The ground was rough here, covered in bulbous rockbuds. Kaladin stepped on the vine from one of them, causing the plant to retract. The bridgemen heaved the bridge up and off their shoulders, then expertly stepped aside, lowering it to the ground. Sixteen other bridge crews lined up with them, setting their bridges down. Behind, Sadeas's heavy cavalry thundered across the plateau toward them.

The Parshendi drew again.

Kaladin gritted his teeth, throwing his weight against one of the wooden bars on the side, helping shove the massive construction across the chasm. He hated this part; the bridgemen were so exposed.

Sadeas's archers kept firing, moving to a focused, disruptive attack intended to force back the Parshendi. As always, the archers didn't seem to mind if they hit bridgemen, and several of those shafts flew dangerously close to Kaladin. He continued to push – sweating, bleeding – and felt a stab of pride for Bridge Four. They were already beginning to move like warriors, light on their feet, moving erratically, making it more difficult for the archers to draw a bead on them. Would Gaz or Sadeas's men notice?

The bridge thumped into place, and Kaladin bellowed the retreat. Bridgemen ducked out of the way, dodging between thick-shafted black Parshendi arrows and lighter green-fletched ones from Sadeas's archers. Moash and Rock hoisted themselves up onto the bridge and ran across it, leaping down beside Kaladin. Others scattered around the back of the bridge, ducking in front of the oncoming cavalry charge.

Kaladin lingered, waving for his men to get out of the way. Once they were all free, he glanced back at the bridge, which bristled with arrows. Not a single man down. A miracle. He turned to run—

Someone stumbled to his feet on the other side of the bridge. Dunny. The youthful bridgeman had a white and green fletched arrow sprouting from his shoulder. His eyes were wide, dazed.

Kaladin cursed, running back. Before he'd taken two steps, a blackhafted arrow took the youth in the other side. He fell to the deck of the bridge, blood spraying the dark wood.

The charging horses did not slow. Frantic, Kaladin reached the side of the bridge, but something pulled him back. Hands on his shoulder. He stumbled, spinning to find Moash there. Kaladin snarled at him, trying to shove the man aside, but Moash – using a move Kaladin himself had taught him – yanked Kaladin sideways, tripping him. Moash threw himself down, holding Kaladin to the ground as heavy cavalry thundered across the bridge, arrows cracking against their silvery armor.

Broken bits of arrow sprinkled to the ground. Kaladin struggled for a moment, but then let himself fall still.

'He's dead,' Moash said, harshly. 'There's nothing you could have done. I'm sorry.'

There's nothing you could have done. . . .

There isn't ever anything I can do. Stormfather, why can't I save them?

The bridge stopped shaking, the cavalry smashing into the Parshendi and making space for the foot soldiers, who clanked across next. The cavalry would retreat after the foot soldiers gained purchase, the horses too valuable to risk in extended fighting.

Yes, Kaladin thought. *Think about the tactics. Think about the battle. Don't think about Dunny.*

He pushed Moash off him, rising. Dunny's corpse was mangled beyond recognition. Kaladin set his jaw and turned, striding away without looking back. He brushed past the watching bridgemen and stepped up to the lip of the chasm, clasping his hands to his forearms behind his back, feet spread. It wasn't dangerous, so long as he stood far down from the bridge. The Parshendi had put away bows and were falling back. The chrysalis was a towering, oval stone mound on the far left side of the plateau.

Kaladin wanted to watch. It helped him think like a soldier, and thinking like a soldier helped him get over the deaths of those near him. The other bridgemen tentatively approached and filled in around him, standing at parade rest. Even Shen the parshman joined them, silently imitating the others. He'd joined every bridge run so far without complaint. He didn't refuse to march against his cousins; he didn't try to sabotage the assault. Gaz was disappointed, but Kaladin wasn't surprised. That was how parshmen were.

Except the ones on the other side of the chasm. Kaladin stared at the fighting, but had difficulty focusing on the tactics. Dunny's death tore at him too much. The lad had been a friend, one of the first to support him, one of the best of the bridgemen.

Each bridgeman dead edged them closer to disaster. It would take weeks to train the men properly. They'd lose half of their number – perhaps even more – before they were anywhere near ready to fight. That wasn't good enough.

Well, you'll have to find a way to fix it, Kaladin thought. He'd made his decision, and had no room for despair. Despair was a luxury.

He broke parade rest and stalked away from the chasm. The other bridgemen turned to look after him, surprised. Kaladin had recently taken to watching entire battles standing like that. Sadeas's soldiers had noticed. Many saw it as bridgemen behaving above their station. A few, however, seemed to respect Bridge Four for the display. He knew there were rumors about him because of the storm; no doubt he was adding to them.

Bridge Four followed, and Kaladin led them across the rocky plateau. He pointedly did not look again at the broken, mangled body on the bridge. Dunny had been one of the only bridgemen to retain any hint of innocence. And now he was dead, trampled by Sadeas, struck by arrows from both sides. Ignored, forgotten, abandoned.

There was nothing Kaladin could do for him. So instead, Kaladin made his way to where the members of Bridge Eight lay, exhausted, on a patch of open stone. Kaladin remembered lying like that after his first bridge runs. Now he barely felt winded.

As usual, the other bridge crews had left their wounded behind as they retreated. One poor man from Eight was crawling toward the others, an arrow through his thigh. Kaladin walked up to him. He had dark brown skin and brown eyes, his thick black hair pulled back into a long, braided tail. Painspren crawled around him. He looked up as Kaladin and the members of Bridge Four loomed over him.

'Hold still,' Kaladin said softly, kneeling and gently turning the man to get a good look at the wounded thigh. Kaladin prodded at it, thoughtful. 'Teft, we'll need a fire. Get out your tinder. Rock, you still have my needle and thread? I'll need that. Where's Lopen with the water?'

The members of Bridge Four were silent. Kaladin looked up from the confused, wounded man.

'Kaladin,' Rock said. 'You know how the other bridge crews have treated us.'

'I don't care,' Kaladin said.

'We don't have any money left,' Drehy said. 'Even pooling our income, we barely have enough for bandages for our own men.'

'I don't care.'

'If we care for the wounded of other bridge crews,' Drehy said, shaking a blond head, 'we'll have to feed them, tend them. . . .'

'I will find a way,' Kaladin said.

'I—' Rock began.

'Storm you!' Kaladin said, standing and sweeping his hand over the plateau. The bodies of bridgemen lay scattered, ignored. 'Look at that! Who cares for them? Not Sadeas. Not their fellow bridgemen. I doubt even the Heralds themselves spare a thought for these.

'I won't stand there and watch while men die behind me. We have to be better than that! We can't look away like the lighteyes, pretending we don't see. This man is one of us. Just like Dunny was.

'The lighteyes talk about honor. They spout empty claims about their nobility. Well, I've only known *one* man in my life who was a true man of honor. He was a surgeon who would help anyone, even those who hated him. Especially those who hated him. Well, we're going to show Gaz, and Sadeas, Hashal, and any other sodden fool who cares to watch, what he taught me. Now go to work and *stop complaining*!'

Bridge Four stared at him with wide, ashamed eyes, then burst into motion. Teft organized a triage unit, sending some men to search for other wounded bridgemen and others to gather rockbud bark for a fire. Lopen and Dabbid rushed off to fetch their litter.

Kaladin knelt down and felt at the wounded man's leg, checking to see how quickly the blood leaked, and determined that he wouldn't need to cauterize. He broke the shaft and wiped the wound with some conicshell mucus for numbing. Then he pulled the wood free, eliciting a grunt, and used his personal set of bandages to wrap the wound.

'Hold this with your hands,' Kaladin instructed. 'And don't walk on it. I'll check on you before we march back to camp.'

'How . . .' the man said. He didn't have even a hint of an accent. Kaladin had expected him to be Azish because of the dark skin. 'How will I get back if I can't walk on the leg?'

'We will carry you,' Kaladin said.

The man looked up, obviously shocked. 'I . . .' Tears formed in his eyes. 'Thank you.'

Kaladin nodded curtly, turning as Rock and Moash brought over another wounded man. Teft had a fire growing; it smelled of pungent wet rockbud. The new man had hit his head and had a long gash in his arm. Kaladin held out a hand for his thread.

'Kaladin, lad,' Teft said with a soft voice, handing him the thread and kneeling. 'Now, don't mark this as complaining, because it ain't. But how many men can we really carry back with us?'

'We've done three before,' Kaladin said. 'Lashed to the top of the bridge. I'll bet we could fit three more and carry another in the water litter.'

'And if we have more than seven?'

'If we bandage them right, some might be able to walk.'

'And if there are still more?'

'Storm it, Teft,' Kaladin said, beginning to sew. 'Then we bring the ones we can and haul the bridge back out again to fetch those we left behind. We'll bring Gaz with us if the soldiers worry that we'll run away.'

Teft was silent, and Kaladin steeled himself for incredulity. Instead, however, the grizzled soldier smiled. He actually seemed a little watery-eyed. 'Kelek's breath. It's true. I never thought . . .'

Kaladin frowned, looking up at Teft and holding a hand to the wound to stanch the bleeding. 'What was that?'

'Oh, nothing.' He scowled. 'Get back to work! That lad needs you.'

Kaladin turned back to his sewing.

'You still carrying a full pouch of spheres with you, like I told you?' Teft asked.

'I can't very well leave them behind in the barracks. But we'll need to spend them soon.'

'You'll do nothing of the sort,' Teft said. 'Those spheres are luck, you hear me? Keep them with you and always keep them infused.'

Kaladin sighed. 'I think there's something wrong with this batch. They won't hold their Stormlight. They fall dun after just a few days, every time. Perhaps it's something to do with the Shattered Plains. It has happened to the other bridgemen too.'

'Odd, that,' Teft said, rubbing his chin. 'This was a bad approach.

Three bridges down. Lots of bridgemen dead. Interesting how we didn't lose anyone.'

'We lost Dunny.'

'But not on the approach. You always run point, and the arrows always seem to miss us. Odd, eh?'

Kaladin looked up again, frowning. 'What are you saying, Teft?'

'Nothing. Get back to that sewing! How many times do I have to tell you?'

Kaladin raised an eyebrow, but turned back to his work. Teft had been acting very strange lately. Was it the stress? A lot of people were superstitious about spheres and Stormlight.

Rock and his team brought three more wounded, then said that was all they'd found. Bridgemen who fell often ended up like Dunny, getting trampled. Well, at least Bridge Four wouldn't have to make a return trip to the plateau.

The three had bad arrow wounds, and so Kaladin left the man with the gash on his arm to them, instructing Skar to keep pressure on the unfinished sewing job. Teft heated a dagger for cauterization; these newcomers had obviously lost a lot of blood. One probably wouldn't make it.

So much of the world is at war, he thought as he worked. The dream had highlighted what others already spoke of. Kaladin hadn't known, growing up in remote Hearthstone, how fortunate his town had been to avoid battle.

The entire world warred, and he struggled to save a few impoverished bridgemen. What good did it do? And yet he continued searing flesh, sewing, saving lives as his father had taught him. He began to understand the sense of futility he'd seen in his father's eyes on those occasional darkened nights when Lirin had turned to his wine in solitude.

You're trying to make up for failing Dunny, Kaladin thought. *Helping these others won't bring him back.*

He lost the one he'd suspected would die, but saved the other four, and the one who'd taken a knock to the head was beginning to wake up. Kaladin sat back on his knees, weary, hands covered in blood. He washed them off with a stream of water from Lopen's waterskins, then reached up, finally remembering his own wound, where the arrow had sliced his cheek.

He froze. He prodded at his skin, but couldn't find the wound. He had felt blood on his cheek and chin. He'd felt the arrow slice him, hadn't he?

He stood up, feeling a chill, and raised his hand to his forehead. What was happening?

Someone stepped up beside him. Moash's now-clean-shaven face exposed a faded scar along his chin. He studied Kaladin. 'About Dunny . . .'

'You were right to do what you did,' Kaladin said. 'You probably saved my life. Thank you.'

Moash nodded slowly. He turned to look at the four wounded men; Lopen and Dabbid were giving them drinks of water, asking their names. 'I was wrong about you,' Moash said suddenly, holding out a hand to Kaladin.

Kaladin took the hand, hesitant. 'Thank you.'

'You're a fool and an instigator. But you're an honest one.' Moash chuckled to himself. 'If you get us killed, it won't be on purpose. Can't say that for some I've served under. Anyway, let's get these men ready for moving.'

54

GIBLETISH

'The burdens of nine become mine. Why must I carry the madness of them all? Oh, Almighty, release me.'

—Dated Palaheses, 1173, unknown seconds pre-death. Subject: a wealthy lighteyes. Sample collected secondhand.

The cold night air threatened that a stretch of winter might soon be coming. Dalinar wore a long, thick uniform coat over trousers and shirt. It buttoned stiffly up the chest and to the collar, and was long in the back and on the sides, coming down to his ankles, flowing at the waist like a cloak. In earlier years, it might have been worn with a takama, though Dalinar had never liked the skirtlike garments.

The purpose of the uniform was not fashion or tradition, but to distinguish him easily for those who followed him. He wouldn't have nearly the problem with the other lighteyes if they would at least wear their colors.

He stepped onto the king's feasting island. Stands had been set up at the sides where the braziers normally stood, each one bearing one of those new fabrials that gave off heat. The stream between the islands had slowed to a trickle; ice had stopped melting in the highlands.

Attendance at the feast tonight was small, though that was mostly manifest on the four islands that were not the king's. Where there was access to Elhokar and the highprinces, people would attend even if the feast were held in the middle of a highstorm. Dalinar walked down the central pathway, and Navani – sitting at a women's dining table – caught his eyes. She turned away, perhaps still remembering his abrupt words to her at their last meeting.

Wit wasn't at his customary place insulting those who walked onto the king's island; in fact, he wasn't to be seen at all. *Not surprising*, Dalinar thought. Wit didn't like to grow predictable; he'd spent several recent feasts on his pedestal doling out insults. Likely he felt he'd played out that tactic.

All nine other highprinces were in attendance. Their treatment of Dalinar had grown stiff and cold since refusing his requests to fight together. As if they were offended by the mere offer. Lesser lighteyes made alliances, but the highprinces were like kings themselves. Other highprinces were rivals, to be kept at arm's length.

Dalinar sent a servant to fetch him food and sat down at the table. His arrival had been delayed while he took reports from the companies he'd called back, so he was one of the last to eat. Most of the others had turned to mingling. To the right, an officer's daughter was playing a serene flute melody to a group of onlookers. To the left, three women had set up sketchpads and were each drawing the same man. Women were known to challenge each other to duels in the way of men with Shardblades, though they rarely used the word. These were always 'friendly competitions' or 'games of talent.'

His food arrived, steamed stagm – a brownish tuber that grew in deep puddles – atop a bed of boiled tallew. The grain was puffed with water, and the entire meal was drenched in a thick, peppery, brown gravy. He slid out his knife and sliced a disk off the end of the stagm. Using his knife to spread tallew over the top, he grasped the vegetable disk between two fingers and began to eat. It had been prepared both spicy and hot this night, probably because of the chill, and tasted good as he chewed, the steam from his plate fogging the air in front of him.

So far, Jasnah had not replied regarding his vision, though Navani claimed she might be able to find something on her own. She was a renowned scholar herself, though her interests had always been more in fabrials. He glanced at her. Was he a fool to offend her as he had? Would it make her use the knowledge of his visions against him?

No, he thought. *She wouldn't be that petty.* Navani *did* seem to care for him, though her affection was inappropriate.

The chairs around him were left empty. He was becoming a pariah, first because of his talk of the Codes, then because of his attempts to get the highprinces to work with him, and finally because of Sadeas's investigation. No wonder Adolin was worried.

Suddenly, someone slid right into the seat beside Dalinar, wearing a black cloak against the chill. It wasn't one of the highprinces. Who would dare—

The figure lowered his hood, revealing Wit's hawklike face. All lines and peaks, with a sharp nose and jaw, delicate eyebrows, and keen eyes. Dalinar sighed, waiting for the inevitable stream of too-clever quips.

Wit, however, didn't speak. He inspected the crowd, his expression intense.

Yes, Dalinar thought. *Adolin is right about this one too.* Dalinar himself had judged the man too harshly in the past. He was not the fool some of his predecessors had been. Wit continued in silence, and Dalinar decided that – perhaps – the man's prank this night was to sit down beside people and unnerve them. It wasn't much of a prank, but Dalinar often missed the point of what Wit did. Perhaps it was terribly clever if one had the mind for it. Dalinar returned to his meal.

'Winds are changing,' Wit whispered.

Dalinar glanced at him.

Wit's eyes narrowed, and he scanned the night sky. 'It's been happening for months now. A whirlwind. Shifting and churning, blowing us round and around. Like a world spinning, but we can't see it because we're too much a part of it.'

'World spinning. What foolishness is this?'

'The foolishness of men who care, Dalinar,' Wit said. 'And the brilliance of those who do not. The second depend on the first – but also exploit the first – while the first misunderstand the second, hoping that the second are more like the first. And all of their games steal our time. Second by second.'

'Wit,' Dalinar said with a sigh. 'I haven't the mind for this tonight. I'm sorry if I'm missing your intent, but I have no idea what you mean.'

'I know,' Wit said, then looked directly at him. 'Adonalsium.'

Dalinar frowned more deeply. 'What?'

Wit searched his face. 'Have you ever heard the term, Dalinar?'

'Ado . . . what?'

'Nothing,' Wit said. He seemed preoccupied, unlike his usual self. 'Nonsense. Balderdash. Figgldygrak. Isn't it odd that gibberish words are often the sounds of other words, cut up and dismembered, then stitched into something like them – yet wholly unlike them at the same time?'

Dalinar frowned.

'I wonder if you could do that to a man. Pull him apart, emotion by emotion, bit by bit, bloody chunk by bloody chunk. Then combine them back together into something else, like a Dysian Aimian. If you do put a man together like that, Dalinar, be sure to name him Gibberish, after me. Or perhaps Gibletish.'

'Is that your name, then? Your real name?'

'No, my friend,' Wit said, standing up. 'I've abandoned my real name. But when next we meet, I'll think of a clever one for you to call me. Until then, Wit will suffice – or if you must, you may call me Hoid. Watch yourself; Sadeas is planning a revelation at the feast tonight, though I know not what it is. Farewell. I'm sorry I didn't insult you more.'

'Wait, you're leaving?'

'I must. I hope to return. I'll do so if I'm not killed. Probably will anyway. Apologize to your nephew for me.'

'He won't be happy,' Dalinar said. 'He's fond of you.'

'Yes, it's one of his more admirable traits,' Wit said. 'Alongside that of paying me, letting me eat his expensive food, and giving me opportunity to make sport of his friends. The cosmere, unfortunately, takes precedence over free food. Watch yourself, Dalinar. Life becomes dangerous, and you're at the center of it.'

Wit nodded once, then ducked into the night. He put his hood up, and soon Dalinar couldn't separate him from the darkness.

Dalinar turned back to his meal. *Sadeas is planning a revelation at the feast tonight, though I know not what it is.* Wit was rarely wrong – though he was almost always odd. Was he really leaving, or would he still be in camp the next morning, laughing at the prank he had played on Dalinar?

No, Dalinar thought. *That wasn't a prank.* He waved over a master-servant in black and white. 'Fetch my elder son for me.'

The servant bowed and withdrew. Dalinar ate the rest of his food in silence, glancing occasionally at Sadeas and Elhokar. They weren't at the dining table any longer, and so Sadeas's wife had joined them. Ialai was a curvaceous woman who reportedly dyed her hair. That indicated foreign blood in her family's past – Alethi hair always bred true, proportionate to how much Alethi blood you had. Foreign blood would mean stray hairs of another color. Ironically, mixed blood was far more common in lighteyes than darkeyes. Darkeyes rarely married foreigners, but the Alethi houses often needed alliances or money from outside.

Food finished, Dalinar stepped down from the king's table onto the island proper. The woman was still playing her melancholy song. She was quite good. A few moments later, Adolin strode onto the king's island. He hurried over to Dalinar. 'Father? You sent for me?'

'Stay close. Wit told me that Sadeas plans to make a storm of something tonight.'

Adolin's expression darkened. 'Time to go, then.'

'No. We need to let this play out.'

'Father—'

'But you *may* prepare,' Dalinar said softly. 'Just in case. You invited officers of our guard to the feast tonight?'

'Yes,' Adolin said. 'Six of them.'

'They have my further invitation to the king's island. Pass the word. What of the King's Guard?'

'I've made sure that some of the ones guarding the island tonight are among those most loyal to you.' Adolin nodded toward a space in the darkness to the side of the feasting basin. 'I think we should position them over there. It'll make a good line of retreat in case the king tries to have you arrested.'

'I still don't think it will come to that.'

'You can't be sure. Elhokar allowed this investigation in the first place, after all. He's growing more and more paranoid.'

Dalinar glanced over at the king. The younger man almost always wore his Shardplate these days, though he didn't have it on now. He seemed continually on edge, glancing over his shoulder, eyes darting from side to side.

'Let me know when the men are in position,' Dalinar said.

Adolin nodded, walking away quickly.

The situation gave Dalinar little stomach for mingling. Still, standing alone and looking awkward was no better, so he made his way to where

Highprince Hatham was speaking with a small group of lighteyes beside the main firepit. They nodded to Dalinar as he joined them; regardless of the way they were treating him in general, they would never turn him away at a feast like this. That simply wasn't done to one of his rank.

'Ah, Brightlord Dalinar,' Hatham said in his smooth, overly polite way. The long-necked, slender man wore a ruffled green shirt underneath a robelike coat, with a darker green silk scarf around the neck. A faintly glowing ruby sat on each of his fingers; they'd each had some of their Stormlight drained away by a fabrial made for the purpose.

Of Hatham's four companions, two were lesser lighteyes and one was a short white-robed ardent Dalinar didn't know. The last was a red-gloved Natan man with bluish skin and stark white hair, two locks dyed a deep red and braided down to hang alongside his cheeks. He was a visiting dignitary; Dalinar had seen him at the feasts. What was his name again?

'Tell me, Brightlord Dalinar,' Hatham said. 'Have you been paying much attention to the conflict between the Tukari and the Emuli?'

'It's a religious conflict, isn't it?' Dalinar asked. Both were Makabaki kingdoms, on the southern coast where trade was plentiful and profitable.

'Religious?' the Natan man said. 'No, I wouldn't say that. All conflicts are essentially economic in nature.'

Au-nak, Dalinar recalled. *That's his name*. He spoke with an airy accent, overextending all of his 'ah' and 'oh' sounds.

'Money is behind every war,' Au-nak continued. 'Religion is but an excuse. Or perhaps a justification.'

'There's a difference?' the ardent said, obviously taking offense at Au-nak's tone.

'Of course,' Au-nak said. 'An excuse is what you make after the deed is done, while a justification is what you offer before.'

'I would say an excuse is something you claim, but do not believe, Nak-ali.' Hatham was using the high form of Au-nak's name. 'While a justification is something you actually believe.' Why such respect? The Natan must have something that Hatham wanted.

'Regardless,' Au-nak said. 'This particular war is over the city of Sesemalex Dar, which the Emuli have made their capital. It's an excellent trade city, and the Tukari want it.'

'I've heard of Sesemalex Dar,' Dalinar said, rubbing his chin. 'The city is quite spectacular, filling rifts cut into the stone.'

'Indeed,' Au-nak said. 'There's a particular composition of the stone there that lets water drain. The design is amazing. It's obviously one of the Dawncities.'

'My wife would have something to say on that,' Hatham said. 'She makes the Dawncities her study.'

'The city's pattern is central to the Emuli religion,' the ardent said. 'They claim it is their ancestral homeland, a gift to them from the Heralds. And the Tukari are led by that god-priest of theirs, Tezim. So the conflict *is* religious in nature.'

'And if the city weren't such a fantastic port,' Au-nak said, 'would they be as persistent about proclaiming the city's religious significance? I think not. They're pagans, after all, so we can't presume their religion has any real importance.'

Talk of the Dawncities had been popular lately among the lighteyes – the idea that certain cities could trace their origins back to the Dawnsingers. Perhaps . . .

'Have any of you heard of a place known as Feverstone Keep?' Dalinar asked.

The others shook their heads; even Au-nak had nothing to say.

'Why?' Hatham asked.

'Just curious.'

The conversation continued, though Dalinar let his attention wander back toward Elhokar and his circle of attendants. When would Sadeas make his announcement? If he intended to suggest that Dalinar be arrested, he wouldn't do it at a feast, would he?

Dalinar forced his attention back to the conversation. He really should pay more heed to what was happening in the world. Once, news of which kingdoms were in conflict had fascinated him. So much had changed since the visions began.

'Perhaps it's not economic or religious in nature,' Hatham said, trying to bring an end to the argument. 'Everyone knows that the Makabaki tribes have odd hatreds of one another.'

'Perhaps,' Au-nak said.

'Does it matter?' Dalinar asked.

The others turned to him.

'It's just another war. If they weren't fighting one another, they'd find others to attack. It's what we do. Vengeance, honor, riches, religion – the reasons all just produce the same result.'

The others fell still, the silence quickly growing awkward.

'Which devotary do you credit, Brightlord Dalinar?' Hatham asked, thoughtful, as if trying to remember something he'd forgotten.

'The Order of Talenelat.'

'Ah,' Hatham said. 'Yes, it makes sense. They do hate arguing over religion. You must find this discussion terribly boring.'

A safe out from the conversation. Dalinar smiled, nodding in thanks to Hatham's politeness.

'The Order of Talenelat?' Au-nak said. 'I always considered that a devotary for the lesser people.'

'This from a Natan,' the ardent said, stuffily.

'My family has always been devoutly Vorin.'

'Yes,' the ardent replied, 'conveniently so, since your family has used its Vorin ties to trade favorably in Alethkar. One wonders if you are equally devout when not standing on our soil.'

'I don't have to be insulted like this,' Au-nak snapped.

He turned and strode away, causing Hatham to raise a hand. 'Nak-ali!' Hatham called, rushing after him anxiously. 'Please, ignore him!'

'Insufferable bore,' the ardent said softly, taking a sip of his wine – orange, of course, as he was a man of the clergy.

Dalinar frowned at him. 'You are bold, ardent,' he said sternly. 'Perhaps foolishly so. You insult a man Hatham wants to do business with.'

'Actually, I belong to Brightlord Hatham,' the ardent said. 'He *asked* me to insult his guest – Brightlord Hatham wants Au-nak to think that he is shamed. Now, when Hatham agrees quickly to Au-nak's demands, the foreigner will assume it was because of this – and won't delay the contract signing out of suspicion that it is proceeding too easily.'

Ah, of course. Dalinar looked after the fleeing pair. *They go to such lengths.*

Considering that, what was Dalinar to think of Hatham's politeness earlier, when he had given Dalinar a reason to explain his apparent distaste for conflict? Was Hatham preparing Dalinar for some covert manipulation?

The ardent cleared his throat. 'I would appreciate it if you did not repeat to anyone what I just told you, Brightlord.' Dalinar noticed Adolin returning to the king's island, accompanied by six of Dalinar's officers, in uniform and wearing their swords.

'Why did you tell me in the first place, then?' Dalinar asked, turning his attention back to the white-robed man.

'Just as Hatham wishes his partner in negotiations to know of his goodwill, I wish you to know of our goodwill toward you, Brightlord.'

Dalinar frowned. He'd never had much to do with the ardents – his devotary was simple and straightforward. Dalinar got his fill of politics with the court; he had little desire to find more in religion. 'Why? What should it matter if you have goodwill toward me?'

The ardent smiled. 'We will speak with you again.' He bowed low and withdrew.

Dalinar was about to demand more, but Adolin arrived, looking after Highprince Hatham. 'What was that all about?'

Dalinar just shook his head. Ardents weren't supposed to engage in politics, whatever their devotary. They'd been officially forbidden to do so since the Hierocracy. But, as with most things in life, the ideal and the reality were two separate things. The lighteyes couldn't help but use the ardents in their schemes, and so – more and more – the devotaries found themselves a part of the court.

'Father?' Adolin asked. 'The men are in place.'

'Good,' Dalinar said. He set his jaw and then crossed the small island. He would see this fiasco finished with, once and for all.

He passed the firepit, a wave of dense heat making the left side of his face prickle with sweat while the right side was still chilled by the autumn cold. Adolin hurried up to walk by him, hand on his side sword. 'Father? What are we doing?'

'Being provocative,' Dalinar said, striding right up to where Elhokar and Sadeas were chatting. Their crowd of sycophants reluctantly parted for Dalinar.

'... and I think that—' The king cut off, glancing at Dalinar. 'Yes, Uncle?'

'Sadeas,' Dalinar said. 'What is the status of your investigation of the cut girth strap?'

Sadeas blinked. He held a cup of violet wine in his right hand, his long, red velvet robe open at the front to expose a ruffled white shirt. 'Dalinar, are you—'

'Your investigation, Sadeas,' Dalinar said firmly.

Sadeas sighed, looking at Elhokar. 'Your Majesty. I was actually planning to make an announcement regarding this very subject tonight. I was going to wait until later, but if Dalinar is going to be so insistent . . .'

'I am,' Dalinar said.

'Oh, go ahead, Sadeas,' the king said. 'You have me curious now.' The king waved to a servant, who rushed to quiet the flutist while another servant tapped the chimes to call for silence. In moments, the people on the island stilled.

Sadeas gave Dalinar a grimace that somehow conveyed the message, 'You demanded this, old friend.'

Dalinar folded his arms, keeping his gaze fixed on Sadeas. His six Cobalt Guardsmen stepped up behind him, and Dalinar noticed that a group of similar lighteyed officers from Sadeas's warcamp were listening nearby.

'Well, I wasn't planning to have such an audience,' Sadeas said. 'Mostly, this was planned for Your Majesty only.'

Unlikely, Dalinar thought, trying to suppress his anxiety. What would he do if Adolin was right and Sadeas charged him with trying to assassinate Elhokar?

It would, indeed, be the end of Alethkar. Dalinar would not go quietly, and the warcamps would turn against one another. The nervous peace that had held them together for the last decade would come to an end. Elhokar would never be able to hold them together.

Also, if it turned to battle, Dalinar would not fare well. The others were alienated from him; he'd have enough trouble facing Sadeas – if several of the others joined against him, he would fall, horribly outnumbered. He could see how Adolin thought it an incredible act of foolishness to have listened to the visions. And yet, in a powerfully surreal moment, Dalinar felt that he'd done the correct thing. He'd never felt it as strongly as at that moment, preparing to be condemned.

'Sadeas, don't weary me with your sense of drama,' Elhokar said. 'They're listening. I'm listening. Dalinar looks like he's ready to burst a vein in his forehead. Speak.'

'Very well,' Sadeas said, giving his wine to a servant. 'My very first task as Highprince of Information was to discover the true nature of the attempt on His Majesty's life during the greatshell hunt.' He waved a hand, motioning to one of his men, who hurried away. Another stepped forward, handing Sadeas the broken leather strap.

'I took this strap to three separate leatherworkers in three different warcamps. Each came to the same conclusion. It was cut. The leather is relatively new, and has been well cared for, as proven by the lack of cracking and flaking in other areas. The tear is too even. Someone slit it.'

Dalinar felt a sense of dread. That was near what he had discovered, but it was presented in the worst possible light. 'For what purpose—' Dalinar began.

Sadeas held up a hand. 'Please, Highprince. First you demand I report, then you interrupt me?'

Dalinar fell still. Around them, more and more of the important lighteyes were gathering. He could sense their tension.

'But when was it cut?' Sadeas said, turning to address the crowd. He did have a flair for the dramatic. 'That was pivotal, you see. I took leave to interview numerous men who were on that hunt. None reported seeing anything specific, though all remembered that there was one odd event. The time when Brightlord Dalinar and His Majesty raced to a rock formation. A time when Dalinar and the king were alone.'

There were whispers from behind.

'There was a problem, however,' Sadeas said. 'One Dalinar himself raised. Why cut the strap on a Shardbearer's saddle? A foolish move. A horseback fall wouldn't be of much danger to a man wearing Shardplate.' To the side, the servant Sadeas had sent away returned, leading a youth with sandy hair bearing only a few hints of black.

Sadeas fished something out of a pouch at his waist, holding it up. A large sapphire. It wasn't infused. In fact, looking closely, Dalinar could see that it was cracked – it wouldn't hold Stormlight now. 'The question drove me to investigate the king's Shardplate,' Sadeas said. 'Eight of the ten sapphires used to infuse his Plate were cracked following the battle.'

'It happens,' Adolin said, stepping up beside Dalinar, hand on his side sword. 'You lose a few in every battle.'

'But eight?' Sadeas asked. 'One or two is normal. But have you ever lost eight in one battle before, young Kholin?'

Adolin's only reply was a glare.

Sadeas tucked away the gemstone, nodding to the youth his men had brought. 'This is one of the grooms in the king's employ. Fin, isn't it?'

'Y ... Yes, brightlord,' the boy stammered. He couldn't be older than twelve.

'What is it you told me earlier, Fin? Please, say it again so that all may hear.'

The darkeyed youth cringed, looking sick. 'Well, Brightlord sir, it was just this: Everyone spoke of the saddle being checked over in Brightlord Dalinar's camp. And I suppose it was, right as that. But I'm the one who prepared His Majesty's horse afore it was turned over to Brightlord Dalinar's men. And I did it, I promise I did. Put on his favorite saddle and everything. But ...'

Dalinar's heart raced. He had to hold himself back from summoning his Blade.

'But what?' Sadeas said to Fin.

'But when the king's head grooms took the horse past on its way to the Highprince Dalinar's camp, it was wearing a different saddle. I swear it.'

Several of those standing around them seemed confused by this admission.

'Aha!' Adolin said, pointing. 'But that happened in the king's palace complex!'

'Indeed,' Sadeas said, raising an eyebrow at Adolin. 'How keen-minded of you, young Kholin. This discovery – mixed with the cracked gemstones – means something. I suspect that whoever attempted to kill His Majesty planted in his Shardplate flawed gemstones that would crack when strained, losing their Stormlight. Then they weakened the saddle girth with a careful slit. The hope would be that His Majesty would fall while fighting a greatshell, allowing it to attack him. The gemstones would fail, the Plate would break, and His Majesty would fall to an "accident" while hunting.'

Sadeas raised a finger as the crowd began to whisper again. 'However, it is important to realize that these events – the switching of the saddle or the planting of the gemstones – must have happened before His Majesty met up with Dalinar. I feel that Dalinar is a very unlikely suspect. In fact, my present guess is that the culprit is someone that Brightlord Dalinar has offended; that someone wanted us all to think he might be involved. It may not have actually been intended to kill His Majesty, just to cast suspicion upon Dalinar.'

The island fell silent, even the whispers dying.

Dalinar stood, stunned. *I . . . I was right!*

Adolin finally broke the quiet. '*What?*'

'All evidence points to your father being innocent, Adolin,' Sadeas said sufferingly. 'You find this surprising?'

'No, but . . .' Adolin's brow furrowed.

Around them, the lighteyes began talking, sounding disappointed. They began to disperse. Dalinar's officers remained standing behind him, as if expecting a surprise strike.

Blood of my fathers . . . Dalinar thought. *What does it mean?*

Sadeas waved for his men to take the groom away, then nodded to Elhokar and withdrew in the direction of the evening trays, where warmed wine sat in pitchers next to toasted breads. Dalinar caught up to Sadeas as the shorter man was filling a small plate. Dalinar took him by the arm, the fabric of Sadeas's robe soft beneath his fingers.

Sadeas looked at him, raising an eyebrow.

'Thank you,' Dalinar said quietly. 'For not going through with it.' Behind them, the flutist resumed her playing.

'For not going through with what?' Sadeas said, setting down his small plate, then prying Dalinar's fingers free. 'I had hoped to make this presentation after I'd discovered more concrete proof that you weren't involved. Unfortunately, pressed as I was, the best I could do was to indicate that it was unlikely you were involved. There will still be rumors, I'm afraid.'

'Wait. You *wanted* to prove me innocent?'

Sadeas scowled, picking up his plate again. 'Do you know what your problem is, Dalinar? Why everyone has begun finding you so tiresome?'

Dalinar didn't reply.

'The presumption. You've grown despicably self-righteous. Yes, I asked Elhokar for this position so I could prove you innocent. Is it so storming difficult for you to believe someone else in this army might do something honest?'

'I . . .' Dalinar said.

'Of course it is,' Sadeas said. 'You've been looking down on us like a man standing atop a single sheet of paper, who therefore thinks himself so high as to see for miles. Well, I think that book of Gavilar's is crem, and the Codes are lies people pretended to follow so that they could justify their shriveled consciences. Damnation, I've got one of those shriveled consciences myself. But I didn't want to see you maligned for this bungled attempt to kill the king. If you'd wanted him dead, you'd have just burned out his eyes and been done with it!'

Sadeas took a drink of his steaming violet wine. 'The problem is, Elhokar kept on and on about that blasted strap. And people started talking, since he was under your protection and you two rode off together like that. Stormfather only knows how they could think *you* would try to have Elhokar assassinated. You can barely bring yourself to kill Parshendi these days.' Sadeas stuffed a small piece of toasted bread in his mouth, then moved to walk away.

Dalinar caught him by the arm again. 'I . . . I owe you a debt. I shouldn't have treated you as I have these six years.'

Sadeas rolled his eyes, chewing his bread. 'This wasn't for you alone. So long as everyone thought you were behind the attempt, nobody would figure out who really tried to have Elhokar killed. And someone *did*, Dalinar. I don't accept eight gemstones cracking in one fight. The strap alone would have been a ridiculous way to attempt an assassination, but with weakened Shardplate . . . I'm half tempted to believe that the surprise arrival of the chasmfiend was orchestrated too. How someone would manage that though, I have no idea.'

'And the talk of me being framed?' Dalinar asked.

'Mostly to give the others something to gossip about while I sort through what's really happening.' Sadeas looked down at Dalinar's hand on his arm. 'Would you let go?'

Dalinar released his grip.

Sadeas set down his plate, straightening his robe and dusting off the shoulder. 'I haven't given up on you yet, Dalinar. I'm probably going to need you before this is all through. I do have to say, though, I don't know what to make of you lately. That talk of you wanting to abandon the Vengeance Pact. Is there any truth to that?'

'I mentioned it, in confidence, to Elhokar as a means of exploring options. So yes, there's truth to it, if you must know. I'm tired of this fighting. I'm tired of these Plains, of being away from civilization, of killing Parshendi a handful at a time. However, I've given up on getting us to retreat. Instead, I want to *win*. But the highprinces won't listen! They all assume that I'm trying to dominate them with some crafty trick.'

Sadeas snorted. 'You'd sooner punch a man in the face than stab him in the back. Blessedly straightforward.'

'Ally with me,' Dalinar said after him.

Sadeas froze.

'You know I'm not going to betray you, Sadeas,' Dalinar said. 'You trust me as the others never can. Try what I've been asking the other highprinces to agree to. Jointly assault plateaus with me.'

'Won't work,' Sadeas said. 'There's no reason to bring more than one army on an assault. I leave half my troops behind each time as it is. There isn't room for more to maneuver.'

'Yes, but think,' Dalinar said. 'What if we tried new tactics? Your quick bridge crews are fast, but my troops are stronger. What if you pushed quickly to a plateau with an advance force to hold off the Parshendi? You could hold until my stronger, but slower, forces arrive.'

That gave Sadeas pause.

'It could mean a Shardblade, Sadeas.'

Sadeas's eyes grew hungry.

'I know you've fought Parshendi Shardbearers,' Dalinar said, seizing on that thread, 'But you've lost. Without a Blade, you're at a disadvantage.' Parshendi Shardbearers had a habit of escaping after entering battles. Regular spearmen couldn't kill one, of course. It took a Shardbearer to kill a Shardbearer. 'I've slain two in the past. I don't often have the opportunity, however, because I can't get to the plateaus quickly enough. You can. Together, we can win more often, and *I* can get you a Blade. We can do this, Sadeas. Together. Like the old days.'

'The old days,' he said idly. 'I'd like to see the Blackthorn in battle again. How would we split the gemhearts?'

'Two-thirds to you,' Dalinar said. 'As you've got twice as good a record at winning assaults as I have.'

Sadeas looked thoughtful. 'And the Shardblades?'

'If we find a Shardbearer, Adolin and I will take him. You win the Blade.' He raised a finger. 'But I win the Plate. To give to my son, Renarin.'

'The invalid?'

'What would you care?' Dalinar said. 'You already have Plate. Sadeas, this could mean *winning* the war. If we start to work together, we could bring the others in, prepare for a large-scale assault. Storms! We might not even need that. We two have the largest armies; if we could find a way to catch the Parshendi on a large enough plateau with the bulk of our troops – surrounding them so they couldn't escape – we might be able to damage their forces enough to bring an end to this all.'

Sadeas mulled it over. Then he shrugged. 'Very well. Send me details via messenger. But do it later. I've already missed too much of tonight's feast.'

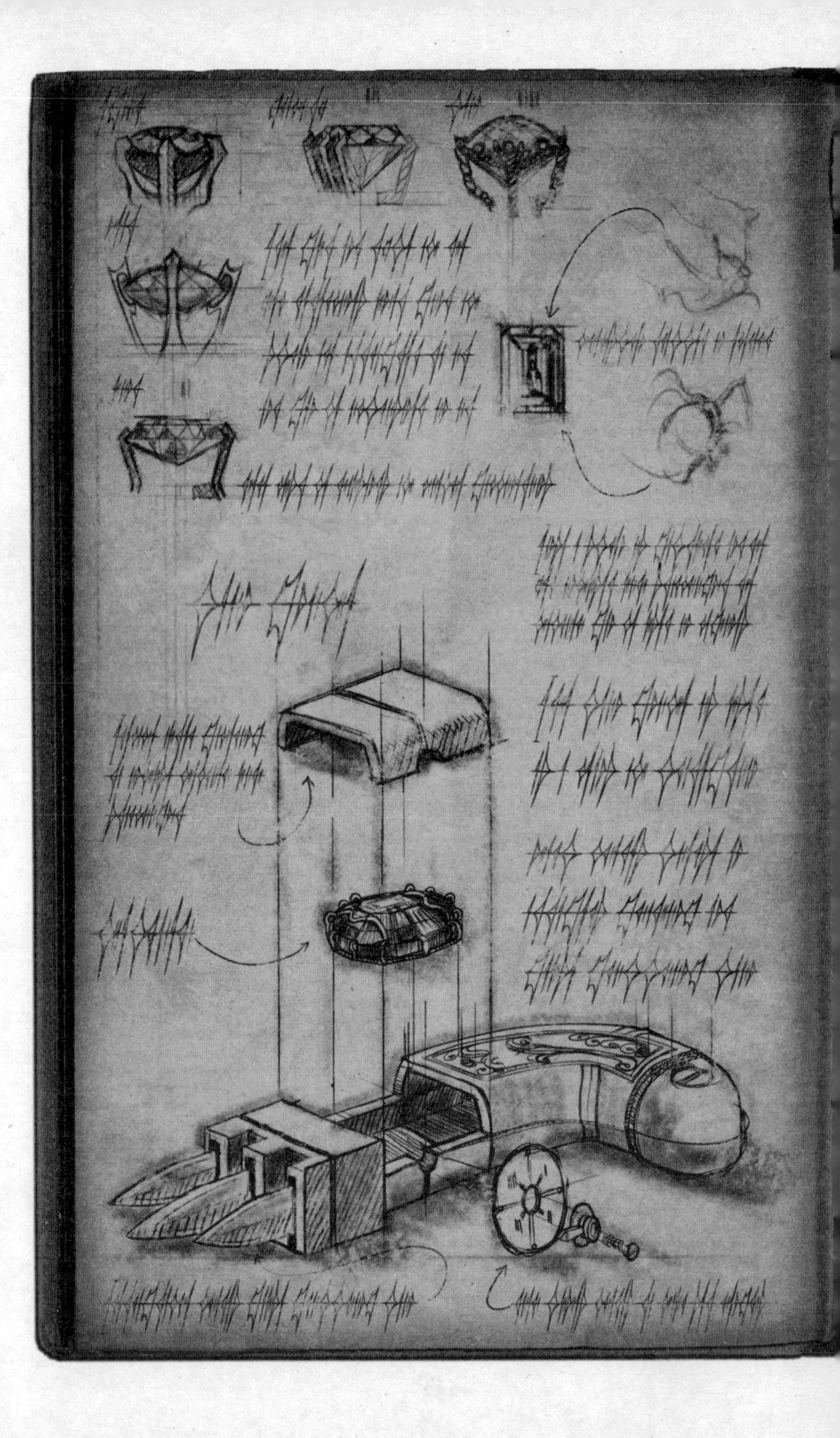

55
AN EMERALD BROAM

'A woman sits and scratches out her own eyes. Daughter of kings and winds, the vandal.'

—Dated Palahevan, 1173, 73 seconds pre-death. Subject: a beggar of some renown, known for his elegant songs.

One week after losing Dunny, Kaladin stood on another plateau, watching a battle proceed. This time, however, he didn't have to save the wounded. They'd actually arrived *before* the Parshendi. A rare but welcome event. Sadeas's army was now holding out at the center of the plateau, protecting the chrysalis while some of his soldiers cut into it.

The Parshendi kept leaping over the line and attacking the men working on the chrysalis. *He's getting surrounded*, Kaladin thought. It didn't look good, which would mean a miserable return trip. Sadeas's men were bad enough when, arriving second, they were rebuffed. Losing the gemheart after arriving first . . . would leave them even more frustrated.

'Kaladin!' a voice said. Kaladin spun to see Rock trotting up. Was someone wounded? 'Have you seen this thing?' The Horneater pointed.

Kaladin turned, following his gesture. Another army was approaching on an adjacent plateau. Kaladin raised eyebrows; the banners flapped blue, and the soldiers were obviously Alethi.

'A little late, aren't they?' Moash asked, standing beside Kaladin.

'It happens,' Kaladin said. Occasionally another highprince would arrive after Sadeas got to the plateau. More often, Sadeas arrived first, and the other Alethi army had to turn around. Usually they didn't get this close before doing so.

'That's the standard of Dalinar Kholin,' Skar said, joining them.

'Dalinar,' Moash said appreciatively. 'They say he doesn't use bridgemen.'

'How does he cross the chasms, then?' Kaladin asked.

The answer soon became obvious. This new army had enormous, siege-tower-like bridges pulled by chulls. They rumbled across the uneven plateaus, often having to pick their way around rifts in the stone. *They must be terribly slow*, Kaladin thought. But, in trade, the army wouldn't have to approach the chasm while being fired on. They could hide behind those bridges.

'Dalinar Kholin,' Moash said. 'They say he's a true lighteyes, like the men from the old days. A man of honor and of oaths.'

Kaladin snorted. 'I've seen plenty of lighteyes with that same reputation, and I've been disappointed by them every time. I'll tell you about Brightlord Amaram sometime.'

'Amaram?' Skar asked. 'The Shardbearer?'

'You've heard of that?' Kaladin asked.

'Sure,' Skar said. 'He's supposed to be on his way here. Everyone's talking about it in the taverns. Were you with him when he won his Shards?'

'No,' Kaladin said softly. 'Nobody was.'

Dalinar Kholin's army approached across the plateau to the south. Amazingly, Dalinar's army came right up to the battlefield plateau.

'He's attacking?' Moash said, scratching his head. 'Maybe he figures that Sadeas will lose, and wants to take a stab at it after he retreats.'

'No,' Kaladin said, frowning. 'He's joining the battle.'

The Parshendi army sent over some archers to fire on Dalinar's army, but their arrows bounced off the chulls without causing any harm. A group of soldiers unhooked the bridges and pushed them into place while Dalinar's archers set up and exchanged fire with the Parshendi.

'Does it seem Sadeas took fewer soldiers with him this run?' Sigzil asked, joining the group watching Dalinar's army. 'Perhaps he planned for this. Could be why he was willing to commit like he did, letting himself get surrounded.'

The bridges could be cranked to lower and extend; there was some marvelous engineering at work. As they began to work, something decidedly strange happened: Two Shardbearers, likely Dalinar and his son, leaped across the chasm and began attacking the Parshendi. The distraction let the soldiers get the large bridges into place, and some heavy cavalry charged across to help. It was a completely different method of doing a bridge assault, and Kaladin found himself considering the implications.

'He really *is* joining the battle,' Moash said. 'I think they're going to work together.'

'It's bound to be more effective,' Kaladin said. 'I'm surprised they haven't tried it before.'

Teft snorted. 'That's because you don't understand how lighteyes think. Highprinces don't just want to win the battle, they want to win it by themselves.'

'I wish I'd been recruited to his army instead,' Moash said, almost reverent. The soldiers' armor gleamed, their ranks obviously well-practiced. Dalinar – the Blackthorn – had done an even better job than Amaram at cultivating a reputation for honesty. People knew of him all the way back in Hearthstone, but Kaladin understood the kinds of corruption a well-polished breastplate could hide.

Though, he thought, *that man who protected the whore on the street, he wore blue. Adolin, Dalinar's son. He seemed genuinely selfless in his defense of the woman.*

Kaladin set his jaw, casting aside those thoughts. He would not be taken in again.

He would *not*.

The fighting grew brutal for a short time, but the Parshendi were overwhelmed – smashed between two opposing forces. Soon, Kaladin's team led a victorious group of soldiers back to the camps for celebration.

◆
◆ ◆

Kaladin rolled the sphere between his fingers. The otherwise pure glass had cooled with a thin line of bubbles permanently frozen along one side. The bubbles were tiny spheres of their own, catching light.

He was on chasm scavenging duty. They'd gotten back from the plateau assault so quickly that Hashal, in defiance of logic or mercy, had sent them down into the chasm that very day. Kaladin continued to turn the sphere in his fingers. Hanging in the very center of it was a large emerald cut in a round shape, with dozens of tiny facets along the sides. A small rim of suspended bubbles clung to the side of the gemstone, as if longing to be near its brilliance.

Bright, crystalline green Stormlight shone from inside the glass, lighting Kaladin's fingers. An emerald broam, the highest denomination of sphere. Worth hundreds of lesser spheres. To bridgemen, this was a fortune. A strangely distant one, for spending it was impossible. Kaladin thought he could see some of the storm's tempest inside that rock. The light was like . . . it was like part of the storm, captured by the emerald. The light wasn't perfectly steady; it just seemed that way compared with the flickering of candles, torches, or lamps. Holding it close, Kaladin could see the light swirling, raging.

'What do we do with it?' Moash asked from Kaladin's side. Rock stood at Kaladin's other side. The sky was overcast, making it darker than usual here at the bottom. The cold weather of late had drawn back to spring, though it was uncomfortably chilly.

The men worked efficiently, quickly gathering spears, armor, boots, and spheres from the dead. Because of the short time given them – and because of the exhausting bridge run earlier – Kaladin had decided to forgo spear practice for the day. They'd load up on salvage instead and stow some of it down beneath, to be used for avoiding punishment next time.

As they'd worked, they'd found a lighteyed officer. He had been quite wealthy. This single emerald broam was worth what a bridgeman slave would make in two hundred days. In the same pouch with it, they'd found a collection of chips and marks that totaled slightly more than another emerald broam. Wealth. A fortune. Simply pocket change to a lighteyes.

'With this we could feed those wounded bridgemen for months,' Moash said. 'We could buy all the medical supplies we could want. Stormfather! We could probably bribe the camp's perimeter guards to let us sneak away.'

'This thing will not happen,' Rock said. 'Is impossible to get spheres out of the chasms.'

'We could swallow them,' Moash said.

'You would choke. Spheres are too big, eh?'

'I'll bet I could do it,' Moash said. His eyes glittered, reflecting the verdant Stormlight. 'That's more money than I've ever seen. It's worth the risk.'

'Swallowing won't work,' Kaladin said. 'You think those guards who watch us in the latrines are there to keep us from fleeing? I'll bet some sodden parshman has to go through our droppings, and I've seen them keep record of who visits and how often. We aren't the first to think of swallowing spheres.'

Moash hesitated, then sighed, crestfallen. 'You're probably right. Storm you, but you are. But we can't just give it to them, can we?'

'Yes, we can,' Kaladin said, closing his fist around the sphere. The glow was bright enough to make his hand shine. 'We'd never be able to spend it. A bridgeman with a full broam? It would give us away.'

'But—' Moash began.

'We give it to them, Moash.' Then he held up the pouch containing the other spheres. 'But we find a way to keep these.'

Rock nodded. 'Yes. If we give up this expensive sphere, they will think us honest, eh? It will disguise the theft, and they will even give us small reward. But how can we do this thing, keeping the pouch?'

'I'm working on that,' Kaladin said.

'Work fast, then,' Moash said, glancing at Kaladin's torch, rammed between two rocks at the side of the chasm. 'We'll need to head back up soon.'

Kaladin opened his hand and rolled the emerald sphere between his fingers. How? 'Have you ever seen anything so beautiful?' Moash asked, staring at the emerald.

'It's just a sphere,' Kaladin said absently. 'A tool. I once held a goblet full of a hundred diamond broams and was told they were mine. Since I never got to spend them, they were as good as worthless.'

'A hundred diamonds?' Moash asked. 'Where . . . how?'

Kaladin closed his mouth, cursing himself. *I shouldn't keep mentioning things like that*. 'Go on,' he said, tucking the emerald broam back into the black pouch. 'We need to be quick.'

Moash sighed, but Rock thumped him on the back good-naturedly and they joined the rest of the bridgemen. Rock and Lopen – using Syl's directions – had led them to a large mass of corpses in red-and-brown uniforms. He didn't know which highprince's men they were, but the bodies were pretty fresh. There were no Parshendi among them.

Kaladin glanced to the side, where Shen – the parshman bridgeman – worked. Quiet, obedient, stalwart. Teft still didn't trust him. A part of Kaladin was glad for that. Syl landed on the wall beside him, standing with her feet planted against the surface and looking up at the sky.

Think, Kaladin told himself. *How do we keep these spheres? There has to be a way.* But each possibility seemed too much of a risk. If they were caught stealing, they'd probably be given a different work detail. Kaladin wasn't willing to risk that.

Silent green lifespren began to fade into existence around him, bobbing around the moss and haspers. A few frillblooms opened up fronds of red and yellow beside his head. Kaladin had thought again and again about Dunny's death. Bridge Four was not safe. True, they'd lost a remarkably small number of men lately, but they were still dwindling. And each bridge run was a chance for total disaster. All it took was one time, with the Parshendi focusing on them. Lose three or four men, and they'd topple. The waves of arrows would redouble, cutting every one of them down.

It was the same old problem, the one Kaladin had beaten his head against day after day. How did you protect bridgemen when everyone wanted them exposed and endangered?

'Hey Sig,' Maps said, walking by carrying an armload of spears. 'You're a Worldsinger, right?' Maps had grown increasingly friendly in the last few weeks, and had proven good at getting the others talking. The balding man reminded Kaladin of an innkeeper, always quick to make his patrons feel at ease.

Sigzil – who was pulling the boots off a line of corpses – gave Rock a straight-lipped glance that seemed to say, 'This is your fault.' He didn't like that others had discovered he was a Worldsinger.

'Why don't you give us a tale?' Maps said, setting down his armload. 'Help us pass the time.'

'I am not a foolish jester or storyteller,' Sigzil said, yanking off a boot. 'I do not "give tales." I spread knowledge of cultures, peoples, thoughts, and dreams. I bring peace through understanding. It is the holy charge my order received from the Heralds themselves.'

'Well why not start spreading then?' Maps said, standing and wiping his hands on his trousers.

Sigzil signed audibly. 'Very well. What is it you wish to hear about?'

'I don't know. Something interesting.'

'Tell us about Brightking Alazansi and the hundred-ship fleet,' Leyten called.

'I am not a storyteller!' Sigzil repeated. 'I speak of nations and peoples, not tavern stories. I—'

'Is there a place where people live in gouges in the ground?' Kaladin said. 'A city built in an enormous complex of lines, all set into the rock as if carved there?'

'Sesemalex Dar,' Sigzil said, nodding, pulling off another boot. 'Yes, it is the capital of the kingdom of Emul, and is one of the most ancient cities in the world. It is said that the city – and, indeed, the kingdom – were named by Jezrien himself.'

'Jezrien?' Malop said, standing and scratching his head. 'Who's that?' Malop was a thick-haired fellow with a bushy black beard and a glyphward tattoo on each hand. He also wasn't the brightest sphere in the goblet, so to speak.

'You call him the Stormfather, here in Alethkar,' Sigzil said. 'Or Jezerezeh'Elin. He was king of the Heralds. Master of the storms, bringer of water and life, known for his fury and his temper, but also for his mercy.'

'Oh,' Malop said.

'Tell me more of the city,' Kaladin said.

'Sesemalex Dar. It is, indeed, built in giant troughs. The pattern is quite amazing. It protects against highstorms, as each trough has a lip at the side, keeping water from streaming in off the stone plain around it. That, mixed with a drainage system of cracks, protects the city from flooding.

'The people there are known for their expert crem pottery; the city is a major waypoint in the southwest. The Emuli are a certain tribe of the Askarki people, and they're ethnically Makabaki – dark-skinned, like myself. Their kingdom borders my own, and I visited there many times in my youth.

'It is a wondrous place, filled with exotic travelers.' Sigzil grew more relaxed as he continued to talk. 'Their legal system is very lenient toward foreigners. A man who is not of their nationality cannot own a home or shop, but when you visit, you are treated as a 'relative who has traveled from afar, to be shown all kindness and leniency.' A foreigner can take dinner at any residence he calls upon, assuming he is respectful and offers a gift of fruit. The people are most interested in exotic fruits. They worship Jezrien, though they don't accept him as a figure from the Vorin religion. They name him the only god.'

'The Heralds aren't gods,' Teft scoffed.

'To you they aren't,' Sigzil said. 'Others regard them differently. The Emuli have what your scholars like to call a splinter religion – containing some Vorin ideas. But to the Emuli, you would be the splinter religion.' Sigzil seemed to find that amusing, though Teft just scowled.

Sigzil continued in more and more detail, talking of the flowing gowns and head-wraps of the Emuli women, the robes favored by the men. The taste of the food – salty – and the way of greeting an old friend – by holding the left forefinger to the forehead and bowing in respect. Sigzil knew an impressive amount about them. Kaladin noticed him smiling wistfully at times, probably recalling his travels.

The details were interesting, but Kaladin was more taken aback by the fact that this city – which he had flown over in his dream weeks ago – was actually real. And he could no longer ignore the strange speed at which he recovered from wounds. Something odd was happening to him. Something supernatural. What if it was related to the fact that everyone around him always seemed to die?

He knelt down to begin rifling the pockets of the dead men, a duty the other bridgemen avoided. Spheres, knives, and other useful objects were kept. Personal mementoes like unburned prayers were left with the bodies. He found a few zircon chips, which he added to the pouch.

Maybe Moash was right. If they could get this money out, could they *bribe* their way free of the camp? That would certainly be safer than fighting. So why was he so insistent on teaching the bridgemen to fight? Why hadn't he given any thought to sneaking the bridgemen out?

He had lost Dallet and the others of his original squad in Amaram's army. Did he think to compensate for that by training a new group of spearmen? Was this about saving men he'd grown to love, or was it just about proving something to himself?

His experience told him that men who could not fight were at a severe disadvantage in this world of war and storms. Perhaps sneaking out would have been the better option, but he knew little of stealth. Besides, if they sneaked away, Sadeas would still send troops after them. Trouble would track them down. Whatever their path, the bridgemen would have to kill to remain free.

He squeezed his eyes shut, remembering one of his escape attempts, when he'd kept his fellow slaves free for an entire week, hiding in the wilderness. They'd finally been caught by their master's hunters. That was when he'd lost Nalma. *None of that has to do with saving them here and now*, Kaladin told himself. *I need these spheres.*

Sigzil was still talking about the Emuli. 'To them,' the Worldsinger said, 'the need to strike a man personally is crass. They wage war in the opposite way from you Alethi. The sword is not a weapon for a leader. A halberd is better, then a spear, and best of all a bow and arrow.'

Kaladin pulled another handful of spheres – skychips – from a soldier's pocket. They were stuck to an aged hunk of sow's cheese, fragrant and moldy. He grimaced, picking the spheres out and washing them in a puddle.

'Spears, used by lighteyes?' Drehy said. 'That's ridiculous.'

'Why?' Sigzil said, sounding offended. 'I find the Emuli way to be interesting. In some countries, it is seen as displeasing to fight at all. To the Shin, for instance, if you must fight a man, then you have already failed. Killing is, at best, a brutish way of solving problems.'

'You're not going to be like Rock and refuse to fight, are you?' Skar asked, shooting a barely veiled glare at the Horneater. Rock sniffed and turned his back on the shorter man, kneeling down to shove boots into a large sack.

'No,' Sigzil said. 'I think we can all agree that other methods have failed. Perhaps if my master knew I still lived . . . but no. That is foolish. Yes, I will fight. And if I have to, the spear seems a favorable weapon, though I honestly would prefer to put more distance between myself and my enemies.'

Kaladin frowned. 'You mean with a bow?'

Sigzil nodded. 'Among my people, the bow is a noble weapon.'

'Do you know how to use one?'

'Alas, no,' Sigzil said. 'I would have mentioned it before now if I had such proficiency.'

Kaladin stood up, opening the pouch and depositing the spheres in with the others. 'Were there any bows among the bodies?'

The men glanced at each other, several of them shaking heads. *Storm it*, Kaladin thought. The seed of an idea had begun to sprout in his mind, but that killed it.

'Gather up some of those spears,' he said. 'Set them aside. We'll need them for training.'

'But we have to turn them in,' Malop said.

'Not if we don't take them with us up out of the chasm,' Kaladin said. 'Each time we come scavenging, we'll save a few spears and stash them down here. It shouldn't take long to gather enough to practice with.'

'How will we get them out when it's time to escape?' Teft asked, rubbing his chin. 'Spears left down here won't do these lads much good once the real fighting starts.'

'I'll find a way to get them up,' Kaladin said.

'You say things like that a lot,' Skar noted.

'Leave off, Skar,' Moash said. 'He knows what he's doing.'

Kaladin blinked. Had *Moash* just defended him?

Skar flushed. 'I didn't mean it like that, Kaladin. I'm just asking, that's all.'

'I understand. It's . . .' Kaladin trailed off as Syl flitted down into the chasm in the form of a curling ribbon.

She landed on a rock outcropping on the wall, taking on her female form. 'I found another group of bodies. They're mostly Parshendi.'

'Any bows?' Kaladin asked. Several of the bridgemen gawked at him until they saw him staring into the air. Then they nodded knowingly to one another.

'I think so,' Syl said. 'It's just down this way. Not too far.'

The bridgemen had mostly finished with these bodies. 'Gather up the things,' Kaladin said. 'I've found us another place to scavenge. We need to gather as much as we can, then stash some in a chasm where it has a good chance of not being washed away.'

The bridgemen picked up their findings, slinging sacks over their shoulders and each man hefting a spear or two. Within moments, they headed down the dank chasm bottom, following Syl. They passed clefts in the ancient rock walls where old, storm-washed bones had gotten lodged, creating a mound of moss-covered femurs, tibia, skulls, and ribs. There wasn't much salvage among them.

After about a quarter-hour, they came to the place Syl had found. A scattered group of Parshendi dead lay in heaps, mixed with the occasional Alethi in blue. Kaladin knelt beside one of the human bodies. He recognized Dalinar Kholin's stylized glyphpair sewn on the coat. Why *had* Dalinar's army joined Sadeas's in battle? What had changed?

Kaladin pointed for the men to begin scavenging from the Alethi while he walked over to one of the Parshendi corpses. It was much fresher than Dalinar's man. They didn't find nearly as many Parshendi corpses as they did Alethi. Not only were there fewer of them in any given battle, but they were less likely to fall to their deaths into the chasms. Sigzil also guessed that their bodies were more dense than human ones, and didn't float or wash away as easily.

Kaladin rolled the body onto its side, and the action elicited a sudden hiss from the back of the group of bridgemen. Kaladin turned to see Shen pushing forward in an uncharacteristic display of passion.

Teft moved quickly, grabbing Shen from behind, placing him in a choke hold. The other bridgemen stood, aghast, though several fell into their stances by reflex.

Shen struggled weakly against Teft's grip. The parshman looked different from his dead cousins; close together, the differences were much more obvious. Shen – like most parshmen – was short and a little plump. Stout, strong, but not threatening. The corpse at Kaladin's feet, however, was muscled and built like a Horneater, easily as tall as Kaladin and far broader at the shoulders. While both had the marbled skin, the Parshendi had those strange red-orange growths of armor on the head, chest, arms, and legs.

'Let him go,' Kaladin said, curious.

Teft glanced at him, then reluctantly did as commanded. Shen scrambled over the uneven ground and gently, but firmly, pushed Kaladin away from the corpse. Shen stood back, as if protecting it from Kaladin.

'This thing,' Rock noted, stepping up beside Kaladin, 'he has done it before. When Lopen and I take him scavenging.'

'He's protective of the Parshendi bodies, gancho,' Lopen added. 'Like he'd stab you a hundred times for moving one, sure.'

'They're all like that,' Sigzil said from behind.

Kaladin turned, raising an eyebrow.

'Parshman workers,' Sigzil explained. 'They're allowed to care for their own dead; it's one of the few things they seem passionate about. They grow irate if anyone else handles the bodies. They wrap them in linen and carry them out into the wilderness and leave them on slabs of stone.'

Kaladin regarded Shen. *I wonder. . . .*

'Scavenge from the Parshendi,' Kaladin said to his men. 'Teft, you'll probably have to hold Shen the whole time. I can't have him trying to stop us.'

Teft shot Kaladin a suffering glance; he still thought they should set Shen at the front of the bridge and let him die. But he did as told, pushing Shen away and getting Moash's help to hold him.

'And men,' Kaladin noted, 'be respectful of the dead.'

'They're Parshendi!' Leyten objected.

'I know,' Kaladin said. 'But it bothers Shen. He's one of us, so let's keep his irritation to a minimum.'

The parshman lowered his arms reluctantly and let Teft and Moash pull him away. He seemed resigned. Parshmen were slow of thought. How much did Shen comprehend?

'Didn't you wish to find a bow?' Sigzil asked, kneeling and slipping a horned Parshendi shortbow out from underneath a body. 'The bowstring is gone.'

'There's another in this fellow's pouch,' Maps said, pulling something out of another Parshendi corpse's belt pouch. 'Might still be good.'

Kaladin accepted the weapon and string. 'Does anyone know how to use one of these?'

The bridgemen glanced at one another. Bows were useless for hunting most shellbeasts; slings worked far better. The bow was really only good for killing other men. Kaladin glanced at Teft, who shook his head. He hadn't been trained on a bow; neither had Kaladin.

'Is simple,' Rock said, rolling over a Parshendi corpse, 'put arrow on string. Point away from self. Pull very hard. Let go.'

'I doubt it will be that easy,' Kaladin said.

'We barely have time to train the lads in the spear, Kaladin,' Teft said. 'You mean to teach some of them the bow as well? And without a teacher who can use one himself?'

Kaladin didn't respond. He tucked the bow and string away in his bag, added a few arrows, then helped the others. An hour later, they marched through the chasms toward the ladder, their torches sputtering, dusk approaching. The darker it grew, the more unpleasant the chasms became. Shadows deepened, and distant sounds – water dripping, rocks falling, wind calling – took on an ominous cast. Kaladin rounded a corner, and a group of many-legged cremlings scuttled along the wall and slipped into a fissure.

Conversation was subdued, and Kaladin didn't take part. Occasionally, he glanced over his shoulder toward Shen. The silent parshman walked head down. Robbing the Parshendi corpses had seriously disturbed him.

I can use that, Kaladin thought. *But dare I?* It would be a risk. A great one. He had already been sentenced once for upsetting the balance of the chasm battles.

First the spheres, he thought. Getting the spheres out would mean he might be able to get out other items. Eventually he saw a shadow above, spanning the chasm. They had reached the first of the permanent bridges. Kaladin walked with the others a little further, until they reached a place where the chasm floor was closer to the top of the plateaus above.

He stopped here. The bridgemen gathered around him.

'Sigzil,' Kaladin said, pointing. 'You know something about bows. How hard do you think it would be to hit that bridge with an arrow?'

'I've occasionally held a bow, Kaladin, but I would not call myself an expert. It shouldn't be too hard, I'd imagine. The distance is what, fifty feet?'

'What's the point?' Moash asked.

Kaladin pulled out the pouch full of spheres, then raised an eyebrow at them. 'We tie the bag to the arrow, then launch it up so that it sticks to the bottom of the bridge. Then when we're on a bridge run, Lopen and Dabbid can hang back to get a drink near that bridge up there. They reach under the wood and pull the arrow off. We get the spheres.'

Teft whistled. 'Clever.'

'We could get all of the spheres,' Moash said eagerly. 'Even the—'

'No,' Kaladin said firmly. 'The lesser ones will be dangerous enough; people might begin wondering where bridgemen are getting so much money.' He would have to buy his supplies from several different apothecaries to hide his influx of money.

Moash looked crestfallen, but the other bridgemen were eager. 'Who wants to try?' Kaladin asked. 'Maybe we should shoot a few practice shots first, then try with the bag. Sigzil?'

'I don't know if I want this on me,' Sigzil said. 'Maybe you should try, Teft.'

Teft rubbed his chin. 'Sure. I guess. How hard can it be?'

'How hard?' Rock asked suddenly.

Kaladin glanced to the side. Rock stood at the back of the group, though his height made him easy to see. He had his arms folded.

'How hard, Teft?' Rock continued. 'Fifty feet is not too far, but is not easy shot. And to do it with bag of heavy spheres tied to it? Ha! You also need to get arrow close to side of bridge, so Lopen can reach. If you miss with this thing, you could lose all spheres. And what if scouts near bridges above see arrow come from chasm? Will think it suspicious, eh?'

Kaladin eyed the Horneater. *Is simple*, he'd said. *Point away from self . . . let go . . .*

'Well,' Kaladin said, watching Rock from the corner of his eye. 'I guess we'll just have to take that chance. Without these spheres, the wounded die.'

'We could wait until the next bridge run,' Teft said. 'Tie a rope to the bridge and toss it over, then tie the bag to it next time. . . .'

'Fifty feet of rope?' Kaladin said flatly. 'It would draw enough attention to buy something like that.'

'Nah, gancho,' Lopen said. 'I have a cousin who works in a place that sells rope. I could get some for you easy, with money.'

'Perhaps,' Kaladin said. 'But you'd still have to hide it in the litter, then hang it down into the chasm without anyone seeing. And to leave it dangling there for several days? It would be noticed.'

The others nodded. Rock seemed very uncomfortable. Sighing, Kaladin took out the bow and several arrows. 'We'll just have to chance this. Teft, why don't you . . .'

'Oh, Kali'kalin's ghost,' Rock muttered. 'Here, give me bow.' He shoved his way through the bridgemen, taking the bow from Kaladin. Kaladin hid a smile.

Rock glanced upward, judging the distance in the waning light. He strung the bowstring, then held out a hand. Kaladin handed him an arrow. He leveled the bow back down the chasm and launched. The arrow flew swiftly, clattering against chasm walls.

Rock nodded to himself, then pointed at Kaladin's pouch. 'We take only five spheres,' Rock said. 'Any more would be too heavy. Is crazy to try with even five. Airsick lowlanders.'

Kaladin smiled, then counted out five sapphire marks – together about two and a half months' worth of pay for a bridgeman – and placed them in a spare pouch. He handed that to Rock, who pulled out a knife and dug a notch into an arrow's shaft near the arrowhead.

Skar folded his arms and leaned against the mossy wall. 'This is stealing, you know.'

'Yes,' Kaladin said, watching Rock. 'And I don't feel the least bit bad about it. Do you?'

'Not at all,' Skar said, grinning. 'I figure once someone is trying to get you killed, all expectations of your loyalty are tossed to the storm. But if someone were to go to Gaz ...'

The other bridgemen suddenly grew nervous, and more than a few eyes darted toward Shen, though Kaladin could see that Skar wasn't thinking of the parshman. If one of the bridgemen were to betray the rest of them, he might earn himself a reward.

'Maybe we should post a watch,' Drehy said. 'You know, make sure nobody sneaks off to talk to Gaz.'

'We'll do no such thing,' Kaladin said. 'What are we going to do? Lock ourselves in the barrack, so suspicious of each other that we never get anything done?' He shook his head. 'No. This is just one more danger. It's a real one, but we can't waste energy spying on each other. So we keep on going.'

Skar didn't look convinced.

'We're Bridge Four,' Kaladin said firmly. 'We've faced death together. We have to trust each other. You can't run into battle wondering if your comrades are going to switch sides suddenly.' He met the eyes of each man in turn. 'I trust you. All of you. We'll make it through this, and we'll do it together.'

There were several nods; Skar seemed placated. Rock finished his work cutting the arrow, then proceeded to tie the pouch tightly around the shaft.

Syl still sat on Kaladin's shoulder. 'You want me to watch the others? Make sure nobody does what Skar thinks they might?'

Kaladin hesitated, then nodded. Best to be safe. He just didn't want the men to have to think that way.

Rock hefted the arrow, judging the weight. 'Near impossible shot,' he complained. Then, in a smooth motion, he nocked the arrow and drew to his cheek, positioning himself directly beneath the bridge. The small pouch hung down, dangling against the wood of the arrow. The bridgemen held their breath.

Rock loosed. The arrow streaked up the side of the chasm wall, almost too fast to follow. A faint click sounded as arrow met wood, and Kaladin held his breath, but the arrow did not pull free. It remained hanging there, precious spheres tied to its shaft, right next to the side of the bridge where it could be reached.

Kaladin clapped Rock on the shoulder as the bridgemen cheered him.

Rock eyed Kaladin. 'I will not use bow to fight. You must know this thing.'

'I promise,' Kaladin said. 'I'll take you if you agree, but I won't force you.'

'I will not fight,' Rock said. 'Is not my place.' He glanced up at the spheres, then smiled faintly. 'But shooting bridge is all right.'

'How did you learn?' Kaladin asked.

'Is secret,' Rock said firmly. 'Take bow. Bother me no more.'

'All right,' Kaladin said, accepting the bow. 'But I don't know if I can promise not to bother you. I may need a few more shots in the future.' He eyed Lopen. 'You really think you can buy some rope without drawing attention?'

Lopen lounged back against the wall. 'My cousin's never failed me.'

'How many cousins do you have, anyway?' Earless Jaks asked.

'A man can never have enough cousins,' Lopen said.

'Well, we need that rope,' Kaladin said, the plan beginning to sprout in his mind. 'Do it, Lopen. I'll make change from those spheres above to pay for it.'

'Light grows so distant. The storm never stops. I am broken, and all around me have died. I weep for the end of all things. He has won. Oh, he has beaten us.'

—Dated Palahakev, 1173, 16 seconds pre-death. Subject: a Thaylen sailor.

Dalinar fought, the Thrill pulsing within him, swinging his Shardblade from atop Gallant's back. Around him, Parshendi fell with eyes burning black.

They came at him in pairs, each team trying to hit him from a different direction, keeping him busy and – they hoped – disoriented. If a pair could rush at him while he was distracted, they might be able to shove him off his mount. Those axes and maces – swung repeatedly – could crack his Plate. It was a very costly tactic; corpses lay scattered around Dalinar. But when fighting against a Shardbearer, every tactic was costly.

Dalinar kept Gallant moving, dancing from side to side, as he swung his Blade in broad sweeps. He stayed just a little ahead of the line of his men. A Shardbearer needed space to fight; the Blades were so long that hurting one's companions was a very real danger. His honor guard would approach only if he fell or encountered trouble.

The Thrill excited him, strengthened him. He hadn't experienced the weakness again, the nausea he had on the battlefield that day weeks ago. Perhaps he'd been worried about nothing.

He turned Gallant just in time to confront two pairs of Parshendi coming at him from behind, singing softly. He directed Gallant with his knees, performing an expert sweeping side-swing, cutting through the necks of two Parshendi, then the arm of a third. Eyes burned out in the first two, and they collapsed. The third dropped his weapon from a hand that grew suddenly lifeless, flopping down, its nerves all severed.

The fourth member of that squad scrambled away, glaring at Dalinar. This was one of the Parshendi who didn't wear a beard, and it seemed that there was something odd about his face. The cheek structure was just a little off. . . .

Was that a woman? Dalinar thought with amazement. *It couldn't have been. Could it?*

Behind him, his soldiers let out cheers as a large number of Parshendi scattered away to regroup. Dalinar lowered his Shardblade, the metal gleaming, gloryspren winking into the air around him. There was another reason for him to stay out ahead of his men. A Shardbearer wasn't just a force of destruction; he was a force of morale and inspiration. The men fought more vigorously as they saw their brightlord felling foe after foe. Shardbearers changed battles.

Since the Parshendi were broken for the moment, Dalinar climbed free of Gallant and dropped to the rocks. Corpses lay unbloodied all around him, though once he approached the place where his men had been fighting, orange-red blood stained the rocks. Cremlings scuttled about on the ground, lapping up the liquid, and painspren wriggled between them. Wounded Parshendi lay staring up into the air, faces masks of pain, singing a quiet, haunting song to themselves. Often just as whispers. They never yelled as they died.

Dalinar felt the Thrill retreat as he joined his honor guard. 'They're getting too close to Gallant,' Dalinar said to Teleb, handing over the reins. The massive Ryshadium's coat was flecked with frothy sweat. 'I don't want to risk him. Have a man run him to the back lines.'

Teleb nodded, waving a soldier to obey the order. Dalinar hefted his Shardblade, scanning the battlefield. The Parshendi force was regrouping. As always, the two-person teams were the focus of their strategy. Each pair would have different weapons, and often one was clean-shaven while the other had a beard woven with gemstones. His scholars had suggested this was some kind of primitive apprenticeship.

Dalinar inspected the clean-shaven ones for signs of any stubble. There was none, and more than a few had a faintly feminine shape to their faces. Could the ones without beards all be women? They didn't appear to have much in the way of breasts, and their builds were like those of men, but the strange Parshendi armor could be masking things. The beardless ones *did* seem smaller by a few fingers, and the shapes of the faces . . . studying them, it seemed possible. Could the pairs be husbands and wives fighting together? That struck him as strangely fascinating. Was it possible that, despite six years of war, nobody had taken the time to investigate the genders of those they fought?

Yes. The contested plateaus were so far out, nobody ever brought back Parshendi bodies; they just set men to pulling the gemstones out of their beards or gathering their weapons. Since Gavilar's death, very little effort had been given to studying the Parshendi. Everyone just wanted them dead, and if there was one thing the Alethi were good at, it was killing.

And you're *supposed to be killing them now*, Dalinar told himself, *not analyzing their culture*. But he did decide to have his soldiers collect a few bodies for the scholars.

He charged toward another section of the battlefield, Shardblade before him in two hands, making certain not to outpace his soldiers. To the south, he could see Adolin's banner flying as he led his division against the Parshendi there. The lad had been uncharacteristically reserved lately. Being wrong about Sadeas seemed to have made him more contemplative.

On the west side, Sadeas's own banner flew proudly, Sadeas's forces keeping the Parshendi from the chrysalis. He'd arrived first, as before, engaging the Parshendi so Dalinar's companies could arrive. Dalinar had considered cutting out the gemheart so the Alethi could retreat, but why end the battle that quickly? He and Sadeas both felt the real point of their alliance was to crush as many Parshendi as possible.

The more they killed, the faster this war would be through. And so far, Dalinar's plan was working. The two armies complemented one another. Dalinar's assaults had been too slow, and he'd allowed the Parshendi to position themselves too well. Sadeas was fast – more so now that he could leave men behind and concentrate fully on speed – and he was frighteningly effective at getting men onto the plateaus to fight, but his men weren't trained as well as Dalinar's. So if Sadeas could arrive first, then hold out long enough for Dalinar to get his men across, the superior training – and superior Shards – of his forces worked like a hammer against the Parshendi, smashing them against Sadeas's anvil.

It was still by no means easy. The Parshendi fought like chasmfiends.

Dalinar crashed against them, swinging out with his Blade, slaying Parshendi on all sides. He couldn't help but feel a grudging respect for the Parshendi. Few men dared assault a Shardbearer directly – at least not without the entire weight of their army forcing them forward, almost against their will.

These Parshendi attacked with bravery. Dalinar spun, laying about him, the Thrill surging within. With an ordinary sword, a fighter focused on controlling his blows, striking and expecting recoil. You wanted quick, rapid strikes with small arcs. A Shardblade was different. The Blade was enormous, yet remarkably light. There was never recoil; landing a blow felt nearly like passing the sword through the air itself. The trick was to control momentum and keep the sword moving.

Four Parshendi threw themselves at him; they seemed to know that working into close quarters was one of the best ways to drop him. If they got too close, the length of his Blade's hilt and the nature of his armor would make fighting more difficult for him. Dalinar spun in a long, waist-high attack, and noted the deaths of Parshendi by the slight tug on the Blade as it passed through their chests. He got all four of them, and felt a surge of satisfaction.

It was followed immediately by nausea.

Damnation! he thought. *Not again!* He turned toward another group of Parshendi as the eyes of the dead burned out and smoked.

He threw himself into another attack – raising his Blade in a twisting swing over his head, then bringing it down parallel to the ground. Six Parshendi died. He felt a spike of regret along with displeasure at the Thrill. Surely these Parshendi – these soldiers – deserved respect, not glee, as they were slaughtered.

He remembered the times when the Thrill had been the strongest. Subduing the highprinces with Gavilar during their youths, forcing back the Vedens, fighting the Herdazians and destroying the Akak Reshi. Once, the thirst for battle had nearly led him to attack Gavilar himself. Dalinar could remember the jealousy on that day some ten years ago, when the itch to attack Gavilar – the only worthy opponent he could see, the man who had won Navani's hand – had nearly consumed him.

His honor guard cheered as his foes dropped. He felt hollow, but he seized the Thrill and got a tight grip on his feelings and emotions. He let the Thrill pulse through him. Blessedly, the sickness went away, which was good, for another group of Parshendi charged him from the side. He executed a Windstance turn, shifting his feet, lowering his shoulder, and throwing his weight behind his Blade as he swung.

He got three in the sweep, but the fourth and final Parshendi shoved past his wounded comrades, getting inside Dalinar's reach, swinging his hammer. His eyes were wide with anger and determination, though he did not yell or bellow. He just continued his song.

His blow cracked into Dalinar's helm. It pushed his head to the side but the Plate absorbed most of the hit, a few tiny weblike lines cracking along its length. Dalinar could see them glowing faintly, releasing Stormlight at the edges of his vision.

The Parshendi was in too close. Dalinar dropped his Blade. The weapon puffed away to mist as Dalinar raised an armored arm and blocked the next hammer blow. Then he swung with his other arm, smashing his fist into the Parshendi's shoulder. The blow tossed the man to the ground. The Parshendi's song cut off. Gritting his teeth, Dalinar stepped up and kicked the man in the chest, throwing the body a good twenty feet through the air. He'd learned to be wary of Parshendi who weren't fully incapacitated.

Dalinar lowered his hands and began to resummon his Shardblade. He felt strong again, passion for battle returning to him. *I shouldn't feel bad for killing the Parshendi*, he thought. *This is right.*

He paused, noticing something. What was that on the next plateau over? It looked like . . .

Like a second Parshendi army.

Several groups of his scouts were dashing toward the main battle lines, but Dalinar could guess the news they brought. 'Stormfather!' he cursed, pointing with his Shardblade. 'Pass the warning! A second army approaches!'

Several men scattered in accordance to his command. *We should have expected this*, Dalinar thought. *We started bringing two armies to a plateau, so they have done the same.*

But that implied that they had limited themselves before. Did they do it because they realized that the battlefields left little room for maneuvering? Or was it for speed? But that didn't make sense – the Alethi had to worry about bridges as choke points, slowing them more and more if they brought more troops. But the Parshendi could jump the chasms. So why commit fewer troops than their all?

Curse it all, he thought with frustration. *We know so little about them!*

He shoved his Shardblade into the rock beside him, placing it intentionally so that it didn't vanish. He began calling out orders. His honor guard formed around him, ushering in scouts and sending out runners. For a short time, he became a tactical general rather than an advance warrior.

It took time to change their battlefield strategy. An army was like a massive chull at times, lumbering along, slow to react. Before his orders could be executed, the new Parshendi force began crossing over onto the north side. That was where Sadeas was fighting. Dalinar couldn't get a good view, and scout reports were taking too long.

He glanced to the side; there was a tall rock formation nearby. It had uneven sides, making it look a little like a pile of boards stacked one atop another. He grabbed his Shardblade in the middle of a report and ran across the stony ground, smashing a few Rockbuds beneath his plated boots. The Cobalt Guard and the messengers followed quickly.

At the rock formation, Dalinar tossed his Blade aside, letting it dissolve to smoke. He threw himself up and grabbed the rock, scaling the formation. Seconds later, he heaved himself up onto its flat top.

The battlefield stretched out below him. The main Parshendi army was a mass of red and black at the center of the plateau, now pressed on two sides by the Alethi. Sadeas's bridge crews waited on a western plateau, ignored, while the new force of Parshendi crossed from the north onto the battlefield.

Stormfather, but they can jump, Dalinar thought, watching the Parshendi span the gap in powerful leaps. Six years of fighting had shown Dalinar that human soldiers – particularly if lightly armored – could outrun Parshendi troops if they had to go more than a few dozen yards. But those thick, powerful Parshendi legs could send them far when they leaped.

Not a single Parshendi lost his footing as they crossed the chasm. They approached the chasm at a trot, then dashed with a burst of speed for about ten feet, launching themselves forward. The new force pushed south, directly into Sadeas's army. Raising a hand against the bright white sunlight, Dalinar found he could make out Sadeas's personal banner.

It was directly in the path of the oncoming Parshendi force; he tended to remain at the back of his armies, in a secure position. Now, that position suddenly became the front lines, and Sadeas's other troops were too slow to disengage and react. He didn't have any support.

Sadeas! Dalinar thought, stepping right up to the lip of the stone, his cape streaming behind him in the breeze. *I need to send him my reserve spearmen—*

But no, they'd be too slow.

The spearmen couldn't get to him. But someone mounted might be able to.

'Gallant!' Dalinar bellowed, throwing himself off the rock formation. He fell to the rocks below, Plate absorbing the shock as he hit, cracking the stone. Stormlight puffed up around him, rising from his armor, and the greaves cracked slightly.

Gallant pulled away from his minders, galloping across the stones at Dalinar's call. As the horse approached, Dalinar grabbed the saddle-holds and heaved himself up and into place. 'Follow if you can,' he bellowed at his honor guard, 'and send a runner to tell my son he now commands our army!'

Dalinar reared Gallant and galloped alongside the perimeter of the battlefield. His guard called for their horses, but they'd have difficulty keeping up with a Ryshadium.

So be it.

Fighting soldiers became a blur to Dalinar's right. He leaned low in the saddle, wind hissing as it blew over his Shardplate. He held a hand out and summoned Oathbringer. It dropped into his hand, steaming and frosted, as he turned Gallant around the western tip of the battlefield. By design, the original Parshendi army lay between his force and Sadeas's. He didn't have time to round them. So, taking a deep breath, Dalinar struck out through the middle of it. Their ranks were spread out because of how they fought.

Gallant galloped through them, and Parshendi threw themselves out of the massive stallion's way, cursing in their melodic language. Hooves beat a thunder upon the rocks; Dalinar urged Gallant on with his knees.

They had to keep momentum. Some Parshendi fighting on the front against Sadeas's force turned and ran at him. They saw the opportunity. If Dalinar fell, he'd land alone, surrounded by thousands of enemies.

Dalinar's heart thumped as he held his Blade out, trying to swipe at Parshendi who came too close. Within minutes, he approached the northwestern Parshendi line. There, his enemies formed up, raising spears and setting them against the ground.

Blast! Dalinar thought. Parshendi had never set spears like that against heavy cavalry before. They were starting to learn.

Dalinar charged the formation, then wheeled Gallant at the last moment, turning parallel to the Parshendi spear wall. He swung his Shardblade out to the side, shearing the tips from their weapons and hitting a few arms. A patch of Parshendi just ahead wavered, and Dalinar took a deep breath, urging Gallant directly into them, shearing off a few spear tips. Another one bounced off his shoulder armor, and Gallant took a long gash on the left flank.

Their momentum carried them forward, trampling over the Parshendi, and with a whinny, Gallant burst free of the Parshendi line just to the side of where Sadeas's main force was engaging the enemy.

Dalinar's heart pumped. He passed Sadeas's force in a blur, galloping toward the back lines, where a churning, disorganized chaos of men tried to react to the new Parshendi force. Men screamed and died, a mess of forest green Alethi and Parshendi in black and red.

There! Dalinar saw Sadeas's banner flap for a moment before falling. He threw himself from Gallant's saddle and hit the stones. The horse turned away, understanding. His wound was bad, and Dalinar would not risk him any further.

It was time for the slaughter to begin again.

He tore into the Parshendi force from the side, and some turned, looks of surprise in their usually stoic black eyes. At times the Parshendi seemed alien, but their emotions were so human. The Thrill rose and Dalinar did not force it down. He needed it too much. An ally was in danger.

It was time to let the Blackthorn loose.

Dalinar punched through the Parshendi ranks. He felled Parshendi like a man sweeping crumbs from the table after a meal. There was no controlled precision here, no careful engagement of a few squads with his honor guard at the back. This was a full-out attack, with all the power and deadly force of a life-long killer enhanced by Shards. He was like a tempest, slashing through legs, torsos, arms, necks, killing, killing, killing. He was a maelstrom of death and steel. Weapons bounced off his armor, leaving tiny cracks. He killed dozens, always moving, forcing his way toward where Sadeas's banner had fallen.

Eyes burned, swords flashed in the sky, and Parshendi sang. The close press of their own troops – bunching up as they hit Sadeas's line – inhibited them. But not Dalinar. He didn't have to worry about striking friends, nor did he have to worry about his weapon getting caught in flesh or stuck in armor. And if corpses got in his way, he sheared through them – dead flesh would cut like steel and wood.

Parshendi blood splashed in the air as he killed, then hacked, then shoved his way through the press. Blade from shoulder to side, back and forth, occasionally turning to sweep at those trying to kill him from behind.

He stumbled on a swath of green cloth. Sadeas's banner. Dalinar spun, searching. Behind him, he'd left a line of corpses that was quickly yet carefully being stepped past by more Parshendi focused on him. Except just to his left. None of the Parshendi there turned toward him.

Sadeas! Dalinar thought, leaping forward, cutting down Parshendi from behind. That revealed a group of them bunched in a circle, beating on something below them. Something leaking Stormlight.

Just to the side lay a large Shardbearer's hammer, fallen where Sadeas had apparently dropped it. Dalinar leaped forward, dropping his Blade and grabbing the hammer. He roared as he slammed it into the group, tossing a dozen Parshendi away from him, then turned and swung again on the other side. Bodies sprayed into the air, hurled backward.

The hammer worked better in such close quarters; the Blade would simply have killed the men, dropping their corpses to the ground, leaving him still pressed and pinned. The hammer, however, flung the bodies away. He leaped into the middle of the area he'd just cleared, positioning himself with one foot on either side of the fallen Sadeas. He began the process of summoning his Blade again and laid about him with the hammer, scattering his enemies.

At the ninth beat of his heart, he threw the hammer into the face of a Parshendi, then let Oathbringer reform in his hands. He fell immediately into Windstance, glancing downward. Sadeas's armor leaked Stormlight from a dozen different breaks and rifts. The breastplate had been shattered completely; broken, jagged bits of metal jutted out, revealing the uniform underneath. Wisps of radiant smoke trailed from the holes.

There was no time to check if he still lived. The Parshendi now saw not one, but two Shardbearers within their grasp, and they threw themselves at Dalinar. Warrior after warrior fell as Dalinar slaughtered them in sweeps, protecting the space just around him.

He couldn't stop them all. His armor took hits, mostly on the arms and back. The armor cracked, like a crystal under too much stress.

He roared, striking down four Parshendi as two more hit him from behind, making his armor vibrate. He spun and killed one, the other barely dancing out of range. Dalinar began to pant, and when he moved quickly, he left trails of blue Stormlight in the air. He felt like a bloodied prey beast trying to fend off a thousand different snapping predators at once.

But he was no chull, whose only protection was to hide. He killed, and the Thrill rose to a crescendo within him. He sensed real danger, a chance of falling, and that made the Thrill surge. He nearly choked on it, the joy, the pleasure, the desire. The danger. More and more blows got through; more and more Parshendi were able to duck or dodge out of the way of his Blade.

He felt a breeze through the back of his breastplate. Cooling, terrible, frightening. The cracks were widening. If the breastplate burst . . .

He screamed, slamming his Blade down through a Parshendi, burning out his eyes, dropping the man without a mark on his skin. Dalinar brought his Blade up, spinning, cutting through the legs of another foe. His insides were a tempest of emotions, and his brow beneath the helm streamed with sweat. What would happen to the Alethi army if both he and Sadeas fell here? Two highprinces dead in the same battle, two sets of Plate and one Blade lost?

It couldn't happen. He wouldn't fall here. He didn't yet know if he was mad or not. He couldn't die until he knew!

Suddenly, a wave of Parshendi died that he hadn't attacked. A figure in brilliant blue Shardplate burst through them. Adolin held his massive Shardblade in a single hand, the metal gleaming.

Adolin swung again, and the Cobalt Guard rushed forward, pouring into the gap Adolin created. The Parshendi song changed tempo, becoming frantic, and they fell back as more and more troops punched through, some in green, others in blue.

Dalinar knelt down, exhausted, letting his Blade vanish. His guard surrounded him, and Adolin's army washed over them all, overrunning the Parshendi, forcing them back. In a few minutes, the area was secure.

The danger was past.

'Father,' Adolin said, kneeling beside him, pulling his helm off. The youth's blond and black hair was disheveled and sweat-slick. 'Storms! You gave me a fright! Are you well?'

Dalinar pulled his own helm free, sweet cooling air washing across his damp face. He took a deep breath, then nodded. 'Your timing is . . . quite good, son.'

Adolin helped Dalinar back to his feet. 'I had to punch through the entire Parshendi army. No disrespect, Father, but what in the storms made you pull a stunt like that?'

'The knowledge that you could handle the army if I fell,' Dalinar said, clapping his son on the arm, their Plate clinking.

Adolin caught sight of the back of Dalinar's Shardplate, and his eyes opened wide.

'Bad?' Dalinar asked.

'Looks like it's held together with spit and twine,' Adolin said. 'You're leaking Light like a wineskin used for archery practice.'

Dalinar nodded, sighing. Already his Plate was feeling sluggish. He'd probably have to remove it before they returned to the camp, lest it freeze on him.

To the side, several soldiers were pulling Sadeas free of his Plate. It was so far gone that the Light had stopped save for a few tiny wisps. It could be fixed, but it would be expensive – regenerating Shardplate generally shattered the gemstones it drew Light from.

The soldiers pulled Sadeas's helm off, and Dalinar was relieved to see his former friend blinking, looking disoriented but largely uninjured. He had a cut on his thigh where one of the Parshendi had gotten him with a sword, and a few scrapes on his chest.

Sadeas looked up at Dalinar and Adolin. Dalinar stiffened, expecting recrimination – this had only happened because Dalinar had insisted on fighting with two armies on the same plateau. That had goaded the

Parshendi into bringing another army. Dalinar should have set proper scouts to watch for that.

Sadeas, however, smiled a wide grin. 'Stormfather, but that was close! How goes the battle?'

'The Parshendi are routed,' Adolin said. 'The last force resisting was the one around you. Our men are cutting the gemheart free at this moment. The day is ours.'

'We win again!' Sadeas said triumphantly. 'Dalinar, once in a while, it appears that senile old brain of yours can come up with a good idea or two!'

'We're the same age, Sadeas.' Dalinar noted as messengers approached, bearing reports from the rest of the battlefield.

'Spread the word,' Sadeas proclaimed. 'Tonight, all my soldiers will feast as if they were lighteyes!' He smiled as his soldiers helped him to his feet, and Adolin moved over to take the scout reports. Sadeas waved away the help, insisting he could stand despite his wound, and began calling for his officers.

Dalinar turned to seek out Gallant and make sure the horse's wound was cared for. As he did, however, Sadeas caught his arm.

'I should be dead,' Sadeas said softly.

'Perhaps.'

'I didn't see much. But I thought I saw you alone. Where was your honor guard?'

'I had to leave it behind,' Dalinar said. 'It was the only way to get to you in time.'

Sadeas frowned. 'That was a terrible risk, Dalinar. Why?'

'You do not abandon your allies on the battlefield. Not unless there's no recourse. It is one of the Codes.'

Sadeas shook his head. 'That honor of yours is going to get you killed, Dalinar.' He seemed bemused. 'Not that I feel like offering a complaint about it this day!'

'If I should die,' Dalinar said, 'then I would do so having lived my life right. It is not the destination that matters, but how one arrives there.'

'The Codes?'

'No. *The Way of Kings*.'

'That storming book.'

'That storming book saved your life today, Sadeas,' Dalinar said. 'I think I'm starting to understand what Gavilar saw in it.'

Sadeas scowled at that, though he glanced at his armor, lying in pieces nearby. He shook his head. 'Perhaps I shall let you tell me what you mean. I'd like to understand you again, old friend. I'm beginning to wonder if I ever really did.' He let go of Dalinar's arm. 'Someone bring me my storming horse! Where are my officers?'

Dalinar left, and quickly found several members of his guard seeing to Gallant. As he joined them, he was struck by the sheer number of corpses on the ground. They ran in a line where he had punched through the Parshendi ranks to get to Sadeas, a trail of death.

He looked back to where he'd made his stand. Dozens dead. Perhaps hundreds.

Blood of my fathers, Dalinar thought. *Did I do that?* He hadn't killed in such numbers since the early days of helping Gavilar unite Alethkar. And he hadn't grown sick at the sight of death since his youth.

Yet now he found himself revolted, barely able to keep his stomach under control. He would not retch on the battlefield. His men should not see that.

He stumbled away, one hand to his head, the other carrying his helm. He should be exulting. But he couldn't. He just . . . couldn't.

You will need luck trying to understand me, Sadeas, he thought. *Because I'm having Damnation's own trouble trying to do so myself.*

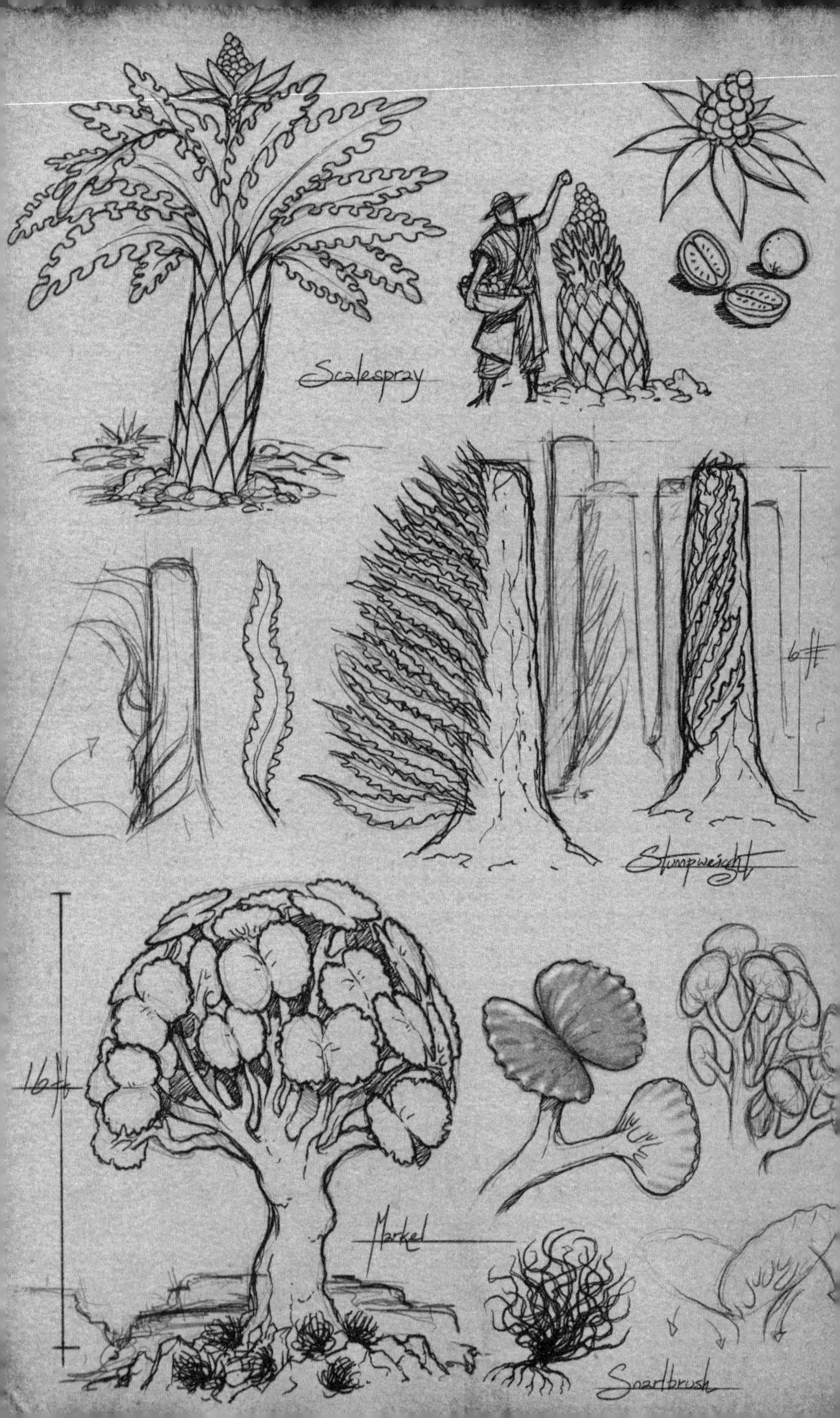

Scalespray
Stumpweight
6ft
16ft
Markel
Snarlbrush

'I hold the suckling child in my hands, a knife at his throat, and know that all who live wish me to let the blade slip. Spill its blood upon the ground, over my hands, and with it gain us further breath to draw.'

—Dated Shashanan, 1173, 23 seconds pre-death. Subject: a darkeyed youth of sixteen years. Sample is of particular note.

'And all the world was shattered!' Maps yelled, back arching, eyes wide, flecks of red spittle on his cheeks. 'The rocks trembled with their steps, and the stones reached toward the heavens. We die! We die!'

He spasmed one last time, and the light faded from his eyes. Kaladin sat back, crimson blood slick on his hands, the dagger he'd been using as a surgical knife slipping from his fingers and clicking softly against the stone. The affable man lay dead on the stones of a plateau, arrow wound in his left breast open to the air, splitting the birthmark he'd claimed looked like Alethkar.

It's taking them, Kaladin thought. *One by one. Open them up, bleed them out. We're nothing more than pouches to carry blood. Then we die, rain it down on the stones like a highstorm's floods.*

Until only I remain. I always remain.

A layer of skin, a layer of fat, a layer of muscle, a layer of bone. That was what men were.

The battle raged across the chasm. It might as well have been another kingdom, for all the attention anyone gave the bridgemen. Die die die, then get out of our way.

The members of Bridge Four stood in a solemn ring around Kaladin. 'What was that he said at the end?' Skar asked. 'The rocks trembled?'

'It was nothing,' said thick-armed Yake. 'Just dying delirium. It happens to men, sometimes.'

'More often lately, it seems,' Teft said. He held his hand to his arm, where he'd hastily wrapped a bandage around an arrow wound. He wouldn't be carrying a bridge anytime soon. Maps's death and Arik's death left them with only twenty-six members now. It was barely enough to carry a bridge. The greater heaviness was very noticeable, and they had difficulty keeping up with the other bridge crews. A few more losses, and they'd be in serious trouble.

I should have been faster, Kaladin thought, looking down at Maps splayed open, his insides exposed for the sun to dry. The arrowhead had pierced his lung and lodged in his spine. Could Lirin have saved him? If Kaladin had studied in Kharbranth as his father had wished, would he have learned enough – known enough – to prevent deaths like this?

This happens sometimes, son. . . .

Kaladin raised shaking bloody hands to his face, gripping his head, as memory consumed him. A young girl, a cracked head, a broken leg, an angry father.

Despair, hate, loss, frustration, horror. How could any man live this way? To be a surgeon, to live knowing that you would be too weak to save some? When other men failed, a field of crops got worms in them. When a surgeon failed, someone died.

You have to learn when to care. . . .

As if he could choose. Banish it, like snuffing a lantern. Kaladin bowed beneath the weight. *I should have saved him, I should have saved him, I should have saved him.*

Maps, Dunny, Amark, Goshel, Dallet, Nalma. Tien.

'Kaladin.' Syl's voice. 'Be strong.'

'If I were strong,' he hissed, 'they would live.'

'The other bridgemen still need you. You promised them, Kaladin. You gave your oath.'

Kaladin looked up. The bridgemen seemed anxious and worried. There were only eight of them; Kaladin had sent the others to look for fallen bridgemen from other crews. They'd found three initially, minor wounds that Skar could care for. No runners had come for him. Either the bridge crews had no other wounded, or those wounded were beyond help.

Maybe he should have gone to look, just in case. But – numb – he could not face yet another dying man he could not save. He stumbled to his feet and walked away from the corpse. He stepped up to the chasm and forced himself to fall into the old stance Tukks had taught him.

Feet apart, hands behind his back, clasping forearms. Straight-backed, staring forward. The familiarity brought him strength.

You were wrong, Father, he thought. *You said I'd learn to deal with the deaths. And yet here I am. Years later. Same problem.*

The bridgemen fell in around him. Lopen approached with a waterskin. Kaladin hesitated, then accepted the skin, washing off his face and hands. The warm water splashed across his skin, then brought welcome coolness as it evaporated. He let out a deep breath, nodding thanks to the short Herdazian man.

Lopen raised an eyebrow, then gestured to the pouch tied to his waist. He had recovered the newest pouch of spheres they'd stuck to the bridge with an arrow. This was the fourth time they'd done that, and had recovered them each without incident.

'Did you have any trouble?' Kaladin asked.

'No, gancho,' Lopen said, smiling widely. 'Easy as tripping a Horneater.'

'I heard that,' Rock said gruffly, standing in parade rest a short distance away.

'And the rope?' Kaladin asked.

'I dropped the whole coil right over the side,' Lopen said. 'But I didn't tie the end to anything. Just like you said.'

'Good,' Kaladin said. A rope dangling from a bridge would have just been too obvious. If Hashal or Gaz caught scent of what Kaladin was planning . . .

And where is *Gaz?* Kaladin thought. *Why didn't he come on the bridge run?*

Lopen gave Kaladin the pouch of spheres, as if eager to be rid of the responsibility. Kaladin accepted it, stuffing it into his trouser pocket.

Lopen retreated, and Kaladin fell back into parade rest. The plateau on the other side of the chasm was long and thin, with steep slopes on the sides. Just as in the last few battles, Dalinar Kholin helped Sadeas's force. He always arrived late. Perhaps he blamed his slow, chull-pulled bridges. Very convenient. His men often had the luxury of crossing without archery fire.

Sadeas and Dalinar won more battles this way. Not that it mattered to the bridgemen.

Many people were dying on the other side of the chasm, but Kaladin didn't feel a thing for them. No itch to heal them, no desire to help. Kaladin could thank Hav for that, for training him to think in terms of 'us' and 'them.' In a way, Kaladin *had* learned what his father had talked about. In the wrong way, but it was something. Protect the 'us,' destroy the 'them.' A soldier had to think like that. So Kaladin hated the Parshendi. They were the enemy. If he hadn't learned to divide his mind like that, war would have destroyed him.

Perhaps it had done so anyway.

As he watched the battle, he focused on one thing in particular to distract himself. How *did* the Parshendi treat their dead? Their actions seemed irregular. The Parshendi soldiers rarely disturbed their dead after they fell; they'd take roundabout paths of attack to avoid dead bodies. And when the Alethi marched over the Parshendi dead, they formed points of terrible conflict.

Did the Alethi notice? Probably not. But he could see that the Parshendi revered their dead – revered them to the extent that they would endanger the living to preserve the corpses of the fallen. Kaladin could use that. He would use that. Somehow.

The Alethi eventually won the battle. Before long, Kaladin and his team were slogging back across the plateau, carrying their bridge, three wounded lashed to the top. They had found only those three, and a part of Kaladin felt sick inside as he realized another part of him was glad. He had already rescued some fifteen men from other bridge crews, and it was straining their resources – even with the money from the pouches – to feed them. Their barrack was crowded with the wounded.

Bridge Four reached a chasm, and Kaladin moved to lower his burden. The process was rote to him now. Lower the bridge, quickly untie the wounded, push the bridge across the chasm. Kaladin checked on the three wounded. Every man he rescued this way seemed bemused at what he'd done, even though he'd been doing it for weeks now. Satisfied that they were all right, he moved to stand at parade rest while the soldiers crossed.

Bridge Four fell in around him. Increasingly, they earned scowls from the soldiers – both darkeyed and lighteyed – who crossed. 'Why do they do that?' Moash said quietly as a passing soldier tossed an overripe pilevine fruit at the bridgemen. Moash wiped the stringy, red fruit from his face, then sighed and fell back into his stance. Kaladin had never asked them to join him, but they did it each time.

'When I fought in Amaram's army,' Kaladin said, 'I dreamed about joining the troops at the Shattered Plains. Everyone knew that the soldiers left in Alethkar were the dregs. We imagined the real soldiers, off fighting in the glorious war to bring retribution to those who had killed our king. Those soldiers would treat their fellows with fairness. Their discipline would be firm. Each would be an expert with the spear, and he would not break rank on the battlefield.'

To the side, Teft snorted quietly.

Kaladin turned to Moash. 'Why do they treat us so, Moash? Because they know they should be better than they are. Because they see discipline in bridgemen, and it embarrasses them. Rather than bettering themselves, they take the easier road of jeering at us.'

'Dalinar Kholin's soldiers don't act like that,' Skar said from just behind Kaladin. 'His men march in straight ranks. There is order in their camp. If they're on duty, they don't leave their coats unbuttoned or lounge about.'

Will I never stop hearing about Dalinar storming Kholin? Kaladin thought.

Men had spoken that way of Amaram. How easy it was to ignore a blackened heart if you dressed it in a pressed uniform and a reputation for honesty.

Several hours later, the sweaty and exhausted group of bridgemen tramped up the incline to the lumberyard. They dumped their bridge in its resting place. It was getting late; Kaladin would have to purchase food immediately if they were going to have supplies for the evening stew. He wiped his hands on his towel as the members of Bridge Four lined up.

'You're dismissed for evening activities,' he said. 'We have chasm duty early tomorrow. Morning bridge practice will have to be moved to late afternoon.'

The bridgemen nodded, then Moash raised a hand. As one, the bridgemen raised their arms and crossed them, wrists together, hands in fists. It had the look of a practiced effort. After that, they trotted away.

Kaladin raised an eyebrow, tucking his towel into his belt. Teft hung back, smiling.

'What was that?' Kaladin asked.

'The men wanted a salute,' Teft said. 'We can't use a regular military salute – not with the spearmen already thinking we're too bigheaded. So I taught them my old squad salute.'

'When?'

'This morning. While you were getting our schedule from Hashal.'

Kaladin smiled. Odd, how he could still do that. Nearby, the other nineteen bridge crews on today's run dropped off their bridges, one by one. Had Bridge Four once looked like them, with those ragged beards and haunted expressions? None of them spoke to one another. Some few glanced at Kaladin as they passed, but they looked down as soon as they saw he was watching. They'd stopped treating Bridge Four with the contempt they'd once shown. Curiously, they now seemed to regard Kaladin's crew as they did everyone else in camp – as people above them. They hastened to avoid his notice.

Poor sodden fools, Kaladin thought. Could he, maybe, persuade Hashal to let him take a few into Bridge Four? He could use the extra men, and seeing those slumped figures twisted his heart.

'I know that look, lad,' Teft said. 'Why is it you always have to help everyone?'

'Bah,' Kaladin said. 'I can't even protect Bridge Four. Here, let me look at that arm of yours.'

'It's not that bad.'

Kaladin grabbed his arm anyway, peeling away the blood-crusted bandage. The cut was long, but shallow.

'We need antiseptic on this,' Kaladin said, noting a few red rotspren crawling around on the wound. 'I should probably sew it up.'

'It's not that bad!'

'Still,' Kaladin said, waving for Teft to follow as he approached one of the rain barrels alongside the lumberyard. The wound was shallow enough that Teft would probably be able to show the others spear thrusts and blocks tomorrow during chasm duty, but that was no excuse for leaving it alone to fester or scar.

At the rain barrel, Kaladin washed out the wound, then called for Lopen – who was standing in the shade beside the barrack – to bring his medical equipment. The Herdazian man gave that salute again, though he did it with one arm, and sauntered away to get the pack.

'So, lad,' Teft said. 'How do you feel? Any odd experiences lately?'

Kaladin frowned, looking up from the arm. 'Storm it, Teft! That's the fifth time in two days you've asked me that. What are you getting at?'

'Nothing, nothing!'

'It *is* something,' Kaladin said. 'What is it you're digging for, Teft? I—'

'Gancho,' Lopen said, walking up, carrying the medical supply pack over his shoulder. 'Here you go.'

Kaladin glanced at him, then reluctantly accepted the pack. He pulled the drawstrings open. 'We'll want to—'

A quick motion came from Teft. Like a punch being thrown.

Kaladin moved by reflex, taking in a sharp breath, moving to a defensive stance, arms up, one hand a fist, the other back to block.

Something blossomed within Kaladin. Like a deep breath drawn in, like a burning liquor injected directly into his blood. A powerful wave pulsed through his body. Energy, strength, awareness. It was like the body's natural alert response to danger, only it was a hundredfold more intense.

Kaladin caught Teft's fist, moving blurringly quick. Teft froze.

'What are you doing?' Kaladin demanded.

Teft was smiling. He stepped back, pulling his fist free. 'Kelek,' he said, shaking his hand. 'That's some grip you've got.'

'Why did you try to strike me?'

'I wanted to see something,' Teft said. 'You're holding that pouch of spheres Lopen gave you, you see, and your own pouch with what we've gathered lately. More Stormlight than you've probably ever carried, at least recently.'

'What does that have to do with anything?' Kaladin demanded. What was that heat inside of him, that burning in his veins?

'Gancho,' Lopen said, his voice awed. 'You're glowing.'

Kaladin frowned. *What is he—*

And then he noticed it. It was very faint, but it was there, wisps of luminescent smoke curling up from his skin. Like steam coming off a bowl of hot water on a cold winter night.

Shaking, Kaladin put the medical pack on the broad rim of the water barrel. He felt a moment of coldness on his skin. What was that? Shocked, he raised his other hand, looking at the wisps streaming off of it.

'What did you do to me?' he demanded, looking up at Teft.

The older bridgeman was still smiling.

'Answer me!' Kaladin said, stepping forward, grabbing the front of Teft's shirt. *Stormfather, but I feel strong!*

'I didn't do anything, lad,' Teft said. 'You've been doing this for a while now. I caught you feeding off Stormlight when you were sick.'

Stormlight. Kaladin hastily released Teft, fishing at the pouch of spheres in his pocket. He yanked it free and pulled it open.

It was dark inside. All five gemstones had been drained. The white light streaming from Kaladin's skin faintly illuminated the inside of the bag.

'Now that's something,' Lopen said from the side. Kaladin spun to find the Herdazian man bending down and looking at the medical pack. Why was that so important?

Then Kaladin saw it. He thought he'd set the pack on the rim of the barrel, but in his haste he'd just pressed it against the side of the barrel. The pack now clung to the wood. Stuck there, hanging as if from an invisible hook. Faintly streaming light, just like Kaladin. As Kaladin watched, the light faded, and the pack slumped free and fell to the ground.

Kaladin raised a hand to his forehead, looking from the surprised Lopen to the curious Teft. Then he glanced around the lumberyard, frantic. Nobody else was looking at them; in the sunlight, the vapors were too faint to see from a distance.

Stormfather . . . what . . . how . . .

He caught sight of a familiar shape above. Syl moved like a blown leaf, tossed this way and that, leisurely, faint.

She did it! Kaladin thought. *What has she done to me?*

He stumbled away from Lopen and Teft, running toward Syl. His footsteps propelled him forward with too much speed. 'Syl!' he bellowed, stopping beneath her.

She zipped down to hover before him, changing from a leaf to a young woman standing in the air. 'Yes?'

Kaladin glanced around. 'Come with me,' he said, hurrying to one of the alleys between barracks. He pressed himself up against a wall, standing in the shade, breathing in and out. Nobody could see him here.

Syl alighted in the air before him, hands behind her back, looking closely at him. 'You're glowing.'

'What have you done to me?'

She cocked her head, then shrugged.

'Syl . . .' he said threateningly, though he wasn't certain what harm he could do a spren.

'I don't know, Kaladin,' she said frankly, sitting down, her legs hanging over the side of the invisible platform. 'I can . . . I can only faintly remember things I used to know so well. This world, interacting with men.'

'But you did do something.'

'*We* have done something. It wasn't me. It wasn't you. But together . . .' She shrugged again.

'That isn't very helpful.'

She grimaced. 'I know. I'm sorry.'

Kaladin raised a hand. In the shade, the light streaming off of him was more obvious. If someone walked by . . . 'How do I get rid of it?'

'Why do you want to get rid of it?'

'Well, because . . . I . . . Because.'

Syl didn't respond.

Something occurred to Kaladin. Something, perhaps, he should have asked long ago. 'You're not a windspren, are you?'

She hesitated, then shook her head. 'No.'

'What are you, then?'

'I don't know. I bind things.'

Bind things. When she played pranks, she made items stick together. Shoes stuck to the ground and made men trip. People reached for their jackets hanging on hooks and couldn't pull them free. Kaladin reached down, picking a stone up off the ground. It was as big as his palm, weathered smooth by highstorm winds and rain. He pressed it against the wall of the barrack and willed his Light into the stone.

He felt a chill. The rock began to stream with luminescent vapors.

When Kaladin pulled his hand away, the stone remained where it was, clinging to the side of the building.

Kaladin leaned close, squinting. He thought he could faintly make out tiny spren, dark blue and shaped like little splashes of ink, clustering around the place where the rock met the wall.

'Bindspren,' Syl said, walking up beside his head; she was still standing in the air.

'They're holding the rock in place.'

'Maybe. Or maybe they're attracted to what you've done in affixing the stone there.'

'That's not how it works. Is it?'

'Do rotspren cause sickness,' Syl said idly, 'or are they attracted to it?'

'Everyone knows they cause it.'

'And do windspren cause the wind? Rainspren cause the rain? Flamespren cause fires?'

He hesitated. No, they didn't. Did they? 'This is pointless. I need to find out how to get rid of this light, not study it.'

'And *why*,' Syl repeated, 'must you get rid of it? Kaladin, you've heard the stories. Men who walked on walls, men who bound the storms to them. Windrunners. Why would you want to be rid of something like this?'

Kaladin struggled to define it. The healing, the way he never got hit, running at the front of the bridge . . . Yes, he'd known something odd was happening. Why did it frighten him so? Was it because he feared being set apart, like his father always was as the surgeon in Hearthstone? Or was it something greater?

'I'm doing what the Radiants did,' he said.

'That's what I just said.'

'I've been wondering if I'm bad luck, or if I've run afoul of something like the Old Magic. Maybe this explains it! The Almighty cursed the Lost Radiants for betraying mankind. What if I'm cursed too, because of what I'm doing?'

'Kaladin,' she said, 'you are *not* cursed.'

'You just said you don't know what's happening.' He paced in the alleyway. To the side, the rock finally plopped free and clattered to the ground. 'Can you say, with all certainty, that what I'm doing might not have drawn bad luck down upon me? Do you know enough to deny it completely, Syl?'

She stood in the air, her arms folded, saying nothing.

'This … thing,' Kaladin said, gesturing toward the stone. 'It isn't natural. The Radiants betrayed mankind. Their powers left them, and they were cursed. Everyone knows the legends.' He looked down at his hands, still glowing, though more faintly than before. 'Whatever we've done, whatever has happened to me, I've somehow brought upon myself their same curse. That's why everyone around me dies when I try to help them.'

'And you think I'm a curse?' she asked him.

'I … Well, you said you're part of it, and …'

She strode forward, pointing at him, a tiny, irate woman hanging in the air. 'So you think I've caused all of this? Your failures? The deaths?'

Kaladin didn't respond. He realized almost immediately that silence might be the worst response. Syl – surprisingly human in her emotions – spun in the air with a wounded look and zipped away, forming a ribbon of light.

I'm overreacting, he told himself. He was just so unsettled. He leaned back against the wall, hand to head. Before he had time to collect his thoughts, shadows darkened the entry to the alleyway. Teft and Lopen.

'Rock talkers!' Lopen said. 'You really shine in shade, gancho!'

Teft gripped Lopen's shoulder. 'He's not going to tell anyone, lad. I'll make certain of it.'

'Yeah, gancho,' Lopen said. 'I swore I'd say nothing. You can trust a Herdazian.'

Kaladin looked at the two, overwhelmed. He pushed past them, running out of the alley and across the lumberyard, fleeing from watching eyes.

⁂

By the time night drew close, the light had long since stopped streaming from Kaladin's body. It had faded like a fire going out, and had only taken a few minutes to vanish.

Kaladin walked southward along the edge of the Shattered Plains, in that transitional area between the warcamps and the Plains themselves. In some areas – like at the staging area near Sadeas's lumberyard – there was a gentle slope leading down between the two. At other points, there was a short ridge, eight or so feet tall. He passed one of these now, rocks to his right, open Plains to his left.

Hollows, crevices, and nooks scored the rock. Some shadowed sections here still hid pools of water from the highstorms days ago. Creatures still scuttled around the rocks, though the cooling evening air would soon drive them to hide. He passed a place pocked with small, water-filled holes; cremlings – multilegged, bearing tiny claws, their elongated bodies plated with carapace – lapped and fed at the edges. A small tentacle snapped out, yanking one down into the hole. Probably a grasper.

Grass grew up the side of the ridge beside him, and the blades peeked from their holes. Bunches of fingermoss sprouted like flowers amid the green. The bright pink and purple fingermoss tendrils were reminiscent of tentacles themselves, waving at him in the wind. When he passed, the timid grass pulled back, but the fingermoss was bolder. The clumps would only pull into their shells if he tapped the rock near them.

Above him, on the ridge, a few scouts stood watch over the Shattered Plains. This area beneath the ridge belonged to no specific highprince, and the scouts ignored Kaladin. He would only be stopped if he tried to leave the warcamps at the southern or northern ends.

None of the bridgemen had come after him. He wasn't certain what Teft had told them. Perhaps he'd said Kaladin was distraught following Maps's death.

It felt odd to be alone. Ever since he'd been betrayed by Amaram and made a slave, he had been in the company of others. Slaves with whom he'd plotted. Bridgemen with whom he'd worked. Soldiers to guard him, slavemasters to beat him, friends to depend on him. The last time he'd been alone had been that night when he'd been tied up for the highstorm to kill him.

No, he thought. *I wasn't alone that night. Syl was there*. He lowered his head, passing small cracks in the ground to his left. Those lines eventually grew into chasms as they moved eastward.

What was happening to him? He wasn't delusional. Teft and Lopen had seen it too. Teft had actually seemed to expect it.

Kaladin *should* have died during that highstorm. And yet, he had been up and walking shortly afterward. His ribs should still be tender, but they hadn't ached in weeks. His spheres, and those of the other bridgemen near him, had consistently run out of Stormlight.

Had it been the highstorm that had changed him? But no, he'd discovered drained spheres before being hung out to die. And Syl . . . she'd as much as admitted responsibility for some of what had happened. This had been going on a long time.

He stopped beside a rock outcropping, resting against it, causing grass to shrink away. He looked eastward, over the Shattered Plains. His home. His sepulcher. This life on them was ripping him apart. The bridgemen looked up to him, thought him their leader, their savior. But he had cracks in him, like the cracks in the stone here at the edges of the Plains.

Those cracks were growing larger. He kept making promises to himself, like a man running a long distance with no energy left. Just a little farther. Run just to that next hill. Then you can give up. Tiny fractures, fissures in the stone.

It's right that I came here, he thought. *We belong together, you and I. I'm like you.* What had made the Plains break in the first place? Some kind of great weight?

A melody began playing distantly, carrying over the Plains. Kaladin jumped at the sound. It was so unexpected, so out of place, that it was startling despite its softness.

The sounds were coming from the Plains. Hesitant, yet unable to resist, he walked forward. Eastward, onto the flat, windswept rock. The sounds grew louder as he walked, but they were still haunting, elusive. A flute, though one lower in pitch than most he'd heard.

As he grew closer, Kaladin smelled smoke. A light was burning out there. A tiny campfire.

Kaladin walked out to the edge of this particular peninsula, a chasm growing from the cracks until it plunged down into darkness. At the very tip of the peninsula – surrounded on three sides by chasm – Kaladin found a man sitting on a boulder, wearing a lighteyes's black uniform. A small fire of rockbud shell burned in front of him. The man's hair was short and black, his face angular. He wore a thin, black-sheathed sword at his waist.

The man's eyes were a pale blue. Kaladin had never heard of a lighteyed man playing a flute. Didn't they consider music a feminine pursuit? Lighteyed men sang, but they didn't play instruments unless they were ardents.

This man was extremely talented. The odd melody he played was alien, almost unreal, like something from another place and time. It echoed down the chasm and came back; it almost sounded like the man was playing a duet with himself.

Kaladin stopped a short distance away, realizing that the last thing he wanted to do now was deal with a brightlord, particularly one who was eccentric enough to dress in black and wander out onto the Shattered Plains to practice his flute. Kaladin turned to go.

The music cut off. Kaladin paused.

'I always worry that I'll forget how to play her,' a soft voice said from behind. 'It's silly, I know, considering how long I've practiced. But these days I rarely give her the attention she deserves.'

Kaladin turned toward the stranger. His flute was carved from a dark wood that was almost black. The instrument seemed too ordinary to belong to a lighteyes, yet the man held it reverently.

'What are you doing here?' Kaladin asked.

'Sitting. Occasionally playing.'

'I mean, why are you here?'

'Why am I here?' the man said, lowering his flute, leaning back and relaxing. 'Why are any of us here? That's a rather deep question for a first meeting, young bridgeman. I generally prefer introductions before theology. Lunch too, if it can be found. Perhaps a nice nap. Actually, practically anything should come before theology. But especially introductions.'

'All right,' Kaladin said. 'And you are . . . ?'

'Sitting. Occasionally playing . . . with the minds of bridgemen.'

Kaladin reddened, turning again to go. Let the fool lighteyes say, and do, what he wished. Kaladin had difficult decisions to think about.

'Well, off with you then,' the lighteyes said from behind. 'Glad you are going. Wouldn't want you too close. I'm rather attached to my Stormlight.'

Kaladin froze. Then he spun. 'What?'

'My spheres,' the strange man said, holding up what appeared to be a fully infused emerald broam. 'Everyone knows that bridgemen are thieves, or at least beggars.'

Of course. He had been talking about spheres. He didn't know about Kaladin's . . . affliction. Did he? The man's eyes twinkled as if at a grand joke.

'Don't be insulted at being called a thief,' the man said, raising a finger. Kaladin frowned. Where had the sphere gone? He had been holding it in that hand. 'I meant it as a compliment.'

'A compliment? Calling someone a thief?'

'Of course. I myself am a thief.'

'You are? What do you steal?'

'Pride,' the man said, leaning forward. 'And occasionally boredom, if I may take the pride unto myself. I am the King's Wit. Or I was until recently. I think I shall probably lose the title soon.'

'The king's what?'

'Wit. It was my job to be witty.'

'Saying confusing things isn't the same as being witty.'

'Ah,' the man said, eyes twinkling. 'Already you prove yourself more wise than most who have been my acquaintance lately. What is it to be witty, then?'

'To say clever things.'

'And what is cleverness?'

'I . . .' Why was he having this conversation? 'I guess it's the ability to say and do the right things at the right time.'

The King's Wit cocked his head, then smiled. Finally, he held out his hand to Kaladin. 'And what is your name, my thoughtful bridgeman?'

Kaladin hesitantly raised his own hand. 'Kaladin. And yours?'

'I've many.' The man shook Kaladin's hand. 'I began life as a thought, a concept, words on a page. That was another thing I stole. Myself. Another time, I was named for a rock.'

'A pretty one, I hope.'

'A beautiful one,' the man said. 'And one that became completely worthless for my wearing it.'

'Well, what do men call you now?'

'Many a thing, and only some of them polite. Almost all are true, unfortunately. You, however, you may call me Hoid.'

'Your name?'

'No. The name of someone I should have loved. Once again, this is a thing I stole. It is something we thieves do.' He glanced eastward, over the rapidly darkening Plains. The little fire burning beside Hoid's boulder shed a fugitive light, red from glimmering coals.

'Well, it was pleasant to meet you,' Kaladin said. 'I will be on my way. . . .'

'Not before I give you something.' Hoid picked up his flute. 'Wait, please.'

Kaladin sighed. He had a feeling that this odd man was not going to let him escape until he was done.

'This is a Trailman's flute,' Hoid said, inspecting the length of dark wood. 'It is meant to be used by a storyteller, for him to play while he is telling a story.'

'You mean to *accompany* a storyteller. Being played by someone else while he speaks.'

'Actually, I meant what I said.'

'How would a man tell a story while playing the flute?'

Hoid raised an eyebrow, then lifted the flute to his lips. He played it differently from flutes Kaladin had seen – instead of holding it down in front of him, Hoid held it out to the side and blew across its top. He tested a few notes. They had the same melancholy tone that Kaladin had heard before.

'This story,' Hoid said, 'is about Derethil and the *Wandersail*.'

He began to play. The notes were quicker, sharper, than the ones he'd played earlier. They almost seemed to tumble over one another, scurrying out of the flute like children racing one another to be first. They were beautiful and crisp, rising and falling scales, intricate as a woven rug.

Kaladin found himself transfixed. The tune was powerful, almost *demanding*. As if each note were a hook, flung out to spear Kaladin's flesh and hold him near.

Hoid stopped abruptly, but the notes continued to echo in the chasm, coming back as he spoke. 'Derethil is well known in some lands, though I have heard him spoken of less here in the East. He was a king during the shadowdays, the time before memory. A powerful man. Commander of thousands, leader of tens of thousands. Tall, regal, blessed with fair skin and fairer eyes. He was a man to envy.'

Just as the echoes faded below, Hoid began to play again, picking up the rhythm. He actually seemed to continue just where the echoing notes grew too soft, as if there had never been a break in the music. The notes grew more smooth, suggesting a king walking through court with his attendants. As Hoid played, eyes closed, he leaned forward toward the fire. The air he blew over the flute churned the smoke, stirring it.

The music grew softer. The smoke swirled, and Kaladin thought he could make out the face of a man in the patterns of smoke, a man with a pointed chin and lofty cheekbones. It wasn't really there, of course. Just imagination. But the haunting song and the swirling smoke seemed to encourage his imagination.

'Derethil fought the Voidbringers during the days of the Heralds and Radiants,' Hoid said, eyes still closed, flute just below his lips, the song echoing in the chasm and seeming to accompany his words. 'When there was finally peace, he found he was not content. His eyes always turned westward, toward the great open sea. He commissioned the finest ship men had ever known, a majestic vessel intended to do what none had dared before: sail the seas during a highstorm.'

The echoes tapered off, and Hoid began playing again, as if alternating with an invisible partner. The smoke swirled, rising in the air, twisting in the wind of Hoid's breath. And Kaladin almost thought he could see an enormous ship in a shipyard, with a sail as large as a building, secured to an arrowlike hull. The melody became quick and clipped, as if to imitate the sounds of mallets pounding and saws cutting.

'Derethil's goal,' Hoid paused and said, 'was to seek the origin of the Voidbringers, the place where they had been spawned. Many called him a fool, yet he could not hold himself back. He named the vessel the *Wandersail* and gathered a crew of the bravest of sailors. Then, on a day when a highstorm brewed, this ship cast off. Riding out into the ocean, the sail hung wide, like arms open to the stormwinds. . . .'

The flute was at Hoid's lips in a second and he stirred the fire by kicking at a piece of rockbud shell. Sparks of flame rose in the air and smoke puffed, swirling as Hoid rotated his head down and pointed the flute's holes at the smoke. The song became violent, tempestuous, notes falling unexpectedly and trilling with quick undulations. Scales rippled into high notes, where they screeched airily.

And Kaladin saw it in his mind's eye. The massive ship suddenly minuscule before the awesome power of a highstorm. Blown, carried out into the endless sea. What had this Derethil hoped or expected to find? A high-storm on land was terrible enough. But on the sea?

The sounds bounced off the echoing walls below. Kaladin found himself sinking down to the rocks, watching the swirling smoke and rising flames.

Seeing the tiny ship captured and held within a furious maelstrom.

Eventually, Hoid's music slowed, and the violent echoes faded, leaving a much gentler song. Like lapping waves.

'The *Wandersail* ran aground and was nearly destroyed, but Derethil and most of his sailors survived. They found themselves on a ring of small islands surrounding an enormous whirlpool, where, it is said, the ocean drains. Derethil and his men were greeted by a strange people with long, limber bodies who wore robes of single color and shells in their hair unlike any that grow back on Roshar.

'These people took the survivors in, fed them, and nursed them back to health. During his weeks of recovery, Derethil studied the strange people, who called themselves the Uvara, the People of the Great Abyss. They lived curious lives. Unlike the people in Roshar – who constantly argue – the Uvara always seemed to agree. From childhood, there were no questions. Each and every person went about his duty.'

Hoid began the music again, letting the smoke rise unhindered. Kaladin thought he could see in it an industrious people, always working. A building rose among them with a figure at the window, Derethil, watching. The music was calming, curious.

'One day,' Hoid said, 'while Derethil and his men were sparring to regain strength, a young serving girl brought them refreshment. She tripped on an uneven stone, dropping the goblets to the floor and shattering them. In a flash, the other Uvara descended on the hapless child and slaughtered her in a brutal way. Derethil and his men were so stunned that by the time they regained their wits, the child was dead. Angry, Derethil demanded to know the cause of the unjustified murder. One of the other natives explained. "Our emperor will not suffer failure."'

The music began again, sorrowful, and Kaladin shivered. He witnessed the girl being bludgeoned to death with rocks, and the proud form of Derethil bowing above her fallen body.

Kaladin knew that sorrow. The sorrow of failure, of letting someone die when he should have been able to do something. So many people he loved had died.

He had a reason for that now. He'd drawn the ire of the Heralds and the Almighty. It had to be that, didn't it?

He knew he should be getting back to Bridge Four. But he couldn't pull himself away. He hung on the storyteller's words.

'As Derethil began to pay more attention,' Hoid said, his music echoing softly to accompany him, 'he saw other murders. These Uvara, these People of the Great Abyss, were prone to astonishing cruelty. If one of their members did something wrong – something the slightest bit untoward or unfavorable – the others would slaughter him or her. Each time he asked, Derethil's caretaker gave him the same answer. "Our emperor will not suffer failure."'

The echoing music faded, but once again Hoid lifted his flute just as it grew too soft to hear. The melody grew solemn. Soft, quiet, like a lament for one who had passed. And yet it was edged with mystery, occasional quick bursts, hinting at secrets.

Kaladin frowned as he watched the smoke spin, making what appeared to be a tower. Tall, thin, with an open structure at the top.

'The emperor, Derethil discovered, resided in the tower on the eastern coast of the largest island among the Uvara.'

Kaladin felt a chill. The smoke images were just from his mind, adding to the story, weren't they? Had he really seen a tower *before* Hoid mentioned it?

'Derethil determined that he needed to confront this cruel emperor. What kind of monster would demand that such an obviously peaceful people kill so often and so terribly? Derethil gathered his sailors, a heroic group, and they armed themselves. The Uvara did not try to stop them, though they watched with fright as the strangers stormed the emperor's tower.'

Hoid fell silent, and didn't turn back to his flute. Instead, he let the music echo in the chasm. It seemed to linger this time. Long, sinister notes.

'Derethil and his men came out of the tower a short time later, carrying a desiccated corpse in fine robes and jewelry. "This is your emperor?" Derethil demanded. "We found him in the top room, alone." It appeared that the man had been dead for years, but nobody had dared enter his tower. They were too frightened of him.

'When he showed the Uvara the dead body, they began to wail and weep. The entire island was cast into chaos, as the Uvara began to burn homes, riot, or fall to their knees in torment. Amazed and confused, Derethil and his men stormed the Uvara shipyards, where the *Wandersail* was being repaired. Their guide and caretaker joined them, and she begged to accompany them in their escape. So it was that Nafti joined the crew.

'Derethil and his men set sail, and though the winds were still, they rode the *Wandersail* around the whirlpool, using the momentum to spin them out and away from the islands. Long after they left, they could see the smoke rising from the ostensibly peaceful lands. They gathered on the deck, watching, and Derethil asked Nafti the reason for the terrible riots.'

Hoid fell silent, letting his words rise with the strange smoke, lost to the night.

'Well?' Kaladin demanded. 'What was her response?'

'Holding a blanket around herself, staring with haunted eyes at her lands, she replied, "Do you not see, Traveling One? If the emperor is dead, and has been all these years, then the murders we committed are not his responsibility. They are our own."'

Kaladin sat back. Gone was the taunting, playful tone Hoid had used earlier. No more mockery. No more quick tongue intended to confuse. This story had come from within his heart, and Kaladin found he could not speak. He just sat, thinking of that island and the terrible things that had been done.

'I think . . .' Kaladin finally replied, licking his dry lips, 'I think that is cleverness.'

Hoid raised an eyebrow, looking up from his flute.

'Being able to remember a story like that,' Kaladin said, 'to tell it with such care.'

'Be wary of what you say,' Hoid said, smiling. 'If all you need for cleverness is a good story, then I'll find myself out of a job.'

'Didn't you say you were already out of a job?'

'True. The king is finally without wit. I wonder what that makes him.'

'Um . . . witless?' Kaladin said.

'I'll tell him you said that,' Hoid noted, eyes twinkling. 'But I think it's inaccurate. One can have a wit, but not a witless. What is a wit?'

'I don't know. Some kind of spren in your head, maybe, that makes you think?'

Hoid cocked his head, then laughed. 'Why, I suppose that's as good an explanation as any.' He stood up, dusting off his black trousers.

'Is the story true?' Kaladin asked, rising too.

'Perhaps.'

'But how would we know it? Did Derethil and his men return?'

'Some stories say they did.'

'But how could they? The highstorms only blow one direction.'

'Then I guess the story is a lie.'

'I didn't say that.'

'No, I said it. Fortunately, it's the best kind of lie.'

'And what kind is that?'

'Why, the kind *I* tell, of course.' Hoid laughed, then kicked out the fire, grinding the last of the coals beneath his heel. It didn't really seem there had been enough fuel to make the smoke Kaladin had seen.

'What did you put in the fire?' Kaladin said. 'To make that special smoke?'

'Nothing. It was just an ordinary fire.'

'But, I saw—'

'What you saw belongs to you. A story doesn't live until it is imagined in someone's mind.'

'What does the story mean, then?'

'It means what you want it to mean,' Hoid said. 'The purpose of a storyteller is not to tell you how to think, but to give you questions to think upon. Too often, we forget that.'

Kaladin frowned, looking westward, back toward the warcamps. They were alight now with spheres, lanterns, and candles. 'It means taking responsibility,' Kaladin said. 'The Uvara, they were happy to kill and murder, so long as they could blame the emperor. It wasn't until they realized there was nobody to take the responsibility that they showed grief.'

'That's one interpretation,' Hoid said. 'A fine one, actually. So what is it you don't want to take responsibility for?'

Kaladin started. 'What?'

'People see in stories what they're looking for, my young friend.' He reached behind his boulder, pulling out a pack and slinging it on his shoulder. 'I have no answers for you. Most days, I feel I never have had any answers. I've come to your land to chase an old acquaintance, but I end up spending most of my time hiding from him instead.'

'You said . . . about me and responsibility . . .'

'Just an idle comment, nothing more.' He reached over, laying a hand on Kaladin's shoulder. 'My comments are often idle. I never can get them to do any solid work. Would that I could make my words carry stones. That would be something to see.' He held out the dark wood flute. 'Here. I've carried her for longer than you'd believe, were I to tell you the truth. Take her for yourself.'

'But I don't know how to play it!'

'Then learn,' Hoid said, pressing the flute into Kaladin's hand. 'When you can make the music sing back at you, then you've mastered it.' He began to walk away. 'And take good care of that blasted apprentice of mine. He really should have let me know he was still alive. Perhaps he feared I'd come to rescue him again.'

'Apprentice?'

'Tell him I graduate him,' Hoid said, still walking. 'He's a full World-singer now. Don't let him get killed. I spent far too long trying to force some sense into that brain of his.'

Sigzil, Kaladin thought. 'I'll give him the flute,' he called after Hoid.

'No you won't,' Hoid said, turning, walking backward as he left. 'It's a gift to *you*, Kaladin Stormblessed. I expect you to be able to play it when next we meet!'

And with that, the storyteller turned and broke into a jog, heading offtoward the warcamps. He didn't move to go up into them, however. His shadowed figure turned to the south, as if he were intending to leave the camps. Where was he going?

Kaladin looked down at the flute in his hand. It was heavier than he had expected. What kind of wood was it? He rubbed its smooth length, thinking.

'I don't like him,' Syl's voice said suddenly, coming from behind. 'He's strange.'

Kaladin spun to find her on the boulder, sitting where Hoid had been a moment ago.

'Syl!' Kaladin said. 'How long have you been here?'

She shrugged. 'You were watching the story. I didn't want to interrupt.' She sat with hands in her lap, looking uncomfortable.

'Syl—'

'I'm behind what is happening to you,' she said, voice soft. 'I'm doing it.'

Kaladin frowned, stepping forward.

'It's both of us,' she said. 'But without me, nothing would be changing in you. I'm ... taking something from you. And giving something in return. It's the way it used to work, though I can't remember how or when. I just know that it was.'

'I—'

'Hush,' she said. 'I'm talking.'

'Sorry.'

'I'm willing to stop it, if you want,' she said. 'But I would go back to being as I was before. That scares me. Floating on the wind, never remembering anything for longer than a few minutes. It's because of this tie between us that I can think again, that I can remember what and who I am. If we end it, I lose that.'

She looked up at Kaladin, sorrowful.

He looked into those eyes, then took a deep breath. 'Come,' he said, turning, walking back down the peninsula.

She flew over, becoming a ribbon of light, floating idly in the air beside his head. Soon they reached the place beneath the ridge leading to the warcamps. Kaladin turned north, toward Sadeas's camp. The cremlings had retreated to their cracks and burrows, but many of the plants still continued to let their fronds float in the cool wind. When he passed, the grass pulled back in, looking like the fur of some black beast in the night, lit by Salas.

What responsibility are you avoiding. . . .

He wasn't avoiding responsibility. He took too much responsibility! Lirin had said it constantly, chastising Kaladin for feeling guilt over deaths he couldn't have prevented.

Though there was one thing he clung to. An excuse, perhaps, like the dead emperor. It was the soul of the wretch. Apathy. The belief that nothing was his fault, the belief that he couldn't change anything. If a man was cursed, or if he believed he didn't have to care, then he didn't need to hurt when he failed. Those failures couldn't have been prevented. Someone or something else had ordained them.

'If I'm not cursed,' Kaladin said softly, 'then why do I live when others die?'

'Because of us,' Syl said. 'This bond. It makes you stronger, Kaladin.'

'Then why can't it make me strong enough to help the others?'

'I don't know,' Syl said. 'Maybe it can.'

If I get rid of it, I'll go back to being normal. For what purpose . . . so I can die with the others?

He continued to walk in the darkness, passing lights above that made vague, faint shadows on the stones in front of him. The tendrils of fingermoss, clumped in bunches. Their shadows seemed arms.

He thought often about saving the bridgemen. And yet, as he considered, he realized that he often framed saving them in terms of saving himself. He told himself he wouldn't *let* them die, because he knew what it would do to him if they did. When he lost men, the wretch threatened to take over because of how much Kaladin hated failing.

Was that it? Was that why he searched for reasons why he might be cursed? To explain his failure away? Kaladin began to walk more quickly.

He was doing something good in helping the bridgemen – but he also was doing something selfish. The powers had unsettled him because of the responsibility they represented.

He broke into a jog. Before long, he was sprinting.

But if it wasn't about *him* – if he wasn't helping the bridgemen because he loathed failure, or because he feared the pain of watching them die – then it would be about *them*. About Rock's affable gibes, about Moash's intensity, about Teft's earnest gruffness or Peet's quiet dependability. What would he do to protect them? Give up his illusions? His excuses?

Seize whatever opportunity he could, no matter how it changed him? No matter how it unnerved him, or what burdens it represented?

He dashed up the incline to the lumberyard.

Bridge Four was making their evening stew, chatting and laughing. The nearly twenty wounded men from other crews sat eating gratefully. It was gratifying, how quickly they had lost their hollow-eyed expressions and begun laughing with the other men.

The smell of spicy Horneater stew was thick in the air. Kaladin slowed his jog, coming to a stop beside the bridgemen. Several looked concerned as they saw him, panting and sweating. Syl landed on his shoulder.

Kaladin sought out Teft. The aging bridgeman sat alone below the barrack's eaves, staring down at the rock in front of him. He hadn't noticed Kaladin yet. Kaladin gestured for the others to continue, then walked over to Teft. He squatted down before the man.

Teft looked up in surprise. 'Kaladin?'

‘What do you know?’ Kaladin said quietly, intense. ‘And how do you know it?’

‘I—’ Teft said. ‘When I was a youth, my family belonged to a secret sect that awaited the return of the Radiants. I quit when I was just a youth. I thought it was nonsense.’

He was holding things back; Kaladin could tell from the hesitation in his voice.

Responsibility. ‘How much do you know about what I can do?’

‘Not much,’ Teft said. ‘Just legends and stories. Nobody really knows what the Radiants could do, lad.’

Kaladin met his eyes, then smiled. ‘Well, we’re going to find out.’

58 THE JOURNEY

'Re-Shephir, the Midnight Mother, giving birth to abominations with her essence so dark, so terrible, so consuming. She is here! She watches me die!'

—Dated Shashabev, 1173, 8 seconds pre-death. Subject: a darkeyed dockworker in his forties, father of three.

'I have a serious loathing of being wrong.' Adolin reclined in his chair, one hand resting leisurely on the crystal-topped table, the other swirling wine in his cup. Yellow wine. He wasn't on duty today, so he could indulge just a tad.

Wind ruffled his hair; he was sitting with a group of other young lighteyes at the outdoor tables of an Outer Market wineshop. The Outer Market was a collection of buildings that had grown up near the king's palace, outside the warcamps. An eclectic mix of people passed on the street below their terraced seating.

'I should think that everyone shares your dislike, Adolin,' Jakamav said, leaning with both elbows on the table. He was a sturdy man, a lighteyes of the third dahn from Highprince Roion's camp. 'Who *likes* being wrong?'

'I've known a number of people who prefer it,' Adolin said thoughtfully. 'Of course, they don't *admit* that fact. But what else could one presume from the frequency of their error?'

Inkima – Jakamav's companion for the afternoon – gave a tinkling laugh. She was a plump thing with light yellow eyes who dyed her hair black. She wore a red dress. The color did not look good on her.

Danlan was also there, of course. She sat on a chair beside Adolin, keeping proper distance, though she'd occasionally touch his arm with her freehand. Her wine was violet. She *did* like her wine, though she seemed to match it to her outfits. A curious trait. Adolin smiled. She looked extremely fetching, with that long neck and graceful build wrapped in a sleek dress. She didn't dye her hair, though it was mostly auburn. There was nothing wrong with light hair. In fact, why was it that they all were so fond of *dark* hair, when light eyes were the ideal?

Stop it, Adolin told himself. *You'll end up brooding as much as Father.*

The other two – Toral and his companion Eshava – were both lighteyes from Highprince Aladar's camp. House Kholin was currently out of favor, but Adolin had acquaintances or friends in nearly all of the warcamps.

'Wrongness can be amusing,' Toral said. 'It keeps life interesting. If we were all right all the time, where would that leave us?'

'My dear,' his companion said. 'Didn't you once claim to me that you were nearly always right?'

'Yes,' Toral said. 'And so if everyone were like me, who would I make sport of? I'd dread being made so mundane by everyone else's competence.'

Adolin smiled, taking a drink of his wine. He had a formal duel in the arena today, and he'd found that a cup of yellow beforehand helped him relax. 'Well, you needn't worry about *me* being right too often, Toral. I was sure Sadeas would move against my father. It doesn't make sense. Why wouldn't he?'

'Positioning, perhaps?' Toral said. He was a keen fellow, known for his refined sense of taste. Adolin always wanted him along when trying wines. 'He wants to look strong.'

'He *was* strong,' Adolin said. 'He gains no more by not moving against us.'

'Now,' Danlan said, voice soft with a breathless quality to it, 'I know that I'm quite new to the warcamps, and my assessment is bound to reflect my ignorance, but—'

'You always say that, you know,' Adolin said idly. He liked her voice quite a bit.

'I always say what?'

'That you're ignorant,' Adolin said. 'However, you're anything but. You're among the most clever women I've met.'

She hesitated, looking oddly annoyed for a moment. Then she smiled. 'You shouldn't say such things – Adolin – when a woman is attempting humility.'

'Oh, right. Humility. I've forgotten that existed.'

'Too much time around Sadeas's lighteyes?' Jakamav said, eliciting another tinkling laugh from Inkima.

'Anyway,' Adolin said. 'I'm sorry. Please continue.'

'I was saying,' Danlan said, 'that I doubt Sadeas would wish to start a war. Moving against your father in such an obvious way would have done that, wouldn't it?'

'Undoubtedly,' Adolin said.

'So perhaps that is why he held himself back.'

'I don't know,' Toral said. 'He could have cast shame on your family without attacking you – he could have implied, for instance, that you'd been negligent and foolish in not protecting the king, but that you hadn't been behind the assassination attempt.'

Adolin nodded.

'That still could have started a war,' Danlan said.

'Perhaps,' Toral said. 'But you have to admit, Adolin, that the Blackthorn's reputation is a little less than . . . impressive of late.'

'And what does that mean?' Adolin snapped.

'Oh, Adolin,' Toral said waving a hand and raising his cup for some more wine. 'Don't be tiresome. You know what I'm saying, and you *also* know I mean no insult by it. Where *is* that serving woman?'

'One would think,' Jakamav added, 'that after six years out here, we could get a decent winehouse.'

Inkima laughed at that too. She was *really* getting annoying.

'My father's reputation is sound,' Adolin said. 'Or have you not been paying attention to our victories lately?'

'Achieved with Sadeas's help,' Jakamav said.

'Achieved nonetheless,' Adolin said. 'In the last few months, my father's saved not only Sadeas's life, but that of the king himself. He fights boldly. Surely you can see that previous rumors about him were absolutely unfounded.'

'All right, all right,' Toral said. 'No need to get upset, Adolin. We can all agree that your father is a wonderful man. But you *were* the one who complained to us that you wanted to change him.'

Adolin studied his wine. Both of the other men at the table wore the sort of outfits Adolin's father frowned upon. Short jackets over colorful silk shirts. Toral wore a thin yellow silk scarf at the neck and another around his right wrist. It was quite fashionable, and looked far more comfortable than Adolin's uniform. Dalinar would have said that the outfits looked silly, but sometimes fashion *was* silly. Bold, different. There was something invigorating about dressing in a way that interested others, moving with the waves of style. Once, before joining his father at the war, Adolin had loved being able to design a look to match a given day. Now he had only two options: summer uniform coat or winter uniform coat.

The serving maid finally arrived, bringing two carafes of wine, one yellow and one deep blue. Inkima giggled as Jakamav leaned over and whispered something in her ear.

Adolin held up a hand to forestall the maid from filling his cup. 'I'm not sure I want to see my father change. Not anymore.'

Toral frowned. 'Last week—'

'I know,' Adolin said. 'That was before I saw him rescue Sadeas. Every time I start to forget how amazing my father is, he does something to prove me one of the ten fools. It happened when Elhokar was in danger too. It's like . . . my father only acts like that when he *really* cares about something.'

'You imply that he doesn't really care about the war, Adolin dear,' Danlan said.

'No,' Adolin said. 'Just that the lives of Elhokar and Sadeas might be more important than killing Parshendi.'

The others took that for an explanation, moving on toward other topics. But Adolin found himself circling the thought. He felt unsettled lately. Being wrong about Sadeas was one cause; the chance that they might actually be able to prove the visions right or wrong was another.

Adolin felt trapped. He'd pushed his father to confront his own sanity, and now – by what their last conversation had established – he had all but agreed to accept his father's decision to step down if the visions proved false.

Everyone hates being wrong, Adolin thought. *Except my father said he'd* rather *be wrong, if it would be better for Alethkar.* Adolin doubted many lighteyes would rather be proven mad than right.

'Perhaps,' Eshava was saying. 'But that doesn't change all of his foolish restrictions. I wish he *would* step down.'

Adolin started. 'What? What was that?'

Eshava glanced at him. 'Nothing. Just seeing if you were attending the conversation, Adolin.'

'No,' Adolin said. 'Tell me what you were saying.'

She shrugged, looking at Toral.

Toral leaned forward. 'You don't think the warcamps are *ignoring* what happens to your father during highstorms, Adolin. Word is that he should abdicate because of it.'

'That would be foolish,' Adolin said firmly. 'Considering how much success he's showing in battle.'

'Stepping down would indeed be an overreaction,' Danlan agreed. 'Though, Adolin, I *do* wish you could get your father to relax all of these foolish restrictions our camp is under. You and the other Kholin men would be able to *truly* join society again.'

'I've tried,' he said, checking the position of the sun. 'Trust me. And now, unfortunately, I have a duel to prepare for. If you'll excuse me.'

'Another of Sadeas's sycophants?' Jakamav asked.

'No,' Danlan said, smiling. 'It's Brightlord Resi. There've been some vocal provocations from Thanadal, and this might serve to shut his mouth.' She looked at Adolin fondly. 'I'll meet you there.'

'Thanks,' he said, rising, doing up the buttons on his coat. He kissed Danlan's freehand, waved to the others, and trotted out onto the street.

That was something of an abrupt departure for me, he thought. *Will they see how uncomfortable the discussion made me?* Probably not. They didn't know him as Renarin did. Adolin liked to be familiar with a large number of people, but not terribly close with any of them. He didn't even know Danlan that well yet. He *would* make his relationship with her last, though. He was tired of Renarin teasing him for jumping in and out of courtships. Danlan was very pretty; it seemed the courtship could work.

He passed through the Outer Market, Toral's words weighing on him. Adolin didn't want to become highprince. He wasn't ready. He liked dueling and chatting with his friends. Leading the army was one thing – but as highprince, he'd have to think of other things. Such as the future of the war on the Shattered Plains, or protecting and advising the king.

That shouldn't have to be our problem, he thought. But it was as his father always said. If they didn't do it, who would?

The Outer Market was far more disorganized than the markets inside Dalinar's warcamp. Here, the ramshackle buildings – mostly built of stone blocks quarried from nearby – had grown up without any specific plan. A large number of the merchants were Thaylen, with their typical caps, vests, and long, wagging eyebrows.

The busy market was one of the few places where soldiers from all ten warcamps mingled. In fact, that had become one of the main functions of the place; it was neutral ground where men and women from different warcamps could meet. It also provided a market that wasn't heavily regulated, though Dalinar had stepped in to provide some rules once the marketplace had begun to show signs of lawlessness.

Adolin nodded to a passing group of Kholin soldiers in blue, who saluted him. They were on patrol, halberds held at their shoulders, helms gleaming. Dalinar's troops kept the peace here, and his scribes watched over it. All at his own cost.

His father didn't like the layout of the Outer Market or its lack of walls. He said that a raid could be catastrophic to it, that it violated the spirit of the Codes. But it had been years since the Parshendi had raided the Alethi side of the Plains. And if they did decide to strike at the warcamps, the scouts and guards would give ample warning.

So what was the point of the Codes? Adolin's father acted as if they were vitally important. Always be in uniform, always be armed, always stay sober. Be ever vigilant while under threat of attack. But there *was* no threat of attack.

As he walked through the market, Adolin looked – really looked – for the first time and tried to see what it was his father was doing.

He could pick out Dalinar's officers easily. They wore their uniforms, as commanded. Blue coats and trousers with silver buttons, knots on the shoulders for rank. Officers who weren't from Dalinar's camp wore all kinds of clothing. It was difficult to pick them out from the merchants and other wealthy civilians.

But that doesn't matter, Adolin told himself again. *Because we're not going to be attacked.*

He frowned, passing a group of lighteyes lounging outside another winehouse. Much as he'd just been doing. Their clothing – indeed, their postures and mannerisms – made them look like they cared only about their revelry. Adolin found himself annoyed. There was a war going on. Almost every day, soldiers died. They did so while lighteyes drank and chatted.

Maybe the Codes weren't just about protecting against the Parshendi. Maybe they were about something more – about giving the men commanders they could respect and rely on. About treating war with the gravity it deserved. Maybe it was about not turning a war zone into a festival. The common men had to remain on watch, vigilant. Therefore, Adolin and Dalinar did the same.

Adolin hesitated in the street. Nobody cursed at him or called for him to move – they could see his rank. They just went around him.

I think I see now, he thought. Why had it taken him so long?

Disturbed, he hurried on his way toward the day's match.

⁂

'"I walked from Abamabar to Urithiru,"' Dalinar said, quoting from memory. '"In this, the metaphor and experience are one, inseparable to me like my mind and memory. One contains the other, and though I can explain one to you, the other is only for me."'

Sadeas – sitting beside him – raised an eyebrow. Elhokar sat on Dalinar's other side, wearing his Shardplate. He'd taken to that more and more, sure that assassins were thirsting for his life. Together, they watched the men dueling down below, at the bottom of a small crater that Elhokar had designated the warcamps' dueling arena. The rocky shelves running around the inside of the ten-foot-tall wall made excellent seating platforms.

Adolin's duel hadn't started yet, and the men who fought right now were lighteyes, but not Shardbearers. Their dull-edged dueling swords were crusted with a white, chalklike substance. When one achieved a hit on the other's padded armor, it would leave a visible mark.

'So, wait,' Sadeas said to him. 'This man who wrote the book . . .'

'Nohadon is his holy name. Others call him Bajerden, though we're not certain whether that was actually his real name or not.'

'He decided to walk from where to where?'

'Abamabar to Urithiru,' Dalinar said. 'I think it must have been a great distance, from the way the story is told.'

'Wasn't he a king?'

'Yes.'

'But why—'

'It's confusing,' Dalinar said. 'But listen. You'll see.' He cleared his throat and continued. '"I strode this insightful distance on my own, and forbade attendants. I had no steed beyond my well-worn sandals, no companion beside a stout staff to offer conversation with its beats against the stone. My mouth was to be my purse; I stuffed it not with gems, but with song. When singing for sustenance failed me, my arms worked well for cleaning a floor or hogpen, and often earned me a satisfactory reward.

'"Those dear to me took fright for my safety and, perhaps, my sanity. Kings, they explained, do not walk like beggars for hundreds of miles. My response was that if a beggar could manage the feat, then why not a king? Did they think me less capable than a beggar?

'"Sometimes I think that I am. The beggar knows much that the king can only guess. And yet who draws up the codes for begging ordinances? Often I wonder what my experience in life – my easy life following the Desolation, and my current level of comfort – has given me of any true experience to use in making laws. If we had to rely on what we knew, kings would only be of use in creating laws regarding the proper heating of tea and cushioning of thrones."'

Sadeas frowned at this. In front of them, the two swordsmen continued their duel; Elhokar watched keenly. He loved duels. Bringing in sand to coat the floor of this arena had been one of his first acts at the Shattered Plains.

'"Regardless,"' Dalinar said, still quoting from *The Way of Kings*, '"I made the trip and – as the astute reader has already concluded – survived it. The stories of its excitements will stain a different page in this narrative, for first I must explain my purpose in walking this strange path. Though I was quite willing to let my family think me insane, I would not leave the same as my cognomen upon the winds of history.

'"My family traveled to Urithiru via the direct method, and had been awaiting me for weeks when I arrived. I was not recognized at the gate, for my mane had grown quite robust without a razor to tame it. Once I revealed myself, I was carried away, primped, fed, worried over, and scolded in precisely that order. Only after all of this was through was

I finally asked the purpose of my excursion. Couldn't I have just taken the simple, easy, and common route to the holy city?"'

'Exactly,' Sadeas interjected. 'He could at the very least have ridden a horse!'

'"For my answer,"' Dalinar quoted, '"I removed my sandals and proffered my callused feet. They were comfortable upon the table beside my half-consumed tray of grapes. At this point, the expressions of my companions proclaimed that they thought me daft, and so I explained by relating the stories of my trip. One after another, like stacked sacks of tallew, stored for the winter season. I would make flatbread of them soon, then stuff it between these pages.

'"Yes, I could have traveled quickly. But all men have the same ultimate destination. Whether we find our end in a hallowed sepulcher or a pauper's ditch, all save the Heralds themselves must dine with the Nightwatcher.

'"And so, does the destination matter? Or is it the path we take? I declare that no accomplishment has substance nearly as great as the road used to achieve it. We are not creatures of destinations. It is the journey that shapes us. Our callused feet, our backs strong from carrying the weight of our travels, our eyes open with the fresh delight of experiences lived.

'"In the end, I must proclaim that no good can be achieved of false means. For the substance of our existence is not in the achievement, but in the method. The Monarch must understand this; he must not become so focused on what he wishes to accomplish that he diverts his gaze from the path he must take to arrive there."'

Dalinar sat back. The rock beneath them had been cushioned and augmented with wooden armrests and back supports. The duel ended with one of the lighteyes – wearing green, as he was subject to Sadeas – scoring a hit on the breastplate of the other, leaving a long white mark. Elhokar clapped his approval, gauntleted hands clanking, and both duelists bowed. The winner's victory would be recorded by the women sitting in the judging seats. They also held the books of dueling code, and would adjudicate disputes or infractions.

'That is the end of your story, I presume,' Sadeas said, as the next two duelists walked out onto the sand.

'It is,' Dalinar said.

'And you have that entire passage memorized?'

'I likely got a few of the words wrong.'

'Knowing you, that means you might have forgotten a single "an" or "the."'

Dalinar frowned.

'Oh, don't be so stiff, old friend,' Sadeas said. 'That was a compliment. Of sorts.'

'What did you think of the story?' Dalinar asked as the dueling resumed.

'It was ridiculous,' Sadeas said frankly, waving for a servant to bring him some wine. Yellow, as it was yet morning. 'He walked all that distance just to make the point that kings should consider the consequences of their commands?'

'It wasn't just to prove the point,' Dalinar said. 'I thought that myself, but I've begun to see. He walked because he wanted to experience the things his people did. He used it as a metaphor, but I think he really wanted to know what it was like to walk that far.'

Sadeas took a sip of his wine, then squinted up at the sun. 'Couldn't we get an awning or something set up out here?'

'I like the sun,' Elhokar said. 'I spend too much time locked away in those caves we call buildings.'

Sadeas glanced at Dalinar, rolling his eyes.

'Much of *The Way of Kings* is organized like that passage I quoted you,' Dalinar said. 'A metaphor from Nohadon's life – a real event turned into an example. He calls them the forty parables.'

'Are they all so ridiculous?'

'I think this one is beautiful,' Dalinar said softly.

'I don't doubt that you do. You always have loved sentimental stories.' He raised a hand. 'That was also intended to be a compliment.'

'Of sorts?'

'Exactly. Dalinar, my friend, you always have been emotional. It makes you genuine. It can also get in the way of levelheaded thinking – but so long as it continues to prompt you to save my life, I think I can live with it.' He scratched his chin. 'I suppose, by definition, I would have to, wouldn't I?'

'I guess.'

'The other highprinces think you are self-righteous. Surely you can see why.'

'I . . .' What could he say? 'I don't mean to be.'

'Well, you do provoke them. Take, for example, the way you refuse to rise to their arguments or insults.'

'Protesting simply draws attention to the issue,' Dalinar said. 'The finest defense of character is correct action. Acquaint yourself with virtue, and you can expect proper treatment from those around you.'

'You see, there,' Sadeas said. 'Who talks like that?'

'Dalinar does,' Elhokar said, though he was still watching the dueling. 'My father used to.'

'Precisely,' Sadeas said. 'Dalinar, friend, the others simply cannot accept that the things you say are serious. They assume it must be an act.'

'And you? What do you think of me?'

'I can see the truth.'

'Which is?'

'That you are a self-righteous prude,' Sadeas said lightly. 'But you come by it honestly.'

'I'm certain you mean that to be a compliment too.'

'Actually, this time I'm just trying to annoy you.' Sadeas raised his cup of wine to Dalinar.

To the side, Elhokar grinned. 'Sadeas. That was quite nearly clever. Shall I have to name you the new Wit?'

'What happened to the old one?' Sadeas's voice was curious, even eager, as if hoping to hear that tragedy had befallen Wit.

Elhokar's grin became a scowl. 'He vanished.'

'Is that so? How disappointing.'

'Bah.' Elhokar waved a gauntleted hand. 'He does this on occasion. He'll return eventually. Unreliable as Damnation itself, that one. If he didn't make me laugh so, I'd have replaced him seasons ago.'

They fell silent, and the dueling continued. A few other lighteyes – both women and men – watched, seated on the benchlike ridges. Dalinar noted with discomfort that Navani had arrived, and was chatting with a group of women, including Adolin's latest infatuation, the auburn-haired scribe.

Dalinar's eyes lingered on Navani, drinking in her violet dress, her mature beauty. She'd recorded his most recent visions without complaint, and seemed to have forgiven him for throwing her out of his rooms so sharply. She never mocked him, never acted skeptical. He appreciated that. Should he thank her, or would she see that as an invitation?

He averted his gaze from her, but found that he couldn't watch the dueling swordsmen without catching sight of her in the corner of his eye. So, instead, he glanced up into the sky, squinting against the afternoon sun. The sounds of metal hitting metal came from below. Behind him, several large snails clung to the rock, waiting for highstorm water.

He had so many questions, so many uncertainties. He listened to *The Way of Kings* and worked to discover what Gavilar's last words had meant. As if, somehow, they held the key to both his madness and the nature of the visions. But the truth was that he didn't know anything, and he couldn't rely on his own decisions. That was unhinging him, bit by bit, point by point.

Clouds seemed less frequent here, in these windswept plains. Just the blazing sun broken by the furious highstorms. The rest of Roshar was influenced by the storms – but here in the East, the feral, untamed highstorms ruled supreme. Could any mortal king hope to claim these lands? There were legends of them being inhabited, of there being more than just unclaimed hills, desolate plains, and overgrown forests. Natanatan, the Granite Kingdom.

'Ah,' Sadeas said, sounding as if he'd tasted something bitter. 'Did he have to come?'

Dalinar lowered his head and followed Sadeas's gaze. Highprince Vamah had arrived to watch the dueling, retinue in tow. Though most of them wore his traditional brown and grey colorings, the highprince himself wore a long grey coat that had slashes cut across it to reveal the bright red and orange silk underneath, matched by the ruffles peeking out of the cuffs and collar.

'I thought you had a fondness for Vamah,' Elhokar said.

'I tolerate him,' Sadeas replied. 'But his fashion sense is absolutely repulsive. Red and orange? Not even a burnt orange, but a blatant, eye-breaking orange. And the rent style hasn't been fashionable for ages. Ah, wonderful, he's sitting directly across from us. I shall be forced to stare at him for the rest of the session.'

'You shouldn't judge people so harshly based on how they look,' Dalinar said.

'Dalinar,' Sadeas said flatly, 'we are highprinces. We *represent* Alethkar. Many around the world view us as a center of culture and influence. Should I not, therefore, have the right to encourage a proper presentation to the world?'

'A proper presentation, yes,' Dalinar said. 'It is right for us to be fit and neat.' *It would be nice if your soldiers, for instance, kept their uniforms clean.*

'Fit, neat, and fashionable,' Sadeas corrected.

'And me?' Dalinar asked, looking down at his simple uniform. 'Would you have me dress in those ruffles and bright colors?'

'You?' Sadeas asked. 'You're completely hopeless.' He raised a hand to forestall objection. 'No, I am unfair. That uniform has a certain . . . timeless quality to it. The military suit, by virtue of its utility, will never be completely out of fashion. It's a safe choice – steady. In a way, you avoid the issue of fashion by not playing the game.' He nodded to Vamah. 'Vamah tries to play, but does so very poorly. And that is unforgivable.'

'I still say you place too much importance on those silks and scarves,' Dalinar said. 'We are soldiers at war, not courtiers at a ball.'

'The Shattered Plains are quickly becoming a destination for foreign dignitaries. It is important to present ourselves properly.' He raised a finger to Dalinar. 'If I am to accept your moral superiority, my friend, then perhaps it is time for you to accept my sense of fashion. One might note that *you* judge people by their clothing even more than I do.'

Dalinar fell silent. That comment stung in its truthfulness. Still, if dignitaries were going to meet with the highprinces on the Shattered Plains, was it too much to ask for them to find an efficient group of warcamps led by men who at least looked like generals?

Dalinar settled back to watch the match end. By his count, it was time for Adolin's bout. The two lighteyes who had been fighting bowed to the king, then withdrew into a tent on the side of the dueling grounds. A moment later, Adolin stepped out onto the sand, wearing his deep blue Shardplate. He carried his helm under his arm, his blond-and-black hair a stylish mess. He raised a gauntleted hand to Dalinar and bowed his head to the king, then put on his helm.

The man who walked out behind him wore Shardplate painted yellow. Brightlord Resi was the only full Shardbearer in Highprince Thanadal's army – though their warcamp had three men who carried only the Blade or the Plate. Thanadal himself had neither. It wasn't uncommon for a highprince to rely on his finest warriors as Shardbearers; it made sound sense, particularly if you were the sort of general who preferred to stay behind the lines and direct tactics. In Thanadal's own princedom, the tradition for centuries had been to appoint the holder of Resi's Shards as something known as the Royal Defender.

Thanadal had recently been vocal about Dalinar's faults, and so Adolin – in a moderately subtle move – had challenged the highprince's star Shardbearer to a friendly bout. Few duels were for Shards; in this case, losing wouldn't cost either man anything other than statistics in the rankings. The match drew an unusual amount of attention, and the small arena filled over the next quarter hour while the duelists stretched and prepared. More than one woman set up a board to sketch or write impressions of the bout. Thanadal himself didn't attend.

The bout began as the highjudge in attendance, Lady Istow, called for the combatants to summon their Blades. Elhokar leaned forward again, intent, as Resi and Adolin circled one another on the sand, Shardblades materializing. Dalinar found himself leaning forward as well, though he did feel a stab of shame. According to the Codes, most duels should be avoided when Alethkar was at war. There was a fine line between sparring for practice and dueling another man for an insult, potentially leaving important officers wounded.

Resi stood in Stonestance, his Shardblade held before him in two hands, point toward the sky, arms all the way extended. Adolin used Windstance, turned sideways slightly, hands before him and elbows bent, Shardblade pointing back over his head. They circled. The winner would be the first one who completely shattered a section of the other's Plate. That wasn't too dangerous; weakened Plate could usually still rebuff a blow, even if it shattered in the process.

Resi attacked first, taking a hopping leap forward and striking by whipping his Shardblade back over his head, then down to his right in a powerful blow. Stonestance focused on that type of attack, delivering the most possible momentum and strength behind each strike. Dalinar found it unwieldy – you didn't need that much power behind a Shardblade on the battlefield, though it was helpful against other Shardbearers.

Adolin jumped back out of the way, Shardplate-enhanced legs giving him a nimbleness that defied the fact that he was wearing over a hundred stoneweights of thick armor. Resi's attack – though well-executed – left him open, and Adolin made a careful strike at his opponent's left vambrace, cracking the forearm plate. Resi attacked again, and Adolin again danced out of the way, then scored a hit on his opponent's left thigh.

Some poets described combat as a dance. Dalinar rarely felt that way about regular combat. Two men fighting with sword and shield would go at one another in a furious rush, slamming their weapons down again and again, trying to get around their opponent's shield. Less a dance, and more like wrestling with weapons.

Fighting with Shardblades, though, *that* could be like a dance. The large weapons took a great deal of skill to swing properly, and Plate was resilient, so exchanges were generally drawn out. The fights were filled with grand motions, wide sweeps. There was a fluidity to fighting with a Shardblade. A grace.

'He's quite good, you know,' Elhokar said. Adolin made a hit on Resi's helm, prompting a round of applause from those watching. 'Better than my father was. Better than even you, Uncle.'

'He works very hard,' Dalinar said. 'He truly loves it. Not the war, not the fighting. The dueling.'

'He could be champion, if he wished it.'

Adolin did wish it, Dalinar knew. But he had refused bouts that would put him within reach of the title. Dalinar suspected that Adolin did it to hold, somewhat, to the Codes. Dueling championships and tournaments were things for those rare times between wars. It could be argued that protecting one's family honor, however, was for all times.

Either way, Adolin didn't duel for ranking, and that made other Shardbearers underestimate him. They were quick to accept duels with him, and some non-Shardbearers challenged him. By tradition, the king's own Shardplate and Blade were available for a large fee to those who both had his favor and the wish to duel a Shardbearer.

Dalinar shivered at the thought of someone else wearing his Plate or holding Oathbringer. It was unnatural. And yet, the lending of the king's Blade and Plate – or before the monarchy had been restored, the lending of a highprince's Blade and Plate – was a strong tradition. Even Gavilar had not broken it, though he had complained about it in private.

Adolin dodged another blow, but he had begun to move into Windstance's offensive forms. Resi wasn't ready for this – though he managed to hit Adolin once on the right pauldron, the blow was a glancing one.

Adolin advanced, Blade sweeping in a fluid pattern. Resi backed away, falling into a parrying posture – Stonestance was one of the few to rely on those.

Adolin batted his opponent's Blade away, knocking it out of stance. Resi reset, but Adolin knocked it away again. Resi grew sloppier and sloppier getting back into stance and Adolin began to strike, hitting him on one side, then on the other. Small, quick blows, meant to unnerve.

They worked. Resi bellowed and threw himself into one of Stonestance's characteristic overhand blows. Adolin handled it perfectly, dropping his Blade to one hand, raising his left arm and taking the blow on his unharmed vambrace. It cracked badly, but the move allowed Adolin to bring his own Blade to the side and strike Resi's cracked left cuisse.

The thigh plate shattered with the sound of ripping metal, pieces blasting away, trailing smoke, glowing like molten steel. Resi stumbled back; his left leg could no longer bear the weight of the Shardplate. The match was over. More important duels might go for two or three broken plates, but that grew dangerous.

The highjudge stood, calling an end. Resi stumbled away, ripping off his helm. His curses were audible. Adolin saluted his enemy, tapping the blunt edge of his Blade to his forehead, then dismissing the Blade. He bowed to the king. Other men sometimes went into the crowd to brag or accept accolades, but Adolin retreated to the preparation tent.

'Talented indeed,' Elhokar said.

'And such a . . . proper lad,' Sadeas said, sipping his drink.

'Yes,' Dalinar said. 'At times, I wish there were peace, simply so that Adolin could dedicate himself to his dueling.'

Sadeas sighed. 'More talk of abandoning the war, Dalinar?'

'That's not what I meant.'

'You keep complaining that you've given up that argument, Uncle,' Elhokar said, turning to regard him. 'Yet you continue to dance around it, speaking longingly of peace. People in the camps call you coward.'

Sadeas snorted. 'He's no coward, Your Majesty. I can attest to that.'

'Why, then?' Elhokar asked.

'These rumors have grown far beyond what is reasonable,' Dalinar said.

'And yet, you do not answer my questions,' Elhokar said. 'If you could make the decision, Uncle, would you have us leave the Shattered Plains? Are you a coward?'

Dalinar hesitated.

Unite them, that voice had told him. *It is your task, and I give it to you.*

Am I a coward? he wondered. Nohadon challenged him, in the book, to examine himself. To never become so certain or high that he wasn't willing to seek truth.

Elhokar's question hadn't been about his visions. And yet, Dalinar had the distinct impression that he *was* being a coward, at least in relation to his desire to abdicate. If he left because of what was happening to him, that would be taking the easy path.

I can't leave, he realized. *No matter what happens. I have to see this through.* Even if he was mad. Or, an increasingly worrisome thought, even if the visions were real, but their origins suspect. *I have to stay. But I also have to plan, to make sure I don't tow my house down.*

Such a careful line to walk. Nothing clear, everything clouded. He'd been ready to run because he liked to make clear decisions. Well, nothing was clear about what was happening to him. It seemed that in making the decision to remain highprince, he placed one important cornerstone into rebuilding the foundation of who he was.

He would not abdicate. And that was that.

'Dalinar?' Elhokar asked. 'Are you . . . well?'

Dalinar blinked, realizing that he had stopped paying attention to the king and Sadeas. Staring off into space like that wouldn't help his reputation. He turned to the king. 'You want to know the truth,' he said. 'Yes, if I could make the order, I would take all ten armies and return to Alethkar.'

Despite what others said, that was not cowardly. No, he'd just confronted cowardice inside of him, and he knew what it was. This was something different.

The king looked shocked.

'I *would* leave,' Dalinar said firmly. 'But not because I wish to flee or because I fear battle. It would be because I fear for Alethkar's stability; leaving this war would help secure our homeland and the loyalty of the highprinces. I would send more envoys and scholars to find out why the Parshendi killed Gavilar. We gave up on that too easily. I still wonder if the assassination was initiated by miscreants or rebels among their own people.

'I'd discover what their culture is – and yes, they do have one. If rebels weren't the cause of the assassination, I'd keep asking until I learned *why* they did it. I'd demand restitution – perhaps their own king, delivered to us for execution in turn – in exchange for granting them peace. As for the gemhearts, I'd speak with my scientists and discover a better method of holding this territory. Perhaps with mass homesteading of the area, securing all of the Unclaimed Hills, we could truly expand our borders and claim the Shattered Plains. I wouldn't *abandon* vengeance, Your Majesty, but I would approach it – and our war here – more thoughtfully. Right now, we know too little to be effective.'

Elhokar looked surprised. He nodded. 'I . . . Uncle, that actually makes sense. Why didn't you explain it before?'

Dalinar blinked. Just several weeks ago, Elhokar had been indignant when Dalinar had merely mentioned the idea of turning back. What had changed?

I don't give the boy enough credit, he realized. 'I have had trouble explaining my own thoughts recently, Your Majesty.'

'Your Majesty!' Sadeas said. 'Surely you wouldn't actually consider—'

'This latest attempt on my life has me unsettled, Sadeas. Tell me. Have you made any progress in determining who put the weakened gems in my Plate?'

'Not yet, Your Majesty.'

'They're trying to kill me,' Elhokar said softly, huddling down in his armor. 'They'll see me dead, like my father. Sometimes I do wonder if we're chasing after the ten fools here. The assassin in white – he was Shin.'

'The Parshendi took responsibility for sending him,' Sadeas said.

'Yes,' Elhokar replied. 'And yet they are savages, and easily manipulated. It would be a perfect distraction, pinning the blame on a group of parshmen. We go to war for years and years, never noticing the real villains, working quietly in my own camp. They watch me. Always. Waiting. I see their faces in mirrors. Symbols, twisted, inhuman . . .'

Dalinar glanced at Sadeas, and the two shared a disturbed look. Was Elhokar's paranoia growing worse, or just more visible? He saw phantom cabals in every shadow, and now – with the attempt on his life – he had proof to feed those worries.

'Retreating from the Shattered Plains could be a good idea,' Dalinar said carefully. 'But not if it is to begin another war with someone else. We must stabilize and unify our people.'

Elhokar sighed. 'Chasing the assassin is only an idle thought right now. Perhaps we won't need it. I hear that your efforts with Sadeas have been fruitful.'

'They have indeed, Your Majesty,' Sadeas said, sounding proud – perhaps a little smug. 'Though Dalinar still insists on using his own slow bridges. Sometimes, my forces are nearly wiped out before he arrives. This would work better if Dalinar would use modern bridge tactics.'

'The waste of life . . .' Dalinar said.

'Is acceptable,' Sadeas said. 'They're mostly slaves, Dalinar. It's an honor for them to have a chance to participate in some small way.'

I doubt they see it in that light.

'I wish you'd at least *try* my way,' Sadeas continued. 'What we've been doing so far has worked, but I worry that the Parshendi will continue to send two armies against us. I don't relish the idea of fighting both on my own before you arrive.'

Dalinar hesitated. That would be a problem. But to give up the siege bridges?

'Well, why not a compromise?' Elhokar said. 'Next plateau assault, Uncle, you let Sadeas's bridgemen help you for the initial march to the contested plateau. Sadeas has plenty of extra bridge crews he could lend you. He could still rush on ahead with a smaller army, but you'd follow more quickly than you have been, using his bridge crews.'

'That would be the same as using my own bridge crews,' Dalinar said.

'Not necessarily,' Elhokar said. 'You've said that the Parshendi can rarely set up and fire on you once Sadeas engages them. Sadeas's men can start the assault as usual, and you can join once he's secured a foothold for you.'

'Yes . . .' Sadeas said, thoughtful. 'The bridgemen *you* use will be safe, and you won't be costing any additional lives. But you'll arrive at the plateau to help me twice as quickly.'

'What if you can't distract the Parshendi well enough?' Dalinar asked. 'What if they still set up archers to fire on my bridgemen when I cross?'

'Then we'll retreat,' Sadeas said with a sigh. 'And we'll call it a failed experiment. But at least we'll have tried. This is how you get ahead, old friend. You try new things.'

Dalinar scratched his chin in thought.

'Oh, go on, Dalinar,' Elhokar said. 'He took your suggestion to attack together. Try it once his way.'

'Very well,' Dalinar said. 'We will see how it works.'

'Excellent,' Elhokar said, standing. 'And now, I believe I'll go congratulate your son. That bout was exciting!'

Dalinar hadn't found it particularly exciting – Adolin's opponent hadn't ever held the upper hand. But that was the best kind of battle. Dalinar didn't buy the arguments about a 'good' fight being a close one. When you won, it was always better to win quickly and with extreme advantage.

Dalinar and Sadeas stood in respect as the king descended the stairlike stone outcroppings toward the sandy floor below. Dalinar then turned to Sadeas. 'I should be leaving. Send me a clerk to detail the plateaus you feel we could try this maneuver on. Next time one of them is up for assault, I'll march my army to your staging area and we'll leave together. You and the smaller, quicker group can go on ahead, and we'll catch up once you're in position.'

Sadeas nodded.

Dalinar turned to climb up the steps toward the ramp out.

'Dalinar,' Sadeas called after him.

Dalinar looked back at the other highprince. Sadeas's scarf fluttered in a gust of wind, his arms folded, the metallic golden embroidery glistening. 'Send me one of your clerks as well. With a copy of that book of Gavilar's. It may amuse me to hear its other stories.'

Dalinar smiled. 'I will do so, Sadeas.'

59
AN HONOR

'Above the final void I hang, friends behind, friends before. The feast I must drink clings to their faces, and the words I must speak spark in my mind. The old oaths will be spoken anew.'

—Dated Betabanan, 1173, 45 seconds pre-death. Subject: a lighteyed child of five years. Diction improved remarkably when giving sample.

Kaladin glared at the three glowing topaz spheres on the ground in front of him. The barrack was dark, empty save for Teft and himself. Lopen leaned in the sunlit doorway, watching with a casual air. Outside, Rock called out commands to the other bridgemen. Kaladin had them working on battle formations. Nothing overt. It would be construed as practice for bridge carrying, but he was actually training them to obey orders and rearrange themselves efficiently.

The three little spheres – only chips – lit the stone ground around themselves in little tan rings. Kaladin focused on them, holding his breath, willing the light into him.

Nothing happened.

He tried harder, staring into their depths.

Nothing happened.

He picked one up, cupping it in his palm, raising it so that he could see the light and nothing else. He could pick out the details of the storm, the shifting, spinning vortex of light. He commanded it, willed it, begged it.

Nothing happened.

He groaned, lying back on the rock, staring at the ceiling.

'Maybe you don't want it badly enough,' Teft said.

'I want it as badly as I know how. It won't budge, Teft.'

Teft grunted and picked up one of the spheres.

'Maybe we're wrong about me,' Kaladin said. It seemed poetically appropriate that the moment he accepted this strange, frightening part of himself, he couldn't make it work. 'It could have been a trick of the sunlight.'

'A trick of the sunlight,' Teft said flatly. 'Sticking a bag to the barrel was a trick of the light.'

'All right. Then maybe it was some odd fluke, something that happened just that once.'

'*And* when you were wounded,' Teft said, '*and* whenever on a bridge run you needed an extra burst of strength or endurance.'

Kaladin let out a frustrated sigh and tapped his head back lightly against the rock floor a few times. 'Well, if I'm one of these Radiants you keep talking about, why can't I do anything?'

'I figure,' the grizzled bridgeman said, rolling the sphere in his fingers, 'that you're like a baby, making his legs work. At first it just kind of happens. Slowly, he figures how to make them move on purpose. You just need practice.'

'I've spent a week staring at spheres, Teft. How much practice can it take?'

'Well, more than you've had, obviously.'

Kaladin rolled his eyes and sat back up. 'Why am I listening to you? You've admitted that you don't know any more than I do.'

'I don't know anything about using the Stormlight,' Teft said, scowling. 'But I know what *should* happen.'

'According to stories that contradict one another. You've told me that the Radiants could fly and walk on walls.'

Teft nodded. 'They sure could. And make stone melt by looking at it. And move great distances in a single heartbeat. And command the sunlight. And—'

'And why,' Kaladin said, 'would they need to both walk on walls *and* fly? If they can fly, why would they bother running up walls?'

Teft said nothing.

'And why bother with either one,' Kaladin added, 'if they can just "move great distances in a heartbeat"?'

'I'm not sure,' Teft admitted.

'We can't trust the stories or legends,' Kaladin said. He glanced at Syl, who had landed beside one of the spheres, staring at it with childlike interest. 'Who knows what is true and what has been fabricated? The only thing we know for certain is this.' He plucked up one of the spheres and held it up in two fingers. 'The Radiant sitting in this room is very, very tired of the color brown.'

Teft grunted. 'You're not a Radiant, lad.'

'Weren't we just talking about—'

'Oh, you can infuse,' Teft said. 'You can drink in the Stormlight and command it. But being a Radiant was more than that. It was their way of life, the things they did. The Immortal Words.'

'The what?'

Teft rolled his sphere between his fingers again, holding it up and staring into its depths. 'Life before death. Strength before weakness. Journey before destination. That was their motto, and was the First Ideal of the Immortal Words. There were four others.'

Kaladin raised an eyebrow. 'Which were?'

'I don't actually know,' Teft said. 'But the Immortal Words – these Ideals – guided everything they did. The four later Ideals were said to be different for every order of Radiants. But the First Ideal was the same for each of the ten: Life before death, strength before weakness, journey before destination.' He hesitated. 'Or so I was told.'

'Yes, well, that seems a little obvious to me,' Kaladin said. 'Life comes before death. Just like day comes before night, or one comes before two. Obvious.'

'You're not taking this seriously. Maybe that's why the Stormlight refuses you.'

Kaladin stood and stretched. 'I'm sorry, Teft. I'm just tired.'

'Life before death,' Teft said, wagging a finger at Kaladin. 'The Radiant seeks to defend life, always. He never kills unnecessarily, and never risks his own life for frivolous reasons. Living is harder than dying. The Radiant's duty is to live.

'Strength before weakness. All men are weak at some time in their lives. The Radiant protects those who are weak, and uses his strength for others. Strength does not make one capable of rule; it makes one capable of service.'

Teft picked up spheres, putting them in his pouch. He held the last one for a second, then tucked it away too. 'Journey before destination. There are always several ways to achieve a goal. Failure is preferable to winning through unjust means. Protecting ten innocents is not worth killing one. In the end, all men die. How you lived will be far more important to the Almighty than what you accomplished.'

'The Almighty? So the knights were tied to religion?'

'Isn't everything? There was some old king who came up with all this. Had his wife write it in a book or something. My mother read it. The Radiants based the Ideals on what was written there.'

Kaladin shrugged, moving over to begin sorting through the pile of bridgemen's leather vests. Ostensibly, he and Teft were here checking those over for tears or broken straps. After a few moments, Teft joined him.

'Do you actually believe that?' Kaladin asked, lifting up a vest, tugging on its straps. 'That anyone would follow those vows, particularly a bunch of lighteyes?'

'They weren't just lighteyes. They were Radiants.'

'They were people,' Kaladin said. 'Men in power always pretend to virtue, or divine guidance, some kind of mandate to "protect" the rest of us. If we believe that the Almighty put them where they are, it's easier for us to swallow what they do to us.'

Teft turned a vest over. It was beginning to tear beneath the left shoulder pad. 'I never used to believe. And then . . . then I saw you infusing Light, and I began to wonder.'

'Stories and legends, Teft,' Kaladin said. 'We want to believe that there were better men once. That makes us think it could be that way again. But people don't change. They are corrupt now. They were corrupt then.'

'Maybe,' Teft said. 'My parents believed in all of it. The Immortal Words, the Ideals, the Knights Radiant, the Almighty. Even old Vorinism. In fact, especially old Vorinism.'

'That led to the Hierocracy. The devotaries and the ardents shouldn't hold land or property. It's too dangerous.'

Teft snorted. 'Why? You think they'd be worse at being in charge than the lighteyes?'

'Well, you've probably got a point there.' Kaladin frowned. He'd spent so long assuming the Almighty had abandoned him, or even cursed him, that it was difficult to accept that maybe – as Syl had said – he'd instead been blessed. Yes, he'd been preserved, and he supposed he should be grateful for that. But what could be worse than being granted great power, yet still being too weak to save those he loved?

Further speculation was interrupted as Lopen stood up straight in the doorway, gesturing covertly to Kaladin and Teft. Fortunately, there wasn't anything to hide anymore. In fact, there hadn't ever been anything to hide, other than Kaladin sitting on the floor and staring at the spheres like an idiot. He set aside the vest and walked to the entrance.

Hashal's palanquin was being carried directly toward Kaladin's barrack, her tall, oft-silent husband walking alongside. The sash at his neck was violet, as was the embroidery on the cuffs of his short, vestlike jacket. Gaz still hadn't reappeared. It had been a week now, and no sign of him. Hashal and her husband – along with their lighteyed attendants – did what he'd once done, and they rebuffed any questions about the bridge sergeant.

'Storm it,' Teft said, stepping up beside Kaladin. 'Those two make my skin itch, same way it does when I know someone's got a knife and is standing behind me.'

Rock had the bridgemen lined up and waiting quietly, as if for inspection. Kaladin walked out to join them, Teft and Lopen following behind. The bearers set the palanquin down in front of Kaladin. Open-sided with only a small canopy on the top, it was little more than an armchair on a platform. Many of the lighteyed women used them in the warcamps.

Kaladin reluctantly gave Hashal a proper bow, prompting the other bridgemen to do so as well. Now was not the time to be beaten for insubordination.

'You have such a well-trained band, bridgeleader,' she said, idly scratching her cheek with a ruby-red nail, her elbow on her armrest. 'So … efficient at bridge runs.'

'Thank you, Brightness Hashal,' Kaladin said, trying – but failing – to keep the stiffness and hostility from his voice. 'May I ask? Gaz hasn't been seen for some days now. Is he well?'

'No.' Kaladin waited for further reply, but she didn't give one. 'My husband has made a decision. Your men are so good at bridge runs that you are a model to the other crews. As such, you will be on bridge duty every day from now on.'

Kaladin felt a chill. 'And scavenging duty?'

'Oh, there will still be time for that. You need to take torches down anyway, and plateau runs never happen at night. So your men will sleep during the day – always on call – and will work the chasms at night. A much better use of your time.'

'Every bridge run,' Kaladin said. 'You're going to make us go on *every one.*'

'Yes,' she said idly, tapping for her bearers to raise her. 'Your team is just too good. It must be used. You'll start full-time bridge duty tomorrow. Consider it an . . . honor.'

Kaladin inhaled sharply to keep himself from saying what he thought of her 'honor.' He couldn't bring himself to bow as she retreated, but she didn't seem to care. Rock and the men started muttering.

Every bridge run. She'd just doubled the rate at which they'd be killed. Kaladin's team wouldn't last another few weeks. They were already so low on members that losing one or two men on an assault would cause them to flounder. The Parshendi would focus on them then, cutting them down.

'Kelek's breath!' Teft said. 'She'll see us dead!'

'It's not fair,' Lopen added.

'We're bridgemen,' Kaladin said, looking at them. 'What made you think that any kind of "fairness" applied to us?'

'She hasn't killed us fast enough for Sadeas,' Moash said. 'You know that soldiers have been beaten for coming to look for you, to see the man who survived the highstorm? He hasn't forgotten about you, Kaladin.'

Teft was still swearing. He pulled Kaladin aside, Lopen following, but the others remained talking among themselves. 'Damnation!' Teft said softly. 'They like to pretend to be evenhanded with the bridge crews. Makes 'em seem fair. Looks like they gave up on that. Bastards.'

'What do we do, gancho?' Lopen asked.

'We go to the chasms,' Kaladin said. 'Just like we're scheduled to. Then make sure we get some extra sleep tonight, as we're apparently going to be staying up all night tomorrow.'

'The men will hate going into the chasms at night, lad,' Teft said.

'I know.'

'But we're not ready for . . . what we need to do,' Teft said, looking to make sure nobody could hear. It was only him, Kaladin, and Lopen. 'It will be another few weeks at least.'

'I know.'

'We won't last another few weeks!' Teft said. 'With Sadeas and Kholin working together, runs happen nearly every day. Just one bad run – one time with the Parshendi drawing a bead on us – and it will all be over. We'll be wiped out.'

'I know!' Kaladin said, frustrated, taking a deep breath and forming fists to keep himself from exploding.

'Gancho!' Lopen said.

'What?' Kaladin snapped.

'It's happening again.'

Kaladin froze, then looked down at his arms. Sure enough, he caught a hint of luminescent smoke rising from his skin. It was extremely faint – he didn't have many gemstones near him – but it was there. The wisps faded quickly. Hopefully the other bridgemen hadn't seen.

'Damnation. What did I do?'

'I don't know,' Teft said. 'Is it because you were angry at Hashal?'

'I was angry before.'

'You breathed it in,' Syl said eagerly, whipping around him in the air, a ribbon of light.

'What?'

'I saw it.' She twisted herself around. 'You were mad, you drew in a breath, and the Light . . . it came too.'

Kaladin glanced at Teft, but of course the older bridgeman hadn't heard. 'Gather the men,' Kaladin said. 'We're going down to our chasm duty.'

'And what about what has happened?' Teft said. 'Kaladin, we can't go on that many bridge runs. We'll be cut to pieces.'

'I'm doing something about it today. Gather the men. Syl, I need something from you.'

'What?' She landed in front of him and formed into a young woman.

'Go find us a place where some Parshendi corpses have fallen.'

'I thought you were going to do spear practice today.'

'That's what the men will be doing,' Kaladin said. 'I'll get them organized first. After that, I have a different task.'

* * *

Kaladin clapped a quick signal, and the bridgemen made a decent arrowhead formation. They carried the spears they'd stashed in the chasm, secured in a large sack filled with stones and stuck in a crevice. He clapped his hands again, and they rearranged into a double-line wall formation. He clapped again, and they formed into a ring with one man standing behind every two as a quick step-in reserve.

The walls of the chasm dripped with water, and the bridgemen splashed through puddles. They were good. Better than they had any right to be, better – for their level of training – than any team he'd worked with.

But Teft was right. They still wouldn't last long in a fight. A few more weeks and he'd have them practiced enough with thrusts and shielding one another that they'd begin to be dangerous. Until then, they were just bridgemen who could move in fancy patterns. They needed more time.

Kaladin had to buy them some.

'Teft,' Kaladin said. 'Take over.'

The older bridgeman gave one of those cross-armed salutes.

'Syl,' Kaladin said to the spren, 'let's go see these bodies.'

'They're close. Come on.' She zipped off down the chasm, a glowing ribbon. Kaladin started after her.

'Sir,' Teft called.

Kaladin hesitated. When had Teft started calling him 'sir'? Odd, how right that felt. 'Yes?'

'You want an escort?' Teft stood at the head of the gathered bridgemen, who were looking more and more like soldiers, with their leather vests and spears held in practiced grips.

Kaladin shook his head. 'I'll be fine.'

'Chasmfiends …'

'The lighteyes have killed any who prowl this close to our side. Besides, if I did run into one, what difference would two or three extra men make?'

Teft grimaced behind his short, greying beard, but offered no further objection. Kaladin continued to follow Syl. In his pouch, he carried the rest of the spheres they'd discovered on bodies while scavenging. They made a habit of keeping some of each discovery and sticking them to bridges, and with Syl helping at scavenging, they now found more than they used to. He had a small fortune in his pouch. That Stormlight – he hoped – would serve him well today.

He got out a sapphire mark for light, avoiding pools of water strewn with bones. A skull protruded from one, wavy green moss growing across the scalp like hair, lifespren bobbing above. Perhaps it should have felt eerie to walk through these darkened slots alone, but they didn't bother Kaladin. This was a sacred place, the sepulcher of the lowly, the burial cavern of bridgemen and spearmen who died by lighteyed edict, spilling blood down the sides of these ragged walls. This place wasn't eerie; it was holy.

He was actually glad to be alone with his silence and the remains of those who had died. These men hadn't cared about the squabbles of those born with lighter eyes than they. These men had cared about their families or – at the very least – their sphere pouches. How many of them were trapped in this foreign land, these endless plateaus, too poor to escape back to Alethkar? Hundreds died each week, winning gems for men who were already rich, winning vengeance for a king long dead.

Kaladin passed another skull, missing its lower jaw, the crown split by an axe's blow. The bones seemed to watch him, curious, the blue Stormlight in his hand giving a haunted cast to the uneven ground and walls.

The devotaries taught that when men died, the most valiant among them – the ones who fulfilled their Callings best – would rise to help reclaim heaven. Each man would do as he had done in life. Spearmen to fight, farmers to work spiritual farms, lighteyes to lead. The ardents were careful to point out that excellence in any Calling would bring power. A farmer would be able to wave his hand and create great fields of spiritual crops. A spearman would be a great warrior, able to cause thunder with his shield and lightning with his spear.

But what of the bridgemen? Would the Almighty demand that all of these fallen rise and continue their drudgery? Would Dunny and the others run bridges in the afterlife? No ardents came to them to test their abilities or grant them Elevations. Perhaps the bridgemen wouldn't be needed in the War for Heaven. Only the very most skilled went there anyway. Others would simply slumber until the Tranquiline Halls were reclaimed.

So do I believe again now? He climbed over a boulder wedged in the chasm. *Just like that?* He wasn't sure. But it didn't matter. He would do the best he could for his bridgemen. If there was a Calling in that, so be it.

Of course, if he did escape with his team, Sadeas would replace them with others who would die in their stead.

I have to worry about what I can do, he told himself. *Those other bridgemen aren't my responsibility.*

Teft talked about the Radiants, about ideals and stories. Why couldn't men actually be like that? Why did they have to rely on dreams and fabrications for inspiration?

If you flee . . . you leave all the other bridgemen to be slaughtered, a voice whispered within him. *There has to be something you can do for them.*

No! he fought back. *If I worry about that, I won't be able to save Bridge Four. If I find a way out, we're going.*

If you leave, the voice seemed to say, *then who will fight for them? Nobody cares. Nobody . . . .*

What was it his father had said all those years ago? He did what he felt was right because someone had to start. Someone had to take the first step.

Kaladin's hand felt warm. He stopped in the chasm, closing his eyes. You couldn't feel any heat from a sphere, usually, but the one in his hand seemed warm. And then – feeling completely natural about it – Kaladin breathed in deeply. The sphere grew cold and a wave of heat shot up his arm.

He opened his eyes. The sphere in his hand was dun and his fingers were crispy with frost. Light rose from him like smoke from a fire, white, pure.

He felt alive with energy. He had no need to breathe – in fact, he held the breath in, trapping the Stormlight. Syl zipped back down the corridor toward him. She twisted around him, then came to rest in the air, taking the form of a woman. 'You did it. What happened?'

Kaladin shook his head, holding his breath. Something was surging within him, like . . .

Like a storm. Raging inside his veins, a tempest sweeping about inside his chest cavity. It made him want to run, jump, yell. It almost made him want to burst. He felt as if he could walk on air. Or walls.

Yes! he thought. He broke into a run, leaping at the side of the chasm. He hit feet-first.

Then bounced off and slammed back into the ground. He was so stunned that he cried out, and he felt the storm within dampen as breath escaped.

He lay on his back as Stormlight rose from him more quickly now that he was breathing. He lay there as the last of it burned away.

Syl landed on his chest. 'Kaladin? What was that?'

'Me being an idiot,' he replied, sitting up and feeling an ache in his back and a sharp pain in his elbow where he'd hit the ground. 'Teft said that the Radiants were able to walk on walls, and I felt so alive. . . .'

Syl walked on air, stepping as if down a set of stairs. 'I don't think you're ready for that yet. Don't be so risky. If you die, I go stupid again, you know.'

'I'll try to keep that in mind,' Kaladin said, climbing to his feet. 'Maybe I'll remove dying from my list of tasks to do this week.'

She snorted, zipping into the air, becoming a ribbon again. 'Come on, hurry up.' She shot off down the chasm. Kaladin collected the dun sphere, then dug into the pouch for another one to provide light. Had he drained them all? No. The others still glowed strongly. He selected a ruby mark, then hurried after Syl.

She led him to a narrow chasm that contained a small group of fresh Parshendi corpses. 'This is morbid, Kaladin,' Syl noted, standing above the bodies.

'I know. Do you know where Lopen went?'

'I sent him scavenging nearby, fetching the things you asked him for.'

'Bring him, please.'

Syl sighed, but zipped away. She always got testy when he made her appear to someone other than him. Kaladin knelt down. Parshendi all looked so similar. That same square face, those blocky – almost rocklike – features. Some had the beards with bits of gemstone tied in them. Those glowed, but not brightly. Cut gemstones held Stormlight better. Why was that?

Rumors in camp claimed that the Parshendi took the wounded humans away and ate them. Rumors also said they left their dead, not caring for the fallen, never building them proper pyres. But that was false. They did care about their dead. They all seemed to have the same sensibility that

Shen did; he threw a fit every time one of the bridgemen so much as touched a Parshendi corpse.

I'd better be right about this, Kaladin thought grimly, slipping a knife off one of the Parshendi bodies. It was beautifully ornamented and forged, the steel lined with glyphs Kaladin didn't recognize. He began to cut at the strange breastplate armor that grew from the corpse's chest.

Kaladin quickly determined that Parshendi physiology was very different from human physiology. Small blue ligaments held the breastplate to the skin underneath. It was attached all the way across. He continued working. There wasn't much blood; it had pooled at the corpse's back or leaked away. His knife wasn't a surgeon's tool, but it did the job just fine. By the time Syl returned with Lopen, Kaladin had gotten the breastplate free and had moved on to the carapace helm. It was harder to remove; it had grown into the skull in places, and he had to saw with the serrated section of the blade.

'Ho, gancho,' Lopen said, a sack slung over his shoulder. 'You don't like them at all, do you?'

Kaladin stood, wiping his hands on the Parshendi man's skirt. 'Did you find what I asked for?'

'Sure did,' Lopen said, letting down the sack and digging into it. He pulled out an armored leather vest and cap, the type that spearmen used. Then he took out some thin leather straps and a medium-sized wooden spearman's shield. Finally came a series of deep red bones. Parshendi bones. At the very bottom of the sack was the rope, the one Lopen had bought and tossed into the chasm, then stashed down below.

'You haven't lost your wits, have you?' Lopen asked, eyeing the bones. 'Because if you have, I've got a cousin who makes this drink for people who've lost their wits, and it might make you better, sure.'

'If I'd lost my wits,' Kaladin said, walking over to a pool of still water to wash off the carapace helm, 'would I say that I had?'

'I don't know,' Lopen said, leaning back. 'Maybe. Guess it doesn't matter if you're crazy or not.'

'You'd follow a crazy man into battle?'

'Sure,' Lopen said. 'If you're crazy, you're a good type, and I like you. Not a killing-people-in-their-sleep type of crazy.' He smiled. 'Besides. We all follow crazies all the time. Do it every day with lighteyes.'

Kaladin chuckled.

'So what's this all for?'

Kaladin didn't answer. He brought the breastplate over to the leather vest, then tied it onto the front with some of the leather straps. He did the same with the cap and the helm, though he eventually had to saw some grooves into the helm with his knife to make it stay.

Once done, Kaladin used the last straps to tie the bones together and attach them to the front of the round wooden shield. The bones rattled as he lifted the shield, but he decided it was good enough.

He took shield, cap, and breastplate and put them all into Lopen's sack. They barely fit. 'All right,' he said, standing up. 'Syl, lead us to the short chasm.' They'd spent some time investigating, finding the best place to launch arrows into the bottom of permanent bridges. One bridge in particular was close to Sadeas's warcamp – so they often traversed it on the way out on a bridge run – and spanned a particularly shallow chasm. Only about forty feet deep, rather than the usual hundred or more.

She nodded, then zipped away, leading them there. Kaladin and Lopen followed. Teft had orders to lead the others back and meet Kaladin at the base of the ladder, but Kaladin and Lopen should be far ahead of them. He spent the hike listening with half an ear as Lopen talked about his extended family.

The more Kaladin thought about what he was planning, the more brazen it seemed. Perhaps Lopen was right to question his sanity. But Kaladin had tried being rational. He'd tried being careful. That had failed; now there wasn't any more time for logic or care. Hashal obviously intended Bridge Four to be exterminated.

When clever, careful plans failed, it was time to try something desperate.

Lopen cut off suddenly. Kaladin hesitated. The Herdazian man had grown pale-faced and frozen in place. What was . . .

Scraping. Kaladin froze as well, a panic rising in him. One of the side corridors echoed with a deep grinding sound. Kaladin turned slowly, just in time to catch sight of something large – no, something *enormous* – moving down the distant chasm. Shadows in the dim light, the sound of chitinous legs scratching on rock. Kaladin held his breath, sweating, but the beast didn't come in their direction.

The scraping grew softer, then eventually faded. He and Lopen stood immobile for a long time after the last sound had vanished.

Finally, Lopen spoke. 'Guess the nearby ones aren't all dead, eh, gancho?'

'Yeah,' Kaladin said. He jumped suddenly as Syl zipped back to find them. He unconsciously sucked in Stormlight as he did so, and when she alighted in the air, she found him sheepishly glowing.

'What is going on?' she demanded, hands on hips.

'Chasmfiend,' Kaladin said.

'Really?' She sounded excited. 'We should chase after it!'

'What?'

'Sure,' she said. 'You could fight it, I'll bet.'

'Syl . . .'

Her eyes were twinkling with amusement. Just a joke. 'Come on.' She zipped away.

He and Lopen stepped more softly now. Eventually Syl landed on the side of the chasm, standing there as if in mockery of when Kaladin had tried to walk up the wall.

Kaladin looked up at the shadow of a wooden bridge forty feet above. This was the shallowest chasm they'd been able to find; they tended to get deeper and deeper the farther eastward you went. More and more, he was certain that trying to escape to the east was impossible. It was too far, and surviving the highstorm floods was too difficult a challenge. The original plan – fighting or bribing the guards, then running – was the best one.

But they needed to live long enough to try that. The bridge above offered an opportunity, if Kaladin could reach it. He hefted his small bag of spheres and his sack full of armor and bones slung over his shoulder. He'd originally intended to have Rock shoot an arrow with a rope tied to it over the bridge, then back down into the chasm. With some men holding one end, another could have climbed up and tied the sack to the bridge's underside.

But that would risk letting an arrow shoot out of the chasm where scouts could see. They were said to be very keen-eyed, as the armies depended on them to spot chasmfiends making chrysalises.

Kaladin thought he had a better way than the arrow. Maybe. 'We need rocks,' he said. 'Fist-size ones. A lot of them.'

Lopen shrugged and began searching about. Kaladin joined him, fishing them out of puddles and pulling them from crevices. There was no shortage of stones in the chasms. In a short time, he had a large pile of rocks in a sack.

He took the pouch of spheres in his hand and tried to think the same way he had earlier, when he'd drawn in the Stormlight. *This is our last chance.*

'Life before death,' he whispered. 'Strength before weakness. Journey before destination.'

The First Ideal of the Knights Radiant. He breathed in deeply, and a thick jolt of power shot up his arm. His muscles burned with energy, with the desire to move. The tempest spread within, pushing at his skin, causing his blood to pump in a powerful rhythm. He opened his eyes. Glowing smoke rose around him. He was able to contain much of the Light, holding it in by holding his breath.

It's like a storm inside me. It felt as if it would rip him apart.

He set the sack with the armor on the ground, but wound the rope around his arm and tied the sack of rocks to his belt. He took out a single fist-size stone and hefted it, feeling its storm-smoothed sides. *This had better work. . . .*

He infused the stone with Stormlight, frost crystallizing on his arm. He wasn't sure how he did it, but it felt natural, like pouring liquid into a cup. Light seemed to pool underneath the skin of his hand, then transfer to the rock – as if he were painting it with a vibrant, glowing liquid.

He pressed the stone to the rock wall. It fixed in place, leaking Stormlight, clinging so strongly that he couldn't pry it free. He tested his weight on it, and it held. He placed another one a little lower, then another a little higher. Then, wishing he had someone to burn him a prayer for success, he started climbing.

He tried not to think about what he was doing. Climbing on rocks stuck to the wall by . . . what? Light? Spren? He kept on going. It was a lot like climbing the stone formations back near Hearthstone with Tien, except that he could make handholds exactly where he wanted.

Should have found some rock dust to cover my hands, he thought, pulling himself up, then taking another stone from his sack and sticking it into place.

Syl walked along beside him, her casual stroll seeming to mock the difficulty of his climb. As he shifted his weight to another rock, he heard an ominous click from below. He risked a glance downward. The first of his rocks had fallen free. The ones near it were leaking Stormlight only faintly now.

The rocks led up toward him like a set of burning footprints. The storm inside him had quieted, though it still blew and raged inside his veins, thrilling and distracting at the same time. What would happen if he ran out of Light before he reached the top?

The next rock fell free. The one beside it followed a few seconds later. Lopen stood on the other side of the chasm bottom, leaning against the wall, interested but relaxed.

Keep moving! Kaladin thought, annoyed at himself for getting distracted. He turned back to his work.

Just as his arms were beginning to burn from the climb, he reached the underside of the bridge. He reached out as two more of his stones fell free. The clatter of each one was louder now, as they fell a much larger distance.

Steadying himself on the bottom of the bridge with one hand, feet still pushing against the highest rocks, he looped the end of the rope around a wooden bridge support. He pulled it around and threaded it through again to make a makeshift knot. He left plenty of extra rope on the short end.

He let the rest of the rope slide free of his shoulder and drop to the floor below. 'Lopen,' he called. Light steamed from his mouth as he spoke. 'Pull it tight.'

The Herdazian did so, and Kaladin held to his end, making the knot firm. Then he took hold of the long section of rope and let himself swing free, dangling from the bottom of the bridge. The knot held.

Kaladin relaxed. He was still steaming light, and – save for the call to Lopen – he'd been holding his breath for a good quarter hour. *That could be handy,* he thought, though his lungs were starting to burn, so he started to breathe normally. The Light didn't leave him altogether, though it escaped faster.

'All right,' Kaladin said to Lopen. 'Tie the other sack to the bottom of the rope.'

The rope wiggled, and a few moments later Lopen called up that it was done. Kaladin gripped the rope with his legs to hold himself in place, then used his hands to pull up the length underneath, hoisting the sack full of armor. Using the rope on the short end of the knot, he slipped his pouch of dun spheres into the sack with the armor, then tied it into place underneath the bridge where – he hoped – Lopen and Dabbid would be able to get to it from above.

He looked down. The ground looked so much more distant than it would have from the bridge above. From this slightly different perspective, everything changed.

He didn't get vertigo from the height. Instead, he felt a little surge of excitement. Something about him had always liked being up high. It felt natural. It was being below – trapped in holes and unable to see the world – that was depressing.

He considered his next move.

'What?' Syl asked, stepping up to him, standing on air.

'If I leave the rope here, someone might spot it while crossing the bridge.'

'So cut it free.'

He looked at her, raising an eyebrow. 'While dangling from it?'

'You'll be fine.'

'That's a forty-foot drop! I'd break bones at the very least.'

'No,' Syl said. 'I feel *right* about this, Kaladin. You'll be fine. Trust me.'

'Trust you? Syl, you've said yourself that your memory is fractured!'

'You insulted me the other week,' she said, folding her arms. 'I think you owe me an apology.'

'I'm supposed to apologize by cutting a rope and dropping forty feet?'

'No, you apologize by trusting me. I told you. I feel right about this.'

He sighed, looking down again. His Stormlight was running out. What else could he do? Leaving the rope would be foolish. Could he tie it in another knot, one he could shake free once at the bottom?

If that type of knot existed, he didn't know how to tie it. He clenched his teeth. Then, as the last of his rocks fell off and clattered to the ground, he took a deep breath and pulled out the Parshendi knife he'd taken earlier. He moved swiftly, before he had a chance to reconsider, and sliced the rope free.

He dropped in a rush, one hand still holding the sliced rope, stomach lurching with the jarring distress of falling. The bridge shot away as if rising, and Kaladin's panicked mind immediately sent his eyes downward. This wasn't beautiful. This was terrifying. It was horrible. He was going to die! He—

It's all right.

His emotions calmed in a heartbeat. Somehow, he knew what to do. He twisted in the air, dropping the rope and hitting the ground with both feet down. He came to a crouch, resting one hand on the stone, a jolt of coldness shooting through him. His remaining Stormlight came out in a single burst, flung from his body in a luminescent smoke ring that crashed against the ground before spreading out, vanishing.

He stood up straight. Lopen gaped. Kaladin felt an ache in his legs from hitting, but it was like that of having leaped four or five feet.

'Like ten crashes of thunder on the mounts, gancho!' Lopen exclaimed. 'That was incredible!'

'Thank you,' Kaladin said. He raised a hand to his head, glancing at the rocks scattered about the base of the wall, then looking up at the armor tied securely up above.

'I told you,' Syl said, landing on his shoulder. She sounded triumphant.

'Lopen,' Kaladin said. 'You think you can get that bundle of armor during the next bridge run?'

'Sure,' Lopen said. 'Nobody will see. They ignore us Herdies, they ignore bridgemen, and they especially ignore cripples. To them, I'm so invisible I should be walking through walls.'

Kaladin nodded. 'Get it. Hide it. Give it to me right before the final plateau assault.'

'They aren't going to like you going into a bridge run armored, gancho,' Lopen said. 'I don't think this will be any different from what you tried before.'

'We'll see,' Kaladin said. 'Just do it.'

'The death is my life, the strength becomes my weakness, the journey has ended.'

—Dated Betabanes, 1173, 95 seconds pre-death. Subject: a scholar of some minor renown. Sample collected secondhand. Considered questionable.

'That is why, Father,' Adolin said, 'you absolutely *cannot* abdicate to me, no matter *what* we discover with the visions.'

'Is that so?' Dalinar asked, smiling to himself.

'Yes.'

'Very well, you've convinced me.'

Adolin stopped dead in the hallway. The two of them were on their way to Dalinar's chambers. Dalinar turned and looked back at the younger man.

'Really?' Adolin asked. 'I mean, I actually *won* an argument with you?'

'Yes,' Dalinar said. 'Your points are valid.' He didn't add that he'd come to the decision on his own. 'No matter what, I will stay. I can't leave this fight now.'

Adolin smiled broadly.

'But,' Dalinar said, raising a finger. 'I have a requirement. I will draft an order – notarized by the highest of my scribes and witnessed by Elhokar – that gives you the right to depose me, should I grow too mentally unstable. We won't let the other camps know of it, but I will not risk letting myself grow so crazy that it's impossible to remove me.'

'All right,' Adolin said, walking up to Dalinar. They were alone in the hallway. 'I can accept that. Assuming you don't tell Sadeas about it. I still don't trust him.'

'I'm not asking you to trust him,' Dalinar said pushing the door open to his chambers. 'You just need to believe that he is capable of changing. Sadeas was once a friend, and I think he can be again.'

The cool stones of the Soulcast chamber seemed to hold the chill of the spring weather. It continued to refuse to slip into summer, but at least it hadn't slid into winter either. Elthebar promised that it would not do so – but, then, the stormwarden's promises were always filled with caveats. The Almighty's will was mysterious, and the signs couldn't always be trusted.

He accepted stormwardens now, though when they'd first grown popular, he'd rejected their aid. No man should try to know the future, nor lay claim to it, for it belonged only to the Almighty himself. And Dalinar wondered how stormwardens could do their research without reading. They claimed they didn't, but he'd seen their books filled with glyphs. Glyphs. They weren't meant to be used in books; they were pictures. A man who had never seen one before could still understand what it meant, based on its shape. That made interpreting glyphs different from reading.

Stormwardens did a lot of things that made people uncomfortable. Unfortunately, they were just so *useful*. Knowing when a highstorm might strike, well, that was just too tempting an advantage. Even though stormwardens were frequently wrong, they were more often right.

Renarin knelt beside the hearth, inspecting the fabrial that had been installed there to warm the room. Navani had already arrived. She sat at Dalinar's elevated writing desk, scribbling a letter; she waved a distracted greeting with her reed as Dalinar entered. She wore the fabrial he had seen her displaying at the feast a few weeks back; the multilegged contraption was attached to her shoulder, gripping the cloth of her violet dress.

'I don't know, Father,' Adolin said, closing the door. Apparently he was still thinking about Sadeas. 'I don't care if he's listening to *The Way of Kings*. He's just doing it to make you look less closely at the plateau assaults so that his clerks can arrange his cut of the gemhearts more favorably. He's manipulating you.'

Dalinar shrugged. 'Gemhearts are secondary, son. If I can reforge an alliance with him, then it's worth nearly any cost. In a way, I'm the one manipulating him.'

Adolin sighed. 'Very well. But I'm still going to keep a hand on my money pouch when he's near.'

'Just try not to insult him,' Dalinar said. 'Oh, and something else. I would like you to take extra care with the King's Guard. If there are soldiers we know for certain are loyal to me, put those in charge of guarding Elhokar's rooms. His words about a conspiracy have me worried.'

'Surely you don't give them credence,' Adolin said.

'Something odd did happen with his armor. This whole mess stinks like cremslime. Perhaps it will turn out to be nothing. For now, humor me.'

'I have to note,' Navani said, 'that I didn't much care for Sadeas back when you, he, and Gavilar were friends.' She finished her letter with a flourish.

'He's not behind the attacks on the king,' Dalinar said.

'How can you be certain?' Navani asked.

'Because it's not his way,' Dalinar said. 'Sadeas never wanted the title of king. Being highprince gives him plenty of power, but leaves him with someone to take the blame for large-scale mistakes.' Dalinar shook his head. 'He never tried to seize the throne from Gavilar, and he's even better positioned with Elhokar.'

'Because my son's a weakling,' Navani said. It wasn't an accusation.

'He's *not* weak,' Dalinar said, 'He's inexperienced. But yes, that does make the situation ideal for Sadeas. He's telling the truth – he asked to be Highprince of Information because he wants very badly to find out who is trying to kill Elhokar.'

'Mashala,' Renarin said, using the formal term for aunt. 'That fabrial on your shoulder, what does it do?'

Navani looked down at the device with a sly smile. Dalinar could see she'd been hoping one of them would ask. Dalinar sat down; the highstorm would be coming soon.

'Oh, this? It's a type of painrial. Here, let me show you.' She reached up with her safehand, pushing a clip that released the clawlike legs. She held it up. 'Do you have any aches, dear? A stubbed toe, perhaps, or a scrape?'

Renarin shook his head.

'I pulled a muscle in my hand during dueling practice earlier,' Adolin said. 'It's not bad, but it does ache.'

'Come over here,' Navani said. Dalinar smiled fondly – Navani was always at her most genuine when playing with new fabrials. It was one of the few times when one got to see her without any pretense. This wasn't Navani the king's mother or Navani the political schemer. This was Navani the excited engineer.

'The artifabrian community is doing some amazing things,' Navani said as Adolin proffered his hand. 'I'm particularly proud of this little device, as I had a hand in its construction.' She clipped it onto Adolin's hand, wrapping the clawlike legs around the palm and locking them into place.

Adolin raised his hand, turning it around. 'The pain is gone.'

'But you can still feel, correct?' Navani said in a self-satisfied way.

Adolin prodded his palm with the fingers of his other hand. 'The hand isn't numb at all.'

Renarin watched with keen interest, bespectacled eyes curious, intense. If only the lad could be persuaded to become an ardent. He could be an engineer then, if he wanted. And yet he refused. His reasons always seemed like poor excuses to Dalinar.

'It's kind of bulky,' Dalinar noted.

'Well, it's just an early model,' Navani said defensively. 'I was working backward from one of those dreadful creations of Longshadow's, and I didn't have the luxury of refining the shape. I think it has a lot of potential. Imagine a few of these on a battlefield to dull the pain of wounded soldiers. Imagine it in the hands of a surgeon, who wouldn't have to worry about his patients' pain while working on them.'

Adolin nodded. Dalinar had to admit, it did sound like a useful device.

Navani smiled. 'This is a special time to be alive; we're learning all kinds of things about fabrials. This, for instance, is a diminishing fabrial – it decreases something, in this case pain. It doesn't actually make the wound any better, but it might be a step in that direction. Either way, it's a completely different type from paired fabrials like the spanreeds. If you could see the plans we have for the future . . .'

'Like what?' Adolin asked.

'You'll find out eventually,' Navani said, smiling mysteriously. She removed the fabrial from Adolin's hand.

'Shardblades?' Adolin sounded excited.

'Well, no,' Navani said. 'The design and workings of Shardblades and Plate are completely different from everything we've discovered. The closest anyone has are those shields in Jah Keved. But as far as I can tell, they use a completely different design principle from true Shardplate. The ancients must have had a wondrous grasp of engineering.'

'No,' Dalinar said. 'I've seen them, Navani. They're ... well, they're ancient. Their technology is primitive.'

'And the Dawncities?' Navani asked skeptically. 'The fabrials?'

Dalinar shook his head. 'I've seen neither. There are Shardblades in the visions, but they seem so out of place. Perhaps they were given directly by the Heralds, as the legends say.'

'Perhaps,' Navani said. 'Why don't—'

She vanished.

Dalinar blinked. He hadn't heard the highstorm approaching.

He was now in a large, open room with pillars running along the sides. The enormous pillars looked sculpted of soft sandstone, with unornamented, granular sides. The ceiling was far above, carved from the rock in geometric patterns that looked faintly familiar. Circles connected by lines, spreading outward from one another ...

'I don't know what to do, old friend,' a voice said from the side. Dalinar turned to see a youthful man in regal white and gold robes, walking with his hands clasped before him, hidden by voluminous sleeves. He had dark hair pulled back in a braid and a short beard that came to a point. Gold threads were woven into his hair and came together on his forehead to form a golden symbol. The symbol of the Knights Radiant.

'They say that each time it is the same,' the man said. 'We are never ready for the Desolations. We should be getting better at resisting, but each time we step closer to destruction instead.' He turned to Dalinar, as if expecting a response.

Dalinar glanced down. He too wore ornamental robes, though not as lavish. Where was he? What time? He needed to find clues for Navani to record and for Jasnah to use in proving – or disproving – these dreams.

'I don't know what to say either,' Dalinar responded. If he wanted information, he needed to act more natural than he had in previous visions.

The regal man sighed. 'I had hoped you would have wisdom to share with me, Karm.' They continued walking toward the side of the room, approaching a place where the wall split into a massive balcony with a stone railing. It looked out upon an evening sky; the setting sun stained the air a dirty, sultry red.

'Our own natures destroy us,' the regal man said, voice soft, though his face was angry. 'Alakavish was a Surgebinder. He should have known better. And yet, the Nahel bond gave him no more wisdom than an ordinary man. Alas, not all spren are as discerning as honorspren.'

'I agree,' Dalinar said.

The other man looked relieved. 'I worried that you would find my claims too forward. Your own Surgebinders were . . . But, no, we should not look backward.'

What's a Surgebinder? Dalinar wanted to scream the question out, but there was no way. Not without sounding completely out of place.

Perhaps . . .

'What do you think should be done with these Surgebinders?' Dalinar asked carefully.

'I don't know if we can force them to do anything.' Their footsteps echoed in the empty room. Were there no guards, no attendants? 'Their power . . . well, Alakavish proves the allure that Surgebinders have for the common people. If only there were a way to encourage them. . . .' The man stopped, turning to Dalinar. 'They need to be better, old friend. We all do. The responsibility of what we've been given – whether it be the crown or the Nahel bond – needs to make *us* better.'

He seemed to expect something from Dalinar. But what?

'I can read your disagreement in your face,' the regal man said. 'It's all right, Karm. I realize that my thoughts on this subject are unconventional. Perhaps the rest of you are right, perhaps our abilities are proof of a divine election. But if this is true, should we not be more wary of how we act?'

Dalinar frowned. That sounded familiar to him. The regal man sighed, walking to the balcony lip. Dalinar joined him, stepping outside. The perspective finally allowed him to look down on the landscape below.

Thousands of corpses confronted him.

Dalinar gasped. Dead filled the streets of the city outside, a city that

Dalinar vaguely recognized. *Kholinar*, he thought. *My homeland*. He stood with the regal man at the top of a low tower, three stories high – a keep of some sort, constructed of stone. It seemed to sit where the palace would someday be.

The city was unmistakable, with its peaked stone formations rising like enormous fins into the air. The windblades, they were called. But they were less weathered than he was accustomed to, and the city around them was very different. Built of blocky stone structures, many of which had been knocked down. The destruction spread far, lining the sides of primitive streets. Had the city been hit by an earthquake?

No, those corpses had fallen in battle. Dalinar could smell the stench of blood, viscera, smoke. The bodies lay strewn about, many near the low wall that surrounded the keep. The wall was broken in places, smashed. And there were rocks of strange shape scattered among the corpses. Stones cut like . . .

Blood of my fathers, Dalinar thought, gripping the stone railing, leaning forward. *Those aren't stones. They're creatures*. Massive creatures, easily five or six times the size of a person, their skin dull and grey like granite. They had long limbs and skeletal bodies, the forelegs – or were they arms? – set into wide shoulders. The faces were lean, narrow. Arrowlike.

'What happened here?' Dalinar asked despite himself. 'It's terrible!'

'I ask myself this same thing. How could we let this occur? The Desolations are well named. I've heard initial counts. Eleven years of war, and nine out of ten people I once ruled are dead. Do we even have kingdoms to lead any longer? Sur is gone, I'm sure of it. Tarma, Eiliz, they won't likely survive. Too many of their people have fallen.'

Dalinar had never heard of those places.

The man made a fist, pounding it softly against the railing. Burning stations had been set up in the distance; they had begun cremating the corpses. 'The others want to blame Alakavish. And true, if he hadn't brought us to war before the Desolation, we might not have been broken this badly. But Alakavish was a symptom of a greater disease. When the Heralds next return, what will they find? A people who have forgotten them yet again? A world torn by war and squabbling? If we continue as we have, then perhaps we *deserve* to lose.'

Dalinar felt a chill. He had thought that this vision must come after his previous one, but prior visions hadn't been chronological. He hadn't seen any Knights Radiant yet, but that might not be because they had disbanded. Perhaps they didn't *exist* yet. And perhaps there was a reason this man's words sounded so familiar.

Could it be? Could he really be standing beside the very man whose words Dalinar had listened to time and time again? 'There is honor in loss,' Dalinar said carefully, using words repeated several times in *The Way of Kings*.

'If that loss brings learning.' The man smiled. 'Using my own sayings against me again, Karm?'

Dalinar felt himself grow short of breath. The man himself. Nohadon. The great king. He was real. Or he had been real. This man was younger than Dalinar had imagined him, but that humble, yet regal bearing ... yes, it was right.

'I'm thinking of giving up my throne,' Nohadon said softly.

'No!' Dalinar stepped toward him. 'You mustn't.'

'I cannot lead them,' the man said. 'Not if this is what my leadership brings them to.'

'Nohadon.'

The man turned to him, frowning. 'What?'

Dalinar paused. Could he be wrong about this man's identity? But no. The name Nohadon was more of a title. Many famous people in history had been given holy names by the Church, before it was disbanded. Even Bajerden wasn't likely to be his real name; that was lost in time.

'It is nothing,' Dalinar said. 'You cannot give up your throne. The people need a leader.'

'They *have* leaders,' Nohadon said. 'There are princes, kings, Soulcasters, Surgebinders. We never lack men and women who wish to lead.'

'True,' Dalinar said, 'but we do lack ones who are good at it.'

Nohadon leaned over the railing. He stared at the fallen, an expression of deep grief – and trouble – on his face. It was so strange to see the man like this. He was so young. Dalinar had never imagined such insecurity, such torment, in him.

'I know that feeling,' Dalinar said softly. 'The uncertainty, the shame, the confusion.'

'You can read me too well, old friend.'

'I know those emotions because I've felt them. I ... I never assumed that you would feel them too.'

'Then I correct myself. Perhaps you don't know me well enough.'

Dalinar fell silent.

'So what do I do?' Nohadon asked.

'You're asking *me*?'

'You're my advisor, aren't you? Well, I should like some advice.'

'I . . . You can't give up your throne.'

'And what should I do with it?' Nohadon turned and walked along the long balcony. It seemed to run around this entire level. Dalinar joined him, passing places where the stone was ripped, the railing broken away.

'I haven't faith in people any longer, old friend,' Nohadon said. 'Put two men together, and they will find something to argue about. Gather them into groups, and one group will find reason to oppress or attack another. Now this. How do I protect them? How do I stop this from happening again?'

'You dictate a book,' Dalinar said eagerly. 'A grand book to give people hope, to explain your philosophy on leadership and how lives should be lived!'

'A book? Me. Write a book?'

'Why not?'

'Because it's a fantastically *stupid* idea.'

Dalinar's jaw dropped.

'The world as we know it has quite nearly been destroyed,' Nohadon said. 'Barely a family exists that hasn't lost half its members! Our best men are corpses on that field, and we haven't food to last more than two or three months at best. And I'm to spend my time writing a book? Who would scribe it for me? All of my wordsmen were slaughtered when Yelignar broke into the chancery. You're the only man of letters I know of who's still alive.'

A *man* of letters? This *was* an odd time. 'I could write it, then.'

'With one arm? Have you learned to write left-handed, then?'

Dalinar looked down. He had both of his arms, though apparently the man Nohadon saw was missing his right.

'No, we need to rebuild,' Nohadon said. 'I just wish there were a way to convince the kings – the ones still alive – not to seek advantage over one another.' Nohadon tapped the balcony. 'So this is my decision. Step down, or do what is needed. This isn't a time for writing. It's a time for action. And then, unfortunately, a time for the sword.'

The sword? Dalinar thought. *From you, Nohadon?*

It wouldn't happen. This man would become a great philosopher; he would teach peace and reverence for others, and would not force men to do as he wished. He would *guide* them to acting with honor.

Nohadon turned to Dalinar. 'I apologize, Karm. I should not dismiss your suggestions right after asking for them. I'm on edge, as I imagine that we all are. At times, it seems to me that to be human is to want that which we cannot have. For some, this is power. For me, it is peace.'

Nohadon turned, walking back down the balcony. Though his pace was slow, his posture indicated that he wished to be alone. Dalinar let him go.

'He goes on to become one of the most influential writers Roshar has ever known,' Dalinar said.

There was silence, save for the calls of the people working below, gathering the corpses.

'I know you're there,' Dalinar said.

Silence.

'What does he decide?' Dalinar asked. 'Did he unite them, as he wanted?'

The voice that often spoke in his visions did not come. Dalinar received no answer to his questions. He sighed, turning to look out over the fields of dead.

'You are right about one thing, at least, Nohadon. To be human is to want that which we cannot have.'

The landscape darkened, the sun setting. That darkness enveloped him, and he closed his eyes. When he opened them, he was back in his rooms, standing with his hands on the back of a chair. He turned to Adolin and Renarin, who stood nearby, anxious, prepared to grab him if he got violent.

'Well,' Dalinar said, 'that was meaningless. I learned nothing. Blast! I'm doing a poor job of—'

'Dalinar,' Navani said curtly, still scribbling with a reed at her paper. 'The last thing you said before the vision ended. What was it?'

Dalinar frowned. 'The last . . .'

'Yes,' Navani said, urgent. 'The very last words you spoke.'

'I was quoting the man I'd been speaking with. "To be human is to want that which we cannot have." Why?'

She ignored him, writing furiously. Once done, she slid off the high-legged chair, hurrying to his bookshelf. 'Do you have a copy of . . . Yes, I thought you might. These are Jasnah's books, aren't they?'

'Yes,' Dalinar said. 'She wanted them cared for until she returned.'

Navani pulled a volume off the shelf. 'Corvana's *Analectics*.' She set the volume on the writing desk and leafed through the pages.

Dalinar joined her, though – of course – he couldn't make sense of the page. 'What does it matter?'

'Here,' Navani said. She looked up at Dalinar. 'When you go into these visions of yours, you know that you speak.'

'Gibberish. Yes, my sons have told me.'

'Anak malah kaf, del makian habin yah,' Navani said. 'Sound familiar?'

Dalinar shook his head, baffled.

'It sounds a lot like what father was saying,' Renarin said. 'When he was in the vision.'

'Not "a lot like," Renarin,' Navani said, looking smug. 'It's exactly the same phrase. That is the last thing you said before coming out of your trance. I wrote down everything – as best I could – that you babbled today.'

'For what purpose?' Dalinar asked.

'Because,' Navani said, 'I thought it might be helpful. And it was. The same phrase is in the *Analectics*, almost exactly.'

'What?' Dalinar asked, incredulous. 'How?'

'It's a line from a song,' Navani said. 'A chant by the Vanrial, an order of artists who live on the slopes of the Silent Mount in Jah Keved. Year after year, century after century, they've sung these same words – songs they claim were written in the Dawnchant by the Heralds themselves. They have the words of those songs, written in an ancient script. But the *meanings* have been lost. They're just sounds, now. Some scholars believe that the script – and the songs themselves – may indeed be in the Dawnchant.'

'And I . . .' Dalinar said.

'You just spoke a line from one of them,' Navani said. 'Beyond that, if the phrase you just gave me is correct, you *translated* it. This could prove the Vanrial Hypothesis! One sentence isn't much, but it could give us the key to translating the entire script. It has been itching at me for a while, listening to these visions. I *thought* the things you were saying had too much order to be gibberish.' She looked at Dalinar, smiling deeply. 'Dalinar, you might just have cracked one of the most perplexing – and ancient – mysteries of all time.'

'Wait,' Adolin said. 'What are you saying?'

'What I'm saying, nephew,' Navani said, looking directly at him, 'is that we have your proof.'

'But,' Adolin said. 'I mean, he could have heard that one phrase . . .'

'And extrapolated an entire language from it?' Navani said, holding up a sheet full of writings. 'This *is not* gibberish, but it's no language that people now speak. I suspect it is what it seems, the Dawnchant. So unless you can think of another way your father learned to speak a dead language, Adolin, the visions are most certainly real.'

The room fell silent. Navani herself looked stunned by what she had said. She shook it off quickly. 'Now, Dalinar,' she said, 'I want you to describe this vision as accurately as possible. I need the exact words you spoke, if you can recall them. Every bit we gather will help my scholars sort through this. . . .'

61

RIGHT FOR WRONG

'In the storm I awaken, falling, spinning, grieving.'

—Dated Kakanev, 1173, 13 seconds pre-death. Subject was a city guardsman.

How can you be so sure it was him, Dalinar?' Navani asked softly.

Dalinar shook his head. 'I just am. That was Nohadon.'

It had been several hours since the end of the vision. Navani had left her writing table to sit in a more comfortable chair near Dalinar. Renarin sat across from him, accompanying them for propriety's sake. Adolin had left to get the highstorm damage report. The lad had seemed very disturbed by the discovery that the visions were real.

'But the man you saw never spoke his name,' Navani said.

'It was him, Navani.' Dalinar stared toward the wall over Renarin's head, looking at the smooth brown Soulcast rock. 'There was an aura of command about him, the weight of great responsibilities. A regality.'

'It could have been some other king,' she said. 'After all, he discarded your suggestion that he write a book.'

'It just wasn't the time for him to write it yet. So much death ... He was cast down by great loss. Stormfather! Nine out of ten people dead in war. Can you imagine such a thing?'

'The Desolations,' Navani said.

Unite the people. ... The True Desolation comes. ...

'Do you know of any references to the Desolations?' Dalinar asked. 'Not the tales ardents tell. Historical references?'

Navani held a cup of warmed violet wine in her hand, beads of condensation on the rim of the glass. 'Yes, but I am the wrong one to ask. Jasnah is the historian.'

'I think I saw the aftermath of one. I . . . I may have seen corpses of Voidbringers. Could that give us more proof?'

'Nothing nearly as good as the linguistics.' Navani took a sip of her wine. 'The Desolations are matters of ancient lore. It could be argued that you imagined what you expected to see. But those words – if we can translate them, nobody will be able to dispute that you are seeing something real.' Her writing board lay on the low table between them, reed and ink set carefully across the paper.

'You intend to tell others?' Dalinar asked. 'Of my visions?'

'How else will we explain what is happening to you?'

Dalinar hesitated. How could he explain? On one hand, it was a relief that he was not mad. But what if some force were trying to mislead him with these visions, using images of Nohadon and the Radiants because he would find them trustworthy?

The Knights Radiant fell, Dalinar reminded himself. *They abandoned us. Some of the other orders may have turned against us, as the legends say.* There was an unsettling edge to all of that. He had another stone in rebuilding the foundation of who he was, but the most important point still remained undecided. Did he trust his visions or not? He couldn't go back to believing them unquestioningly, not now that Adolin's challenges had raised real worries in his head.

Until he knew their source, he felt he shouldn't spread knowledge of them.

'Dalinar,' Navani said, leaning forward. 'The warcamps speak of your episodes. Even the wives of your officers are uncomfortable. They think you fear the storms, or that you have some disease of the mind. This will vindicate you.'

'How? By making me into some kind of mystic? Many will think that the breeze of these visions blows too close to prophecy.'

'You see the past, Father,' Renarin said. 'That is not forbidden. And if the Almighty sends them, then how could men question?'

'Adolin and I both spoke with ardents,' Dalinar replied. 'They said it was very unlikely that this would come from the Almighty. If we do decide the visions are to be trusted, many will disagree with me.'

Navani settled back, sipping her wine, safehand lying across her lap. 'Dalinar, your sons told me that you once sought the Old Magic. Why? What did you ask of the Nightwatcher, and what curse did she give you in return?'

'I told them that shame is my own,' Dalinar said. 'And I will not share it.'

The room fell silent. The flurries of rain following the highstorm had ceased falling on the roof. 'It might be important,' Navani finally said.

'It was long ago. Long before the visions began. I don't think it's related.'

'But it could be.'

'Yes,' he admitted. Would that day never stop haunting him? Was not losing all memory of his wife enough?

What did Renarin think? Would he condemn his father for such an egregious sin? Dalinar forced himself to look up and meet his son's bespectacled eyes.

Curiously, Renarin didn't seem bothered. Just thoughtful.

'I'm sorry you had to discover my shame,' Dalinar said, looking to Navani.

She waved indifferently. 'Soliciting the Old Magic is offensive to the devotaries, but their punishments for the act are never severe. I assume that you didn't have to do much to be cleansed.'

'The ardents asked for spheres to give the poor,' Dalinar said. 'And I had to commission a series of prayers. None of that removed the effects or my sense of guilt.'

'I think you'd be surprised at how many devout lighteyes turn to the Old Magic at one point in their lives or another. The ones who can make their way to the Valley, at least. But I *do* wonder if this is related.'

'Aunt,' Renarin said, turning to her. 'I have recently asked for a number of readings about the Old Magic. I agree with his assessment. This does not feel like the work of the Nightwatcher. She gives curses in exchange for granting small desires. Always one curse and one desire. Father, I assume you know what both of those things are?'

'Yes,' he said. 'I know exactly what my curse was, and it does not relate to this.'

'Then it is unlikely that the Old Magic is to blame.'

'Yes,' Dalinar said. 'But your aunt is right to question. The truth is, we don't have any proof that this came from the Almighty either. Something wants me to know of the Desolations and the Knights Radiant. Perhaps we should start asking ourselves why that is.'

'What *were* the Desolations, Aunt?' Renarin asked. 'The ardents talk of the Voidbringers. Of mankind, and the Radiants, and of fighting. But what were they really? Do we know anything specific?'

'There are folklorists among your father's clerks who would serve you better in this matter.'

'Perhaps,' Dalinar added, 'but I'm not sure which of them I can trust.'

Navani paused. 'Fair enough. Well, from what I understand, there are no primary accounts remaining. This was long, long ago. I do recall that the myth of Parasaphi and Nadris mentions the Desolations.'

'Parasaphi,' Renarin said. 'She's the one who searched out the seed-stones.'

'Yes,' Navani replied. 'In order to repopulate her fallen people, she climbed the peaks of Dara – the myth changes, listing different modern mountain ranges as the true peaks of Dara – to find stones touched by the Heralds themselves. She brought them to Nadris on his deathbed and harvested his seed to bring life to the stones. They hatched forth ten children, which she used to found a new nation. Marnah, I believe it was called.'

'Origin of the Makabaki,' Renarin said. 'Mother told me that story when I was a child.'

Dalinar shook his head. 'Born from rocks?' The old stories rarely made much sense to him, although the devotaries had canonized many of them.

'The story mentions the Desolations at the beginning,' Navani said. 'Giving them credit for having wiped out Parasaphi's people.'

'But what *were* they?'

'Wars.' Navani took a sip of wine. 'The Voidbringers came again and again, trying to force mankind off Roshar and into Damnation. Just as they once forced mankind – and the Heralds – out of the Tranquiline Halls.'

'When were the Knights Radiant founded?' Dalinar asked.

Navani shrugged. 'I don't know. Perhaps they were some military group from a specific kingdom, or perhaps they were originally a mercenary band. That would make it easy to see how they could eventually become tyrants.'

'My visions don't imply that they were tyrants,' he said. 'Perhaps that is the true purpose of the visions. To make me believe lies about the Radiants. Making me trust them, perhaps trying to lead me to mimic their downfall and betrayal.'

'I don't know,' Navani said, sounding skeptical. 'I don't think you've seen anything untrue about the Radiants. The legends tend to agree that the Radiants weren't always so bad. As much as the legends agree on anything, at least.'

Dalinar stood and took her nearly empty cup, then walked over to the serving table and refilled it. Discovering that he was not mad should have helped clear things up, but instead left him more disturbed. What if the Voidbringers were behind the visions? Some stories he heard said that they could possess the bodies of men and make them do evil. Or, if they *were* from the Almighty, what was their purpose?

'I need to think on all of this,' he said. 'It has been a long day. Please, if I could be left to my own thoughts now.'

Renarin rose and bowed his head in respect before heading to the door. Navani rose more slowly, sleek dress rustling as she set her cup on the table, then walked over to fetch her pain-drinking fabrial. Renarin left, and Dalinar walked to the doorway, waiting as Navani approached. He didn't intend to let her trap him alone again. He looked out the doorway. His soldiers were there, and he could see them. Good.

'Aren't you pleased at all?' Navani asked, lingering beside the doorway near him, one hand on the frame.

'Pleased?'

'You aren't going mad.'

'And we don't know if I'm being manipulated or not,' he said. 'In a way, we have more questions now than we had before.'

'The visions are a blessing,' Navani said, laying her freehand on his arm. 'I feel it, Dalinar. Don't you see how wonderful this is?'

Dalinar met her eyes, light violet, beautiful. She was so thoughtful, so clever. How he wished he could trust her completely.

She has shown me nothing but honor, he thought. *Never speaking a word to anyone else of my intention to abdicate. She hasn't so much as tried to use my visions against me*. He felt ashamed that he'd once worried that she might.

She was a wonderful woman, Navani Kholin. A wonderful, amazing, *dangerous* woman.

'I see more worries,' he said. 'And more danger.'

'But Dalinar, you're having experiences scholars, historians, and folklorists could only dream about! I envy you, although you claim to have seen no fabrials of note.'

'The ancients didn't have fabrials, Navani. I'm certain of it.'

'And that changes everything we thought we understood about them.'

'I suppose.'

'Stonefalls, Dalinar,' she said, sighing. 'Does nothing bring you to passion any longer?'

Dalinar took a deep breath. 'Too many things, Navani. My insides feel like a mass of eels, emotions squirming over one another. The truth of these visions is unsettling.'

'It's exciting,' she corrected. 'Did you mean what you said earlier? About trusting me?'

'I said that?'

'You said you didn't trust your clerks, and you asked me to record the visions. There's an implication in that.'

Her hand was still on his arm. She reached out with her safehand and closed the door to the hallway. He almost stopped her, but he hesitated. Why?

The door clicked closed. They were alone. And she was so beautiful. Those clever, excitable eyes, alight with passion.

'Navani,' Dalinar said, forcing down his desire. 'You're doing it again.' Why did he let her?

'Yes, I am,' she said. 'I'm a stubborn woman, Dalinar.' There didn't seem to be any playfulness in her tone.

'This is not proper. My brother . . .' He reached for the door to open it again.

'Your brother,' Navani spat, expression flashing with anger. 'Why must everyone always focus on him? Everyone always worries so much about the man who died! He's not here, Dalinar. He's gone. I miss him. But not half as much as you do, it appears.'

'I honor his memory,' Dalinar said stiffly, hesitating, hand on the door's latch.

'That's fine! I'm happy you do. But it's been *six years*, and all anyone can see me as is the wife of a dead man. The other women, they humor me with idle gossip, but they won't let me into their political circles. They think I'm a relic. You wanted to know why I came back so quickly?'

'I—'

'I *returned*,' she said, 'because I have no home. I'm expected to sit out of important events because my husband is dead! Lounge around, pampered but ignored. I make them uncomfortable. The queen, the other women at court.'

'I'm sorry,' Dalinar said. 'But I don't—'

She raised her freehand, tapping him on the chest. 'I won't take it from you, Dalinar. We were friends before I even *met* Gavilar! You still know me as me, not some shadow of a reign that crumbled years ago. Don't you?' She looked at him, pleading.

Blood of my fathers, Dalinar thought with shock. *She's crying*. Two small tears.

He had rarely seen her so sincere.

And so he kissed her.

It was a mistake. He knew it was. He grabbed her anyway, pulling her into a rough, tight embrace and pressing his mouth to hers, unable to contain himself. She melted against him. He tasted the salt of her tears as they ran down to her lips and met his.

It lasted long. Too long. Wonderfully long. His mind screamed at him, like a prisoner chained in a cell and forced to watch something horrible. But a part of him had wanted this for decades – decades spent watching his brother court, marry, and then hold the only woman that the young Dalinar had ever wanted.

He'd told himself he would never allow this. He had denied himself feelings for Navani the moment Gavilar had won her hand. Dalinar had stepped aside.

But the taste of her – the smell of her, the warmth of her pressed against him – was too sweet. Like a blossoming perfume, it washed away the guilt. For a moment, that touch banished everything. He couldn't remember his fear at the visions, his worry about Sadeas, his shame at past mistakes.

He could only think of her. Beautiful, insightful, delicate yet strong at once. He clung to her, something he could hold on to as the rest of the world churned around him.

Eventually, he broke the kiss. She looked up at him, dazed. Passionspren, like tiny flakes of crystalline snow, floated down in the air around them. Guilt flooded him again. He tried gently to push her away, but she clung to him, holding on tight.

'Navani,' he said.

'Hush.' She pressed her head against his chest.

'We can't—'

'Hush,' she said, more insistently.

He sighed, but let himself hold her.

'Something is going wrong in this world, Dalinar,' Navani said softly. 'The king of Jah Keved was assassinated. I heard it just today. He was killed by a Shin Shardbearer in white clothing.'

'Stormfather!' Dalinar said.

'Something's going on,' she said. 'Something bigger than our war here, something bigger than Gavilar. Have you heard of the twisted things men say when they die? Most ignore it, but surgeons are talking. And stormwardens whisper that the highstorms are growing more powerful.'

'I have heard,' he said, finding it difficult to get the words out, intoxicated by her as he was.

'My daughter seeks something,' Navani said. 'She frightens me sometimes. She's so intense. I honestly believe she's the most intelligent person I've ever known. And the things she searches for . . . Dalinar, she believes that something very dangerous is near.'

The sun approaches the horizon. The Everstorm comes. The True Desolation. The Night of Sorrows. . . .

'I need you,' Navani said. 'I've known it for years, though I feared it would destroy you with guilt, so I fled. But I couldn't stay away. Not with the way they treat me. Not with what is happening to the world. I'm terrified, Dalinar, and I need you. Gavilar was not the man everyone thought him to be. I was fond of him, but he—'

'Please,' Dalinar said, 'don't speak ill of him.'

'Very well.'

Blood of my fathers! He couldn't get her scent out of his head. He felt paralyzed, holding to her like a man clinging to a stone in the stormwinds.

She looked up at him. 'Well, let it be said – then – that I was fond of Gavilar. But I'm more than fond of you. And I'm tired of waiting.'

He closed his eyes. 'How can this work?'

'We'll find a way.'

'We'll be denounced.'

'The warcamps already ignore me,' Navani said, 'and they spread rumors and lies about you. What more can they do to us?'

'They'll find something. As of yet, the devotaries do not condemn me.'

'Gavilar is dead,' Navani said, resting her head back against his chest. 'I was never unfaithful while he lived, though the Stormfather knows I had ample reason. The devotaries can say what they wish, but *The Arguments* do not forbid our union. Tradition is not the same as doctrine, and I will not hold myself back for fear of offending.'

Dalinar took a deep breath, then forced himself to open his arms and pull back. 'If you had hoped to soothe my worries for the day, then this didn't help.'

She folded her arms. He could still feel where her safehand had touched him on the back. A tender touch, reserved for a family member. 'I'm not here to soothe you, Dalinar. Quite the opposite.'

'Please. I *do* need time to think.'

'I won't let you put me away. I won't ignore that this happened. I won't—'

'Navani,' he gently cut her off, 'I will not abandon you. I promise.'

She eyed him, then a wry smile crept onto her face. 'Very well. But you began something today.'

'*I* began it?' he asked, amused, elated, confused, worried, and ashamed at the same time.

'The kiss was yours, Dalinar,' she said idly, pulling open the door and entering his antechamber.

'You seduced me to it.'

'What? Seduced?' She glanced back at him. 'Dalinar, I've never been more open and honest in my life.'

'I know,' Dalinar said, smiling. 'That was the seductive part.' He closed the door softly, then let out a sigh.

Blood of my fathers, he thought, *why can't these things ever be simple?*

And yet, in direct contrast with his thoughts, he felt as if the entire world had somehow become more right for having gone wrong.

62
THREE GLYPHS

'The darkness becomes a palace. Let it rule! Let it rule!'

–Kakevah 1173, 22 seconds pre-death. A darkeyed Selay man of unknown profession.

'You think one of those will save us?' Moash asked, scowling as he looked at the prayer tied about Kaladin's upper right arm.

Kaladin glanced to the side. He stood at parade rest as Sadeas's soldiers crossed their bridge. The chilly spring air felt good, now that he'd started working. The sky was bright, cloudless, and the stormwardens promised that no highstorm was near.

The prayer tied on his arm was simple. Three glyphs: wind, protection, beloved. A prayer to Jezerezeh – the Stormfather – to protect loved ones and friends. It was the straightforward type his mother had preferred. For all her subtlety and wryness, whenever she'd knitted or written a prayer, it had been simple and heartfelt. Wearing it reminded him of her.

'I can't believe you paid good money for that,' Moash said. 'If there are Heralds watching, they don't pay any mind to bridgemen.'

'I've been feeling nostalgic lately, I guess.' The prayer was probably meaningless, but he'd had reason to start thinking more about religion lately. The life of a slave made it difficult for many to believe that anyone, or anything, was watching. Yet many bridgemen had grown more religious during their captivity. Two groups, opposite reactions. Did that mean some were stupid and others were callous, or something else entirely?

'They're going to see us dead, you know,' Drehy said from behind. 'This is it.' The bridgemen were exhausted. Kaladin and his team had been forced to work the chasms all night. Hashal had put strict requirements on them, demanding an increased amount of salvage. In order to meet the quota, they'd forgone training to scavenge.

And then today they'd been awakened for a morning chasm assault after only three hours of sleep. They were drooping as they stood in line, and they hadn't even reached the contested plateau yet.

'Let it come,' Skar said quietly from the other side of the line. 'They want us dead? Well, I'm not going to back down. We'll show them what courage is. They can hide behind our bridges while we charge.'

'That's no victory,' Moash said. 'I say we attack the soldiers. Right now.'

'Our own troops?' Sigzil said, turning his dark-skinned head and looking down the line of men.

'Sure,' Moash said, eyes still forward. 'They're going to kill us anyway. Let's take a few of them with us. Damnation, why not charge Sadeas? His guard won't expect it. I'll bet we could knock down a few and grab their spears, then be on to killing lighteyes before they cut us down.'

A couple of bridgemen murmured their assent as the soldiers continued to cross.

'No,' Kaladin said. 'It wouldn't accomplish anything. They'd have us dead before we could so much as inconvenience Sadeas.'

Moash spat. 'And this will accomplish something? Damnation, Kaladin, I feel like I'm already dangling from the noose!'

'I have a plan,' Kaladin said.

He waited for the objections. His other plans hadn't worked.

No one offered a complaint.

'Well then,' Moash said. 'What is it?'

'You'll see today,' Kaladin said. 'If it works, it will buy us time. If it fails, I'll be dead.' He turned to look down the line of faces. 'In that case, Teft has orders to lead you on an escape attempt tonight. You're not ready, but at least you'll have a chance.' That was far better than attacking Sadeas as he crossed.

Kaladin's men nodded, and Moash seemed content. As contrary as he'd been originally, he had grown equally loyal. He was hotheaded, but he was also the best with the spear.

Sadeas approached, riding his roan stallion, wearing his red Shardplate, helm on but visor up. By chance, he crossed on Kaladin's bridge, though – as always – he had twenty to choose from. Sadeas didn't give Bridge Four so much as a glance.

'Break and cross,' Kaladin ordered after Sadeas was over. The bridgemen crossed their bridge, and Kaladin gave the orders for them to pull it behind them, then lift.

It felt heavier than it ever had before. The bridgemen broke into a trot, rounding the army column and hustling to reach the next chasm. In the distance behind, a second army – one in blue – was following them, crossing using some of Sadeas's other bridge crews. It looked like Dalinar Kholin had given up his bulky mechanical bridges, and was now using Sadeas's own bridge crews to cross. So much for his 'honor' and not sacrificing bridgeman lives.

In his pouch, Kaladin carried a large number of infused spheres, obtained from the moneychangers in exchange for a greater quantity of dun spheres. He hated taking that loss, but he needed the Stormlight.

They reached the next chasm quickly. It would be the next-to-last one, according to the word he'd gotten from Matal, Hashal's husband. The soldiers began checking their armor, stretching, anticipationspren rising in the air like small streamers.

The bridgemen set their bridge and stepped back. Kaladin noted Lopen and silent Dabbid approaching with their stretcher, waterskins and bandages inside. Lopen had hitched the stretcher to a hook at his waist, making up for his missing arm. The two moved among the members of Bridge Four, giving them water.

As he passed Kaladin, Lopen nodded toward the large bulge at the stretcher's center. The armor. 'When do you want it?' Lopen asked softly, lowering the litter, then handing Kaladin a waterskin.

'Right before we run the assault,' Kaladin replied. 'You did well, Lopen.'

Lopen winked. 'A one-armed Herdazian is still twice as useful as a no-brained Alethi. Plus, so long as I've got one hand, I can still do this.' He covertly made a rude gesture toward the marching soldiers.

Kaladin smiled, but was growing too nervous to feel mirth. It had been a long time since he'd gotten jitters going into a battle. He thought Tukks had beaten that out of him years ago.

'Hey,' a sudden voice called, 'I need some of that.'

Kaladin spun to see a soldier walking over. He was exactly the type of man Kaladin had known to avoid back in Amaram's army. Darkeyed but of modest rank, he was naturally large, and had probably gotten promoted by sheer virtue of size. His armor was well maintained but the uniform beneath was stained and wrinkled, and he kept the sleeves rolled up, exposing hairy arms.

At first, Kaladin assumed that the man had seen Lopen's gesture. But the man didn't seem mad. He shoved Kaladin aside, then pulled the waterskin away from Lopen. Nearby, the soldiers waiting to cross had noticed. Their own water crews were much slower, and more than a few of the waiting men eyed Lopen and his waterskins.

It would set a terrible precedent to let the soldiers take their water – but that was a tiny problem compared with the greater one. If those soldiers swarmed around the litter to get water, they'd discover the sack full of armor.

Kaladin moved quickly, snatching the waterskin from the soldier's hand. 'You have your own water crews.'

The soldier looked at Kaladin, as if completely unable to believe that a bridgeman was standing up to him. He scowled darkly, lowering his spear to his side, its butt against the ground. 'I don't want to wait.'

'How unfortunate,' Kaladin said, stepping right up to the man, meeting him eye to eye. Silently, he cursed the idiot. If it turned into a scuffle ...

The soldier hesitated, even more astonished to see such an aggressive threat from a bridgeman. Kaladin wasn't as thick-armed as this man, but he was a finger or two taller. The soldier's uncertainty showed in his face.

Just back down, Kaladin thought.

But no. Backing down from a bridgeman while his squad was watching? The man made a fist, knuckles cracking.

Within seconds, the entire bridge crew was there. The soldier blinked as Bridge Four formed around Kaladin in an aggressive inverted wedge pattern, moving naturally – smoothly – as Kaladin had trained them. Each one made fists, giving the soldier ample chance to see that the heavy lifting had trained these men to a physical level beyond that of the average soldier.

The man glanced back at his squad, as if looking for support.

'Do you want to spark a fight now, friend?' Kaladin asked softly. 'If you hurt the bridgemen, I wonder who Sadeas will make run this bridge.'

The man glanced back at Kaladin, was silent for a moment, then scowled, cursed, and stalked away. 'Probably full of crem anyway,' he muttered, rejoining his team.

The members of Bridge Four relaxed, though they received more than a few appreciative looks from the other soldiers in line. For once, there was something other than scowls. Hopefully they wouldn't realize that a squad of bridgemen had quickly and accurately made a battle formation commonly used in spear fighting.

Kaladin waved for his men to stand down, nodding his thanks. They fell back, and Kaladin tossed the recovered waterskin back to Lopen.

The shorter man smirked wryly. 'I'll keep a tighter grip on these things from now on, gancho.' He eyed the soldier who had tried to take the water.

'What?' Kaladin asked.

'Well, I've got a cousin in the water crews, you see,' Lopen said. 'And I'm thinking that he might owe me a favor on account of this one time I helped his sister's friend escape a guy looking for her. . . .'

'You *do* have a lot of cousins.'

'Never enough. You bother one of us, you bother us all. That's something you strawheads never seem to get. No offense or anything, gancho.'

Kaladin raised an eyebrow. 'Don't make trouble for the soldier. Not today.' *I'll make enough of that myself here soon.*

Lopen sighed, but nodded. 'All right. For you.' He held up a waterskin. 'You sure you don't want any?'

Kaladin didn't; his stomach was too unsettled. But he made himself take the waterskin back and drink a few mouthfuls.

Before long, the time came to cross and pull the bridge up for the last run. The assault. Sadeas's soldiers were forming ranks, lighteyes riding back and forth, calling orders. Matal waved Kaladin's crew forward. Dalinar Kholin's army had fallen behind, coming more slowly because of his larger numbers.

Kaladin took his place at the very front of his bridge. Ahead, the Parshendi were lined up with bows on the edge of their plateau, staring down the oncoming assault. Were they singing already? Kaladin thought he could hear their voices.

Moash was on Kaladin's right, Rock on his left. Only three on the death-line, because of how shorthanded they were. He'd put Shen in the very back, so he wouldn't see what Kaladin was about to do.

'I'm going to duck out from underneath once we start moving,' Kaladin told them. 'Rock, you take over. Keep them running.'

'Very well,' Rock said. 'It will be hard to carry without you. We have so few men, and we are very weak.'

'You'll manage. You'll have to.'

Kaladin couldn't see Rock's face, not positioned under the bridge as they were, but his voice sounded troubled. 'This thing you will try, is dangerous?'

'Perhaps.'

'Can I help?'

'I'm afraid not, my friend. But it strengthens me to hear you ask.'

Rock didn't get a chance to reply. Matal yelled for the bridge crews to go. Arrows shot overhead to distract the Parshendi. Bridge Four broke into a run.

And Kaladin ducked down and dashed out in front of them. Lopen was waiting to the side, and he tossed Kaladin the sack of armor.

Matal screamed at Kaladin in a panic, but the bridge crews were already in motion. Kaladin focused on his goal, protecting Bridge Four, and sucked in sharply. Stormlight flooded him from the pouch at his waist, but he didn't draw too much. Just enough to give him a jolt of energy.

Syl zipped in front of him, a ripple in the air, nearly invisible. Kaladin whipped the tie off the sack, pulling out the vest and throwing it awkwardly over his head. He ignored the ties at the side, getting on the helm as he leaped over a small rock formation. The shield came last, clattering with red Parshendi bones in a crisscross pattern on the front.

Even while donning the armor, Kaladin easily stayed far ahead of the heavily laden bridge crews. His Stormlight-infused legs were quick and sure.

The Parshendi archers directly ahead of him abruptly stopped singing. Several of them lowered their bows, and though it was too distant to make out their faces, he could sense their outrage. Kaladin had expected this. He'd hoped for it.

The Parshendi left their dead. Not because they were uncaring, but because they found it a terrible offense to move them. Merely touching the dead seemed a sin. If that was the case, a man desecrating corpses and wearing them into battle would be far, far worse.

As Kaladin grew closer, a different song started among the Parshendi archers. A quick, violent song, more chant than melody. Those who had lowered their bows raised them.

And they tried with everything they had to kill him.

Arrows flew at him. Dozens of them. They weren't fired in careful waves. They flew individually, rapidly, wildly, each archer loosing at Kaladin as quickly as he could. A swarm of death bore down on him.

Pulse racing, Kaladin ducked to the left, leaping off a small outcropping. Arrows sliced the air around him, dangerously close. But while infused with the Stormlight, his muscles reacted quickly. He dodged between arrows, then turned in the other direction, moving erratically.

Behind, Bridge Four came into range, and not a single arrow was fired at them. Other bridge crews were ignored as well, many of the archers focusing on Kaladin. The arrows came more swiftly, spraying around him, bouncing off his shield. One sliced open his arm as it shot past; another snapped against his helm, nearly knocking it free.

The arm wound leaked Light, not blood, and to Kaladin's amazement it slowly began to seal up, frost crystallizing on his skin and Stormlight draining from him. He drew in more, infusing himself to the cusp of glowing visibly. He ducked, he dodged, he jumped, he ran.

His battle-trained reflexes delighted in the newfound speed, and he used the shield to knock arrows out of the air. It was as if his body had longed for this ability, as if it had been born to take advantage of the Stormlight. During the earlier part of his life, he had lived sluggish and impotent. Now he was healed. Not acting beyond his capacities – no, finally *reaching* them.

A flock of arrows sought his blood, but Kaladin spun between them, taking another slice on the arm but deflecting the others with shield or breastplate. Another flight came, and he brought his shield up, worried that he was going to be too slow. However, the arrows changed course, arcing toward his shield, slamming into it. Drawn to it.

I'm pulling them to it! He remembered dozens of bridge runs, with arrows slamming into the wood near where his hands had clung to the support bars. Always just missing him.

How long have I been doing this? Kaladin thought. *How many arrows did I draw to the bridge, pulling them away from me?*

He didn't have time to think about that. He kept moving, dodging. He felt arrows whish through the air, heard them zip, felt the splinters as they hit stone or shield and broke. He'd hoped that he would distract some of the Parshendi from firing on his men, but he'd had no idea how strong a reaction he'd get.

Part of him exulted in the thrill of ducking, dodging, and blocking the hail of arrows. He started to slow, however. He tried to suck in Stormlight, but none came. His spheres were drained. He panicked, still dodging, but then the arrowfalls began to slacken.

With a start, Kaladin realized that the bridge crews had parted around him, leaving a space for him to keep dodging while they passed him and set their burdens. Bridge Four was in place, cavalry charging across to attack the archers. Despite that, some of the Parshendi continued to fire on Kaladin, enraged. The soldiers cut these Parshendi down easily, sweeping the ground of them and making room for Sadeas's foot soldiers.

Kaladin lowered his shield. It bristled with arrows. He barely had time to take a fresh breath of air as the bridgemen reached him, calling out with joy, nearly tackling him in their excitement.

'You fool!' Moash said. 'You storming fool! What was that? What were you thinking?'

'Was incredible,' Rock said.

'You should be dead!' Sigzil said, though his normally stern face was split by a smile.

'Stormfather,' Moash added, pulling an arrow from Kaladin's vest at the shoulder. 'Look at these.'

Kaladin looked down, shocked to find a dozen arrow holes in the sides of his vest and shirt where he'd narrowly avoided being hit. Three arrows stuck from the leather.

'Stormblessed,' Skar said. 'That's all there is to it.'

Kaladin shrugged off their praise, his heart still pounding. He was numb. Amazed that he'd survived, cold from the Stormlight he'd consumed, exhausted as if he'd run a rigorous obstacle course. He looked to Teft, raising an eyebrow, nodding toward the pouch at his waist.

Teft shook his head. He'd watched; the Stormlight rising from Kaladin hadn't been visible to those observing, not in the light of day. Still, the way Kaladin had dodged would have looked incredible, even without the obvious light. If there had been stories about him before, they would grow greatly following this.

He turned to look at the passing troops. As he did, he realized something. He still had to deal with Matal. 'Fall into line, men,' he said.

They obeyed reluctantly, falling into place around him in a double rank. Ahead, Matal stood beside their bridge. He looked concerned, as well he should. Sadeas was riding up. Kaladin steeled himself, remembering how his previous victory – when they'd run with the bridge on its side – had been turned on its head. He hesitated, then hurried over toward the bridge where Sadeas was going to ride past Matal. Kaladin's men followed.

Kaladin arrived as Matal bowed to Sadeas, who wore his glorious red Shardplate. Kaladin and the bridgemen bowed as well.

'Avarak Matal,' Sadeas said. He nodded toward Kaladin. 'This man looks familiar.'

'He is the one from before, Brightlord,' Matal said, nervous. 'The one who . . .'

'Ah yes,' Sadeas said. 'The "miracle." And you sent him forward as a decoy like that? One would think that you would be hesitant to dare such measures.'

'I take full responsibility, Brightlord,' Matal said, putting the best face on it.

Sadeas regarded the battlefield. 'Well, luckily for you, it worked. I suppose I'll have to promote you now.' He shook his head. 'Those savages practically ignored the assault force. All twenty bridges set, most with nary a casualty. It seems like a waste, somehow. Consider yourself commended. Most remarkable, the way that boy dodged . . .' He kicked his horse into motion, leaving Matal and the bridgemen behind.

It was the most backhanded promotion Kaladin had ever heard, but that would do. Kaladin smiled broadly as Matal turned to him, eyes enraged.

'You—' Matal sputtered. 'You could have gotten me executed!'

'Instead I got you promoted,' Kaladin said, Bridge Four forming up around him.

'I should see you strung up anyway.'

'It's been tried,' Kaladin said. 'Didn't work. Besides, you know that from now on Sadeas is going to expect me to be out there distracting the archers. Good luck getting any other bridgeman to try that.'

Matal's face grew red. He turned and stalked away to check on the other bridge crews. The two nearest – Bridge Seven and Bridge Eighteen – stood looking toward Kaladin and his team. All twenty bridges had been set?

Hardly any casualties?

Stormfather, Kaladin thought. *How many archers were firing at me?*

'You did it, Kaladin!' Moash exclaimed. 'You found the secret. We need to make this work. Expand it.'

'I'll bet I could dodge those arrows, if that were all I was doing,' Skar said. 'With enough armor . . .'

'We should have more than one,' Moash agreed. 'Five or so, running around drawing the Parshendi attacks.'

'The bones,' Rock said, folding his arms. 'This is what made it work. The Parshendi were so mad that they ignored bridge crew. If all five wear the bones of Parshendi . . .'

That made Kaladin consider something. He looked back, searching through the bridgemen. Where was Shen?

There. He was sitting on the rocks, distant, staring forward. Kaladin approached with the others. The parshman looked up at him, face a mask of pain, tears streaking his cheeks. He looked at Kaladin and shuddered visibly, turning away, closing his eyes.

'He sat down like that the moment he saw what you'd done, lad,' Teft said, rubbing his chin. 'Might not be good for bridge runs anymore.'

Kaladin pulled the carapace-tied helm off his head, then ran his fingers through his hair. The carapace stuck to his clothing stank faintly, even though he'd washed it off down below. 'We'll see,' Kaladin said, feeling a twist of guilt. Not nearly enough to overshadow the victory of protecting his men, but enough to dampen it, at least. 'For now, there are still many bridge crews that got fired upon. You know what to do.'

The men nodded, trotting off to search for the wounded. Kaladin set one man to watch over Shen – he wasn't sure what else to do with the parshman – and tried not to show his exhaustion as he put his sweaty, carapace-covered cap and vest in Lopen's litter. He knelt down to go through his medical equipment, in case it was needed, and found that his hand was shaking and quivering. He pressed it down against the ground to still it, breathing in and out.

Cold, clammy skin, he thought. *Nausea. Weakness*. He was in shock.

'You all right, lad?' Teft asked, kneeling down beside Kaladin. He still wore a bandage on his arm from the wound he'd taken a few bridge runs back, but it wasn't enough to stop him from carrying. Not when there were too few as it was.

'I'll be fine,' Kaladin said, taking out a waterskin, holding it in a quivering hand. He could barely get the top off.

'You don't look—'

'I'll be fine,' Kaladin said again, drinking, then lowering the water. 'What's important is that the men are safe.'

'You going to do this every time. Whenever we go to battle?'

'Whatever keeps them safe.'

'You're not immortal, Kaladin,' Teft said softly. 'The Radiants, they could be killed, just like any man. Sooner or later, one of those arrows will find your neck instead of your shoulder.'

'The Stormlight heals.'

'The Stormlight helps your body heal. That's different, I'm thinking.' Teft laid a hand on Kaladin's shoulder. 'We can't lose you, lad. The men need you.'

'I'm not going to avoid putting myself in danger, Teft. And I'm not going to leave the men to face a storm of arrows if I can do something about it.'

'Well,' Teft said, 'you are going to let a few of us go out there with you. The bridge can manage with twenty-five, if it has to. That leaves us a few extra, just like Rock said. And I'll bet some of those wounded from the other crews we saved are well enough to begin helping carry. They won't dare send them back to their own crews, not so long as Bridge Four is doing what you did today, and helping the whole assault work.'

'I . . .' Kaladin trailed off. He could imagine Dallet doing something like this. He'd always said that as sergeant, part of his job was to keep Kaladin alive. 'All right.'

Teft nodded, rising.

'You were a spearman, Teft,' Kaladin said. 'Don't try to deny it. How did you end up here, in these bridge crews?'

'It's where I belong.' Teft turned away to supervise the search for wounded.

Kaladin sat down, then lay back, waiting for the shock to wear off. To the south, the other army – flying the blue of Dalinar Kholin – had arrived. They crossed to an adjacent plateau.

Kaladin closed his eyes to recover. Eventually, he heard something and opened his eyes. Syl sat cross-legged on his chest. Behind her, Dalinar Kholin's army had begun an assault onto the battlefield, and they managed to do so without getting fired on. Sadeas had the Parshendi cut off.

'That was amazing,' Kaladin said to Syl. 'What I did with the arrows.'

'Still think you're cursed?'

'No. I know I'm not.' He looked up at the overcast sky. 'But that means the failures were all just me. I let Tien die, I failed my spearmen, the slaves I tried to rescue, Tarah ...' He hadn't thought of her in some time. His failure with her had been different from the others, but a failure it was nonetheless. 'If there's no curse or bad luck, no god above being angry at me – I have to live with knowing that with a little more effort – a little more practice or skill – I could have saved them.'

Syl frowned more deeply. 'Kaladin, you need to get over this. Those things aren't your fault.'

'That's what my father always used to say.' He smiled faintly. "Overcome your guilt, Kaladin. Care, but not too much. Take responsibility, but don't blame yourself." Protect, save, help – but know when to give up. They're such precarious ledges to walk. How do I do it?'

'I don't know. I don't know any of this, Kaladin. But you're ripping yourself apart. Inside and out.'

Kaladin stared at the sky above. 'It was wondrous. I was a storm, Syl. The Parshendi couldn't touch me. The arrows were nothing.'

'You're too new to this. You pushed yourself too hard.'

'"Save them," Kaladin whispered. '"Do the impossible, Kaladin. But don't push yourself too hard. But also don't feel guilty if you fail." Precarious ledges, Syl. So narrow ...'

Some of his men returned with a wounded man, a square-faced Thaylen fellow with an arrow in the shoulder. Kaladin went to work. His hands were still shaking slightly, but not nearly as badly as they had been.

The bridgemen clustered around, watching. He'd started training Rock, Drehy, and Skar already, but with all of them watching, Kaladin found himself explaining. 'If you put pressure here, you can slow the blood flow. This isn't too dangerous a wound, though it probably doesn't feel too good . . .' – the patient grimaced his agreement – '. . . and the real problem will come from infection. Wash the wound to make sure there aren't any slivers of wood or bits of metal left, then sew it. The muscles and skin of the shoulder here are going to get worked, so you need a strong thread to hold the wound together. Now . . .'

'Kaladin,' Lopen said, sounding worried.

'Wha?' Kaladin said, distracted, still working.

'Kaladin!'

Lopen had called him by his name, rather than saying *gancho*. Kaladin stood up, turning to see the short Herdazian man standing at the back of the crowd, pointing at the chasm. The battle had moved farther north, but a group of Parshendi had punched through Sadeas's line. They had bows.

Kaladin watched, stunned, as the group of Parshendi fell into formation and nocked. Fifty arrows, all pointed at Kaladin's crew. The Parshendi didn't seem to care that they were exposing themselves to attack from behind. They seemed focused on only one thing.

Destroying Kaladin and his men.

Kaladin screamed the alarm, but he felt so sluggish, so tired. The bridgemen around him turned as the archers drew. Sadeas's men normally defended the chasm to keep Parshendi from pushing over the bridges and cutting off their escape. But this time, noticing that the archers weren't trying to drop the bridges, the soldiers didn't hasten to stop them. They left the bridgemen to die, instead cutting off the Parshendi route to the bridges themselves.

Kaladin's men were exposed. Perfect targets. *No*, Kaladin thought. *No! It can't happen like this. Not after—*

A force crashed into the Parshendi line. A single figure in slate-grey armor, wielding a sword as long as many men were tall. The Shardbearer swept through the distracted archers with urgency, slicing into their ranks. Arrows flew toward Kaladin's team, but they were loosed too early, aimed poorly. A few came close as the bridgemen ducked for cover, but nobody was hit.

Parshendi fell before the sweeping Blade of the Shardbearer, some toppling into the chasm, others scrambling back. The rest died with burned-out eyes. In seconds, the squad of fifty archers had been reduced to corpses.

The Shardbearer's honor guard caught up with him. He turned, armor seeming to glow as he raised his Blade in a salute of respect toward the bridgemen. Then he charged off in another direction.

'That was him,' Drehy said, standing up. 'Dalinar Kholin. The king's uncle!'

'He saved us!' Lopen said.

'Bah.' Moash dusted himself off. 'He just saw a group of undefended archers and took the chance to strike. Lighteyes don't care about us. Right, Kaladin?'

Kaladin stared at the place where the archers had stood. In one moment, he could have lost it all.

'Kaladin?' Moash said.

'You're right,' Kaladin found himself saying. 'Just an opportunity taken.'

Except, why raise the Blade toward Kaladin?

'From now on,' Kaladin said, 'we pull back farther after the soldiers cross. They used to ignore us after the battle began, but they won't any longer. What I did today – what we're all going to be doing soon – will make them mighty angry. Angry enough to be stupid, but also angry enough to see us dead. For now, Leyten, Narm, find good scouting points and watch the field. I want to know if any Parshendi make moves toward that chasm. I'll get this man bandaged and we'll pull back.'

The two scouts ran off, and Kaladin turned back to the man with the wounded shoulder.

Moash knelt beside him. 'An assault against a prepared foe without any bridges lost, a Shardbearer coincidentally coming to our rescue, Sadeas himself complimenting us. You almost make me think I should get one of those armbands.'

Kaladin glanced down at the prayer. It was stained with blood from a slice on his arm that the vanishing Stormlight hadn't quite been able to heal.

'Wait to see if we escape.' Kaladin finished his stitching. 'That's the real test.'

'I wish to sleep. I know now why you do what you do, and I hate you for it. I will not speak of the truths I see.'

—Kakashah 1173, 142 seconds pre-death. A Shin sailor, left behind by his crew, reportedly for bringing them ill luck. Sample largely useless.

'You see?' Leyten turned the piece of carapace over in his hands. 'If we carve it up at the edge, it encourages a blade – or in this case an arrow – to deflect away from the face. Wouldn't want to spoil that pretty grin of yours.'

Kaladin smiled, taking back the piece of armor. Leyten had carved it expertly, putting in holes for leather straps to affix it to the jerkin. The chasm was cold and dark at night. With the sky hidden, it felt like a cavern. Only the occasional sparkle of a star high above revealed otherwise.

'How soon can you have them done?' he asked Leyten.

'All five? By the end of the night, likely. The real trick was discovering how to work it.' He knocked on the carapace with the back of his knuckles. 'Amazing stuff. Nearly as hard as steel, but half the weight. Hard to cut or break. But if you drill, it shapes easily.'

'Good,' Kaladin said. 'Because I don't want five sets. I want one for each man in the crew.' Leyten raised an eyebrow.

'If they're going to start letting us wear armor,' Kaladin said, 'every one gets a suit. Except Shen, of course.' Matal had agreed to let them leave him behind on the bridge runs; he wouldn't even look at Kaladin now.

Leyten nodded. 'All right, then. Better get me some help, though.'

'You can use the wounded men. We'll cart out as much carapace as we can find.'

His success had translated to an easier time for Bridge Four. Kaladin had pled that his men needed time to find carapace, and Hashal – not knowing any better – had reduced the scavenging quota. She was already pretending – quite smoothly – that the armor had been her idea the entire time, and was ignoring the question of where it had come from in the first place. When she met Kaladin's eyes, however, he saw worry. What else would he try? So far, she hadn't dared remove him. Not while he brought her so much praise from Sadeas.

'How did an apprentice armorer end up as a bridgeman anyway?' Kaladin asked as Leyten settled back down to work. He was a thick-armed man, stout and oval-faced with light hair. 'Craftsmen don't usually get thrown away.'

Leyten shrugged. 'When a piece of armor breaks and a lighteyes takes an arrow in the shoulder, someone has to take the blame. I'm convinced my master keeps an extra apprentice especially for those kinds of situations.'

'Well, his loss is our good fortune. You're going to keep us alive.'

'I'll do my best, sir.' He smiled. 'Can't do much worse on the armor than you did yourself, though. It's amazing that breastplate didn't fall off halfway through!'

Kaladin patted the bridgeman on the shoulder, then left him to his work, surrounded by a small ring of topaz chips; Kaladin had gotten permission to bring them, explaining his men needed light to work on the armor. Nearby, Lopen, Rock, and Dabbid were returning with another load of salvage. Syl zipped ahead, leading them.

Kaladin walked down the chasm, a garnet sphere looped in a small leather carrier at his belt for light. The chasm branched here, making a large triangular intersection – a perfect place for spear training. Wide enough to give the men room to practice, yet far enough from any permanent bridges that scouts weren't likely to hear echoes.

Kaladin gave the initial instructions each day, then let Teft lead the practice. The men worked by sphere light, small piles of diamond chips at the corners of the intersection, barely enough to see by. *Never thought I'd envy those days practicing beneath the hot sun back in Amaram's army*, he thought.

He walked up to gap-toothed Hobber and corrected his stance, then showed him how to put his weight behind his spear thrusts. The bridgemen were progressing quickly, and the fundamentals were proving their merit. Some were training with the spear and the shield, practicing stances where they held lighter spears up beside the head with the shield raised.

The most skilled were Skar and Moash. In fact, Moash was surprisingly good. Kaladin walked to the side, watching the hawk-faced man. He was focused, eyes intense, jaw set. He moved in attack after attack, the dozen spheres giving him an equal number of shadows.

Kaladin remembered feeling such dedication. He'd spent a year like that, after Tien's death, driving himself to exhaustion each day. Determined to get better. Determined never to let another person die because of his lack of skill. He'd become the best in his squad, then the best in his company. Some said he'd been the best spearmen in Amaram's army.

What would have happened to him, if Tarah hadn't coaxed him out of his single-minded dedication? Would he have burned himself out, as she'd claimed?

'Moash,' Kaladin called.

Moash paused, turning toward Kaladin. He didn't fall out of stance.

Kaladin waved him to approach, and Moash reluctantly trotted over. Lopen had left a few waterskins for them, hanging by their cords from a cluster of haspers. Kaladin pulled a skin free, tossing it to Moash. The other man took a drink, then wiped his mouth.

'You're getting good,' Kaladin said. 'You're probably the best we have.'

'Thanks,' Moash said.

'I've noticed you keep training when Teft lets the other men take breaks. Dedication is good, but don't work yourself ragged. I want you to be one of the decoys.'

Moash smiled broadly. Each of the men had volunteered to be one of the four who would join Kaladin distracting the Parshendi. It was amazing. Months ago, Moash – along with the others – had eagerly placed the new or the weak at the front of the bridge to catch arrows. Now, to a man, they volunteered for the most dangerous jobs.

Do you realize what you could have in these men, Sadeas? Kaladin thought. *If you weren't so busy thinking of how to get them killed?*

'So what is it for you?' Kaladin said, nodding toward the dim practice ground. 'Why do you work so hard? What is it you hunt?'

'Vengeance,' the other man said, face somber.

Kaladin nodded. 'I lost someone once. Because I wasn't good enough with the spear. I nearly killed myself practicing.'

'Who was it?'

'My brother.'

Moash nodded. The other bridgemen, Moash included, seemed to regard Kaladin's 'mysterious' past with reverence.

'I'm glad I trained,' Kaladin said. 'And I'm glad you're dedicated. But you have to be careful. If I'd gotten myself killed by working so hard, it wouldn't have meant anything.'

'Sure. But there's a difference between us, Kaladin.'

Kaladin raised an eyebrow.

'You wanted to be able to save someone. Me, I want to kill somebody.'

'Who?'

Moash hesitated, then shook his head. 'Maybe I'll say, someday.' He reached out, grabbing Kaladin on the shoulder. 'I'd surrendered my plans, but you've returned them to me. I'll guard you with my life, Kaladin. I swear it to you, by the blood of my fathers.'

Kaladin met Moash's intense eyes and nodded. 'All right, then. Go help Hobber and Yake. They're still off on their thrusts.'

Moash jogged off to do as told. He didn't call Kaladin 'sir,' and didn't seem to regard him with the same unspoken reverence as the others. That made Kaladin more comfortable with him.

Kaladin spent the next hour helping the men, one by one. Most of them were overeager, throwing themselves into their attacks. Kaladin explained the importance of control and precision, which won more fights than chaotic enthusiasm. They took it in, listening. More and more, they reminded him of his old spear squad.

That set him thinking. He remembered how he had felt when originally proposing the escape plan to the men. He'd been looking for something to do – a way to fight, no matter how risky. A chance. Things had changed.

He now had a team he was proud of, friends he had come to love, and a possibility – perhaps – for stability.

If they could get the dodging and armor right, they might be reasonably safe. Maybe even as safe as his old spear squad had been. Was running still the best option?

'That is a worried face,' a rumbling voice noted. Kaladin turned as Rock walked up and leaned against the wall near him, folding powerful forearms. 'Is the face of a leader, say I. Always troubled.' Rock raised a bushy red eyebrow.

'Sadeas will never let us go, particularly not now that we're so prominent.' Alethi lighteyes considered it reprehensible for a man to let slaves escape; it made him seem impotent. Capturing those who ran away was essential to save face.

'You said this thing before,' Rock said. 'We will fight the men he sends after us, will seek Kharbranth, where there are no slaves. From there, the Peaks, to my people who will welcome us as heroes!'

'We might beat the first group, if he's foolish and sends only a few dozen men. But after that he'll send more. And what of our wounded? Do we leave them here to die? Or do we take them with us and go that much more slowly?'

Rock nodded slowly. 'You are saying that we need a plan.'

'Yes,' Kaladin said. 'I guess that's what I'm saying. Either that, or we stay here . . . as bridgemen.'

'Ha!' Rock seemed to take it as a joke. 'Despite new armor, we would die soon. We make ourselves targets!'

Kaladin hesitated. Rock was right. The bridgemen would be used, day in and day out. Even if Kaladin slowed the death toll to two or three men a month – once, he would have considered that impossible, but now it seemed within reach – Bridge Four as it was currently composed would be gone within a year.

'I will talk with Sigzil about this thing,' Rock said, rubbing his chin between the sides of his beard. 'We will think. There must be a way to escape this trap, a way to disappear. A false trail? A distraction? Perhaps we can convince Sadeas that we have died during bridge run.'

'How would we do that?'

'Don't know,' Rock said. 'But we will think.' He nodded to Kaladin and sauntered off toward Sigzil. The Azish man was practicing with the others. Kaladin had tried speaking to him about Hoid, but Sigzil – typically closemouthed – hadn't wanted to discuss it.

'Hey, Kaladin!' Skar called. He was part of an advanced group that was going through Teft's very carefully supervised sparring. 'Come spar with us. Show these rock-brained fools how it's really done.' The others began calling for him as well.

Kaladin waved them down, shaking his head.

Teft trotted over, a heavy spear on one shoulder. 'Lad,' he said quietly, 'I think it would be good for their morale if you showed them a thing or two yourself.'

'I've already given them instruction.'

'With a spear you knocked the head off of. Going very slowly, with lots of talk. They need to see it, lad. See you.'

'We've been through this, Teft.'

'Well, so we have.'

Kaladin smiled. Teft was careful not to look angry or belligerent – he looked as if he were having a normal conversation with Kaladin. 'You've been a sergeant before, haven't you?'

'Never mind that. Come on, just show them a few simple routines.'

'No, Teft,' Kaladin said, more seriously.

Teft eyed him. 'You going to refuse to fight on the battlefield, just like that Horneater?'

'It's not like that.'

'Well what is it like?'

Kaladin reached for an explanation. 'I'll fight when the time comes. But if I let myself get back into it now, I'll be too eager. I'll push to attack now. I'll have trouble waiting until the men are ready. Trust me, Teft.'

Teft studied him. 'You're scared of it, lad.'

'What? No. I—'

'I can see it,' Teft said. 'And I've seen it before. Last time you fought for someone, you failed, eh? So now you hesitate to take it up again.'

Kaladin paused. 'Yes,' he admitted. But it was more than that. When he fought again, he would have to become that man from long ago, the man who had been called Stormblessed. The man with confidence and strength. He wasn't certain he could be that man any longer. That was what scared him.

Once he held that spear again, there would be no turning back.

'Well.' Teft rubbed his chin. 'When the time comes, I hope you're ready. Because this lot will need you.'

Kaladin nodded and Teft hurried back to the others, giving some kind of explanation to mollify them.

64

A MAN OF EXTREMES

'They come from the pit, two dead men, a heart in their hands, and I know that I have seen true glory.'

—Kakashah 1173, 13 seconds pre-death. A rickshaw puller.

I couldn't decide if you were interested or not,' Navani said softly to Dalinar as they slowly walked around the grounds of Elhokar's raised field palace. 'Half the time, you seemed like a flirt – offering hints at courtship, then backing away. The other half of the time, I was certain I had misread you. And Gavilar was so direct. He always did prefer to seize what he wished.'

Dalinar nodded thoughtfully. He wore his blue uniform, while Navani was in a subdued maroon dress with a thick hem. Elhokar's gardeners had begun to cultivate the plant life here. To their right, a twisting length of yellow shalebark rose to waist height, like a railing. The stonelike plant was overgrown by small bunches of haspers with pearly shells slowly opening and closing as they breathed. They looked like tiny mouths, silently speaking in rhythm with one another.

Dalinar and Navani's pathway took a leisurely course up the hillside. Dalinar strolled with hands clasped behind his back. His honor guard and Navani's clerks followed behind. A few of them looked perplexed at the amount of time Dalinar and Navani were spending with one another.

How many of them suspected the truth? All? Part? None? Did it matter?

'I didn't mean to confuse you, all those years ago,' he said, voice soft to keep it from prying ears. 'I had intended to court you, but Gavilar expressed a preference for you. So I eventually felt I had to step aside.'

'Just like that?' Navani asked. She sounded offended.

'He didn't realize that I was interested. He thought that by introducing you to him, I was indicating that he should court you. That was often how our relationship worked; I would discover people Gavilar should know, then bring them to him. I didn't realize until too late what I had done in giving you to him.'

'"Giving" me? Is there a slave's brand on my forehead of which I've been unaware?'

'I did not mean—'

'Oh hush,' Navani said, her voice suddenly fond. Dalinar stifled a sigh; though Navani had matured since their youth, her moods always *had* changed as quickly as the seasons. In truth, that was part of her allure.

'Did you often step aside for him?' Navani asked.

'Always.'

'Didn't that grow tiresome?'

'I didn't think about it much,' Dalinar said. 'When I did . . . yes, I was frustrated. But it was Gavilar. You know how he was. That force of will, that air of natural entitlement. It always seemed to surprise him when someone denied him or when the world itself didn't do as he wished. He didn't force me to defer – it was simply how life was.'

Navani nodded in understanding.

'Regardless,' Dalinar said, 'I apologize for confusing you. I . . . well, I had difficulty letting go. I fear that – on occasion – I let too much of my true feelings slip out.'

'Well, I suppose I can forgive that,' she said. 'Though you did spend the next two decades making certain I thought you hated me.'

'I did nothing of the sort!'

'Oh? And how else was I to interpret your coldness? The way you would often leave the room when I arrived?'

'Containing myself,' Dalinar said. 'I had made my decision.'

'Well, it looked a lot like hatred,' Navani said. 'Though I did wonder several times what you were hiding behind those stony eyes of yours. Of course, then *Shshshsh* came along.'

As always, when the name of his wife was spoken, it came to him as the sound of softly rushing air, then slipped from his mind immediately. He could not hear, or remember, the name.

'She changed everything,' Navani said. 'You truly seemed to love her.'

'I did,' Dalinar said. Surely he had loved her. Hadn't he? He could remember nothing. 'What was she like?' He quickly added, 'I mean, in your opinion. How did you see her?'

'Everyone loved *Shshshsh*,' Navani said. 'I tried hard to hate her, but in the end, I could only be mildly jealous.'

'You? Jealous of her? Whatever for?'

'Because,' Navani said. 'She fit you so well, never making inappropriate comments, never bullying those around her, always so calm.' Navani smiled. 'Thinking back, I really should have been able to hate her. But she was just so nice. Though she wasn't very . . . well . . .'

'What?' Dalinar asked.

'Clever,' Navani said. She blushed, which was rare for her. 'I'm sorry, Dalinar, but she just wasn't. She wasn't a fool, but . . . well . . . not everyone can be cunning. Perhaps that was part of her charm.'

She seemed to think that Dalinar would be offended. 'It's all right,' he said. 'Were you surprised that I married her?'

'Who could be surprised? As I said, she was perfect for you.'

'Because we were matched intellectually?' Dalinar said dryly.

'Hardly. But you *were* matched in temperament. For a time, after I got over trying to hate her, I thought that the four of us could be quite close. But you were so stiff toward me.'

'I could not allow any further . . . lapses to make you think that I was still interested.' He said the last part awkwardly. After all, wasn't that what he was doing now? Lapsing?

Navani eyed him. 'There you go again.'

'What?'

'Feeling guilty. Dalinar, you are a wonderful, honorable man – but you really are quite prone to self-indulgence.'

Guilt? As self-indulgence? 'I never considered it that way before.'

She smiled deeply.

'What?' he asked. 'You really are genuine, aren't you, Dalinar?'

'I try to be,' he said. He glanced over his shoulder. 'Though the nature of our relationship continues to perpetuate a kind of lie.'

'We've lied to nobody. Let them think, or guess, what they wish.'

'I suppose you are right.'

'I usually am.' She fell silent for a moment. 'Do you regret what we have—'

'No,' Dalinar said sharply, the strength of his objection surprising him. Navani just smiled. 'No,' Dalinar continued, more gently. 'I do not regret this, Navani. I don't know how to proceed, but I am *not* going to let go.'

Navani hesitated beside a growth of small, fist-size rockbuds with their vines out like long green tongues. They were grouped almost like a bouquet, growing on a large oval stone placed beside the pathway.

'I suppose it's too much to ask for you to not feel guilty,' Navani said. 'Can't you let yourself bend, just a little?'

'I'm not certain if I can. Particularly not now. Explaining why would be difficult.'

'Could you try to? For me?'

'I . . . Well, I'm a man of extremes, Navani. I discovered that when I was a youth. I've learned, repeatedly, that the only way to control those extremes is to dedicate my life to something. First it was Gavilar. Now it's the Codes and the teachings of Nohadon. They're the means by which I bind myself. Like the enclosure of a fire, meant to contain and control it.'

He took a deep breath. 'I'm a weak man, Navani. I really am. If I give myself a few feet of leeway, I burst through all of my prohibitions. The momentum of following the Codes these years after Gavilar's death is what keeps me strong. If I let a few cracks into that armor, I might return to the man I once was. A man I never want to be again.'

A man who had contemplated murdering his own brother for the throne – and for the woman who had married that brother. But he couldn't explain that, didn't dare let Navani know what his desire for her had once almost driven him to do.

On that day, Dalinar had sworn that he would never hold the throne himself. That was one of his restraints. Could he explain how she, without trying, pried at those restraints? How it was difficult to reconcile his long-fermenting love for her with his guilt at finally taking for himself what he'd long ago given up for his brother?

'You are not a weak man, Dalinar,' Navani said.

'I am. But weakness can imitate strength if bound properly, just as cowardice can imitate heroism if given nowhere to flee.'

'But there's nothing in Gavilar's book that prohibits us. It's just tradition that—'

'It feels wrong,' Dalinar said. 'But please, don't worry; I do enough worrying for both of us. I will find a way to make this work; I just ask your understanding. It will take time. When I display frustration, it is not with you, but with the situation.'

'I suppose I can accept that. Assuming you can live with the rumors. They're starting already.'

'They won't be the first rumors to plague me,' he said. 'I'm starting to worry less about them and more about Elhokar. How will we explain to him?'

'I doubt he'll notice,' Navani said, snorting softly, resuming her walk. He followed. 'He's so fixated on the Parshendi and, occasionally, the idea that someone in camp is trying to kill him.'

'This might feed into that,' Dalinar said. 'He could read a number of conspiracies out of the two of us entering a relationship.'

'Well, he—'

Horns began sounding loudly from below. Dalinar and Navani stopped to listen and identify the call.

'Stormfather,' Dalinar said. 'That's the *Tower itself* where a chasmfiend has been seen. It's one of the plateaus Sadeas has been watching.' Dalinar felt a surge of excitement. 'Highprinces have failed every time to win a gemheart there. It will be a major victory if he and I can do it together.'

Navani looked troubled. 'You're right about him, Dalinar. We *do* need him for our cause. But keep him at arm's length.'

'Wish me the wind's favor.' He reached toward her, but then stopped himself. What was he going to do? Embrace her here, in public? That would set off the rumors like fire across a pool of oil. He wasn't ready for that yet. Instead, he bowed to her, then hastened off to answer the call and collect his Shardplate.

It wasn't until he was halfway down the path that he paused to consider Navani's choice of words. She had said 'We need him' for 'our cause.'

What was their cause? He doubted that Navani knew either. But she had already started to think of them as together in their efforts.

And, he realized, so did he.

◆
◆ ◆

The horns called, such a pure and beautiful sound to signify the imminence of battle. It caused a frenzy in the lumberyard. The orders had come down. The Tower was to be assaulted again – the very place where Bridge Four had failed, the place where Kaladin had caused a disaster.

Largest of the plateaus. Most coveted.

Bridgemen ran this way and that for their vests. Carpenters and apprentices rushed out of the way. Matal shouted orders; an actual run was the only time he did that without Hashal. Bridgeleaders, showing a modicum of leadership, bellowed for their teams to line up.

A wind whipped the air, blowing wood chips and bits of dried grass into the sky. Men yelled, bells rang. And into this chaos strode Bridge Four, Kaladin at their head. Despite the urgency, soldiers stopped, bridgemen gaped, carpenters and apprentices stilled.

Thirty-five men marched in rusty orange carapace armor, expertly crafted by Leyten to fit onto leather jerkins and caps. They'd cut off arm guards and shin guards to complement the breastplates. The helms were built from several different headpieces, and had been ornamented – at Leyten's insistence – with ridges and cuts, like tiny horns or the edges of a crab's shell. The breastplates and guards were ornamented as well, cut into toothlike patterns, each one reminiscent of a saw blade. Earless Jaks had bought blue and white paint and drawn designs across the orange armor.

Each member of Bridge Four carried a large wooden shield strapped – tightly now – with red Parshendi bones. Ribs, for the most part, shaped in spiral patterns. Some of the men had tied finger bones to the centers so they would rattle, and others had attached sharp protruding ribs to the sides of their helms, giving them the look of fangs or mandibles.

The onlookers watched with amazement. It wasn't the first time they'd seen this armor, but this would be the first run where every man of Bridge Four had it. All together, it made an impressive sight.

Ten days, with six bridge runs, had allowed Kaladin and his team to perfect their method. Five men to be decoys with five more in the front holding shields and using only one arm to support the bridge. Their numbers were augmented by the wounded they'd saved from other crews, now strong enough to help carry.

So far – despite six bridge runs – there hadn't been a single fatality. The other bridgemen were whispering about a miracle. Kaladin didn't know about that. He just made certain to keep a full pouch of infused spheres with him at all times. Most of the Parshendi archers seemed to focus on him. Somehow, they could tell that he was the center of all this.

They reached their bridge and formed up, shields strapped to rods on the sides to await use. As they hefted their bridge, a spontaneous round of cheering rose up from the other crews.

'That's new,' Teft said from Kaladin's left.

'Guess they finally realized what we are,' Kaladin said.

'And what's that?'

Kaladin settled the bridge onto his shoulders. 'We're their champions. Bridge forward!'

They broke into a trot, leading the way down from the staging yard, ushered by cheers.

⁂

My father is not insane, Adolin thought, alive with energy and excitement as his armorers strapped on his Shardplate.

Adolin had stewed over Navani's revelation for days. He'd been wrong in such a horrible way. Dalinar Kholin *wasn't* growing weak. He *wasn't* getting senile. He *wasn't* a coward. Dalinar had been right, and Adolin had been wrong. After much soul searching, Adolin had come to a decision.

He was *glad* that he'd been wrong.

He grinned, flexing the fingers of his Plated hand as the armorers moved to his other side. He didn't know what the visions meant, or what the implications of those visions would be. His father was some kind of prophet, and that was daunting to consider.

But for now, it was enough that Dalinar was not insane. It was time to trust him. Stormfather knew, Dalinar had earned that right from his sons.

The armorers finished with Adolin's Shardplate. As they stepped away, Adolin hurried out of the armoring room into the sunlight, adjusting to the combined strength, speed, and weight of the Shardplate. Niter and five other members of the Cobalt Guard hastened up, one bringing Sureblood to him. Adolin took the reins, but led the Ryshadium at first, wanting more time to adapt to his Plate.

They soon entered the staging area. Dalinar, in his Shardplate, was conferring with Teleb and Ilamar. He seemed to tower over them as he pointed eastward. Already, companies of soldiers were moving out onto the lip of the Plains.

Adolin strode up to his father, eager. In the near distance, he noticed a figure riding down along the eastern rim of the warcamps. The figure wore gleaming red Shardplate.

'Father?' Adolin said, pointing. 'What's he doing here? Shouldn't he be waiting for us to ride to his camp?'

Dalinar looked up. He waved for a groom to bring Gallant, and the two of them mounted. They rode down to intercept Sadeas, trailed by a dozen members of the Cobalt Guard. Did Sadeas want to call off the assault? Was he worried about failing against the Tower again?

Once they drew close, Dalinar pulled up. 'You should be moving, Sadeas. Speed will be important, if we're to get to the plateau before the Parshendi take the gemheart and go.'

The highprince nodded. 'Agreed, in part. But we need to confer first. Dalinar, this is the Tower we're assaulting!' He seemed eager.

'Yes, and?'

'Damnation, man!' Sadeas said. 'You're the one who told me we needed to find a way to trap a large force of Parshendi on a plateau. The Tower is *perfect*. They always bring a large force there, and two sides are inaccessible.'

Adolin found himself nodding. 'Yes,' he said. 'Father, he's right. If we can box them in and hit them hard . . .' The Parshendi normally fled when they took large losses. That was one of the things extending the war so long.

'It could mean a turning point in the war,' Sadeas said, eyes alight. 'My scribes estimate that they have no more than twenty or thirty thousand troops left. The Parshendi will commit ten thousand here – they always do. But if we can corner and kill all of them, we could nearly *destroy* their ability to wage war on these Plains.'

'It'll work, Father,' Adolin said eagerly. 'This could be what we've been waiting for – what *you've* been waiting for. A way to turn the war, a way to deal enough damage to the Parshendi that they can't afford to keep fighting!'

'We need troops, Dalinar,' Sadeas said. 'Lots of them. How many men could you field, at maximum?'

'On short notice?' Dalinar said. 'Eight thousand, perhaps.'

'It will have to do,' Sadeas said. 'I've managed to mobilize about seven thousand. We'll bring them all. Get your eight thousand to my camp, and we'll take every one of my bridge crews and march together. The Parshendi will get there first – it's inevitable with a plateau that close to their side – but if we can be fast enough, we can corner them on the plateau. Then we'll show them what a *real* Alethi army is capable of!'

'I won't risk lives on your bridges, Sadeas,' Dalinar said. 'I don't know that I can agree to a completely joint assault.'

'Bah,' Sadeas said. 'I've got a new way of using bridgemen, one that doesn't cost nearly as many lives. Their casualties have dropped to almost nothing.'

'Really?' Dalinar said. 'Is it because of those bridgemen with armor? What made you change?'

Sadeas shrugged. 'Perhaps you're getting through to me. Regardless, we need to go now. Together. With as many troops as they'll have, I can't risk engaging them and waiting for you to catch up. I want to go together and assault as closely together as we can manage. If you're still worried about the bridgemen, I can attack first and gain a foothold, then let you cross without risking bridgeman lives.'

Dalinar looked thoughtful.

Come on, Father, Adolin thought. *You've been waiting for a chance to hit the Parshendi hard. This is it!*

'Very well,' Dalinar said. 'Adolin, send messengers to mobilize the Fourth through Eighth Divisions. Prepare the men to march. Let's end this war.'

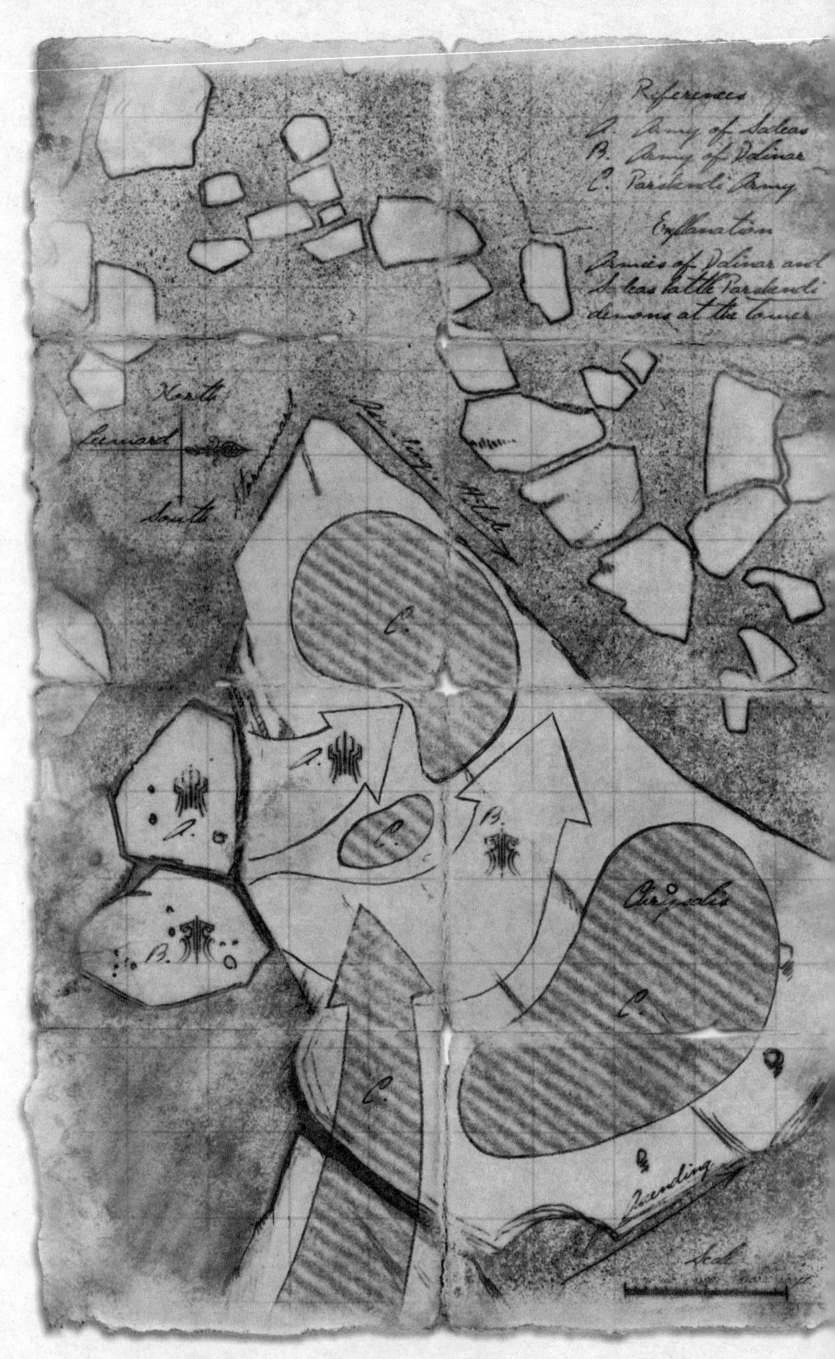

Map of the Battle of the Tower, drawn and labeled by Navani Kholin, circa 1173.

'I see them. They are the rocks. They are the vengeful spirits. Eyes of red.'

—Kakakes 1173, 8 seconds pre-death. A darkeyed young woman of fifteen. Subject was reportedly mentally unstable since childhood.

Several hours later, Dalinar stood with Sadeas on a rock formation overlooking the Tower itself. It had been a hard, long march. This was a distant plateau, as far eastward as they had ever struck. Plateaus beyond this point were impossible to take. The Parshendi could arrive so quickly that they had the gemheart out before the Alethi arrived. Sometimes that happened with the Tower as well.

Dalinar searched. 'I see it,' he said, pointing. 'They don't have the gemheart out yet!' A ring of Parshendi were pounding on the chrysalis. Its shell was like thick stone, however. It was still holding.

'You should be glad you're using my bridges, old friend.' Sadeas shaded his face with a gauntleted hand. 'Those chasms might be too wide for a Shardbearer to jump.'

Dalinar nodded. The Tower was enormous; even its huge size on the maps didn't do it justice. Unlike other plateaus, it wasn't level – instead, it was shaped like an enormous wedge that dipped toward the west, pointing a large cliff face in the stormward direction. It was too steep –

and the chasms too wide – to approach from the east or south. Only three adjacent plateaus could provide staging areas for assaults, all along the western or southwestern side.

The chasms between these plateaus were unusually large, almost too wide for the bridges to span. On the nearby staging plateaus, thousands upon thousands of soldiers in blue or green were gathered, one color per plateau. Combined, they made for a larger force than Dalinar had ever seen brought against the Parshendi.

The Parshendi numbers were as large as anticipated. There were at least ten thousand of them lining up. This would be a full-scale battle, the kind Dalinar had been hoping for, the kind that would let them pit a huge number of Alethi against a large Parshendi force.

This *could* be it. The turning point in the war. Win this day, and everything would change.

Dalinar shaded his eyes as well, helm under his arm. He noted with satisfaction that Sadeas's scouting crews were crossing to adjacent plateaus where they could watch for Parshendi reinforcements. Just because the Parshendi had brought so many at first didn't mean that there were no other Parshendi forces waiting to flank them. Dalinar and Sadeas wouldn't be taken by surprise again.

'Come with me,' Sadeas said. 'Let us assault them together! A single grand wave of attack, across forty bridges!'

Dalinar looked down at the bridge crews; many of their members were lying exhausted on the plateau. Awaiting – likely dreading – their next task. Very few of them wore the armor Sadeas had spoken of. Hundreds of them would be slaughtered in the assault if they attacked together. But was that any different from what Dalinar did, asking his men to charge into battle to seize the plateau? Weren't they all part of the same army?

The cracks. He couldn't let them get wider. If he was going to be with Navani, he had to prove to himself he could remain firm in the other areas. 'No,' he said. 'I will attack, but only after you've made a landing point for my bridge crews. Even that is more than I should allow. Never force your men to do as you yourself would not.'

'You do charge the Parshendi!'

'I'd never do it carrying one of those bridges,' Dalinar said. 'I'm sorry, old friend. It's not a judgment of you. It is what I must do.'

Sadeas shook his head, pulling on his helmet. 'Well, it will have to do.

We still planning on dining together tonight to discuss strategy?'

'I assume so. Unless Elhokar has a fit for both of us missing his feast.'

Sadeas snorted. 'He's going to have to grow accustomed to it. Six years of feasting every night is growing tedious. Besides, I doubt he'll feel anything but elation after we win this day and leave the Parshendi down a full third of their soldiers. See you on the battlefield.'

Dalinar nodded and Sadeas jumped off the rock formation, dropping down to the surface below and joining his officers. Dalinar lingered, looking over at the Tower. It was not only larger than most plateaus, it was rougher, covered with lumpish rock formations of hardened crem. The patterns were rolling and smooth, yet very uneven – like a field full of short walls covered by a blanket of snow.

The eastern tip of the plateau rose to a point overlooking the Plains. The two plateaus they'd use were on the middle of the west side; Sadeas would take the northern one and Dalinar would assault from one just below it, once Sadeas had cleared a landing for him.

We need to push the Parshendi to the southeast, Dalinar thought, rubbing his chin, *corner them there*. Everything hinged on that. The chrysalis was up near the top, so the Parshendi were already situated in a good position for Dalinar and Sadeas to push them back against the cliff edge. The Parshendi would probably allow this, as it would give them the high ground.

If a second Parshendi army came, it would be separated from the others. The Alethi could focus on the Parshendi trapped atop the Tower while holding a defensive formation against the new arrivals. It *would* work.

He felt himself growing excited. He hopped down to a shorter outcropping, then walked down a few steplike clefts to reach the plateau floor, where his officers waited. He then rounded the rock formation, investigating Adolin's progress. The young man stood in his Shardplate, directing the companies as they crossed Sadeas's mobile bridges onto the southern staging plateau. In the near distance, Sadeas's men were forming up for the assault.

That group of armored bridgemen stood out, preparing at the front center of the formation of bridge crews. Why *were* they allowed armor? Why not the others as well? It looked like Parshendi carapace. Dalinar shook his head. The assault began, bridge crews running out ahead of Sadeas's army, approaching the Tower first.

'Where would you like to make our assault, Father?' Adolin asked, summoning his Shardblade and resting it on his pauldron, sharp side up.

'There,' Dalinar said, pointing to a spot on their staging plateau. 'Get the men ready.'

Adolin nodded, shouting the orders.

In the distance, bridgemen began to die. *Heralds guide your paths, you poor men*, Dalinar thought. *As well as my own.*

⁂

Kaladin danced with the wind.

Arrows streamed around him, passing close, nearly kissing him with their painted scragglebark fletching. He had to let them get close, had to make the Parshendi feel they were near to killing him.

Despite four other bridgemen drawing their attention, despite the other men of Bridge Four behind armored with the skeletons of fallen Parshendi, most of the archers focused on Kaladin. He was a symbol. A living banner to destroy.

Kaladin spun between arrows, slapping them away with his shield. A storm raged inside him, as if his blood had been sucked away and replaced with stormwinds. It made his fingertips tingle with energy. Ahead, the Parshendi sang their angry, chanting song. The song for one who blasphemed against their dead.

Kaladin stayed at the front of the decoys, letting the arrows fall close. Daring them. Taunting them. Demanding they kill him until the arrows stopped falling and the wind stilled.

Kaladin came to rest, breath held to contain the storm within. The Parshendi reluctantly fell back before Sadeas's force. An enormous force, as far as plateau assaults went. Thousands of men and thirty-two bridges. Despite Kaladin's distraction, five bridges had been dropped, the men carrying them slaughtered.

None of the soldiers rushing across the chasm had made any specific effort to attack the archers firing on Kaladin, but the weight of numbers had forced them away. A few gave Kaladin loathing gazes, making an odd gesture by cupping a hand to the right ear and pointing at him before finally retreating.

Kaladin released his breath, Stormlight pulsing away from him. He had to walk a very fine line, drawing in enough Stormlight to stay alive, but not so much that it was visible to the watching soldiers.

The Tower rose ahead of him, a slab of stone that dipped toward the west. The chasm was so wide that he'd worried the men would drop the bridge into the chasm as they tried to place it. On the other side, Sadeas had arrayed his forces in a cupping shape, pushing the Parshendi back away, trying to give Dalinar an opening.

Perhaps attacking this way served to protect Dalinar's pristine image. He wouldn't make bridgemen die. Not directly, at least. Never mind that he stood on the backs of the men who had fallen to get Sadeas across. Their corpses were his true bridge.

'Kaladin!' a voice called from behind.

Kaladin spun. One of his men was wounded. *Storm it!* he thought, dashing up to Bridge Four. There was enough Stormlight still pulsing in his veins to stave off exhaustion. He'd grown complacent. Six bridge runs without a casualty. He should have realized it couldn't last. He pushed through the collected bridgemen to find Skar on the ground, holding his foot, red blood seeping between his fingers.

'Arrow in the foot,' Skar said through gritted teeth. 'In the storming foot! Who gets hit in the foot?'

'Kaladin!' Moash called urgently. The bridgemen split as Moash brought Teft in, an arrow sprouting from his shoulder between carapace breastplate and arm.

'Storm it!' Kaladin said, helping Moash set Teft down. The older bridgeman looked dazed. The arrow had dug deep into the muscle. 'Somebody get pressure on Skar's foot and wrap it until I can look at it. Teft, can you hear me?'

'I'm sorry, lad,' Teft mumbled, eyes glassy. 'I'm . . .'

'You're all right,' Kaladin said, hurriedly taking some bandages from Lopen, then nodding grimly. Lopen would heat a knife for cauterizing. 'Who else?'

'Everyone else is accounted for,' Drehy said. 'Teft was trying to hide his wound. He must have taken it when we were shoving the bridge across.'

Kaladin pressed gauze against the wound, then gestured for Lopen to hurry with the heated knife. 'I want our scouts watching. Make sure the Parshendi don't try a stunt like they did a few weeks back! If they jump across that plateau to get at Bridge Four, we're dead.'

'Is all right,' Rock said, shading his eyes. 'Sadeas is keeping his men in this area. No Parshendi will get through.'

The knife came, and Kaladin held it hesitantly, a curl of smoke rising from its length. Teft had lost too much blood; there was no risking a sewing. But with the twist of the knife, Kaladin risked some bad scarring. That could leave the aging bridgeman with a stiffness that would hurt his ability to wield a spear.

Reluctantly, Kaladin pressed the knife into the wound, the flesh hissing and blood drying to black crisps. Painspren wiggled out of the ground, sinewy and orange. In a surgery, you could sew. But on the field, this was often the only way.

'I'm sorry, Teft.' He shook his head as he continued to work.

⁂

Men began to scream. Arrows hit wood and flesh, sounding like distant woodsmen swinging axes.

Dalinar waited beside his men, watching Sadeas's soldiers fight. *He had better give us an opening*, he thought. *I'm starting to hunger for this plateau.*

Fortunately, Sadeas quickly gained his footing on the Tower and sent a flanking force over to carve out a section of land for Dalinar. They didn't get entirely into place before Dalinar started moving.

'One of you bridges, come with me!' he bellowed, barreling to the forefront. He was followed by one of the eight bridge teams Sadeas had lent him.

Dalinar needed to get onto that plateau. The Parshendi had noticed what was happening and had begun to put pressure on the small company in green and white that Sadeas had sent to defend his entry area. 'Bridge crew, there!' Dalinar said, pointing.

The bridgemen hustled into place, looking relieved that they wouldn't be asked to place their bridge under fire of arrows. As soon as they got it into position, Dalinar charged across, the Cobalt Guard following. Just ahead, Sadeas's men broke.

Dalinar bellowed, closing his gauntleted hands around Oathbringer's hilt as the sword formed from mist. He crashed into the surging Parshendi line with a wide, two-handed sweep that dropped four men. The Parshendi began to chant in their strange language, singing their war song. Dalinar kicked a corpse aside and began to attack in earnest, frantically defending the foothold Sadeas's men had gained him. Within minutes, his soldiers surged around him.

With the Cobalt Guard watching his back, Dalinar waded into the battle, breaking enemy ranks as only a Shardbearer could. He tore pockets through the Parshendi front lines, like a fish leaping from a stream, cutting back and forth, keeping his enemies disorganized. Corpses with burned eyes and slashed clothing made a trail behind him. More and more Alethi troops filled in the holes. Adolin crashed through a group of Parshendi nearby, his own squad of Cobalt Guardsmen a safe distance behind. He brought his whole army across – he needed to ascend quickly, pinning the Parshendi back so they couldn't escape. Sadeas was to watch the northern and western edges of the Tower.

The rhythm of the battle sang to Dalinar. The Parshendi chanting, the soldiers grunting and yelling, the Shardblade in his hands and the surging power of the Plate. The Thrill rose within him. Since the nausea didn't strike him, he carefully let the Blackthorn free, and felt the joy of dominating a battlefield and the disappointment at lacking a worthy foe.

Where were the Parshendi Shardbearers? He had seen that one in battle weeks ago. Why had he not reappeared? Would they commit so many men to the Tower without sending a Shardbearer?

Something heavy hit his armor, banging off it, causing a small puff of Stormlight to escape between the joints along his upper arm. Dalinar cursed, raising an arm to protect his face while scanning the near distance. *There*, he thought, picking out a nearby rock formation where a group of Parshendi stood swinging enormous rock slings with two hands. The head-size stones crashed into Parshendi and Alethi alike, though Dalinar was obviously the target.

He growled as another one hit, smashing against his forearm, sending a soft jolt through the Shardplate. The blow was strong enough to send a small array of cracks through his right vambrace.

Dalinar growled and threw himself into a Plate-enhanced run. The Thrill surged more strongly through him, and he rammed his shoulder into a group of Parshendi, scattering them, then spun with his Blade and cut down those too slow to get out of his way. He dodged to the side as a hail of stones fell where he'd been standing, then leaped onto a low boulder. He took two steps and jumped for the ledge where the rock-throwers were standing.

He grabbed its edge with one hand, holding his Blade with the other. The men atop the small ridge stumbled back, but Dalinar heaved himself up just high enough to swing. Oathbringer cut at their legs, and four men tumbled to the ground, feet dead. Dalinar dropped the Blade – it vanished – and used both hands to heave himself onto the ridge.

He landed in a crouch, Plate clanking. Several of the remaining Parshendi tried to swing their slings, but Dalinar grabbed a pair of head-size stones from a pile – easily palming them in his gauntleted hands – and flung them at the Parshendi. The stones hit with enough force to toss the slingmen off the formation, crushing their chests.

Dalinar smiled, then began throwing more stones. As the last Parshendi fell off the ledge, Dalinar spun, summoning Oathbringer and looking over the battlefield. A spear wall of blue and reflective steel struggled against black and red Parshendi. Dalinar's men did well, pressing the Parshendi up to the southeast, where they would be trapped. Adolin led this effort, Shardplate gleaming.

Breathing deeply from the Thrill now, Dalinar held his Shardblade up above his head, reflecting sunlight. Below, his men cheered, sending up calls that rose above the Parshendi war chant. Gloryspren sprouted around him.

Stormfather, but it felt good to be winning again. He threw himself offthe rock formation, for once not taking the slow and careful way down. He fell amid a group of Parshendi, crashing to the stones, blue Stormlight rising from his armor. He spun, slaying, remembering years spent fighting alongside Gavilar. Winning, conquering.

He and Gavilar had created something during those years. A solidified, cohesive nation out of something fractured. Like master potters reconstructing a fine ceramic that had been dropped. With a roar, Dalinar cut through the line of Parshendi, to where the Cobalt Guard was fighting to catch up to him. 'We press them!' he bellowed. 'Pass the word! All companies up the side of the Tower!'

Soldiers raised spears and runners went to deliver his orders. Dalinar spun and charged into the Parshendi, pushing himself – and his army – forward. To the north, Sadeas's forces were stalled. Well, Dalinar's force would do the work for him. If Dalinar could spear forward here, he could slice the Parshendi in half, then crush the northern side against Sadeas and the southern side against the cliff edge.

His army surged forward behind him, and the Thrill bubbled within. It was power. Strength greater than Shardplate. Vitality greater than youth. Skill greater than a lifetime of practice. A fever of power. Parshendi after Parshendi fell before his Blade. He couldn't cut their flesh, yet he sheared through their ranks. The momentum of their attacks often carried their corpses stumbling past him even as their eyes burned. The Parshendi started to break, running away or falling back. He grinned behind his near-translucent visor.

This was life. This was control. Gavilar had been the leader, the momentum, and the essence of their conquest. But Dalinar had been the warrior. Their opponents had surrendered to Gavilar's rule, but the Blackthorn – he was the man who had scattered them, the one who had dueled their leaders and slain their best Shardbearers.

Dalinar screamed at the Parshendi, and their entire line bent, then shattered. The Alethi surged forward, cheering. Dalinar joined his men, charging at their forefront to run down the Parshendi warpairs fleeing to the north or south, trying to join larger groups who held there.

He reached a pair. One turned to hold him off with a hammer, but Dalinar cut him down in passing, then grabbed the other Parshendi and threw him down with a twist of the arm. Grinning, Dalinar raised his Blade high over his head, looming over the soldier.

The Parshendi rolled awkwardly, holding his arm, no doubt shattered as he was thrown down. He looked up at Dalinar, terrified, fearspren appearing around him.

He was only a youth.

Dalinar froze, Blade held above his head, muscles taut. Those eyes . . . that face . . . Parshendi might not be human, but their features – their expressions – were the same. Save for the marbled skin and the strange growths of carapace armor, this boy could have been a groom in Dalinar's stable. What did he see above him? A faceless monster in impervious armor? What was this youth's story? He would only have been a boy when Gavilar was assassinated.

Dalinar stumbled backward, the Thrill vanishing. One of the Cobalt Guardsmen passed by, casually ramming a sword into the Parshendi boy's neck. Dalinar raised a hand, but it was over too quickly for him to stop. The soldier didn't notice Dalinar's gesture.

Dalinar lowered his hand. His men were rushing around him, rolling over the fleeing Parshendi. The majority of the Parshendi still fought, resisting Sadeas on one side and Dalinar's force on the other. The eastern plateau edge was just a short distance to Dalinar's right – he had come up against the Parshendi force like a spear, slicing it through the center, splitting it off to the north and south.

Around him lay the dead. Many of them had fallen face-down, taken in the back by spears or arrows from Dalinar's forces. Some Parshendi were still alive, though dying. They hummed or whispered to themselves a strange, haunting song. The one they sang as they waited to die.

Their whispered songs rose like the curses of spirits on Soul's March. Dalinar had always found the death song the most beautiful of all he had heard from the Parshendi. It seemed to cut through the grunts, clangs, and screams of the nearby battle. As always, each Parshendi's song was in perfect time with that of his fellows. It was as if they could all hear the same melody somewhere far away, and sang along through sputtering, bloodied lips, with rasping breath.

The Codes, Dalinar thought, turning toward his fighting men. *Never ask of your men a sacrifice you wouldn't make yourself. Never make them fight in conditions you would refuse to fight in yourself. Never ask a man to perform an act you wouldn't soil your own hands doing.*

He felt sick. This wasn't beautiful. This wasn't glorious. This wasn't strength, power, or life. This was revolting, repellent, and ghastly.

But they killed Gavilar! he thought, searching for a way to overcome the sickness he suddenly felt.

Unite them . . . .

Roshar had been united, once. Had that included the Parshendi?

You don't know if you can trust the visions or not, he told himself, his honor guard forming up behind him. *They could be from the Nightwatcher or the Voidbringers. Or something else entirely.*

In that moment, the objections felt weak. What had the visions wanted him to do? Bring peace to Alethkar, unite his people, act with justice and honor. Could he not judge the visions based on that?

He raised his Shardblade to his shoulder, walking solemnly among the fallen toward the northern line, where the Parshendi were trapped between his men and Sadeas's. His sickness grew stronger.

What was *happening* to him?

'Father!' Adolin's shout was frantic.

Dalinar turned toward his son, who was running to him. The young man's Plate was sprayed with Parshendi blood, but as always his Blade gleamed.

'What do we do?' Adolin asked, panting.

'About what?' Dalinar asked.

Adolin turned, pointing to the southwest – toward the plateau south of the one from which Dalinar's army had begun their assault over an hour ago. There, leaping across the wide chasm, was an enormous second army of Parshendi.

Dalinar slammed his visor up, fresh air washing across his sweaty face. He stepped forward. He'd anticipated this possibility, but someone should have given warning. Where were the scouts? What was—

He felt a chill.

Shaking, he scrambled toward one of the smooth, bulging formations of rock that were plentiful on the Tower.

'Father?' Adolin said, running after him.

Dalinar climbed, seeking the top of the formation, dropping his Shardblade. He crested the rise and stood looking northward over his troops and the Parshendi. Northward, toward Sadeas. Adolin climbed up beside him, gauntleted hand slapping up his visor.

'Oh no . . .' he whispered.

Sadeas's army was retreating across the chasm to the northern staging plateau. Half of it was across already. The eight groups of bridgemen he'd lent Dalinar had pulled back and were gone.

Sadeas was abandoning Dalinar and his troops, leaving them surrounded on three sides by Parshendi, alone on the Shattered Plains. And he was taking all of his bridges with him.

'That chanting, that singing, those rasping voices.'

—Kaktach 1173, 16 seconds pre-death. A middle-aged potter. Reported seeing strange dreams during highstorms during the last two years.

Kaladin wearily unwrapped Skar's wound to inspect his stitches and change the bandage. The arrow had hit on the right side of the ankle, deflecting off the knob of the fibula and scraping down through the muscles on the side of the foot.

'You were very lucky, Skar,' Kaladin said, putting on the new bandage. 'You'll walk on this again, assuming you do *not* put weight on it until it's healed. We'll have some of the men carry you back to camp.'

Behind them, the screaming, pounding, pulsing battle raged on. The fighting was distant now, focused on the eastern edge of the plateau. To Kaladin's right, Teft drank as Lopen poured water into his mouth. The older man scowled, taking the waterskin from Lopen with his good hand. 'I'm not an invalid,' he snapped. He'd gotten over his initial dizziness, though he was weak.

Kaladin sat back, feeling drained. When Stormlight faded away, it left him exhausted. That should pass soon; it had been over an hour since the initial assault. He carried a few more infused spheres in his pouch; he forced himself to resist the urge to suck in their Light.

He stood up, meaning to gather some men to carry Skar and Teft toward the far side of the plateau, just in case the battle went poorly and they had to retreat. That wasn't likely; the Alethi soldiers had been doing well the last time he'd checked.

He scanned the battlefield again. What he saw made him freeze.

Sadeas was retreating.

At first, it seemed so impossible that Kaladin couldn't accept it. Was Sadeas bringing his men around to attack in another direction? But no, the rear guard was already across the bridges, and Sadeas's banner was approaching. Was the highprince wounded?

'Drehy, Leyten, grab Skar. Rock and Peet, you take Teft. Hustle to the western side of the plateau in preparation to flee. The rest of you, get into bridge positions.'

The men, only now noticing what was going on, responded with anxiety.

'Moash, you're with me,' Kaladin said, hastening toward their bridge.

Moash hurried up beside Kaladin. 'What's going on?'

'Sadeas is pulling out,' Kaladin said, watching the tide of Sadeas's men in green slide away from the Parshendi lines like wax melting. 'There's no reason to. The battle's barely begun, and his forces were winning. I can only think that Sadeas must have been wounded.'

'Why would they withdraw the entire army for that?' Moash said. 'You don't think he is . . .'

'His banner still flies,' Kaladin said. 'So he's probably not dead. Unless they left it up to keep the men from panicking.'

He and Moash reached the side of the bridge. Behind, the rest of the crew hastened to form a line. Matal was on the other side of the chasm, speaking with the commander of the rear guard. After a quick exchange, Matal crossed and began to run down the line of bridge crews, calling for them to prepare to carry. He glanced at Kaladin's team, but saw they were already ready, and so hurried on.

To Kaladin's right, on the adjacent plateau – the one where Dalinar had launched his assault – the eight lent bridge crews pulled away from the battlefield, crossing over to Kaladin's plateau. A lighteyed officer Kaladin didn't recognize was giving them orders. Beyond them, farther to the south, a new Parshendi force had arrived, and was pouring onto the Tower.

Sadeas rode up to the chasm. The paint on his Shardplate gleamed in the sun; it didn't bear a single scratch. In fact, his entire honor guard was unharmed. Though they had gone over to the Tower, they had disengaged the enemy and come back. Why?

And then Kaladin saw it. Dalinar Kholin's force, fighting on the upper middle slope of the wedge, was now surrounded. This new Parshendi force was flooding into sections that Sadeas had held, supposedly protecting Dalinar's retreat.

'They're abandoning him!' Kaladin said. 'This was a trap. A setup. Sadeas is leaving Highprince Kholin – and all of his soldiers – to die.' Kaladin scrambled around the end of the bridge, pushing through the soldiers who were coming off it. Moash cursed and followed.

Kaladin wasn't certain why he elbowed his way up to the next bridge – bridge ten – where Sadeas was crossing. Perhaps he needed to see for certain that Sadeas wasn't wounded. Perhaps he was still stunned. This was treachery on a grand scale, terrible enough that it made Amaram's betrayal of Kaladin seem almost trivial.

Sadeas trotted his horse across the bridge, the wood clattering. He was accompanied by two lighteyed men in regular armor, and all three had their helms under their arms, as if they were on parade.

The honor guard stopped Kaladin, looking hostile. He was still close enough to see that Sadeas was, indeed, completely unharmed. He was also close enough to study Sadeas's proud face as he turned his horse and looked back at the Tower. The second Parshendi force swarmed Kholin's army, trapping them. Even without that, Kholin had no bridges. He could not retreat.

'I told you, old friend,' Sadeas said, voice soft but distinct, overlapping the distant screams. 'I said that honor of yours would get you killed someday.' He shook his head.

Then he turned his horse, trotting it away from the battlefield.

◆
◆ ◆

Dalinar cut down a Parshendi warpair. There was always another to replace it. He set his jaw, falling into Windstance and taking the defensive, holding his little rise in the hillside and acting as a rock over which the oncoming Parshendi wave would have to break.

Sadeas had planned this retreat well. His men hadn't been having trouble; they'd been ordered to fight in a way that they could easily disengage. And he had a full forty bridges to retreat across. Together, that made his abandonment of Dalinar happen quickly, by the scale of battles. Though Dalinar had immediately ordered his men to push forward, hoping to catch Sadeas while the bridges were still set, he hadn't been nearly quick enough. Sadeas's bridges were pulling away, the entirety of his army now across.

Adolin fought nearby. They were two tired men in Plate facing an entire army. Their armor had accumulated a frightening number of cracks. None were critical yet, but they did leak precious Stormlight. Wisps of it rose like the songs of dying Parshendi.

'I warned you not to trust him!' Adolin bellowed as he fought, cutting down a pair of Parshendi, then taking a wave of arrows from a team of archers who had set up nearby. The arrows sprayed against Adolin's armor, scratching the paint. One caught in a crack, widening it.

'I told you,' Adolin continued to yell, lowering his arm from his face and slicing into the next pair of Parshendi just before they landed their hammers on him. 'I said he was an eel!'

'I know!' Dalinar yelled back.

'We walked right into this,' Adolin continued, shouting as if he hadn't heard Dalinar. 'We let him take away our bridges. We let him get us onto the plateau before the second wave of Parshendi arrived. We let him control the scouts. We even *suggested* the attack pattern that would leave us surrounded if he didn't support us!'

'I know.' Dalinar's heart twisted inside of him.

Sadeas was carrying out a premeditated, carefully planned, and very thorough betrayal. Sadeas hadn't been overwhelmed, hadn't retreated for safety – though that was undoubtedly what he would claim when he got back to camp. A disaster, he'd say. Parshendi everywhere. Attacking together had upset the balance, and – unfortunately – he'd been forced to pull out and leave his friend. Oh, perhaps some of Sadeas's men would talk, tell the truth, and other highprinces would undoubtedly know what really happened. But nobody would challenge Sadeas openly. Not after such a decisive and powerful maneuver.

The people in the warcamps would go along with it. The other high-princes were too displeased with Dalinar to raise a fuss. The only one who might speak up was Elhokar, and Sadeas had his ear. It wrenched

Dalinar's heart. Had it all been an act? Could he really have misjudged Sadeas so completely? What of the investigation clearing Dalinar? What of their plans and reminiscences? All lies?

I saved your life, Sadeas. Dalinar watched Sadeas's banner retreat across the staging plateau. Among that distant group, a rider who wore crimson Shardplate turned and looked back. Sadeas, watching Dalinar fighting for his life. That figure paused for a moment, then turned around and rode on.

The Parshendi were surrounding the forward position where Dalinar and Adolin fought just ahead of the army. They were overwhelming his guard. He jumped down and slew another pair of enemies, but earned another blow to his forearm in the process. The Parshendi swarmed around him, and Dalinar's guard began to buckle.

'Pull away!' he yelled at Adolin, then began to back toward the army proper.

The youth cursed, but did as ordered. Dalinar and Adolin retreated back behind the front line of defense. Dalinar pulled off his cracked helm, panting. He'd been fighting nonstop long enough to get winded, despite his Shardplate. He let one of the guardsmen hand him a waterskin, and Adolin did the same. Dalinar squirted the warm water into his mouth and across his face. It had the metallic taste of stormwater.

Adolin lowered his waterskin, swishing the water in his mouth. He met Dalinar's eyes, his face haunted and grim. He knew. Just as Dalinar did. Just as the men likely did. There would be no surviving this battle. The Parshendi left no survivors. Dalinar braced himself, waiting for further accusations from Adolin. The boy had been right all along. And whatever the visions were, they had misled Dalinar in at least one respect. Trusting Sadeas had brought them to doom.

Men died just a short distance away, screaming and cursing. Dalinar longed to fight, but he needed to rest himself. Losing a Shardbearer because of fatigue would not serve his men.

'Well?' Dalinar demanded of Adolin. 'Say it. I have led us to destruction.'

'I—'

'This is *my* fault,' Dalinar said. 'I should never have risked our house for those foolish dreams.'

'No,' Adolin said. He sounded surprised at himself for saying it. 'No, Father. It's not your fault.'

Dalinar stared at his son. That was not what he'd expected to hear.

'What would you have done differently?' Adolin asked. 'Would you stop trying to make something better of Alethkar? Would you become like Sadeas and the others? No. I wouldn't have you become that man, Father, regardless of what it would gain us. I wish to the Heralds that we hadn't let Sadeas trick us into this, but I will not blame you for his deceit.'

Adolin reached over, gripping Dalinar's Plate-covered arm. 'You are right to follow the Codes. You were right to try to unite Alethkar. And I was a fool for fighting you on it every step along the path. Perhaps if I hadn't spent so much time distracting you, we would have seen this day coming.'

Dalinar blinked, dumbfounded. This was *Adolin* speaking those words? What had changed in the boy? And why did he say this now, at the dawn of Dalinar's greatest failure?

And yet, as the words hung in the air, Dalinar felt his guilt evaporating, blown away by the screams of the dying. It *was* a selfish emotion.

Would he have had himself change? Yes, he could have been more cautious. He could have been warier of Sadeas. But would he have given up on the Codes? Would he have become the same pitiless killer he'd been as a youth?

No.

Did it matter that the visions had been wrong about Sadeas? Was he ashamed of the man that they, and the readings from the book, had made him become? The final piece fell into place inside of him, the final cornerstone, and he found that he was no longer worried. The confusion was gone. He knew what to do, at long last. No more questions. No more uncertainty.

He reached up, gripping Adolin's arm. 'Thank you.'

Adolin nodded curtly. He was still angry, Dalinar could see, but he chose to follow Dalinar – and part of following a leader was supporting him even when the battle turned against him.

Then they released one another and Dalinar turned to the soldiers around them. 'It is time for us to fight,' he said, voice growing louder. 'And we do so not because we seek the glory of men, but because the other options are worse. We follow the Codes not because they bring gain, but because we loathe the people we would otherwise become. We stand here on this battlefield alone because of who we are.'

The members of the Cobalt Guard standing in a ring began to turn, one at a time, looking toward him. Beyond them, reserve soldiers – lighteyed and dark – gathered closer, eyes terrified, but faces resolute.

'Death is the end of all men!' Dalinar bellowed. 'What is the measure of him once he is gone? The wealth he accumulated and left for his heirs to squabble over? The glory he obtained, only to be passed on to those who slew him? The lofty positions he held through happenstance?

'No. We fight here because we understand. The end is the same. It is the *path* that separates men. When we taste that end, we will do so with our heads held high, eyes to the sun.'

He held out a hand, summoning Oathbringer. 'I am not ashamed of what I have become,' he shouted, and found it to be true. It felt so strange to be free of guilt. 'Other men may debase themselves to destroy me. Let them have their glory. For I will retain mine!'

The Shardblade formed, dropping into his hand.

The men did not cheer, but they *did* stand taller, straight-backed. A little of the terror retreated. Adolin shoved his helm on, his own Blade appearing in his hand, coated in condensation. He nodded.

Together they charged back into the battle.

And so I die, Dalinar thought, crashing into the Parshendi ranks. There he found peace. An unexpected emotion on the field of battle, but all the more welcome for that.

He did, however, discover one regret: He was leaving poor Renarin as Kholin highprince, in over his head and surrounded by enemies grown fat on the flesh of his father and brother.

I never did deliver that Shardplate I promised him, Dalinar thought. *He will have to make his way without it. Honor of our ancestors protect you, son.*

Stay strong – and learn wisdom more quickly than your father did.

Farewell.

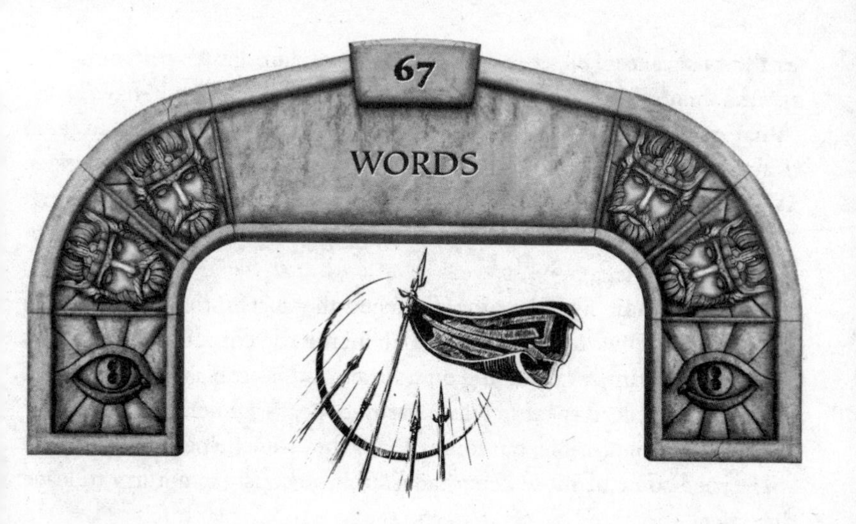

'Let me no longer hurt! Let me no longer weep! Dai-Gonarthis! The Black Fisher holds my sorrow and consumes it!'

—Tanatesach 1173, 28 seconds pre-death. A darkeyed female street juggler. Note similarity to sample 1172–89.

Bridge Four lagged behind the rest of the army. With two wounded and four men needed to carry them, the bridge weighed them down. Fortunately, Sadeas had brought nearly every bridge crew on this run, including eight to lend to Dalinar. That meant the army didn't need to wait for Kaladin's team in order to cross.

Exhaustion saturated Kaladin, and the bridge on his shoulders seemed made of stone. He hadn't felt so tired since his first days as a bridgeman. Syl hovered in front of him, watching with concern as he marched at the head of his men, sweat drenching his face, struggling over the uneven ground of the plateau.

Ahead, the last of Sadeas's army was bunched along the chasm, crossing. The staging plateau was nearly empty. The sheer awful audacity of what Sadeas had done twisted at Kaladin's insides. He thought what had been done to him had been horrible. But here, Sadeas callously condemned thousands of men, lighteyed and dark. Supposed allies. That betrayal seemed to weigh as heavily on Kaladin as the bridge itself. It pressed on him, made him gasp for breath.

Was there no hope for men? They killed those they should have loved. What good was it to fight, what good was it to win, if there was no difference between ally and enemy? What was victory? Meaningless. What did the deaths of Kaladin's friends and colleagues mean? Nothing. The entire world was a pustule, sickeningly green and infested with corruption.

Numb, Kaladin and the others reached the chasm, though they were too late to help with the transfer. The men he'd sent ahead were there, Teft looking grim, Skar leaning on a spear to support his wounded leg. A small group of dead spearmen lay nearby. Sadeas's soldiers retrieved their wounded, when possible, but some died as they were helped along. They'd abandoned some of those here; Sadeas was obviously in a hurry to leave the scene.

The dead had been left with their equipment. Skar had probably gotten his crutch there. Some poor bridge crew would have to cross all the way back here at a later date to salvage from these, and from Dalinar's fallen.

They set their bridge down, and Kaladin wiped his brow. 'Don't place the bridge across the chasm,' he told the men. 'We'll wait until the last of the soldiers have crossed, then carry it over on one of the other bridges.' Matal eyed Kaladin and his team, but didn't order them to set their bridge. He realized that by the time they got it into position, they'd have to pull it up again.

'Isn't that a sight?' Moash said, stepping up beside Kaladin, looking back.

Kaladin turned. The Tower rose behind them, sloped in their direction. Kholin's army was a circle of blue, trapped in the middle of the slope after trying to push down and get to Sadeas before he left. The Parshendi were a dark swarm with specks of red from their marbled skins. They pressed at the Alethi ring, compressing it.

'Such a shame,' Drehy said from beside their bridge, sitting on its lip. 'Makes me sick.'

Other bridgemen nodded, and Kaladin was surprised to see the concern in their faces. Rock and Teft joined Kaladin and Moash, all wearing their Parshendi-carapace armor. He was glad they'd left Shen back in the camp. He'd have been catatonic at the sight of it all.

Teft cradled his wounded arm. Rock raised a hand to shade his eyes and shook his head, looking eastward. 'Is a shame. A shame to Sadeas. A shame to us.'

'Bridge Four,' Matal called. 'Come on!'

Matal was waving for them to cross Bridge Six's bridge and leave the staging plateau. An idea came to Kaladin suddenly. A fantastic idea, like a blooming rockbud in his mind.

'We'll follow with our own bridge, Matal,' Kaladin called. 'We only just got to the chasm. We need to sit for a few minutes.'

'Cross now!' Matal yelled.

'We'll just fall further behind!' Kaladin retorted. 'You want to explain to Sadeas why he has to hold the entire army for one miserable bridge crew? We've got our bridge. Let my men rest. We'll catch up to you later.'

'And if those savages come after you?' Matal demanded.

Kaladin shrugged.

Matal blinked, then seemed to realize how badly he wanted that to happen. 'Suit yourself,' he called, rushing across bridge six as the other bridges were pulled up. In seconds, Kaladin's team was alone beside the chasm, the army retreating westward.

Kaladin smiled broadly. 'I can't believe it, after all that worrying ... Men, we're free!'

The others turned to him, confused.

'We'll follow in a short while,' Kaladin said eagerly, 'and Matal will assume we're coming. We fall farther and farther behind the army, until we're out of sight. Then we'll turn north, use the bridge to cross the Plains. We can escape northward, and everyone will just assume the Parshendi caught us and slaughtered us!'

The other bridgemen regarded him with wide eyes.

'Supplies,' Teft said.

'We have these spheres,' Kaladin said, pulling out his pouch. 'A wealth of them, right here. We can take the armor and weapons from the dead over there and use those to defend ourselves from bandits. It will be hard, but we *won't be chased*!'

The men were starting to grow excited. However, something gave Kaladin pause. *What of the wounded bridgemen back in the camp?*

'I'll have to stay behind,' Kaladin said.

'*What?*' Moash demanded.

'Someone will need to,' Kaladin said. 'For the good of our wounded in camp. We can't abandon them. And if I stay behind, I can support the story. Wound me and leave me on one of the plateaus. Sadeas is *sure* to send scavengers back. I'll tell them my crew was hunted down in retribution for desecrating the Parshendi corpses, our bridge tossed into the chasm. They'll believe it; they've seen how the Parshendi hate us.'

The crew was all standing now, shooting glances at one another. Uncomfortable glances.

'We're not leaving without you,' Sigzil said. Many of the others nodded.

'I'll follow,' Kaladin said. 'We can't leave those men behind.'

'Kaladin, lad—' Teft began.

'We can talk about me later,' Kaladin interrupted. 'Maybe I'll go with you, then sneak back into camp later to rescue the wounded. For now, go salvage from those bodies.'

They hesitated.

'It's an order, men!'

They moved, offering no further complaint, rushing to pilfer from the corpses Sadeas had abandoned. That left Kaladin alone beside the bridge.

He was still unsettled. It wasn't just the wounded back in camp. What was it, then? This was a fantastic opportunity. The type he'd have practically killed to get during his years as a slave. The chance to vanish, presumed dead? The bridgemen wouldn't have to fight. They were free. Why, then, was he so anxious?

Kaladin turned to survey his men, and was shocked to see someone standing beside him. A woman of translucent white light.

It was Syl, as he'd never seen her before, the size of an ordinary person, hands clasped in front of her, hair and dress streaming to the side in the wind. He'd had no idea she could make herself so large. She stared eastward, her expression horrified, eyes wide and sorrowful. It was the face of a child watching a brutal murder that stole her innocence.

Kaladin turned and slowly looked in the direction she was staring. Toward the Tower.

Toward Dalinar Kholin's desperate army.

The sight of them twisted his heart. They fought so hopelessly. Surrounded. Abandoned. Left alone to die.

We have a bridge, Kaladin realized. *If we could get it set . . .* Most of the Parshendi were focused on the Alethi army, with only a token reserve force down at the base near the chasm. It was a small enough group that perhaps the bridgemen could contain them.

But no. That was idiocy. There were thousands of Parshendi soldiers blocking Kholin's path to the chasm. And how would the bridgemen set their bridge, with no archers to support them?

Several of the bridgemen returned from their quick scavenge. Rock joined Kaladin, staring eastward, expression becoming grim. 'This thing is terrible,' he said. 'Can we not do something to help?'

Kaladin shook his head. 'It would be suicide, Rock. We'd have to run a full assault without an army to support us.'

'Couldn't we just go back a little of the way?' Skar asked. 'Wait to see if Kholin can cut his way down to us? If he does, then we could set our bridge.'

'No,' Kaladin said. 'If we stayed out of range, Kholin would assume us to be scouts left by Sadeas. We'll have to charge the chasm. Otherwise he'd never come down to meet us.'

That made the bridgemen pale.

'Besides,' Kaladin added. 'If we did somehow save some of those men, they'd talk, and Sadeas would know we still live. He'd hunt us down and kill us. By going back, we'd throw away our chance at freedom.'

The other bridgemen nodded at that. The rest had gathered, carrying weapons. It was time to go. Kaladin tried to squelch the feeling of despair inside him. This Dalinar Kholin was probably just like the others. Like Roshone, like Sadeas, like any number of other lighteyes. Pretending virtue but corrupted inside.

But he has thousands of darkeyed soldiers with him, a part of him thought. *Men who don't deserve this terrible fate. Men like my old spear crew.*

'We owe them nothing,' Kaladin whispered. He thought he could see Dalinar Kholin's banner, flying blue at the front of his army. 'You got them into this, Kholin. I won't let my men die for you.' He turned his back on the Tower.

Syl still stood beside him, facing eastward. It made his very soul twist in knots to see that look of despair on her face. 'Are windspren attracted to wind,' she asked softly, 'or do they make it?'

'I don't know,' Kaladin said. 'Does it matter?'

'Perhaps not. You see, I've remembered what kind of spren I am.'

'Is this the time for it, Syl?'

'I bind things, Kaladin,' she said, turning and meeting his eyes. 'I am honorspren. Spirit of oaths. Of promises. And of nobility.'

Kaladin could faintly hear the sounds of the battle. Or was that just his mind, searching for something he knew to be there?

Could he hear the men dying?

Could he see the soldiers running away, scattering, leaving their warlord alone?

Everyone else fleeing. Kaladin kneeling over Dallet's body.

A green-and-burgundy banner, flying alone on the field.

'I've been here before!' Kaladin bellowed, turning back toward that blue banner.

Dalinar always fought at the front.

'What happened last time?' Kaladin yelled. 'I've learned! I won't be a fool again!'

It seemed to crush him. Sadeas's betrayal, his exhaustion, the deaths of so many. He was there again for a moment, kneeling in Amaram's mobile headquarters, watching the last of his friends being slaughtered, too weak and hurt to save them.

He raised a trembling hand to his head, feeling the brand there, wet with his sweat. 'I owe you nothing, Kholin.'

And his father's voice seemed to whisper a reply. *Somebody has to start, son. Somebody has to step forward and do what is right*, because *it is right. If nobody starts, then others cannot follow.*

Dalinar had come to help Kaladin's men, attacking those archers and saving Bridge Four.

The lighteyes don't care about life, Lirin had said. *So I must. So we must. So you must . . . .*

Life before death.

I've failed so often. I've been knocked to the ground and trod upon.

Strength before weakness.

This would be death I'd lead my friends to . . .

Journey before destination.

. . . death, and what is right.

'We have to go back,' Kaladin said softly. 'Storm it, we *have* to go back.'

He turned to the members of Bridge Four. One by one, they nodded. Men who had been the dregs of the army just months before – men who had once cared for nothing but their own skins – took deep breaths, tossed away thoughts for their own safety, and nodded. They would follow him.

Kaladin looked up and sucked in a deep breath. Stormlight rushed into him like a wave, as if he'd put his lips up to a highstorm and drawn it into himself.

'Bridge up!' he commanded.

The members of Bridge Four cheered their agreement, grabbing their bridge and hoisting it high. Kaladin pulled on a shield, grabbing the straps in his hand.

Then he turned, raising it high. With a shout, he led his men in a charge back toward that abandoned blue banner.

◆
◆ ◆

Dalinar's Plate leaked Stormlight from dozens of small breaks; no major piece had escaped damage. Light rose above him like steam from a cauldron, lingering as Stormlight did, slowly diffusing.

The sun beat down upon him, baking him as he fought. He was so tired. It hadn't been long since Sadeas's betrayal, not as time was counted in battles. But Dalinar had pushed himself hard, staying at the very front, fighting side by side with Adolin. His Plate had lost much Stormlight. It was growing heavier, and lent him less power with each swing. Soon it would weigh him down, slowing him so the Parshendi could swarm over him.

He'd killed many of them. So many. A frightening number, and he did it without the Thrill. He was hollow inside. Better that than pleasure.

He hadn't killed nearly enough of them. They focused on Dalinar and Adolin; with Shardbearers on the front line, any breach would soon be patched by a man in gleaming armor and a deadly Blade. The Parshendi had to bring him and Adolin down first. They knew it. Dalinar knew it. Adolin knew it.

Stories spoke of battlefields where the Shardbearers were the last ones standing, pulled down by their enemies after long, heroic fights. Completely unrealistic. If you killed the Shardbearers first, you could take their Blades and turn them against the enemy.

He swung again, muscles lagging with fatigue. Dying first. It was a good place to be. *Ask nothing of them you wouldn't do yourself*. . . . Dalinar stumbled on the rocks, his Shardplate feeling as heavy as regular armor.

He could be satisfied with the way he'd handled his own life. But his men . . . he had failed them. Thinking of the way he had stupidly led them into a trap, that sickened him.

And then there was Navani.

Of all the times to finally begin courting her, Dalinar thought. *Six years wasted. A lifetime wasted. And now she'll have to grieve again.*

That thought made him raise his arms and steady his feet on the stone. He fought off the Parshendi. Struggling on. For her. He would not let himself fall while he still had strength.

Nearby, Adolin's armor leaked as well. The youth was extending himself more and more to protect his father. There had been no discussion of trying, perhaps, to leap the chasms and flee. With chasms so wide, the chances were slim – but beyond that, they would not abandon their men to die. He and Adolin had lived by the Codes. They would die by the Codes.

Dalinar swung again, staying at Adolin's side, fighting in that just-out-of-reach tandem way of two Shardbearers. Sweat streamed down his face inside his helm, and he shot a final glance toward the disappearing army. It was just barely visible on the horizon. Dalinar's current position gave him a good view down to the west.

Let that man be cursed for . . .

For . . .

Blood of my fathers, what is that*?*

A small force was moving across the western plateau, running toward the Tower. A solitary bridge crew, carrying their bridge.

'It can't be,' Dalinar said, stepping back from the fighting, letting the Cobalt Guard – what was left of them – rush in to defend him. Distrusting his eyes, he pushed his visor up. The rest of Sadeas's army was gone, but this single bridge crew remained. Why?

'Adolin!' he bellowed, pointing with his Shardblade, a surge of hope flooding his limbs.

The young man turned, tracing Dalinar's gesture. Adolin froze. 'Impossible!' he yelled. 'What kind of trap is that?'

'A foolish one, if it is a trap. We are already dead.'

'But why would he send one back? What purpose?'

'Does it matter?'

They hesitated for a moment amid the battle. Both knew the answer.

'Assault formations!' Dalinar yelled, turning back to his troops.

Stormfather, there were so few of them left. Less than half of his original eight thousand.

'Form up,' Adolin called. 'Get ready to move! We're going to punch through them, men. Gather everything you've got. We've got one chance!'

A slim one, Dalinar thought, pulling his visor down. *We'll have to cut through the rest of the Parshendi army.* Even if they reached the bottom, they'd probably find the crew dead, their bridge cast into the chasm. The Parshendi archers were already forming up; there were more than a hundred of them. It would be a slaughter.

But it was a hope. A tiny, precious hope. If his army was going to fall, it would do so while trying to seize that hope.

Raising his Shardblade high, feeling a surge of strength and determination, Dalinar charged forward at the head of his men.

⁂

For the second time in one day, Kaladin ran toward an armed Parshendi position, shield before him, wearing armor cut from the corpse of a fallen enemy. Perhaps he should have felt revolted at what he'd done in creating his armor. But it was no worse than what the Parshendi had done in killing Dunny, Maps, and that nameless man who had shown Kaladin kindness on his first day as a bridgemen. Kaladin still wore that man's sandals.

Us and them, he thought. That was the only way a soldier could think of it. For today, Dalinar Kholin and his men were part of the 'us.'

A group of Parshendi had seen the bridgemen approaching and was setting up with bows. Fortunately, it appeared that Dalinar had seen Kaladin's band as well, for the army in blue was beginning to cut its way toward rescue.

It wasn't going to work. There were too many Parshendi, and Dalinar's men would be tired. It was another disaster. But for once, Kaladin charged into it with eyes wide open.

This is my choice, he thought as the Parshendi archers formed up. *It's not some angry god watching me, not some spren playing tricks, not some twist of fate.*

It's me. I chose *to follow Tien.* I chose *to charge the Shardbearer and save Amaram.* I chose *to escape the slave pits. And now, I* choose *to try to rescue these men, though I know I will probably fail.*

The Parshendi loosed their arrows, and Kaladin felt an exaltation. Tiredness evaporated, fatigue fled. He wasn't fighting for Sadeas. He wasn't working to line someone's pockets. He was fighting to protect.

The arrows zipped at him and he swung his shield in an arc, spraying them away. Others came, shooting this way and that, seeking his flesh. He stayed just ahead of them, leaping as they shot for his thighs, turning as they shot for his shoulders, raising his shield when they shot for his face. It wasn't easy, and more than a few arrows got close to him, scoring his breastplate or shin guards. But none hit. He was doing it. He was—

Something was wrong.

He spun between two arrows, confused.

'Kaladin!' Syl said, hovering nearby, back to her smaller form. 'There!'

She pointed toward the other staging plateau, the one nearby that Dalinar had used for his assault. A large contingent of Parshendi had jumped across to that plateau and were kneeling down, raising bows. Pointed not at him, but right at Bridge Four's unshielded flank.

'No!' Kaladin screamed, Stormlight escaping from his mouth in a cloud. He turned and ran back across the rocky plateau toward the bridge crew. Arrows launched at him from behind. One took his backplate square on, but skidded aside. Another hit his helm. He leaped over a rocky rift, dashing with all the speed his Stormlight could lend him.

The Parshendi at the side were drawing. There were at least fifty of them. He was going to be too late. He was going to—

'Bridge Four!' he bellowed. 'Side carry right!'

They hadn't practiced that maneuver in weeks, but their training was manifest as they obeyed without question, dropping the bridge to their side just as the archers loosed. The flight of arrows hit the bridge's deck, bristling across the wood. Kaladin let out a relieved breath, reaching the bridge team, who had slowed to carry the bridge on the side.

'Kaladin!' Rock said, pointing.

Kaladin spun. The archers behind, on the Tower, were drawing for a large volley.

The bridge crew was exposed. The archers loosed.

He yelled again, screaming out, Stormlight infusing the air around him as he threw every bit of it he had into his shield. The scream echoed in his ears; the Stormlight burst from him, his clothing freezing and cracking.

Arrows darkened the sky. Something *hit* him, an extended impact that tossed him backward into the bridgemen. He struck hard, grunting as the force continued to push upon him.

The bridge ground to a halt, the men stopping.

All fell still.

Kaladin blinked, feeling completely drained. His body hurt, his arms tingled, his back ached. There was a sharp pain in his wrist. He groaned, opening his eyes, stumbling as Rock's hands caught him from behind.

A muted thump. The bridge being set down. *Idiots!* Kaladin thought. *Don't set it down . . . . Retreat . . . .*

The bridgemen crowded around him as he slipped to the ground, overwhelmed by having expended too much Stormlight. He blinked at what he held before him, attached to his bleeding arm.

His shield was *covered* in arrows, dozens of them, some splitting the others. The bones crossing the shield's front had shattered; the wood was in splinters. Some of the arrows had gone through and hit his forearm. That was the pain.

Over a hundred arrows. An entire volley. Pulled into a single shield.

'By the Brightcaller's rays,' Drehy said softly. 'What . . . what was . . .'

'It was like a fountain of light,' Moash said, kneeling beside Kaladin. 'Like the sun itself burst from you, Kaladin.'

'The Parshendi . . .' Kaladin croaked, and let go of the shield. The straps were broken, and as he struggled to stand, the shield all but disintegrated, falling to pieces, scattering dozens of broken arrows at his feet. A few remained stuck in his arm, but he ignored the pain, looking across at the Parshendi.

The groups of archers on both plateaus froze in stunned postures. The ones in front began to call to one another in a language Kaladin didn't understand. 'Neshua Kadal!' They stood up.

And then they fled.

'What?' Kaladin said.

'I don't know,' Teft said, cradling his own wounded arm. 'But we're getting you to safety. Blast this arm. Lopen!'

The shorter man brought Dabbid, and they ushered Kaladin away to a more secure location toward the center of the plateau. He held his arm, numb, his exhaustion so deep that he could barely think.

'Bridge up!' Moash called. 'We've still got a job to do!'

The rest of the bridgemen grimly ran back to their bridge, hoisting it up. On the Tower, Dalinar's force was fighting its way through the Parshendi toward the possible safety of the bridge crew. *They must be taking such heavy losses . . .* Kaladin thought numbly.

He stumbled and fell to the ground; Teft and Lopen pulled Kaladin into a sheltered hollow, joining Skar and Dabbid. Skar's foot bandage reddened with seeping blood, the spear he'd been using as a staff resting beside him. *Thought I told him . . . to stay off that foot. . . .*

'We need spheres,' Teft said. 'Skar?'

'He asked for them this morning,' the lean man said. 'Gave him everything I had. I think most of the men did the same.' Teft cursed softly, pulling the remaining arrows from Kaladin's arm, then wrapping it with bandages.

'Is he going to be all right?' Skar asked.

'I don't know,' Teft said. 'I don't know anything. Kelek! I'm an idiot. Kaladin. Lad, can you hear me?'

'It's . . . just shock . . .' Kaladin said.

'You're looking strange, gancho,' Lopen said nervously. 'White.'

'Your skin is ashen, lad,' Teft said. 'It looks like you did something to yourself back there. I don't know . . . I . . .' He cursed again, smacking his hand against the stone. 'I should have listened. Idiot!'

They'd laid him on his side, and he could barely see the Tower. New groups of Parshendi – ones who hadn't seen Kaladin's display – were making for the chasm, bearing weapons. Bridge Four arrived and set down their bridge. They unstrapped their shields and hurriedly retrieved spears from the sacks of salvage tied at the bridge's side. Then the men went to their positions pushing at the sides, preparing to slide the bridge across the gap.

The Parshendi teams didn't have bows. They formed up to wait, weapons out. There were easily three times as many as there were bridgemen, and more were coming.

'We've got to go help,' Skar said to Lopen and Teft.

The other two nodded, and all three – two wounded and one missing an arm – climbed to their feet. Kaladin tried to do likewise, but he fell back down, legs too weak to hold him.

'Stay, lad,' Teft said, smiling. 'We'll handle it just fine.' They gathered some spears from a stock Lopen had put in his litter, then hobbled out to join the bridge crew. Even Dabbid joined them. He hadn't spoken since being wounded on that first bridge run, so long ago.

Kaladin crawled up to the lip of the depression, watching them. Syl landed on the stone beside him. 'Storming fools,' Kaladin muttered. 'Shouldn't have followed me. Proud of them anyway.'

'Kaladin . . .' Syl said.

'Is there anything you can do?' He was so *storming* tired. 'Something to make me stronger?'

She shook her head.

A short distance ahead, the bridgemen began to push. The bridge's wood scraped loudly as it crossed the rocks, moving out over the chasm toward the waiting Parshendi. They began singing that harsh battle song, the one they did whenever they saw Kaladin in his armor.

The Parshendi looked eager, angry, deadly. They wanted blood. They would cut into the bridgemen and rip them apart, then drop the bridge – and their corpses – into the void beneath.

It's happening again, Kaladin thought, dazed and overwhelmed. He found himself curling up, drained and shaken. *I can't get to them. They'll die. Right in front of me. Tukks. Dead. Nelda. Dead. Goshel. Dead. Dallet. Cenn. Maps. Dunny. Dead. Dead. Dead . . .*

Tien.

Dead.

Lying huddled in a hollow in the rock. The sounds of battle ringing in the distance. Death surrounding him.

In a moment, he was there again, on that most horrible of days.

⁂

Kaladin stumbled through the cursing, screaming, fighting chaos of war, clinging to his spear. He'd dropped his shield. He needed to find a shield somewhere. Shouldn't he have a shield?

It was his third real battle. He'd been in Amaram's army only a few months, but already Hearthstone seemed a world away. He reached a hollow of rock and crouched down, pushing his back to it, breathing in and out, fingers slick on the spear's shaft. He was shaking.

He'd never realized how idyllic his life had been. Away from war. Away from death. Away from those screams, the cacophony of metal on metal,

metal on wood, metal on flesh. He squeezed his eyes shut, trying to block it out.

No, he thought. *Open your eyes. Don't let them find you and kill you that easily.*

He forced his eyes open, then turned and peeked out over the battlefield. It was a complete mess. They fought on a large hillside, thousands of men on either side, intermixing and killing. How could anyone keep track of anything in this insanity?

Amaram's army – Kaladin's army – was trying to hold the hilltop. Another army, also Alethi, was trying to take it from them. That was all Kaladin knew. The enemy seemed more numerous than his own army.

He'll be safe, Kaladin thought. *He will be!*

But he had trouble convincing himself. Tien's stint as a messenger boy hadn't lasted long. Recruitment was down, he'd been told, and every hand that could hold a spear was needed. Tien and the other older messenger boys had been organized into several squads of deep reserves.

Dalar said those wouldn't ever be used. Probably. Unless the army was in serious danger. Did being surrounded atop a steep hill, their lines in chaos, constitute serious danger?

Get to the top, he thought, looking up the incline. Amaram's banner still flew up there. Their soldiers must be holding. All Kaladin could see was a churning mess of men in orange and the occasional bit of forest green.

Kaladin took off at a run up the side of the hill. He didn't turn as men shouted at him, didn't check to see which side they were from. Patches of grass pulled down in front of him. He stumbled over a few corpses, dashed around a couple of scraggly stumpweight trees, and avoided places where men were fighting.

There, he thought, noting a group of spearmen ahead, standing in a line, watching warily. Green. Amaram's colors. Kaladin scrambled up to them, and the soldiers let him pass.

'Which squad are you from, soldier?' said a stocky lighteyed man with the knots of a low captain.

'Dead, sir,' Kaladin forced out. 'All dead. We were in Brightlord Tashlin's company, and—'

'Bah,' the man said, turning to a runner. 'Third report we've had that Tashlin is down. Somebody warn Amaram. East side is weakening by degrees.' He looked to Kaladin. 'You, off to the reserves for reassignment.'

'Yes, sir,' Kaladin said, numb. He glanced down the way he'd come. The incline was littered with corpses, many of them in green. Even as he watched, a group of three stragglers rushing for the top was intercepted and slaughtered.

None of the men at the top moved to help them. Kaladin could have fallen just as easily, within yards of safety. He knew that it was probably important, strategically, that these soldiers in the line maintain their positions. But it seemed so heartless.

Find Tien, he thought, trotting off toward the reserves field on the north side of the wide hilltop. Here, however, he found only more chaos. Groups of dazed men, bloodied, getting sorted into new squads and sent back out onto the field. Kaladin moved through them, searching for the squad that had been created out of the messenger boys.

He found Dalar first. The lanky, three-fingered sergeant of the reserves stood beside a tall post bearing a pair of flapping triangular banners. He was assigning newly made squads to fill out losses in the companies fighting below. Kaladin could still hear the yells.

'You,' Dalar said, pointing at Kaladin. 'Squad reassignment is in that direction. Get moving!'

'I need to find the squad made from messenger boys,' Kaladin said.

'Why in Damnation do you want to do that?'

'How should I know?' Kaladin said, shrugging, trying to remain calm. 'I just follow orders.'

Dalar grunted. 'Brightlord Sheler's company. Southeast side. You can—'

Kaladin was already running. This wasn't supposed to happen. Tien was supposed to stay safe. Stormfather. It hadn't even been *four months* yet!

He made his way to the southeast side of the hill and searched out a banner flapping a quarter of the way down the incline. The stark black glyphpair read *shesh lerel* – Sheler's company. Surprised at his own determination, Kaladin brushed past the soldiers guarding the hilltop and found himself on the battlefield again.

Things looked better over here. Sheler's company was holding its ground, although assaulted by a wave of enemies. Kaladin dashed down the incline, skidding in places, sliding on blood. His fear had vanished. It had been replaced by worry for his brother.

He arrived at the company line just as enemy squads were assaulting. He tried to scramble farther behind the lines to search for Tien, but he was caught in the wave of attacks. He stumbled to the side, joining a squad of spearmen.

The enemy was on them in a second. Kaladin held his spear in two hands, standing at the edge of the other spearmen and trying not to get in their way. He didn't really know what he was doing. He barely knew enough to use his shieldmate for protection. The exchange happened quickly, and Kaladin made only a single thrust. The enemy was rebuffed, and he managed to avoid taking a wound.

He stood, panting, gripping his spear.

'You,' an authoritative voice said. A man was pointing at Kaladin, knots at his shoulders. The squadleader. 'About time my team got some of those reinforcements. For a time there, I thought Varth was going to get every man. Where's your shield?'

Kaladin scrambled to grab one off a fallen soldier nearby. As he was working, the squadleader swore behind him. 'Damnation. They're coming again. Two prongs this time. We can't hold like this.'

A man in a green messenger's vest scrambled over a nearby rock formation. 'Hold against the east assault, Mesh!'

'What about that wave to the south?' the squadleader – Mesh – bellowed.

'It's handled for now. Hold east! Those are your orders!' The messenger scrambled on, delivering a similar message to the next squad in line. 'Varth. Your squad is to hold east!'

Kaladin got up with his shield. He needed to go find Tien. He couldn't—

He stumbled to a stop. There, in the next squad down the line, stood three figures. Younger boys, looking small in their armor and holding their spears uncertainly. One was Tien. His team of reserves had obviously been split apart to fill holes in other squads.

'Tien!' Kaladin screamed, falling out of line as the enemy troops came upon them. Why were Tien and the other two positioned in the *middle front* of the squad formation? They barely knew how to hold a spear!

Mesh yelled after Kaladin, but Kaladin ignored him. The enemy was upon them in a moment, and Mesh's squad broke, losing their discipline and turning to a more frenzied, unorganized resistance.

Kaladin felt something like a thump against his leg. He stumbled, hitting the ground, and realized with shock that he'd been stabbed with a spear. He felt no pain. Odd.

Tien! he thought, forcing himself up. Someone loomed above him, and Kaladin reacted immediately, rolling as a spear came down for his heart. His own spear was back in his hands before he realized he'd grabbed it, and he whipped it upward.

Then he froze. He'd just driven his spear through the enemy soldier's neck. It had happened so quickly. *I just killed a man.*

He rolled over, letting the enemy drop to his knees as Kaladin yanked his spear free. Varth's squad was back a little farther. The enemy hit it a little while after attacking where Kaladin had been. Tien and the other two were still in the front.

'Tien!' Kaladin yelled.

The boy looked toward him, eyes opening wide. He actually smiled. Behind him, the rest of the squad pulled back. Leaving the three untrained boys exposed.

And, sensing weakness, the enemy soldiers descended on Tien and the others. There was an armored lighteyes at their front, in gleaming steel. He swung a sword.

Kaladin's brother fell just like that. One eyeblink and he was standing there, looking terrified. The next he was on the ground.

'*No!*' Kaladin screamed. He tried to get to his feet, but slipped to his knees. His leg didn't work right.

Varth's squad hurried forward, attacking the enemies – who had been distracted with Tien and the other two. They'd placed the untrained at the front to stop the momentum of the enemy attack.

'No, no, no!' Kaladin screamed. He used his spear to hoist himself to his feet, then stumbled forward. It couldn't be what he thought. It couldn't be over that quickly.

It was a miracle that nobody struck Kaladin down as he stumbled the rest of the distance. He barely thought about it. He just watched where Tien had fallen. There was thunder. No. Hooves. Amaram had arrived with his cavalry, and they were sweeping through the enemy lines.

Kaladin didn't care. He finally reached the spot. There, he found three corpses: young, small, lying in a hollow in the stone. Horrified, numb, Kaladin reached out his hand and rolled over the one that was facedown.

Tien's dead eyes stared upward.

Kaladin continued to kneel beside the body. He should have bound his wound, should have moved back to safety, but he was too numb. He just knelt.

'About time he rode down here,' a voice said.

Kaladin looked up, noting a group of spearmen gathering nearby, watching the cavalry.

'He wanted them to bunch up against us,' one of the spearmen said. He had knots on the shoulders. Varth, their squadleader. Such keen eyes the man had. Not a brutish lout. Lean, thoughtful.

I should feel anger, Kaladin thought. *I should feel . . . something.*

Varth looked down at him, then at the bodies of the three dead messenger boys.

'You bastard,' Kaladin hissed. 'You put them in front.'

'You work with what you have,' Varth said, nodding to his team, then pointing at a fortified position. 'If they give me men who can't fight, I'll find another use for them.' He hesitated as his team marched away. He seemed regretful. 'Gotta do what you can to stay alive, son. Turn a liability into an advantage whenever you can. Remember that, if you live.'

With that, he jogged off.

Kaladin looked down. *Why couldn't I protect him?* he thought, looking at Tien, remembering his brother's laugh. His innocence, his smile, his excitement at exploring the hills outside Hearthstone.

Please. Please let me protect him. Make me strong enough.

He felt so weak. Blood loss. He found himself slumping to the side, and with tired hands, he tied off his wound. And then, feeling terribly vacant inside, he lay down beside Tien and pulled the body close.

'Don't worry,' Kaladin whispered. When had he started to cry? 'I'll bring you home. I'll protect you, Tien. I'll bring you back. . . .'

He held the body into the evening, long past the end of the battle, clinging to it as it slowly grew cold.

⁂

Kaladin blinked. He wasn't in that hollow with Tien. He was on the plateau.

He could hear men dying in the distance.

He hated thinking of that day. He almost wished he'd never gone looking for Tien. Then he wouldn't have had to watch. Wouldn't have had to kneel there, powerless, as his brother was slaughtered.

It was happening again. Rock, Moash, Teft. They were all going to die. And here he lay, powerless again. He could barely move. He felt so *drained.*

'Kaladin,' a voice whispered. He blinked. Syl was hovering in front of him. 'Do you know the Words?'

'All I wanted to do was protect them,' he whispered.

'That's why I've come. The Words, Kaladin.'

'They're going to die. I can't save them. I—'

Amaram slaughtered his men in front of him.

A nameless Shardbearer killed Dallet.

A lighteyes killed Tien.

No.

Kaladin rolled over and forced himself to his feet, wavering on weak legs.

No!

Bridge Four hadn't set its bridge yet. That surprised him. They were still pushing it across the chasm, the Parshendi crowding up on the other side, eager, their song becoming more frantic. His delusions had seemed like hours, but had passed in just a few heartbeats.

NO!

Lopen's litter was in front of Kaladin. A spear rested amid the drained water bottles and ragged bandages, steel head reflecting sunlight. It whispered to him. It terrified him, and he loved it.

When the time comes, I hope you're ready. Because this lot will need you.

He seized the spear, the first real weapon he had held since his display in the chasm so many weeks ago. Then he started to run. Slowly at first. Picking up speed. Reckless, his body exhausted. But he did not stop. He pushed forward, harder, charging toward the bridge. It was only halfway across the chasm.

Syl shot out in front of him, looking back, worried. 'The *Words*, Kaladin!'

Rock cried out as Kaladin ran onto the bridge as it was moving. The wood wobbled beneath him. It was out over the chasm, but hadn't reached the other side.

'Kaladin!' Teft yelled. 'What are you doing?'

Kaladin screamed, reaching the end of the bridge. Finding a tiny surge of strength somewhere, he raised his spear and threw himself off the end of the wooden platform, launching into the air above the cavernous void.

Bridgemen cried out in dismay. Syl zipped about him with worry. Parshendi looked up with amazement as a lone bridgeman sailed through the air toward them.

His drained, worn-out body barely had any strength left. In that moment of crystallized time, he looked down on his enemies. Parshendi with their marbled red and black skin. Soldiers raising finely crafted weapons, as if to cut him from the sky. Strangers, oddities in carapace breastplates and skullcaps. Many of them wearing beards.

Beards woven with glowing gemstones.

Kaladin breathed in.

Like the power of salvation itself – like rays of sunlight from the eyes of the Almighty – Stormlight exploded from those gemstones. It surged through the air, pulled in visible streams, like glowing columns of luminescent smoke. Twisting and turning and spiraling like tiny funnel clouds until they slammed into him.

And the storm came to life again.

Kaladin hit the rocky ledge, legs suddenly strong, mind, body, and blood *alive* with energy. He fell into a crouch, spear under his arm, a small ring of Stormlight expanding from him in a wave, pushed down to the stones by his fall. Stunned, the Parshendi shied away, eyes widening, song faltering.

A trickle of Stormlight closed the wounds on his arm. He smiled, spear held before him. It was as familiar as the body of a lover long lost.

The Words, a voice said, urgent, as if directly into his mind. In that moment, Kaladin was amazed to realize that he knew them, though they'd never been told to him.

'I will protect those who cannot protect themselves,' he whispered.

The Second Ideal of the Knights Radiant.

⁂

A *crack* shook the air, like an enormous clap of thunder, though the sky was completely clear. Teft stumbled back – having just set the bridge in place – and found himself gaping with the rest of Bridge Four. Kaladin *exploded* with energy.

A burst of whiteness washed out from him, a wave of white smoke. Stormlight. The force of it slammed into the first rank of Parshendi, tossing them backward, and Teft had to hold his hand up against the vibrancy of the light.

'Something just changed,' Moash whispered, hand up. 'Something important.'

Kaladin raised his spear. The powerful light began to subside, retreating. A more subdued glow began to steam off his body. Radiant, like smoke from an ethereal fire.

Nearby, some of the Parshendi fled, though others stepped up, raising weapons in challenge. Kaladin spun into them, a living storm of steel, wood, and determination.

'They named it the Final Desolation, but they lied. Our gods lied. Oh, how they lied. The Everstorm comes. I hear its whispers, see its stormwall, know its heart.'

—Tanatanes 1173, 8 seconds pre-death. An Azish itinerant worker. Sample of particular note.

Soldiers in blue yelled, screaming war cries to encourage themselves. The sounds were like a roaring avalanche behind Adolin as he swung his Blade in wild swings. There was no room for a proper stance. He had to keep moving, punching through the Parshendi, leading his men toward the western chasm.

His father's horse and his own were still safe, carrying some wounded through the back ranks. The Shardbearers didn't dare mount, though. In these close quarters, the Ryshadium would be chopped down and their riders dropped.

This was the type of battlefield maneuver that would have been impossible without Shardbearers. A rush against superior numbers? Made by wounded, exhausted men? They should have been stopped cold and crushed.

But Shardbearers could not be stopped so easily. Their armor leaking Stormlight, their six-foot Blades flashing in wide swaths, Adolin and

Dalinar shattered the Parshendi defenses, creating an opening, a rift. Their men – the best-trained in the Alethi warcamps – knew how to use it. They formed a wedge behind their Shardbearers, prying the Parshendi armies open, using spearman formations to cut through and keep going forward.

Adolin moved at almost a jog. The incline of the hill worked in their favor, giving them better footing, letting them rumble down the slope like charging chulls. The chance to survive when all had been thought lost gave the men a surge of energy for one last dash toward freedom.

They took enormous casualties. Already, Dalinar's force had lost another thousand of his four, probably more. But it didn't matter. The Parshendi fought to kill, but the Alethi – this time – fought to live.

◆
◆ ◆

Living Heralds above, Teft thought, watching Kaladin fight. Just moments ago, the lad had looked near death, skin a dull grey, hands shaking. Now he was a shining whirlwind, a storm wielding a spear. Teft had known many a battlefield, but he had never seen anything remotely like this. Kaladin held the ground before the bridge by himself. White Stormlight streamed from him like a blazing fire. His speed was incredible, nearly inhuman, and his precision – each thrust of the spear hit a neck, side, or other unarmored target of Parshendi flesh.

It was more than the Stormlight. Teft had only a fragmentary recollection of the things his family had tried to teach him, but those memories all agreed. Stormlight did not grant skill. It could not make a man into something he was not. It enhanced, it strengthened, it invigorated.

It perfected.

Kaladin ducked low, slamming the butt against the leg of a Parshendi, dropping him to the ground, and came up to block an axe swing by catching the haft with that of his spear. He let go with one hand, sweeping the tip of the spear up under the arm of the Parshendi and ramming it into his armpit. As that Parshendi fell, Kaladin pulled his spear free and slammed the end into a Parshendi head that had gotten too close. The butt of the spear shattered with a spray of wood, and the Parshendi's carapace helm exploded.

No, this wasn't just Stormlight. This was a master of the spear with his capacity enhanced to astonishing levels.

The bridgemen gathered around Teft, amazed. His wounded arm didn't seem to hurt as much as it should. 'He's like a part of the wind itself,' Drehy said. 'Pulled down and given life. Not a man at all. A spren.'

'Sigzil?' Skar asked, eyes wide. 'You ever seen anything like this?'

The dark-skinned man shook his head.

'Stormfather,' Peet whispered. 'What ... what *is* he?'

'He's our bridgeleader,' Teft said, snapping out of his reverie. On the other side of the chasm, Kaladin barely dodged a blow from a Parshendi mace. 'And he needs our help! First and second teams, you take the left side. Don't let the Parshendi get around him. Third and fourth teams, you're with me on the right! Rock and Lopen, you be ready to pull back any wounded. The rest of you, wrinkled wall formation. Don't attack, just stay alive and keep them back. And Lopen, toss him a spear that isn't broken!'

◆ ◆ ◆

Dalinar roared, striking down a group of Parshendi swordsmen. He charged over their bodies, running up a short incline and throwing himself in a leap, dropping several feet into the Parshendi below, sweeping out with his Blade. His armor was an enormous weight upon his back, but the energy of his struggle kept him going. The Cobalt Guard – the straggling members who were left – roared and leaped off the incline behind him.

They were doomed. Those bridgemen would be dead by now. But Dalinar blessed them for their sacrifice. It might have been meaningless as an end, but it had changed the journey. *This* was how his soldiers should fall – not cornered and frightened, but fighting with passion.

He would not slide quietly into the dark. No indeed. He shouted his defiance again as he smashed into a group of Parshendi, whirling and hauling his Shardblade in a circling sweep. He stumbled through the patch of dead Parshendi, their eyes burning as they fell.

And Dalinar burst out onto open stone.

He blinked, stunned. *We did it*, he thought in disbelief. *We cut all the way through*. Behind him, soldiers roared, their tired voices sounding nearly as amazed as he felt. Just ahead of him, a final group of Parshendi lay between Dalinar and the chasm. But their backs were turned to him. Why were they—

The bridgemen.

The *bridgemen* were fighting. Dalinar gaped, lowering Oathbringer with numb arms. That little force of bridgemen held the bridgehead, fighting desperately against the Parshendi who were trying to force them back.

It was the most amazing, most *glorious* thing Dalinar had ever seen.

Adolin let out a whoop, breaking through the Parshendi to Dalinar's left. The younger man's armor was scratched, cracked, and scored, and his helm had shattered, leaving his head dangerously exposed. But his face was exultant.

'Go, go,' Dalinar bellowed, pointing. 'Give them support, storm it! If those bridgemen fall, we're all dead!'

Adolin and the Cobalt Guard dashed forward. Gallant and Sure-blood, Adolin's Ryshadium, galloped past, carrying three wounded each. Dalinar hated to have left so many wounded on the slopes, but the Codes were clear. In this case, protecting the men he could save was more important.

Dalinar turned to strike at the main body of Parshendi to his left, making certain the corridor remained open for his troops. Many of the soldiers scrambled toward safety, though several squads proved their mettle by forming up at the sides to keep fighting, opening the gap wider. Sweat had soaked through the brow rag attached to Dalinar's helm, and drops of it fell, overwhelming his eyebrows and falling into his left eye. He cursed, reaching to open his visor – then froze.

The enemy troops were parting. There, standing among them, was a seven-foot-tall giant of a Parshendi in gleaming silver Shardplate. It fit as only Plate could, having molded to his large stature. His Shardblade was wicked and barbed, like flames frozen into metal. He raised it to Dalinar in a salute.

'Now?' Dalinar bellowed incredulously. '*Now* you come?'

The Shardbearer stepped forward, steel boots clanking on stone. The other Parshendi backed away.

'Why not earlier?' Dalinar demanded, hurriedly setting himself into Windstance, blinking his left eye against the sweat. He stood near the shadow of a large, oblong rock formation shaped like a book on its side. 'Why wait out the entire battle only to attack now? When . . .'

When Dalinar was about to get away. Apparently the Parshendi Shardbearer had been willing to let his fellows throw themselves at Dalinar when it seemed obvious he would fall. Perhaps they let the regular soldiers try to win Shards, as was done in human armies. Now that Dalinar might escape, the potential loss of a Plate and Blade was too great, and so the Shardbearer had been sent to fight him.

The Shardbearer stepped up, speaking in the thick Parshendi language. Dalinar didn't understand a word of it. He raised his Blade and fell into stance. The Parshendi said something further, then grunted and stepped forward, swinging.

Dalinar cursed to himself, still blinded in his left eye. He dodged back, swinging his Blade and slapping the enemy's weapon. The parry shook Dalinar inside his armor. His muscles responded sluggishly. Stormlight still leaked from cracks in his armor, but it was abating. It wouldn't be much longer before the Plate stopped responding.

The Parshendi Shardbearer attacked again. His stance was unfamiliar to Dalinar, but there was something practiced about it. This wasn't a savage playing with a powerful weapon. He was a trained Shardbearer. Dalinar was once again forced to parry, something Windstance wasn't intended to do. His weight-laden muscles were too sluggish to dodge, and his Plate was too cracked to risk letting himself get hit.

The blow nearly threw him out of stance. He clenched his teeth, throwing weight behind his weapon and intentionally overcorrecting as the Parshendi's next blow came. The Blades met with a furious clang, throwing off a shower of sparks like a bucket of molten metal dashed into the air.

Dalinar recovered quickly and threw himself forward, trying to slam his shoulder into his enemy's chest. The Parshendi was still full of power, however, his Plate uncracked. He got out of the way and quite nearly hit Dalinar on the back.

Dalinar twisted just in time. Then he turned and leaped onto a small rock formation, then stepped to a higher ledge and managed to reach the top. The Parshendi followed, as Dalinar had hoped. The precarious footing raised the stakes – which was just fine with him. A single blow could ruin Dalinar. That meant taking risks.

As the Parshendi neared the top of the formation, Dalinar attacked, using the advantage of surer footing and high ground. The Parshendi didn't bother dodging. He took a hit to the helm, which cracked, but gained a chance to swing at Dalinar's legs.

Dalinar leaped backward, feeling painfully sluggish. He barely got out of the way, and wasn't able to get in a second strike as the Parshendi climbed atop the formation.

The Parshendi man made an aggressive thrust. Setting his jaw, Dalinar raised his forearm to block and stepped into the attack, praying to the Heralds that his forearm plate would deflect the blow. The Parshendi sword connected, shattering the Plate, sending a shock up Dalinar's arm. The gauntlet on his fist suddenly felt like a lead weight, but Dalinar kept moving, swinging his sword for his own attack.

Not at the Parshendi's armor, but at the stone beneath him.

Even as the molten shards of Dalinar's forearm plate sprayed in the air, he sheared through the rock shelf under his opponent's feet. The entire section broke free, sending the Shardbearer tumbling backward toward the ground. He hit with a crash.

Dalinar slammed his fist – the one with the broken armguard – into the ground and released the gauntlet. It unlatched and he pulled his hand free into the air, sweat making it feel cold. He left the gauntlet – it wouldn't work properly now that the forearm piece was gone – and roared as he swung his Blade single-handed. He sliced through another chunk of the rock and sent it falling down toward the Shardbearer.

The Parshendi stumbled to his feet, but the rock smashed down on top of him, sending out a splash of Stormlight and a deep cracking sound. Dalinar climbed down, trying to get to the Parshendi while he was still. Unfortunately, Dalinar's right leg was dragging, and when he reached the ground, he walked in a limp. If he took the boot off, he wouldn't be able to hold up the rest of the Shardplate.

He gritted his teeth, stopping as the Parshendi stood up. He'd been too slow. The Parshendi's armor, though cracked in several places, was nowhere near as strained as Dalinar's. Impressively, he'd managed to retain his Shardblade. He leveled his armored head at Dalinar, eyes hidden behind the slit in the helm. Around them, the other Parshendi watched silently, forming a ring, but not interfering.

Dalinar raised his Blade, holding it in one gauntleted hand and one bare one. The breeze was cold on his clammy, exposed hand.

There was no use running. He fought here.

⁂

For the first time in many, many months, Kaladin felt fully awake and alive.

The beauty of the spear, whistling in the air. The unity of body and mind, hands and feet reacting instantly, faster than thoughts could be formed. The clarity and familiarity of the old spear forms, learned during the most terrible time in his life.

His weapon was an extension of himself; he moved it as easily and instinctively as he did his fingers. Spinning, he cut through the Parshendi, bringing retribution to those who had slaughtered so many of his friends. Repayment for each and every arrow loosed at his flesh.

With Stormlight making an ecstatic pulse within him, he felt a rhythm to the battle. Almost like the beat of the Parshendi song.

And they did sing. They'd recovered from seeing him drink in the Stormlight and speak the Words of the Second Ideal. They now attacked in waves, fervently trying to get to the bridge and knock it free. Some had leaped to the other side to attack from that direction, but Moash had led bridgemen to respond there. Amazingly, they held.

Syl twirled around Kaladin in a blur, riding the waves of Stormlight that rose from his skin, moving like a leaf on the winds of a storm. Enraptured. He'd never seen her like this before.

He didn't break his attacks – in a way, there was only *one* attack, as each strike flowed directly into the next. His spear never stopped, and together with his men, he pushed the Parshendi back, accepting each challenge as they stepped forward in pairs.

Killing. Slaughtering. Blood flew in the air and the dying groaned at his feet. He tried not to pay too much attention to that. They were the enemy. Yet the sheer glory of what he did seemed at odds with the desolation he caused.

He was protecting. He was saving. Yet he was killing. How could something so terrible be so beautiful at the same time?

He ducked the swing of a fine silvery sword, then brought his spear around to the side, crushing ribs. He spun the spear, shattering its already fractured length against the side of the Parshendi's comrade. He threw the remains at a third man, then caught a new spear as Lopen tossed it to him. The Herdazian was collecting them from the fallen Alethi nearby to give to Kaladin when needed.

When you engaged a man, you learned something about him. Were your enemies careful and precise? Did they bully their way forward, aggressive and domineering? Did they spout curses to make you enraged? Were they ruthless, or did they leave an obviously incapacitated man to live?

He was impressed by the Parshendi. He fought dozens of them, each with a slightly different style of combat. It seemed they were sending only two or four at him at a time. Their attacks were careful and controlled, and each pair fought as a team. They seemed to respect him for his skill.

Most telling, they seemed to back away from fighting Skar or Teft, who were wounded, instead focusing on Kaladin, Moash, and the other spearmen who showed the most skill. These were not the wild, uncultured savages he had been led to expect. These were professional soldiers who held to an honorable battlefield ethic he had found absent in most of the Alethi. In them, he found what he'd always hoped he would find in the soldiers of the Shattered Plains.

That realization rocked him. He found himself *respecting* the Parshendi as he killed them.

In the end, the storm within drove him forward. He had chosen a course, and these Parshendi would slaughter Dalinar Kholin's army without a moment's regret. Kaladin had committed himself. He would see himself and his men through it.

He wasn't certain how long he fought. Bridge Four held out remarkably well. Surely they didn't fight for very long, otherwise they would have been overwhelmed. Yet the multitude of wounded and dying Parshendi around Kaladin seemed to indicate hours.

He was both relieved and oddly disappointed when a figure in Plate broke through the Parshendi ranks, releasing a flood of soldiers in blue. Kaladin reluctantly stepped back, heart thumping, the storm within dampened. The light had stopped streaming off his skin noticeably. The continual supply of Parshendi with gems in their braids had kept him fueled during the early part of the fight, but the later ones had come to him without gemstones. Another indication that they weren't the simpleminded subhumans the lighteyes claimed they were. They'd seen what he was doing, and even if they hadn't understood it, they'd countered it.

He had enough Light to keep him from collapsing. But as the Alethi pushed back the Parshendi, Kaladin realized how timely their arrival had been.

I need to be very careful with this, he thought. The storm within made him thirst for motion and attack, but using it drained his body. The more of it he used, and the faster he used it, the worse it was when he ran out.

Alethi soldiers took up perimeter defense on both sides of the bridge, and the exhausted bridgemen fell back, many sitting down and holding wounds. Kaladin hurried over to them. 'Report!'

'Three dead,' Rock said grimly, kneeling beside bodies he'd laid out. Malop, Earless Jaks, and Narm.

Kaladin frowned in sorrow. *Be glad the rest live*, he told himself. It was easy to think. Hard to accept. 'How are the rest of you?'

Five more had serious wounds, but Rock and Lopen had seen to them. Those two were learning quite well from Kaladin's instruction. There was little more Kaladin could do for the wounded. He glanced at Malop's body. The man had taken an axe cut to the arm, severing it and splintering the bone. He'd died from blood loss. If Kaladin hadn't been fighting, he might have been able to—

No. No regrets for the moment.

'Pull back across,' he said to the bridgemen, pointing. 'Teft, you're in command. Moash, you strong enough to stay with me?'

'Sure am,' Moash said, a grin on his bloody face. He looked excited, not exhausted. All three of the dead had been on his side, but he and the others had fought remarkably well.

The other bridgemen retreated. Kaladin turned to inspect the Alethi soldiers. It was like looking into a triage tent. Every man had a wound of some sort. The ones at the center stumbled and limped. Those at the outsides still fought, their uniforms bloodied and torn. The retreat had dissolved into chaos.

He made his way through the wounded, waving for them to cross the bridge. Some did as he said. Others stood about, looking dazed. Kaladin rushed up to one group that seemed better off than most. 'Who's in command here?'

'It ...' The soldier's face had been cut across the cheek. 'Brightlord Dalinar.'

'Immediate command. Who's your captain?'

'Dead,' the man said. 'And my companylord. And his second.'

Stormfather, Kaladin thought. 'Across the bridge with you,' he said, then moved on. 'I need an officer! Who's in command of the retreat?'

Ahead, he could make out a figure in scratched blue Shardplate, fighting at the front of the group. That would be Dalinar's son Adolin. He was busy holding the Parshendi off; bothering him would not be wise.

'Over here,' a man called. 'I've found Brightlord Havar! He's commander of the rear guard!'

Finally, Kaladin thought, rushing through the chaos to find a bearded lighteyed man lying on the ground, coughing blood. Kaladin looked him over, noting the enormous gut wound. 'Who's his second?'

'Dead,' said the man beside the commander. He was lighteyed.

'And you are?' Kaladin asked.

'Nacomb Gaval.' He looked young, younger than Kaladin.

'You're promoted,' Kaladin said. 'Get these men across the bridge as quickly as possible. If anyone asks, you've been given a field commission as commander of the rear guard. If anyone claims to outrank you, send them to me.'

The man started. 'Promoted ... Who are you? Can you *do* that?'

'Someone needs to,' Kaladin snapped. 'Go. Get to work.'

'I—'

'*Go!*' Kaladin bellowed.

Remarkably, the lighteyed man saluted him and began yelling for his squad. Kholin's men were wounded, battered, and dazed, but they were well trained. Once someone took command, orders passed quickly. Squads crossed the bridge, falling into marching formations. Likely, in the confusion, they clung to these familiar patterns.

Within minutes, the central mass of Kholin's army was flowing across the bridge like sand in an hourglass. The ring of fighting contracted. Still, men screamed and died in the anarchic tumult of sword against shield and spear against metal.

Kaladin hurriedly pulled the carapace off his armor – enraging the Parshendi didn't feel wise at the moment – then moved among the wounded, looking for more officers. He found a couple, though they were dazed, wounded, and out of breath. Apparently, those who were still battleworthy were leading the two flanks who held back the Parshendi.

Trailed by Moash, Kaladin hurried to the central front line, where the Alethi seemed to be holding the best. Here, finally, he found someone in command: a tall, stately lighteyes with a steel breastplate and matching helm, his uniform a darker shade of blue than the others. He directed the fighting from just behind the front lines.

The man nodded to Kaladin, yelling to be heard over the sounds of battle. 'You command the bridgemen?'

'I do,' Kaladin said. 'Why aren't your men moving across the bridge?'

'We are the Cobalt Guard,' the man said. 'Our duty is to protect Brightlord Adolin.' The man pointed toward Adolin in his blue Shardplate just ahead. The Shardbearer seemed to be pushing toward something.

'Where's the highprince?' Kaladin yelled.

'We're not sure.' The man grimaced. 'His guardsmen have vanished.'

'You *have* to pull back. The bulk of the army is across. If you remain here, you'll be surrounded!'

'We will not leave Brightlord Adolin. I'm sorry.'

Kaladin looked around. The groups of Alethi fighting at the flanks were barely holding their ground, but they wouldn't fall back until ordered.

'Fine,' Kaladin said, raising his spear and pushing his way through to the front line. Here, the Parshendi fought with vigor. Kaladin cut down one by the neck, spinning into the middle of a group, flashing out with his spear. His Stormlight was nearly gone, but these Parshendi had gemstones in their beards. Kaladin breathed in – just a little, so as to not reveal himself to the Alethi soldiers – and launched into a full attack.

The Parshendi fell back before his furious assault, and the few members of the Cobalt Guard around him stumbled away, looking stunned. In seconds, Kaladin had a dozen Parshendi on the ground around him, wounded or dead. That opened a gap, and he tore through, Moash on his heels.

A lot of the Parshendi were focused on Adolin, whose blue Shardplate was scraped and cracked. Kaladin had never seen a suit of Shardplate in such a terrible state. Stormlight rose from those cracks in much the way it steamed from Kaladin's skin when he held – or used – a lot of it.

The fury of a Shardbearer at war gave Kaladin pause. He and Moash stopped just outside of the man's fighting range, and the Parshendi ignored the bridgemen, trying with obvious desperation to take down the Shardbearer. Adolin cut down multiple men at once – but, as Kaladin had seen only once before, his Blade did not slice flesh. Parshendi eyes burned and blackened, and dozens fell dead, Adolin collecting corpses around him like ripened fruit falling from a tree.

And yet, Adolin was obviously struggling. His Shardplate was more than just cracked – there were holes in parts. His helm was gone, though he'd replaced it with a regular spearman's cap. His left leg limped, nearly dragging. That Blade of his was deadly, but the Parshendi drew closer and closer.

Kaladin didn't dare step into range. 'Adolin Kholin!' he bellowed.

The man kept fighting.

'Adolin Kholin!' Kaladin yelled again, feeling a little puff of Stormlight leave him, his voice booming.

The Shardbearer paused, then looked back at Kaladin. Reluctantly, the Shardbearer pulled back, letting the Cobalt Guard – using the path opened by Kaladin – rush forward and hold back the Parshendi.

'Who are you?' Adolin demanded, reaching Kaladin. His proud, youthful face was slick with sweat, his hair a matted mess of blond mixed with black.

'I'm the man who saved your life,' Kaladin said. 'I need you to order the retreat. Your troops can't fight any longer.'

'My father is out there, bridgeman,' Adolin said, pointing with his overly large Blade. 'I saw him just moments ago. His Ryshadium went for him, but neither horse nor man has returned. I'm going to lead a squad to—'

'You are going to *retreat*!' Kaladin said, exasperated. 'Look at your men, Kholin! They can barely keep their feet, let alone fight. You're losing dozens by the minute. You need to get them out.'

'I won't abandon my father,' Adolin said stubbornly.

'For the peace of . . . If you fall, Adolin Kholin, these men have *nothing*. Their commanders are wounded or dead. You can't go to your father; you can barely walk! I repeat, *get your men to safety*!'

The young Shardbearer stepped back, blinking at Kaladin's tone. He looked northeastward, toward where a figure in slate grey suddenly appeared on a rock outcropping, fighting against another figure in Shardplate. 'He's so close. . . .'

Kaladin took a deep breath. 'I'll go for him. You lead the retreat. Hold the bridge, but only the bridge.'

Adolin glared at Kaladin. He took a step, but something in his armor gave out, and he stumbled, going to one knee. Teeth gritted, he managed to rise. 'Captainlord Malan,' Adolin bellowed. 'Take your soldiers, go with this man. Get my father out!'

The man Kaladin had spoken to earlier saluted crisply. Adolin glared at Kaladin again, then hefted his Shardblade and stalked with difficulty toward the bridge.

'Moash, go with him,' Kaladin said.

'But—'

'Do it, Moash,' Kaladin said grimly, glancing toward the outcropping where Dalinar fought. Kaladin took a deep breath, tucked his spear under his arm, and dashed off at a dead run.

The Cobalt Guard yelled at him, trying to keep up, but he didn't look back. He hit the line of Parshendi attackers, turned and tripped two with his spear, then leaped over the bodies and kept going. Most Parshendi in this patch were distracted by Dalinar's fight or the battle to get to the bridge; the ranks were thin here between the two fronts.

Kaladin moved quickly, drawing in more Light as he ran, dodging and scrambling around Parshendi who tried to engage him. Within moments, he'd reached the place where Dalinar had been fighting. Though the rock shelf was now empty, a large group of Parshendi were gathered around its base. *There*, he thought, leaping forward.

⁂

A horse whinnied. Dalinar looked up in shock as Gallant charged into the open ring of ground the watching Parshendi had made. The Ryshadium had come to him. How . . . where . . .? The horse should have been free and safe on the staging plateau.

It was too late. Dalinar was on one knee, beaten down by the enemy Shardbearer. The Parshendi kicked, smashing his foot into Dalinar's chest, throwing him backward.

A blow to the helm followed. Another. Another. The helm exploded, and the force of the blows left Dalinar dazed. Where was he? What was happening? Why was he pinned by something so heavy?

Shardplate, he thought, struggling to rise. *I'm wearing ... my Shardplate. ...*

A breeze blew across his face. Head blows; you had to be careful of head blows, even when wearing Plate. His enemy stood over him, looming, and seemed to inspect him. As if searching for something.

Dalinar had dropped his Blade. The common Parshendi soldiers surrounded the duel. They forced Gallant back, making the horse whinny. He reared. Dalinar watched him, vision swimming.

Why didn't the Shardbearer just finish him? The Parshendi giant leaned down, then spoke. The words were thickly accented, and Dalinar's mind nearly dismissed them. But here, up close, Dalinar realized something. He understood what was being said. The accent was nearly impenetrable, but the words were in *Alethi*.

'It *is* you,' the Parshendi Shardbearer said. 'I have found you at last.'

Dalinar blinked in surprise.

Something disturbed the back ranks of the watching Parshendi soldiers. There was something familiar about this scene, Parshendi all around, Shardbearer in danger. Dalinar had lived it before, but from the other side.

That Shardbearer couldn't be talking to him. Dalinar had been hit too hard on the head. He must be delusional. What was that disturbance in the ring of Parshendi watchers?

Sadeas, Dalinar found himself thinking, his mind confused. *He's come to rescue me, as I rescued him.*

Unite them. ...

He'll come, Dalinar thought. *I know he will. I will gather them. ...*

The Parshendi were yelling, moving, twisting. Suddenly, a figure exploded through them. Not Sadeas at all. A young man with a strong face and long, curling black hair. He carried a spear.

And he was glowing.

What? Dalinar thought, dazed.

❖

Kaladin landed in the open circle. The two Shardbearers were at the center, one on the ground, Stormlight trailing faintly from his body. Too faintly. Considering the number of cracks, his gemstones must be almost spent. The other – a Parshendi, judging by the size and shape of the limbs – was standing over the fallen one.

Great, Kaladin thought, dashing forward before the Parshendi soldiers could collect their wits and attack him. The Parshendi Shardbearer was bent down, focused on Dalinar. The Parshendi's Plate was leaking Stormlight through a large fissure in the leg.

So – memory flashing back to the time he rescued Amaram – Kaladin got in close and slammed his spear into the crack.

The Shardbearer screamed and dropped his Blade in surprise. It puffed to mist. Kaladin whipped his spear free and dodged backward. The Shardbearer swung toward him with a gauntleted fist, but missed. Kaladin jumped in and – throwing his full strength behind the blow – rammed his spear into the cracked leg armor again.

The Shardbearer screamed even louder, stumbling, then fell to his knees. Kaladin tried to pull his spear free, but the man crumpled on top of it, snapping the shaft. Kaladin dodged back, now facing a ring of Parshendi, empty-handed, Stormlight streaming from his body.

Silence. And then, they began speaking again, the words they'd said before. 'Neshua Kadal!' They passed it among themselves, whispering, looking confused. Then they began to chant a song he'd never heard before.

Good enough, Kaladin thought. So long as they weren't attacking him. Dalinar Kholin was moving, sitting up. Kaladin knelt down, commanding most of his Stormlight into the stony ground, retaining just enough to keep him going, but not enough to make him glow. Then he hurried over to the armored horse at the side of the ring of Parshendi.

The Parshendi shied away from him, looking terrified. He took the reins and quickly returned to the highprince.

◆
◆ ◆

Dalinar shook his head, trying to clear his mind. His vision still swam, but his thoughts were re-forming. What had happened? He'd been hit on the head, and . . . and now the Shardbearer was down.

Down? What had caused the Shardbearer to fall? Had the creature really talked to him? No, he must have imagined that. That, and the young spearman glowing. He wasn't doing so now. Holding Gallant's reins, the young man waved at Dalinar urgently. Dalinar forced himself to his feet. Around them, the Parshendi were muttering something unintelligible.

That Shardplate, Dalinar thought, looking at the kneeling Parshendi. *A Shardblade . . . I could fulfill my promise to Renarin. I could . . .*

The Shardbearer groaned, holding his leg with a gauntleted hand. Dalinar itched to finish the kill. He took a step forward, dragging his unresponsive foot. Around them, the Parshendi troops watched silently. Why didn't they attack?

The tall spearman ran up to Dalinar, pulling Gallant's reins. 'On your horse, lighteyes.'

'We should finish him. We could—'

'On your horse!' the youth commanded, tossing the reins at him as the Parshendi troops turned to engage a contingent of approaching Alethi soldiers.

'You're supposed to be an honorable one,' the spearman snarled. Dalinar had rarely been spoken to in such a way, particularly by a darkeyed man. 'Well, your men won't leave without *you*, and *my* men won't leave without *them*. So you *will* get on your horse and we *will* escape this deathtrap. Do you understand?'

Dalinar met the young man's eyes. Then nodded. Of course. He was right; they had to leave the enemy Shardbearer. How would they get the armor out, anyway? Tow the corpse all the way?

'Retreat!' Dalinar bellowed to his soldiers, pulling himself into Gallant's saddle. He barely made it, his armor had so little Stormlight left.

Steady, loyal Gallant sprang into a gallop down the corridor of escape his men had bought for him with their blood. The nameless spearman dashed behind him, and the Cobalt Guard fell in around them. A larger force of his troops was ahead, on the escape plateau. The bridge still stood, Adolin waiting anxiously at its head, holding it for Dalinar's retreat.

With a rush of relief, Dalinar galloped across the wooden deck, reaching the adjoining plateau. Adolin and the last of his troops filed along behind him.

He turned Gallant, looking eastward. The Parshendi crowded up to the chasm, but did not give chase. A group of them worked on the chrysalis atop the plateau. It had been forgotten by all sides in the furor. They had never followed before, but if they changed their mind now, they could harry Dalinar's force all the way back to the permanent bridges.

But they didn't. They formed ranks and began to chant another of their songs, the same one they sang every time the Alethi forces retreated. As Dalinar watched, a figure in cracked, silvery Shardplate and a red cape stumbled to their forefront. The helm had been removed, but it was too distant to make out any features on the black and red marbled skin. Dalinar's erstwhile foe raised his Shardblade in a motion that was unmistakable. A salute, a gesture of respect. Instinctively, Dalinar summoned his Blade, and ten heartbeats later raised it to salute in return.

The bridgemen pulled the bridge across the chasm, separating the armies.

'Set up triage,' Dalinar bellowed. 'We don't leave anyone behind who has a chance at living. The Parshendi will not attack us here!'

His men let out a shout. Somehow, escaping felt like more of a victory than any gemheart they'd won. The tired Alethi troops divided into battalions. Eight had marched to battle, and they became eight again – though several had only a few hundred members remaining. Those men trained for field surgery looked through the ranks while the remaining officers got survivor counts. The men began to sit down among the painspren and exhaustionspren, bloodied, some weaponless, many with torn uniforms.

On the other plateau, the Parshendi continued their odd song.

Dalinar found himself focusing on the bridge crew. The youth who had saved him was apparently their leader. Had he fought down a *Shardbearer*? Dalinar hazily remembered a quick, sharp encounter, a spear to the leg. Clearly the young man was both skilled and lucky.

The bridgeman's team acted with far more coordination and discipline than Dalinar would have expected of such lowly men. He could wait no longer. Dalinar nudged Gallant forward, crossing the stones and passing wounded, exhausted soldiers. That reminded him of his own fatigue, but now that he had a chance to sit, he was recovering, his head no longer ringing.

The leader of the bridge crew was seeing to a man's wound, and his fingers worked with expertise. A man trained in field medicine, among *bridgemen*?

Well, why not? Dalinar thought. *It's no odder than their being able to fight so well.* Sadeas had been holding out on him.

The young man looked up. And, for the first time, Dalinar noticed the slave brands on his forehead, hidden by the long hair. The youth stood, posture hostile, folding his arms.

'You are to be commended,' Dalinar said. 'All of you. Why did your highprince retreat, only to send you back for us?'

Several of the bridgemen chuckled.

'He didn't send us back,' their leader said. 'We came on our own. Against his wishes.'

Dalinar found himself nodding, and he realized that this was the only answer that made sense. 'Why?' Dalinar asked. 'Why come for us?'

The youth shrugged. 'You allowed yourself to get trapped in there quite spectacularly.'

Dalinar nodded tiredly. Perhaps he should have been annoyed at the young man's tone, but it was only the truth. 'Yes, but *why* did you come? And how did you learn to fight so well?'

'By accident,' the young man said. He turned back to his wounded.

'What can I do to repay you?' Dalinar asked.

The bridgeman looked back at him. 'I don't know. We were going to flee from Sadeas, disappear in the confusion. We might still, but he'll certainly hunt us down and kill us.'

'I could take your men to my camp, make Sadeas free you from your bondage.'

'I worry that he wouldn't let us go,' the bridgeman said, eyes haunted. 'And I worry that your camp would offer no safety at all. This move today by Sadeas. It will mean war between you two, will it not?'

Would it? Dalinar had avoided thinking of Sadeas – survival had taken his focus – but his anger at the man was a seething pit deep within. He *would* exact revenge on Sadeas for this. But could he allow war between the princedoms? It would shatter Alethkar. More than that, it would destroy the Kholin house. Dalinar didn't have the troops or the allies to stand against Sadeas, not after this disaster.

How would Sadeas respond when Dalinar returned? Would he try to finish the job, attacking? *No*, Dalinar thought. *No, he did it this way for a reason.* Sadeas had not engaged him personally. He had abandoned Dalinar, but by Alethi standards, that was another thing entirely. He didn't want to risk the kingdom either.

Sadeas wouldn't want outright war, and Dalinar couldn't *afford* outright war, despite his seething anger. He formed a fist, turning to look at the spearman. 'It will not turn to war,' Dalinar said. 'Not yet, at least.'

'Well, if that's the case,' the spearman said, 'then by taking us into your camp, you commit robbery. The king's law, the Codes my men always claim you uphold, would demand that you return us to Sadeas. He *won't* let us go easily.'

'I will take care of Sadeas,' Dalinar said. 'Return with me. I vow that you will be safe. I promise it with every shred of honor I have.'

The young bridgeman met his eyes, searching for something. Such a hard man he was for one so young.

'All right,' the spearman said. 'We'll return. I can't leave my men back at camp and – with so many men now wounded – we don't have the proper supplies to run.'

The young man turned back to his work, and Dalinar rode Gallant in search of a casualty report. He forced himself to contain his rage at Sadeas. It was difficult. No, Dalinar could not let this turn to war – but neither could he let things go back to the way they had been.

Sadeas had upset the balance, and it could never be regained. Not in the same way.

'All is withdrawn for me. I stand against the one who saved my life. I protect the one who killed my promises. I raise my hand. The storm responds.'

—Tanatanev 1173, 18 seconds pre-death. A darkeyed mother of four in her sixty-second year.

Navani pushed her way past the guards, ignoring their protests and the calls of her attending ladies. She forced herself to remain calm. She *would* remain calm! What she had heard was just rumor. It *had* to be.

Unfortunately, the older she grew, the worse she became at maintaining a brightlady's proper tranquility. She hastened her step through Sadeas's warcamp. Soldiers raised hands toward her as she passed, either to offer her aid or to demand she halt. She ignored both; they'd never dare lay a finger on her. Being the king's mother gained one a few privileges.

The camp was messy and poorly laid out. Pockets of merchants, whores, and workers made their homes in shanties built on the leeward sides of barracks. Drippings of hardened crem hung from most leeward eaves, like trails of wax left to pour over the side of a table. It was a distinct contrast to the neat lines and scrubbed buildings of Dalinar's warcamp.

He will be fine, she told herself. *He'd* better *be fine!*

It was a testament to her disordered state that she barely considered constructing a new street pattern for Sadeas in her head. She made her way directly to the staging area, and arrived to find an army that hardly looked as if it had been to battle. Soldiers without any blood on their uniforms, men chatting and laughing, officers walking down lines and dismissing the men squad by squad.

That should have relieved her. This didn't *look* like a force that had just suffered a disaster. Instead, it made her even more anxious.

Sadeas, in unmarred red Shardplate, was speaking with a group of officers in the shade of a nearby canopy. She stalked up to the canopy, but here a group of guards managed to bar her way, forming up shoulder to shoulder while one went to inform Sadeas of her arrival.

Navani folded her arms impatiently. Perhaps she should have taken a palanquin, as her attending ladies had suggested. Several of them, looking beleaguered, were just arriving at the staging area. A palanquin would be faster in the long run, they had explained, as it would leave time for messengers to be sent so Sadeas could receive her.

Once, she had obeyed such proprieties. She could remember being a young woman, playing the games expertly, delighting in ways to manipulate the system. What had that gotten her? A dead husband whom she'd never loved and a 'privileged' position in court that amounted to being put out to pasture.

What would Sadeas do if she just started screaming? The king's own mother, bellowing like an axehound whose antenna had been twisted? She considered it as the soldier waited for a chance to announce her to Sadeas.

From the corner of her eye, she noticed a youth in a blue uniform arriving in the staging area, accompanied by a small honor guard of three men. It was Renarin, for once bearing an expression other than calm curiosity. Wide-eyed and frantic, he hurried up to Navani.

'Mashala,' he pled in his quiet voice. 'Please. What have you heard?'

'Sadeas's army returned without your father's army,' Navani said. 'There is talk of a rout, though it doesn't look as if these men have been through one.' She glared at Sadeas, giving serious contemplation to throwing a fit. Fortunately, he finally spoke with the soldier and then sent him back.

'You may approach, Brightness,' the man said, bowing to her.

'About time,' she growled, shoving past and passing underneath the canopy. Renarin joined her, walking more hesitantly.

'Brightness Navani,' Sadeas said, clasping his hands behind his back, imposing in his crimson Plate. 'I had hoped to bring you the news at your son's palace. I suppose that a disaster like this is too large to contain. I express my condolences at the loss of your brother.'

Renarin gasped softly.

Navani steeled herself, folding her arms, trying to quiet the screams of denial and pain that came from the back of her mind. This was a pattern. She often saw patterns in things. In this case, the pattern was that she could never possess anything of value for long. It was always snatched from her just when it began to look promising.

Quiet, she scolded herself. 'You will explain,' she said to Sadeas, meeting his gaze. She'd practiced that look over the decades, and was pleased to see that it discomfited him.

'I'm sorry, Brightness,' Sadeas repeated, stammering. 'The Parshendi overwhelmed your brother's army. It was folly to work together. Our change in tactics was so threatening to the savages that they brought every soldier they could to this battle, surrounding us.'

'And so you *left* Dalinar?'

'We fought hard to reach him, but the numbers were simply overpowering. We had to retreat lest we lose ourselves as well! I would have continued fighting, save for the fact that I saw your brother fall with my own eyes, swarmed by Parshendi with hammers.' He grimaced. 'They began carrying away chunks of bloodied Shardplate as prizes. Barbaric monsters.'

Navani felt cold. Cold, numb. How could this happen? After finally – *finally* – making that stone-headed man see her as a woman, rather than as a sister. And now . . .

And now . . .

She set her jaw against the tears. 'I don't believe it.'

'I understand that the news is difficult.' Sadeas waved for an attendant to fetch her a chair. 'I wish I had not been forced to bring it to you. Dalinar and I . . . well, I have known him for many years, and while we did not always see the same sunrise, I considered him an ally. And a friend.' He cursed softly, looking eastward. 'They will pay for this. I will *see* that they pay.'

He seemed so earnest that Navani found herself wavering. Poor Renarin, pale-faced and wide-eyed, seemed stunned beyond the means to speak. When the chair arrived, Navani refused it, so Renarin sat, earning a glance of disapproval from Sadeas. Renarin grasped his head in his hands, staring at the ground. He was trembling.

He's highprince now, Navani realized.

No. *No.* He was only highprince if she accepted the idea that Dalinar was dead. And he wasn't. He couldn't be.

Sadeas had all of the bridges, she thought, looking down at the lumberyard.

Navani stepped out into the late-afternoon sunlight, feeling its heat on her skin. She walked up to her attendants. 'Brushpen,' she said to Makal, who carried a satchel with Navani's possessions. 'The thickest one. And my burn ink.'

The short, plump woman opened the satchel, taking out a long brushpen with a knob of hog bristles on the end as wide as a man's thumb. Navani took it. The ink followed.

Around her, the guards stared as Navani took the pen and dipped it into the blood-colored ink. She knelt, and began to paint on the stone ground.

Art was about creation. That was its soul, its essence. Creation and order. You took something disorganized – a splash of ink, an empty page – and you built something from it. Something from nothing. The *soul* of creation.

She felt the tears on her cheeks as she painted. Dalinar had no wife and no daughters; he had nobody to pray for him. And so, Navani painted a prayer onto the stones themselves, sending her attendants for more ink. She paced off the size of the glyph as she continued its border, making it enormous, spreading her ink onto the tan rocks.

Soldiers gathered around, Sadeas stepping from his canopy, watching her paint, her back to the sun as she crawled on the ground and furiously dipped her brushpen into the ink jars. What was a prayer, if not creation? Making something where nothing existed. Creating a wish out of despair, a plea out of anguish. Bowing one's back before the Almighty, and forming humility from the empty pride of a human life.

Something from nothing. True creation.

Her tears mixed with the ink. She went through four jars. She crawled, holding her safehand to the ground, brushing the stones and smearing ink on her cheeks when she wiped the tears. When she finally finished, she knelt back before a glyph twenty paces long, emblazoned as if in blood. The wet ink reflected sunlight, and she fired it with a candle; the ink was made to burn whether wet or dry. The flames burned across the length of the prayer, killing it and sending its soul to the Almighty.

She bowed her head before the prayer. It was only a single character, but a complex one. *Thath*. Justice.

Men watched quietly, as if afraid of spoiling her solemn wish. A cold breeze began blowing, whipping at pennants and cloaks. The prayer went out, but that was fine. It wasn't meant to burn long.

'Brightlord Sadeas!' an anxious voice called.

Navani looked up. Soldiers parted, making way for a runner in green. He hurried up to Sadeas, beginning to speak, but the highprince grabbed the man by the shoulder in a Shardplate grip and pointed, gesturing for his guards to make a perimeter. He pulled the messenger beneath the canopy.

Navani continued to kneel beside her prayer. The flames left a black scar in the shape of the glyph on the ground. Someone stepped up beside her – Renarin. He went to one knee, resting a hand on her shoulder. 'Thank you, Mashala.'

She nodded, standing, her freehand sprinkled with drops of red pigment. Her cheeks were still wet with tears, but she narrowed her eyes, looking through the press of soldiers toward Sadeas. His expression was thunderous, face growing red, eyes wide with anger.

She turned and pushed her way through the press of soldiers, scrambling up to the rim of the staging field. Renarin and some of Sadeas's officers joined her in staring out over the Shattered Plains.

And there they saw a creeping line of men limping back toward the warcamps, led by a mounted man in slate-grey armor.

◆
◆ ◆

Dalinar rode Gallant at the head of two thousand six hundred and fifty-three men. That was all that remained of his assault force of eight thousand.

The long trek back across the plateaus had given him time to think. His insides were still a tempest of emotions. He flexed his left hand as he rode; it was now encased by a blue-painted Shardplate gauntlet borrowed from Adolin. It would take days to regrow Dalinar's own gauntlet. Longer, if the Parshendi tried to grow a full suit from the one he had left. They would fail, so long as Dalinar's armorers fed Stormlight to his suit. The abandoned gauntlet would degrade and crumble to dust, a new one growing for Dalinar.

For now, he wore Adolin's. They had collected all of the infused gemstones among his twenty-six hundred men and used that Stormlight to recharge and reinforce his armor. It was still scarred with cracks. Healing as much damage as it had sustained would take days, but the Plate was in fighting shape again, if it came to that.

He needed to make certain it didn't. He intended to confront Sadeas, and he wanted to be armored when he did. In fact, he *wanted* to storm up the incline to Sadeas's warcamp and declare formal war on his 'old friend.' Perhaps summon his Blade and see Sadeas dead.

But he wouldn't. His soldiers were too weak, his position too tenuous. Formal war would destroy him and the kingdom. He had to do something else. Something that protected the kingdom. Revenge would come. Eventually. Alethkar came first.

He lowered his blue-gauntleted fist, gripping Gallant's reins. Adolin rode a short distance away. They'd repaired his armor as well, though he now lacked a gauntlet. Dalinar had refused the gift of his son's gauntlet at first, but had given in to Adolin's logic. If one of them was going to go without, it should be the younger man. Inside Shardplate, their differences in age didn't matter – but outside of it, Adolin was a young man in his twenties and Dalinar an aging man in his fifties.

He still didn't know what to think of the visions, and their apparent failure in telling him to trust Sadeas. He'd confront that later. One step at a time.

'Elthal,' Dalinar called. The highest-ranked officer who had survived the disaster, Elthal was a limber man with a distinguished face and a thin mustache. His arm was in a sling. He'd been one of those to hold the gap alongside Dalinar during the last part of the fight.

'Yes, Brightlord?' Elthal asked, jogging over to Dalinar. All of the horses save the two Ryshadium were carrying wounded.

'Take the wounded to my warcamp,' Dalinar said. 'Then tell Teleb to bring the entire camp to alert. Mobilize the remaining companies.'

'Yes, Brightlord,' the man said, saluting. 'Brightlord, what should I tell them to prepare for?'

'Anything. But hopefully nothing.'

'I understand, Brightlord,' Elthal said, leaving to follow the orders.

Dalinar turned Gallant to march over to the group of bridgemen, still following their somber leader, a man named Kaladin. They'd left their bridge as soon as they'd reached the permanent bridges; Sadeas could send for it eventually.

The bridgemen stopped as he approached, looking as tired as he felt, then arranged themselves in a subtly hostile formation. They clung to their spears, as if certain he'd try to take them away. They had saved him, yet they obviously didn't trust him.

'I'm sending my wounded back to my camp,' Dalinar said. 'You should go with them.'

'You're confronting Sadeas?' Kaladin asked.

'I must.' *I have to know why he did what he did.* 'I will buy your freedom when I do.'

'Then I'm staying with you,' Kaladin said.

'Me too,' said a hawk-faced man at the side. Soon all of the bridgemen were demanding to stay.

Kaladin turned to them. 'I should send you back.'

'What?' asked an older bridgeman with a short grey beard. 'You can risk yourself, but we can't? We have men back in Sadeas's camp. We need to get them out. At the very least, we need to stay together. See this through.'

The others nodded. Again, Dalinar was struck by their discipline. More and more, he was certain Sadeas had nothing to do with that. It was this man at their head. Though his eyes were dark brown, he held himself like a brightlord.

Well, if they wouldn't go, Dalinar wouldn't force them. He continued to ride, and soon close to a thousand of Dalinar's soldiers broke off and marched south, toward his warcamp. The rest of them continued toward Sadeas's camp. As they drew closer, Dalinar noticed a small crowd gathering at the final chasm. Two figures in particular stood at their forefront. Renarin and Navani.

'What are *they* doing in Sadeas's warcamp?' Adolin asked, smiling through his fatigue, edging Sureblood up beside Dalinar.

'I don't know,' Dalinar said. 'But the Stormfather bless them for coming.' Seeing their welcome faces, he began to feel it sink in – finally – that he had survived the day.

Gallant crossed the last bridge. Renarin was there waiting, and Dalinar rejoiced.

For once, the boy was displaying outright joy. Dalinar swung free from the saddle and embraced his son.

'Father,' Renarin said, 'you live!'

Adolin laughed, swinging out of his own saddle, armor clanking. Renarin pulled out of the embrace and grabbed Adolin on the shoulder, pounding the Shardplate lightly with his other hand, grinning widely. Dalinar smiled as well, turning from the brothers to look at Navani. She stood with hands clasped before her, one eyebrow raised. Her face, oddly, bore a few small smears of red paint.

'You weren't even worried, were you?' he said to her.

'Worried?' she asked. Her eyes met his, and for the first time, he noticed their redness. 'I was terrified.'

And then Dalinar found himself grabbing her in an embrace. He had to be careful as he was in Shardplate, but the gauntlets let him feel the silk of her dress, and his missing helm let him smell the sweet floral scent of her perfumed soap. He held her as tightly as he dared, bowing his head and pressing his nose into her hair.

'Hmm,' she noted warmly, 'it appears that I was missed. The others are watching. They'll talk.'

'I don't care.'

'Hmm . . . It appears I was *very much* missed.'

'On the battlefield,' he said gruffly, 'I thought I would die. And I realized it was all right.'

She pulled her head back, looking confused.

'I have spent too much of my time worrying about what people think, Navani. When I thought my time had arrived, I realized that all my worrying had been wasted. In the end, I was pleased with how I had lived my life.' He looked down at her, then mentally unlatched his right gauntlet, letting it drop to the ground with a clank. He reached up with that callused hand, cupping her chin. 'I had only two regrets. One for you, and one for Renarin.'

'So, you're saying you can just die, and it would be all right?'

'No,' he said. 'What I'm saying is that I faced eternity, and I saw peace there. That will change how I live.'

'Without all of the guilt?'

He hesitated. 'Being me, I doubt I'll banish it entirely. The end was peace, but living ... that is a tempest. Still, I see things differently now. It is time to stop letting myself be shoved around by lying men.' He looked up, toward the ridge above, where more soldiers in green were gathering. 'I keep thinking of one of the visions,' he said softly, 'the latest one, where I met Nohadon. He rejected my suggestion that he write down his wisdom. There's something there. Something I need to learn.'

'What?' Navani asked.

'I don't know yet. But I'm close to figuring it out.' He held her close again, hand on the back of her head, feeling her hair. He wished for the Plate to be gone, to not be separated from her by the metal.

But the time for that had not yet come. Reluctantly, he released her, turning to the side, where Renarin and Adolin were watching them uncomfortably. His soldiers were looking up at Sadeas's army, gathering on the ridge.

I can't let this come to bloodshed, Dalinar thought, reaching down and putting his hand into the fallen gauntlet. The straps tightened, connecting to the rest of the armor. *But I'm also not going to slink back to my camp without confronting him.* He at least had to know the purpose of the betrayal. All had been going so well.

Besides, there was the matter of his promise to the bridgemen. Dalinar walked up the slope, bloodstained blue cloak flapping behind him. Adolin clanked up next to him on one side, Navani keeping pace on the other. Renarin followed, Dalinar's remaining sixteen hundred troops marching up as well.

'Father ...' Adolin said, looking at the hostile troops.

'Don't summon your Blade. This will not come to blows.'

'Sadeas abandoned you, didn't he?' Navani asked quietly, eyes alight with anger.

'He didn't just abandon us,' Adolin spat. 'He set us up, then betrayed us.'

'We survived,' Dalinar said firmly. The way ahead was becoming clearer. He knew what he needed to do. 'He won't attack us here, but he might try to provoke us. Keep your sword as mist, Adolin, and don't let our troops make any mistakes.'

The soldiers in green parted reluctantly, holding spears. Hostile. To the side, Kaladin and his bridgemen walked near the front of Dalinar's force.

Adolin didn't summon his Blade, though he regarded Sadeas's troops around them with contempt. Dalinar's soldiers couldn't have felt easy about being surrounded by enemies once again, but they followed him onto the staging field. Sadeas stood ahead. The treacherous highprince waited with arms folded, still wearing his Shardplate, curly black hair blowing in the breeze. Someone had burned an enormous *thath* glyph on the stones here, and Sadeas stood at its center.

Justice. There was something magnificently appropriate about Sadeas standing there, treading upon justice.

'Dalinar,' Sadeas exclaimed, 'old friend! It appears that I overestimated the odds against you. I apologize for retreating when you were still in danger, but the safety of my men came first. I'm certain you understand.'

Dalinar stopped a short distance from Sadeas. The two faced each other, collected armies tense. A cold breeze whipped at a canopy behind Sadeas.

'Of course,' Dalinar said, his voice even. 'You did what you had to do.'

Sadeas relaxed visibly, though several of Dalinar's soldiers muttered at that. Adolin silenced them with pointed glances.

Dalinar turned, waving Adolin and his men backward. Navani gave him a raised eyebrow, but retreated with the others when he urged her. Dalinar looked back at Sadeas, and the man – looking curious – waved his own attendants back.

Dalinar walked up to the edge of the *thath* glyph, and Sadeas stepped forward until only inches separated them. They were matched in height. Standing this close, Dalinar thought he could see tension – and anger – in Sadeas's eyes. Dalinar's survival had ruined months of planning.

'I need to know why,' Dalinar asked, too quietly for any but Sadeas to hear.

'Because of my oath, old friend.'

'*What?*' Dalinar asked, hands forming fists.

'We swore something together, years ago.' Sadeas sighed, losing his flippancy and speaking openly. 'Protect Elhokar. Protect this kingdom.'

'That's what I was doing! We had the same purpose. And we were fighting together, Sadeas. It was *working*.'

'Yes,' Sadeas said. 'But I'm confident I can beat the Parshendi on my own now. Everything we've done together, I can manage by splitting my army into two – one to race on ahead, a larger force to follow. I had to take this chance to remove you. Dalinar, can't you see? Gavilar died because of his weakness. *I* wanted to attack the Parshendi from the start, conquer them. He insisted on a treaty, which led to his death. Now you're starting to act just like him. Those same ideas, the same ways of speaking. Through you they begin to infect Elhokar. He dresses like you. He talks of the Codes to me, and of how perhaps we should enforce them through all the warcamps. He's beginning to think of *retreating*.'

'And so you'd have me think this an act of honor?' Dalinar growled.

'Not at all,' Sadeas said, chuckling. 'I have struggled for years to become Elhokar's most trusted advisor – but there was always you, distracting him, holding his ear despite my every effort. I won't pretend this was only about honor, though there was an element of that to it. In the end, I just wanted you gone.'

Sadeas's voice grew cold. 'But you *are* going insane, old friend. You may name me a liar, but I did what I did today as a mercy. A way of letting you die in glory, rather than watching you descend further and further. By letting the Parshendi kill you, I could protect Elhokar from you and turn you into a symbol to remind the others what we're really doing here. Your death might have become what finally united us. Ironic, if you consider it.'

Dalinar breathed in and out. It was hard not to let his anger, his indignation, consume him. 'Then tell me one thing. Why not pin the assassination attempt on me? Why clear me, if you were only looking to betray me later on?'

Sadeas snorted softly. 'Bah. Nobody would *really* believe that you tried to kill the king. They'd gossip, but they wouldn't believe it. Blaming you too quickly would have risked implicating myself.' He shook his head. 'I think Elhokar knows who tried to kill him. He's admitted as much to me, though he won't give me the name.'

What? Dalinar thought. *He knows? But . . . how? Why not tell us who?*

Dalinar adjusted his plans. He wasn't certain if Sadeas was telling the truth, but if he was, he could use this.

'He knows it wasn't you,' Sadeas continued. 'I can read that much in him, though he doesn't realize how transparent he is. Blaming you would have been pointless. Elhokar would have defended you, and I might very well have lost the position of Highprince of Information. But it *did* give me a wonderful opportunity to make you trust me again.'

Unite them. . . . The visions. But the man who spoke to Dalinar in them had been dead wrong. Acting with honor *hadn't* won Sadeas's loyalty. It had just opened Dalinar up to betrayal.

'If it means anything,' Sadeas said idly, 'I'm fond of you. I really am. But you are a boulder in my path, and a force working – without realizing it – to destroy Gavilar's kingdom. When the chance came along, I took it.'

'It wasn't simply a convenient opportunity,' Dalinar said. 'You set this up, Sadeas.'

'I planned, but I'm often planning. I don't always act on my options. Today I did.'

Dalinar snorted. 'Well, you've shown me something today, Sadeas – shown it to me by the very act of trying to remove me.'

'And what was that?' Sadeas asked, amused.

'You've shown me that I'm still a threat.'

⁂

The highprinces continued their low-pitched conversation. Kaladin stood to the side of Dalinar's soldiers, exhausted, with the members of Bridge Four.

Sadeas spared a glance for them. Matal stood in the crowd, and had been watching Kaladin's team the entire time, red-faced. Matal probably knew that he would be punished as Lamaril had been. They should have learned. They should have killed Kaladin at the start.

They tried, he thought. *They failed.*

He didn't know what had happened to him, what had gone on with Syl and the words in his head. It seemed that Stormlight worked better for him now. It had been more potent, more powerful. But now it was gone, and he was *so* tired. Drained. He'd pushed himself, and Bridge Four, too far. Too hard.

Perhaps he and the others should have gone to Kholin's camp. But Teft was right; they needed to see this through.

He promised, Kaladin thought. *He promised he would free us from Sadeas.*

And yet, where had the promises of lighteyes gotten him in the past?

The highprinces broke off their conference, separating, stepping back from one another.

'Well,' Sadeas said loudly, 'your men are obviously tired, Dalinar. We can speak later about what went wrong, though I think it is safe to assume that our alliance has proven unfeasible.'

'Unfeasible,' Dalinar said. 'A kind way of putting it.' He nodded toward the bridgemen. 'I will take these bridgemen with me to my camp.'

'I'm afraid I cannot part with them.'

Kaladin's heart sank.

'Surely they aren't worth much to you,' Dalinar said. 'Name your price.'

'I'm not looking to sell.'

'I will pay sixty emerald broams per man,' Dalinar said. That drew gasps from the watching soldiers on both sides. It was easily twenty times the price of a good slave.

'Not for a thousand each, Dalinar,' Sadeas said. Kaladin could see the deaths of his bridgemen in those eyes. 'Take your soldiers and go. Leave my property here.'

'Do not press me on this, Sadeas,' Dalinar said.

Suddenly, the tension was back. Dalinar's officers lowered hands to swords, and his spearmen perked up, gripping the hafts of their weapons.

'Do not press you?' Sadeas asked. 'What kind of threat is that? *Leave* my camp. It's obvious that there is nothing more between us. If you try to steal my property, I will have every justification in attacking you.'

Dalinar stood in place. He looked confident, though Kaladin saw no reason why. *And another promise dies*, Kaladin thought, turning away. In the end, for all his good intentions, this Dalinar Kholin was the same as the others.

Behind Kaladin, men gasped in surprise.

Kaladin froze, then spun around. Dalinar Kholin was holding his massive Shardblade; it dripped beads of water from having just been summoned. His armor steamed faintly, Stormlight rising from the cracks.

Sadeas stumbled back, eyes wide. His honor guard drew their swords. Adolin Kholin reached his hand to the side, apparently beginning to summon his own weapon.

Dalinar took one step forward, then drove his Blade point-first into the middle of the blackened glyph on the stone. He took a step back. 'For the bridgemen,' he said.

Sadeas blinked. Muttering voices fell silent, and the people on the field seemed too stunned, even, to breathe.

'*What?*' Sadeas asked.

'The Blade,' Dalinar said, firm voice carrying in the air. 'In exchange for your bridgemen. All of them. Every one you have in camp. They become mine, to do with as I please, never to be touched by you again. In exchange, you get the sword.'

Sadeas looked down at the Blade, incredulous. 'This weapon is worth fortunes. Cities, palaces, *kingdoms*.'

'Do we have a deal?' Dalinar asked.

'Father, no!' Adolin Kholin said, his own Blade appearing in his hand. 'You—'

Dalinar raised a hand, silencing the younger man. He kept his eyes on Sadeas. '*Do we have a deal?*' he asked, each word sharp.

Kaladin stared, unable to move, unable to think.

Sadeas looked at the Shardblade, eyes full of lust. He glanced at Kaladin, hesitated just briefly, then reached and grabbed the Blade by the hilt. '*Take* the storming creatures.'

Dalinar nodded curtly, turning away from Sadeas. 'Let's go,' he said to his entourage.

'They're worthless, you know,' Sadeas said. 'You're of the ten fools, Dalinar Kholin! Don't you see how mad you are? This will be remembered as the most ridiculous decision ever made by an Alethi highprince!'

Dalinar didn't look back. He walked up to Kaladin and the other members of Bridge Four. 'Go,' Dalinar said to them, voice kindly. 'Gather your things and the men you left behind. I will send troops with you to act as guards. Leave the bridges and come swiftly to my camp. You will be safe there. You have my word of honor on it.'

He began to walk away.

Kaladin shook off his numbness. He scrambled after the highprince, grabbing his armored arm. 'Wait. You— That— *What just happened?*'

Dalinar turned to him. Then, the highprince laid a hand on Kaladin's shoulder, the gauntlet gleaming blue, mismatched with the rest of his slate-grey armor. 'I don't know what has been done to you. I can only guess what your life has been like. But know this. You will not be bridgemen in my camp, nor will you be slaves.'

'But . . .'

'What is a man's life worth?' Dalinar asked softly.

'The slavemasters say one is worth about two emerald broams,' Kaladin said, frowning.

'And what do you say?'

'A life is priceless,' he said immediately, quoting his father.

Dalinar smiled, wrinkle lines extending from the corners of his eyes. 'Coincidentally, that is the exact value of a Shardblade. So today, you and your men sacrificed to buy me twenty-six hundred priceless lives. And all I had to repay you with was a single priceless sword. I call that a bargain.'

'You really think it was a good trade, don't you?' Kaladin said, amazed.

Dalinar smiled in a way that seemed strikingly paternal. 'For my honor? Unquestionably. Go and lead your men to safety, soldier. Later tonight, I will have some questions for you.'

Kaladin glanced at Sadeas, who held his new Blade with awe. 'You said you'd take care of Sadeas. This was what you intended?'

'This wasn't taking care of Sadeas,' Dalinar said. 'This was taking care of you and your men. I still have work to do today.'

⁂

Dalinar found King Elhokar in his palace sitting room.

Dalinar nodded once more to the guards outside, then closed the door. They seemed troubled. As well they should; his orders had been irregular. But they would do as told. They wore the king's colors, blue and gold, but they were Dalinar's men, chosen specifically for their loyalty.

The door shut with a snap. The king was staring at one of his maps, wearing his Shardplate. 'Ah, Uncle,' he said, turning to Dalinar. 'Good. I had wanted to speak with you. Do you know of these rumors about you and my mother? I realize that nothing untoward could be happening, but I *do* worry about what people think.'

Dalinar crossed the room, booted feet thumping on the rich rug. Infused diamonds hung in the corners of the room, and the carved walls had been set with tiny chips of quartz to sparkle and reflect the light.

'Honestly, Uncle,' Elhokar said, shaking his head. 'I'm growing very intolerant of your reputation in camp. What they are saying reflects poorly on me, you see, and ...' He trailed off as Dalinar stopped about a pace from him. 'Uncle? Is everything all right? My door guards reported some kind of mishap with your plateau assault today, but my mind was full of thoughts. Did I miss anything vital?'

'Yes,' Dalinar said. Then he raised his leg and kicked the king in the chest.

The strength of the blow tossed the king backward against his desk. The fine wood shattered as the heavy Shardbearer crashed through it. Elhokar hit the floor, his breastplate slightly cracked. Dalinar stepped up to him, then delivered another kick to the king's side, cracking the breastplate again.

Elhokar began shouting in panic. 'Guards! To me! Guards!'

Nobody came. Dalinar kicked again, and Elhokar cursed, catching his boot. Dalinar grunted, but bent down and grabbed Elhokar by the arm, then yanked him to his feet, tossing him toward the side of the room. The king stumbled on the rug, crashing through a chair. Round lengths of wood scattered, splinters spraying out.

Wide-eyed, Elhokar scrambled to his feet. Dalinar advanced on him.

'What has gone wrong with you, Uncle?' Elhokar yelled. 'You're mad! Guards! Assassin in the king's chamber! Guards!' Elhokar tried to run for the door, but Dalinar threw his shoulder against the king, tossing the younger man to the ground again.

Elhokar rolled, but got a hand under himself and climbed to his knees, the other hand to the side. A puff of mist appeared in it as he summoned his Blade.

Dalinar kicked the king's hand just as the Shardblade dropped into it. The blow knocked the Blade free, and it dissolved back to mist immediately.

Elhokar frantically swung a fist at Dalinar, but Dalinar caught it, then reached down and hauled the king to his feet. He pulled Elhokar forward and slammed his fist into the king's breastplate. Elhokar struggled, but Dalinar repeated the move, smashing his gauntlet against the Plate, cracking the steel casings around his fingers, making the king grunt.

The next blow shattered Elhokar's breastplate in an explosion of molten shards.

Dalinar dropped the king to the floor. Elhokar struggled to rise again, but the breastplate was a focus for the Shardplate's power. Losing it left arms and legs heavy. He went to one knee beside the squirming king. Elhokar's Shardblade formed again, but Dalinar grabbed the king's wrist and smashed it against the stone floor, knocking the Blade free yet again. It vanished into mist.

'Guards!' Elhokar squealed. 'Guards, guards, *guards*!'

'They won't come, Elhokar,' Dalinar said softly. 'They're my men, and I left them with orders not to enter – or let anyone else enter – no matter what they heard. Even if that included pleas for help from you.'

Elhokar fell silent.

'They are my men, Elhokar,' Dalinar repeated. 'I trained them. I placed them there. They've always been loyal to me.'

'Why, Uncle? What are you doing? Please, tell me.' He was nearly weeping.

Dalinar leaned down, getting close enough to smell the king's breath.

'The girth on your horse during the hunt,' Dalinar said quietly. 'You cut it yourself, didn't you?'

Elhokar's eyes grew wider.

'The saddles were switched before you came to my camp,' Dalinar said. 'You did that because you didn't want to ruin your favorite saddle when it flew free of the horse. You were planning for it to happen; you *made* it happen. That's why you've been so certain that the girth was cut.'

Cringing, Elhokar nodded. 'Someone was trying to kill me, but you wouldn't believe! I . . . I worried it might be you! So I decided . . . I . . .'

'You cut your own strap,' Dalinar said, 'to create a visible, obvious-seeming attempt on your life. Something that would get me or Sadeas to investigate.'

Elhokar hesitated, then nodded again.

Dalinar closed his eyes, breathing out slowly. 'Don't you realize what you did, Elhokar? You brought suspicion on me from across the camps! You gave Sadeas an opportunity to destroy me.' He opened his eyes, looking down at the king.

'I had to know,' Elhokar whispered. 'I couldn't trust anyone.' He groaned beneath Dalinar's weight.

'What of the cracked gemstones in your Shardplate? Did you place those too?'

'No.'

'Then maybe you did uncover something,' Dalinar said with a grunt. 'I guess you can't be completely blamed.'

'Then you'll let me up?'

'No.' Dalinar leaned down farther. He laid a hand against the king's chest. Elhokar stopped struggling, looking up in terror. 'If I push,' Dalinar said, 'you die. Your ribs crack like twigs, your heart is smashed like a grape. Nobody would blame me. They all whisper that the Blackthorn should have taken the throne for himself years ago. Your guard is loyal to me. There would be nobody to avenge you. Nobody would care.'

Elhokar breathed out as Dalinar pressed his hand down just slightly.

'Do you understand?' Dalinar asked quietly.

'No!'

Dalinar sighed, then released the younger man and stood up. Elhokar inhaled with a gasp.

'Your paranoia may be unfounded,' Dalinar said, 'or it may be well founded. Either way, you need to understand something. I am not your enemy.'

Elhokar frowned. 'So you're not going to kill me?'

'Storms, no! I love you like a son, boy.'

Elhokar rubbed his chest. 'You . . . have very odd paternal instincts.'

'I spent years following you,' Dalinar said. 'I gave you my loyalty, my devotion, and my counsel. I swore myself to you – promising myself, *vowing* to myself, that I would never covet Gavilar's throne. All to keep my heart loyal. Despite this, you don't trust me. You pull a stunt like that one with the girth, implicating me, giving your own enemies position against you without knowing it.'

Dalinar stepped toward the king. Elhokar cringed.

'Well, now you know,' Dalinar said, voice hard. 'If I'd wanted to kill you, Elhokar, I could have done it a dozen times over. A *hundred* times over. It appears you won't accept loyalty and devotion as proof of my honesty. Well, if you act like a child, you get treated like one. You know now, for a fact, that I don't want you dead. For if I did, I would have crushed your chest and been done with it!'

He locked eyes with the king. 'Now,' Dalinar said, '*do you understand*?'

Slowly, Elhokar nodded.

'Good,' Dalinar said. 'Tomorrow, you're going to name me Highprince of War.'

'What?'

'Sadeas betrayed me today,' Dalinar said. He walked over to the broken desk, kicking at the pieces. The king's seal rolled out of its customary drawer. He picked it up. 'Nearly six thousand of my men were slaughtered. Adolin and I barely survived.'

'What?' Elhokar said, forcing himself up to a sitting position. 'That's impossible!'

'Far from it,' Dalinar said, looking at his nephew. 'He saw a chance to pull out, letting the Parshendi destroy us. So he did it. A very Alethi thing to do. Ruthless, yet still allowing him to feign a sense of honor or morality.'

'So . . . you expect me to bring him to trial?'

'No. Sadeas is no worse, and no better, than the others. Any of the highprinces would betray their fellows, if they saw a chance to do it without risking themselves. I intend to find a way to unite them in more than just name. Somehow. Tomorrow, once you name me Highprince of War, I will give my Plate to Renarin to fulfill a promise. I've already given away my Blade to fulfill a different one.'

He walked closer, meeting Elhokar's eyes again, then gripped the king's seal in his hand. 'As Highprince of War, I will enforce the Codes in all ten camps. Then I'll coordinate the war effort directly, determining which armies get to go on which plateau assaults. All gemhearts will be won by the Throne, then distributed as spoils by you. We'll change this from a competition to a real war, and I'll use it to turn these ten armies of ours – and their leaders – into real soldiers.'

'Stormfather! They'll kill us! The highprinces will revolt! I won't last a week!'

'They won't be pleased, that's for certain,' Dalinar said. 'And yes, this will involve a great deal of danger. We'll have to be much more careful with our guard. If you're right, someone is already trying to kill you, so we should be doing that anyway.'

Elhokar stared at him, then looked at the broken furniture, rubbing his chest. 'You're *serious*, aren't you?'

'Yes.' He tossed the seal to Elhokar. 'You're going to have your scribes draw up my appointment right after I leave.'

'But I thought you said it was wrong to force men to follow the Codes,' Elhokar said. 'You said that the best way to change people was to live right, and then let them be influenced by your example!'

'That was before the Almighty lied to me,' Dalinar said. He still didn't know what to think of that. 'Much of what I told you, I learned from *The Way of Kings*. But I didn't understand something. Nohadon wrote the book at the end of his life, *after* creating order – after forcing the kingdoms to unite, after rebuilding lands that had fallen in the Desolation.

'The book was written to embody an ideal. It was given to people who already had momentum in doing what was right. That was my mistake. Before any of this can work, our people need to have a minimum level of honor and dignity. Adolin said something to me a few weeks back, something profound. He asked me why I forced my sons to live up to such high expectations, but let others go about their errant ways without condemnation.

'I have been treating the other highprinces and their lighteyes like adults. An adult can take a principle and adapt it to his needs. But we're not ready for that yet. We're children. And when you're teaching a child, you *require* him to do what is right until he grows old enough to make his own choices. The Silver Kingdoms didn't *begin* as unified, glorious bastions of honor. They were trained that way, raised up, like youths nurtured to maturity.'

He strode forward, kneeling down beside Elhokar. The king continued to rub his chest, his Shardplate looking strange with the central piece missing.

'We're going to make something of Alethkar, nephew,' Dalinar said softly. 'The highprinces gave their oaths to Gavilar, but now ignore those oaths. Well, it's time to stop letting them. We're going to win this war, and we're going to turn Alethkar into a place that men will envy again. Not because of our military prowess, but because people here are safe and because justice reigns. We're going to do it – or you and I are going to die in the attempt.'

'You say that with eagerness.'

'Because I finally know exactly what to do,' Dalinar said, standing up straight. 'I was trying to be Nohadon the peacemaker. But I'm not. I'm the Blackthorn, a general and a warlord. I have no talent for backroom politicking, but I am very good at training troops. Starting tomorrow, every man in each of these camps will be mine. As far as I'm concerned, they're all raw recruits. Even the highprinces.'

'Assuming I make the proclamation.'

'You will,' Dalinar said. 'And in return, I promise to find out who is trying to kill you.'

Elhokar snorted, beginning to remove his Shardplate piece by piece. 'After that announcement goes out, discovering who's trying to kill me will become easy. You can put every name in the warcamps on the list!'

Dalinar's smile widened. 'At least we won't have to guess, then. Don't be so glum, nephew. You learned something today. Your uncle doesn't want to kill you.'

'He just wants to make me a target.'

'For your own good, son,' Dalinar said, walking to the door. 'Don't fret too much. I've got some plans on how, exactly, to keep you alive.' He opened the door, revealing a nervous group of guards keeping at bay a nervous group of servants and attendants.

'He's just fine,' Dalinar said to them. 'See?' He stepped aside, letting the guards and servants in to attend their king.

Dalinar turned to go. Then he hesitated. 'Oh, and Elhokar? Your mother and I are now courting. You'll want to start growing accustomed to that.'

Despite everything else that had happened in the last few minutes, this got a look of pure astonishment from the king. Dalinar smiled and pulled the door closed, walking away with a firm step.

Most everything was still wrong. He was still furious at Sadeas, pained by the loss of so many of his men, confused at what to do with Navani, dumbfounded by his visions, and daunted by the idea of bringing the war-camps to unity.

But at least now he had something to work with.

PART FIVE

The Silence Above

SHALLAN • DALINAR • KALADIN
SZETH • WIT

Shallan lay quietly in the bed of her little hospital room. She'd cried herself dry, then had actually retched into the bedpan, over what she had done. She felt miserable.

She'd betrayed Jasnah. And Jasnah knew. Somehow, disappointing the princess felt worse than the theft itself. This entire plan had been foolish from the start.

Beyond that, Kabsal was dead. Why did she feel so sick about *that*? He'd been an assassin, trying to kill Jasnah, willing to risk Shallan's life to achieve his goals. And yet, she missed him. Jasnah hadn't seemed surprised that someone would want to kill her; perhaps assassins were a common part of her life. She likely thought Kabsal a hardened killer, but he'd been sweet with Shallan. Could that all really have been a lie?

He had to be somewhat sincere, she told herself, curled up on her bed. *If he didn't care for me, why did he try so hard to get me to eat the jam?*

He had handed Shallan the antidote first, rather than taking it himself.

And yet, he did *take it eventually*, she thought. *He put that fingerful of jam into his mouth. Why didn't the antidote save him?*

This question began to haunt her. As it did, something else struck her, something she would have noticed earlier, had she not been distracted by her own guilt.

Jasnah had eaten the bread.

Arms wrapped around herself, Shallan sat up, pulling back to the bed's headboard. *She ate it, but she wasn't poisoned*, she thought. *My life makes no sense lately. The creatures with the twisted heads, the place with the dark sky, the Soulcasting . . . and now this.*

How had Jasnah survived? How?

With trembling fingers, Shallan reached to the pouch on the stand beside her bed. Inside, she found the garnet sphere that Jasnah had used to save her. It gave off weak light; most had been used in the Soulcasting. It was enough light to illuminate her sketchpad sitting beside the bed. Jasnah probably hadn't even bothered to look through it. She was so dismissive of the visual arts. Next to the sketchpad was the book Jasnah had given her. The *Book of Endless Pages*. Why had she left that?

Shallan picked up the charcoal pencil and flipped through to a blank page in her sketchbook. She passed several pictures of the symbol-headed creatures, some set in this very room. They lurked around her, always. At some times, she thought she saw them out of the corners of her eyes. At others, she could hear them whispering. She hadn't dared speak back to them again.

She began to draw, fingers unsteady, sketching Jasnah on that day in the hospital. Sitting beside Shallan's bed, holding the jam. Shallan hadn't taken a distinct Memory, and wasn't as accurate as if she had, but she remembered well enough to draw Jasnah with her finger stuck into the jam. She had raised that finger to smell the strawberries. Why? Why put her finger into the jam? Wouldn't raising the jar to her nose have been enough?

Jasnah hadn't made any faces at the scent. In fact, Jasnah hadn't mentioned that the jam had spoiled. She'd just replaced the lid and handed back the jar.

Shallan flipped to another blank page and drew Jasnah with a piece of bread raised to her lips. After eating it, she'd grimaced. Odd.

Shallan lowered her pen, looking at that sketch of Jasnah, piece of bread pinched between her fingers. It wasn't a perfect reproduction, but it was close enough. In the sketch, it looked like the piece of bread was *melting*. As if it were squished unnaturally between Jasnah's fingers as she put it into her mouth.

Could it . . . could it be?

Shallan slid out of the bed, gathering the sphere and carrying it in her hand, sketchpad tucked under her arm. The guard was gone. Nobody seemed to care what happened to her; she was being shipped off in the morning anyway.

The stone floor was cold beneath her bare feet. She wore only the white robe, and felt almost naked. At least her safehand was covered. There was a door to the city outside at the end of the hallway, and she stepped through it.

She crossed quietly through the city, making her way to the Ralinsa, avoiding dark alleyways. She walked up toward the Conclave, long red hair blowing free behind her, drawing more than a few strange looks and stares. It was so late at night that nobody on the roadway cared enough to ask if she wanted help.

The master-servants at the entrance to the Conclave let her pass. They recognized her, and more than a few asked if she needed help. She declined, walking alone down to the Veil. She passed inside, then looked up at the walls full of balconies, some of them lit with spheres.

Jasnah's alcove was occupied. Of course it was. Always working, Jasnah was. She'd be particularly bothered by having lost so much time over Shallan's presumed suicide attempt.

The lift felt rickety beneath Shallan's feet as the parshmen lifted her up to Jasnah's level. She rode in silence, feeling disconnected from the world around her. Walking around through the palace – through the *city* – in only a robe? Confronting Jasnah Kholin *again*? Hadn't she learned?

But what did she have to lose?

She walked down the familiar stone hallway to the alcove, weak violet sphere held before her. Jasnah sat at her desk. Her eyes looked uncharacteristically fatigued, dark circles underneath, her face stressed. She looked up and stiffened as she saw Shallan. 'You are not welcome here.'

Shallan walked in anyway, surprised by how calm she felt. Her hands should be shaking.

'Don't make me call the soldiers to get rid of you,' Jasnah said. 'I could have you thrown in prison for a hundred years for what you did. Do you have any idea what—'

'The Soulcaster you wear is a fake,' Shallan said quietly. 'It was a fake the whole time, even before I made the swap.'

Jasnah froze.

'I wondered why you didn't notice the switch,' Shallan said, sitting in the room's other chair. 'I spent weeks confused. Had you noticed, but decided to keep quiet in order to catch the thief? Hadn't you Soulcast in all that time? It didn't make any sense. Unless the Soulcaster I stole was a decoy.'

Jasnah relaxed. 'Yes. Very clever of you to realize that. I keep several decoys. You're not the first to try to steal the fabrial, you see. I keep the real one carefully hidden, of course.'

Shallan took out her sketchpad and searched through for a specific picture. It was the image she'd drawn of the strange place with the sea of beads, the floating flames, the distant sun in a black, black sky. Shallan regarded it for a moment. Then she turned it and held it up for Jasnah.

The look of utter shock Jasnah displayed was nearly worth the night spent feeling sick and guilty. Jasnah's eyes bulged and she sputtered for a moment, trying to find words. Shallan blinked, taking a Memory of that. She couldn't help herself.

'Where did you find that?' Jasnah demanded. 'What book described that scene to you?'

'No book, Jasnah,' Shallan said, lowering the picture. 'I visited that place. The night when I accidentally Soulcast the goblet in my room to blood, then covered it up by faking a suicide attempt.'

'Impossible. You think I'd believe–'

'There *is* no fabrial, is there, Jasnah? There's no Soulcaster. There never has been. You use the fake "fabrial" to distract people from the fact that you have the power to Soulcast on your own.'

Jasnah fell silent.

'I did it too,' Shallan said. 'The Soulcaster was tucked away in my safe-pouch. I wasn't touching it – but that didn't matter. It was a fake. What I did, I did without it. Perhaps being near you has changed me, somehow. It has something to do with that place and those creatures.'

Again, no reply.

'You suspected Kabsal of being an assassin,' Shallan said. 'You knew immediately what had happened when I fell; you were expecting poison, or at least were aware that it was possible. But *you* thought the poison was in the jam. You Soulcast it when you opened the lid and pretended to smell it. You didn't know how to re-create strawberry jam, and when you tried, you made that vile concoction. You thought to get rid of poison. But you inadvertently Soulcast away the *antidote*.

'You didn't want to eat the bread either, just in case there was something in it. You always refused it. When I convinced you to take a bite, you Soulcast it into something else as you put it in your mouth. You said you're terrible at making organic things, and what you created was revolting. But you got rid of the poison, which is why you didn't succumb to it.'

Shallan met her former mistress's eyes. Was it the fatigue that made her so indifferent to the consequences of confronting this woman? Or was it her knowledge of the truth? 'You did all that, Jasnah,' Shallan finished, 'with a *fake* Soulcaster. You hadn't spotted my swap yet. Don't try to tell me otherwise. I took it on the night when you killed those four thugs.'

Jasnah's violet eyes showed a glimmer of surprise.

'Yes,' Shallan said, 'that long ago. You didn't replace it with a decoy. You didn't know you'd been tricked until I got out the fabrial and let you save me with it. It's all a lie, Jasnah.'

'No,' Jasnah said. 'You're just delusional from your fatigue and the stress.'

'Very well,' Shallan said. She stood up, clutching the dim sphere. 'I guess I'll have to show you. If I can.'

Creatures, she said in her head. *Can you hear me?*

Yes, always, a whisper came in response. Though she'd hoped to hear it, she still jumped.

Can you return me to that place? she asked.

You need to tell me something true, it replied. *The more true, the stronger our bond.*

Jasnah is using a fake Soulcaster, Shallan thought. *I'm sure that's a truth.*

That's not enough, the voice whispered. *I must know something true about you. Tell me. The stronger the truth, the more hidden it is, the more powerful the bond. Tell me. Tell me. What are you?*

'What am I?' Shallan whispered. 'Truthfully?' It was a day for confrontation. She felt strangely strong, steady. Time to speak it. 'I'm a murderer. I killed my father.'

Ah, the voice whispered. *A powerful truth indeed . . . .*

And the alcove vanished.

Shallan fell, dropping into that sea of dark glass beads. She struggled, trying to stay at the surface. She managed it for a moment. Then something tugged on her leg, pulling her down. She screamed, slipping beneath the surface, tiny beads of glass filling her mouth. She panicked. She was going to—

The beads above her parted. Those beneath her surged, bearing her upward, out to where someone stood, hand outstretched. Jasnah, back to the black sky, face lit by nearby hovering flames. Jasnah grasped Shallan's hand, pulling her upward, onto something. A raft. *Made* from the beads of glass. They seemed to obey Jasnah's will.

'Idiot girl,' Jasnah said, waving. The sea of beads to the left split, and the raft lurched, bearing them sideways toward a few flames of light. Jasnah shoved Shallan into one of the small flames, and she fell backward off the raft.

And hit the floor of the alcove. Jasnah sat where she had been, eyes closed. A moment later, she opened them, giving Shallan an angry look.

'Idiot girl!' Jasnah repeated. 'You have no *idea* how dangerous that was. Visiting Shadesmar with only a single dim sphere? Idiot!'

Shallan coughed, feeling as if she still had beads in her throat. She stumbled to her feet, meeting Jasnah's gaze. The other woman still looked angry, but said nothing. *She knows that I have her*, Shallan realized. *If I spread the truth . . .*

What would it mean? She had strange powers. Did that make Jasnah some kind of Voidbringer? What would people say? No wonder she'd created the decoy.

'I want to be part of it,' Shallan found herself saying.

'Excuse me?'

'Whatever you're doing. Whatever it is you're researching. I want to be part of it.'

'You have no idea what you're saying.'

'I know,' Shallan said. 'I'm ignorant. There's a simple cure for that.' She stepped forward. 'I want to *know*, Jasnah. I want to be your ward in truth. Whatever the source of this thing you can do, I can do it too. I want you to train me and let me be part of your work.'

'You stole from me.'

'I know,' Shallan said. 'And I'm sorry.'

Jasnah raised an eyebrow.

'I won't excuse myself,' Shallan said. 'But Jasnah, I came here intending to steal from you. I was planning it from the beginning.'

'That's supposed to make me feel better?'

'I planned to steal from Jasnah the bitter heretic,' Shallan said. 'I didn't realize I'd come to regret the need for that theft. Not just because of you, but because it meant leaving *this*. What I've come to love. Please. I made a mistake.'

'A large one. Insurmountable.'

'Don't make a larger one by sending me away. I can be someone you don't have to lie to. Someone who knows.'

Jasnah sat back.

'I stole the fabrial on the night you killed those men, Jasnah,' Shallan said. 'I'd decided I couldn't do it, but you convinced me that truth was not as simple as I thought it. You've opened a box full of storms in me. I made a mistake. I'll make more. I need you.'

Jasnah took a deep breath. 'Sit down.'

Shallan sat.

'You will never lie to me again,' Jasnah said, raising a finger. 'And you will never steal from me, or anyone, again.'

'I promise.'

Jasnah sat for a moment, then sighed. 'Scoot over here,' she said, pulling open a book.

Shallan obeyed as Jasnah took out several sheets filled with notes. 'What is this?' Shallan asked.

'You wanted to be part of what I'm doing? Well, you'll need to read this.' Jasnah looked down at the notes. 'It's about the Voidbringers.'

71
RECORDED IN BLOOD

Szeth-son-son-Vallano, Truthless of Shinovar, walked with bowed back, carrying a sack of grain down off the ship and onto the docks of Kharbranth. The City of Bells smelled of a fresh ocean morning, peaceful yet excited, fishermen calling to friends as they prepared their nets.

Szeth joined the other porters, carrying his sack through the twisting streets. Perhaps another merchant might have used a chull cart, but Kharbranth was infamous for its crowds and its steep walkways. A line of porters was an efficient option.

Szeth kept his eyes down. Partially to imitate the look of a worker. Partially to lower his gaze from the blazing sun above, the god of gods, who watched him and saw his shame. Szeth should not have been out during the day. He should have hidden his terrible face.

He felt his every step should leave a bloody footprint. The massacres he'd committed these months, working for his hidden master . . . He could hear the dead scream every time he closed his eyes. They grated against his soul, wearing it to nothing, haunting him, consuming him.

So many dead. So very many dead.

Was he losing his mind? Each time he carried out an assassination, he found himself blaming the victims. He cursed them for not being strong enough to fight back and kill him.

During each of his slaughters, he wore white, just as he had been commanded.

One foot in front of the other. Don't think. Don't focus on what you've done. On what you're . . . going to do.

He had reached the last name on the list: Taravangian, the king of Kharbranth. A beloved monarch, known for building and maintaining hospitals in his city. It was known as far away as Azir that if you were sick, Taravangian would take you in. Come to Kharbranth and be healed. The king loved all.

And Szeth was going to kill him.

At the top of the steep city, Szeth lugged his sack with the other porters around to the back of the palace structure, entering a dim stone corridor. Taravangian was a simpleminded man. That should have made Szeth feel more guilty, but he found himself consumed by loathing. Taravangian would not be smart enough to prepare for Szeth. Fool. Idiot. Would Szeth never face a foe strong enough to kill him?

Szeth had come to the city early and taken the job as a porter. He had needed to research and study, for the instructions commanded him – for once – not to kill anyone else in performing this assassination. Taravangian's murder was to be done quietly.

Why the difference? The instructions stated that he was to deliver a message. 'The others are dead. I've come to finish the job.' The instructions were explicit: Make certain Taravangian heard and acknowledged the words before harming him.

This was looking like a work of vengeance. Someone had sent Szeth to hunt down and destroy the men who had wronged him. Szeth laid his sack down in the palace larder. He turned automatically, following the shuffling line of porters back down the hallway. He nodded toward the servants' privy, and the portermaster waved for him to go ahead. Szeth had made this same haul on several occasions, and could be trusted – presumably – to do his business and catch up.

The privy didn't smell half as foul as he had anticipated. It was a dark room, cut into the underground cavern, but a candle burned beside a man standing at the pissing trough. He nodded to Szeth, tying up the front of his trousers and wiping his fingers on the sides as he walked to the door. He took his candle, but kindly lit a leftover stub before withdrawing.

As soon as he was gone, Szeth infused himself with Stormlight from his pouch and laid his hand on the door, performing a Full Lashing between it and the frame, locking it closed. His Shardblade came out next. In the palace, everything was built downward. Trusting the maps he'd purchased, he knelt and carved a square of rock from the floor, wider at the bottom. As it began to slide down, Szeth infused it with Stormlight, performing half a Basic Lashing upward, making the rock weightless.

Next, he Lashed himself upward with a subtle Lashing that left him weighing only a tenth his normal weight. He leapt onto the rock, and his lessened weight pushed the rock down slowly. He rode it down into the room below. Three couches with plush violet cushions lined the walls, sitting beneath fine silver mirrors. The lighteyes' privy. A lamp burned with a small flame in the sconce, but Szeth was alone.

The stone thumped softly to the floor, and Szeth leaped off. He shed his clothing, revealing a black and white master-servant's outfit underneath. He took a matching cap from the pocket and slipped it on, reluctantly dismissed his Blade, then slipped into the hallway and quickly Lashed the door shut.

These days, he rarely gave a thought to the fact that he walked on stone. Once, he would have revered a corridor of rock like this. Had that man once been him? Had he ever revered anything?

Szeth hurried onward. His time was short. Fortunately, King Taravangian kept a strict schedule. Seventh bell: private reflection in his study. Szeth could see the doorway into the study ahead, guarded by two soldiers.

Szeth bowed his head, hiding his Shin eyes and hurrying up to them. One of the men held out his hand wardingly, so Szeth grabbed it, twisting, shattering the wrist. He smashed his elbow into the man's face, throwing him back against the wall.

The man's stunned companion opened his mouth to yell, but Szeth kicked him in the stomach. Even without a Shardblade, he was dangerous, infused with Stormlight and trained in kammar. He grabbed the second guard by the hair and slammed his forehead against the rock floor. Then he rose and kicked open the door.

He walked into a room well illuminated by a double row of lamps on the left. Crammed bookcases covered the right wall from floor to ceiling. A man sat cross-legged on a small rug directly ahead of Szeth. The man looked out an enormous window cut through the rock, staring at the ocean beyond.

Szeth strode forward. 'I have been instructed to tell you that the others are dead. I've come to finish the job.' He raised his hands, Shardblade forming.

The king did not turn.

Szeth hesitated. He had to make certain the man acknowledged what had been said. 'Did you hear me?' Szeth demanded, striding forward.

'Did you kill my guards, Szeth-son-son-Vallano?' the king asked quietly.

Szeth froze. He cursed and stepped backward, raising his Blade in a defensive stance. Another trap?

'You have done your work well,' the king said, still not facing him. 'Leaders dead, lives lost. Panic and chaos. Was this your destiny? Do you wonder? Given that monstrosity of a Shardblade by your people, cast out and absolved of any sin your masters might require of you?'

'I am not absolved,' Szeth said, still wary. 'It is a common mistake stonewalkers make. Each life I take weighs me down, eating away at my soul.'

The voices . . . the screams . . . spirits below, I can hear them howling . . . .

'Yet you kill.'

'It is my punishment,' Szeth said. 'To kill, to have no choice, but to bear the sins nonetheless. I am Truthless.'

'Truthless,' the king mused. 'I would say that you know much truth. More than your countrymen, now.' He finally turned to face Szeth, and Szeth saw that he had been wrong about this man. King Taravangian was no simpleton. He had keen eyes and a wise, knowing face, rimmed with a full white beard, the mustaches drooping like arrow points. 'You have seen what death and murder do to a man. You could say, Szeth-son-son-Vallano, that you bear great sins for your people. You understand what they cannot. And so you have truth.'

Szeth frowned. And then it began to make sense. He knew what would happen next, even as the king reached into his voluminous sleeve and withdrew a small rock that glittered in the light of two dozen lamps. 'You were always him,' Szeth said. 'My unseen master.'

The king set the rock on the ground between them. Szeth's Oathstone.

'You put your own name on the list,' Szeth said.

'In case you were captured,' Taravangian said. 'The best defense against suspicion is to be grouped with the victims.'

'And if I'd killed you?'

'The instructions were explicit,' Taravangian said. 'And, as we have determined, you are *quite* good at following them. I probably needn't say it, but I order you *not* to harm me. Now, did you kill my guards?'

'I do not know,' Szeth said, forcing himself to drop to one knee and dismissing his Blade. He spoke loudly, trying to drown out the screams that he thought – for certain – must be coming from the upper eaves of the room. 'I knocked them both unconscious. I believe I cracked one man's skull.'

Taravangian breathed out, sighing. He rose, stepping to the doorway. Szeth glanced over his shoulder to note the aged king inspecting the guards and checking their wounds. Taravangian called for help, and other guards arrived to see to the men.

Szeth was left with a terrible storm of emotions. This kindly, contemplative man had sent him to kill and murder? He had caused the screams?

Taravangian returned.

'Why?' Szeth asked, voice hoarse. 'Vengeance?'

'No.' Taravangian sounded very tired. 'Some of those men you killed were my dear friends, Szeth-son-son-Vallano.'

'More insurance?' Szeth spat. 'To keep yourself from suspicion?'

'In part. And in part because their deaths were necessary.'

'Why?' Szeth asked. 'What could it possibly have served?'

'Stability. Those you killed were among the most powerful and influential men in Roshar.'

'How does that help stability?'

'Sometimes,' Taravangian said, 'you must tear down a structure to build a new one with stronger walls.' He turned around, looking out over the ocean. 'And we are going to need strong walls in the coming years. Very, very strong walls.'

'Your words are like the hundred doves.'

'*Easy to release, difficult to keep*,' Taravangian said, speaking the words in Shin.

Szeth looked up sharply. This man spoke the Shin language and knew his people's proverbs? Odd to find in a stonewalker. Odder to find in a murderer.

'Yes, I speak your language. Sometimes I wonder if the Lifebrother himself sent you to me.'

'To bloody myself so that you wouldn't have to,' Szeth said. 'Yes, that sounds like something one of your Vorin gods would do.'

Taravangian fell silent. 'Get up,' he finally said.

Szeth obeyed. He would always obey his master. Taravangian led him to a door set into the side of the study. The aged man pulled a sphere lamp off the wall, lighting a winding stairwell of deep, narrow steps. They followed it down and eventually came to a landing. Taravangian pushed open another door and entered a large room that wasn't on any of the palace maps that Szeth had purchased or bribed a look at. It was long, with wide railings on the sides, giving it a terraced look. Everything was painted white.

It was filled with beds. Hundreds and hundreds of them. Many were occupied.

Szeth followed the king, frowning. An enormous hidden room, cut into the stone of the Conclave? People bustled about wearing white coats. 'A hospital?' Szeth said. 'You expect me to find your humanitarian efforts a redemption for what you have commanded of me?'

'This is not humanitarian work,' Taravangian said, walking forward slowly, white-and-orange robes rustling. Those they passed bowed to him with reverence. Taravangian led Szeth to an alcove of beds, each with a sickly person in it. There were healers working on them. Doing something to their arms.

Draining their blood.

A woman with a writing clipboard stood near the beds, pen held, waiting for something. What?

'I don't understand,' Szeth said, watching in horror as the four patients grew pale. 'You're killing them, aren't you?'

'Yes. We don't need the blood; it is merely a way to kill slowly and easily.'

'Every one of them? The people in this room?'

'We try to select only the worst cases to move here, for once they are brought to this place, we cannot let them leave if they begin to recover.' He turned to Szeth, eyes sorrowful. 'Sometimes we need more bodies than the terminally sick can provide. And so we must bring the forgotten and the lowly. Those who will not be missed.'

Szeth couldn't speak. He couldn't voice his horror and revulsion. In front of him, one of the victims – a man in his younger years – expired.

Two of those remaining were children. Szeth stepped forward. He had to stop this. He had to—

'You will still yourself,' Taravangian said. 'And you will return to my side.'

Szeth did as his master commanded. What were a few more deaths? Just another set of screams to haunt him. He could hear them now, coming from beneath beds, behind furniture.

Or I could kill him, Szeth thought. *I could stop this.*

He nearly did it. But honor prevailed, for the moment.

'You see, Szeth-son-son-Vallano,' Taravangian said. 'I did not send you to do my bloody work for me. I do it here, myself. I have personally held the knife and released the blood from the veins of many. Much like you, I know I cannot escape my sins. We are two men of one heart. This is one reason why I sought you out.'

'But *why*?' Szeth said.

On the beds, a dying youth started speaking. One of the women with the clipboards stepped forward quickly, recording the words.

'The day was ours, but they took it,' the boy cried. 'Stormfather! You cannot have it. The day is ours. They come, rasping, and the lights fail. Oh, Stormfather!' The boy arched his back, then fell still suddenly, eyes dead.

The king turned to Szeth. 'It is better for one man to sin than for a people to be destroyed, wouldn't you say, Szeth-son-son-Vallano?'

'I . . .'

'We do not know why some speak when others do not,' Taravangian said. 'But the dying see something. It began seven years ago, about the time when King Gavilar was investigating the Shattered Plains for the first time.' His eyes grew distant. 'It is coming, and these people see it. On that bridge between life and the endless ocean of death, they view something. Their words might save us.'

'You are a monster.'

'Yes,' Taravangian said. 'But I am the monster who will save this world.' He looked at Szeth. 'I have a name to add to your list. I had hoped to avoid doing this, but recent events have made it inevitable. I cannot let him seize control. It will undermine everything.'

'Who?' Szeth asked, wondering if anything at all could horrify him further.

'Dalinar Kholin,' Taravangian said. 'I'm afraid it must be done quickly, before he can unite the Alethi highprinces. You will go to the Shattered Plains and end him.' He hesitated. 'It must be done brutally, I'm afraid.'

'I have rarely had the luxury of working otherwise,' Szeth said, closing his eyes.

The screams greeted him.

'Before I read,' Shallan said, 'I need to understand something. You Soulcast my blood, didn't you?'

'To remove the poison,' Jasnah said. 'Yes. It acted extremely quickly; as I said, it must have been a very concentrated form of the powder. I had to Soulcast your blood several times as we got you to vomit. Your body continued to absorb the poison.'

'But you said you aren't good with organics,' Shallan said. 'You turned the strawberry jam into something inedible.'

'Blood isn't the same,' Jasnah said, waving her hand. 'It's one of the Essences. You'll learn this, should I actually decide to teach you Soulcasting. For now, know that the pure form of an Essence is quite easy to make; the eight kinds of blood are easier to create than water, for instance. Creating something as complex as strawberry jam, however – a mush made from a fruit I'd never before tasted or smelled – was well beyond my abilities.'

'And the ardents,' Shallan said. 'Those who Soulcast? Do they actually use fabrials, or is it all a hoax?'

'No, Soulcasting fabrials are real. Quite real. So far as I know, everyone else who does what I – what *we* – can do uses a fabrial to accomplish it.'

'What of the creatures with the symbol heads?' Shallan asked. She flipped through her sketches, then held up an image of them. 'Do you see them too? How are they related?'

Jasnah frowned, taking the image. 'You see beings like this? In Shadesmar?'

'They appear in my drawings,' Shallan said. 'They're around me, Jasnah. You don't see them? Am I—'

Jasnah held up a hand. 'These are a type of spren, Shallan. They *are* related to what you do.' She tapped the desk softly. 'Two orders of the Knights Radiant possessed inherent Soulcasting ability; it was based on their powers that the original fabrials were designed, I believe. I had assumed that you . . . But no, that obviously wouldn't make sense. I see now.'

'What?'

'I will explain as I train you,' Jasnah said, handing back the sheet. 'You will need a greater foundation before you can grasp it. Suffice it to say that each Radiant's abilities were tied to the spren.'

'Wait, *Radiants*? But—'

'I will explain,' Jasnah said. 'But first, we must speak of the Voidbringers.'

Shallan nodded. 'You think they'll return, don't you?'

Jasnah studied her. 'What makes you say that?'

'The legends say the Voidbringers came a hundred times to try to destroy mankind,' Shallan continued. 'I . . . read some of your notes.'

'You *what*?'

'I was looking for information on Soulcasting,' Shallan confessed.

Jasnah sighed. 'Well, I suppose it is the least of your crimes.'

'I can't understand,' Shallan said. 'Why are you bothering with these stories of myths and shadows? Other scholars – scholars I know you respect – consider the Voidbringers to be a fabrication. Yet you chase stories from rural farmers and write them down in your notebook. Why, Jasnah? Why do you have faith in this when you reject things that are so much more plausible?'

Jasnah looked over her sheets of paper. 'Do you know the real difference between me and a believer, Shallan?'

Shallan shook her head.

'It strikes me that religion – in its essence – seeks to take natural events and ascribe supernatural causes to them. I, however, seek to take supernatural events and find the *natural* meanings behind them. Perhaps that is the final dividing line between science and religion. Opposite sides of a card.'

'So . . . you think . . .'

'The Voidbringers had a natural, real-world correlate,' Jasnah said firmly. 'I'm certain of it. Something *caused* the legends.'

'What was it?'

Jasnah handed Shallan a page of notes. 'These are the best I've been able to find. Read them. Tell me what you think.'

Shallan scanned the page. Some of the quotes – or at least the concepts – were familiar to her from what she'd read already.

Suddenly dangerous. Like a calm day that became a tempest.

'They were real,' Jasnah repeated.

Beings of ash and fire.

'We fought with them,' Jasnah said. 'We fought so often that men began to speak of the creatures in metaphor. A hundred battles – ten tenfolds . . .'

Flame and char. Skin so terrible. Eyes like pits of blackness. Music when they kill.

'We defeated them . . .' Jasnah said.

Shallan felt a chill.

'. . . but the legends lie about one thing,' Jasnah continued. 'They claim we chased the Voidbringers off the face of Roshar or destroyed them. But that's not how humans work. We don't throw away something we can use.'

Shallan rose, walking to the edge of the balcony, looking out at the lift, which was slowly being lowered by its two porters.

Parshmen. With skin of black and red.

Ash and fire.

'Stormfather . . .' Shallan whispered, horrified.

'We didn't destroy the Voidbringers,' Jasnah said from behind, her voice haunted. 'We *enslaved* them.'

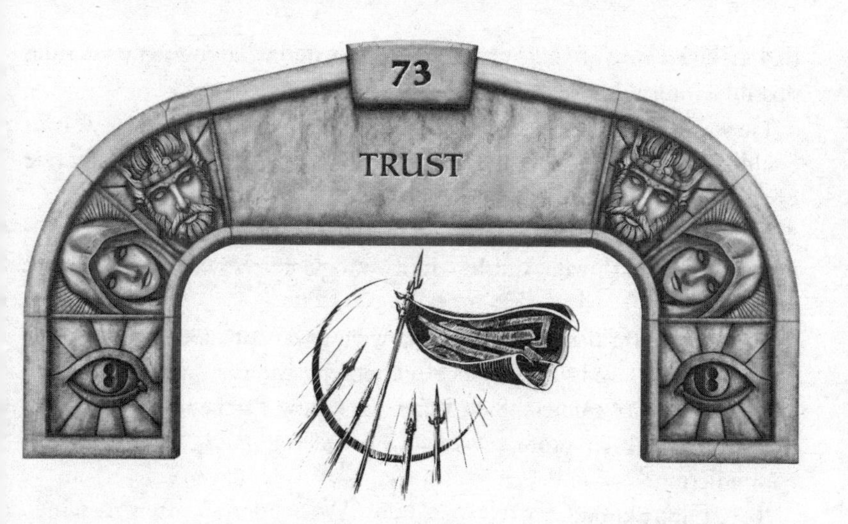

73
TRUST

The chill spring weather might finally have slipped back into summer. It was still cool at night, but not uncomfortably so. Kaladin stood on Dalinar Kholin's staging ground, looking eastward over the Shattered Plains.

Ever since the betrayal, the rescue, and the fulfilling of Kholin's oath, Kaladin had found himself nervous. Freedom. Bought with a Shardblade. It seemed impossible. His every life experience taught him to expect a trap.

He clasped his hands behind him; Syl sat on his shoulder.

'Dare I trust him?' he asked softly.

'He's a good man,' Syl said. 'I've watched him. Despite that *thing* he carried.'

'That thing?'

'The Shardblade.'

'What do you care about it?'

'I don't know,' she said, wrapping her arms around herself. 'It just feels *wrong* to me. I hate it. I'm glad he got rid of it. Makes him a better man.'

Nomon, the middle moon, began to rise. Bright and pale blue, bathing the horizon in light. Somewhere, out across the Plains, was the Parshendi Shardbearer that Kaladin had fought. He'd stabbed the man in the leg from behind. The watching Parshendi had not interfered with the duel and had avoided attacking Kaladin's wounded bridgemen, but Kaladin had attacked one of their champions from the most cowardly position possible, interfering with a fight.

He was bothered by what he'd done, and that frustrated him. A warrior couldn't worry about who he attacked or how. Survival was the only rule of the battlefield.

Well, survival and loyalty. And he sometimes let wounded enemies live if they weren't a threat. And he saved young soldiers who needed protection. And . . .

And he'd never been good at doing what a warrior should.

Today, he'd saved a highprince – another lighteyes – and along with him thousands of soldiers. Saved them by killing Parshendi.

'Can you kill to protect?' Kaladin asked out loud. 'Is that a self-contradiction?'

'I . . . I don't know.'

'You acted strangely in the battle,' Kaladin said. 'Swirling around me. After that, you left. I didn't see much of you.'

'The killing,' she said softly. 'It hurt me. I had to go.'

'Yet you're the one who prompted me to go and save Dalinar. You wanted me to return and kill.'

'I know.'

'Teft said that the Radiants held to a standard,' Kaladin said. 'He said that by their rules, you shouldn't do terrible things to accomplish great ones. Yet what did I do today? Slaughter Parshendi in order to save Alethi. What of that? They aren't innocent, but neither are we. Not by a faint breeze or a stormwind.'

Syl didn't reply.

'If I hadn't gone to save Dalinar's men,' Kaladin said, 'I would have allowed Sadeas to succeed in a terrible betrayal. I'd have let men die who I could have saved. I'd have been sick and disgusted with myself. I also lost three good men, bridgemen who were mere breaths away from freedom. Are the lives of the others worth that?'

'I don't have the answers, Kaladin.'

'Does anyone?'

Footsteps came from behind. Syl turned. 'It's him.'

The moon had just risen. Dalinar Kholin, it appeared, was a punctual man.

He stepped up beside Kaladin. He carried a bundle under his arm, and he had a military air about him, even without his Shardplate on. In fact, he was more impressive without it. His muscular build indicated that he did not rely on his Plate to give him strength, and the neatly pressed uniform indicated a man who understood that others were inspired when their leader looked the part.

Others have looked just as noble, Kaladin thought. But would any man trade a *Shardblade* just to keep up appearances? And if they would, at what point did the appearance become reality?

'I'm sorry to make you meet me so late,' Dalinar said. 'I know it has been a long day.'

'I doubt I could have slept anyway.'

Dalinar grunted softly, as if he understood. 'Your men are seen to?'

'Yes,' Kaladin said. 'Quite well, actually. Thank you.' Kaladin had been given empty barracks for the bridgemen and they had received medical attention from Dalinar's best surgeons – they'd gotten it *before* the wounded lighteyed officers had. The other bridgemen, the ones who weren't from Bridge Four, had accepted Kaladin immediately, without any deliberation on the matter, as their leader.

Dalinar nodded. 'How many, do you suspect, will take my offer of a purse and freedom?'

'A fair number of the men from other crews will. But I'll wager an even larger number won't. Bridgemen don't think of escape or freedom. They wouldn't know what to do with themselves. As for my own crew . . . Well, I have a feeling that they'll insist on doing whatever I do. If I stay, they'll stay. If I go, they'll go.'

Dalinar nodded. 'And what will you do?'

'I haven't decided yet.'

'I spoke to my officers.' Dalinar grimaced. 'The ones who survived. They said that you gave orders to them, took charge like a lighteyes. My son still feels bitter about the way your . . . conversation with him went.'

'Even a fool could see he wasn't going to be able to get to you. As for the officers, most were in shock or run ragged. I merely nudged them.'

'I owe you my life twice over,' Dalinar said. 'And that of my son and my men.'

'You paid that debt.'

'No,' Dalinar said. 'But I've done what I can.' He eyed Kaladin, as if sizing him up, judging him. 'Why did your bridge crew come for us? Why, really?'

'Why did you give up your Shardblade?'

Dalinar held his eyes, then nodded. 'Fair enough. I have an offer for you. The king and I are about to do something very, very dangerous. Something that will upset all the warcamps.'

'Congratulations.'

Dalinar smiled faintly. 'My honor guard has nearly been wiped out, and the men I do have are needed to augment the King's Guard. My trust is stretched thin these days. I need someone to protect me and my family. I want you and your men for that job.'

'You want a bunch of bridgemen as bodyguards?'

'The elite ones as bodyguards,' Dalinar said. 'Those in your crew, the ones you trained. I want the rest as soldiers for my army. I have heard how well your men fought. You trained them without Sadeas's knowing, all while running bridges. I'm curious to see what you could do with the right resources.' Dalinar turned away, glancing northward. Toward Sadeas's camp. 'My army is depleted. I'm going to need every man I can get, but everyone I recruit is going to be suspect. Sadeas will try to send spies into our camp. And traitors. And assassins. Elhokar thinks we won't last a week.'

'Stormfather,' Kaladin said. 'What are you planning?'

'I'm going to take away their games, fully expecting them to react like children losing their favored toy.'

'These children have armies and Shardblades.'

'Unfortunately.'

'And *this* is what you want me to protect you from?'

'Yes.'

No quibbling. Straightforward. There was much to respect about that.

'I'll augment Bridge Four to become the honor guard,' Kaladin said. 'And train the rest as a spearman company. Those in the honor guard get paid like it.' Generally, a lighteyes's personal guard got triple a standard spearman's wage.

'Of course.'

'And I want space to train,' Kaladin said. 'Full right of requisition from the quartermasters. I get to set my men's schedule, and we appoint our own sergeants and squadleaders. We don't answer to any lighteyes but yourself, your sons, and the king.'

Dalinar raised an eyebrow. 'That last one is a little ... irregular.'

'You want me to guard you and your family?' Kaladin said. 'Against the other highprinces and their assassins, who might infiltrate your army and your officers? Well, I can't be in a position where any lighteyes in the camp can order me around, now can I?'

'You have a point,' Dalinar said. 'You realize, however, that in doing this I would essentially be giving you the same authority as a lighteyes of fourth dahn. You'd be in charge of a thousand former bridgemen. A full battalion.'

'Yes.'

Dalinar thought for a moment. 'Very well. Consider yourself appointed to the rank of captain – that's as high as I dare appoint a darkeyes. If I named you battalionlord, it would cause a whole mess of problems. I'll let it be known, however, that you're outside the chain of command. You don't order around lighteyes of lesser rank than you, and lighteyes of higher rank have no authority over you.'

'All right,' Kaladin said. 'But these soldiers I train, I want them assigned to patrolling, not plateau runs. I hear you've had several full battalions hunting bandits, keeping the peace in the Outer Market, that sort of thing. That's where my men go for one year, at least.'

'Easy enough,' Dalinar said. 'You want time to train them before throwing them into battle, I assume.'

'That, and I killed a lot of Parshendi today. I found myself regretting their deaths. They showed me more honor than most members of my own army have. I didn't like the feeling, and I want some time to think about it. The bodyguards I train for you, we'll go out onto the field, but our primary purpose will be protecting you, not killing Parshendi.'

Dalinar looked bemused. 'All right. Though you shouldn't have to worry. I don't plan to be on the front lines much in the future. My role is changing. Regardless, we have a deal.'

Kaladin held out a hand. 'This is contingent on my men agreeing.'

'I thought you said that they'd do what you did.'

'Probably,' Kaladin said. 'I command them, but I don't own them.'

Dalinar reached out, taking his hand, shaking it by the light of the rising sapphire moon. Then he took the bundle out from underneath his arm. 'Here.'

'What is this?' Kaladin said, taking the bundle.

'My cloak. The one I wore to battle today, washed and patched.'

Kaladin unfurled it. It was of a deep blue, with the glyphpair of *khokh* and *linil* sewn into the back in white embroidery.

'Each man who wears my colors,' Dalinar said, 'is of my family, in a way. The cloak is a simple gift, but it is one of the few things I can offer that has any meaning. Accept it with my gratitude, Kaladin Stormblessed.'

Kaladin slowly refolded the cloak. 'Where did you hear that name?'

'Your men,' Dalinar said. 'They think very highly of you. And that makes *me* think very highly of you. I need men like you, like all of you.' He narrowed his eyes, looking thoughtful. 'The whole kingdom needs you. Perhaps all of Roshar. The True Desolation comes. . . .'

'What was that last part?'

'Nothing,' Dalinar said. 'Please, go get some rest, Captain. I hope to hear good news from you soon.'

Kaladin nodded and withdrew, passing the two men who acted as Dalinar's guard for the night. The hike back to his new barracks was a short one. Dalinar had given him one building for each of the bridge crews. Over a thousand men. What was he going to do with so many? He'd never commanded a group larger than twenty-five before.

Bridge Four's barrack was empty. Kaladin hesitated outside the doorway, looking in. The barrack was furnished with a bunk and locking chest for each man. It seemed a palace.

He smelled smoke. Frowning, he rounded the barrack to find the men sitting around a firepit in the back, relaxing on stumps or stones, waiting as Rock cooked them a pot of stew. They were listening to Teft, who sat with his arm bandaged, speaking quietly. Shen was there; the quiet parshman sat at the very edge of the group. They'd recovered him, along with their wounded, from Sadeas's camp.

Teft cut off as soon as he saw Kaladin, and the men turned, most of them bearing bandages of some sort. *Dalinar wants* these *for his bodyguards?* Kaladin thought. They were a ragged bunch indeed.

As it happened, however, he seconded Dalinar's choice. If he were going to put his life in someone's hands, he'd choose this group.

'What are you doing?' Kaladin asked sternly. 'You should all be resting.'

The bridgemen glanced at each other.

'It just . . .' Moash said. 'It didn't feel right to go to sleep until we'd had a chance to . . . well, do this.'

'Hard to sleep on a day like this, gancho,' Lopen added.

'Speak for yourself,' Skar said, yawning, wounded leg resting up on a stump. 'But the stew is worth staying up for. Even if he does put rocks in it.'

'I do not!' Rock snapped. 'Airsick lowlanders.'

They'd left a place for Kaladin. He sat down, using Dalinar's cloak as a cushion for his back and head. He gratefully took a bowl of stew that Drehy handed him.

'We've been talking about what the men saw today,' Teft said. 'The things you did.'

Kaladin hesitated, spoon to his mouth. He'd nearly forgotten – or maybe he'd intentionally forgotten – that he'd shown his men what he could do with Stormlight. Hopefully Dalinar's soldiers hadn't seen. His Stormlight had been faint by then, the day bright.

'I see,' Kaladin said, his appetite fleeing. Did they see him as different? Frightening? Something to be ostracized, as his father had been back in Hearthstone? Worse yet, something to be worshipped? He looked into their wide eyes and braced himself.

'It was *amazing*!' Drehy said, leaning forward.

'You're one of the Radiants,' Skar said, pointing. 'I believe it, even if Teft says you aren't.'

'He isn't *yet*,' Teft snapped. 'Don't you listen?'

'Can you teach me to do what you did?' Moash cut in.

'I'll learn too, gancho,' Lopen said. 'You know, if you're teaching and all.'

Kaladin blinked, overwhelmed, as the others chimed in.

'What can you do?'

'How does it feel?'

'Can you fly?'

He held up a hand, stanching the questions. 'Aren't you alarmed by what you saw?'

Several of the men shrugged.

'It kept you alive, gancho,' Lopen said. 'The only thing I'd be alarmed about is how irresistible the women would find it. "Lopen," they'd say, "you only have one arm, but I see that you can glow. I think that you should kiss me now."'

'But it's strange and frightening,' Kaladin protested. 'This is what the Radiants did! Everyone knows they were traitors.'

'Yeah,' Moash said, snorting. 'Just like everyone knows that the light-eyes are chosen by the Almighty to rule, and how they're always noble and just.'

'We're Bridge Four,' Skar added. 'We've been around. We've lived in the crem and been used as bait. If it helps you survive, it's good. That's all that needs to be said about it.'

'So can you teach it?' Moash asked. 'Can you show us how to do what you do?'

'I ... I don't know if it *can* be taught,' Kaladin said, glancing at Syl, who bore a curious expression as she sat on a nearby rock. 'I'm not certain what *it* is.'

They looked crestfallen.

'But,' Kaladin added, 'that doesn't mean that we shouldn't try.'

Moash smiled.

'Can you do it?' Drehy asked, fishing out a sphere, a small glowing diamond chip. 'Right now? I want to see it when I'm expecting it.'

'It's not a feastday sport, Drehy,' Kaladin said.

'Don't you think we deserve it?' Sigzil leaned forward on his stone.

Kaladin paused. Then, hesitantly, he reached out a finger and touched the sphere. He inhaled sharply; drawing in the Light was becoming more and more natural. The sphere faded. Stormlight began to trickle from Kaladin's skin, and he breathed normally to make it leak faster, making it more visible. Rock pulled out a ragged old blanket – used for kindling – and tossed it over the fire, disturbing the flamespren and making a few moments of darkness before the flames chewed through.

In that darkness, Kaladin glowed, pure white Light rising from his skin.

'Storms ...' Drehy breathed.

'So, what *can* you do with it?' Skar asked, eager. 'You didn't answer.'

'I'm not entirely certain what I can do,' Kaladin said, holding his hand up in front of him. It faded in a moment, and the fire burned through the blanket, lighting them all again. 'I've only known about it for sure for a few weeks. I can draw arrows toward me and can make rocks stick together. The Light makes me stronger and faster, and it heals my wounds.'

'How *much* stronger does it make you?' Sigzil said. 'How much weight can the rocks bear after you stick them together, and how long do they remain bonded? How much faster do you get? Twice as fast? A quarter again as fast? How far away can an arrow be when you draw it toward you, and can you draw other things as well?'

Kaladin blinked. 'I . . . I don't know.'

'Well, it seems pretty important to know that kind of stuff,' Skar said, rubbing his chin.

'We can do tests,' Rock folded his arms, smiling. 'Is good idea.'

'Maybe it will help us figure out how we can do it too,' Moash noted.

'Is not thing to learn.' Rock shook his head. 'Is of the *holetental*. For him only.'

'You don't know that for certain,' Teft said.

'You don't know for certain I don't know for certain.' Rock wagged a spoon at him. 'Eat your stew.'

Kaladin held up his hands. 'You can't tell anyone about this, men. They'll be frightened of me, maybe think I'm related to the Voidbringers or the Radiants. I need your oaths on this.'

He looked at them, and they nodded, one by one.

'But we want to help,' Skar said. 'Even if we can't learn it. This thing is part of you, and you're one of us. Bridge Four. Right?'

Kaladin looked at their eager faces and couldn't stop himself from nodding. 'Yes. Yes, you can help.'

'Excellent,' Sigzil said. 'I'll prepare a list of tests to gauge speed, accuracy, and the strength of these bonds you can create. We'll have to find a way to determine if there's anything else you can do.'

'Throw him off cliff,' Rock said.

'What good will that do?' Peet asked.

Rock shrugged. 'If he has other abilities, this thing will make them come out, eh? Nothing like falling from cliff to make a man out of a boy!'

Kaladin regarded him with a sour expression, and Rock laughed. 'It will be small cliff.' He held up his thumb and forefinger to indicate a tiny amount. 'I like you too much for large one.'

'I think you're joking,' Kaladin said, taking a bite of his stew. 'But just to be safe, I'm sticking you to the ceiling tonight to keep you from trying any experiments while I'm asleep.'

The bridgemen chuckled.

'Just don't glow too brightly while we're trying to sleep, eh, gancho?' Lopen said.

'I'll do my best.' He took another spoonful of stew. It tasted better than usual. Had Rock changed the recipe?

Or was it something else? As he settled back to eat, the other bridgemen began chatting, speaking of home and their pasts, things that had once been taboo. Several of the men from other crews – wounded whom Kaladin had helped, even just a few lonely souls who were still awake – wandered over. The men of Bridge Four welcomed them, handing over stew and making room.

Everyone looked as exhausted as Kaladin felt, but nobody spoke of turning in. He could see why, now. Being together, eating Rock's stew, listening to the quiet chatter while the fire crackled and popped, sending dancing flakes of yellow light into the air . . .

This was more relaxing than sleep could be. Kaladin smiled, leaning back, looking upward toward the dark sky and the large sapphire moon. Then he closed his eyes, listening.

Three more men were dead. Malop, Earless Jaks, and Narm. Kaladin had failed them. But he and Bridge Four had protected hundreds of others. Hundreds who would never have to run a bridge again, would never have to face Parshendi arrows, would never have to fight again if they didn't want to. More personally, twenty-seven of his friends lived. Partially because of what he'd done, partially because of their own heroism.

Twenty-seven men lived. He'd finally managed to save someone.

For now, that was enough.

Shallan rubbed her eyes. She'd read through Jasnah's notes – at least the most important ones. Those alone had made a large stack. She still sat in the alcove, though they'd sent a parshman to get her a blanket to wrap around herself, covering up the hospital robe.

Her eyes burned from the night spent crying, then reading. She was exhausted. And yet she also felt alive.

'It's true,' she said. 'You're right. The Voidbringers are the parshmen. I can see no other conclusion.'

Jasnah smiled, looking oddly pleased with herself, considering that she'd only convinced one person.

'So what next?' Shallan asked.

'That has to do with your previous studies.'

'My studies? You mean your father's death?'

'Indeed.'

'The Parshendi attacked him,' Shallan said. 'Killed him suddenly, without warning.' She focused on the other woman. 'That's what made you begin studying all of this, isn't it?'

Jasnah nodded. 'Those wild parshmen – the Parshendi of the Shattered Plains – are the key.' She leaned forward. 'Shallan. The disaster awaiting us is all too real, all too terrible. I don't need mystical warnings or theological sermons to frighten me. I'm downright terrified in my own right.'

'But we have the parshmen tamed.'

'Do we? Shallan, think of what they do, how they're regarded, how often they're used.' Shallan hesitated. The parshmen were pervasive. 'They serve our food,' Jasnah continued. 'They work our storehouses. They tend our *children*. There isn't a village in Roshar that doesn't have some parshmen. We ignore them; we just expect them to be there, doing as they do. Working without complaint.

'Yet one group turned suddenly from peaceful friends to ferocious warriors. Something set them off. Just as it did hundreds of years ago, during the days known as the Heraldic Epochs. There would be a period of peace, followed by an invasion of parshmen who – for reasons nobody understood – had suddenly gone mad with rage. *This* was what was behind mankind's fight to keep from being "banished to Damnation." This was what nearly ended our civilization. These were the terrible, repeated cataclysms that were so frightening men began to speak of them as Desolations.

'We've nurtured the parshmen. We've integrated them into every part of our society. We depend on them, never realizing that we've harnessed a highstorm waiting to explode. The accounts from the Shattered Plains speak of these Parshendi's ability to communicate among themselves, allowing them to sing their songs in unison when far apart. Their minds are connected, like spanreeds. Do you realize what that means?'

Shallan nodded. What would happen if every parshman on Roshar suddenly turned against his masters? Seeking freedom, or worse – vengeance? 'We'd be devastated. Civilization as we know it could collapse. We have to *do* something!'

'We are,' Jasnah said. 'We're gathering facts, making certain we know what we think we know.'

'And how many facts do we need?'

'More. Many more.' Jasnah glanced at the books. 'There are some things about the histories I don't yet understand. Tales of creatures fighting alongside the parshmen, beasts of stone that might be some kind of greatshell, and other oddities that I think may have truth to them. But we've exhausted what Kharbranth can offer. Are you still certain you want to delve into this? It is a heavy burden we will bear. You won't be returning to your estates for some time.'

Shallan bit her lip, thinking of her brothers. 'You'd let me go now, after what I know?'

'I won't have you serving me while thinking of ways to escape.' Jasnah sounded exhausted.

'I can't just abandon my brothers.' Shallan's insides twisted again. 'But this is bigger than them. Damnation – it's bigger than *me* or *you* or any of us. I have to help, Jasnah. I can't walk out on this. I'll find some other way to help my family.'

'Good. Then go pack our things. We're leaving tomorrow on that ship I chartered for you.'

'We're going to Jah Keved?'

'No. We need to get to the center of it all.' She looked at Shallan. 'We're going to the Shattered Plains. We need to find out if the Parshendi were ever ordinary parshmen, and if so, what set them off. Perhaps I am wrong about this, but if I am right, then the Parshendi could hold the key to turning ordinary parshmen into soldiers.' Then, grimly, she continued. 'And we need to do it before someone else does, then uses it against us.'

'Someone else?' Shallan asked, feeling a sharp stab of panic. 'There are others looking for this?'

'Of course there are. Who do you think went to so much trouble trying to have me assassinated?' She reached into a stack of papers on her desk. 'I don't know much about them. For all I know, there are many groups searching for these secrets. I know of one for certain, however. They call themselves the Ghostbloods.' She pulled out a sheet. 'Your friend Kabsal was one. We found their symbol tattooed on the inside of his arm.'

She set the sheet down. On it was a symbol of three diamonds in a pattern, overlapping one another.

It was the same symbol that Nan Balat had shown her weeks ago. The symbol worn by Luesh, her father's steward, the man who had known how to use the Soulcaster. The symbol worn by the men who had come, pressuring her family to return it. The men who had been financing Shallan's father in his bid to become highprince.

'Almighty above,' Shallan whispered. She looked up. 'Jasnah, I think . . . I think my *father* might have been a member of this group.'

The highstorm winds began to blow against Dalinar's complex, powerful enough to make rocks groan. Navani huddled close to Dalinar, holding to him. She smelled wonderful. It felt . . . humbling to know how terrified she'd been for him.

Her joy at having him back was enough to dampen, for now, her fury at him for how he'd treated Elhokar. She would come around. It had needed to be done.

As the highstorm hit in force, Dalinar felt the vision coming on. He closed his eyes, letting it take him. He had a decision to make, a responsibility. What to do? These visions had lied to him, or had at least misled him. It seemed that he couldn't trust them, at least not as explicitly as he once had.

He took a deep breath, opened his eyes, and found himself in a place of smoke.

He turned about, wary. The sky was dark and he stood on a field of dull, bone-white rock, jagged and rough, extending in all directions. Off into eternity. Amorphous shapes made of curling grey smoke rose from the ground. Like smoke rings, only in other shapes. Here a chair. There a rockbud, with vines extended, curling to the sides and vanishing. Beside him appeared the figure of a man in uniform, silent and vaporous, rising lethargically toward the sky, mouth open. The shapes melted and distorted as they climbed higher, though they seemed to hold their forms longer than they should. It was unnerving, standing on the boundless plain, pure darkness above, smoke figures rising all around.

It wasn't like any vision he'd seen before. It was . . .

No, wait. He frowned, stepping back as the figure of a tree burst from the ground close to him. *I have seen this place before. In the first of my visions, so many months ago.* It was fuzzy in his mind. He'd been disoriented, the vision vague, as if his mind hadn't learned to accept what it was seeing. In fact, the only thing he remembered distinctly was—

'You must unite them,' a powerful voice boomed.

—was the voice. Speaking to him from all around, causing the smoke figures to fuzz and distort.

'Why did you lie to me?' Dalinar demanded of the open darkness. 'I did what you said, and I was betrayed!'

'Unite them. The sun approaches the horizon. The Everstorm comes. The True Desolation. The Night of Sorrows. You must prepare. Build of your people a fortress of strength and peace, a wall to resist the winds. Cease squabbling and unite.'

'I need answers!' Dalinar said. 'I don't trust you any longer. If you want me to listen to you, you'll need to—'

The vision changed. He spun about, finding that he was still on an open plain of rock, but the normal sun was in the sky. The stone field looked like an ordinary one on Roshar.

It was very odd for one of the visions to set him in a place without others to talk to and interact with. Though, for once, he wore his own clothing. The sharp blue Kholin uniform.

Had this happened before, the other time he'd been in that place of smoke? Yes . . . it had. This was the first time he'd been taken to somewhere he'd been before. Why?

He carefully scanned the scenery. Since the voice didn't speak to him again, he began to walk, passing cracked boulders and broken bits of shale, pebbles and rocks. There were no plants, not even rockbuds. Just an empty landscape filled with broken stones.

Eventually, he spotted a ridge. Getting to high ground felt like a good idea, though the hike seemed to take hours. The vision did not end. Time was often odd in these visions. He continued to hike up the side of the rock formation, wishing he had his Shardplate to strengthen him. Finally at the top, he walked over to the edge to look down below.

And there he saw Kholinar, his home, the capital city of Alethkar.

It had been destroyed.

The beautiful buildings had been shattered. The windblades were cast down. There were no bodies, just broken stone. This wasn't like the vision he had seen before, with Nohadon. That wasn't the Kholinar of the distant past; he could see the rubble of his own palace. But there was no rock formation like the one he stood on near Kholinar in the real world. Always before, these visions had shown him the past. Was this now a vision of the future?

'I cannot fight him any longer,' the voice said.Dalinar jumped, glancing to the side. A man stood there. He had dark skin and pure white hair. Tall, thick of chest but not massive, he wore exotic clothing of a strange cut: loose, billowing trousers and a coat that came down only to his waist. Both seemed made of gold.

Yes ... this very thing had happened before, in his very first vision. Dalinar could remember it now. 'Who are you?' Dalinar demanded. 'Why are you showing me these visions?'

'You can see it there,' the figure said, pointing. 'If you look closely. It begins in the distance.'

Dalinar glanced in that direction, annoyed. He couldn't make out anything specific. 'Storm it,' Dalinar said. 'Won't you answer my questions for once? What is the good of all of this if you just speak in riddles?'

The man didn't answer. He just kept pointing. And ... yes, something *was* happening. There was a shadow in the air, approaching. A wall of darkness. Like a highstorm, only *wrong*.

'At least tell me this,' Dalinar said. 'What time are we seeing? Is this the past, the future, or something else entirely?'

The figure didn't answer immediately. Then he said, 'You're probably wondering if this is a vision of the future.'

Dalinar started. 'I just ... I just asked ...'

This was familiar. Too familiar.

He said that exact thing last time, Dalinar realized, feeling a chill. *This all happened. I'm seeing the same vision again.*

The figure squinted at the horizon. 'I cannot see the future completely. Cultivation, she is better at it than I. It's as if the future is a shattering window. The further you look, the more pieces that window breaks into.

The near future can be anticipated, but the distant future . . . I can only guess.'

'You can't hear me, can you?' Dalinar asked, feeling a horror as he finally began to understand. 'You never could.'

Blood of my fathers . . . he's not ignoring me. He can't see me! He doesn't speak in riddles. It just seems that way because I took his responses as cryptic answers to my questions.

He didn't tell me to trust Sadeas. I . . . I just assumed . . .

Everything seemed to shake around Dalinar. His preconceptions, what he'd thought he'd known. The ground itself.

'That is what could happen,' the figure said, nodding into the distance. 'It's what I fear will happen. It's what he wants. The True Desolation.'

No, that wall in the air wasn't a highstorm. It wasn't rain making that enormous shadow, but blowing dust. He remembered this vision in full, now. It had ended here, with him confused, staring out at that oncoming wall of dust. This time, however, the vision continued.

The figure turned to him. 'I am sorry to do this to you. By now I hope that what you've seen has given you a foundation to understand. But I can't know for certain. I don't know who you are, or how you have found your way here.'

'I . . .' What to say? Did it matter?

'Most of what I show you are scenes I have seen directly,' the figure said. 'But some, such as this one, are born out of my fears. If I fear it, then you should too.'

The land was trembling. The wall of dust was being caused by something. Something approaching.

The ground was falling away.

Dalinar gasped. The very rocks ahead were shattering, breaking apart, becoming dust. He backed away as everything began to shake, a massive earthquake accompanied by a terrible roar of dying rocks. He fell to the ground.

There was an awful, grinding, terrifying moment of nightmare. The shaking, the destruction, the sounds of the land itself seeming to die.

Then it was past. Dalinar breathed in and out before rising on unsteady legs. He and the figure stood on a solitary pinnacle of rock. A little section that – for some reason – had been protected. It was like a stone pillar a few paces wide, rising high into the air.

Around it, the land was *gone*. Kholinar was gone. It had all fallen away into unplumbed darkness below. He felt vertigo, standing on the tiny bit of rock that – impossibly – remained.

'What is this?' Dalinar demanded, though he knew that the being couldn't hear him.

The figure looked about, sorrowful. 'I can't leave much. Just these few images, given to you. Whoever you are.'

'These visions . . . they're like a journal, aren't they? A history you wrote, a book you left behind, except I don't read it, I see it.'

The figure looked into the sky. 'I don't even know if anyone will ever see this. I am gone, you see.'

Dalinar didn't respond. He looked over the pinnacle's sheer edge, down at a void, horrified.

'This isn't just about you either,' the figure said, raising his hand into the air. A light winked out in the sky, one that Dalinar hadn't realized was there. Then another winked out as well. The sun seemed to be growing dimmer.

'It's about all of them,' the figure said. 'I should have realized he'd come for me.'

'Who are you?' Dalinar asked, voicing the words to himself.

The figure still stared into the sky. 'I leave this, because there must be something. A hope to discover. A chance that someone will find what to do. Do you wish to fight him?'

'Yes,' Dalinar found himself saying, despite knowing that it didn't matter. 'I don't know who he is, but if he wants to do *this*, then I will fight him.'

'Someone must lead them.'

'I will do it,' Dalinar said. The words just came out.

'Someone must unite them.'

'I will do it.'

'Someone must protect them.'

'I will do it!'

The figure was silent for a moment. Then he spoke in a clear, crisp voice. 'Life before death. Strength before weakness. Journey before destination. Speak again the ancient oaths and return to men the Shards they once bore.' He turned to Dalinar, meeting his eyes. 'The Knights Radiant must stand again.'

'I cannot comprehend how that can be done,' Dalinar said softly. 'But I will try.'

'Men must face them together,' the figure said, stepping up to Dalinar, placing a hand on his shoulder. 'You cannot squabble as in times past. He's realized that you, given time, will become your own enemies. That he doesn't *need* to fight you. Not if he can make you forget, make you turn against one another. Your legends say that you won. But the truth is that we lost. And we are losing.'

'Who are you?' Dalinar asked again, voice softer.

'I wish I could do more,' repeated the figure in gold. 'You might be able to get him to choose a champion. He is bound by some rules. All of us are. A champion could work well for you, but it is not certain. And ... without the Dawnshards ... Well, I have done what I can. It is a terrible, terrible thing to leave you alone.'

'Who are you?' Dalinar asked again. And yet, he thought he knew.

'I am ... *I was* ... God. The one you call the Almighty, the creator of mankind.' The figure closed his eyes. 'And now I am dead. Odium has killed me. I am sorry.'

'Can you feel it?' Wit asked of the open night. 'Something just changed. I believe that's the sound the world makes when it pisses itself.'

Three guards stood just inside the thick wooden city gates of Kholinar. The men regarded Wit with worry.

The gates were closed, and these men were of the night watch, a somewhat inappropriate title. They didn't spend time 'watching' so much as chatting, yawning, gambling, or – in tonight's case – standing uncomfortably and listening to a crazy man.

That crazy man happened to have blue eyes, which let him get away with all kinds of trouble. Perhaps Wit should have been bemused by the stock these people put in something as simple as eye color, but he had been many places and seen many methods of rule. This didn't seem any more ridiculous than most others.

And, of course, there was a reason the people did what they did. Well, there was usually a reason. In this case, it just happened to be a good one.

'Brightlord?' one of the guards asked, looking at where Wit sat on his boxes. They'd been piled there and left by a merchant who had tipped the night watchmen to make certain nothing was stolen. To Wit, they simply made a convenient perch. His pack sat beside him, and on his knees he was tuning his enthir, a square, stringed instrument. You played it from above, plucking its strings while it sat on your lap.

'Brightlord?' the guard repeated. 'What are you doing up there?'

'Waiting,' Wit said. He looked up, glancing eastward. 'Waiting for the storm to arrive.' That made the guards more uncomfortable. A highstorm was not predicted this night.

Wit began playing the enthir. 'Let us have a conversation to pass the time. Tell me. What is it that men value in others?'

The music played toward an audience of silent buildings, alleys, and worn cobblestones. The guards didn't respond to him. They didn't seem to know what to make of a black-clad, lighteyed man who entered the city just before evening fell, then sat on boxes beside the gates playing music.

'Well?' Wit asked, pausing the music. 'What do you think? If a man or woman were to have a talent, which would be the most revered, best regarded, considered of the most worth?'

'Er . . . music?' one of the men finally said.

'Yes, a common answer,' Wit said, plucking at a few low notes. 'I once asked this question of some very wise scholars. What do men consider the most valuable of talents? One mentioned artistic ability, as you so keenly guessed. Another chose great intellect. The final chose the talent to invent, the ability to design and create marvelous devices.'

He didn't play a specific tune on the enthir, just plucks here and there, an occasional scale or fifth. Like chitchat in string form.

'Aesthetic genius,' Wit said, 'invention, acumen, creativity. Noble ideals indeed. Most men would pick one of those, if given the choice, and name them the greatest of talents.' He plucked a string. 'What beautiful liars we are.'

The guards glanced at each other; the torches burning in brackets on the wall painted them with orange light.

'You think I'm a cynic,' Wit said. 'You think I'm going to tell you that men claim to value these ideals, but secretly prefer base talents. The ability to gather coin or to charm women. Well, I *am* a cynic, but in this case, I actually think those scholars were honest. Their answers speak for the souls of men. In our hearts, we want to believe in – and would choose– great accomplishment and virtue. That's why our lies, particularly to ourselves, are so beautiful.'

He began to play a real song. A simple melody at first, soft, subdued. A song for a silent night when the entire world changed.

One of the soldiers cleared his throat. 'So what *is* the most valuable talent a man can have?' He sounded genuinely curious.

'I haven't the faintest idea,' Wit said. 'Fortunately, that wasn't the question. I didn't ask what was most valuable, I asked what *men value most*. The difference between those questions is at once both tiny and as vast as the world itself.'

He kept plucking his song. One did not strum an enthir. It just wasn't done, at least not by people with any sense of propriety.

'In this,' Wit said, 'as in all things, our actions give us away. If an artist creates a work of powerful beauty – using new and innovative techniques – she will be lauded as a master, and will launch a new movement in aesthetics. Yet what if another, working independently with that exact level of skill, were to make the same accomplishments the very next month? Would she find similar acclaim? No. She'd be called derivative.

'Intellect. If a great thinker develops a new theory of mathematics, science, or philosophy, we will name him wise. We will sit at his feet and learn, and will record his name in history for thousands upon thousands to revere. But what if another man determines the same theory on his own, then delays in publishing his results by a mere week? Will he be remembered for his greatness? No. He will be forgotten.

'Invention. A woman builds a new design of great worth – some fabrial or feat of engineering. She will be known as an innovator. But if someone with the same talent creates the same design a year later – not realizing it has already been crafted – will *she* be rewarded for her creativity? No. She'll be called a copier and a forger.'

He plucked at his strings, letting the melody continue, twisting, haunting, yet with a faint edge of mockery. 'And so,' he said, 'in the end, what must we determine? Is it the *intellect* of a genius that we revere? If it were their artistry, the beauty of their mind, would we not laud it regardless of whether we'd seen their product before?

'But we don't. Given two works of artistic majesty, otherwise weighted equally, we will give greater acclaim to the one who did it *first*. It doesn't matter what you create. It matters what you create *before anyone else*.

'So it's not the beauty itself we admire. It's not the force of intellect. It's not invention, aesthetics, or capacity itself. The greatest talent that we think a man can have?' He plucked one final string. 'Seems to me that it must be nothing more than novelty.'

The guards looked confused.

The gates shook. Something pounded on them from outside.

'The storm has come,' Wit said, standing up.

The guards scrambled for spears left leaning beside the wall. They had a guardhouse, but it was empty; they preferred the night air.

The gate shook again, as if something enormous were outside. The guards yelled, calling to the men atop the wall. All was chaos and confusion as the gate boomed yet a third time, powerful, shaking, vibrating as if hit with a boulder.

And then a bright, silvery blade rammed between the massive doors, slicing upward, cutting the bar that held them closed. A Shardblade.

The gates swung open. The guards scrambled back. Wit waited on his boxes, enthir held in one hand, pack over his shoulder.

Outside the gates, standing on the dark stone roadway, was a solitary man with dark skin. His hair was long and matted, his clothing nothing more than a ragged, sacklike length of cloth wrapping his waist. He stood with head bowed, wet, ratty hair hanging down over his face and mixing with a beard that had bits of wood and leaves stuck in it.

His muscles glistened, wet as if he'd just swum a great distance. To his side, he carried a massive Shardblade, point down, sticking about a finger's width into the stone, his hand on the hilt. The Blade reflected torchlight; it was long, narrow, and straight, shaped like an enormous spike.

'Welcome, lost one,' Wit whispered.

'Who are you!' one of the guards called, nervous, as one of the other two ran to give the alert. A Shardbearer had come to Kholinar.

The figure ignored the question. He stepped forward, dragging his Shardblade, as if it weighed a great deal. It cut the rock behind him, leaving a tiny groove in the stone. The figure walked unsteadily, and nearly tripped. He steadied himself against the gate door, and a lock of hair moved from the side of his face, exposing his eyes. Dark brown eyes, like a man of the lower class. Those eyes were wild, dazed.

The man finally noticed the two guards, who stood, terrified, with spears leveled at him. He raised his empty hand toward them. 'Go,' he said raggedly, speaking perfect Alethi, no hint of an accent. 'Run! Raise the call! Give the warning!'

'Who are you?' one of the guards forced out. 'What warning? Who attacks?'

The man paused. He raised a hand to his head, wavering. 'Who am I?

I … I am Talenel'Elin, Stonesinew, Herald of the Almighty. The Desolation has come. Oh, God … it has come. And I have failed.'

He slumped forward, hitting the rocky ground, Shardblade clattering down behind him. It did not vanish. The guards inched forward. One prodded the man with the butt of his spear.

The man who had named himself a Herald did not move.

'What is it we value?' Wit whispered. 'Innovation. Originality. Novelty. But most importantly … timeliness. I fear you may be too late, my confused, unfortunate friend.'

THE END OF

Book One of

THE STORMLIGHT ARCHIVE

ENDNOTE

"Above silence, the illuminating storms—dying storms—
illuminate the silence above."

The above sample is noteworthy as it is a ketek, a complex form of holy Vorin poem. The ketek not only reads the same forward and backward (allowing for alteration of verb forms) but is also divisible into five distinct smaller sections, each of which makes a complete thought.

The complete poem must form a sentence that is grammatically correct and (theoretically) poignant in meaning. Because of the difficulty in constructing a ketek, the structure was once considered the highest and most impressive form of all Vorin poetry.

The fact that this one was uttered by an illiterate, dying Herdazian in a language he barely spoke should be of particular note. There is no record of this particular ketek in any repository of Vorin poetry, so it is very unlikely that the subject was merely repeating something he once heard. None of the ardents we showed it to had any knowledge of it, though three did praise its structure and ask to meet the poet.

We leave it to His Majesty's mind, on a strong day, to puzzle out the meaning of why the storms might be important, and what the poem may mean by indicating that there is silence both above and below said storms.

—Joshor, Head of His Majesty's Silent Gatherers, Tanatanev 1173

ARS ARCANUM

THE TEN ESSENCES AND THEIR HISTORICAL ASSOCIATIONS

NUMBER	GEMSTONE	ESSENCE	BODY FOCUS	SOULCASTING PROPERTIES	PRIMARY / SECONDARY DIVINE ATTRIBUTES
1 Jes	Sapphire	Zephyr	Inhalation	Translucent gas, air	Protecting / Leading
2 Nan	Smokestone	Vapor	Exhalation	Opaque gas, smoke, fog	Just / Confident
3 Chach	Ruby	Spark	The Soul	Fire	Brave / Obedient
4 Vev	Diamond	Lucentia	The Eyes	Quartz, glass, crystal	Loving / Healing
5 Palah	Emerald	Pulp	The Hair	Wood, plants, moss	Learned / Giving
6 Shash	Garnet	Blood	The Blood	Blood, all non-oil liquid	Creative / Honest
7 Betab	Zircon	Tallow	Oil	All kinds of oil	Wise / Careful
8 Kak	Amethyst	Foil	The Nails	Metal	Resolute / Builder
9 Tanat	Topaz	Talus	The Bone	Rock and stone	Dependable / Resourceful
10 Ishi	Heliodor	Sinew	Flesh	Meat, flesh	Pious / Guiding

The preceding list is an imperfect gathering of traditional Vorin symbolism associated with the Ten Essences. Bound together, these form the Double Eye of the Almighty, an eye with two pupils representing the creation of plants and creatures. This is also the basis for the hourglass shape that was often associated with the Knights Radiant.

Ancient scholars also placed the ten orders of Knights Radiant on this list, alongside the Heralds themselves, who each had a classical association with one of the numbers and Essences.

I'm not certain yet how the ten levels of Voidbinding or its cousin the Old Magic fit into this paradigm, if indeed they can. My research suggests that, indeed, there should be another series of abilities that is even more esoteric than the Voidbindings. Perhaps the Old Magic fits into those, though I am beginning to suspect that it is something entirely different.

ON THE CREATION OF FABRIALS

Five groupings of fabrial have been discovered so far. The methods of their creation are carefully guarded by the artifabrian community, but they appear to be the work of dedicated scientists, as opposed to the more mystical Surgebindings once performed by the Knights Radiant.

ALTERING FABRIALS

Augmenters: These fabrials are crafted to enhance something. They can create heat, pain, or even a calm wind, for instance. They are powered – like all fabrials – by Stormlight. They seem to work best with forces, emotions, or sensations.

The so-called half-shards of Jah Keved are created with this type of fabrial attached to a sheet of metal, enhancing its durability. I have seen fabrials of this type crafted using many different kinds of gemstone; I am guessing that any one of the ten Polestones will work.

Diminishers: These fabrials do the opposite of what augmenters do, and generally seem to fall under the same restrictions as their cousins. Those artifabrians who have taken me into confidence seem to believe that even greater fabrials are possible than what have been created so far, particularly in regard to augmenters and diminishers.

PAIRING FABRIALS

Conjoiners: By infusing a ruby and using methodology that has not been revealed to me (though I have my suspicions), you can create a conjoined pair of gemstones. The process requires splitting the original ruby. The two halves will then create parallel reactions across a distance. Spanreeds are one of the most common forms of this type of fabrial.

Conservation of force is maintained; for instance, if one is attached to a heavy stone, you will need the same strength to lift the conjoined fabrial that you would need to lift the stone itself. There appears to be some sort of process used during the creation of the fabrial that influences how far apart the two halves can go and still produce an effect.

Reversers: Using an amethyst instead of a ruby also creates conjoined halves of a gemstone, but these two work in creating *opposite* reactions. Raise one, and the other will be pressed downward, for instance.

These fabrials have only just been discovered, and already the possibilities for exploitation are being conjectured. There appear to be some unexpected limitations to this form of fabrial, though I have not been able to discover what they are.

WARNING FABRIALS

There is only one type of fabrial in this set, informally known as the Alerter. An Alerter can warn one of a nearby object, feeling, sensation, or phenomenon. These fabrials use a heliodor stone as their focus. I do not know whether this is the only type of gemstone that will work, or if there is another reason heliodor is used.

In the case of this kind of fabrial, the amount of Stormlight you can infuse into it affects its range. Hence the size of gemstone used is very important.

WINDRUNNING AND LASHINGS

Reports of the Assassin in White's odd abilities have led me to some sources of information that, I believe, are generally unknown. The Windrunners were an order of the Knights Radiant, and they made use of two primary types of Surgebinding. The effects of these Surgebindings were known – colloquially among the members of the order – as the Three Lashings.

BASIC LASHING: GRAVITATIONAL CHANGE

This type of Lashing was one of the most commonly used Lashings among the order, though it was not the easiest to use. (That distinction belongs to the Full Lashing below.) A Basic Lashing involved revoking a being's or object's spiritual gravitational bond to the planet below, instead temporarily linking that being or object to a different object or direction.

Effectively, this creates a change in gravitational pull, twisting the energies of the planet itself. A Basic Lashing allowed a Windrunner to run up walls, to send objects or people flying off into the air, or to create similar effects. Advanced uses of this type of Lashing would allow a Windrunner to make himself or herself lighter by binding part of his or her mass upward. (Mathematically, binding a quarter of one's mass upward would halve a person's effective weight. Binding half of one's mass upward would create weightlessness.)

Multiple Basic Lashings could also pull an object or a person's body downward at double, triple, or other multiples of its weight.

FULL LASHING: BINDING OBJECTS TOGETHER

A Full Lashing might seem very similar to a Basic Lashing, but they worked on very different principles. While one had to do with gravitation, the other had to do with the force (or Surge, as the Radiants called them) of adhesion – binding objects together as if they were one. I believe this Surge may have had something to do with atmospheric pressure.

To create a Full Lashing, a Windrunner would infuse an object with Stormlight, then press another object to it. The two objects would become bound together with an extremely powerful bond, nearly impossible to break. In fact, most materials would themselves break before the bond holding them together would.

REVERSE LASHING: GIVING AN OBJECT A GRAVITATIONAL PULL

I believe this may actually be a specialized version of the Basic Lashing. This type of Lashing required the least amount of Stormlight of any of the three Lashings. The Windrunner would infuse something, give a mental command, and create a *pull* to the object that yanked other objects toward it.

At its heart, this Lashing created a bubble around the object that imitated its spiritual link to the ground beneath it. As such, it was much harder for the Lashing to affect objects touching the ground, where their link to the planet was strongest. Objects falling or in flight were the easiest to influence. Other objects could be affected, but the Stormlight and skill required were much more substantial.